Tom Holt was born in 1961 and started writing at an early age (his first book, *Poems by Tom Holt*, was published when he was thirteen). As a child he was fascinated by ancient Greek history and mythology, and went on to read ancient history at Oxford; after which he appears to have broken at least one mirror, since he spent the next seven years working as a solicitor. Best known for his own unique brand of comic fantasy, he has also written two sequels to E. F. Benson's Lucia series, and a highly acclaimed historical novel, *The Walled Orchard*, to which *Alexander at the World's End* is, in some respects, a sequel.

Tom Holt is married with one daughter and lives in Chard, Somerset.

By Tom Holt

ALEXANDER
AT THE WORLD'S END

TOM HOLT

An *Abacus* Book

First published in Great Britain by Little, Brown and Company 1999
This edition published by Abacus 2000

A CIP catalogue record for this book
is available from the British Library.

ISBN 0 349 11315 7

Typeset by Solidus (Bristol) Limited
Printed and bound in Great Britain by
Mackays of Chatham PLC, Chatham, Kent

Abacus
A Division of
Little, Brown and Company (UK)
Brettenham House
Lancaster Place
London WC2E 7EN

For Gharlane
My imaginary friend

'Here are set forth the histories of Herodotus of Halicarnassus, that men's actions may not in time be forgotten, nor things great and wonderful accomplished both by Greeks and foreigners . . .'

Herodotus

'Let us begin by committing ourselves to the truth, to see it like it is and to tell it like it is, to find the truth, to speak the truth and live with the truth. That's what we'll do.'

Richard M. Nixon

Olbia
Antolbia
Chersonesus
Istrus
Odessus
Macedonia
Thracia
Pella
Olynthus
Cranieus
Thebes
Corinth
Lydia
Phrygia
Cappadocia
Armenia
Athens
Sardis
Sparta
Ephesus
Issus
Mesopotamia
Gaugamela
Arbela
Cyprus
Assyria
Tyre
Babylon
Libya
Alexandria
Shrine of Ammon
Egypt
ARABIA
Thebes
Nile

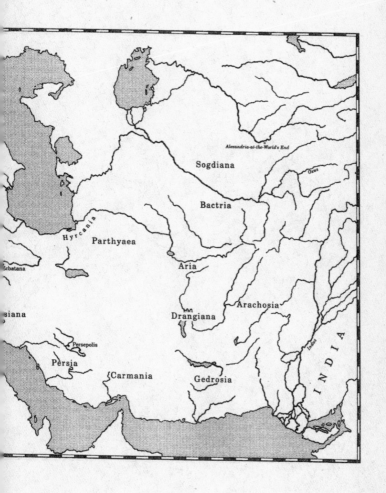

Alexandria-at-the-World's End

Sogdiana

Bactria

Oxus

Hyrcania

Parthyaea

Aria

Arachosia

Ecbatana

Drangiana

Indus

Persepolis

INDIA

Persia

Carmania

Gedrosia

siana

CHAPTER ONE

Written in Alexandria-at-the-End-of-the-World* in Sogdiana in the twenty-third year after the foundation of the city, the seventy-third year of my life, by Euxenus the son of Eutychides, of the deme of Pallene.

Consider Alexander, and consider me. Both of us came a long way to die, but my journey wasn't like his; mine led me out of vast tracts of folly and into a small village on the borders of wisdom.

Once, when I was young, I believed in democracy. When I was a little older, I believed in oligarchy, government by the enlightened few; after that, in monarchy, the rule of the philosopher-king. Now I believe only in drainage, public sanitation and clean water.

Oh, yes; I've come a lot further than Alexander.

'My father used to say,' I told you once, 'that the greatest misfortune a man can know is to bury his own son. Of course, he was quoting from one of those mouldy old tragedians my grandfather Eupolis knocked around with at one time, but the sentiment is commonplace enough. My father, a remarkably fortunate man, never got to put this to the test. The consequences for his sons, all seven of us, were accordingly catastrophic.'

You looked puzzled, my young friend. 'Sorry,' you said, 'I don't quite follow. How could it have been any better for any of you if some of you had died?'

---

*Iskander, about 50 miles north-east of Tashkent.

You remember the conversation, Phryzeutzis, I'm sure. We were standing in the shade of the gatehouse watching them put up the scaffolding for building the first of the rainwater tanks, which goes to show how long ago it was. As I recall, it was as hot as a smithy that day, even in the shade. I confess I was in one of my more garrulous moods. As usual, I was talking about myself. Most of it was probably going right over your head.

'Over the course of my excessively long life,' I explained, 'I've made something of a study of luck, in roughly the same way as a three-legged cat studies the habits of mice, and I believe I've detected a pattern in the way it operates. Take, for example, the history of my family over the past few generations. It's a wonderful illustration of my theory. You can keep the score if you like.'

'Excuse me?' you said.

'Keep score. Count up instances of good luck versus instances of bad luck, and tell me who wins in the end.'

'All right,' you said.

'Here goes, then. Now then, let's see. My great-grandfather (who died long before I was born) was a nothingish sort of man who lived an uneventful life in Pallene, fairly but not very near the glorious city of Athens—'

'Athens,' you repeated. 'In Greece, right?'

'In Greece,' I confirmed. 'In his day, Athens was the greatest power in Greece, the only place in the world ruled by a democracy, the home of the finest poets, painters, philosophers, scientists and the like that the world has ever seen.'

'Ah, yes,' you said. 'You've mentioned it before.'

Of course, we didn't know each other so well in those days.

'Anyway,' I said, 'he farmed his land, voted in Assembly when he could spare the time, went to the Festivals, raised a family, got on with his life in a reasonably efficient manner and probably went to his grave wondering when the show was going to start. He was neither rich nor poor, famous nor infamous, and though he died on active service in the early stages of the Great Peloponnesian War against Sparta, I don't suppose he made a big deal about it; I picture him dying unobtrusively somewhere, probably of dysentery after drinking bad water, rather than falling ostentatiously among the clash of arms. He was, by any definition, a lucky man, although his good fortune lay entirely in the fact that he had no luck of any kind, good or bad.'

'You're losing me again,' you said.

'Am I? Sorry. You'll get the hang of it as I go along, I expect. Now then,' I went on, 'my grandfather Eupolis, on the other hand, had far more than his share of luck. Having survived the plague that wiped out a large slice of the population of Athens—'

'Good luck,' you said, folding down a finger on your right hand.

'Quite so,' I said, 'except that it disfigured him for life.'

'Bad luck,' you said firmly, folding down a finger on your left hand.

'Anyway,' I continued, 'because of the plague he inherited substantial amounts of property by virtue of being the only one left –'

'Good luck,' you said. 'I guess,' you added.

'– But found himself bereft of family at an early age –'

You frowned sympathetically. Of course, at that time I didn't know about your family history. 'Bad luck,' you said.

'– And went on to contract a disastrously unhappy marriage –'

You nodded. 'More bad luck,' you said.

I smiled. 'Not long after that,' I said, swatting away an unusually persistent fly, 'he took part in the ill-fated Athenian invasion of Sicily, where the whole of our army was massacred—'

'Still more bad luck,' you pointed out. 'I'll run out of fingers soon.'

'The whole of our army,' I repeated, 'except for him—'

'Ah,' you said cheerfully. 'Good luck at last.'

'Him and his deadliest enemy—'

'Oh. Properly speaking, that's more bad luck, isn't it?'

'Absolutely,' I replied. 'A good man loves his friends and hates his enemies. After a series of hair-raising adventures – lots and lots of luck; a jumble of good and bad, like the junk lots at the end of a public auction – he made it back to Athens (good luck) only to be charged with sacrilegious treason and put on trial for his life (bad luck), escaping by a hair's breadth—'

'Good luck?' you suggested hopefully.

I nodded. 'You could say that,' I replied, 'though from what I can gather, pure fluke would be nearer the mark. After that,' I added, 'he continued the distinguished career as a writer of comic drama that he'd begun before the War interrupted it. He lived to see the fall of the great Athenian democracy (bad luck), which with good reason he detested (so good luck really), survived his shrewish and deceitful wife (good luck), whom he'd been devoted to (bad luck) and died at a ripe old age (good luck) after choking on a fishbone (bad luck), survived by one son, my father Eutychides.'

'Sorry,' you said. 'I lost count some time back. But I think it was pretty evenly matched.'

I shrugged. 'In Greek,' I explained, 'Eutychides means "son of a lucky man". Grandfather had his faults, Heaven knows, but you couldn't fault his keen sense of irony.'

You smiled, and offered me the pitcher of water. You were laughing.

'What's the joke?' I said.

'Nothing,' you replied. 'Have a drink. You need to drink more in this hot weather.'

'Never mind that,' I said. 'Tell me what I said that was so confoundedly funny. Usually when I make a joke you just stare at me with a half-witted expression on your face.'

'All right,' you said. 'Though it isn't funny, just – well, curious. Sounds to me,' you said, 'that your grandfather had luck the way we have rats in our barn.'

While I think of it, maybe I should just explain at this point why I'm not writing this in Greek. I should be, I know. After all, Greek is now the common language of the known civilised world, whereas this barbarous Scytho-Sogdanian dialect, which is so obscure it hasn't even got a name, has never previously been used for writing and probably won't be used again; as witness the fact that I'm having to use the Greek alphabet to write it down in, notwithstanding that there aren't Greek letters for half the peculiar noises these people (sorry; you people) make with your mouths. If there's a reason, it's because I simply don't want to be an Athenian any more, or even a Greek of any description. In which case, you ask, why are you doing something so absurdly, quintessentially Greek as writing a book – 'sitting talking to yourself with a stick and a bit of sheepskin,' as my neighbours call it – which nobody will want or be able to read? To which I immediately reply that I wish I knew. I do, honestly. My excuse, however, is that it behoves those of us who have seen momentous events to record them for the benefit of generations yet unborn, so that the deeds of great men shall not be wholly forgotten, and the mistakes of the past shall not unwittingly be repeated in the future. Or something like that.

Where have we got to? Oh, yes, my father, and luck.

I had another discussion with you about this, Phryzeutzis (if that's your damn name; it sounds more like a dog being sick than anything I'd call a name, but Phryzeutzis is the nearest I can get to it in Greek letters), a month or so back, if you remember; and since you're probably going to be the only reader this book ever has, I can't think why I'm painfully transcribing it here. But I did make some rather brilliant points, as I recall, and I expressed myself with more than usual clarity, succinctness and wit; and anyway, most of the time you were watching a beetle climbing up the doorframe and not paying proper attention, so here it is again, for you to read and digest at your leisure.

'My father,' I told you, as we watched them digging the big trench for the main drain I was insisting on (very sweetly, they were humouring an old man), 'was a stolid man; solid bronze all the way through and never claimed to be anything else. He never wore a thin coating of silver and pretended to be a drachma.'

You turned your head and looked at me. 'What's a drachma?' you asked.

'It's an Athenian coin,' I replied. 'They were always made of pure silver, but at the end of the War we were so poor we took to making them out of bronze and coating them in silver. Didn't fool anybody.'

'Ah,' you said. 'This is money we're talking about, yes?'

'That's right,' I said, nodding.

'The little round metal buttons with a horse on one side and Alexander on the other.'

(You didn't say 'Alexander', of course; you can't pronounce Alexander, you poor savage. You said something like Zgunda. But I knew who you meant.)

'Correct,' I replied, rather grumpily. 'Except that in those days, they didn't have Alexander on them anywhere, they had Athena, Goddess of Wisdom, eternal patron of Athens.'

'I see,' you replied, optimistically in my opinion. 'Athena is the giver of wisdom, and you Athenians were especially fond of her.'

'That's it.'

'Why?'

You have this aggravating habit of asking difficult questions. Not *difficult*, of course, in the sense that sixteen multiplied by four take away six divided by three is difficult; awkward to explain to one of your limited intelligence is probably a better way of putting it.

'Well,' I said, 'because we Athenians honour wisdom above all things.'

'Oh.' You looked puzzled. 'Strange.' You didn't choose to amplify that rather odd remark; instead you asked me whether stolid was a good or a bad thing to be.

I thought about that for a moment. 'Neither, really,' I said. 'Or both. Of course, he was lucky—'

You laughed, for some reason. 'Sorry,' you said. 'Please, go on.'

'He was lucky,' I continued, slightly annoyed at the interruption, 'to be living during an uncharacteristically peaceful time in Athenian history. Well, I say peaceful; it wasn't. We were caught up in a series of nasty little wars – us against the Spartans—'

'Just a moment,' you said. 'I thought you told me the war was over by his time.'

That's your trouble, you never pay attention. '*The* War, yes. That finished when Father was seventeen. The wars against Sparta in his day were just wars. We were also fighting the Persians, and with the Persians against the Spartans, and with the Thebans against the Spartans, and with the Spartans against the Thebans—'

'Why?' you asked.

'What? Because we were at war, of course.'

'Yes, but why? What was the war about?' You looked so worried it was almost comical. 'It must have been pretty complicated, if your enemies kept becoming your friends and the other way around.'

I frowned. 'I can't remember,' I said. 'Mostly, I think, it was about who owned which cities. The cities of the various empires, I mean.'

You nodded; then something else bothered you. 'Athens had an empire, then?' you asked.

'Sort of. Well, we were protecting them against the others, you see. Except when they rebelled.'

'And then you protected them against themselves?'

'Pretty much. You see, the Spartans and the Thebans and the Persians were picking on our cities, trying to take away their freedom, so we had to prevent that. And sometimes our cities wanted to go over to the enemy, so we had to prevent that too.'

'I see,' you said, though I think you were probably lying. 'And you were protecting them because you were a democracy.'

'That's it. We believed that no man should be superior to another.'

'Right. And that's why you had an empire. I think I get the idea. But all these wars,' you went on, 'they must have made life terribly difficult for you and your family, when you were growing up.'

I smiled and shook my head. 'Oh, no,' I said, 'it wasn't anything like the War. Actually, it was a fairly good time to be an Athenian. We had the democracy back again – the Spartans abolished it at the end of the War, but when we threw out the Thirty Tyrants—'

'They were Spartans, then.'

'No,' I said patiently, 'they were Athenians. Anyway, after we'd got rid of them, and when we'd started rebuilding the empire and tribute-money was coming in from the cities of the empire, it was almost like it had been back in Grandfather's day.'

You closed your eyes for a moment. 'You mean, during the War?'

'Well, yes. But the War wasn't all fighting, there were big gaps in it when life wasn't too bad. And in Father's time, too, we were really quite prosperous, thanks to the state-owned silver mines. In fact, a few years before I was born we were able to pay people just to sit in Assembly and listen to the debates.'

You were suitably impressed by that; or so I thought. 'You mean, people wouldn't go to the debates unless they were paid? I thought Assembly was where you did the democracy.'

I sighed. 'This is why it's so hard for me to teach you anything,' I said. 'You keep wandering off the point. And the point is, life wasn't so bad after the War, in my father's day. Nothing much was going on; not like it was during the War.'

You gave me an odd look when I said that, presumably because you still hadn't grasped what I was trying to tell you. Maybe it's just as well I'm writing all this down for you. You'll be able to read it through slowly and carefully and finally get it all straight in your mind.

'You were telling me about your father,' you said.

'Yes indeed.' I smiled fondly. 'He was a man for his time, really. He cared about his property and his family and that was about it. And he had seven sons.'

'Ah,' you said, 'I think you said something about that once before, when we were talking about luck that time. You seemed to think that was bad luck.'

'No,' I answered slowly, so you'd be able to follow, 'that was good luck. Well, his good luck, anyway. A large family is a sign of the gods' blessing. No, we were the ones who had the bad luck, after he died. You see, back home, when a man dies all his property doesn't just go to his eldest son, it's divided equally between all his sons, because that's much fairer, you see.'

'Ah,' you said. 'Democracy.'

I laughed. 'You could call it that, I suppose. But the upshot of it was that Father's property, divided seven ways, didn't come to very much for each of us. In fact, it wasn't enough to keep a pig alive. Now do you see the point I was making? Father had good luck, pretty well all his life; but as soon as he died, the bad luck started for us. None of us could make a living, so we had to give up farming and find something else to do. And that, basically, is how I ended up in Macedonia, with King Philip and Prince Alexander.'

The plain truth of the matter is that my childhood was far too pleasant to be memorable. Not, of course, that I thought it was pleasant at the time. I seemed to spend most of my time hiding from people; my six elder brothers, all trying to palm their chores off on me, or my father, or the latest in a long succession of teachers and tutors. I got to be quite good at hiding, but not nearly good enough. I learned a lot of basic strategy that way – never hide in a tree, because once they spot you there's nowhere else to run to; the last place they'll think of looking is the place where they've just looked, and so on – and I got plenty of fresh air and exercise. But the lesson I never did learn was that it's stupid to waste a whole day hiding rather than do a morning's work. That's simple commercial good sense, not spending a day to earn a morning; but in all the courses of tuition my father arranged for me (and he was fanatical about education, for reasons I'll explain in a moment), simple good sense was never part of the curriculum. Like so many things in my life, I never got around to learning that until I was far too old for it to be of any use to me.

Thinking about it, I may have made it sound as if the inevitable division of my father's property into seven worthless shares came as a dreadful shock that dawned on us some time between the moment of his death and the morning after the funeral. Far from it; even when he was a relatively young man with only four sons, Father was obsessed by it, virtually to the exclusion of everything else. It coloured his whole life, and so hard did he try to find some workable solution to the problem that he neglected a great many other things, and so made the situation far worse.

It's worth mentioning at this point that we Greeks (or at least we Athenians, back in those days; I keep using this magic new word 'Greeks' as if it actually means something, but it doesn't. And what I know about the rest of the Greeks, the ones who weren't Athenians, could be written on the back of a potsherd with a rusty spearhead) had very strict views on how an honest man should make his living. Basically, he grew it, or for choice watched it grow, while other people did the actual hoeing and planting and pruning. The ideal was that a man inherited enough land from his father to grow enough food to qualify him for a respectable place in society – we divided people up into classes, according to how many measures of produce, wet and dry, their land produced in a year; so many measures and you could vote, so many more and you could fight for your country, and if your estate was big enough to produce five hundred measures a year, it stood to reason that there was no way you'd be able to eat all that stuff yourself without dying of chronic obesity, so you were obliged to use the surplus for the good of the community, by fitting out a warship for the fleet or financing the production of a play at one of the Festivals. That's how come the Athenians of old had the best fleet in Greece, invented the Drama and never seemed to put on weight.

Best of all, of course, was having enough money to be able to afford enough slaves to do all the fieldwork for you. Failing that, it was considered honourable, if tiresome, to work in the fields yourself, and some fairly rich men (Grandfather Eupolis, for example) quite enjoyed fooling about in the dust with a mattock or a pruning-knife. As far as earning a living went, though, that was it. Anybody who worked for someone else, even if he was a free man, felt that he was no better off than a slave. Nearly all the craftsmen and artisans, the smiths and carpenters and potters and wheel-wrights and so forth, had their four or five scruffy acres of vines interplanted with barley and so could imagine they were really gentlemen farmers who happened to make door-hinges or sandals for a hobby. Merchants saw themselves as farmers who whiled away the parts of the year when nothing much was doing on the land by renting a space on a ship and taking a pleasure-cruise to Egypt or Italy, fetching along a few jars of wine or oil or honey just to help defray expenses. And the people who simply had no land at all, not even enough to lie down on without trespassing, had no choice but to admit that they were good-for-nothing outcasts from society and try to make a living out of politics.

Actually, that wasn't too hard at all. What with payment for attending Assembly and payment for sitting on juries (and we were such a savagely litigious nation that the demand for jurors usually outstripped the supply of layabouts by an alarming degree), a man could eat reasonably well and feed his family just by sitting on a stone bench all day, listening to the flower of Athenian oratory (a science in which we're still unsurpassed in all the world; wonder why?) and doing his civic duty. If that wasn't enough, however, there always used to be the third means by which Athens provided for her less fortunate children, namely the three obols a day she paid a man to sit in a warship and pull an oar. Since it was the moral effect of so many fine warships cruising up and down their coast-lines that encouraged our loyal allies on the islands to part with the tribute money that paid for the juries and the Assemblies, the third option was necessary to provide for the other two; hence, I suppose, all those wars. At any rate, we Athenians proudly declare to all who'll listen that Athens is the only place in the world where a man can make a living sitting on his bum being entertained by pro-fessional orators. It's a proud boast, and one that nobody before or since has ever sought to emulate, for some reason.

So it was understood that I and my brothers wouldn't actually starve, whatever happened. But there's more to life than just staying alive, the gods know; and so my poor father fretted himself half to death trying to dream up schemes whereby all eight of us would be able to live like gentlemen without having to listen to speeches. He was an ingenious man, my father, I'll give him that. One way round the property qualifications was to own a workshop or a factory. Some of the greatest Athenians of the past had done precisely that; Nicias the General, Cleon the Orator, Hyperbolus and so on. It was respectable, so long as you simply owned the building and the slaves and didn't actually dirty your own hands.

So Father snooped around looking for promising businesses to invest in, in the hope that in time they'd grow successful enough to do one of us boys as his share of the inheritance. Sadly, the only businesses my father could afford to buy into were either failing or doomed from the start. Offhand I can recall the franchise in the state-owned silver mines (he bought the concession on the only chunk of rock in Laurium that *didn't* have any silver in it); the trumpet factory (how many trumpets a year do you think a city the size of Athens consumes, for pity's sake?); the sandal-making shop that would have got the contract to supply sandals to a large contingent of the Athenian army, if that contingent hadn't been the one decimated by the Thebans at Mantinea; the charcoal-burning yard on Lemnos, which he bought shortly before Lemnos was taken away from us by the Spartans, and which he sold for the price of a second-hand hat a month or so before we got it back again . . . If he'd only kept the money he poured into these disasters and laid it aside in a temple, there'd probably have been enough to buy three of us a merchant ship each. As it was, his prudence and foresight left us when he died with nothing but the land, the stock and the farm instruments; even some of the slaves had had to be sold to cover his liabilities from a joint-venture trading scheme involving a shipload of prime Euxine timber that hit a submerged rock somewhere near Byzantium.

But at least he'd seen to it that I had an education, though I'm not sure a bit and brace and a set of chisels wouldn't have been more useful. Father had got it into his head at an early stage in my development that I was going to be the clever one, and it's perfectly true to say that Athens has always appreciated cleverness, more so than any city in Greece. Unfortunately, cleverness is a bit like sulphur or charcoal; producing the stuff is all very well, but the by-products can make the whole district uninhabitable. Athenian cleverness is nasty stuff to be around, like tar or nitre, and people who make their living in the cleverness industry – law, philosophy and politics, as if there was any difference between them – tend to die young. Accordingly I wasn't too keen on the idea, in spite of Father's insistence, which is why I kept running away and hiding.

There were three ways you could earn a living by making speeches. First, there was good old-fashioned informing, though that was going out of fashion even then. Basically, an informer made it his business to bring actions at law against those who allegedly betrayed or injured the State. If they got a conviction, they were awarded a fat slice of the convicted man's property, while the remainder went to the Treasury to pay for such things as jurors' wages. Good, honest work; but for some reason a degree of stigma went with the job, and there was always a slight risk of having your throat cut on a dark night.

Writing speeches was far more socially acceptable, though it didn't pay quite as well. We Athenians are tolerant people; we understand that not everybody is blessed with an inspired turn of phrase, and sometimes it's not very fair to pitch a honey-tongued professional informer against a doddery old farmer in a talking match to the death. It was, therefore, open to the defendant to pay someone to write his speech for him.

Slightly more prestigious was teaching philosophy, with special reference to ethics, morality and how to turn these lofty concepts arse-about-face in the course of a public address. Since a fair number of the practitioners of this art were gentlemen who studied and taught the subject either as a hobby or for wickedness, rather than as a commercial proposition, my father decided that this was the least degrading of the three options and looked around for someone to apprentice me to.

And that, to cut a long story short, is how I came to be involved with Diogenes, the Yapping Dog, quite possibly the most unpleasant and distasteful person I've ever known. He had no original ideas, nothing to say, no redeeming qualities of any kind except a certain flair for meretricious annoyance and self-advertisement, and a complete and total lack of fear. He's dead now, of course; and if I were Hercules or Theseus or some other hero from the old stories and could go down to Hell and bring back just one soul with me, it'd be Diogenes'.

Dear gods, I remember with appalling vividness the day my father took me to meet him for the first time. Being my father, he'd formulated his cunning scheme and set his heart on it as being the definitive answer to the problem of what to do about Euxenus, before stopping to consider the one basic practicality on which the success of the project depended, namely money. A last-minute glance at the household accounts made him revise quite drastically his choice of who I was to be apprenticed to. Up to that point, my father's criteria for selection had been reputation, valuable contacts, proven rates of success, et cetera. Came the day, however, and it all boiled down to who would be prepared to take me on for the money available, and the choice suddenly dwindled down to one.

That was the time when Diogenes was running his celebrated (or notorious) living-in-a-barrel gimmick. The idea was to show up the mindless materialism of us regular folks by dispensing with any vestige of luxury and retaining only the barest of essentials; to wit, one upended oil-jar, with a sort of hole-cum-door smashed in the side for him to crawl in and out of. It was a marvellous attention-grabber, which he exploited shamelessly by rolling this confounded thing from pitch to pitch, wherever there was likely to be a large, good-natured crowd, and squatting in it looking all haggard and unworldly until he'd attracted a substantial enough audience to justify a performance. Of course, he didn't actually sleep in the wretched thing. As soon as the show was over, he'd dump it somewhere and either sneak back to his own warm, cosy house or (more usually) spend the night with one of his devoted female disciples whose husband happened to be out of town. The remarkable thing was that nobody (except me, of course) ever seemed to notice that the whole thing was a racket. In retrospect, I think it was because everybody wanted him to be genuine, and so assumed he was, without question.

Come to think of it, nearly everything about the Yapping Dog was a lie, and a strange kind of lie at that; he went out of his way to make himself seem far worse than he actually was. When he stood up straight and combed his hair and washed (I think he did all three simultaneously about five times in his entire life) he was a reasonably tall, well-proportioned man, quite good-looking in a bland sort of a way; but somehow or other he managed to make himself look like a scrawny, ugly little dwarf. I think he smeared soot under his eyes to make them look sunken and hollow, and his deformed crouch was a masterpiece of histrionics, though he undoubtedly suffered for his art. As his accredited pupil, I was allowed to watch when nobody else was looking, and he stood up and stretched his sorely abused spine with a quite heart-rending groan.

Anyway. Diogenes was on duty in his jar when we found him (he was never hard to track down, at least during working hours). He was sitting in the shade, half in and half out of the jar, with his other celebrated prop, the lantern (which he lit and carried round in broad daylight, claiming to be looking for an honest man. Great line. If anybody can tell me what it means, I'd be ever so grateful) and nibbling at a crust of stale bread which he kept handy at all times.

'Diogenes,' my father said.

'Get lost.'

My father (stolid, respectable, robustly healthy, a great eater of garlic and onions) didn't know what to make of that, so he pretended he hadn't heard. 'Diogenes,' he repeated.

'Didn't you hear what I just said? Gods, it must be awful to be deaf as well as stupid. Go away, you're ruining the view.'

My father, a born straight man, turned round to see what he was talking about. 'What view?' he said. 'There's just a wall.'

'So?'

Now, being a boy of tender years, I'd instinctively guessed what Diogenes' game was within a minute of first setting eyes on him – after all, his entire persona was little more than Bad Boy – and as far as I was concerned, the best of luck to him. But I also knew my father, who was as straightforward as they come; insult him to his face three times and he'd just look confused, but try it a fourth time and you'd be going home with your teeth in your hat. For some reason I decided it wouldn't be good if Father broke the strange man's neck, so I intervened.

'Come on,' I said. 'We've come to the wrong place. This isn't Diogenes the philosopher, it's only a chicken.'

'Be quiet,' said my father automatically; he always said 'Be quiet' when one of us spoke, right up till we were grown men. But Diogenes leaned forward a little and raised one grubby eyebrow.

'What did you call me?' he said.

'A chicken,' I repeated.

'You think I look like a chicken?'

I nodded. 'A featherless biped. Sorry we disturbed you.'

Now that, of course, was the most outrageous flattery, but I'd guessed (correctly) that Diogenes craved flattery almost as much as money. To explain: once, when Diogenes was going through one of his periodic picking-on-great-men phases – 'monstering', he used to call it – he took to showing up at the public lectures staged by the celebrated Plato (student of Socrates, Founder of the Academy, greatest living philosopher; a nasty bastard who picked his nose while eating dinner). Once, when Plato was lecturing on 'What Is Man?' and got to the bit where he contrasted/compared Man with other animals, he used this phrase 'featherless biped', and Diogenes took a fancy to the expression. At the next lecture, therefore, Diogenes sat in the front row, waited till Plato used The Phrase, stood up and threw a plucked chicken onto the middle of the stage.

'There you go,' he said in a loud voice. 'Plato's Man.'

I know; it loses a lot in the telling. Probably you had to be there. But that was the end of Plato's public lectures for several months, and the poor fellow found it hard to get about during daylight for the crowds of small boys who'd materialise out of nowhere and follow him about going 'Ter-*wuck*-wuck-wuck!' and waggling their arms up and down. If it had been anybody else, I'd have felt sorry for him.

Anyway, the flattery did the job. 'I'll talk to you,' he said to me. 'You're obviously the brains of the family. What do you want?'

My father cleared his throat. 'Diogenes, I want you to consider taking my boy here as your apprentice. Of course, I'm willing—'

'What did he just say?' Diogenes interrupted.

'He wants you to consider taking me as your apprentice,' I said.

'Ah. Right.' Diogenes smiled, and scratched himself ostentatiously. That was another thing about him; all his disgusting habits were so obviously affectations that I, for one, was never offended by them. 'He should have said so himself. All right, how much?'

My father mentioned a sum of money. Diogenes looked at me pointedly. I repeated what Father had said. Diogenes spat.

'Try again,' he said. 'Dammit, I wouldn't even teach you philosophy for that.'

My father, who was controlling his temper so ferociously that I was afraid his neck would snap, pointed out pleasantly enough that that was in fact what he wanted me to learn.

'Huh?' Diogenes grunted.

I repeated what Father had said, word for word. 'The hell with that,' Diogenes replied. 'Any bloody fool can teach philosophy. In fact, *only* a bloody fool can teach philosophy. What I teach is how to be human, for which my rates are rather more than your man there is willing to pay. Sorry, kid.'

To be honest, I was starting to get a little bit tired of Diogenes' cabaret act. Either Father was going to stand there and take it, which wasn't right since he'd done nothing to deserve it, or else pretty soon he was going to kick Diogenes halfway to Boeotia, and I didn't want that to happen, either. 'Suit yourself, then,' I replied. 'You'd have made a lousy pupil anyway.'

Diogenes looked at me, and I recognised the look; recognition, together with a warning: *This is my pitch, keep off!* He ignored the feed line, and yawned. 'But,' he said, 'I do occasionally do charity work. All right, then.' He stood up, three quarters upright so as to be shorter than my father. 'You gods,' he droned, in best hiring-fair fashion, with one hand uplifted, 'witness that I take this boy as my apprentice and in return for his service and the woefully inadequate sum agreed upon by the parties hereto I undertake to teach him how to be a featherless biped and a good dog, amen.' Then he looked my father straight in the eye and held out his hand for the money.

'Good,' he said, after he'd counted it (twice). 'We start tomorrow, first light, sharp. Bring your own lunch.'

On the way home, Father was unusually silent. Normally he'd think aloud as we walked together.

'Euxenus,' he said at last, 'there's a lot you can learn from that man.'

I was surprised. In fact, I was surprised that he'd made the deal at all. 'Yes, Father,' I said.

'That man,' (and Diogenes was always *that man* in our household from that day forth), 'is very good at what he does. In fact, that's probably the best investment I'll ever make on behalf of you boys.'

The remarkable thing about my father – that stolid, misguided man – was that from time to time he was entirely right.

CHAPTER TWO

Curiously enough, the first day I spent as an apprentice human being under the tuition of the celebrated Diogenes was also the day on which a minor tribal chieftain in the far north of Greece was killed in a battle with some neighbouring bunch of savages. The man's name was Perdiccas, and he had been the ruler of a district called Macedonia.

Perdiccas was the second of the three sons of King Amyntas. He'd achieved the throne by murdering his elder brother Alexander in the normal course of business, and would undoubtedly have been a highly satisfactory ruler by Macedonian standards if only he'd had the chance. He was survived by a son and a younger brother, who was appointed regent until Perdiccas' son came of age. Predictably enough, the boy died not long after, and Amyntas' youngest son, Philip, became king. He was twenty-three years old.

Eight years earlier, the brilliant and successful Theban general Pelopidas, finding himself at something of a loose end between massacres, amused himself for a while by persecuting the northern primitives. Anxious to get rid of him without parting with anything of value, King Perdiccas offered him his younger brother as a hostage, and so off young Philip went to Thebes for three years as a guest of Pelopidas and his even more brilliant and successful colleague, the Theban commander-in-chief Epaminondas, a man regarded by his contemporaries as the most innovative and clear-sighted military thinker of his day. It was Epaminondas who virtually reinvented the art of war by changing the criteria of victory. Previously, you won a battle by taking possession of the battlefield, piling up a great heap of the enemy's discarded arms and armour, and dedicating the spoils to your regional patron god; it was Epaminondas who demonstrated to the world that the best way to win a battle is to kill as many of the enemy as you can, and the hell with piles of shiny helmets and breastplates. The novelty of this approach wasn't lost on impressionable young Philip, and since he wasn't a proper Greek anyway and accordingly lacked the true Hellenic feel for a truly beautiful and satisfying heap of verdigrised armour, he set himself to contemplating the new Theban approach to war with a view to mastering it and if possible improving it further.

Well, Philip served his apprenticeship, I served mine. That first morning, I showed up for work bright and early, with my wax tablets for making notes and my lunch in a goatskin bag on my shoulder, to find that Diogenes wasn't there. For some reason, this didn't come as a total surprise to me. As I think I mentioned earlier, I'd observed at our first encounter that although Diogenes was beyond doubt very dirty and scruffy, it was a comfortable, really rather cosy sort of dirtiness and scruffiness that looked as if it was designed to give a firm feel of authenticity without causing distress or inconvenience to the man who had to live in it. It certainly wasn't the sort of miserable, demoralising squalor you'd expect from, say, sleeping rough in a broken old storage jar.

(Very perceptive of me. Diogenes' appearance was quite the work of art, and when I got to know him better I found that he took longer over his face, clothes and hair every morning than the most fastidious society hostess.)

I sat down in the shade and waited, and in due course Diogenes showed up, rolling his damned jar like Sisyphus in the stories. You could hear him coming from quite a distance, because the jar made a sort of grumbling, grinding noise like the distant sound of an olive-press. It was a hot day, and when he finally came into view Diogenes was sweating freely.

'Don't just stand there,' he panted, catching sight of me, 'come and help me with this bloody thing.'

I carefully put down my satchel and ran over. He'd managed to get the thing stuck in a rut in the road, and it took both of us a fair deal of cursing and shoving to work it loose. When at last we'd managed to stow it where he wanted it to go, he flopped down on the ground and told me to go and fetch some water, which I did.

'That's better,' he said, wiping his beard and handing me the cup. 'All right then, let's get a few things straight before we start on this apprenticeship thing.' He looked at me for a moment, and shook his head. 'You're a smart kid, I can tell you that by looking at you, so I won't waste my time or energy trying to impress you. Actually, I've been giving this business a bit of thought and I do believe there are a few things I can teach you, beyond all the meaningless bullshit I do for money. That's assuming you want to learn,' he added. 'Because if you don't, you can bugger off and amuse yourself all day, I'll keep your father's money and we'll both be happy.'

I thought for a moment. 'I don't mind learning,' I replied, 'so long as it's interesting and useful. My father thinks I should be a philosopher.'

Diogenes nodded. 'Very worthy aspiration. Haven't a clue what it means. Have you?'

'A lover of wisdom,' I replied. 'At least, that's what the word means literally.'

Diogenes rested the back of his head against the wall of the jar, which was comfortably warm, and closed his eyes. 'A lover of wisdom,' he repeated. 'Which begs a nice pair of questions: what's wisdom, and is it something you can love?'

'Excuse me?' I said.

'Oh, come on,' Diogenes replied. 'Fairly basic stuff, this. All right, let's take the second bit first; only because the first one's too hard for me, mind. Lover of wisdom; well, I assume you know what love is.'

'More or less,' I said.

'All right. So, there are things you can love – beautiful people, the city you live in, your parents and children – and there's other things you can't, like a mattock-handle or cutting your toenails or cleaning caked mud off a ploughshare. You can appreciate a well-made mattock-handle, if it's a nice straight-grained piece of ash that's been properly shaped and smoothed so it won't blister your hands, but I defy anybody who isn't crazy or very, very sad to be in love with a mattock-handle. Now then, can you spot the difference?'

'I think so,' I said. 'A mattock-handle is meant to be useful, in a practical sort of way. The other things you said are more – well, inspirational.'

Diogenes nodded. 'Sounds good to me,' he said. 'And the same goes for my other two examples, I guess. Cutting your toenails makes walking more comfortable, and cleaning mud off a plough-share makes ploughing easier. Beautiful men and women, the city and your friends and relations, on the other hand, can be useless or even downright aggravating and you'll still love them. All right so far?'

'I think so,' I said.

'Mphm.' His voice was getting lower and slower, and I thought he was about to fall asleep. 'So if philosophy's the love of wisdom, wisdom's something that's capable of being loved. We appreciate and value useful things but we love things that inspire us without necessarily being useful and quite often aren't; in fact, bearing in mind the vast amount of unhappiness and pain caused by love in this life, it's a reasonable observation that anything capable of being loved is also capable of making your life thoroughly miserable, whereas if your mattock-handle rubs your hands and you've got any sense, you mend it or sling it and get a new one. Conclusion, there-fore: wisdom is more likely to be a pain in the bum than anything useful. Is that a sensible thing for a young man to spend his time learning?'

I shook my head. 'I suppose not,' I said.

Diogenes opened his eyes and sat up. 'You suppose damn right,' he said, with an unexpected degree of animation. 'Oh, I know a bit about wisdom, you see, and I could teach you some if you really wanted me to. I could teach you to understand a little of human nature by studying history, and then you'd begin to see what a mess we humans make of things whenever we try living in cities and organising each other's lives. Now that's inspirational stuff; you get this sort of heady, dizzy feeling that comes with moments of great insight. But all it'll do is depress you and make you want to pack in trying to be a good citizen and go live in a jar. Instead, I suggest you take my word for it when I tell you that wisdom – which is just another way of saying "the truth" – isn't something you want any truck with. Keep well clear of it; sell it to other people if it'll make you a drachma, by all means, but don't think of trying it yourself. No, what I imagine you want to learn is something useful and helpful, the sort of thing that'll earn you a living and keep you safe and warm in later life. What do you think?'

'That sounds eminently reasonable,' I said.

'Good, because it so happens that that's what I'm eminently qualified to teach you. I can teach you the opposite of wisdom, which is folly, and the opposite of truth, which is lying. Deal?'

I looked at him gravely. 'Deal,' I said.

'Good lad.' He looked round to see who was passing by, then looked back at me. 'All right,' he said, 'what do you want to be when you grow up?'

'I'm sorry?' I replied, puzzled.

'You heard me,' Diogenes repeated. 'What do you want to do for the rest of your life? Farmer? Speechmaker? Mercenary soldier? Do you want to be the man who goes round with a mop and a bit of rag cleaning out the baths when everyone's gone home? Or would you rather be the King of Persia, say, or the Dictator of Syracuse?'

I smiled. 'It isn't as easy as that,' I said. 'There's some things I can't be, however much I'd like to.'

Diogenes frowned. 'Why not?' he said. 'You're not thinking clearly. All right, let's be scientific about this. What do you, me, the blind man who sells sausages outside the Theatre of Dionysus and the Persian governor of Ionia all have in common?'

I scratched my head. 'I don't know,' I admitted.

'For a start,' Diogenes replied, 'they're all featherless bipeds.'

I assumed that was a joke, but he was serious. 'Well, of course they are,' I replied. 'They're all people. Human beings. But then, so's everybody.'

'True,' said Diogenes. 'So's everybody.' He stood up, not bothering to crouch. I hadn't realised how tall he was. 'And if they gave out prizes for meaningless generalisations like they do for plays, they'd be draping both of us in garlands right now. The hell with this, let's go and earn some money. It's not as worthy or admirable as sitting in the shade all day talking drivel, but—' He suddenly crouched down beside me and lowered his voice. 'Can you keep a secret?'

'Of course.'

'It's more fun.'

I looked at him. 'I'm not sure I agree,' I replied.

He sighed, crossed his legs and sat down in the dust. 'That's the trouble with you people, no sense of wonder, no appreciation of magic and the supernatural. That's why your vision's so limited.'

I frowned. 'Sorry,' I said, 'I'm confused. I thought you were talking about money, not magic.'

'I was.' He lowered his voice again; later I came to recognise that stage whisper of his as a sign that I was about to be made a fool of. 'All right, how about this? Suppose I was to tell you that there's a special magical talisman, an artefact with the power to make people give you anything you want, do whatever you tell them to. Interested?'

'I would be,' I replied. 'If I thought such a thing existed.'

'Oh, it does,' Diogenes said. 'And what's more, I've got one.'

'Really?' I was young, remember. 'I don't believe you.'

'All right, I'll prove it to you.' He jumped up and started to walk away. I had to run to keep up with him.

'Where are we going?' I asked.

'You'll see.'

As we walked, he kept on about the extraordinary powers of this talisman of his. Not only could it make people obey you, so that they could refuse you nothing; it could even make them like you. Love you, even. In spite of myself, I was getting interested; but Diogenes was walking so quickly that I didn't have enough breath to ask questions with. With his special magical artefact, he continued, he could move mountains – literally, he could cause a mountain to be taken from one place and put down in another. He could create cities, destroy them; he could feed and clothe all the starving poor, or he could enslave a whole nation; the virtue of its magic was such that it could carry him across the sea, take him to the most remote corners of the world, from the Isles of Tin in the far west to the furthest reaches of Sogdiana . . .

We'd stopped in front of a baker's shop.

'But to start with,' he said, 'let's do something easy. Watch carefully. I'm going to make the baker give me a loaf of bread.'

'All right,' I replied.

He nodded resolutely, walked over to the baker's window and tapped on the sill.

'Good morning,' he said, 'I'd like a quarter-measure loaf. Wheat, not barley.'

'There you go,' the baker replied. 'One obol.'

Diogenes opened his mouth, fished out a coin (we used to carry our small change in our mouths back then) and put it down on the sill. 'Thanks,' he said, and walked back to where I was standing.

'Satisfied?' he said.

'But you didn't do any magic,' I protested. 'You *bought* the loaf.'

'That's right,' Diogenes replied. 'With my magic talisman.'

I didn't say anything; didn't seem to be much point. After all, that was just *silly*.

'You'd be amazed,' he went on, talking with his mouth full as we walked back to where he'd left the jar, 'at how much magic we're all capable of.'

'Really,' I said, sulking.

'Oh, yes. For instance, I can make water go uphill.'

I frowned. 'Really? No fooling?'

'No fooling. Of course, I need my magic talisman.'

I could feel a headache coming on. 'Oh, no,' I replied. 'You can't pay water to flow uphill.'

'No, but you can buy a jar to carry it in.'

That was so silly that I was about to say something rude. But I didn't. In fact, I didn't say anything.

'Magic,' Diogenes went on, 'is easy. Just like most things in life. The trick lies in persuading people that they're difficult.'

I stopped where I was. 'All right,' I said. 'I think I can see what you're getting at. You're saying that . . .' I paused, trying to find the right words. 'What a thing is depends first of all on how we define it. You defined magic as being able to make people do things, but you didn't exclude paying them money from the definition. That's how you were able to trick me.'

He shook his head. 'No trick,' he said. 'You made it difficult for yourself, that's all.'

'But,' I insisted, 'some things really are difficult, because – well, they just are.'

He smiled. 'Really? Name one.'

'All right.' I thought for a moment. 'Flying through the air.'

He shook his head. 'No. I can do that.'

'Oh, yes?'

'Honestly. I give you my word. Put me on a mountain or on the top of the old tower in the Potters' Quarter, and I promise you I can fly through the air.'

He said it so convincingly that for a moment I believed him. 'Really?'

'Oh, yes.' He grinned. 'Just not for very long, that's all.'

My brother Eudaemon loved playing soldiers. I can picture him now, with his wooden sword and the shield my father made for him out of a torn cloak stretched over a vine-sapling frame, charging up and down the rows in the small vineyard on the slopes of Parnes, chasing invisible Spartans. Well, I say they were invisible, and for sure I can't see them any more, but in those days they were as plain as day (I was five at the time, and Eudaemon was seven). The difference between us was that while Eudaemon sallied forth to meet them, one small boy against a thousand fire-breathing hoplites, I tended to hide behind the old fig-tree until they'd gone.

My father's attitude towards my brother's martial aspirations tended to vary from day to day, depending on circumstances. For instance, when Eudaemon soundly defeated a phalanx of newly planted olive saplings (they outnumbered him thirty-five to one but eventually he overcame and beheaded them all), Father chased him three times round the terrace and broke his stick over Eudaemon's shoulders when he finally caught up with him. On the other hand, when one of our neighbours asked Eudaemon what he wanted to be when he grew up and Eudaemon immediately answered 'a soldier', Father nodded sagely and said there were far worse careers for an ambitious young man of good family. Later, I found out the reason for that reaction, and it's a salutary lesson for anybody who tends to read books.

It was many years later, after Father's death, and we were going through the box he kept his books in (he had well over twenty of the wretched things) with a view to sharing them out between us and maybe selling any that were worth money. While the rest of us browsed happily, snatching the rolls out of each other's hands and reading bits aloud in silly voices, Eudaemon grimly worked his way through all of them till he found the one he was looking for, then stuffed it inside his tunic and hurried away. Well, naturally we couldn't let that pass without finding out what it was that meant so much to our dear brother (we assumed it must be something with naughty bits in) and we left off fighting over the other books and persecuted Eudaemon until we'd managed to get the book from him. But it wasn't dirty poetry or anything like that; it was a scruffy and well-used copy of Xenophon's *Persian Campaign*, a most dangerous and pernicious thing as I'll explain in a moment. Anyway, we tried teasing Eudaemon about this, but he got so angry and so violent that we had to give it back to him before he hurt somebody.

You, my ignorant young friend, don't know the celebrated Xenophon from a stick of rhubarb, so I'd better tell you a little bit about him; because if anybody was to blame for all the things that eventually happened, it may well have been him. Xenophon was a mercenary soldier, one of those sad, nasty people who were unaccountably still alive at the end of the War – sorry; the Great Peloponnesian War – and lacked the patience to wait around at home till the next war began. Instead they went toddling off to Persia to fight for young Prince Cyrus against his brother, the rightful king. Of course, it was a complete and utter fiasco, Cyrus' army was beaten; his Greek mercenaries, about ten thousand of them who survived the war, found themselves stranded deep in the heart of the Persian Empire, which at that time stretched from the Greek border as far as the edge of the known world; as if that wasn't enough, all the Greek army's senior officers were lured to a banquet by the local Persian representatives and murdered. Awkward, to say the least. At this point, our hero Xenophon (an Athenian, needless to say) was elected commander-in-chief by his fellow desperadoes and proceeded to march them home, from Cunaxa, where the Tigris meets the Euphrates, across deserts and mountains and all manner of other romantic and godforsaken terrain, through Media, Armenia, Pontus, Paphlagonia (it goes without saying that we had only the vaguest notion where the blazes any of these places were, but that didn't matter; they sounded fantastic) until finally reaching the Bosporus, which was effectively home. Every step of the way, according to Xenophon's insidious little book, they fought and made mincemeat out of hordes of Persian warriors, shrugging off their vastly superior numbers like an ox dispersing a cloud of flies with a shake of his head and a contemptuous flick of his tongue.

All this happened about fifteen years before I was born, and if it hadn't been for Xenophon's unfortunately compelling way with words, it'd have gone the way of all the other battles and wars in which foreigners have beaten Greeks and been forgotten about and buried. No such luck. To my father's generation, who'd grown up at the lowest point of the War and lived through our defeat and the fall of the democracy, Xenophon's escapade was incredibly significant and inspirational. If Greeks stopped killing Greeks, they said, and started killing Persians instead, there was no limit to what we could do. All the wealth and power of the Great King's empire could be ours. The Persians were weak, effete, apples ripe and hanging heavy on the branch waiting to be picked or fall of their own accord. And so forth. It didn't help matters that Xenophon's pirate band was made up of men from all over Greece, Athenians and Spartans and Boeotians, deadliest of enemies during the War but now comrades-in-arms taking on the whole world and winning . . .

If it made sensible grown-ups go a bit crazy, think of the effect this tripe had on my poor brother, with his vine-prop spear and his home-made scrap-leather helmet with a single tatty crow's feather for a plume. Apparently my father had been polluting his brain with it for years, reading it to him as a special treat in return for extra chores and double shifts breaking up clods of earth on the terraces. It's easy enough to imagine the scene; there's Eudaemon with his mattock, too big and heavy for a boy his age but that's all part of the challenge; every recalcitrant chunk of dirt and tree-root is the head of a Persian soldier, a Mossynoician peltast or a Bactrian-camel-rider or even an Immortal of the King's own guard. And every blow would send a shudder of pain down through his elbows, jarring his spine and making his head ring, until his eyes glazed over with berserk fury and he slashed wildly at the ground, striking great showers of sparks off stones and never ceasing from smiting and smiting until at last he missed his aim completely and knocked the head off the mattock against the trunk of a tree . . .

You're reading this, Phryzeutzis, and wondering why on earth I'm making such a big deal out of this. Among your people, you're about to remind me, a boy practises every day with his bow as soon as he's old enough to string it on his own. By the time he's twelve years old he rides with the fighting men when they go cattle-rustling; by fourteen he'll either have killed some other miserable little kid or been killed himself. Yes. Well.

I suppose it's different for you – I mean us – here at the end of the world. You don't recognise childhood as a sovereign nation among the ages of Man. Children are just adults who haven't finished growing yet; the fact that they can't do as much work is offset by the fact that they need less food, and so they're tolerated until they're fit to be deployed, so to speak. It's a different attitude from ours, theirs, the Athenian way of looking at things, and I'm too old now to care whether it's better or worse. Let's just say that since Eudaemon was a little Athenian boy, and little Athenians don't have to bring home the severed head of an enemy warrior in order to prove they've graduated to adulthood (we have a little ceremony with music and cakes and an embroidered tunic instead), then I hold by my assertion that encouraging his obsession was the wrong thing to do.

Where was I? Oh, yes. Eudaemon wanted to be a soldier; so Father set about trying to find a soldier to apprentice him to. Now, we Athenians didn't have anything like a standing army (the navy was different, as I think I explained earlier) and we were getting into the pernicious habit of hiring mercenaries whenever we needed people killing in bulk, rather than putting on bronze underwear and doing the job ourselves. I think that was what my father had in mind when he talked about soldiering being a worthwhile career for a young man of good family; true enough, some mercenaries were making good money, and somehow or other professional soldiering managed to escape the working-for-someone-else stigma (probably because the average mercenary worked for himself first and whoever was paying him a poor second).

Anyway, there was one mercenary living near us, an extraordinary fellow by the name of Bias – an appropriate name, it means 'violence'. He was a sight to see, Bias was, on a fine spring morning. In retrospect, I suppose he was a walking advertisement for his own prowess. He used to go down to the market every morning in his fanciest armour – mirror-polished Boeotian helmet, corselet of gleaming gilded scales, silver-plated greaves clipped round the calves of his legs, and a whacking great Thracian cavalry sabre bouncing up and down on his hip, regardless of whether or not carrying arms in public happened to be illegal that week. People used to stop and stare at him as he bought his pint of sprats (he tended to carry them home in his helmet) and if anybody was so ill-advised as to stop him and admire a particular item of his outfit, he'd gladly spend an hour or so telling them the whole gory history of where he'd acquired the piece, who it had formerly belonged to and how, in graphic detail, he'd killed the previous owner. All Bias' clobber was taken from the bodies of his slain foes, of course, prizes of war (or, if you prefer, second-hand); the idea being, I suppose, to advertise his excellence in his chosen profession and designed to create opportunities for sales pitches. I remember when I was a kid skipping along behind him trying to spot the hole in the backplate whose previous incumbent he'd reportedly kebabbed with a javelin at no fewer than forty paces; there was no trace of a puncture-mark or a brazed-on patch, so I guess he must have had it invisibly mended.

In due course my father apprenticed Eudaemon to this remarkable person. Money changed hands, and Eudaemon went to live at Bias' house. Now, it occurred to me that, for someone who made his living fighting in wars, Bias spent an unconscionable percentage of his time at home in Athens, where there weren't any. For all his splendid outfits and stirring tales of valour, Bias never actually seemed to do any fighting, and therefore didn't seem to me to be a suitable person to teach our kid the warrior's trade. I mentioned this to Father and got a thick ear for my pains, appropriately enough. But time went on, and whenever Eudaemon was allowed home for a visit (he lived about two hundred yards away) I got the impression from what he told us that he was receiving a first-class education in the noble arts of armour-polishing, sword-burnishing, cloak-darning and cleaning mildew off leather, but that was about as far as it went. Eudaemon, of course, was fiercely loyal, as you'd expect a soldier to be. According to him, a man's got to look after his kit if he expects his kit to look after him, and no soldier's worth a damn who doesn't spend a substantial number of his waking hours bulling up metal and waxing leather. As it happened, this was confirmed by my father's recollections of his brief period of military service, many years earlier, which he spent either polishing his gear or getting it covered in mud while digging miles of trenches across a flat, uninhabited plain many miles from where the fighting was taking place; so he accepted the Bias/Eudaemon version of the military curriculum without question, and got annoyed with anybody who suggested that he was being taken for a sucker.

Nevertheless, rumours of the scepticism that was rife in the lesser members of our household seemed to have reached Bias, because he started giving Eudaemon lessons in military theory. All of these came out of a remarkable book (I wish I still had my copy, but it went the way of all flesh last year, when I needed some thin rawhide to mend a broken hoe) by a man called Aeneas the Tactician, whose qualifications for pontificating about the art of war seemed to consist solely of having written this same book. What Aeneas lacked in hands-on experience, however, he more than made up for in imagination. His book (and, therefore, Bias' lessons) positively teemed with cunning schemes and devilish contraptions for winning wars at a stroke and bringing the boys home before harvest. There were ox-powered troop-ships and mechanical gadgets that hurled rocks, there were dastardly ploys for deceiving the enemy (unless, of course, they'd also read Aeneas' book), there were stratagems and counter-stratagems and counter-counter-stratagems for the really advanced student. And, best of all, there were the bees.

Oh, gods, the bees.

Imagine you're trapped in a city under siege, with seventy thousand men camping out under your battlements, vowing to slaughter every living thing inside the walls. They have archers and battering-rams and siege-towers, not to mention plenty of food and drink. You, on the other hand, have a first-generation copy of Aeneas the Tactician, so there isn't anything to worry about really. Every day the enemy shoot and bombard and hammer away; you repel every attempt, sword in one hand and book of instructions in the other. Eventually, the enemy get depressed. Some of them start talking loudly about going home. Their general is getting worried, and consults his chief engineer.

No problem, the engineer replies. We can't climb over the walls or bash them down, so what we'll do is we'll dig a tunnel under the walls and then collapse it, bringing the walls tumbling down. The general smiles broadly and off the engineer goes, requisitioning buckets and organising shift rosters; and the next thing you know, your sleep is troubled by a sort of underground scratching noise, which is too loud to be cockroaches and too quiet for an earthquake.

Just in time, you figure out what's going on, and immediately consult The Book. Sure enough, there's the answer. It's wonderful. It goes like this.

First, find out as best you can where the enemy tunnel is. Then, dig a tunnel of your own to intercept it. When you're nearly through into the enemy's main shaft, you stop and go round the city collecting up all the hives of bees you can possibly find, stunning the vicious little creatures by puffing smoke at them with a portable brazier and a pair of bellows. Then you take the hives of drowsy but evil-tempered bees down your tunnel, break through into next door, sling in the beehives and seal the hole up quick. In due course the bees wake up with a foul hangover and set about finding someone to blame for their injuries. Since ten standard beehives contain something of the order of five million bees, life in the enemy's mines is likely to be unbearably exciting for quite some time. Once you've given your black-and-yellow-arsed allies a chance to do their stuff, you open the hole up again and flood the mines with smoke, enabling your men to get into the enemy's diggings and cave in the tunnels, leaving them the whole lousy job to do again.

I remember that the first time Eudaemon told us about this, I laughed so much I had to go outside and take deep breaths of cold night air to regain my composure, much to my brother's irritation. What, he wanted to know, was so damn funny about a thoroughly ingenious, utterly foolproof military manoeuvre? I replied that if he couldn't see the joke, I wasn't going to be able to explain it to him, and we left it at that. I may even have apologised, under duress, for my lack of proper respect. Of course, the next time I came across Aeneas' book – well, that'll keep.

So there we were, the sons of Eutychides, all apprenticed to our various vocations, all quietly chugging along with them to humour our father and not really giving much thought to the future. I knew, of course, that what I was learning from the illustrious Diogenes wasn't, in purely commercial terms, worth spit. I assume Eudaemon realised the same thing, deep down in his liver, and the same for the others as they played at surveying or banking or trading in exotic spices. It didn't matter really, because Father was fit and healthy and in due course we'd each marry a girl with enough of a dowry to make up the difference between our inheritances and what we'd need to bring in a decent living.

Time passed, though, and one by one all the gullible heiresses in our part of Attica married other people. This was annoying; it meant that our brides would be from more distant regions, which would mean a lot of traipsing about the countryside going from holding to holding – five acres in Pallene, seven more out as far as Marathon maybe, two more over Phyle way; grandfather Eupolis' inheritance had been scattered enough as it was without the further headache of subdividing it and then matching up the bits with more far-flung snippets. Before you ask, there was no question of selling inconveniently situated land and buying other land to take its place. In those days, that simply wasn't done; it'd be like selling the members of your family you didn't happen to get on with and buying someone else's sweet-natured aunt. Land, after all, was for ever; it was people who came and went. It was thinking like this that made the relatively straightforward task of making a living in Attica such a complex and difficult matter, and led the Athenians as a nation to turn their back on self-sufficient agriculture and dabble in world domination instead.

Came the time, however, when even the girls of our age in Acharnae and the back end of the Mesogaia were all married, but not to any of us. Naturally enough, we started to ask why. Generally speaking, Athenian fathers are only too delighted to get their daughters off their hands as quickly as possible, only just stopping short of giving them away, one free with every five jars of olives. It turned out, however, that my father, and our family in general, had acquired such an unhealthy reputation for eccentricity (because of my father's knack of apprenticing his sons to world-famous dead-heads) that nobody wanted to know us, let alone marry into our obviously jinxed house. Perhaps it would have been different if my mother had been alive (she died when I was three). She'd been the daughter of a very prestigious and respectable family – you could tell how grand they were from the fact that most of them were in political exile at any given moment – and I'm sure her people's solid reputation would have gone a long way towards undoing the damage. But once she died her family didn't want to know us, so that was no help. And of course the more obvious it became that we weren't going to be able to marry our way out of trouble, the more feverishly my father schemed and contrived to make sure we'd all be provided for. I tell you, he reminded me of a boy trying to untangle a ball of wool; the more he tugged and yanked at it, the tighter the tangles became, and the harder he pulled. It's something of a miracle, in fact, that we managed to keep things together as long as we did.

In the event, my father died as stolidly and disastrously as he'd lived. He was stung by a wasp during the olive harvest, and fell out of a tree. It was a singularly fatuous way for him to die; there wasn't any call for him to go shinning up trees at his age, but the slave whose job it was had bruised his knee and gone limping home, and Father was worried in case the wind blew the olives down (we were late with the olives that year, for some reason), leaving them on the ground, spoiling. So, being Father, he clambered up into the branches with his long stick for knocking the olives down, and he'd already cleared all the ones worth having; all that were left were a few small, hard specimens up in the high, thin branches, but (being Father) he was determined to show up the malingering slave by doing a thorough job. The wasp stung the back of his left hand, the one he was holding onto the branch with; I suppose he automatically let go, and went crashing down in a tangle of twigs and foliage, landing awkwardly and breaking his leg.

Now, that wasn't enough to kill him, Heaven knows; but he was alone out there, unable to move, with the sun setting, which meant that all our sensible neighbours had left the terraces and started home. And of course it would have to be the one night in the year when we had a freak rainstorm.

Normally, of course, we'd have realised something was wrong when he failed to come home, and gone out to see what the matter was. But of course we had a house at Phyle (house is an overstatement; it had been a house back in Grandfather Eupolis' day, but by that point it was four walls and a vague recollection of the shape of a roof, which we patched up with trimmings and branches whenever we had occasion to use it, for example during the olive harvest) and we naturally assumed that Father had decided to sleep there rather than trudge all the way back to Pallene.

He was still very much alive the next morning, when our loathsome neighbour Demonax found him and (grudgingly, we assume) helped him down the hill to our roofless, tumbledown house. That, however, was the limit of neighbourly charity as far as Demonax was concerned; he had olives to get in, and if Eutychides was fool enough to go falling out of trees and breaking legs, he should be grateful for a shoulder to lean on as far as the house, where undoubtedly the slave or one of the maids would show up before noon. So he left him there, wrapped in his sopping wet cloak, either failing to notice or failing to care that Father was developing a rare old fever.

Well, the slave with the bad knee tottered back up to the olive grove, saw that Father wasn't there, assumed he'd gone home and set about getting in the rest of the olives. He knew he was in trouble for sloping off the previous day, and was anxious to regain a bit of lost favour by putting in a full day's work. It was only by chance that he stayed so late at his work that he decided to stop over at the house himself; where he found my father, half off his head with fever, apparently having a heated argument with Grandfather Eupolis about the merits of Euripides' play *The Trojan Women*.

By this time, of course, it was too late in the day to think about trying to get him home, or even finding help. So Father had to spend the night there, with nothing to eat (the slave had only taken his own lunch with him, and of course he'd eaten that) and precious little in the way of warmth or comfort. As soon as it was light, the slave set off to find help. He made the mistake of hammering on Demonax's door. Our neighbour replied that he'd already wasted enough valuable time larking about with the old fool, and he had better things to do, etc. By the time the slave gave up and left, encouraged on his way by Demonax's two unspeakably ferocious dogs, it was already mid-morning, and by the time the slave had gone back home, found someone who'd listen to him (my feckless brother Euthyphron; hardly the person you'd choose to turn to in a crisis), organised a makeshift litter and some bearers, and slogged back out to Phyle, it was dark again.

By now Father was in terrible shape, so Euthyphron decided to take him home in the dark. I suppose it wasn't his fault that it rained again; it rains so rarely in Attica that the risk was practically negligible. But he'd been going back and forth to Phyle since he was a little kid, he shouldn't have got lost and spent the whole night wandering up and down, round and round in circles, until he finally blundered into the house at Pallene, soaked to the skin, about an hour before dawn.

Even after all that, you'd have expected Father to pull through. True, he had dreadful congestion in his lungs by this stage, as well as the fever, but this was Attica, where as a rule people generally don't die of a broken leg. We called for a doctor, and he came; a short, fat, busy little man from Halicarnassus who drained off an alarming amount of Father's blood in a series of little bronze dishes while mumbling prayers to Asclepius in a sing-song voice that nearly drove me round the bend. His considered opinion was that the real cause of the illness was the wasp-sting. Some people, he said, react very badly to being stung, and that's just how it goes. We pointed out that we kept bees, and Father had been stung more times than he'd eaten salted fish, but the doctor shook his head and said that bee-stings and wasp-stings had quite different effects and attacked different humours in the body. Then he siphoned off another jugful of Father's blood just to be on the safe side, charged us a drachma, and went home.

But we didn't imagine for a moment that he was going to die; we knew he was very ill, but the worst we anticipated was the inconvenience of having to hang around the house listening to him argue (with incredible bitterness, most of the time) with the ghost of his dead father when we all had work to do. I suppose the apprehension set in when we realised that none of us knew how the estate, the family business, actually worked. Oh, we knew about its component parts, but Father had always kept a firm and exclusive grip on the overall management of it all, and we didn't have a clue what needed to be done. Slaves and day-labourers kept turning up at the door wanting to be told what they should be doing, and we didn't know. It was utterly thoughtless of Father, we told each other, to be lying there raving like a loon when there was so much work to be done that only he could do. We knew whose fault it would be when he recovered and found that everything was in a total mess; there'd be no point trying to explain . . .

And then one of us raised the possibility – I don't think anybody said it in so many words – of what would happen if he didn't recover; what if he died, and left us all alone? At first that didn't bear thinking about, and besides, he wasn't going to die, so stop being so damn morbid. But time went on, and although his slanging match with our late grandfather grew steadily more vitriolic (we could only hear one side of it, of course, but we remembered Eupolis and were sure that at the very least he was giving as good as he got), his voice was getting steadily weaker. He didn't recognise any of us, or even seem to be aware that there was anybody there except his own father. When he started telling the old man that it was his neglect and mental cruelty that killed our grandmother Phaedra, we were all so embarrassed we got up and left the room.

He died on the seventh day of the fever, in the middle of a stream of abuse. It was the first time we'd ever heard him use that sort of language, or express himself so passionately about anything. In fact, after Grandfather died, I can't remember Father ever mentioning him (aside, of course, from this occasion) in anything except a vaguely respectful tone such as you'd use about some minor god you believed in but didn't actually know very much about.

Well, soon enough I expect to see him again – both of them, in fact – on the other side of the blind river, that drab and featureless place where we Greeks go when we die. I'll be able to ask them both what it was that passed between them that was important enough to blot out everything else from Father's mind in the last hours of his life. I've often speculated idly about what on earth it might have been. The prospect of satisfying my curiosity on this point is, in fact, about the only thing that reconciles me to the thought of death, which in all other respects has nothing to recommend it whatsoever.

CHAPTER THREE

▨▨▨▨▨▨▨▨▨▨▨▨▨▨▨▨▨▨▨▨▨▨

Athenian children, my illiterate young friend, are plagued from their earliest years by the poet Homer. For reasons which I have never and will never understand, we're required to learn vast acreages of his dreary masterpieces by heart, and anybody who can't or won't is immediately dismissed out of hand as perverse or just plain stupid. 'Ignorant little ratbag, doesn't even know his Homer,' they say, and reinforce their reproof with the backs of their hands.

Bizarre. After all, there's nothing in the *Iliad* and next to nothing in the *Odyssey* that's of any practical value to anybody; quite the reverse, in fact. Four-fifths of the *Iliad* is endlessly repetitive battle scenes, describing a style of fighting that would get you killed in less time than it takes to blow your nose if you tried it on a modern battlefield, and the rest of it's an extremely dubious, if not down-right blasphemous, take on the lifestyle and morals of our gods. There's some stuff about shipbuilding and carpentry in general in the *Odyssey*, I grant you; but as a guide-book it's been proven use-less time after time. The gods only know how many poor fools have set off to find all the wonderful places that Homer firmly asserts are out there, somewhere between Troy and Ithaca; according to those of them who've made it back in one piece, Homer got it wrong. As simple as that.

But there was one bit in the *Iliad* that made one hell of an impression on me when I was a small boy; in fact, it scared me stiff, and still does. I'm not talking about those comically gory descriptions of spearpoints coming out through the backs of people's skulls. They just make me giggle. The bit I'm talking about is the scene where Hector's off to join the fighting and Andromache, his wife, is urging him not to go. What'll become of me and the kids, she says, if you get yourself killed? There's nothing worse in all the world than the fate of a woman whose husband's killed in war. Suddenly, she's left on her own, with nobody to protect her. At best, the people she thought were her friends ignore her, at worst they come sniffing round like wild dogs looking for easy prey. And if the city falls, what has she got to look forward to but slavery and degradation at the hands of the people who killed her husband?

That sense of loneliness, of no longer being protected against the world by someone who you thought you could rely on to be there; I know how that feels. That's how we felt, my brothers and I, when our father died. For all our splendid and expensive educations, we hadn't got a clue what we were supposed to do. It was like looking down as you walk along and seeing that there isn't any ground, that in fact you're walking on thin air over a damn great chasm. All we knew was that with Father gone we were in deep trouble – we knew that because he'd been telling us so ever since we were children. Now, in spite of his best efforts, the very catastrophe he'd worked all his life to avoid had come about, and we were the ones who were going to have to deal with it.

My brother Eudaemon dealt with the problem by running away. He left without telling anybody on the morning after the funeral, taking with him my father's armour and sword (no great loss; after forty years of neglect they consisted of nine parts verdigris, one part force of habit) and all the badly hidden money, just enough to pay for a passage on a ship, if you didn't mind sleeping on top of the cargo. We tried to find out where he'd gone, and a friend of the family reported hearing that the mighty Bias (who vanished from sight at the same time, to the great sorrow of various creditors) had joined an army being raised by Philomelus of Phocia against the Thebans. It seemed logical to assume that Eudaemon had gone with him, and when we heard a while later that Philomelus and a large part of his army had been wiped out, we shot out urgent messages begging for news and offering a cash reward for any information, but no replies were forthcoming, not even obvious lies.

My brother Eugenes, easily summed up by the phrase 'hatefully pragmatic', pointed out that at least this meant one less brother to share the estate with. With Eudaemon gone, he explained as we sat under the old fig tree outside the back door at Pallene, we would now have just over seventeen acres each rather than barely fifteen.

'For gods' sakes,' interrupted my brother Eudemus (the sensitive one; apprenticed to Lysias the banker, and the only one of us with any real prospect of being able to make a decent living), 'that's a disgusting thing to say.'

'I'm just trying to be practical,' Eugenes replied irritably. 'Somebody's got to be, after all. Dammit, if it'd bring him back I'd willingly hand over my entire share to the King of the Centaurs, but it won't. He's gone, we're still here. And maybe, just maybe, that could make it possible to keep the family together, so that the rest of us won't have to go out risking our lives halfway across the world—'

'Do you really think so?' interrupted my brother Euthyphron. You may remember, he was the one who coped so remarkably badly with the job of getting my father home from Phyle. There was no malice in him, but he was an idiot.

'Well,' Eugenes replied, 'it's conceivable. Let's look at this scientifically, shall we?' He fished a wax tablet and a stylus out of the fold of his tunic. 'Now then, last year we got an average return of eleven medimni per acre on barley, twenty metretes per acre for the vines and two metretes for the olives. Very roughly, and not allowing for interplanting barley in the vineyards, we've got thirty acres suitable for barley, seventy acres of vineyards and twenty of olives and other general rubbish – Grandfather's beans, the great lupin experiment, other junk like that. Split seven ways –' he paused for a moment, scowling and counting on his fingers '– split seven ways, we each get four and a quarter acres of the barley fields, ten each of vines and two and three quarters of the leftovers, making a total of seventeen acres. Everybody with me so far?'

Eudemus was about to make another formal protest at the distastefulness of this conversation, but the rest of us shushed him. This was interesting.

'All right then,' Eugenes went on. 'Here's the good bit. Four and a quarter of barley at eleven medimni the acre is forty-seven medimni. Ten of vines at twenty metretes, that's easy enough, two hundred metretes. Two and three quarters at two, wet or dry – probably over-optimistic, but it doesn't make much odds anyhow – call it five and a half measures for ready money. Add those all up –' another pause while he did just that '– and the total for each one of us,' he announced triumphantly, 'is two hundred and fifty-two and a half measures each, wet and dry. Not enough for Cavalry class, sure, but we'll easily qualify for Heavy Infantry, and there's no shame in that, none at all.'

We looked at each other like men rescued at the last minute from a shipwreck. 'That's amazing,' said my brother Eumenes, more commonly known inside the family as The Human Weasel. 'Even splitting the estate up like that, we're all still rich. And that's all because Eudaemon took it into his head to totter off and get himself killed?'

'Hardly,' broke in my brother Eudorus. 'If Eudaemon was still here, we'd have fifteen each, not seventeen. By Eugenes' reckoning, we'd all still be producing enough to make Heavy Infantry. And there's the point. Father wasn't stupid, he could do sums just as well as Eugenes can, probably better. And he still thought we were done for. So what's changed?'

That was typical Eudorus; hence his nickname Apometeorus, that which descends upon one from a great height. He took a delight in exterminating optimism wherever he happened to find it, like a man clearing his barns of rats. The worst thing was, he was always right.

'I don't see that,' Eugenes replied. 'It's a matter of simple arithmetic.'

Eudorus shook his head. 'No, it's not,' he said. 'You're basing your argument on a false premise. Euxenus, you're the tame philosopher. Explain to your brother what a false premise is.'

Eudorus, I need hardly add, was also the eldest, which probably accounts for his pessimistic nature. He'd lived longer than any of us with Father's obsessive conviction that we were all headed for ineluctable destitution and poverty, and so it was a fundamental article of faith with him.

'I know what a false premise is, thank you very much,' Eugenes said. 'I just don't think I'm guilty of one, that's all.'

Eudorus sighed. He had the knack of making a noise just like an icy winter wind sighing through the eaves. 'All right,' he said, 'let me

explain it to you so you'll know better in future. You're basing all
these clever calculations of yours on these figures for average yield.
Would you mind telling me how you arrived at those figures? I
mean, is there any solid basis for them, or did the Muses tell them
to you in a dream when you were herding goats on Parnes?'

There was a slight crackle in the air, evidence of Eugenes painfully keeping his temper. 'Simple,' he said. 'I looked up last year's
census in Father's accounts, divided the yield figures by the acreages, and got the figure for the average that way.'

Eudorus nodded. 'Splendid,' he said. 'Obviously it didn't occur
to you that – to take an example at random – the long five-acre at
Pallene regularly gives us sixteen measures of wheat to the acre,
while Old Rocky at Phyle barely gives us six in a good year. Now
you tell me, brother. Which of us gets the five-acre, and who gets
stuck with Old Rocky?'

Needless to say, there was a loud and confused chorus of replies
to that question. Eudorus shut us all up with a ferocious scowl, and
went on.

'Another point,' he said. 'We get sixteen measures per acre off
the five-acre because we manure it properly. We can do that because we've got nine mules. We can afford to keep nine mules
because we've got a hundred and twenty acres. Now, if each of us
has seventeen acres, it stands to reason – or at least, it does in the
version of reality where I'm compelled to live – that we can't each
keep nine mules. In fact, we'll be hard put to it to keep one. And
what about labour? We get good yields because we plough three
times and we harrow and we break up the clods and we make sure
the terraces are kept up. When I say "we", of course, I'm referring to
the slaves; the slaves which our father, with typical fat-headed
generosity and respect for tradition, set free in his will. No slaves, no
work-force, no triple ploughing. Result: reduced yields. Face it,
brothers, the old man knew what he was talking about. This family's
finished in agriculture, and there's no two ways about it.'

There was a long, wretched silence; an invariable sign that
Eudorus had been talking. 'All right, then,' Eumenes piped up. 'If
you're so damned clever, you tell us what we should be doing.'

Eudorus sighed again, and I instinctively pulled my cloak up to
my ears to ward off the freezing cold wind. 'It's pretty obvious,
actually,' he said. 'But you're not going to like it.'

'You don't say,' Eugenes muttered.

(It's just occurred to me, my Scythian friend; I'll bet you're completely and utterly bemused by the fact that all my brothers' names begin Eu-. I'm afraid you're just going to have to live with it; we did. Once an Athenian family gets it into its collective head to have a tradition like that, you're stuck with it. Be grateful that at least all the names are different. In one of the oldest and grandest Athenian families, all the men were called either Callias or Hipponicus, and had been for a thousand carefully recorded years.)

'What we've got to do,' Eudorus went on, ignoring him, 'is this. The land is split between four of us – four only, no more. The other three will have to make shift for themselves as best they can. I know it's hard, but it's the only thing we can do. It's that, or sitting on juries for a living.'

This time, the post-Eudorus silence was very long and quite deadly. Eventually, Euthyphron, of all people, cleared his throat nervously and said, 'I agree with Eudorus.'

'Of course you do,' Eudorus said. 'Because I'm right, and we all know it. Now, how are we going to do this? I propose we draw straws, but we can fish for pebbles in a hat if anybody's got strong feelings on the matter.'

(You'll have noticed, I'm sure, that nobody once thought of suggesting that we do the really obvious thing, namely not split the estate up at all, just carry on living together as we'd always done with our nine mules and their abundant manure. Well, it's probably really obvious to you, and it's become really obvious to me now that I'm an old man who's seen the whole world and devoted his life to philosophy. But back then we were young. More to the point, we were young Athenians. It would never have occurred to us in ten thousand years not to divide up the estate, because that was what happened when a father died. Even Eudorus' suggestion was outrageously radical, the sort of desperate expedient people are forced into in the worst of extremes, like when starving men in a dungeon must either turn cannibal or die.)

In the end, we fished for pebbles in a hat. There were four black pebbles and three white ones. I have my white pebble still. A clever man I met in Propontis some years later managed to drill a hole through it, using a tiny sliver of sapphire as a drill-bit, so I could wear it on a string round my neck. I'd hate to lose it; after all, it's the only bit of my father's land I ever got to keep for my own, so I've had to make the most of it. Does that sound bitter, Phryzeutzis or whatever your barbarian name is? Of course it does, because I am bitter. I'm as angry and wretched and full of hate now as I was all those years ago, when I opened my fingers and looked down and saw a white pebble in the palm of my hand. There are still some mornings when I wake up out of a dream about home and realise where I really am, and start crying and crying until my chest hurts and I can scarcely breathe. I'm afraid that's what it means to be an Athenian, you see. We have this absurd devotion to our rocky, barren, evil-natured, dry, thin-soiled, infertile, poxy little armpit of a country, and that's what makes us so terribly dangerous when we're defending it and so utterly dangerous when we're deprived of it. There's an old story about the time when Xerxes the Great King of Persia invaded Greece with a million men, the hour of our greatest glory when we silly little Greeks killed his soldiers by the hundred thousand and threw him back across the Hellespont. After the great battle at Plataea, so the story goes, the Spartan king captured the Persian general's luggage and broke it open. He'd never seen the like; gold and silver tableware, silk and furs and tapestries, precious stones and ivory and sandalwood and all the legendary wealth of Asia, heaped up in obscene confusion on the floor of the general's tent. According to the story, King Pausanias stood staring at all this stuff for quite some time; then he scratched his head, turned to his second-in-command and said, 'It doesn't make sense.'

'What doesn't?' the other man said.

'These people have all this wealth,' he said, 'all this gold and stuff, all these *things*. Why in the gods' names should they risk their lives to come all this way and try to take our miserable, poverty-stricken little country away from us?'

(A good story, that; for all I know, it may even be true. Remember it, please; keep in your mind the expression on those thin Greek faces at the sight of all that luxury, that Oriental plunder. It might help you understand a bit of what comes after.)

On the day my father died, Queen Olympias of Macedon gave birth to a son.

In fact, it was a busy day all round. On that day, King Philip of Macedon won a battle; the Macedonian general Parmenio won another battle; King Philip's prize racehorse won its event at the Olympic Games; and in Ephesus, the world-famous temple of Artemis burned to the ground.

Philip and Olympias named their son Alexander. It wasn't the best-omened name they could possibly have chosen. The first King Alexander had collaborated shamelessly with the invaders during the Great War against Persia, and the second Alexander had reigned for barely a year. Shortly before she gave birth, Olympias (who came from the barbarous tribes of Illyria and kept live snakes as pets) was struck by lightning during a freak thunderstorm. It was a miracle she wasn't killed and didn't lose the baby. For many years, King Philip suspected the boy wasn't his son at all, and Olympias didn't help matters much by dropping heavy hints that the father of her child was a god, either Zeus himself or one of those strange and faintly ridiculous Illyrian gods-of-drinking-a-lot-and-falling-over, in whose honour the secret order to which Olympias belonged staged jolly little orgies, at which they drank themselves silly, danced naked round a campfire and tore living things (human beings, if they could catch any) into small pieces before stewing them in a cauldron and eating them.

I don't remember hearing about the birth of an heir to the Macedonian throne at the time; reasonably enough, I think. True, even that early in his career, Philip was starting to show signs of being a strong, innovative king with an apparently endless appetite for war and conquest, but it was still easily possible to ignore him. If you'd have asked me or my brothers to say who the King of Macedon was on that tiresomely eventful day, it's quite likely that we wouldn't have known.

'No more money,' Diogenes said with a sigh, 'no more lessons. Sorry.'

I was shocked. We'd spent so much time together, had so many long-winded debates about abstruse philosophical issues, that I honestly believed we shared some kind of bond of friendship. Besides, what had he actually taught me that anybody would possibly want to know? Nothing. And there had been a great deal of money, over the years.

'I'm sorry you feel that way,' I replied stiffly. 'I was under the impression that we'd gone past that stage.'

Diogenes raised one eyebrow. 'Really? How strange. Anyway, not much I can do about it now, not if there's no more money. Pity. I don't like leaving a job almost but not quite finished.'

That was a bit too much for me to let pass without comment. 'Come on, now,' I said. 'Admit it, you've taken me and my family for suckers. You haven't taught me anything.'

Diogenes scowled at me so ferociously I thought he was going to burst into flames. 'You little bastard,' he said. 'You ungrateful little snot. I've taught you everything you know about being human, and this is the thanks I get.'

'Not quite,' I said icily. 'You've had enough *thanks* from my family to buy a warship.'

He stood up. 'I don't think there's anything more to be said,' he replied. 'I forgive you for your disgusting behaviour; after all, your father's just died, so I suppose I have to make allowances. I'm just rather sad to see how little of what I've taught you has actually managed to penetrate that thick layer of bricks you call your skull. I'm disappointed, Euxenus, bitterly disappointed.'

And with that he walked away, a perfect study in sorrowful contempt. Fortunately, there weren't any stones or bits of broken pot lying about, or I'd have committed a crime against philosophy.

So there I was, a young man in his twentieth year, with no land, no skill or profession, no apparent means of earning a living; in precisely the situation my father had spent his life trying to avoid. If I'd had in my hand the money he'd spent on my education, I'd have been comfortably set up for life.

Having nothing better to do, I wandered through the streets towards the market-place, just as any Athenian in my position would do. There was once a Scythian, one of your countrymen, who lived in Athens for a while and then went home. When his neighbours asked him what was the most remarkable thing he'd seen in the Great City, he replied, 'The market-place.'

'Oh,' they said. 'What's that?'

'Well,' answered this Scythian – Anacharsis, his name was – 'it's a large open space in the middle of town set aside for respectable people to swindle each other in.'

A bit harsh, but there's an element of truth in it. Certainly, the market-place is one of the places in the City where Athenians go to get the better of each other, along with the Law-Courts and

Assembly. Come to think of it, quite a few of the landmarks of Athens are dedicated to the Athenian passion for doing down one's fellow citizens.

I sat down under the shade of an awning and tried to think of a way of earning some money. The prospects weren't encouraging. I had no goods to sell and no trade or profession to offer. Until the next census I was theoretically a member of the highest class of Athenian society, the *pentacosiomedimni* or Five-hundred-measure-men, eligible for the supreme offices of state; but my total wealth came to just under seven drachmas plus whatever somebody might be persuaded to pay me for my shoes . . .

True enough. But, outside our family, who knew about it? No reason why anybody should. In the eyes of my fellow citizens I was still a man of wealth and leisure. Once I'd grasped that, I didn't need to ask myself, *What would Diogenes do if he were in my place?* I already knew.

For an obol I bought one of those little jars of cheap, disgusting wine, and drank the contents to bolster my nerve. Then I looked around for a group of people, any group of people. As it happened, there were ten or so likely-looking types standing about reading the latest three-days-rations list; so I picked up my empty jar, wandered over and sat down under the list.

'Hey, you,' someone said. 'Get out of the way!'

I ignored him. He said it again. I looked up with a frown.

'Do you mind?' I said. 'I'm trying to concentrate here.'

The man who'd yelled at me looked puzzled. 'What do you mean?' he said. 'You're just sitting there.'

I deepened my frown into a scowl. 'Are you blind as well as stupid?' I replied. 'What do you think this is?' And I pointed to the jar.

'It's a jar.'

I sneered at him. 'It's a jar,' I repeated. 'For gods' sakes. If I was as unobservant as you, I'd climb the old tower in the Potters' Quarter and jump off, just to save myself further humiliation. Assuming I could find it, that is.'

Instead of getting angry, the man just looked more curious; like-wise the others with him. 'All right,' he said, 'what's so special about the damn jar?'

I grinned. 'It's not the jar, you fool,' I replied. 'It's what's in it.' I paused and furrowed my brows. 'Why am I telling you this, anyway? It's none of your business, go away.'

'Like hell I will,' the man said. 'This is the Market Square and I'm an Athenian citizen. Tell me what you've got in the jar.'

I shook my head. 'Certainly not,' I told him. 'You want one, go find your own. This one's mine.' I made a show of standing up and getting ready to leave; at once, the crowd (which had grown already) clustered round to stop me.

'Tell us what's in the jar,' the man said urgently. 'Go on, we aren't going to take it off you or anything. We just want to know what it is.'

'I'll bet you do,' I said angrily. 'But if you think I'm sharing my birthright with the likes of you, you're badly mistaken. Go to hell.'

The word 'birthright' caught their attention. Someone at the back called out, 'I know him, that's Eutychides' boy. You know, Eutychides from Pallene, the one who just died.'

'Thank you so much for reminding me,' I said bitterly. 'As you correctly pointed out, my father died a few days ago, and yes, this jar's my portion of his estate. Now go away and leave me in peace with my property, before I take you to law.'

Another one of them leaned forward for a closer look. 'Eutychides the Five-hundred-measure-man? And all you got was that little jar?'

I nodded. 'And what's in the jar. I won't warn you again, who-ever you are. Bugger off, before I do you an injury.'

There were about thirty people in the crowd by now; I judged that to be a sufficient number.

'Go on,' someone called out. 'Tell us what you've got in the jar, you rich bastard.'

I couldn't have asked for anything better if I'd written his lines myself. 'Who are you calling a bastard?' I answered angrily, taking care not to contradict the word 'rich'. The point wasn't wasted.

'You going to tell us what's in the jar, or what?'

'All right.' I sighed, and sat down again. 'All right. If you all promise to clear off and leave me in peace, I'll tell you. Satisfied?'

There was a general murmur of agreement, and they started sitting down too, with a certain degree of elbowing and shoving from those who wanted a better view. Thank the gods, I muttered to myself, for the abiding curiosity of the Athenians.

'My grandfather Eupolis,' I said, 'was a great friend of the cele-brated philosopher Socrates – probably the wisest man the world has ever known.' I paused for a moment. 'I take it you people have at least heard of Socrates?'

'Of course we have,' someone said impatiently. 'Get on with it, will you?'

'And if you've heard of Socrates,' I went on, 'you'll know about his tame demon, the one he talked about at his trial?'

(*Tame demon* is the best translation I can manage into this brutal, crack-jaw language of yours, Phryzeutzis; the Greek is *daimonion ti*, and it also means something like 'tiny piece of the essence of divinity'. But tame demon was what I wanted these people to think about.)

'Sure we do,' someone said.

'Right,' I went on with a nod. 'Well, after Socrates had been tried and sentenced to death, my grandfather went to visit him in prison, and took him a basket of figs and a little jug of wine. They talked for a while, and then Socrates asked my grandfather if he'd like to take the tame demon. Now, my grandfather was incredibly excited at this, because of course it was the demon who lived inside Socrates' ear and whispered to him all the incredible bits of wisdom that made him so famous.

'"Hang on, though," my grandfather said. "Will he stay with me? Or will he try and run away?"

'Socrates nodded. "Oh, he's utterly devoted to me," he replied. "He won't want to live with anyone else after I'm gone. If you want to take him, you'll have to find something to shut him up in, to stop him escaping." My grandfather looked round and saw the empty wine-jar. "Will this do?" he asked; and between them they managed to coax the demon out of Socrates' ear and into the jar. This jar,' I added, holding it up, 'where it remains to this day. Of course,' I went on, 'the demon hated being cooped up in a jar, so it always refused to say a single word to my grandfather, or my father after him. But when I was a little kid of about seven, I was playing in the house one day and I thought I heard a voice from inside this funny little jar.

'"Hello," I said. "Who's there?"'

'Well, to cut a long story short, the demon and I became friends; I didn't know anything about Socrates or any of that stuff, and the demon was fed up with sulking in a jar for years on end, not to mention as lonely as hell. So he was prepared to talk to me, though not to anybody else. And now that my father's dead and we've shared out his property, I've taken the demon as my portion. After all,' I added, 'it's worth a damn sight more than all the rest put together.'

There was a long, impressed silence; then someone said, 'I can see why that jar's a wonderful thing, but how come it's valuable? I mean, what use is a tame demon?'

I laughed. 'Are you kidding?' I said. 'A real live demon? *Socrates'* demon? The demon responsible for all the wisdom of the wisest man who ever lived?'

'Fair enough,' the man conceded. 'Actually, I did hear tell once that the demon used to tell Socrates where treasure was buried.'

I shook my head vigorously; last thing I wanted was a reputation for finding buried treasure. That way, I'd have people following me and bashing me over the head every time I dug a hole to shit in. 'Don't talk rubbish,' I said. 'Tell me, when did anyone ever see Socrates with any money? No, the sort of treasure the demon helped him find was a sight more valuable than mere silver. After all,' I added, 'it's an *Athenian* demon.'

That got a good laugh. Oh, sure enough, Athenians are as fond of money as the next man; they've sacked enough cities and sold enough children in search of it, Heaven knows. But ask the average Athenian you meet in the square which he values more, silver or wisdom, and when he says wisdom, there's a fair chance he means it. Or thinks he means it, anyway. Of course, what he calls love of wisdom is just this same curiosity. You've seen a cat sniffing at a pot lying on its side, tentatively reaching inside with its paw, then kicking at it, trying to get it to roll. That's how we Athenians regard the whole world; we can't let it alone, we have to keep on prying and poking and sniffing and batting at it to try to find out what's *really* inside. It's been our greatest strength and our undoing, this forever-yearning-after-some-new-thing, as the celebrated Thucydides put it. You can't honestly call it wisdom – personally, I'd define wisdom as knowing when to leave well alone – but you can see how the confusion arises.

'That demon,' somebody said, 'can you ask it questions?'

'Of course,' I replied.

'All right,' the man said. 'I'll ask you a question and you ask the demon, and you can tell me what he says.'

I shook my head and tried to look rich and objectionable. 'Why should I?' I said.

'I'll pay you.'

I looked offended. 'Get lost,' I said.

'I'll pay you three obols.'

'For three obols,' I answered, 'I wouldn't ask my demon what colour the jar is.'

'All right,' the man said. 'Four.'

'Go to hell.'

'Five.'

I hesitated, just for a third of a heartbeat. 'No way.'

'All right,' the man said, 'one drachma. A drachma for just one question.'

I looked down at the jar. I bit my lip. I frowned. I looked at the jar again. 'A drachma?' I repeated.

'A silver drachma.'

I sighed. 'Oh, all right,' I said, and held out my hand for the money. 'All right, what's the question?'

The man cleared his throat. 'Ask the demon,' he said, 'whether my new business venture's going to be a success.'

I took a deep breath, closed my eyes and lay down with my left ear pressed against the side of the jar. I stayed there without moving for so long that my left arm and both my legs went to sleep.

'Well?' the man asked eventually.

'Shut up,' I snapped.

'Sorry.'

When I couldn't stand the discomfort any longer I sat up, groaned (no need to fake that) and opened my eyes. 'You ready?' I said.

'Yes.'

'All right.' And I recited –

'*Woe to the neck of the dog, to the sharp steel claws of the eagle!*
Woe to the land where the pig is preferred to the natural son!
Further repent your grief, as the rays of the sun curl upwards;
Behold as the stone peels back, revealing the olive within.'

There was a long silence.

(Admit it, Phryzeutzis, you're impressed; it sounds just like the sort of thing the oracles of the gods come out with, and it doesn't mean *anything*. Or rather, it could mean anything you want it to, which is the secret of a truly great oracle. Let me confess: I was only able to do this sort of thing because my brother Euthyphron and I used to spend hours making the stuff up as a game when we were kids. He was better at it than me, so you can see how good he was.)

'That's amazing,' the man said eventually. 'How the hell did you know that?'

I shrugged my shoulders. 'I haven't got a clue what you're talking about,' I said. 'It wasn't me, remember, it was the demon. Did it make any sense to you? It sounded like complete rubbish to me.'

'Oh, no,' the man said vehemently; and he went on to explain. The dog, he said, was the Egyptian god Anubis, and that referred to the stake he was thinking of buying in a partnership trading wine for Egyptian wheat. The steel claws of the eagle were arrowheads (steel heads; eagle equals feathers equals the fletchings on the arrow) and arrows mean archers, and archers mean the King of Persia, because he's shown as a running archer on the backs of his coins; Egypt was a possession of the Persian Empire; so beware of Persian intervention against Greek trading interests in Egypt. The bit about the pig, the man said, was brilliant; it referred to Judaea, where they don't eat pork but where the Persian governor had just had to execute his own son for joining a conspiracy – hence the pig survives, but the son doesn't; the pig is preferred. Now, so far the oracle seemed to be advising him against the venture; but then it said *repent your grief*, followed by the bit about the olive being inside the stone, instead of the other way round – in other words, ignore your misgivings and do the opposite of what you were intending to do, namely not go ahead with the project. 'That's absolutely amazing,' the man repeated. 'Thank you. Now I *understand*!'

For about two heartbeats I just sat there with my mouth open, staring. I was dumbstruck. (For example, the pig and son bit – I just put that in because it sounded good; in Greek, pig is *huos* and son is *huios*. I didn't even know Judaea had a Persian governor.) 'You see?' I somehow managed to croak. 'Didn't I tell you?'

In the end I had to refuse their money and go away, to somewhere I could lie down in the shade and rest my aching head. I made fifteen drachmas in a couple of hours, but it was hard work;

not making up the drivel, but listening to the poor fools explaining why it was so absolutely right.

Mind you, the odd thing was that it *was* right, as often as not. For example, the man with the trading venture to Egypt made a point of seeking me out when he got back and giving me twenty drachmas and a solid silver bowl embossed with lions and goats; he'd got rid of all his stock and quadrupled his money, in spite of being quite viciously persecuted by Persian customs officials. He wasn't the only one to get an apparently spot-on oracle, not by a long way.

I think the gods have a sick sense of humour. I think that's how we know they exist.

CHAPTER FOUR

᪲᪲᪲᪲᪲᪲᪲᪲᪲᪲᪲᪲᪲᪲᪲᪲᪲᪲

'Now you've got some money again,' Diogenes said, 'we can continue with your education.'

We were sitting outside my house in the City, enjoying the sun. I'd had a busy morning – woken up at the crack of dawn by a nervous merchant, one of my regular customers, who hadn't been able to sleep after hearing a rumour about Italian pirates infesting the straits of Rhegium; next, another merchant (two thirds of my customers were merchants, either individual traders or shipowners) wanting to know if there was going to be any call for bone-handled bath-oil scrapers, because he knew where there was a consignment of twelve gross going cheap; a lovelorn middle-aged widow, desperate to know if her handsome young boyfriend was only after her money; another merchant... Not that I was complaining, far from it. By luck or innate shrewdness I'd stumbled on the secret of making money by fraudulent prophecy. It was quite simple: give the impression that you don't need the money and you actually find the whole business of forecasting the future both irksome and distasteful, and you'll have them queuing up outside your door.

'That's very kind of you,' I replied, smothering a yawn, 'but now that I've got the money I don't need the education.'

'Oh, really?'

'Really. Just ask yourself which one of us lives in a jar, and you'll see what I mean.'

Of course, Diogenes didn't really live in a jar, as I think I mentioned earlier. That said, he didn't live in a large, comfortable house a hundred yards back from the Painted Cloister, either; he had a cosy but definitely cramped little house just up the hill from the Mint, unhappily downwind of the Areopagus tannery. 'You forget,' he said, 'I choose to live in a jar. I'm like a snail, I carry my house with me wherever I go.'

'And you leave a trail of slime to show where you've been. Yes, it's a good analogy.' I poured more wine into his cup. 'I'll be honest, though, I owe it all to you. You taught me how to lie and cheat. I'm just better at it than you are, that's all.'

Diogenes smiled. 'Don't you believe it,' he said. 'If all I was interested in was money, I'd be so rich by now the Great King would be coming to me asking for a loan. That's the trouble with you, you judge people by your own pathetic standards.'

I nodded. 'That's right,' I said. 'Actually, though, you've raised an interesting point there. How shall I put it? We both share the same basic philosophy, yes?'

'The one you stole from me. Agreed.'

'The one my father bought from you.'

'Hired, not bought.'

'Whatever,' I said. 'We both accept the truth of the contention that a man can be whatever he can deceive his neighbours into believing he is; that's the fundamental credo of the Mysteries of the Yapping Dog. Now, I use this truth to take money away from fools. So do you, but only to a very limited extent. What is it you *do* want, Diogenes?'

He lifted his hat, wiped his forehead and put his hat back on his head. 'To teach,' he said. 'To disseminate the truth, both by word and example. It's all I care about. And that's the difference between you and me, Yapping Pup. You cheat people out of money in order to live and prosper. I do it to punish them, and by punishment to teach them. I don't swindle a man out of a drachma. I fine him a drachma for being gullible enough to pay me money.'

'Like you punished my father?'

He shook his head. 'That really bothers you, doesn't it? And yet he's one of the people I gave good value to; I showed you how to make a good living, which is exactly what he wanted.'

I thought for a moment. 'But you're such a useless teacher,' I said. 'Teachers show people how to lead better, more virtuous lives; how to be better citizens, how to be better at their chosen trade or vocation, how to be morally better—'

Diogenes made a rude noise, something he was very good at. 'That's not teaching,' he said contemptuously, 'that's propagating a lie. Teaching is showing people the truth.'

I smiled. 'And the truth is?'

'That human beings are basically foolish, wicked and cruel. That human aspirations are vanity, and human values of good and evil are shallow and false. That, when all is said and done, human beings are no better than the gods.' He finished off his wine and helped himself to some more. 'I'd have thought you'd have known that, a clever boy like you.'

'That's just Yapping Dog talk,' I said. 'Save it for the customers.'

He shook his head. 'Take it or leave it,' he said. 'Doesn't bother me. I tell the truth as I see it. You're perfectly entitled to be wrong if you want to; after all, this is a democracy.'

An ox-cart rumbled past, dangerously overloaded with jars of dried figs. I could see its axles bowing in the middle, so that the wheels slanted inwards. 'So you're saying that basically we're all no better than animals or gods, and anybody who pretends otherwise is a liar. And yet you taught me that I could be anything I wanted, anything at all. Even a god, I seem to remember you saying once.'

Diogenes nodded. 'That's right,' he said. 'Provided you lie convincingly enough. Use your logic, boy. If all human pretensions are lies, why be cheapskate and petty and lie on a small scale, when you could equally well tell big lies; Olympian lies that make you so tall you can reach out and scoop up handfuls of cloud? That's the point of what I'm telling you. Recognising the truth is all very well, but it doesn't get you anywhere, it's just depressing.'

'I'd agree with you there,' I said, 'if I thought it was the truth.'

'Be quiet and listen, you're getting free education here. I must be mad, telling you this for nothing. In fact, that's why you don't believe me, I guess. People never believe anything they haven't paid money for.'

'You're drifting away from the point.'

'Am I? Oh, yes. The point is,' he went on, closing his eyes and leaning back against the doorpost, 'that when enough people believe a lie, it becomes a sort of half-truth. It's like the way they build causeways in harbours; they cut down a hundred thousand trees, sharpen the ends and hammer them into the silt, all crammed up so close together that you can walk across them, even drive a cart. The causeway works; it does the job of dry land where dry land isn't but where dry land ought to be. Build a house on a causeway and pretty soon you'll forget that you aren't on dry land. But you're not. Your house is resting on the tops of twenty thousand log-ends jammed into the mud; and sooner or later that mud's going to wash away or subside, and your house is going to fall into the water.' He sighed. 'You ram a hundred thousand false ideas into people's minds, you'll get a structure firm enough to stand on, for a while. But it isn't real, and in the end it'll turn out badly, no way round that.'

'Not necessarily,' I said. 'If you do a proper job, make sure the foundations are really firm—'

'Then your house may stand for a thousand years,' he yawned drowsily. 'And people will come to rely on it so much that when it eventually falls in, they won't be expecting anything of the sort and so they'll all be drowned. But you'll be dead and long gone, so it won't bother you; sure, as far as you're concerned, the causeway gets the job done. It's true during your lifetime but it turns back into a lie for your great-great-great-grandchildren.' He opened his eyes and grinned. 'Now that's something you should be able to grasp, of all people.'

I shook my head. 'Doesn't follow,' I said. 'You're referring to Grandfather Eupolis inheriting all that property from people who died in the plague, and you're saying it's a lie that he was rich, because his grandchildren are back to being poor again. But Eupolis was rich; we've just fallen on hard times since.'

'Whatever.' Diogenes leaned back and let his hat drop down over his eyes. 'Maybe you're right and I'm wrong. Be reasonable; you can't expect me to use true arguments when I'm not getting paid. It's like the people who have speeches written for lawsuits; if they were telling the truth, they wouldn't need a lawyer.'

I'd been in the fortune-telling business for over a year by this time. As you'll have gathered, it was being kind to me. Still, I wasn't happy with it. I was caught in that strange little fold of society, people with money but no land, and I didn't like it at all. Most people in my position, my merchants and ship-owners and factory-owners, felt the same way, but there wasn't anything we could do about it. In spite of the fact that we had more silver money than many Knights, even some Five-hundred-measurers, we still counted as Oarsmen class; we couldn't hold political office or be on the Council, all we could do was speak and vote in Assembly. Now, in Grandfather's time, that was enough; Assembly ruled everything, and men like the celebrated Cleon effectively ran the City that way, holding no office but getting their way simply by making speeches that people liked listening to. Back then, in fact, it was a positive handicap to hold office, because if you did, you could be held accountable and put to death if something went wrong in the City's affairs, whereas someone who just spoke his mind in an Assembly debate was as free as the wind. Things had changed since then, though. There wasn't any specific law or statute you could point to, but the centre of gravity had definitely shifted; and people like myself were shut out, and didn't like it one bit. Not that it mattered a damn, of course; there were so few of us, and the share of the City's wealth that we controlled was negligible.

A substantial proportion of the unhappiness and evil in the world today is the fault of a man by the name of Dion, who was for many years the chamberlain, or chief adviser or grand vizier or what have you, of the mighty and absurd dictator Dionysius I of Syracuse.

Dion was, by all accounts, a noble and virtuous man with the soul of a poet and the mind of a philosopher; but I can't really explain about Dion without first telling you a bit about Dionysius, who's much more fun to talk about anyhow.

Dionysius was a ferocious, jolly man who seized power in Syracuse, the wealthiest city in Sicily, after a bloodbath and divided his time thereafter between screwing money out of his unfortunate subjects and writing plays, which he submitted to the Inspectors of Plays and Warships in Athens in the hope that one of them would be presented at the world-famous Dramatic Festivals.

There's a family connection here, of course, though I don't suppose you'll understand a word of what I'm about to tell you, poor ignorant Phryzeutzis. Here's a grossly simplified explanation.

We Athenians invented Drama. Drama is where a whole bunch of people dress up in masks and fancy costumes and get up on a platform in a special building called a theatre, and pretend to be someone else; invariably characters from our rich Greek heritage of myth and legend. In the course of this deception, they recite poetry which purports to be what the characters in the story say to each other, but which is in fact written well in advance by a poet and given to them to learn by heart. Most of the people who take part in these affairs are members of the chorus – there are about twenty of them and they all say the same words simultaneously (we're expected to believe that people did that sort of thing, back in our mythical past) – but the four most skilful poetry-reciters pretend to be the protagonists in the story, and they're allowed to speak on their own.

Dramas, or plays as they're also known, are staged twice a year in Athens, at two religious Festivals called the Lenaea and the Great Dionysia. For three days, every Athenian who can spare the time sits on a hard stone bench from dawn to dusk watching the actors and listening to the poetry; every day there are three tragedies (sad stories, which end with half the people dead and the rest utterly miserable) and one comedy (funny stories – *intentionally* funny stories – in which nobody dies, but unpopular people get beaten up with huge padded sticks fashioned to represent the male reproductive organ). My grandfather Eupolis was, according to himself, probably the greatest of all the Athenian comic poets; and to be fair to him, he did win the first prize on a number of occasions.

Dionysius, however, wrote tragedies – purportedly unfunny plays – which was appropriate for a Syracusan. In Sicily, you see, although they're utterly provincial and not really proper Greeks, they've always been mad keen on Athenian Drama; so much so that when Eupolis was stranded in Sicily as one of the very few survivors of the huge Athenian army sent to conquer Syracuse in the Great Peloponnesian War (they failed, miserably, and nearly all of them died; served them right, it must be said, since the invasion was utterly unprovoked and only undertaken in the hope of accumulating enough plunder from the obscenely rich Sicilians to help pay for Athens' war with Sparta), he managed to survive and escape capture in the heart of enemy territory thanks to his ability to recite by heart large chunks of the latest tragedies, as performed at the Festivals he'd himself written comedies for.

Dionysius was, by all accounts, a pretty competent writer of plays. But he wasn't Athenian, he was the ruler of a city that had more or less directly caused the defeat of Athens in the War, his philosophy of government was directly opposite to Athenian ideas of democracy, and on top of all that he was without question one of the nastiest pieces of work ever to hold power in a human community. As a result, his plays were always turned down flat by the Inspectors and never performed.

This annoyed Dionysius, but it didn't stop him writing; quite the reverse. Instead of having his plays performed in Athens, however, he had to make do with reading them aloud to his assembled courtiers, who were supposed to sit still and listen attentively, and then tell him how good they were afterwards.

Which brings us on to Dion. Now, Dion really did like poetry; he genuinely liked Dionysius' poetry. He'd have liked it even if Dionysius hadn't been his master and a psychotic killer. But one evening, during a reading of Dionysius' masterpiece *Iolaus*, Dion made the mistake of falling asleep. Dionysius noticed, and flew into a murderous rage. At first he ordered his guards to cut Dion's head off there and then; he changed his mind just in time, but only because it occurred to him that beheading was too quick and easy a death for someone capable of nodding off during a recital of the greatest tragedy ever. So instead, he sentenced him to hard labour for life in the stone quarries.

When this story was first told in Athens, a lot of people suddenly went all silent and thoughtful at the mention of the stone quarries of Syracuse. That's because it was those same quarries where the men taken prisoner by the Syracusans during the War ended up; suffice to say, none of them ever came back. Not one.

Somehow or other, though, Dion managed to survive in the quarries for three years, at the end of which time Dionysius relented, pardoned him and had him cleaned up, given a decent meal and brought back in honour to the royal court. And to celebrate his old friend's pardon and return, Dionysius announced, he was going to hold a grand banquet and read them all his latest play, *Niobe In Chains*.

Dion, looking rather thin and rather frail, had the seat of honour for the feast and the subsequent recital. Well, to cut a long story short he sat quietly through the first half-hour of the play-reading and then stood up and started to walk slowly towards the door.

'Hey,' roared Dionysius, looking up from his roll. 'Where the hell do you think you're going?'

'Back to the stone quarries,' Dion replied.

That was Dion; noble, fearless, a champion of truth and integrity, thick as a brick. Dionysius stared at him speechlessly for a couple of heartbeats; then he roared with laughter, tore up the manuscript and made Dion his chief minister. When Dionysius was on his deathbed (as a result, so they say, of the lethal dose of raw wine he gulped down to celebrate the news that finally one of his plays had been *accepted* by the Athenian Inspectors) he made him regent and Lord Protector during the infancy of the utterly worthless crown prince, who in due course became King Dionysius II.

The younger Dionysius was said by those who knew him well to be so bland and ineffectual a man that if you dissolved him in water and drank him, you'd hardly notice the taste; in consequence, Syracuse was ruled by the noble Dion, who announced as soon as the old reprobate had been safely reduced to charcoal on his funeral pyre that the bad times were over at last and henceforth Syracuse was going to be run along the lines of the most perfect state, namely the theoretical Republic devised and written about at interminable length by the celebrated Athenian philosopher Plato.

That's right: Plato, the featherless biped, Diogenes' habitual victim. Plato had been a pupil of Socrates, the legendary wizard whose little demon I pretended to keep imprisoned in my jar. After Socrates' death (he was convicted on twelve counts of being generally guilty, and quite properly executed; according to Eupolis, he was a veritable human toad) Plato set up a thinking shop called the Academy, where rich young men went to learn wisdom and stuff, at highly competitive rates. When not lecturing or putting up with Diogenes, he wrote books of philosophy, including this same *Republic* that Dion admired so much. In this celebrated work, he set out his idea of the perfect society; and to be fair to him, he did have a few good ideas. For example, in Plato's Republic, poetry was illegal. No poets were allowed inside the City, and all books of poetry were to be called in and publicly burned; specifically including (and this is why I've always had a soft spot for the old fool) Homer.

The main thrust of Plato's work, though, was that democracy isn't a terribly good idea (it was, after all, a democracy that executed Socrates). Instead, Plato's state was ruled by a king; but not just any king. Plato's king had to be a philosopher; in fact, he had to be a philosopher who was more or less bullied into being a king against his will.

Something tells me that it was this, rather than the stuff about outlawing poetry or abolishing families and replacing them with state-hired nannies, that appealed to Dion. According to Plato, the king/philosopher was to be supreme ruler, advised and guided by a select group of other philosophers who governed the people, who were to be treated more or less as slaves. I can see Dion reading this stuff and thinking *Yes!* Do away with ruthless oppression of the citizen body by a drunken, intemperate madman and replace it with ruthless oppression of the citizen body by a load of philosophers. Just the thing, and utterly Syracusan.

So Dion sent a messenger to Athens begging Plato to come to Syracuse and help set up the perfect society; and if he could bring along a couple of dozen other philosophers, so much the better. To his eternal credit, Diogenes, when asked, refused to go; but he was one of the very few who stayed behind. It was, Diogenes said, like the lancing of a monumental boil, as all the philosophers left Athens in a fleet of hastily chartered bulk timber freighters, sailing west to found the perfect society among the people who'd massacred their grandfathers.

For some reason, they didn't even ask me. But they made a special point of inviting Plato's most devoted and brilliant pupil, a man of my own age by the name of Aristotle; and that's why Dion's ghost deserves to rot for ever at the bottom of the Great Shit Lake in Hell, with giant seals gnawing his testicles. Aristotle; that sad, bewildered, ill-used, misunderstood, brilliant, pedantic little man, the cause of so much evil.

He wasn't Athenian, of course; he was the son of a doctor from a little place called Stagira, up north somewhere, and when he was young his father went to work for King Amyntas of Macedon, the father of the King Philip I've already mentioned. But young Aristotle knew what he wanted to be when he grew up, and when he was seventeen he made the long and dangerous journey south (oh, I can picture him, that thin, nervous, fastidious traveller, suffering the torments of the damned from dusty, rutted tracks and flea-infested mattresses) to sign up with Plato's Academy. There he stayed, not even paying any fees because he was so brilliant and so admiring, until the time came for the whole circus to move to Syracuse.

They had several good years there, playing perfect societies, until finally the Syracusan people (who'd put up with Dionysius, but who found that the one thing they couldn't take was too much per-fection) threw them out with prejudice and stuck young Dionysius on the throne. Dion escaped with his life, most of his philosophers and a new perspective on what was really needed for a truly perfect society, namely young Dionysius' head on a pole in the middle of the market square. Despite several attempts, he never quite attained this state of grace; but he did finally manage, with the help of some non-philosophical mercenaries recruited from the pirate bands of Rhegium, to throw young Dionysius out, make himself king and rule in absolute, blood-soaked perfection for a year or so before someone with a bad attitude towards wisdom in general slit his throat for him and brought Dionysius back, quite possibly (know-ing the Syracusans) in the misguided belief that he'd turn out to be as good a playwright as his old man.

Aristotle followed his master Plato home, of course, and for a while there wasn't quite so much talk about perfect societies and philosopher kings as there had been. Plato, in fact, never recovered from his bad experience. He lived to be nearly ninety, but he grew steadily dottier as he grew older, so much so that even Diogenes stopped teasing him. Aristotle stuck by him, out of loyalty and love and because the Academy was still a thoroughly sound commercial concern, until he died; but all the while Aristotle was thinking long, hard thoughts about such matters as human society and perfection and the sort of low-down, dirty little bastards who'd chased him out of cosy Syracuse. It was at this time that he evolved his theory of Natures, which states that every living thing has its own Nature, which defines its existence. You are, in other words, what you're born as; and everybody who isn't born a philosopher or a seeker after perfection is by nature a slave (*physei doulos*; it sounds so much neater in Greek).

Bear with me, Phryzeutzis; even after all this time, I'm still a devoutly yapping dog, or a Cynic as we came to call ourselves when we wanted to be a little bit more respectable (the word sounds impressive but it just means 'doggy'). None of it ought to have mattered, you see; it should just have been word-games, entertainments with lies, like King Dionysius' plays. It was Alexander who made the evil possible, but the fact remains, if it hadn't been for Dion, there wouldn't have been an Alexander, and I would be home now, in Athens, instead of here at the end of the world.

You know Pigface (I can't remember his real name and I couldn't pronounce it if I could), the big, burly man who trudges round the villages with that enormous basket on his back selling bits and pieces of trash to the country people? Well, he passed through this morning just before dawn (I expect you were still fast asleep, you layabout) and I saw that he had a few Athenian-made scent bottles in with the rest of his junk; I could only just see the necks, poking up out of the straw and felt they were wrapped in, but I'd recognise Attic ware at night down a mineshaft. Well; I guess that means the place is still there, or it was a few months ago, when those pots began their commercial odyssey. I don't suppose the man who made them ever imagined they'd end up out here, right on the pie-crust of the world. You could say the same about me, too, of course.

There are parts of your life that move slowly, like goats going back up the hill after they've been milked – childhood, of course, and bad experiences, like being in the army or a nasty illness – and there are other parts that skim by, like swallows or kingfishers. As often as not they're the good times, or else those parts of your life where one day was just like another, you had somewhere to sleep and enough to eat, and you were like a man with an old mule yoked up to his cart, letting him find his own way home.

My years as a jobbing oracle to the wealthy and gullible traders of Attica passed like that – zip, all gone, and before I knew it I'd stopped being a cocky kid and weathered into a minor landmark, a very small part of Athens. What happened to me during that time, I wonder? Well, I did get married.

Her name was Myrrhine, and the thing that most attracted me to her was four acres of mature vines in the Mesogaia. They were good vines; south-facing, well dug-in and laid out so as to leave enough room to plant useful raps of barley between the rows (which not only supplements your cereals yield and makes the most use of

precious land, but also slows the growth of the vines and so produces better grapes). Her father even threw in the complete set of
vine-props – a worthwhile consideration at the time, when good,
seasoned ash prop-shafts were at a premium, what with all the good
timber being used up by the spear-makers. Also included in the deal
were two big wicker baskets for harvesting the grapes. I couldn't
persuade him to include the pressing-vat, but I got it at cost, with
a pruning and grafting knife on top as luck-money (but it was
worthless; the blade was bent and I never could get it to keep an
edge).

Myrrhine herself – well, she was sixteen when we got married,
and I was eight years older. Her father was solid Heavy Infantry
class, with one serving son (the other had been killed in the Theban
war) and an honest enough man according to his lights. Certainly,
nothing he told me about Myrrhine was a lie.

She ate. Non-stop. Incessantly. You don't see fat people in Attica
as a rule; those of us who can afford to get fat don't, because your
upper classes of society have all been taught the Athenian doctrine
of beauty. It's a linguistic thing, I fancy; our word for 'beautiful' is
also the word for 'good', and 'ugly' also means 'bad', and the words
also have political meanings that you simply can't bleach out of
them – *kalos* means beautiful, good and upper class, *aischros* is ugly,
bad, common. In consequence, we can't imagine things being any
other way, because we can't find the words to express it. I tell you, it
plays merry hell with light comedy; the best-loved and most-used
plot in modern comedy is rich boy meets lovely peasant girl, they
fall in love, his dad won't let them marry, your variation on the
theme here, and at the end it turns out that she's not a peasant after
all, she's a rich man's daughter who was snatched from her cradle
by an eagle or stolen by pirates or some such trash – it's got to be
that way, or else if she's an Oarsman's daughter, how can she
possibly be pretty?

Yes, I know I'm hedging round the subject. It's deliberate. I feel
really uncomfortable telling you about this, because it's a part of my
life I'm not particularly proud of. Not that I did anything wrong. I
married her for the dowry, and I was the only husband they could
get for her, even with five acres. I fulfilled my part of the bargain by
taking her off her father's hands and keeping her housed, clothed
and fed (the latter element being no trifle, I'm here to tell you). She

didn't expect anything more out of the arrangement and that was just as well. I wasn't cruel or horrible. I just kept out of her way, which wasn't a problem for me. I took to giving consultations on the steps of Hephaestus' temple, and when I wasn't working I was out at the vineyard – that is, I spent about as much time at home as the average Athenian husband, who gets up an hour before dawn and goes out to the fields, comes home when it's getting dark and very soon afterwards goes to sleep.

But I know I made a bad job of the marriage, and it was for the simple reason that outside of the dowry, she didn't interest me in the least. The gods alone know what she found to do all day; we had a houseboy for the domestic chores, and she simply couldn't spin or weave to save her life, though she tried so desperately hard (but wool costs money, and she wasted so much of it I had to stop her trying). I think most of the time she just sat and ate, great handfuls of the coarse, dry barley bread I bought in the hope that it would discourage her (but no; even the stale ends I got cheap were always gone by the time I got home), washed down with a substantial proportion of the yield of her dowry. She had a little bird in a cage for a while, but one day I came home and it wasn't there any more. The houseboy tried to convince me she'd eaten it, but my guess is she let it out for a fly round the room and it got away. That'd be entirely possible; she was the clumsiest person I ever knew, except for Aristotle of Stagira.

She lived to the age of nineteen and died in childbirth; poor girl, she desperately wanted a baby, it was the only thing she ever asked of me, and it killed her, as everybody said it would. They told me that because she was so obese, her heart would never stand the strain of labour. Unforgivably, my main reaction when they told me she was dead was exasperation (*serves her right, she should have listened*), followed immediately by the numb despair caused by the knowledge that if she died childless the dowry reverted to her father.

So that was my career in husbandry, so to speak, and a fine mess I made of it. Diogenes summed it up perfectly. 'You put in just the right amount of effort,' he said, as we walked back together from the funeral, 'but you made a mess of the proportions. If you'd spent a bit more effort on the girl and a bit less on the vineyard, you'd be a father and a man of property today instead of a—'

'Thank you,' I interrupted. 'And thank you very much for waiting till now to point it out to me.'

He shrugged. 'I was thinking of her,' he said. 'She's gone safely home now. It'd have been wrong to keep her here just to spare you from feeling guilty.'

I didn't speak to Diogenes for a week after that; but for once I believe he was being sincere, not just trying to be annoying for effect. I don't know; where the monstering stopped and the philosophy began, I don't think even he knew most of the time.

What else did I do during that time? Well, I became a philosopher. Sounds grand, doesn't it? But in Athens in those days you were a philosopher by default; if you could tell your right from your left without tying a hank of straw to your left foot and you weren't a total recluse, sooner or later you'd find yourself talking philosophy with someone or other, in the queue at the cheap fish stall or while you were waiting for your shoes to be mended.

In Eupolis' day it had been plays; all Athenians were crazy about the theatre, they followed it avidly, the way you people follow the horse-races and the archery leagues and the cockfights, only more so – there's much more to discuss and argue over in Drama than there is in cockfighting. But the love of the theatre gradually petered out after the War. They stopped writing Eupolis' kind of comedy, the topical satires, and turned to the wishy-washy love-stories we're stuck with nowadays, while tragedy died for lack of interest, because everything had already been said. So the Athenians, always yearning for something new, turned their enthusiasm towards philosophy, and soon enough they were even starting to get it muddled up with religion, which made it even more addictive.

Now, philosophy for its own sake interests me about as much as watching iron rust, but I am (as you may have noticed) a garrulous sort, fond of nothing so much as the sound of my own voice, and since I was one of the Founders of the Cynic school of philosophy, the pupil of the one and only Yapping Dog, I'd have had a hard time steering clear of philosophical debates even if I'd been born mute or half-witted. Diogenes thought it was all desperately amusing, of course; it was clear proof of the validity of his theory of self-fulfilling bullshit, and he did everything he could to encourage it, sending earnest young men to follow me about writing down my maxims and apothegms on those little portable wax tablets that fit so neatly into the palm of your left hand, and attributing to me some of his wittiest and most profound (not to mention outrageous and blasphemous) sayings. I had the privilege of perfect strangers thronging round me in the street and not knowing whether they were going to fall at my feet or knock out my teeth. Still, it was very good for business and I'll be perfectly honest, I enjoyed it. Political and social philosophy was my forte, since you didn't need to know any arithmetic or geometry and you didn't have to go traipsing round naming species of plants or measuring shadows or finding out what causes volcanoes.

But I shouldn't, I really shouldn't ever have started taking it seriously. It was, after all, mere self-fulfilling bullshit, and I ought to have been on my guard about the self-fulfilling part. But it's such seductive stuff; you wouldn't be human if you didn't have your own pet theories on how to create the perfect society. Everybody does it; you do, Phryzeutzis, I've heard you. 'The world'd be a better place if we could all just get along together,' I've heard you say, and that's political philosophy, of the most pernicious and dangerous sort, I might add. Oh, it doesn't matter fleabites if it's just you saying it; but if someone who people listen to comes out with something like that – the triter the better, because it's easier to understand – it becomes invested with a thick furry pelt of profundity, and the idiot proposer of the notion gets a reputation for marvellously uncluttered vision and cutting clean through to the heart of the matter. And if the next thing he happens to say in an unguarded moment is along the lines of, 'The world'd be a better place if we lined up those damned Thebans and shoved 'em off a cliff,' next thing you know, the City's filled with men in armour trying to find where their regiment's supposed to be mustering, and you can't buy olives because the navy commissioners have bought the lot for the Fleet. Not to mention, of course, all the deaths and amputated legs and burned-out houses. Wonderful stuff, political philosophy; like strong wine, only cheaper.

But of course you know it'll never do any harm if it's you saying it, because first you're not important enough for anybody to take any notice of, and second, *you'd* never be irresponsible enough to say anything dangerous or inflammatory, like the other fools do. Oh, no. Never meant anything by it. Just harmless philosophy, that's all.

★

Of course, working conditions can colour your view of any trade or vocation. Think of the poor charcoal-burner, who spends his life with red eyes and tears running down his face, or the wretched man who works all day in the lime-kilns; or the sword-grinder, whose snot and spit come out like wet mortar because of all the fine grit-dust he breathes in as he sits behind his grinding-wheel. What about the scorched and blistered hands of the smith, or the shredded fingertips of the leatherworker, or the red-raw palms of the oars-man? The seamstress ends up blind, the potter's knees wear out, the tanner gets tanned himself, and as for the miserable creatures who work in the mines – well, if they were mules you'd have knocked them on the head and cut them up for the dogs years ago, out of simple humanity. The farmer, of course, plies many different trades and each one mutilates a different bit of him, from the top of his sunburned head to the verrucas on his feet after he's trodden the season's grapes, by way of his permanently stooped shoulders and hopelessly twisted back.

Worst afflicted of all, it goes without saying, is the poor bloody philosopher, who must exercise his calling at dinner-parties and drinking-parties, or huddled in the dust under the shade of a tree or a tall building. When he isn't being stuffed like a barn-yard pig with rich food, his host is trying to soak him to death in neat wine; and some of the couches you find yourself lying on are just instruments of torture in disguise, like the celebrated bed of Procrustes in the old fable. Gods help you if you fall asleep after a heavy dinner on the average Athenian dining-room couch; you'll wake up feeling as if someone had cut off your head while you were asleep and then stuck it back on with fish-glue without taking proper care to see if the seams were lined up just right.

But the physical pain and discomfort's nothing compared with the mental agony of a really protracted, seventeen-course dinner where your host fancies himself as a bit of a philosopher, and you daren't sit up and point out his deplorable errors of logic unless you want to find yourself out in the street before they've even brought in the mullet baked in cream cheese.

(Now, I've noticed, Phryzeutzis, that in these parts, the host of a feast or banquet provides all the food himself. The greater the ostentatious expense, the rule seems to be, the greater the prestige.

Foolish, of course, but logical. Where I come from, though, the tradition was different. At an Athenian party, all the host provided was the wine – but gods help him if it ran out – and it was up to the guests to produce the food. That's why you'd sometimes see those solemn little processions, headed by a kitchen slave bearing a huge dish covered over with a towel, as a gourmet shipped his dinner across central Athens in the cool of the early evening.)

And yet, just as pure refined silver comes out of the hell of the mines, so true philosophy somehow drains out of the endless boozy nights we philosophers spend in the course of our arduous vocation. I can best illustrate this, I think, by telling you about a dinner party I went to in Athens when I was just beginning to be recognised as a force to be reckoned with in the cut-throat arena of political theory.

Our host was a man called Memnides, a relentlessly generous patron of the sciences who'd made a lot of money in the Black Sea grain trade over the years. There were always one or two house philosophers lounging around at his place, mostly the philosophical equivalent of punch-drunk old boxers whose bodies and reactions are shot but who can still make a fight of it out of sheer technique and experience; men like Speusippus and Erastus, who'd been minor-league sparring partners of the likes of Plato, hard to injure as they'd long since spat out their last remaining tooth. Then there'd be young garlic-primed fighting-cocks like me, some new discovery from out of town, like Coriscus or Aristotle, and always at least one true heavyweight champion, such as Diogenes—

All these names are whizzing over your head like the first volley of arrows on a blustery day, when the archers are still trying to gauge elevation and windage. Don't worry about it; most of them live now only in the minds of old men like me with memories like a miser's barn, where nothing that's truly useless ever gets thrown away. And as for the few you'd be expected to have heard of if you were an Athenian, the truth is that fame and glory attach themselves almost at random in philosophy, with no more regard for merit or originality in their choice of target than a seagull's droppings falling from a great height. There were always plenty more to take the places of the ones who went down and stayed down, and quite soon you stopped trying to tell them apart and just thought of them by the categories they fell into – Platonist, Peripatetic, Cynic, what have you.

As was his custom, Memnides chose the starting point of the debate, and then let it go where it wanted, provided it didn't leave a trail of blood and bone all over the furniture. Because Diogenes and I were there, Memnides selected a topic that was pretty well certain to be political whichever way it decided to drift.

'If I was the Great King,' he said, 'and I was to say to you, here's five thousand families and enough money and goods to start a colony, where would you go and how'd you go about setting it up? Coriscus, your city's a fairly recent foundation, you should have some pretty clear insights into the process. What do you reckon?'

The part of me that wasn't groaning, *Ye gods, not again!* was happy enough at the choice of subject. It was one that the conscientious philosopher practised daily, the way a musician practises scales; as he trimmed his vines or dug over his trenches, he'd be polishing up his opening remarks or racking his brains for a new and original take on the stock elements of the argument. As it happened, this was a topic that had always appealed to me, in spite of its bone-crushing banality. It was one of the few subjects in political theory that actually interested me, but I tried my best not to let my enthusiasm get in the way of my professionalism.

'Well,' said Coriscus (the out-of-towner, you may remember, and as such the only man present who might conceivably have something new to say), 'I reckon we've got the balance just about right in . . .' (damned if I can remember the name of the place; it's nothing but a pile of overgrown masonry now anyhow, after it got under the feet of an advancing army in some war or other). 'We believe that we have the perfect blend of the three systems of government, monarchy, oligarchy and democracy. It all happened quite by chance, of course, but we found long since that there wasn't really anything we could do to improve on what good fortune had given us.'

'Really?' Memnides said. 'This sounds interesting. What happened?'

Coriscus smiled. 'A rockslide, would you believe,' he said. 'We built our Council Chamber on the south-facing side of our Citadel Rock, our version of your Acropolis, if you like. It's a sort of miniature mountain right in the middle of town with sheer cliffs on three sides, wonderful for defence and with a natural spring on top. Unfortunately there was some sort of fault in the rock where we built the

Chamber, because one day, quite without warning, it fell off the edge into the Basket-Weavers' Market with the whole Council still in it.'

Diogenes grinned. 'You're making this up,' he said. 'It sounds too good to be true.'

'You'd believe me if you could see the Citadel Rock,' Coriscus replied. 'Really, we should have seen it coming, but we didn't and that was that. Our entire government was wiped out in under a minute, and there was nobody left with the authority to hold elections or co-opt an inner council or nominate archons or anything like that.

'Well, once we'd hunted through the rubble and cleared up and buried the dead – quite a lengthy business, I'm afraid, we specialise rather in basket-making – we realised what a fix we were in. To make matters worse, we've always had something of a history of infighting, ever since foundation times. Originally, you see, the land all belonged to the descendants of the founding families, and they didn't let go without a fight. There were still enough of them left to form a substantial and influential lobby for returning to the original constitution, which was an oligarchy, of course.'

'I trust you didn't, though,' someone interrupted. 'That'd have been a retrograde step, surely.'

Coriscus nodded. 'Oh, we couldn't have had that,' he replied. 'The Geomoroi – that's what we called the founding families – were so unpopular with the trading community, we'd have had civil war. We do a lot of trade, being up there on the Black Sea, so there were enough merchants to make a difference.'

'So what did you decide?' Memnides prompted.

Coriscus held out his cup for a refill. 'I was coming to that,' he said. 'But first I'd better just mention how we arrived at our decision. After all, it has some bearing on what we decided, and proper scientific method—'

'Yes, yes,' someone interrupted. 'Get on with it. This sounds interesting.'

Memnides' young nephew took the empty cup over to the mixing-bowl and filled it up. When he'd returned with it, Coriscus carried on.

'Pretty well everybody was on the scene by this time,' he said, 'so the few of us who were still thinking straight sneaked round with the red ropes—'

'Oh, you did that too?' Aristotle broke in, scrabbling in his sleeve for those tablets of his, which go with him everywhere. 'That's interesting.'

(They were referring to the long ropes dipped in red paint which the Athenian city watch used to stretch across the market-place and then slowly carry forward just before Assembly time, to herd people out of the market square and into Assembly. Anybody who was dilatory about going to do his duty as a citizen got a broad red stripe across his backside and had to endure the wit of his friends and acquaintances until the paint wore off. In the old days, democracy in Athens was *compulsory*; in fact, once when we'd just come out of a pretty nasty minor civil war, the Council decreed that anybody who hadn't supported either faction in the recent bloodbath should be heavily fined and deprived of his rights as a citizen. Apathy, you see, just isn't our way.)

'Anyway,' Coriscus continued, trying not to be vexed at the interruption, 'once everybody was all together, one of the priests of Dionysus – he was the nearest thing we had to a figure of authority – got up and said that we were all going to stay where we were until we agreed by an overwhelming majority on adopting a new form of constitution. And to encourage our deliberations, he was going to post six of his temple guards round the well; anybody attempting to draw water from it before the debate closed would be thrown down it, by order of the god.

'It was a hot day, and the temple guards looked like they meant business; so it was a singularly constructive and orderly debate.

'I won't bore you with the order of speeches or the detailed arguments – or at least I will, but not now; I'm going to write them all down one of these days, because some of them were pretty good. Suffice it to say, we took a vote just after mid-afternoon and got the necessary majority, and this is what we decided.

'The first proposal was for a monarchy. Nobody wanted that at first, but some of the arguments in favour – continuity, consistency, a legislature that was above party squabbling or private or factional interests – were hard to deny. It was agreed that it would be nice to incorporate the good features of monarchy, provided we could dispose of the drawbacks.

'Next, someone proposed democracy; full democracy, Athenian style. This was a very popular suggestion at first, until we started hearing the downside; ill-informed decisions based on the whim of the mob, irrational mood-swings, the tendency of the many to prey on the few unless restrained from doing so, the dangers of apathy and so on. Again, we had to face up to the facts and agree that a pure democracy – with all due respect to present company – would be a very uncomfortable place to live in, rather like building a house on the rim of an active volcano.

'Someone put forward oligarchy, a proposal that got support from the usual vociferous minority. Well, we weren't having that; but we had to agree whether we liked it or not that oligarchy does have a few things going for it, such as continuity and consistency again, the fact that the ruling group are, as it were, professional rulers rather than amateurs and so can be expected to do the right thing as opposed to the thing that'll be popular – most of the benefits of monarchy, but without the risk of placing all your lives and property in the hands of just one man.

'The obvious flaws in each of these that hadn't yet been aired were then discussed – quite fervently, at times – and once again some points were raised that we just couldn't ignore, even though we didn't like many of them on an intuitive level. They were all quite basic – kings have nothing at all to keep them in line; oligarchies have peer pressure but are much more likely to encourage corruption and the growth of monopolies; democracies tend to eat their children, like absent-minded sows. One man put up the idea of an elected oligarchy, combining the two more favourable systems – once every three years or so Assembly elects a Council of two or three hundred, who rule the city like oligarchs until it's time for the next election. The man who'd suggested it couldn't seem to understand why we were all laughing, though several people tried to explain that yes, he'd developed a very neat fusion of the two concepts, but he'd also unerringly picked out the worst parts of both, and the result would be a perpetual shambles, with gangs of Council members fighting each other tooth and nail for the good opinion of the voters, which would obviously be far more significant to them than the welfare of city or people. It would be an even worse version of the rule of the great demagogues, Cleon and Hyperbolus and Theramenes and their kind, who'd effectively destroyed the City not once but many times. Eventually the man got the message; he apologised for wasting our time and sat down again.

'And then someone came up with a really good idea, or rather a series of ideas linked by a common theme: absolute power tempered by fear of death.

'First, at the top of the heap, would be the kings. Not king singular; there'd be two of them, like in Sparta, one Big King who'd lead the army in war and one Little King who'd mind the store during his absence. Each king would be able to veto anything the other one proposed; five vetos against him and the offender would be dragged up to the top of Citadel Rock and chucked off, without mercy or appeal. Every ten years the Council would have the right to execute or exile either or both of them, but only in respect of things they'd done off their own hook, without the Council's endorsement.

'Now, for the Council, which was to be made up of the five hundred richest citizens, we borrowed another Athenian idea, the Lawsuit of Illegality –'

(Ah, yes, the *graphe paranomon*; if someone proposes an enactment that, if passed, would change the constitution, he can be prosecuted and, if found guilty, put to death. On the other hand, if he's acquitted and the prosecutor got less than a certain percentage of the votes of the jury, then the prosecutor is put to death instead. The Athenian constitution hasn't been fiddled with much over the centuries, for some reason.)

'– which we adapted slightly so that any councillor could challenge any other councillor's proposals, with the hemlock or the long drop awaiting the loser; the counterbalance being that every five years Assembly could impeach and execute any councillors who'd been guilty of fudging up secret deals to avoid open confrontations that could get one or both parties killed. In addition, the kings and the councillors could raise any taxes they liked, but each year they had to present accounts to Assembly to show that all the money was accounted for and explain what it had been spent on, and if the accounts weren't accepted, either king and the treasurer of the Council would die.

'Finally, public office was to be compulsory, on pain of death; so, if you were next in line to inherit the throne or a seat on the Council you had no choice but to accept. This has the tremendous advantage that at any given time, at least nine-tenths of the Government are only there under protest, and the chances of power ever falling into the hands of somebody who wants it are kept to an acceptable minimum.'

There was a long silence.

'And it actually works, does it?' someone eventually asked. 'I mean, you really do run your city like that?'

'For the last hundred and twenty years,' Coriscus replied.

'I see,' Aristotle murmured, rubbing his chin with his left hand and writing furiously with his right. 'And may I ask, how many kings and councillors, in round numbers, have been put to death during that time?'

Coriscus smiled and picked up his cup. 'None,' he said.

CHAPTER FIVE

King Philip of Macedon started off his reign with a series of hard, difficult wars against the seemingly inexhaustible supply of savage and barbarous races who filled up the mountainous wastes to the north and west of his kingdom – Illyrians, Thracians, Thessalians, Triballians, Paeonians and Getae. Much to everyone's surprise he beat them all and, more surprising still, instead of burning their villages, killing the men and selling the women and children as slaves, he turned as many of these apparently sub-human creatures as he possibly could into good Macedonians, or at least the nearest imitation he could get.

Mildly interesting to an Athenian observer; we relish strange tales from the hills, and of course at that time we made it our business to stay *au fait* with the latest reports from the region because we had valuable colonies up there, inhabited by real Athenians who'd left Athens for reason of business or health.

We started to take a little more notice when Philip, having run out of hairy tribesmen to slaughter and tame, turned south. It's a long story and rather a sad one if you're an Athenian. The short version is that he began by appointing himself the guardian of Apollo – we'd always assumed that Apollo, being a god, was big enough and ugly enough to look after himself, but apparently not; it came to Philip's attention that some impious wretches from the city of Phocis had annexed the sacred shrine and oracle of Delphi, helped themselves to the huge reserves of money deposited there

(Apollo is honorary banker to the cities of Greece, something I've always found most odd. After all, he's a *god*; not the sort of person you'd trust to look after your cloak in the baths, let alone your life's savings) and were behaving in a generally disrespectful manner. By the time he managed to wangle an excuse for intervening, the man who'd masterminded the coup was dead and his henchmen scattered, but nevertheless Philip ploughed steadfastly on, beat the Phocians to a pulp, scooped up a couple of valuable cities that had been carelessly left lying about, and somehow wandered sixty or so miles further south until he came up against the Athenian army at the celebrated narrow pass of Thermopylae. We'd rushed our forces up there to protect our colonies, mines and other valuables, just in case Philip absent-mindedly slipped them up his sleeve, as guests sometimes palm spoons at dinner-parties; on this occasion he took the hint and proceeded no further. Nevertheless, anybody who hadn't heard of Philip before was well aware of him now, and we were in the uncomfortable position of people who've acquired an antisocial and boisterous new neighbour, whose children steal apples from the home orchard and whose dog chases the sheep.

No matter, we thought; all except a man by the name of Demosthenes, a professional lawyer with a speech impediment who started saying worrying things in Assembly not long after Philip's picnic in Thessaly. Demosthenes had a fine turn of phrase and it was a treat to listen to him on a warm, lazy morning when there wasn't much else to do. There was always a splendid turnout when we knew he was planning to speak; but we didn't really take any notice. After all, the idea of the wild and woolly Philip being a serious threat to Athens was a fantasy, as imaginative and amusing as that old comedy by Aristophanes where women take over the government of Athens and start voting in Assembly. We Athenians love comic fantasy.

Not long ago I met a man who told me a story he'd heard about young Alexander, Philip's son; according to this man, the incident referred to must have taken place about this time. I'm convinced it's either wholly or partly false – you'll see why in due course – but there may be a grain of truth in it, so I'll pass it on, and you can make up your own mind.

Background, Phryzeutzis: you probably know by now that we

Greeks tell stories about a mighty hero called Hercules, the son of Zeus Himself. In the stories, the first sign that Hercules was going to be a mighty hero was when a couple of snakes crawled into his cot a few days after he was born and tried to sting him, whereupon he strangled them with his bare hands. Now, according to what this man told me, Philip's wife Olympias felt that her son deserved a proper start in life just as much as Hercules, and arranged for a couple of fangless, elderly snakes to be turned loose in the bed where Alexander was sleeping; the idea was that the young prince (who was old enough to throttle snakes, and undoubtedly knew the story) would take the point, recognise a good public-relations opportunity when he saw one, scrag the unfortunate snakes and let the goddess Rumour do the rest. The plan worked just fine, up to a point. The snakes did their part, following a carefully laid trail of live ants trapped in runny honey up the side of the bed and on to the prince's pillow; Alexander noticed them and, quick as lightning, snatched a dagger from under his pillow (which nobody knew was there) and slashed the heads off the snakes before you could say 'garlic'. So far, so good.

Unfortunately, Alexander's next step was to storm into the great hall of the palace, fling the headless remains down at his mother's feet, and in a very loud voice demand to know why she'd seen fit to try to murder him. This put Olympias in a rather awkward position – she couldn't tell the truth for fear of looking extremely silly, but the evidence of the dead snakes and the trail of ants and honey did seem to point towards an assassination attempt. Accordingly, Olympias was forced to frame a minor Macedonian nobleman and his wife and have them put to death on the spot, which annoyed Philip when he heard about it and caused a coolness between them that lasted for some time.

As I said a moment ago, you'll soon see why I don't accept this story as the whole truth. But that picture of the young Alexander, stalking past the astonished nobles with a pair of dead snakes dragging behind him where most kids his age would be trailing a wooden horse on a string or some other favourite toy – that I can believe in; and if it isn't true, it should be. So, by including it in this book of mine, I've given it a certain degree of truth and thereby, I guess, improved history.

*

Athenians of my generation play a memory-game, a sort of reminiscence competition. 'Where were you and what were you doing when you first heard about Olynthus?' they ask each other. 'Pruning my vines,' says one. 'In the market square.' 'In Assembly, of course.' 'You remember that brothel in Tripod Street? Well, I was just coming out of there when I met my cousin, and he told me . . .' But it's true enough; everybody remembers hearing the news. It was one of those moments – rare enough, thank the gods – when you feel the outside world bursting through the walls we all build to keep it out of our personal lives, like a flood battering down a sea-wall; a moment when you realise you're suddenly ankle-deep in history, and the level is all set to rise faster than you can run.

I was in Pallene, of all places, helping my brother Euthyphron. Gods alone know what I was doing there; but Euthyphron had sounded so pathetic when I bumped into him in the street, moaning about how impossible it was for a man on his own to cope with all the work that had to be done in the height of summer on a miserably rocky, strung-out holding like his. I offered to change places with him there and then; he pretended he hadn't heard me.

'You remember the mountain terraces,' he sighed, leaning on his walking-stock like an old man of seventy (he's a year younger than me). 'Three ploughings in summer, minimum; really, three's the absolute minimum, you need to go four if you expect to do any good. Fewer than three and come autumn you're just wasting good seed-corn.'

'I couldn't agree more,' I replied. 'Which begs the question, why are you here in the City rather than back home working?'

Now, I didn't remember Euthyphron as being particularly hard of hearing, but something must have happened to him since I left home, because he had great difficulty hearing a lot of what I said to him.

'As if that's not bad enough,' he went on, 'the damn plough's virtually clapped out – the share-iron's thin as a leaf at the point and you remember where Father mended the break in the drawbar by wrapping it round with rawhide? Well, that's starting to peel off, but where am I going to get rawhide from this time of year? Just my luck, of course, to get the old knackered spare and not the—'

'My heart bleeds,' I interrupted. 'Of course, it simply hasn't occurred to you to get a new one made.'

He must have heard that all right, because he turned his head like a crow looking up from a carcass and gave me that special look of scorn that's reserved for a working farmer talking to a landless townsman.

'It's all right for you,' he said. 'Oh, yes, you've done very nicely for yourself, you've forgotten what it's like actually working for a living. Well, I'm here to tell you, I just haven't got that much coined money, that's all; not with a wife and four daughters to provide for, and the roof on the old barn needing fixing – but I just didn't have the time to do it, so I had to hire a carpenter; do you have any idea . . .'

I'd been about to offer to buy him a new plough anyway, as a peace offering; but the way he put it, I realised that it wouldn't be a gift so much as blood-money to appease the wrath of twenty generations of sturdy Attic yeomen whom I'd foully betrayed by turning my back on the land in favour of a life of Persian luxury. Bless him, though, he didn't hold it against me. As a reward (though really I was just doing my belated duty) he allowed me to help with the ploughing and so re-establish contact with the better part of myself that I'd walled up in some dark recess of my mind; while Euthyphron played with the new plough down on the home enclosures, he let me take the old, rickety heirloom up onto the high terraces, where the stones are the size of a man's head and have always seemed to me to grow faster than the grapes.

'*Please* be careful with it,' he said, almost pleadingly, as I yoked in the oxen. 'If that split in the sole opens out any further, the whole thing'll only be fit for firewood.'

So there I was, right up high like an eagle, nursing that decrepit heap of a plough through the dust-thin topsoil of a terrace no wider than the width of my own shoulders, when our neighbour came running past down the hill.

I'd known Chaereas all my life – twenty-six years, in case you're interested – and in all that time I'd never seen him run. It'd never have occurred to me that he was capable of it. As far as I was concerned, Chaereas slouched – quick slouch in the mornings, agonisingly slow slouch come evening, when he dragged his weary bones home again (and politeness demanded that if I met him on the track I had to walk the rest of the way with him, at his pace; and you know how exhausting it can be, deliberately walking slowly). Yet here he was, racing down the hill like a stag with the hounds at his heels. I let go of the handlebar, took my foot off the footplate and watched, dumbfounded.

'Chaereas?' I called out.

'Can't stop.' He'd seen the plough directly in front of him, but he was going too fast to slow down; instead he soared over it with a mighty leap, like a prize-winning hurdler at the Games. A man twenty years younger would have been proud of that jump.

'Chaereas!' I yelled down the hill after him. 'What the hell's going on?'

'The Macedonians,' he called back. 'They're coming! Run!'

By that point he was too far away to hear me, but I couldn't leave it at that. I left the plough and team standing – the great thing about nine-year-old oxen is that they stay put – and followed after him as quickly as I dared go, which wasn't nearly fast enough. I didn't catch up with him, in fact, until I reached the village, where I saw him huddled in a crowd around a couple of other neighbours of ours, who were saying something about Philip of Macedon . . .

It shouldn't have come as such a shock, really. Philip had been playing war in Chalcidice for some time, threatening and harassing our colonies and allies up there into leaving us and joining him; but for some reason we still hadn't been able to work up enough enthusiasm to send an army and sort him out. I think it was because of what happened at Thermopylae, where, if you recall, the sight of an Athenian army holding the pass had sent him scuttling away like a fox who's seen the sheepdog. Sooner or later we'd make a proper show of force, instead of sending a few cut-price mercenaries, and he'd bolt off back to his mountains and his mead-hall and his week-long drinking matches with the tribal warrior-chieftains. He was, after all, just a Macedonian; they may look a bit like proper Greeks, but that didn't mean a thing. A savage is a savage is a savage; and when you stand up to them, they run. Everybody knew that.

The news that broke that summer day in my twenty-sixth year was that Philip of Macedon had stormed Olynthus, the principal city of Chalcidice and a loyal friend of Athens; once inside, he'd ordered a general massacre, after which he'd rounded up the ten thousand or so survivors and marched them off in slave-irons to be sold abroad.

A lot of speeches were made around that time; very good speeches, most of them, packed with memorable phrases. But what immediately comes to mind when I think of that day is old Chaereas hurdling my father's beat-up second-best plough, with a look of terror on his face as if the Great King and ninety thousand of his archers were treading down the backs of his heels. 'They're coming!' he'd said, but he was a bit behind the times. They'd already arrived, and we hadn't even noticed.

Extraordinary times bring to the fore extraordinary men; and the fall of Olynthus was no exception. In her hour of need, Athens turned to me, Euxenus son of Eutychides of the deme of Pallene, a man extraordinarily ill-suited to the task assigned to me.

We were quite a party, the Athenian embassy to Philip; there was Aeschines, who'd been an actor before he turned to politics; there was Demosthenes, a lawyer; there was Philocrates, an earnest and utterly terrified little man who understood Philip so well that he should never have been allowed to join the party, let alone lead it – whenever he was in the man's presence, he watched Philip with the motionless resignation of a fledgeling bird on the ground watching a polecat, because he *knew*, beyond the faintest shadow of a doubt, that it was only a matter of time . . .

There were ten ambassadors. Correction; there were nine ambassadors and me. When I canvassed my family and friends for possible explanations of why I'd been chosen, I got a wide selection of plausible replies, but no overall consensus. My sister-in-law Praxagora reckoned they'd chosen me because Philip had a habit of killing messengers, and who else was so uniquely expendable? My brother Eudorus, who was also a professional actor, opined that I'd been included as official scapegoat, a complete nobody on whom Aeschines and Demosthenes could dump the blame when the whole mission came to nothing. Diogenes grinned and said they must have chosen me to lull Philip into a true sense of security. Anyway, I went.

Before I tell you about this momentous event in my life, I'll just pause for a moment or two and indulge in a little narcissistic mirror-gazing. In my twenty-sixth year I was one of the tallest men in Athens. Between the ages of thirteen and seventeen I'd sprouted at an unbelievable rate – people told me they used to stand there and watch me getting taller, until it made them feel all dizzy and faint. It was my excessive height, according to some, that made me go bald at a relatively early age. That high up, they said, you can't expect anything to grow except a little moss and the most tenacious species of rockflower. Now, most of the other freaks of altitude I've met have made up for it by being thin and stringy, as if they'd been made out of wax and stretched when they were three parts set. Not me. In spite of the fact that I'd given up farm work at a relatively early age and never took any exercise that I could possibly avoid, I had broad shoulders and forearms as thick as some men's calves. I could pick up great big oil-jars that took two ordinary men to shift – I didn't, as a rule, but I could have if I'd wanted to – and from the age of thirteen onwards, fights and aggravation were things that happened to other people, not to me. Looking back, of course, this was a handicap.

That said, I was a pretty feeble specimen when it came to anything involving stamina. My diminutive brother Eumenes, for instance, could walk under my outstretched arm without ducking and if we walked together he had to trot to keep up with my great shambling strides. But if we happened to be walking uphill, it wouldn't be long before he'd be tapping his foot impatiently, waiting for me to catch up. Eumenes, of course, was a farmer.

When an Athenian asks you, 'What does so-and-so look like?' what he means is, 'Is he good-looking?' That's essential information for an Athenian, because of this beautiful-good/ugly-bad thing I've touched on before. We reckon that beauty is like a seal, pressed into the soft wax of our faces when we're born, so that for ever afterwards people will be able to tell at a glance whether we're good or bad. By that criterion, I was sort of middling-nothingish, which I suppose is fair enough (but I still don't believe in the general rule). Baldness is regarded as a sort of amusing eccentricity-cum-folly in Athens, like absent-mindedness, wearing outlandish or inappropriate clothes or mild kleptomania; people made it plain that though they didn't condone it, they didn't really hold it against me either.

(I can see you smiling, Phryzeutzis; you think that because I can't see you doing it, I won't know. But it's true; when I was younger, I was a very tall man, and if I could only get this pathetic excuse for a back of mine to straighten out, I could prove it to you. All right, don't believe me if you don't want to; but the only man I ever met who was noticeably taller than me was Hephaestion the Macedonian, Alexander's friend; the one the Persian queen assumed must be Alexander, because he was the tallest man in the room. And no, I don't know why I'm making such an issue of it. I suppose it's because it's really the only respect in which I've excelled my fellow men and so in spite of myself I'm really rather proud of it, deep down, even though it was none of my doing.)

Philocrates was supposed to brief us on the ship, so that we'd arrive in Macedon fully informed and up to date, ready for anything that the man already widely acknowledged as the world's greatest living negotiator might have lined up for us. But Philocrates was seasick. Desperately seasick. In fact, he was so wholeheartedly and continuously seasick that he set me thinking seriously about the theory of reincarnation, as proposed by the great Pythagoras and endorsed fairly recently by the celebrated Plato. I'd never had much time for it myself; but watching Philocrates hurling second-hand food with tremendous force into the Aegean, the Straits of Euboea, the Gulf of Pasagae and the Thracian Sea, I found myself reconsidering my position on the issue. It was fairly obvious that Philocrates had already chucked up every morsel of food he'd ever eaten in his life before we were even clear of Cape Sunium, so everything he vomited after that must have been stuff he'd eaten in previous incarnations.

Of my other co-ambassadors, Demosthenes and Aeschines disagreed so completely and so violently that I couldn't face asking either of them for fear of starting off a war that'd have made the Olynthus campaign seem like a polite difference of opinion by comparison; and none of the others seemed all that better-informed than I was. So much, then, for the series of introductory lectures on the present crisis, Macedonian culture and heritage and King Philip's bargaining style. However, as one of my colleagues pointed out, it doesn't require a significant amount of preparation or background knowledge to squeal for mercy, so it didn't really make much odds.

Obviously, Phryzeutzis, you've never seen a ship in your life, and I expect you're pulling all sorts of muscles in your imagination just trying to picture in your mind what one of these extraordinary contraptions looks like. Try this. Imagine a fairly deep, round clay bowl that's still wet from the wheel; but you don't know that, so you pick it up and your fingers cave in two of the sides, leaving you with something that looks a bit like a pear split longwise. Sticking up out of the middle is the trunk of a tall tree, stripped of its branches. Tied to the top of this tree and at right-angles to it is another, smaller beam of wood, from which hangs the linen bag used to catch the wind – that's the sail. Front and back there's two posts sticking up, like the head and tail of a goat; on either side of the goat's tail, there are two broad wooden planks on the end of poles, which trail in the water. The helmsman – the man who tries to make the boat go where it's supposed to be going – drags on these planks to make the boat change direction (try holding your hand out flat, thumb upwards; then plunge it into water and push sideways. You'll feel your hand shoving water out of the way, but not immediately. Pushing against the water is how you steer the ship). That's it, basically. The whole thing is made out of wooden planks, fitted together closely enough to be watertight; it's horribly fragile, and when the wind blows on the sea and stirs it up, the boat is tossed up and down, it can turn over or get swamped, or it can be blown against a rock, which'll smash it to pieces. Imagine trying to float down the river inside an upturned parasol, and you'll get the basic idea.

No wonder, then, that sailors – people who make their living crossing the world in these things – are a nervous bunch, prone to irrational fears and superstitions. All Greeks are superstitious to some extent, but sailors are quite obsessive about it, and in particular they pay great attention to dreams, bad language and sneezing. Sneeze when you're walking up the gangplank and there's a good chance they'll refuse to get on board – unless, of course, your head happens to be facing to the right at the time, in which case they take it as a good omen. Sailors are as foul-mouthed as the next man when they're on land, but once the ship is under way they'll throw you over the side if you say 'Damn!' or 'To the crows with you'. (A crow in the rigging, by the way, is recognised as the worst omen of all, so if someone sees a black shape drifting through the air towards the ship, everybody stops what they're doing and crowds on to the deck, stamping and whistling and throwing nuts and handfuls of olives and anything else that happens to come to hand.) But it's dreams above all that they're interested in. There you are, sleeping peacefully on the deck just as the sun's about to come up, and some clown of a sailor comes and digs you in the ribs with his toe and demands to know what you've been dreaming about. I asked one of the sailors on that voyage to explain to me what all the various dreams meant; it took him a full hour. I can only remember snippets of it – a goat means big waves, especially a black goat; a pig means a storm so violent that your chances of survival are minimal. Owls mean pirates. A dream about seagulls, on the other hand, also foreshadows a disaster, but of a non-lethal variety – the ship will probably sink, but nobody will drown. Dreaming about flying on your back or crossing the sea on foot mean good luck – try to remember how many times you've dreamed of flying on your back, and you'll begin to appreciate the fundamental pessimism of your average sailor. Oh, yes, and dancing on board ship is right out; they'll chuck you overboard so hard you'll probably bounce.

I'm only telling you all this because it explains how I came to hear about Aeschines' dream. Now, I think I've already mentioned that Aeschines was a professional actor before he found he could make a better living out of politics; he was a good actor, too, specialising in winsome young girls, long-winded old crones and messengers reporting bloody murder. I don't know; maybe all those years of cramming his mind with all that poetry, all that vivid and striking imagery, had done something to him. Perhaps he was like that anyway, which was what prompted him to take up acting in the first place. Anyway, on the third morning, when we were within sight of the town of Pasagae (or where Pasagae had until recently been, before Philip played rough games with it), I overheard him talking to one of the sailors, an incorrigible dream monitor.

'Never set eyes on the place in my life,' he was saying, 'but I knew it was Pasagae as if I'd lived there since I was a boy. Strange feeling, actually.'

The sailor nodded. 'And when you saw it just now, was it like what you'd seen in your dream?'

'I've no idea,' Aeschines replied. 'That is, no, it didn't look anything like what we're looking at now. But that's because what we're looking at now is a heap of fallen walls and ashes.'

I don't think the sailor liked the way this story was going. 'Well?' he said. 'What happened?'

Aeschines frowned. 'I'm not sure, really,' he said. 'Oh, I can remember the dream quite clearly, and it seemed to be making perfect sense while I was having it. Now, though—'

Just then the sailor looked up and caught sight of me; I saw him seeing me, but by then it was too late to make an unobtrusive exit, which is something that needs a good deal of notice and forward planning on something as small and confined as a ship. I should explain that somehow or other, the crew had got wind of the way I made my living – and, being extremely superstitious, they believed it wholesale, all the stuff about the little demon who lived in a jar.

'Euxenus,' the sailor called out. 'Come over here. I need you to explain a dream.'

Obviously he'd forgotten that he'd spent all that time the previous day telling me how to interpret dreams. Anyway, there was no point in arguing. I fetched the jar out of my luggage and went over to join them.

'I was standing in the market square at Pasagae,' Aeschines said, 'talking to some people I apparently knew, when a dog suddenly appeared out of nowhere and started running in and out of the stalls, pulling them down and killing people. I could hear the screams. It was awful.'

The sailor had turned a revolting green colour. 'Go on,' I said to Aeschines, in a nice calm voice. 'This is quite interesting.'

'Well,' Aeschines went on, 'pretty soon the dog had smashed up the whole town and rounded up all the sheep and it was herding them into a pen – by this point we were in Pella, except it was also Athens; you'll just have to take my word on that, I *knew* – when a lion jumped out and swatted it over the head, and it fell over. Then the lion led the sheep across the Hellespont into Asia – only they weren't sheep any more, they were bees, and the lion – he'd stopped being a lion but it was still him – was marching up and down the rows inspecting wings and stings, like they were soldiers on parade, then packing them up into hives and loading them on a man's back until he could hardly stagger. After that they both flew away east; and I knew they went a very long way, but I was there waiting for them at the other end. When they got there, the number of hives was enormous; and I was standing in the gateway of a city, desperately trying to get the gate shut to stop them getting in; but it was one of those dreams, you know, the sort where the gate won't budge even though there's nothing obstructing it, and every time you look up the people who're after you are closer and closer. Anyway, they lined up all the hives in front of my gate and pulled off the doors; and all these hundreds of thousands of dead bees came tumbling out. There weren't any live ones left at all. Then the lion was dead too, and I was standing in Assembly back home, and I could smell the lion's dead body, all the way from Asia. I looked round for somebody to ask what was going on, but everybody was running on the spot and wouldn't talk to me. I tried to make them listen but they pushed me over and started kicking me as I lay there. And that's when you' – the sailor – 'woke me up. Well?' he concluded, looking at me. 'Have you the faintest idea what that means?'

'Yes,' I replied. 'You want to lay off eating that strong cheese last thing at night. It's indigestion, that's all.'

Neither of them thought that was funny, but at least I wasn't asked to interpret any more dreams. When we made landfall the next day without shipwreck, pirates, mutiny or manifestations of divine anger, I'll swear the superstitious man was disappointed. There's no pleasing some people.

It's a long but not too arduous journey from the mouth of the river Axius to Pella, where Philip's palace was. He'd sent a troop of cavalry to escort us, with spare horses for us to ride; Macedonians don't walk anywhere if they can help it. At this point in my life I'd had mercifully little to do with horses; my father owned one because he was obliged to do so, by law, being in theory a member of the Athenian Cavalry by virtue of his wealth and political status. Its name was Chestnut, and it ate a king's ransom in barley and lived in a stable in Pallene, and if I was naughty as a boy, he threatened to feed me to it. I regarded this as a pretty terrifying threat. A man sitting on a horse is a long way off the ground, and I couldn't see the point in taking that sort of risk. Now you, Phryzeutzis, and all your bone-idle countrymen are perfectly at home aboard the horrible things, which I regard as proof that in spite of appearances to the contrary, at heart you're all still ignorant savages.

Nevertheless, we were supposed to be diplomats, and refusing to go anywhere near the dreadful creatures would probably have caused grave offence, so we rode from the coast up to Pella. I did a wonderful impersonation of a sack of oats slung over the back of a donkey.

Macedonia is divided into two parts, highlands and lowlands.

The mountains form a double horseshoe, hemming in the rich, pleasant farmlands above the Gulf of Thermai. Pella was in the plains, and it wasn't in the least what I'd been expecting. We Athenians reckoned we knew about the Macedonians; they were brutal, drunken hooligans who lived in mountain passes and dressed in goatskins. That was true enough of the highlanders; but Philip's family were lowlanders, and although they dutifully maintained old national customs like blood-feuds and succession by right of assassination, they'd been doing their best to improve themselves for several generations. Philip's grandfather, for instance, had hired the great and perpetually unpopular Athenian dramatist Euripides to be his court poet, and he did it only partly to annoy the hell out of the highland tribal chiefs (who had to sit still and listen when they'd far rather have been out in the fresh air killing something; having read the collected works of Euripides, I can't blame them. So would I).

Be that as it may; we'd been expecting some kind of long-house built out of tree-trunks, and what we found was a fantasy in white and painted marble, although the mosaic-pattern cobbles were a bit on the garish side for my taste. Actually, I had a head start on my fellow ambassadors. I happen to like dogs, even big, enthusiastic ones, and they like me. As we made our way through King Philip's courtyard, there were dogs everywhere, the pride and joy of the highland barons. When they saw an Athenian who didn't immediately cringe away and try to climb the nearest wall when something the size of a horse, with a lolling pink tongue and teeth like shipwright's nails, planted two enormous forepaws on his shoulders, they were intrigued. I was, as far as they were concerned, in; and I hadn't said a word yet.

It wasn't long before I found out where they'd got their ideas from about what Athenians are like; but I'll come to that in a minute.

Gods forgive me for saying this, but I found I quite liked the Macedonians. Partly, I'm sure, it was relief at finding they weren't grunting savages who wore the neck-bones of their enemies as hair decorations. To a certain extent, besides that, I was ashamed of the attitude of my fellow diplomats, who acted from the start as if they expected to be stuck on spits like thrushes and roasted whole for dinner – Demosthenes was the worst offender, as you'd expect, given that his whole life was devoted to convincing the City that Philip was evil incarnate and the Macedonians were his attendant demons, but all of them except me were appallingly rude from start to finish. I could also try to rationalise by saying that the rather free-and-easy informality of Philip's court appealed to me in my Yapping Dog persona.

Excuses, excuses. I couldn't help liking them. They were just like those enormous dogs of theirs; all it took was a little friendliness and a little fortitude, just enough to show that you weren't afraid of them, and they went from growling mastiffs to big soft puppies in no time at all. The difference was, they were prepared to like us if we liked them, particularly if we showed even the slightest inclination to treat them as 'proper' Greeks – which they weren't, let's face it, but I'm not so sure that's necessarily a bad thing. That was almost the first thing I picked up on, that grudging awe of us just because we were Athenians. They regarded us, I think, the way we regard the gods; we acknowledge that they're probably wiser than us, undoubtedly a hell of a lot stronger, and we most certainly don't *like* them. We disapprove of them, and we console ourselves for being inferior in every other respect with the satisfying knowledge that morally, we're far superior to the whole lot of them. I could feel that same moral superiority, as of straightforward, simple folk confronted with sophisticated decadence, being held up against me like a shield. I felt they had a point, at that. So I went along with it.

Excuse me for a moment, but that reminds me of Diogenes . . . We were walking through the Potters' Quarter one day when I was still quite young, and he pointed out a rather dashing young man in the latest fashions, hair curled and scented, beard neatly trimmed right back.

'What do you reckon?' he said, loudly enough that people could hear.

'I think he looks very smart,' I said.

Diogenes shook his head. 'Affectation,' he replied.

A little later, we passed the Academy, and Diogenes stopped and pointed out a fairly well-known foreign philosopher who happened to be visiting the City from one of the islands. He was an impressive spectacle; very plainly dressed in coarse homespun wool, with bare feet and a long grey beard, clean but uncombed and untrimmed.

'What do you reckon?' he said.

'Affectation?'

'You're learning.'

I nodded, and we walked on a bit further until we came to a well. I stopped, dipped the bucket, drew it up and pointed at it. 'What do you reckon?' I said.

He looked down and caught sight of his reflection. 'Point taken,' he said, and we walked on.

So yes, the Macedonians' pose of primitive manly virtues was just as much an affectation as our culture and sophistication; but so what? Show me a man with no affectations whatsoever, and I'll show you a dead body.

I don't remember much about the room where we first met Philip, except that it seemed to be full of Philip, with not much space for anything else.

Actually, he was a short man, neither slight nor stocky; you'll see a hundred men like him if you walk from the City to the hill when the farmers are out pruning or bashing up the clods with mattocks. But Philip was like a beautiful woman, his face was his fortune; and if you cast your mind back to that conversation we had about good luck and bad luck, King Philip's face is an excellent illustration of my point. It was his appearance that made him undoubtedly the most skilful negotiator and manipulator of men's hearts and minds that I've ever met in my life.

King Philip was incredibly ugly. Actually, you could see quite clearly that once he'd been quite strikingly good-looking; but he'd lost his right eye in some battle, and the scarring was quite revolting. The eye itself was still partly visible, just the white bit of it, turned upwards as if he was trying to look at something perched on his left shoulder, and the seams of the scar that ran down from the forehead, across the eyesocket and down the cheek almost to the corner of his mouth looked like a child's first attempts at moulding in clay, where he's pressed two edges together and tried unsuccessfully to smooth them over into a join.

Now, you can imagine the effect of that on an Athenian (beauty equals good, remember, and ugliness equals evil); ruggedly handsome in left profile, hideously ugly in right. Now, as if that bizarre dichotomy wasn't bad enough, there was the fact that you couldn't help staring, no matter how hard you tried. It wasn't something you could ignore or get used to; you had to stare. And it was obvious – he made it obvious – that he knew you were staring, and that it wounded him deeply, the horror and the pity, all the pathos of a handsome man suddenly reduced to a monster. He never said anything; he just met your eyes and looked at you with his one good eye.

Absolutely invincible negotiating technique, and he exploited it to the full; in fact, it *was* his negotiating technique, happily dropped into his lap by indulgent Fortune. Without it, I don't suppose he'd have been half the diplomat he was, and diplomacy was easily as important a factor as force in his incredible success. It helped, of course, that he had a soft, quite musical voice that made his northern accent a pleasant thing to listen to rather than a jarring, scraping pain.

So Philip filled the room; there was no time or space to look at anything else, because everything tightened down into that one mutilated eye. There were other Macedonians there, of course, big noble-looking men with hairy black arms and a vague impression of beautiful but fierce women, but every time we met Philip it was like we were alone with him, not even conscious of each other. For a negotiating team, this was a distinct disadvantage.

He trashed us, needless to say. No bluster, no raised voice – when he wanted to shout us down, he simply spoke a little more quietly, so that we had to shut up in order to hear what he was saying. He never mumbled, though. I swear you could have heard Philip of Macedon whispering on the other side of the straits of Euboea. That's not to say he didn't make threats. He was all threat, he radiated danger as the sun radiates light, and everyone who stood where he shone knew he was in danger of his life. It was a very immediate, physical danger – you knew for certain that if you happened to say precisely the wrong thing, he'd jump up out of his chair, draw his sword (he was always armed, usually with a broad, blue Thracian steel sabre) and crack your skull open before you could even move; and he'd do it and get away with it because he was Philip, from whom nobody and nothing in the world was safe.

Apart from that he was a pleasant enough man, and I rather liked him.

All the time we were there, there was no respite. When we

weren't negotiating (I use the term for convenience only; we negotiated in the same way as a roast quail negotiates with the man
who's eating it) we were being entertained, either with intimidating
quantities of food – meat, meat and more meat, as much of it in one
meal as the average Athenian sees in a year – and lethal doses of
strong, neat wine, or with very high-class recitals of music and
poetry performed by expensive imported artists, which Philip obviously enjoyed almost as much as the heavy banqueting. He was, I
should point out at this stage, a ferocious drinker; one of those
dangerous drunks who doesn't show it on the surface one bit. The
only difference I could see, in fact, was that when he was drunk he
was more inclined to extremes of both cruelty and humanity,
though there was no way of knowing which you'd get.

For instance; one evening, when the boozing had reached the
stage where our hosts were too fuddled to notice and be offended
by the fact that we'd stopped trying to match them flagon for flagon
quite some time ago, a man and a woman came storming into the
dining hall, with a sleepy-looking guard chasing after them. Before
they could be caught and slung out, Philip raised his hand to signify
that he was prepared to listen to what they had to say, whereupon
the man launched into an incredibly complicated story about a
disputed parcel of land about the size of a large hat that adjoined his
and the woman's properties, a hole deliberately drilled in a lead
water-pipe to steal water from a private supply, an errant goat that
turned up a week later with the woman's brand mysteriously in
place of the original mark, and I don't know what else. About four
minutes into this, the woman joined in, although from what little I
could follow she was talking about unlawful lopping of the low
branches of a tree growing just her side of the boundary, a vine
trampled and broken by a stray donkey, some extremely arcane
stuff about the man's son's friend's dog killing somebody else's
neighbour's daughter's tame polecat – I'll be honest with you, I gave
up on that one at quite an early stage.

I was surprised at how long Philip just sat there and took all this.
I kept expecting him to blow his top with impatience and order the
guards to throw both of them down the nearest well – but at that
time, you see, I didn't know how seriously Philip took his duties as
supreme arbiter, or how strong was the tradition that the King of
Macedon's subjects had a right to an audience, at any time of day or

night, when circumstances justified it. Eventually, though, he'd had enough. He started to speak in that low, calm voice I've been telling you about, but by now the two litigants were so engrossed in their tales of the other's iniquities that they went on yammering and ignored him completely. I braced myself for the sight of blood on the floor; instead, I heard Philip banging on the table with his cup.

'All right,' he said. 'That'll do. Now then, I won't pretend I followed what you two were saying. I don't suppose it'd have made any difference if I had. The plain fact is, you're both rotten neighbours and I'm damned glad I don't have to live next door to either one of you. Ready? Good. My judgement is that you will both be fined one drachma, and you will both go away and not come bothering me again. Understood?'

The woman shook her head. 'That's not good enough,' she said. 'I want justice.'

'Tough,' Philip snapped. 'I haven't got any. You'll have to make do with Law, instead.'

But the woman wasn't having any of that. 'All right,' she said, 'I'm lodging an appeal.'

Philip frowned. 'Don't talk soft,' he said, 'I'm the King, the fountain of all justice. Who else is there for you to appeal to?'

'To Philip, of course; Philip when he's sober.'

Philip was having a good day; the woman got her appeal, and got judgement in her favour, too. But the silent three or four heartbeats after she'd said that was the longest three or four heartbeats I can ever remember, and when it was over I checked my reflection in a polished silver plate to see if my beard had gone white while I'd been waiting.

As soon as the two litigants had been shooed away again, everybody started talking at once. Philip was pouring himself a stiff drink, probably feeling he'd earned it. I was just starting to relax when I heard raised voices from up on Philip's table, a man's voice and a woman's.

The woman was Philip's wife, Queen Olympias. The man was Aristotle.

What's he doing here? I asked myself, feeling a bit like the man in the old story who dies and goes to the Islands of the Blessed only to find when he gets there that his mother-in-law's there too.

The argument they were having was a wonderful illustration of diametrically opposed slanging-match techniques. Queen Olympias was yelling at the top of her extremely powerful lungs. Aristotle, on the other hand, was waiting till she had to stop and draw breath and then carrying on where he'd left off, ignoring everything she'd said and talking in his most monotonous, plonking tone of voice. Philip rolled his eyes (an alarming sight, I assure you) then belted the table with his fist so hard that cups and jugs fell over on all sides.

'You two,' he murmured. 'Pack it in.'

Did I say just now that everybody in the world was afraid of Philip? Everybody bar one. Whether or not Philip was afraid of Olympias, on the other hand, is a moot point. I don't think he was; he tolerated her, because killing her would cause more problems than it would solve and besides, he was on-and-off in love with her – fascinated would be a better word – probably for the same reason, that she wasn't afraid of him.

They'd met when they were both very young, at a weird religious bash in her home territory in the wilds (the very wilds) of Illyria. Olympias' people were snake-worshippers, and she was as keen as mustard on the whole snake thing. Why Philip was up there getting initiated into a snake cult, the gods only know; he was about as religious as my neighbour Philemon's old mule and besides, the snake people weren't even his gods. It was lust at first sight for him – ten or so years later, she was still a sight to see, although a lot of wine and honey-cakes had passed through the gates of her teeth in that time, and there was quite a lot more of her in every direction. What she saw in him I don't know, could have been any one of many things or maybe the snakes told her to marry him. In any event, the outcome of all this had been a splurge of diplomatically useful daughters and a son, by the name of Alexander.

Aristotle, I quickly gathered from the text of the slanging-match, was up here as the boy's tutor, and whatever it was that he was teaching the lad, Olympias didn't hold with it. Not one bit.

I won't try to reproduce the way Olympias spoke; Greek wasn't her native language and she hadn't bothered to clean up her accent or her grammar. So I'll translate it a bit and put down what she would have said if she'd been able to; after all, I'm pretending to be a historian, and that's what historians do.

'Evil, that's what he is.' Those were the first words of hers I actually made out. 'He's poisoning my son's mind with his Athenian lies. If you were any sort of a father, you'd throw him in the river instead of paying him good money to –'

Philip stood up, crossed the floor to where she was standing in three long strides, and slapped her across the face so hard that she stumbled backwards and sat down heavily, jarring her back against a table. Everybody stopped talking; but I rather got the impression that this wasn't the first time that Philip had done something like this, not by a long way.

'– Teach our son all this blasphemous Athenian trash,' Olympias carried on as if nothing had happened (though she dabbed blood from her cheek and upper lip with her sleeve as she spoke). 'I'm telling you for the last time, if you don't do something about it then I will, so don't say I didn't warn you.'

Philip growled, softly and with considerable menace; it was a characteristic noise of his, one which I think he made without even realising it. 'You lay one finger on that man and I'll kill you,' he replied, his voice only just audible even in the deathly hush. 'Now get out of my sight. Go and sleep it off somewhere you can't be seen.'

Olympias stood up, spat with great force on the ground between Philip's feet, and hobbled out of the audience chamber. For his part, Philip breathed out slowly, then turned to Aristotle and nodded.

'I apologise for my wife,' he said. 'I wish I could say it won't happen again, but I respect the truth too much for that. I'll assign you a guard for the next three days or so; after that she'll lose interest, she'll be trying to get at me some other way.'

Aristotle smiled, very thinly, and thanked him. Something told me that he wasn't in the least reassured. I can't say I blame him.

'That said,' Philip went on, 'I'd be interested to know – what exactly have you been teaching the boy that she's taken such an exception to? She was saying something about blasphemy, wasn't she?'

'Quite so,' Aristotle replied nervously. 'But I really can't imagine why she found it so offensive. Today we were considering animals, and I was pointing out that every living thing has its own nature, to which it cannot help but be faithful – dogs bark and wag their tails, birds sing and lay their eggs in nests, snakes hiss and crawl on their bellies in the dirt—'

'Snakes,' Philip repeated. 'You told him snakes were animals.'

'I believe so,' Aristotle replied. 'I mentioned various examples in today's lesson; not necessarily the ones I gave you just now, but quite possibly the same. Snakes are quite an obvious—'

'I see,' Philip interrupted. 'What else did you say about snakes?'

Aristotle paused for a moment, frowning. 'Let me see,' he said. 'I mentioned the fact that their jaws are flexible, not fixed; that they shed their skins repeatedly during their lifetimes; that they can extend and retract their tongues; that the eyes of a decapitated snake close of their own accord forty minutes after death, and likewise the severed head of a poisonous snake will still bite and discharge its poison an hour after being struck from the trunk—'

'I didn't know that,' Philip broke in. 'Is that true?'

'Oh, yes,' Aristotle replied confidently. 'I've observed it myself, and it's recorded by good authorities.' He frowned. 'Would that have offended her, do you think?'

'I doubt it,' Philip replied. 'Quite the reverse, in fact. Anything that suggests that snakes don't die the way other animals do ought to please her no end. What else did you say?'

Aristotle tugged at his beard – he actually did do that, the only person I ever met who did. 'I honestly can't remember,' he replied. 'Oh, yes, I pointed out that the snake, contrary to popular belief, is in fact deaf, and can only detect sounds by feeling vibrations transmitted through the—'

'What did you just say?'

Aristotle gave him a startled look. 'Snakes are deaf,' he repeated. 'They have no ears. Therefore they cannot hear in the way that—'

'Ah.' Philip nodded. 'That'll be it, then. You see, she sings to her snakes for an hour every morning and evening. That's how she prays to them. You implied that they can't hear her prayers.'

'Well, properly speaking they can't—'

'And if they can't hear her prayers,' Philip went on, 'they can't hear her telling them the names of the people she's put curses on. Which means the curses won't work.' He smiled. 'Actually, I'm surprised she confined herself to shouting at you.'

'Really,' Aristotle said, rather disdainfully.

Philip nodded. 'I wouldn't have, if I was her. Anyway,' he went on, as Aristotle cringed visibly, 'no harm done. But if I were you, I'd check my bed carefully before getting into it for a week or so, just to be on the safe side. You might see if the housekeeper's got some of that fine-mesh Persian gauze, to make a canopy out of, in case someone bores a hole in the ceiling and drops something down on top of you. It'd be highly appropriate if the snakes punished you for your wicked slanders, don't you think?'

Aristotle had gone ever such a funny colour. 'It hadn't occurred to me—' he began, but Philip didn't let him finish. 'Apparently not,' Philip said. 'Which surprises me, you being a philosopher and a wise man generally, and knowing how she feels about snakes. Well, it only goes to show; we can all learn something new every day, no matter how clever we are.'

CHAPTER SIX

‘Alexander,’ the Macedonian told me, ‘is the king’s son. What more needs to be said?’

I frowned. I’d been trying to find out more about the boy, simply because Aristotle was his tutor and I didn’t like Aristotle. If it turned out that young Alexander was violent, unruly and big for his age, and that he regularly set booby-traps for his teachers or threw the writing-tablets at them or stabbed them with the pen when they said he’d got something wrong, it would have delighted my soul and brightened my day, since a good man delights as much in the discomfiture of an enemy as in the good fortune of a friend.

‘All right,’ I said. ‘But apart from that; what’s he like? Is he quiet? Noisy? Does he climb trees? Does he go for long walks on his own and keep pet frogs in jars, or is he more into playing with other kids of his own age? It must be strange,’ I went on, ‘being the King’s son. Where I come from, either they’re in school or they’re out on the hill with the goats or scaring birds off the planted fields. I don’t suppose the King’s son does that sort of thing.’

The Macedonian looked at me as if I was asking detailed questions about his mother’s sex life. ‘The King’s son learns the arts of war and government,’ he said stiffly. ‘As is fitting. He is accompanied by the sons of noblemen, who will grow up at his side and in time become his trusted ministers and captains in war. He also learns such noble accomplishments as hunting, falcony, athletics, dancing and music, although,’ he added, ‘it’s not proper for a nobleman to play or sing *too* well, just enough to be able to join in the singing at the banquet without disgracing himself. And of course he learns to honour the gods of his country.'

'Right,' I said, trying to imagine Aristotle giving falconry lessons. 'Well, I agree that that's just the sort of thing a king's son ought to know.'

The Macedonian raised an eyebrow. 'You do?' he said.

I shrugged. 'Why not?' I said. 'My father sent me out to look after the goats so I could learn about keeping livestock and in due course become a farmer. Every man trains his son to take over his trade or occupation. It's just common sense.'

'Oh.' The Macedonian – a middle-aged nobleman called Parmenio, one of Philip's chief advisers – shrugged. 'I'm surprised to hear you say that, you being an Athenian. And,' he added, with the tiniest curl of his lip, 'a philosopher, so I gather. I thought you had different ideas.'

'Oh, yes?' I said. 'You're thinking of Aristotle, aren't you?'

Parmenio nodded. 'Yes,' he admitted. I grinned.

'You don't want to go judging the rest of us by him,' I said. 'And besides, he isn't even a proper Athenian, he's from Stagira. Really, he's one of you more than he's one of us.'

Parmenio shook his head. 'I don't think so,' he said. 'You should hear the things he's cramming into that boy's head. I don't hold with it, I'm telling you.' He wrinkled his forehead, aware that he was talking to a foreigner and, by rights, an enemy. 'However,' he said, 'since the King feels it's appropriate—'

'I'm sure Philip has his reasons,' I said. 'My guess is, he feels it's important for his son to understand the way the Athenian mind works, the way it's important for a hunter to understand the mind of the deer.'

Parmenio wasn't very keen on that analogy. *Subtle and perfidious Athenian,* I could see him thinking, as if the words were inscribed on his forehead. 'It's not my concern,' he said. 'And neither,' he added sternly, 'with due respect, is it yours.'

'Oh, quite,' I replied. 'Just idle curiosity, that's all.'

I went away with an image in my mind of a crown prince with all the individuality of a coin-blank, in between being punched out of the silver sheet and hammered between the forming dies to give it its shape. In fact, I used that comparison when I was talking to

Lysicles, one of my fellow ambassadors, later on that day.

'It's a well-known syndrome,' Lysicles replied, lying back on his couch and dropping a grape into his mouth. 'Great men's sons never amount to anything. All through their early years they're completely overshadowed by their fathers, like weedy little plants growing under big trees. Everybody tries so hard to turn them into exact copies of the Old Man that they never learn the ability to think for themselves. I expect you'll find this young Alexander's a little tiny Philip, like the wee clay figures the Egyptians put in tombs; an exact copy, but much smaller in every respect. It's a well-known fact; the more illustrious the father, the feebler the son. That's why great empires ebb and flow like rivers,' he added, stifling a belch. 'Up one generation, down the next. Take the Persians,' he went on. 'First there's Cyrus. Cyrus the Great. Carves out a mighty empire, conquers half the world. And who does he have for a son? Hydaspes, of whom virtually nothing is known. His son? Darius the wet-slap. Darius, who we beat the shit out of. And who does he have for a son? Xerxes. The moral: a great conqueror, an empire-builder like Cyrus, has a weak son and a pathetic grandson and great-grandson.'

I thought for a moment before answering. 'Possibly,' I said. 'Though I'm not quite so sure. I mean, it's true that our great-great-grandfathers beat King Darius' army—'

'You bet your life,' Lysicles yawned.

'But,' I went on, 'not before he'd burned Chalcis and Eretria and trampled over most of Greece without anybody daring to oppose him. And as I recall, the first thing he had to do when he became king was put down major rebellions in pretty well every province of the empire, which he succeeded in doing in just over a year—'

'If he'd been anything they'd never have rebelled in the first place. And remember, the Scythians beat him too. And they're just savages.'

'True,' I admitted. 'But in their country it snows half the year, and the rest of the time it's so hot you die of thirst in a day if you don't know where the wells are. I sort of got the impression he realised Scythia just wasn't worth the effort and came home again.'

'He was weak,' Lysicles replied firmly. 'A strong king'd never have risked his prestige starting a war he knew he couldn't win.

Nothing buggers up a king's prestige like losing a war. Look at Xerxes.'

I was only arguing for devilment's sake. 'Xerxes burned Athens to the ground,' I pointed out, the voice of sweet reason and pure truth. 'Not to mention a whole bunch of other cities. And he got back home again with most of his army intact. Sure, we won a few battles, but maybe it was the same as Darius and Scythia. Maybe he realised Greece just wasn't worth the effort.'

Lysicles smiled. 'If I were you,' he said, 'I'd be a bit careful talking about Xerxes' war around these parts. Might be a sore topic.'

That was a good point. Back in those days, when King Xerxes invaded Greece with his huge army, the King of Macedon voluntarily joined the Persian Empire rather than try to fight – a perfectly sensible decision on his part under the circumstances, since he'd have stood no chance at all, but one which had been a source of endless embarrassment to the Macedonians ever since. Sure enough, as soon as it became apparent that, against all the odds, the Greek allies were winning the war and Xerxes was going home, the Macedonian King did his best to set matters straight by betraying the Persian order of battle to the Greek general staff on the night before the decisive battle of Plataea; a helpful act, but not desperately honourable. (Who was that famous general who once said, 'I've nothing against treachery; it's traitors I don't like'?)

Come to think of it, the King of Macedon in those days was also called Alexander. A family name, presumably.

I left Lysicles to catch up on his sleep (I never knew anybody who needed as much sleep as he did) and wandered out into the fresh air. It happened to be one of the few afternoons on that mission that we actually had to ourselves; Philip had been called away, and Parmenio, who was supposed to keep us entertained and busy when Himself wasn't about, loathed pointless socialising almost as much as he loathed Athenians. The respite came just in time for me; I've never liked being indoors terribly much at the best of times. I strolled round a courtyard, found a side door that opened onto an alley and walked up it until I came to another courtyard, where someone was halfway through building a house. There were piles of stone blocks, all neatly cut, shaped and stacked, scaffolding, ropes, orphan tools and all the other junk you find heaped up on building sites, but there was nobody about. I sat down on a heap of blocks, yawned and stretched my arms, taking sincere delight in the absence of human voices. Then I noticed movement behind a pile of timber. I sat still and waited.

It turned out that there was a boy behind the pile. He was so engrossed in what he was doing that he didn't realise I was there. I stood and watched him.

He didn't look very much like either his father or his mother; even so, I had no trouble recognising him. He may have been a thumb-joint taller than most boys his age, certainly no more than that. He had a long, straight nose, full lips like a girl's, and big eyes. His hair was naturally curly. Both his knees and elbows were scabbed with recent grazes, and he had a big purple bruise on his right forearm.

He'd found a nest of wild bees among the stones, and was studying it carefully. From time to time he poked at it with a long stick, until a scouting party of bees came buzzing out to see what the matter was. As they emerged from between the stones and started to fly, he flicked them out of the air with the split end of his stick, snapping them down with a short, brisk jerk of the wrist. The speed of his reactions and his eye/hand co-ordination were little short of phenomenal.

'Been stung yet?' I asked.

He didn't jump or even look round, just went on concentrating on the job in hand as he replied. 'Seven times,' he said. 'Twice on the arm, three times on the leg, once on the neck and once on the face.'

'Does it hurt much?'

'Yes.'

I smiled, but he wasn't paying me any attention. 'Then why do it?' I asked.

'Because they stung my dog yesterday.'

'Good reason,' I said. 'It's the mark of a good man to avenge his friends and dependants. But why do it that way? Why not smoke them out?'

He narrowed his eyebrows without taking his eye off the bee he was tracking. 'I hadn't thought of it,' he admitted.

'Did you try and think of a better way?' I asked. 'Or does the exercise of skill and speed please you so much that you don't want to find one?'

'I don't understand.'

'No reason to suppose you would,' I conceded. 'After all, you're what, ten?'

'Nine,' he replied. 'And seven months.'

I got up and walked round to where he could see me, provided he could be bothered to look.

'You're an Athenian,' he said. 'One of the ambassadors.'

'That's right,' I replied. 'But I used to be a farmer, and when I was your age we had a swarm of wild bees nest in a cavity between the doorframe and the front door. Nearly drove us out of the house for a couple of days, until my father smoked them out.'

'How did he do it?' Alexander asked.

'With a brazier,' I replied, 'one of those little portable ones on a tripod, like they make in Corinth. He cooked up some damp kindling until it was smoking well, then he stood the tripod in the doorway and puffed the smoke up into the nest with a pair of bellows he'd borrowed from our neighbour the smith. That made them all drowsy and sleepy, and we were able to bundle them into an empty hive we'd got handy – we'd lost a swarm the year before, and this way we were able to replace it for free.'

Alexander thought about that, and let a bee go by unswatted. 'Didn't you all get stung while you were doing it?' he said.

'Once or twice,' I answered him. 'Not nearly as much as seven times. Of course, we knew to muffle ourselves up in cloaks and blankets.'

I could see him digesting the information, the way a cormorant digests a whole fish; you can see the shape of it in his long neck as it goes down. 'So you took bad luck and made it into good luck,' he said thoughtfully. 'That's clever.'

'That's wisdom,' I said, 'which comes from knowledge and experience. Instead of fighting our enemies and destroying them, at the cost to ourselves of many painful stings, we overwhelmed them with our superior wisdom and added them to our household. We got a good load of honey from that swarm for many years.'

He dropped the stick. 'You're saying that killing the bees is the wrong thing to do. I could be capturing them and making them work for me.'

I nodded. 'You've got it,' I said. 'And you won't get stung so much, either. It's brave to fight in the forefront of the battle, but you shouldn't do it unless it achieves a useful end. As it is, every bee you kill is one less to bring you honey. You're wasting resources.'

He frowned. 'But they stung my dog,' he said. 'Oughtn't they to be punished for it?'

'By captivity,' I said, 'not death. And anyway, the bee that did the actual stinging is dead already; you can't punish him where he's gone.'

Alexander smiled. 'You make it sound like bees go to the Elysian Fields when they die,' he said.

'Well, why not? They have flowers there, don't they? In which case, it stands to reason they have bees.'

'Now you're making fun of me,' Alexander said, in a tone of voice that suggested that that wasn't a prudent course of action.

'Not at all,' I said. 'Bees aren't a laughing matter. We have the best bees of all, back where I live, in Attica. Of course. I expect you've heard of the Hyblaean strain.'

'No,' he admitted. 'But Aristotle's going to teach me all about the different varieties and breeds of animals and birds. He knows all about that sort of thing.'

'I bet.'

'Sorry?'

'Doesn't matter. So,' I continued, 'what are you going to do? Are you going to continue the war, or make peace on favourable terms?'

Alexander thought for a moment. 'Oh, make peace,' he said. 'Trouble is, I haven't got a hive to put them in.'

'Ah, well,' I said, 'that's no excuse. We farmers, when we haven't got something we need, we go away and make it.'

'How do you make a beehive?' he asked.

'Out of strips of bark,' I told him, 'which you sew together with bits of trailing ivy. Or if you prefer, you can use osiers, like you'd use for weaving baskets. Anyway, once you've got the shell, so to speak, the next step is to line it with clay. Then finally you add a loop to hang it from, and there you are. Keeps the frost and the birds out, but you can still get in when it's time to rob them of their honey.'

'Thank you,' Alexander said. 'Which is better, the bark or the osiers? I know where there's a big old apple tree we could strip some bark off, but osiers might be a problem.'

'There,' I said, 'you've answered your own question.'

He smiled. 'So I have,' he said. 'All right, I'll get the bark, and you—'

I held up my hands. 'Whoa!' I interrupted. 'So I've been conscripted, have I?'

'You've got to help me make it,' Alexander said, with an odd note of urgency in his voice. 'Where's the point in knowing how to do something if you don't go and do it?'

I shrugged. 'What's wrong with knowledge for its own sake?' I said. 'No, don't bother with that, it'll be quicker to make the beehive. All right, you want me to look for some ivy, I suppose.'

'Yes,' Alexander said.

'And a needle,' I added. 'Got to have a needle for the sewing. Before you ask, I can make one out of wood, that's no problem.'

Alexander was a remarkably quick study. If he had a fault, it was impatience; he wanted very much to be able to do a thing without having to go through the humiliation – I'm sure he saw it as that – of having to learn, of being subservient to another who happened to have a piece of knowledge he hadn't acquired yet; he wanted to gulp down knowledge like a sick man gulps down medicine, to be able to take it and immediately be in a perfect state of being able to do whatever the task was, without any intermediate stage of half-knowledge or apprenticeship. I'd say, 'This is how you do such-and-such,' and he'd interrupt and say, 'Yes, I know,' when fairly obviously he didn't. But he was amazingly sharp and quick, and his level of concentration was astounding for a human being that age.

'There,' he said, regarding the finished article with a satisfied look on his face, 'that's good, isn't it?'

'It'll do,' I said. 'It'd have been even better if we'd waited for the clay to dry properly like I told you, but it'll get the job done. Now I suppose you want to smoke out the bees.'

He looked at me. 'Of course,' he said. 'Otherwise there wouldn't be any point making the hive. Come on, we'll ask the priest in the small temple if we can borrow his portable brazier. He'll say yes, he knows me well enough. We can ask for some of that thick smelly incense; that'll make good smoke.'

I laughed. 'That's an interesting thought,' I replied, 'using expensive imported incense to smoke out bees. You can ask if you like, but I wouldn't hold your breath if I were you. I think you'll have to wait until you're a great warrior and you've conquered the

Spice Islands beyond the Great Ocean before you can go using the stuff that freely.'

Of course, that made him all the more determined to get the incense, and so of course he did. Best quality stuff, too; it smelt disgusting, all sweet and cloying.

'That'll do fine,' I said. 'If it has this effect on us, think what it'll do to the bees.'

We also requisitioned a small shovel and a slab of potsherd, for scooping the dazed bees up with. As we put these items with the rest of the kit, I saw that Alexander was looking at them nervously. I asked him why.

'I was thinking of that story,' he replied.

'Which one?' I asked him. 'There's several, you know.'

He looked at me oddly, and I suddenly realised: *no sense of humour*. Oh, well, nobody's perfect. 'The one about the Lydians,' he said. 'You know, where they went to fight the Persians, and they were so sure they were going to win that they took along a whole bunch of chains and collars and stuff to chain the prisoners up in, and after the battle they ended up wearing them themselves. I think a lot about that story,' he added.

'You do? Well, fair enough. I don't think the bees are going to chain us up and make us go round collecting honey from flowers.'

'I didn't mean it *literally*,' he said patiently. 'It just feels a bit like – what's that expression?'

'Tempting Providence?'

He nodded. 'That's the one. But I suppose we need to scoop them up quickly while they're still groggy from the smoke, so we'd better take this stuff with us.'

Gods; it had been years since I'd last smoked out bees, and I wasn't quite sure I'd remember how to do it. There's quite a knack to it, mostly getting the smoke to go in the nest. In the event, Alexander appropriated the bellows and clung onto them so tightly that I didn't even bother suggesting that I should handle that part of the operation. Interesting sidelight here; a few years later, I asked him if he remembered this episode and he said yes, of course. During the conversation, this issue of him having to be the one who did the difficult bit came up, and he said he'd insisted because he'd worked out that the bellows-operator was far more likely to get stung if things went wrong than the man holding the tripod; if there was a risk of danger, a front rank to be fought in, then it was up to him to take the position of most danger, because he was the leader. He quoted me those famous lines of Homer, the ones people who don't know any Homer tend to spout at you out of context –

Tell me, Glaucus, why are we honoured among the Lycians
With thrones and banquets and the respect due to gods?
Because we always take our stand in the front rank of the fighting . . .

– Except that he'd got it wrong, or else whoever taught it to him knew a different version; he'd somehow managed to incorporate into it that other famous bit about Glaucus the Lycian, so that his third line went –

Because we are always the best, excelling all other men . . .

–Which isn't the same at all. But when I tried to tell him this, he wouldn't believe me; he said that obviously the Homer we had in Athens wasn't the real Homer, and if one of us was wrong, it was me; it stood to reason that the Macedonians would know the real Homer, because he was descended on his mother's side from Achilles himself. He clearly took this all so seriously that I resisted the urge to point out that, following his system of logic, if I was ever in a lawsuit I'd know more about the law than anybody else because an ancestor of mine successfully proposed a measure in Assembly—

(Which is true, believe it or not; a decree abolishing certain trade tariffs imposed on citizens of Locris Opuntia trading in Athenian markets, passed shortly after King Xerxes' war. A futile piece of legislation, since the tariffs were on commodities the Locrians didn't deal in; but never let it be said that our family hasn't scratched its name in a corner of the wall of history.)

Anyway; the bees didn't stand a chance. One whiff of that nauseating incense and they fell out of the nest into our shovel like dung from a cow's backside, everything going exactly according to plan and no unforeseen contingencies arising. I mention this in my role as historian, because I think it's the first recorded instance of Alexander's unbelievable luck, the same elemental force that made it possible for him to walk into Babylon, the world's most forti-fied city, without striking a blow, or conquer unconquerable Egypt without having to fight a single battle. Alexander was always lucky; a quality he shared, in pretty well exactly the same way, with my father.

'Right,' I said, as we ladled the last squirming dollop of bees into the hive. 'We've captured them. Now what do we do with them?'

He looked at me as if I'd just asked him why he breathed. 'Take them to my father, of course,' he said.

'Fine.' I nodded slowly. 'Tell you what,' I said. 'You take them to him. You don't have to mention my name, tell him you caught them all by yourself. I'm not sure I want to be in the picture when you plonk down a hundred thousand hungover bees on your father's dining-table.'

'I can't do that,' Alexander replied, shocked. 'I can't take the credit for something I haven't done. Where'd be the point in that?'

I sighed. The concept of diplomatic immunity was known in Macedon, but only in the category of quaint and impractical foreign customs, along with the Hyperborean savages who worship the souls of fish, or the Hyrcanian ascetics who believe that painting themselves with the urine of pregnant sheep makes them invulnerable to arrows. 'You did all the hard work,' I pointed out. 'Not to mention all the difficult tactical planning. I just advised on the technical aspects. If you storm a city who gets the praise, you or the man who built the battering-ram?'

'Both of us,' Alexander replied firmly. 'I led, and you helped. Glory,' he added, reciting carefully, 'is the only commodity that seems to increase the more you spread it around.'

I'd heard a similar version of that saying; it started *Glory and dogshit are the two commodities* . . . 'Think,' I urged him. 'By the time your father gets back, those bees will have woken up, and they aren't going to be pleased about how they've been treated. Besides, unless you give them a chance to settle down in their new home, there's a good chance they'll just up sticks and move on, and there's no knowing where they'll go after that.'

Alexander thought about it. 'That makes sense, I suppose,' he conceded. 'Perhaps you'd better give the hive to me. I'll find a place for it and then take my father to see it once he gets back.'

My excuse for going along with the proposal – well, there were three of them. First, young Alexander seemed like a serious, thoughtful young fellow, not inclined to mischief. Second, it reduced the risk of my being blamed for a swarm of bees being turned loose in a packed dining-hall. Third, by this point what I really wanted to do was put space between me and the soon-to-revive bees. 'Up to you,' I said. 'He's your father, and they're now your bees. But if it all goes horribly wrong, I've never set eyes on you before. Understood?'

'You mean you'd want me to lie to my father?'

'Yes.'

He was profoundly unimpressed by the idea, but eventually we agreed that he'd limit the assignation of blame to 'one of the Athenians', whose name he didn't quite catch. To make it true, I had to mumble my name two or three times under my breath so he'd be able to say with a clean conscience that he hadn't been able to make my name out when I told it to him.

I left Alexander and walked away. As soon as I was out of sight, Alexander took his trophy and scuttled off into the town, where lived an old man and his wife who'd once been Philip's chief steward and housekeeper respectively. In this capacity they'd somehow earned the young prince's extreme displeasure.

Now here's the difference between Alexander as a young boy and countless tens of thousands of other bright, imaginative lads of his age. Any boy worth the name could have scrambled up onto the old couple's roof and dropped the hive down the smokehole. It took the future hero of the Granicus to bar all the doors and windows from the outside first (silently and unassisted), so the poor fools were trapped in there, facing an angry phalanx of bee-stings with nowhere to run.

Didn't quite work out that way, however. The hive got stuck, about a forearm's length down the hole, and wouldn't go any further; nor could it be fished back out again. For all I know it's still there; assuming that whoever's got that cottage now doesn't mind a roomful of smoke every time he tries lighting a fire.

So when Philip got home, there was no magnificent trophy of the bee-hunt to delight his warrior heart. What he did get, however, was a glowing account of the merits of one of the Athenian ambassadors, with special reference to his skill both as a teacher and as a military engineer.

I didn't know about that, of course. The first I heard was when two officers of the household (translate: two hulking great Macedonians in armour) turned up at the door of my quarters telling me that I had to go with them at once, and not answering my pleas for further information.

I knew it had to be something to do with Alexander, since I hadn't done anything else on my own since I'd been there. The picture of Philip smashing Queen Olympias in the face stuck in my mind as firmly as that damned beehive in the chimney, and by the time I reached Philip's audience chamber I was fine-honing my philosopher's deathbed speech – a tradition started by the illustrious Socrates ('Don't forget, Crito, we owe a cock to Asclepius,' whatever that's supposed to mean; hence the customary obscurity of these utterances).

When I got there, I found Philip (filling the room as usual), the Queen, Alexander, an old man with a shiny bald head, and Aristotle. Of course, as soon as I saw Aristotle I more or less gave up hope – the most I could expect was that my deathbed words would make it back to Athens, probably in heavily garbled form, unless they turned out to be good enough for him to plagiarise.

'Thank you for joining us,' Philip said politely. 'Now, to come straight to the point—'

'Do you keep a snake in a bottle?' Queen Olympias interrupted.

For a brief moment I shut my eyes, since I didn't particularly want to see a repeat performance of the Queen of Macedon trying to learn how to fly; but there was no chunky, solid sound of bone against bone, and I opened them again. Olympias was glaring at me.

'Do you keep a snake in a bottle?' she repeated.

Olympias wasn't quite the formidable presence that her husband was; nevertheless, she could have stapled a seven-ply shield to an oak door just by scowling at it. This was, I judged, no time for finely honed Athenian evasiveness. 'No,' I said.

'Oh.' She didn't look happy. 'I'd heard you did.'

I contemplated trying to explain, but decided not to. For all I knew, conjuring the spirits of the dead into small non-returnable wine jars was grounds for crucifixion in those parts; or perhaps it was fraudulently pretending to conjure ghosts into jars that was the capital offence. I had no idea; and it's a good general rule of thumb that if you haven't got the faintest idea what's going on, the truth's as good as anything else. At that, the bald-headed type looked up at me (up to that point he'd been studying the straps of his sandals).

'Don't you claim to speak to the immortal part of the soul of Socrates, which you keep sealed in a jar?' he said, in a loud, high, clear voice. 'I gather that's how you earn your living.'

Gods in Heaven, I thought, are there any of these damned Macedonians who *aren't* expert interrogators? Who was going to cross-examine me next, I wondered? The cook's dog?

'That's true,' I said.

'Thought so,' crowed Olympias, bashing the arm of her chair with her balled fist. 'I told you he keeps a snake in a bottle.'

I suppose I should have seen that one creeping up on me. Olympias' people believe that snakes are the spirits of the dead; they're immortal and they go from body to body, shedding the old one when it's worn out just as a regular snake sheds its skin. I reckoned it'd be best if I kept my face shut, and that's what I did.

'I see,' Philip said, after a moment. 'Well, that seems to cover it. Right?' he added, looking back over his shoulder at Olympias. She nodded. The old man grinned. Aristotle looked as if he'd woken up out of a nightmare about being marooned on an island inhabited by cannibals to find it was all horribly true. 'That's all right, then,' Philip said. 'In that case, I'd like to offer you a job as my son's tutor.'

I felt – well, imagine how you'd feel after you'd been wandering in the desert for two days, slowly dying of thirst, and then someone sneaked up behind you, knocked you down and started drowning you in a shallow pool of fresh spring water. My fears about being tortured to death flocked out of my mind like an audience leaving the theatre, only to find themselves sharing a narrow gateway with a whole lot of new fears about offending Philip by refusing his offer, which were all trying to crowd in.

'I'm honoured,' I stalled. 'This is truly a great distinction—'

'He means no,' Olympias grunted, chewing on a stray curl of hair that had crept out from behind her ear. 'Offer him money. If he won't take the job, see if he'll sell the snake.'

'Olympias,' Philip purred (and it wasn't a domestic cat kind of purr). 'Euxenus,' he went on, 'please don't be afraid to speak your mind. As I'm sure you know, my son already has two highly qualified tutors; my cousin Leonidas,' (the bald man nodded very slightly), 'and your celebrated compatriot Aristotle, both of whom enjoy my fullest confidence. The Queen, however,' he went on, his voice hardening a little, 'feels that another perspective, perhaps one that encompasses more of the spiritual, mystic side—'

'Tell him we want the snake,' Olympias rumbled, in that remarkably deep voice of hers. 'I don't care a damn about the Athenian, but I want that snake for my son.'

You know, it was almost worth all the terror and embarrassment just to watch Aristotle squirm. He was hating this, I could see. I formed a hasty assessment of my position. I could refuse altogether, and risk having to be persuaded to change my mind – Philip had a staff of full-time persuaders; he recruited them from among his cavalry farriers, on the grounds of physical strength and familiarity with the use and properties of red-hot metal – or I could sell them the empty jar and risk assassination on the grounds of having swindled the royal house of Macedon. Or I could take the job. The last choice had the fringe benefit of a number of chances to dump on the celebrated Aristotle, not to mention the prospect of a chance of getting a closer look at that damned map, which had become something of an obsession with me . . .

The map that invariably lay across Philip's knees whenever we'd had meetings with him looked to be (and was, as I was able to confirm later on) very old, with a long and remarkable history; turns out it was one of the maps made by Aristagoras of Miletus, who governed the city in the old days when it was part of the Persian empire. He sent out maps, among the first ever seen in Greece, with his requests for aid from the mainland in the great rebellion against Persian rule; they impressed the hell out of everyone except the Spartans, who actually took the trouble to read them and work out how far away Miletus was. Other cities, including Athens, sent token contingents or other forms of aid and comfort to the rebellion; after it had been utterly crushed, the Persian King, Darius, sent a punitive expedition to deal with the mainland states who'd taken part, and destroyed two great cities, Chalcis and Eretria. The Athenians managed to defeat the expedition at the celebrated battle of Marathon, and it was the need to avenge this defeat that led King Xerxes to invade Greece with his vast, unwieldy army of a million men, after which it became an established principle in the Greek mind that Greece would never be safe until the Persian Empire was overthrown. So, as you can see, Phryzeutzis, Aristagoras' pretty sheets of engraved bronze had a lot to answer for, one way or another; and here one of them was, in the possession of the King of Macedon, another mighty conqueror. The fact that he used it more as a dinner-tray cum writing-desk than as a whetstone for his aspirations was neither here nor there.

'I shall be honoured to accept,' I said.

'Oh, good,' Philip replied, with a very slight trace of a yawn. 'Have a word with Leonidas here later on today; he'll make the arrangements and sort you out, tell you how everything's set up. It's, um, a pleasure to welcome you to our household.' He sighed, and gave Olympias a mildly poisonous look. 'You and your potted snake,' he added.

At this point, I suppose I ought to say a few words . . .

Don't sigh like that, Phryzeutzis; quite probably this is the bit you actually want to hear. After all, most people who learn that I knew Alexander when I was younger can't wait for me to tell them: what was he like, what was he *really* like?

And, over the years, I've learned a little speech which I can recite mindlessly, the way the herald recites the formal part of the law without knowing or caring much what he's saying. Probably you've heard it yourself, I can't remember. Anyway, I recite the speech and they go away again, feeling that they've somehow folded the fabric of history back on itself, so that their present has in some way touched the past. It makes them happy, and stops them bothering me.

You, I feel, deserve something better. Now, let's analyse the question; when you ask me, 'What was he *really* like?', what you're asking (whether you realise it or not) is, 'What did you think about him?' – because that's the only way that question can ever be answered when one mortal man talks to another. What did I think of him? That way, Alexander is filtered through me, like whey strained through fine cloth.

You want a straight answer, Phryzeutzis? I'll give you one. I know, I've been putting this off since I started telling you this story, because it's quite difficult for me to say this. But without this rather essential piece of information, you won't be able to make an awful lot of sense of what I have to say about the man later, or indeed what I say about myself. So; here goes.

I have no opinion about Alexander one way or the other; and

that's a deliberate decision on my part, one that's cost me a lot of peace over the years. Let me give you an analogy – it's what we Athenians do best, they say, the subtle art of talking about something else instead of what we've been asked about.

Suppose you lived in the valley on the river-bank, and one year the rains were so heavy that the whole plain flooded, washing out your house and crops and leaving you destitute. Now suppose you lived near the desert, and one year it didn't rain at all, parching your land, killing your stock and driving you out to make your living begging in the streets of some city. In one case, you curse the rain because it keeps falling; in the other, you curse it for not falling at all.

But cursing the rain is pointless, Phryzeutzis; it can't hear you, it's a force of nature, something beyond benevolence or malice. Blame someone if you must – the king, for not building a dam or an embankment; your father, for settling on the edge of the desert; your neighbour, for blocking the drains or bleeding off water from the spring that feeds your well. Blame human beings, whose actions and decisions you can at least understand; blame the rain and you just look ridiculous.

Alexander was a force of nature; he was a force of history. Think about him dispassionately for a moment. Think of the hole you'd make in history if you cut him out of it, like a carpenter fret-sawing a pattern out of a brass sheet to inlay into a piece of wood; see if anybody or anything else would fit in that hole, so as not to destroy the integrity of history. I think you'll be surprised.

First, Alexander would've been nobody if he hadn't been Philip's son. Philip took the old Macedon and changed it out of all recognition, made it the greatest power in Greece. By the same token, Philip couldn't have done this if the great cities of Greece – Athens, Sparta, Thebes, Corinth – hadn't bled themselves weak and silly with their own incessant wars, hadn't grown weak and lazy and fat, and most of all *tired*, so that they couldn't be bothered any more. The same goes for Persia; if the Persian empire hadn't been on its last legs anyway, if the Persian king had been anything like as good a soldier as his predecessors— Look at it another way. All round this Alexander-shaped hole we've sawed out of history are these factors that made him possible, and the more you look at them, the more important they become, the smaller Alexander gets. It's quite possible that if Alexander had died when he was a week old, Macedonians or Greeks or both would still have overthrown the Great King and taken his empire. It may have taken them longer; then again, they may have made a more thorough job.

Now we've reduced Alexander, let's grind him flat. As a man, Alexander had his faults. Lots of them. He had no depth or breadth of feeling or understanding – insofar as he had a sense of humour I'll swear he learned it by rote, as he learned many skills that he reckoned a great man ought to have. He had no sense of pleasure beyond the gratifications of succeeding in his task; he was hardly interested in sex, in beauty of any kind, in anything that wasn't needed for the work in hand; he selected the qualities that made him up like a man packing for a long journey, taking with him only the things he knew he'd need. In a sense, Alexander was painfully flat; look at him face on, he was so broad he blocked out the light; look at him sideways, you'd hardly know he was there.

That's Alexander, then; a flat shape in history, like a country sawn out of one of Aristagoras' sheet-bronze maps; an image representing a substantive thing, not the thing itself. Now, this flattening effect is something I reckon happens to all Great Men to a certain extent. What they do starts to replace what they are, until there's nothing left except the shape of their achievements in history. But Alexander, being Philip's son, was born that way; he was brought up and trained to be the conqueror of the world, to finish what Philip had started. More than that; Philip was an enormous man, both in his place in history and in himself – I've said, I think, how he seemed to fill any room he was in, making anybody else seem incidental and irrelevant. Alexander was both bigger and smaller than his father. Alexander – well, it's possible to convince oneself that he was a god; rather harder to believe that he was ever a human being. You'd have to crush a dozen Alexanders in an olive-press before you could extract enough humanity to make up an ordinary person. As a human being, he was *tiny*.

Most of all, though – well, we're considering what I thought of him; and when you look back, as I frequently have, there he always is, in the background of my life, following me about like a sausage-maker's dog. He was born on the day my father died. As soon as he was old enough to be of any account, he sort of welled up out of the ground and enveloped me, as if I'd put my foot in quicksand or an enormous cow-pat. Afterwards – well, we'll come to that. This is going to sound a little crazy, bearing in mind our respective fortunes and place in history; but over the years I came to regard Alexander as my shadow – a flat, dark thing that was always beside me, a step behind or in front depending on which direction the sun was shining but always there, matching my every move in another dimension, following or leading me; dammit, a part of me but completely separate, not like me at all.

Shall I tell you something I've never told anyone before, Phryzeutzis? I plan on being better than Alexander some day, greater than Alexander, better remembered, ever so much more loved. Because I *am* better than him – I cast him, my shadow, in a sense I made him in my image, but I am a whole man, he was only ever flat and dark, made unnaturally long and wide by the angle of the sun behind me. I shall beat him yet, Phryzeutzis, by virtue of leaving behind me something of value, by improving the lives of countless thousands of people who haven't even been born yet. Gods, I've beaten him already, haven't I? You doubt that, ask yourself this: which one of us is still alive?

Sorry. Got a bit carried away there. Yapping Dog philosophy; we creep up on the statues of great men at dead of night and chop off their balls with a cold chisel. Serves you right for asking.

First on the agenda: to tell Philocrates, the leader of the embassy, that I wouldn't be going back to Athens with him.

I didn't get the response I'd expected. Unrealistically, I'd hoped for something like *You can't do that, Athens needs you, your insight, your clarity of vision*. Didn't get that. I'd been afraid of *You bastard, you're betraying your city for a fistful of dirty Macedonian silver*. Didn't get that either. I'd have happily settled for *It's probably for the best, it means there'll be at least one pro-Athenian voice at Philip's court* or *It's your life, mate, and if you think this is where your work lies, then go to it and the best of luck*. Huh.

In fact, the conversation went something like this:

'Philocrates,' I said, 'I won't be going back with you. Philip's asked me to tutor his son, and I've accepted.'

Philocrates, who looked as if he hadn't really been listening, blinked a couple of times. 'What? Oh, all right,' he said. 'Thanks for letting me know. I'll see if we can get a refund on your fare.'

I'd scribbled a note to my brother Eudemus, the banker, entrusting my property in Athens to his care and hinting at what would happen to him if it wasn't all present and correct when I returned. Philocrates looked at it as if I'd just handed him a live rat, then promised faithfully to deliver it and tucked it away in a fold of his gown. As it turned out, Eudemus did well by me; he let my house to a foreign merchant and invested my money in a grain-ship making the run between Athens and the Black Sea, which brought in a reasonable return and managed not to hit any rocks, an unusual state of affairs for a ship as heavily insured as a grain-freighter.

Next, I went to see Leonidas. Remember him? He was the ancient, bald cousin of King Philip who'd ambushed me with a trick question when I was being auditioned. On my way to see him I ran into a Macedonian guard officer I'd somehow managed to strike up some sort of proto-friendship with (we both liked dogs and the poetry of Semonides of Amorgos, and we'd sat next to each other for an evening at some damned banquet or other). I asked him if he could tell me anything about the man.

'Leonidas?' my friend said. 'Sure.' Then he hesitated for a moment. 'Leonidas the Prince's tutor?' he asked.

'That's right. Older man, bald, the King's cousin—'

'Ah, yes. Him.' My friend lowered his voice a little. 'Better known around the court as either the Clayball or the Old Felt Hat; they're both apt enough, because they're both things you can mould into any shape that fits.'

'I see,' I said. 'So he's – adaptable? Versatile?'

My friend smiled. 'You could say that,' he replied. 'Or you could say he's a devious, slippery old bastard who's spent a lifetime around the court and hasn't been killed yet – which, for a Macedonian of royal blood, is a remarkable and somewhat disreputable achievement. Over the years, so they say, he's changed tack more often than a clipper sailing up and down the forks of Chalcidice.'

'Ah,' I said.

My friend put a massive hand on my shoulder by way of silent commiseration. 'I don't know what your business with Leonidas is,' he said, 'but whatever it is, don't turn your back on him for a split second. And whatever you do, don't try to get between him and the Prince. Those who do tend to have accidents – you know, falling down flights of steps in the dark, accidentally drowning in shallow rivers, that sort of thing. I imagine he believes Philip's on the way out so he's making sure of his influence over the Prince, as a form of insurance for his old age. The gods only know how your friend Aristotle's managed to last this long without ending up at the foot of some cliff.'

Precisely what I needed to hear; I almost went dashing off after Philocrates to beg him not to cancel my berth on the boat home. But (I reasoned) if I were to run out on them now, King Philip and the Queen wouldn't be best pleased with me either; so I had the choice, antagonise someone who was well on his way to being the most powerful man in Greece, or make a deadly enemy of one of his most trusted advisers. Broad as it's long, really, I concluded.

So I went to see Leonidas.

I found him in a corner of a shield-maker's workshop in the armoury. He was sitting on a low three-legged stool, scraping little scraps of parchment with a well-worn block of pumice.

'Economy,' he said, before I had a chance to ask him what he was doing. 'I scrounge bits and pieces of waste parchment from the shield-menders – they use it for wrapping the handles – and scrape them down till they're fit to write on. Then, when they're all filled up, I bring them back here, borrow a stone and clean them off again. Make all the ink, too, and melt the wax for the writing tablets. Never chuck anything away if I can help it. All the time I've been running the school, haven't had to ask the King for an obol for equipment.'

I believed him. He had the appearance of a man who bought a really expensive luxury cloak thirty years ago and still expects to get a further twenty years' wear out of it. Just the sort of man, in fact, to be obsessive about details.

'Excuse me,' I was eventually able to say, after I'd sat through a long sermon on the divine right of kings. 'Are you expecting me? I'm Euxenus, the new tutor.'

He looked up at me and grinned. He still had all his own teeth (and at his age too).

'I know,' he said. 'I was there, remember? You're the snake-charmer. You use a tame snake? Heard tell they're easier to train than a dog, those snakes, if you find one big enough. Folks round here have 'em to keep the rats down.'

I decided not to rise to any of that. 'Someone said something about a school,' I replied. 'Is this it?'

He laughed. 'Not even close,' he said. 'School's not in Pella, it's over to Mieza, day and a half's ride south-west of here, in Midas' Garden. That's vineyard and orchard country.' He was talking to me as if I was a hard-working but backwards ten-year-old. 'So you're going to come and teach, are you? What?'

I hadn't the faintest idea; my brief from King Philip had been to teach, that was all. 'Oh, I can teach anything,' I replied. 'I'm an Athenian scientist, to us the whole world is our—'

'I do Homer,' said Leonidas, 'and music and accounting. Aristotle –' he didn't actually gob and spit when he said the name, but the contempt in his voice was unmistakable and communicated with splendid economy '– Aristotle, he does geography and politics and rhetoric, abstract mathematics, natural sciences, all that. We've got a trainer who does athletics and drill. What does that leave that you can teach?'

'Logic,' I replied firmly. 'And ethics. And land management,' I added, suddenly remembering the one thing I did know a little bit about. But Leonidas shook his head.

'I do land management,' he said, 'under accounting. And Aristotle does it under geography and politics. What're you going to do it under?'

I looked him in the eye for a moment. He was beginning to get on my nerves, something that many people try to do but very few manage to achieve. 'All right,' I said, 'you tell me. And before you say anything else, I didn't ask for this job. Queen Olympias had me sent for, under the mistaken belief that I can do snake magic. If you want to go to their majesties and tell them I'm surplus to requirements, you go right ahead.' He didn't move or speak, so I went on. 'All right,' I said, 'you're in charge of this school, you tell me what I can do to help.'

He rubbed his chin, on which grew the longest, straggliest beard you ever saw in your life. It seemed to drip off his face like a slow leak in a water-pipe. 'All right,' he said. 'You can do astronomy, medicine, military history and literature, except,' he added sternly, 'Homer. I do Homer. Sound good to you?'

'Sure,' I replied. 'Especially Homer. I never could be doing with Homer.'

He looked at me as if I'd just boasted of raping his mother. 'That's settled, then,' he said. 'Now I guess you want to hear about the school.'

I nodded and sat down, or rather I perched on the edge of a workbench. 'That'd probably be a good idea,' I said.

He sighed, picked out another scrap of parchment and went on with his endless slow polishing.

'You being Athenian,' he said, 'you don't know about Macedonian ways. Well?'

'Not a lot,' I admitted. 'So I'd be grateful for any—'

'In Macedon,' Leonidas interrupted, 'we believe in loyalty. Most important thing of all. So when the heir to the throne's still just a kid, we choose other kids his age, noblemen's sons, to be his life companions – they grow up together, get educated together, each one of them knows what he's going to be when he grows up. Makes sense that way. Always worked, in the past. And that's who the school's for – Prince Alexander and the companions.'

I nodded. 'It does sound like a good idea,' I replied. 'It's always struck me as odd that in my country, the most important work of all, running the city, is the only work nobody's ever trained for. I mean,' I went on, not allowing the old vulture to interrupt me, 'shoemakers' sons learn their trade from childhood, and likewise carpenters, poets and scent-bottle painters. Nobody learns government until it's too late, and even then the only people we've got who profess to teach it are men like me, who've never held power in their lives.'

Leonidas smirked at me. 'And that qualifies you to come here and teach it,' he said. 'Don't follow.'

'Ah,' I replied, 'but you're forgetting something. We Athenians can teach ourselves anything. And we do. But it's in spite of the way we bring up our children, not because of it. Well, that's not strictly true either. When we're young we're taught to have enquiring minds. Once you have one of those, you can learn anything.'

'Except Homer,' Leonidas said, studying the parchment scrap in his hand. 'Homer, you've just got to sit down and learn by heart.'

'There I agree with you,' I replied. 'All right, you've told me about the general idea of the school. Now tell me about the kids.'

He grunted, and settled himself a little more comfortably on his stool. 'Well, aside from the Prince, there's Hephaestion. Good kid, not the quickest but he tries harder than the rest so he keeps up. Harpalus, he's a bright kid, too bright even; mustard for figuring, he'll be treasurer or chancellor one day. Ptolemy's bright but doesn't try. Callas is a good boy, but thick. Cleitus, he's the pick of the bunch for brains and character together, but the Prince doesn't like him. He likes Philotas – that's Parmenio's son; you came across Parmenio? Thought you might have. Philip wouldn't be half what he is today without Parmenio, though nobody understands that except me. Pity his son's an arsehole, but that can't be helped, and maybe he'll grow out of it. There's others too, but you keep an eye on them and the rest won't matter.'

'And Alexander?' I said. 'What about him?'

Leonidas looked me in the eye. 'Met him?' I nodded. 'Then you'll already know. He's what we'll all make of him, no more and no less.' He stood up, and although he was just a little old man and I was half as tall again and probably twice his bulk, I felt myself shrinking back. 'That's why this job's *important*, boy. That's why if you don't do it right, I'll kill you. Got that?'

I blinked a couple of times. 'I think so,' I replied. 'No pressure or anything; just do a good job, and I get to stay alive.'

'That's it exactly,' Leonidas confirmed, sitting down again. I could see now that he was Philip's cousin. 'Like you just said, no pressure.'

This is the way things happen, Phryzeutzis; this goes some way towards explaining why things are as they are. Because there had been a time when I was destitute and desperate enough to make my living pretending to talk to a ghost in an empty wine-jar, I found myself in Mieza, one of four men charged with responsibility for building the next king of Macedon, King Philip's heir. Because of the empty jar, and the swarm of wild bees choosing to nest in the foundations of that building, and Queen Olympias' snake fetish; trivia, unpredictable scraps of the-way-things-happen, too random and inconsequential to be dignified with a grand name like destiny or fate, or even luck. Go further back, and you'll see the moment when I chose the wrong coloured pebble when my brothers and I were casting lots for who stayed and who went away. Go further back and there's my father, dying an unnecessary death in the steading at Phyle because a slave had hurt his leg and was afraid of being thought a malingerer. All these diverging possibilities; hold a dried leaf up to the light so that it becomes transparent and you can see the veins, how they branch and fork, all derived from one stem but ending up divided into countless small choices. Well, I was just one of these random sequences of cause and effect; Aristotle was another, so was Leonidas, so was Philip – gods alone know how many of them there were, whether they were all equally important, or some more so than others. Don't know, don't care. The only possible conclusion is that nothing was anybody's fault, simply because the fault must go right back, from the frayed ends of the vein back into the stem, from the stem to the branch, from the branch to the tree, from the tree to the root, from the root to the seed, from the seed to the tree.

So why do I feel bad about it, Phryzeutzis?

Consider, if you will, the difference between men and gods. Oh, I'm not talking about your gods, I'm talking about *proper* gods, the ones I grew up with; Zeus and Hera and Athena and Apollo and Ares. Now a god is much, much stronger than a man, and he lives for ever, and nothing can harm him – he's like a city, if you like, or a way of governing cities; and the point about a god is, he doesn't care. Doesn't give a damn. Nobody can call him to account, punish him, threaten him or frighten him, and because he lives for ever he's got no purpose or meaning to his existence. A god lives for his pleasure, his entertainment, for himself. Like a city, a god exists to exist; simply continuing to be there is all that's expected of him, all he can really achieve. Now take a man; weak, fragile and mortal. He can be called to account, punished, threatened, frightened; to him, right and wrong and good and evil are very meaningful things; and because his life is so short and lacking in value, he needs to believe it has a meaning. So there we have it. Virtuous, honourable, conscientious mortals and amoral, careless gods. Zeus doesn't give a damn, and I do.

And guess which one of us decides what happens.

This is the way things happen, Phryzeutzis. This is the way things are.

CHAPTER SEVEN

◫◫◫◫◫◫◫◫◫◫◫◫◫◫◫◫◫◫◫◫◫◫◫

I remember my last day as an Athenian ambassador, the day before I became a Macedonian teacher.

Demosthenes the Athenian, in his own opinion and that of several others the greatest orator of his time, had been working on his speech ever since we left Athens. He was going to make just one speech – one honey of a speech, one sledgehammer, battering-ram, warship-beak, grandmother and -father of all speeches speech. After hearing it, Philip would immediately curl up like an over-turned woodlouse and die. If by some astounding miracle or divine intervention Philip managed to live on an hour or so after Demosthenes had made his speech, he was going to spend his last agonising minutes in this life apologising to the Athenian people and forswearing every last inch of Athenian territory, every last stool and jar and bowl and blacksmith's apron he'd stolen from them. Once the Macedonians had heard Demosthenes' speech, they'd all form up in column and march off a cliff into the sea. Compared with being on the wrong end of Demosthenes' speech, being hit by Zeus' thunderbolt was a tickle under the chin with the very tip of a long, soft feather. It was going to be, we got the impression, some speech.

Naturally, we begged Demosthenes for previews, but he wouldn't let us hear so much as a word. We implored. We cajoled. We threatened. We tried guessing – 'Hey, Demosthenes, my friend here reckons you'll say "and" at some point in your speech. Is that right?' All in vain. As soon as we started on at him, he'd withdraw to a corner of the deck or the inn, cover his head with his gown and ignore us until we went away. Now there aren't many places to hide on a ship, so he even took to climbing up into the rigging or burrowing down between the jars in the cargo hold, like a mouse. Obviously, we couldn't wait to hear this speech.

Well, the days went by; no speech. We reached Pella; no speech. Day followed day, negotiating session merged into negotiating session; we conceded everything that Philip wanted and got nothing in return; no speech. It was like the hot, thundery weather of late summer, when you look up at the sky every morning and you know it'll rain today, but it doesn't; it's hot and tense and even the goats in the pen and the mules in the stable get restless and quarrelsome, but still no rain and no thunder. No speech.

Then we worked it out; he was waiting for the final day of the talks, to ensure that he got maximum effect. There Philip'd be, nicely relaxed and off guard after his diplomatic triumphs, imagining that it was all over and he could tick Athens off his list of Things To Do Today; then, at the last minute, Demosthenes would pop up like the god at the end of a tragic play and blow Philip into wind-strewn chaff, right when he imagined he was safe. We couldn't help admiring the audacity of the plan, to say nothing of the firm grasp of tactics and the insights into Philip's personality – after all, it was broadly based on Philip's celebrated battlefield manoeuvre of letting his enemy breach his line and pass through the middle of his forces, the better to cut them off and surround them at the very last moment. Fitting, we thought. Brilliant, even. Not to mention inspirational and a tremendous morale-booster.

And the moment came. It was after we'd officially concluded the embassy's business and made our last concession – we'd been quite open-handed about it, giving away big raw cutlets of our national endowment, since we knew for certain that once Demosthenes had made his speech, we'd get 'em all back again – and we were just about to plunge into yet another drab, long-winded Macedonian court ceremonial when Demosthenes reared up on his hind legs, cleared his throat and began to speak.

'Gentlemen,' he began. 'Were it not for the fact that—'

—And he froze. Either he'd forgotten the words or he'd been seized with a near-fatal dose of stage fright. Whichever it was, he couldn't move, not even enough to open his mouth. He was like one of the many statues of Demosthenes about to make a speech, the ones that at one time were put up all over the place as a symbol of anti-Macedonian feeling, except that a lot of those statues were pretty lifelike and at that precise moment Demosthenes, frankly, wasn't. I couldn't help but be reminded of that old story about Perseus and the head of Medusa the Gorgon, which was so incredibly ugly that it turned whoever looked at it to stone – interesting parallel, that, given the way Philip looked.

For a long while, nobody moved, and there's a fair chance we'd all be there still, all turned to stone, if it hadn't been for Philip. As soon as he'd got over his initial bewilderment and he'd worked out what had happened, he leaned forward a little in his chair and tapped Demosthenes on the arm, just above the elbow.

'It's all right,' he said. 'It happens to all of us now and again. Now, try taking a deep breath, and start again.'

Demosthenes looked at him, breathed in and began to shake.

'Try just telling us your name,' Philip said. 'Just say something, to break the ice. Come on, you can do it.'

'D-d,' Demosthenes mumbled. 'D-d-*d*.'

'All right,' Philip said. 'Now try looking straight past me at the back of the room. Pick a point, something you can fix your eyes on; lamp-sconce, ornament, a particular pattern in a tapestry, doesn't matter what. Just look straight at it, and tell it your name. Out loud. Go on.'

Demosthenes' eyes locked onto something, and he gasped for a moment like a stranded fish.

'D-d-d-demos,' he said. 'D-d-d-d-*mosthnes*.'

Philip clapped his hands together. 'Well done,' he said. 'All right, this is good, we're making progress. Again – and this time, a bit more slowly and fluently.'

Demosthenes, of course, never made his speech. Philip coaxed and coached him to the point where he could say his name, his father's name and his city and deme, then let him off the hook.

'I'm disappointed, though,' Philip said, as Demosthenes sat down, staring at the ground between his feet. 'I've been looking forward to hearing a Demosthenes speech ever since the conference began. You'll have to come back another time, when you're feeling a bit better.'

★

The embassy left for home. I stayed.

I hadn't planned it, gods know. I'd never before shown any inclination to want to leave Attica – quite the opposite, in fact. It wasn't as if I was unhappy there, or that the job at Macedon was anything wonderful. On the other hand, I didn't have any cause not to stay; no family worth speaking of (at least, none who'd talk to me), no debts, no obligations. It was like dying, and being reborn, though as what remained to be seen.

Later the same day I found myself in a cart headed for the village of Mieza. It was a big, heavy farm-cart, and the rear offside wheel squeaked. In the cart with me were Leonidas and Alexander, who I'd already met; Parmenio's sons Philotas and Nicanor; another boy called Menippus, about whom I remember nothing at all; and the principal of the school, Lysimachus. We went for the rest of that day in stony silence, nobody daring to say a thing in front of the stranger (me), and put up for the night in a small, comfortable inn about halfway between Pella and Mieza. When the innkeeper saw us, and the two Thracian cavalrymen we had as outriders, he went white as a sheet and dashed back inside; a few seconds later, his wife and son emerged, looking equally panic-stricken, and started unloading our kit without a word.

It was unnerving, that silence. I was beginning to wonder what on earth I'd walked into. Was it some really ancient, bizarre custom, that the young hope of Macedon went everywhere in complete silence, broken only during lessons? As an Athenian, I wasn't sure I could stand that. Athenians talk. All the time. The surest way to drive an Athenian mad is to shut him up in a confined space on his own and deprive him of conversation; and even then he'll talk to himself, disagree, shout, lose patience, start a fight . . . But that theory, mercifully, proved false; I could hear them whispering to each other when they thought I couldn't hear, though I couldn't make out anything of what they were saying. I wanted to break the silence myself by talking to one of them, asking a simple question and defying them to break all the rules of polite conduct by not answering; but I had an attack of Demosthenes' fever and couldn't bring myself to say a word. Dinner, consisting of bread, cheese, cold sausage and a pleasantly sweet, strong, neat wine, went down in silence except for wordless demolition noises, and we were shown our sleeping quarters in dumb show and left alone for the night.

I tried to put it all out of my mind; instead, I asked myself why Aristotle wasn't with the party. That thought, however, wasn't conducive to sweet dreams. I kept remembering episodes from mythology where the victim is sent on a mission by the wicked king to a distant town or province bearing a sealed letter which contains instructions for his own execution. The big mystery, why I'd been offered the job in the first place, didn't seem such a mystery after all. Aristotle had been here – what, two years? Five? I couldn't remember offhand, but long enough, surely, to have wormed his way into the King's confidence and affection. I could picture the scene; the throne-room, dark except for the ambivalent light of one smoking lamp. Aristotle approaches the royal presence and whispers for a moment in Philip's ear. The Athenian herald, Euxenus. What of it, my friend? Do you know him? Know him! Why, your majesty, I hate him above all mortals, as would you if only you knew . . . Tell me more, Aristotle, tell me more . . . Philip nods; his one eye burns fiercely in the gloom. I see, he says quietly, I see. Well, we'll have to do something about that, won't we? Leave it to me, my friend. Aristotle bows deeply; thank you, your majesty, you can't know how long I've dreamt of vengeance . . . Think nothing of it, my good and faithful servant. The man's as good as dead.

Well, you know how it is when you're lying awake in the middle of the night, fretting. You can imagine anything, any kind of horror, and convince yourself that it's true. And guilty conscience had something to do with it, of course—

What, I never told you, Phryzeutzis? Well, I'd better tell you now, otherwise this whole business of Aristotle and me isn't going to make a whole lot of sense. Yes, the wretched man had every reason to hold a grudge against me, after what I'd done to him. It's not a story I like telling, mainly because it puts me in a bad light; but what the hell, this is History.

Actually, it was all Diogenes' fault; at least, he put me up to it.

Aristotle collected cities; that is, he was compiling a huge database of the constitutions of Greek city-states, with the aim of reducing all this data down and using it to compile the authoritative, all-time Number One best model constitution for a Greek city. He was quite serious about the project; he'd been to all manner of out-of-the-way places, asking questions and getting under the feet of the city fathers, and whenever a stranger from a city he hadn't distilled and bottled yet arrived in Athens he'd scamper off with his tablets and stylus and be asking detailed questions about procedures for the co-option of council members to replace a deceased Superintendent of Drains before the unfortunate traveller had had a chance to shake the dust out of his cloak.

For some reason Diogenes and I found this noble project unbearably amusing; so we decided to sabotage it. Aristotle had never met me or heard of me; so Diogenes saw to it that a rumour went round concerning the arrival in Athens of a citizen of Escoracaschia (meaning, loosely translated, 'Pissoffsville'; there's advanced Athenian wit for you), the furthest-flung Greek colony in the world.

That citizen, of course, was me. We hired a room in a cheap inn, bought some raggedy old travelling clothes in the market, and waited. Sure enough, along came Aristotle, tablets in hand, imploring me to spare him just an hour or so of my time . . .

'Sho' nuff,' I replied, in the corniest stage-Doric accent I could muster. 'Mighty civil of you to take an interest in us plain folks from Hyperborea, you bein' a book-learned gennelmun an' all.'

Then I told him all about my native city; how it lies on the southern tip of an island that lies opposite the north-eastern coast of Europe, an island so distant and remote that for half the year it rains nearly every day, and great banks of fog sweep down from the hills and cover everything, so that between the driving rain and the impenetrable mist day was as obscure as night, and instead of using our eyes to find our way about we used our noses, planting aromatic herbs at strategic points as beacons to guide us to our fields and villages; how the said rain and fog makes it impossible for us to tell each other apart except at very close quarters, with the result that we long ago ceased trying, and now no longer differentiate between other men's families and wives and our own; how, in consequence, we don't recognise such concepts as ownership and property but hold everything in common, so that a man who blunders in out of the rain sits down in front of the hearth and makes that house his home, until such time as the wind and the rain stave in the roof and send him on his travels again; how there is no crime or wickedness in our city because, when you're soaked to the skin and coughing your lungs up all the time, you simply don't have the energy to start fights or plot against your neighbour (and since you haven't the faintest idea who your neighbour's going to be from one day to the next, there really isn't much point); how, in short, thanks to the unremitting violence of nature and the utter savagery of our environment, we live in a sort of earthly paradise with neither poverty nor excessive wealth, without crime or discord, freed from the snares and delusions of the flesh and the petty aspirations and ambitions of the natives of happier climes. In fact (I added, picking up a jug of water), being this far south, in this unwholesome and decadent land of sunshine and warm earth, my heart ached for the feel of cold rain dripping down between my neck and collar, the comforting dampness of a leaky boot, the spiritual solace of a lungful of phlegm – at which point I solemnly upended the jug of water over my head, closed my eyes and relaxed my face into a beatific vision of contentment.

And Aristotle believed it. He fell for it, this dedicated man of science, this pre-eminent logician, like a stranger off an Egyptian grain-freighter who meets a man in the market square offering to sell him the Acropolis for five hundred drachmas. He took the whole thing so seriously that it frightened me; but I didn't dare tell him, the joke had gone too far. So he thanked me profusely, folded his tablets carefully away, and scuttled off like a startled crab to write up his notes and incorporate them into his work in progress.

So taken was he by the world-view of the good people of Escoracaschia Ap' Eschatois ('Pissoffsville At The End Of The World', to give it its official designation) that he wrote up a monograph on the subject and announced that he would deliver it as a public lecture, admission one obol. Then he sent to discover whether by any lucky chance Oumeleresas son of Oudemiapolis ('Come-off-it, son of No-such-city'; subtlety our speciality) was still in Athens and might possibly be prepared to attend the lecture and answer questions from the audience.

At this point I told Diogenes that the joke had gone far enough and I wanted nothing more to do with it. No power on earth, I told him, would induce me to get up on a platform in front of people who probably knew me and make a public exhibition of myself. Absolutely not. No point even considering the idea.

So there I was, on the platform, doing my best to shade my face under the brim of an impossibly broad, floppy hat that Diogenes had dug up somewhere for me; and there was Aristotle, declaiming his monograph to a painfully large audience with all the passion of one who has long sought and finally found.

It was a long time before somebody laughed, and even then it was just one snigger; a soft, muffled snort, the sound made by a man who's got a gathered handful of cloak stuffed in his mouth and still can't stop himself from laughing. But once that noise had broken the silence, others followed in a torrent, like water coming through a compromised dam, until the whole crowd were roaring their heads off – and there was Aristotle, his nose buried in his manuscript, not looking up, still carefully reading. When the noise was so loud he could no longer hear his own voice he looked up, with an expression of bewilderment and sorrow on his face that would have melted a heart of stone.

'What's the m-matter?' he said. 'Why are you laughing?'

Not the best thing to say, under the circumstances. I tell you, if my celebrated grandfather Eupolis the comic poet had ever managed to get a laugh like that, he'd have prayed to Apollo to shoot him dead on the spot, since life could hold nothing better for him if he lived to be a thousand. Aristotle, meanwhile, was on his feet, waving his hands in my direction and yelling that if they didn't believe him, here was a citizen of the city, in person, who'd confirm that every word he'd said was absolutely true.

Whereupon I stood up and took off my hat, and the whole crowd went quiet. I looked at them, and then at Aristotle; and some evil god put words into my mouth that I've repented ever since.

'All right, boss,' I said. 'Now can I have my three drachmas?'

That was when they started throwing things – fruit, mostly, some chunks of sausage, a few stones and shards of pottery. About the only life-threatening thing that got thrown was the leg off a small bronze tripod, and I entirely agree that it was right and proper that it hit me a glancing blow on the side of the head and sent me down like a sacrificial bull when the priest whacks its neck with a big axe. The next thing I knew, therefore, was opening my eyes to Diogenes' malevolent grin and the worst headache, bar two, I've ever had in a long and headache-prone life.

And that, Phryzeutzis, is why I was afraid Aristotle might have arranged an obscure and bloody death for me, out in the wilds of the Macedonian countryside, where it could be blamed on renegade Illyrians or bears. It was, you'll agree, a singularly obnoxious thing to do (quite apart from the humiliation and shame, he'd spent a sizeable portion of his ready cash on having a hundred copies of the monograph made for immediate sale, all of which ended up as fish-wrap and shield-grip padding), and if I'd been Aristotle I wouldn't have rested until the man responsible for such an outrage was paying his three obols to Charon the Ferryman for his one-way ride across the River of Death.

Anyway; dawn broke, and there I was, still awake, still largely unmurdered, and wishing very hard that I was safely back in Attica, where if someone wants to kill you they falsely accuse you of treason in the Law-Courts and the whole thing is done in a calm, civilised manner. I sneaked out into the courtyard, hid in a doorway until I saw the landlord's son going by with a bucket of oats for the mules, jumped out on him and grabbed him by both arms.

'All right,' I said. 'What's going on? Why won't anybody talk to me?'

But the poor lad just stared at me and made a soft whimpering noise, so I let him go and sat down on the mounting block, feeling very confused; at which point, someone behind me cleared his throat.

'Morning,' said Leonidas. 'You're up early. Trouble sleeping?'

I nodded. 'Tell me,' I said, 'what is it with you people, or with me? Why won't anybody talk to me?'

Leonidas grinned. 'They're scared,' he said.

I blinked. 'Scared?'

'Terrified.'

'Of me?'

'Of the snake.'

I opened my mouth, but no sound came out.

'By now,' Leonidas went on, 'word's reached all four corners of Macedon; beware of the Athenian wizard and his familiar spirit. Superstitious people. Almost as bad as the Thessalians. Mind you,' he added darkly, 'Thessalians have good reason to be superstitious, every third one of 'em's a witch.'

For all I knew that was meant to be a joke, but I didn't feel like laughing (and besides; from what I gather, it's true). 'That's crazy,' I said. 'Look, how many times do I have to tell you people this, there is no snake, repeat, no snake, in my goddamned jar. Understood?'

Leonidas shook his head slowly. 'You say there isn't,' he replied. 'Queen Olympias says there is. Who do people believe? Need you ask?'

'Oh, for . . .' I'd had enough. 'Wait there,' I said, 'and don't move. I'll be back.' I stomped off, fetched the jar and stomped back. 'Now then,' I said, 'you're to be my witness. I'm releasing the neck of the jar, I'm lifting off the lid. There now, as you can plainly see, there is no . . .'

And that was when I dropped the jar (fortunately it landed in a big pile of horseshit and didn't break); about a tenth of a second after, this dinky little black and green snake popped its head out of the jar and stuck its tongue out at me.

Excuse me. I have this thing about snakes. Never could be doing with the horrible creatures.

'You were saying?' Leonidas said, without batting an eyelid.

The snake wound itself out of the jar and slithered away among the straw. I didn't move a muscle.

'You're a brave man,' Leonidas went on. 'One tiny nip from that and you'd be dead before you could blink an eye.'

Just what I wanted to hear. After about a minute I managed to get a grip on myself, and I was just about to explain that it was either a practical joke, an attempt on my life by Aristotle, part of some political chicanery involving Queen Olympias, a really bizarre coincidence or a trick of the light, when I noticed that Prince Alexander was standing in the doorway looking at me. Marvellous. The perfect way to start the day.

'My ancestor Hercules strangled two snakes while he was still in his cot,' Alexander said.

Leonidas smiled at him. 'Hercules,' he said. 'Fancy. I'd heard that was you.'

Alexander gave him a look that'd have made a Scythian feel homesick. 'No,' he replied, 'it was Hercules.'

'Ah, well,' Leonidas replied. 'I expect if you'd had snakes in your cot, you'd have strangled them right enough.'

I managed to get my legs moving and used them, having first picked my jar out of the horse dung. It was a bad enough day already without eavesdropping on whatever private feud there was between Leonidas and Alexander. Another time I'd have lapped it up like a dog slurping up spilt wine – inside information's always useful, as my father told me often enough – but right then I wasn't in the mood. I stomped back inside, wiped off the jar with a handful of loose straw and got my kit ready for the next stage of the journey.

And yet, I thought. There are worse fates that can befall a man than unexpected miracles that prove conclusively that he's not a charlatan and a rogue, especially when he is a charlatan and a rogue and he's just about to start a new job. The best odds said that Olympias arranged for the snake to be there; except, since she presumably wanted me there to counterbalance Philip's basically non-snake-oriented tutorial corps at the Mieza school, why would she have given orders for a deadly poisonous snake to be hidden in my jar, just where it was most likely to give me a nip as I carelessly opened it? I'd be no good to her dead; so, unless it was some kind of primitive ritual thing – ordeal by serpent, to judge whether I was worthy of the task, etc. – that effectively knocked that theory on the head, leaving me with the Aristotle's Revenge version. It made sense, after all. By arranging for Euxenus the purported snake-charmer to die at the fangs of his own stooge, he'd be able to spice his revenge with ridicule and contempt on a par with what I'd exposed him to all those years ago.

And Aristotle wasn't on the cart with the rest of us . . .

I gave it up as a bad job, picked up my luggage and took my place on the cart. As before, conversation stopped dead as soon as I appeared – I remember thinking, you poor fools, what a boring day you've got ahead of you and it's all your own fault. Then, as the cart started to roll, Alexander got up and came and sat beside me.

'Is it true?' he said. 'That you've got one of the sacred serpents in a jar?'

I sighed. 'Maybe,' I said. 'Maybe not.'

Alexander didn't like that answer. 'I asked you a civil question,' he said. 'Is it true?'

'All right,' I replied. 'If you'd asked me that question an hour ago, I'd have said no. But just now I happened to open the jar and yes, there was a dirty great snake in it. Terrified the life out of me. I can only imagine someone put it there for a joke.'

Alexander nodded. 'That's right,' he said, 'only it wasn't a joke. I put it there.'

At that moment I came perilously close to changing the course of history. 'You put it there,' I repeated.

'I just said so, didn't I?'

'Fine.' I took a deep breath. 'Would you mind telling me why?'

'To see how you'd react when you found it, of course. I wanted to see if you're a fake or a real wizard.'

'I see. And what conclusion did you reach?'

Alexander smiled. 'If you'd been a fake, the snake would've bitten you. So obviously you're a wizard.'

'You think I'm a wizard?'

'Isn't that what I just said?'

'Right. That's settled, then, I'm a wizard. Get out of my face before I turn you into a rat.'

Alexander didn't like that either. 'How dare you talk to me like that?' he said angrily.

'Ah, but I can talk how I like to whoever I like. I'm a wizard, remember. Officially.'

'Yes, but even wizards only have one neck.'

What a marvellous way, I thought, to begin our relationship of teacher and pupil. 'If, on the other hand,' I replied, 'I'm not a wizard, then of course I wouldn't dare to speak to your majesty in such a disrespectful manner. Well? Am I still a wizard?'

At that moment I happened to catch sight of old Leonidas. He was smirking. I didn't like that much, either. *Athenian, go home*, seemed to be the message, and I had the uncomfortable feeling that I was stuck in the middle of a group of very stupid, primitive people, all of whom were cleverer than me.

'If you aren't a wizard,' Alexander said, 'the snake would have bitten you.'

I nodded. 'Maybe it did,' I answered. 'Maybe it bit me and I didn't die, because I'm a wizard.'

Just then the boy Hephaestion leaned forward and smiled. He had one of those good-natured I-know-I'm-thick-so-forgive-me smiles that can solve all sorts of problems, up to and including treason and murder. 'Maybe he's a different sort of wizard,' he said. 'Not the sort of wizard the snake's used to, but still a wizard. By the way, what *is* a wizard, exactly?'

I felt as if I'd just been arrested and the arresting officer took another look at me and said, 'Sorry, mistaken identity,' and let me go. I could also feel a dirty great big cue sitting up and begging me to follow it up.

'Now there's a sensible question,' I said. 'Anybody? What's a wizard?'

Nicanor, Parmenio's younger son, held up his hand. 'Someone who can do magic,' he said.

'All right,' I said, 'let's start from there. So what's magic?'

His brother Philotas, a stocky, broad-faced kid sitting with his back to the driver, held up his hand. 'Magic is what gives you power over people,' he said.

'Good answer,' I said, 'but enlarge on it a bit. Otherwise King Philip's a magician. Not,' I added, 'that I'm saying he isn't. But carry on, please.'

Philotas thought for a moment. 'You use magic to make people do what you want,' he said. 'If you aren't a king or something. Kings and people like that have authority.'

'I see,' I replied. 'In that case, let me show you some magic. Here, hold out your hand.'

Philotas looked at me with grave suspicion but did as I said.

'Here you are,' I said, reaching in my mouth for a single obol and putting it in his hand. 'A magic charm for you. Go into a baker's shop, tell him to give you a loaf of bread and hand him the magic charm. He'll do exactly what you tell him to.'

There was a moment of puzzled silence; then somebody laughed. From memory I think it was Hephaestion. Everybody laughed then; not so much because it was a funny joke but because the tension was released. Everybody, that is, except Alexander. He just looked at me.

'So you are a wizard,' he said quietly.

'Yes,' I replied. 'And I learned wizardry from a very great and powerful wizard in Athens, by the name of Diogenes. He taught me to cast spells on people so that they'd believe anything I told them was true; and if people believe something's true, then pretty soon it is true.'

Alexander shook his head. 'That's nonsense,' he said.

'Really?' I raised an eyebrow. 'All right. Suppose you believed I was the King of Macedon. Suppose everybody in Macedon believed it. Wouldn't that make it true?'

He shook his head. 'No,' he replied. 'It'd make it a lie that everybody believed.'

'That's a first-rate definition of the truth,' I said.

'No it isn't,' he replied.

I nodded approvingly. 'Congratulations,' I said. 'Correct answer. You've successfully mastered the first thing I needed to teach you before you can become a wizard too.'

'But I don't want to become a wizard,' Alexander said. 'Wizardry's all about lies and deception.'

'Fine. So what do you want to be when you grow up?'

Alexander shrugged. 'I want to be a god,' he said, as if stating the blindingly obvious. 'Gods do magic, but the magic they do is real.'

It wasn't a bad place to be. In fact, it was a wonderful place, in a self-conscious sort of way. Rolling hills neatly dressed in vineyards and orchards, like a well-muscled man in well-cut clothes; a well-behaved lowlands climate, with the mountains behind like a painted backdrop in the theatre; it felt as if it had been modelled in clay as the perfect setting for the happiest days of your life, and then handed over to a work-gang of giants, who set about bashing rocks and diverting rivers according to the architect's plans.

Well, it was better than Attica; most places are. Attica is a hard country, all rock and dust, everything there is an effort. Mieza was no effort at all.

Nothing could start until Aristotle arrived, so Alexander led his schoolmates off into the hills to hunt things, while I settled into the quarters that Principal Lysimachus had assigned to me. At first, I thought I was being shown round the schoolhouse itself, or some royal hunting lodge; it was a huge house by Attic standards, with a front room as big as any in Athens and a back room almost as big. The furniture was amazing; I learned later that it was all stuff that had accumulated at the palace in Pella over the years – diplomatic gifts, spur-of-the-moment purchases that had seemed like a good idea at the time, that sort of thing; there was a gold-plated tripod stand and an Egyptian painted couch and an ivory folding chair and a huge, huge silvered bronze mixing-bowl that must have held five gallons, embossed with scenes of heroic carnage on one side and amorous centaurs persecuting scantily clad women on the other. There was a cedarwood footstool upholstered with genuine Tyrian purple, worth a fortune in spite of the large scorch-mark on one side where someone had left it too close to the fire. The overall effect was so overwhelming that I shoved most of it over to one side of the room and set up a sort of camp on the other with a plain wooden stool and a low plank table I found in the outhouse.

In the same outhouse I found a box; a heavy olivewood chest with a smashed lock, which I dragged out into the light and opened up. It was full of books; nineteen genuine books, all rather sticky and tacky after spending so long in contact with the olivewood, but all perfectly legible providing you were careful about unrolling them. Gods only know how they got there; my best guess is that they were another diplomatic gift, of the how-lovely-what-is-it? variety, which had been put away out of sight, rediscovered some time later and jemmied open in the vain hope that such a robust locked box must contain something worth having. Then the connection books-school formed in someone's mind and they were shipped up here, out of the way of the men and horses.

My excitement at this discovery waned just a little when I discovered that eleven of them were Homer; four *Iliad*s, three *Odyssey*s, two *Homeric Hymns* and two *Cypria*s. Even so, that left eight proper books, of which only one (the collected plays of my grandfather Eupolis) had been nibbled by mice into a state of total uselessness. The other seven were: the poems of Archilochus; a long-forgotten epic poem about Hercules by Panyasis; selections from Aristotle; Thucydides' *History of the War*, mercifully abridged; a seventy-year-old pamphlet by someone called Chrysippus suggesting improvements to the franchising system for exploiting Athenian mining interests at Laurium; an anonymous commentary on military tactics in Homer, seeking to prove their relevance to modern-day warfare; and my ill-fated brother Eudaemon's preferred bedside reading, Aeneas the Tactician's monograph on the art of war. I flicked through this chance accumulation of dross, took the Archilochus and Chrysippus pamphlet for myself, earmarked the selections from Aristotle for mending leaky boots, and dumped the rest in the front room for the use of my young and impressionable charges.

Practicalities were all taken care of with typical Macedonian robust efficiency. Meals happened four times a day, monolithic affairs involving huge slabs of roast meat, cheeses the size of cartwheels and enormous baskets of coarse barley bread, washed down with raw red wine mixed half-and-half. On special days, I gathered, there were olives, maybe the occasional fig. Laundry was in the hands of three gigantic troll-women, who reminded me alarmingly of the Three Wise Witches – the ones who live at the end of the world and share one eye, one ear and one tongue between them. There was an issue of clothing once a month; one cloak, one tunic, one pair of sandals, ditto boots, one hat, all of them fairly recent cast-offs from the nobs in Pella. For some reason I kept getting Philip's hats and Parmenio's tunics; the royal hats all had a thick band of grease just inside the brim, and Parmenio apparently spilt more wine down his front than he ever managed to get into his face. Once I got a stunningly beautiful silk shawl embroidered with countless blue and red snakes, heavily scented with saffron and violets and heavily stained in one corner with a dark brown stuff that was, beyond any shadow of doubt, human blood, which raised all sorts of interesting speculations in my mind as to what Queen Olympias' duties as high priestess of the snake cult actually involved. The boots were standard army issue, but the sandals were soft and comfortable, if several sizes too big. In fact, everything in Macedon was several sizes too big, from the crockery to the lifestyle to the country itself – too big for me, and I'm no dwarf, remember; extremely curious, that, because I met very few Macedonians who were taller or broader than me, but all their clothes seemed to have been made for the elder brothers of the Titans.

Aristotle arrived, eventually; at which point Lysimachus came to see me.

I don't know to this day whether Lysimachus was a Macedonian with a speech impediment or an offcomer who'd been in Macedon too long. As a general rule I had no trouble at all understanding the Macedonians, but whatever dialect or accent Lysimachus spoke in gave me endless problems, which was awkward when he was notifying me of timetable changes or amendments to the curriculum. He was a long, thin, harassed-looking man with a tiny little nose and enormous eyes, and loud noises made him jump even when he knew they were coming well in advance. When the school first started up and the young Alexander, banished here against his will from the royal court in Pella, manifested his displeasure by refusing to have anything to do with the proceedings, Lysimachus finally managed to coax him into co-operating by setting up a vast and intricate role-playing game, in which Alexander was the young Achilles, and Lysimachus took the role of Achilles' aged and decrepit old tutor, Phoenix. At first, the whole school had to be run in accordance with the rules of the Homer game; everybody was assigned a role to play and had to stay in character every minute of every day. By the time I arrived this requirement had been relaxed considerably, so that we only had to be our Homeric counterparts at morning assembly and after the plates had been cleared away following the evening meal. Even those two occasions were too much for me; because I'd arrived late on the scene, the only role still open for me was that of the wily Ulysses, a character I've loathed and despised ever since I was a small child. Besides which, I'm hopeless at acting. I feel like an idiot, pretending to be someone I'm not. But Lysimachus, by necessity, had taken real pains to *be* Phoenix, which argues a latent genius for histrionics on his part. After all, Phoenix as written by Homer has all the character and individuality of a small root; in order to *be* such a shallow and ill-defined personality so intensively and for so long, Lysimachus must have had an imagination capable of bending thick iron bars.

When not being Phoenix, Lysimachus was a pedantic, worried man with a small gift for administration and a disturbing habit of bursting into tears whenever things started to go wrong. In later years Alexander demonstrated a genuine fondness for the poor old fool, which was in keeping with his habit of being very kind to simple, humble folks who agreed fervently with every word he said.

I can picture you looking at me, Phryzeutzis, and grinning lopsidedly; here's this little man, you're thinking, taking every opportunity he can to snipe at the great Alexander now that he's dead and gone. Maybe, maybe. I never claimed that I liked the boy, even at the height of my period of hero-worship. But the main reason I assume my mask of Yapping Dog, first class, when I start talking about him is that – well, in part I'm responsible. And if I was writing this in Greek you'd understand better, because we use the same word for 'responsible' and 'guilty'. I only helped shape one small part of Alexander's character, and my motives for doing what I did were always, always for the best. I genuinely wanted to prepare the boy – and the rest of them too – for a useful career of service as rulers of their country; I wasn't conducting a controlled experiment in creating a philosopher-king, or angling for power behind the throne when the Prince came into his own, or even doing what was necessary to earn money. I was trying to help.

The fact that the world would be a better place if I'd died at birth is something I have to live with. I feel responsible, but not guilty.

Anyway.

Lysimachus came to see me, and he told me about the curriculum, and what I was supposed to be doing, when and where, and a lot of useful stuff like that, for which I was properly grateful. When he'd finished briefing me, he stood up to go, then turned round, sat down again, leaned forward and grabbed me by both elbows.

'Now listen to me,' he said. 'You're an Athenian . . .'

'I know,' I replied, trying to tug my arms free without being too obvious about it.

'You're an Athenian,' he repeated. 'I admire the Athenians. Your Drama, your poetry, your philosophy – I admire it all. Athens is a great nation. You have given so much to all of Greece.'

'Thank you,' I said.

'And that's why I'm warning you,' he went on, ignoring me. 'You don't know these people the way I do, you don't know how their minds work or how they live their lives. You don't understand. So it's *very important* that you remember what I'm telling you now. Yes?'

I nodded, mostly in the hope that he'd finish quickly and go away. He'd recently been eating onions. I could tell.

'All right,' he said. 'Now listen. Macedon is a kingdom, a monarchy. You don't understand how a monarchy works. In a monarchy, there isn't any right or wrong or good or evil, there's only two things: what He wants and what He doesn't. In a monarchy there isn't any such word as *Why?* In a monarchy, if He says the sky's green, it's green. If He says, Kill my firstborn son, it's done. If He says, Bring me the head of the murdering bastard who killed my son, that's done too. No wrong. No why. Just "Yes, sir" and that's all. You need to remember that, here, being an Athenian.'

'I'll bear it in mind,' I replied, struggling to keep a straight face. 'Thank you ever so much for sharing it with me.'

Lysimachus stared at me for a moment, as if he was trying to decode some abstruse cypher. 'Just remember,' he said. 'And be careful. Aside from Him, there is no law in Macedon.'

I nodded. 'We have heaps and heaps of law in Athens,' I said. 'No justice, but plenty of law. We've got so much we have to hire people to remember it for us. I think I might rather like it here.'

He shook his head. 'You be careful. In Macedon, people are murdered by the State.'

'Ah.' I smiled. 'It's different back home. In Athens, scores of people are killed by the State every year, but it's never murder. What's the matter, Lysimachus? Why are you trying to frighten me away?'

He shook his head vehemently. Small things were thrown clear of his hair. 'Stay if you want. Stay as long as you like. Just remember, that's all.'

I jerked my arms free and stood up. 'You bet,' I said. 'I'll remember.'

And I have.

CHAPTER EIGHT

෭෦෭෦෭෦෭෦෭෦෭෦෭෦෭෦෭෦෭෦෭෦෭෦෭෦෭෦

Philip of Macedon, so the story goes, was arguing with young Alexander one day.

'What's the point of me learning all this political theory and literature and stuff?' the Prince asked. 'I'm not going to need it when I'm King.'

'Don't you believe it,' Philip said. 'Being King isn't about who you are, it's about what you are. And don't forget, we're not Persians or Egyptians, we're Macedonians. If they accept you as their King it won't be because I'm who I am, it'll be because you're who you are.'

Heartwarming, isn't it? Not to mention completely untrue. On those occasions when Philip did talk to the young Alexander, it was more a case of, 'Get the hell out of here, can't you see I'm busy?'

I should know; I was there. And that's what makes it so bizarre when I hear these delightful little vignettes of family life at Pella. They're fairy-tales, the lot of them, little bite-sized chunks out of myth and legend, and as everybody knows, myth and legend deal with long ago and far away, not something that happened quite recently in places where I happened to be at the time. How dare they do this to parts of my life? I feel like a man who comes home from buying sprats in the fish market and finds that his house has been taken over and turned into a shrine to some god or hero who happens to have the same name as him; and the custodians of the shrine won't let him go into his house and get anything, not even a clean tunic.

★

The first lesson of the first day was military history.

Truly is it said: the best way to learn about something you're completely ignorant of is to teach it to somebody else. And the key to that, of course, is admitting your ignorance to yourself.

Even more truly is it said: when you don't know spit, bullshit.

They were sitting in a circle under a fig tree. It was a hot day, about mid-morning, and apart from the flies it was quiet and peaceful. I walked across the courtyard and they all stopped talking and stared at me. Strong men have been known to die of less.

But I'm not a strong man; so I sat down with my back to the trunk of that excellent tree, pulled my hat down over my eyes and said, 'Military history.' Nobody spoke. I counted to twenty under my breath.

'All right,' I said. 'Here's some military history for you. Iphicrates of Athens, who was a friend of my father, was pitching camp in the middle of friendly territory. He ordered his men to dig a ditch and build a palisade round the camp. "Why bother?" someone asked. "It's not as if anybody's going to attack us here." Whereupon Iphicrates shook his head. "Don't you believe it," he said. "The worst thing a general can ever say is, Hell, I never expected *that*." And that, gentlemen, is why we learn military history. Understood?'

There was a short, polite silence. then someone asked, 'Did your father really know Iphicrates?'

That threw me. I had only the sketchiest notion of who Iphicrates was – short, scruffy-looking man who came to dinner once, behaved obnoxiously to the flute-girl and fell asleep face down in a plate of thinly sliced smoked eel – but this terrible child was obviously rather more familiar with the great man's career than I was. 'Yes,' I replied. 'Now then, can somebody give me three reasons why the Phoenician colonists in Carthage would beat the crap out of the Phoenicians in Phoenicia if ever there was a war between them?'

A longer silence this time; they were all looking at Alexander, and he was thinking it over. 'You,' I said, pointing to a thin-faced kid on my right. 'Any ideas?'

The boy looked startled, but recovered well. 'The Carthaginians hire mercenaries,' he said. 'Mercenaries fight for money, not honour, so they fight to win the battle.'

I nodded. 'Correct,' I said. 'You – Hephaestion, isn't it? – what do you think?'

Hephaestion rubbed the tip of his nose with the back of his wrist. 'The Carthaginians have fought a lot of wars on land against Greeks,' he said. 'The Phoenicians of Tyre haven't, so they haven't had the opportunity or the incentive to learn.'

'All right,' I said. 'Alexander, what's the third reason?'

Alexander looked at me before answering. 'If there was a war between Carthage and Tyre,' he said, 'it would be because Tyre was trying to establish its authority over a former colony, and Carthage would be fighting for its freedom. So the Carthaginians would have more to lose, and they'd fight harder.'

I nodded again. 'That's a good answer,' I said. 'But it contradicts what your friend here just said about the Carthaginians hiring mercenaries. Don't you agree with that?'

Alexander looked up, and then down again. 'I agree with it,' he said. 'But the men running the war would still be Carthaginians, even if the soldiers were mercenaries. Put together determined generals and trained, competent men and you're likely to win.'

I sat up. 'That's good,' I said. 'Clearly you all know a lot of the basics already. But what you don't know, I'll wager, is the great secret of military history; and you don't know it because although every successful general who ever lived knows this secret, none of them ever mention it. Not even to their brothers or their lovers or their sons. Would you like to know what this secret is?'

Intrigued silence this time. Eventually Hephaestion said, 'Yes, please.'

'All right, listen carefully.' I waited till they were all gazing earnestly at me. 'The secret is this. Out of every hundred battles, ninety-nine of them are lost by the loser, not won by the winner. Ninety-nine battles out of a hundred go the way they do because one of the commanders makes a bloody awful mistake, which costs him the day and thousands of his men their lives. Now then; name me some battles and I'll prove that I'm right.'

'Plataea,' someone called out.

'Delium,' said Philotas.

'Marathon.'

'That one where Brasidas was surrounded in Thessaly.'

By good fortune – and because the rule, which is not my own

observation, happens to be true – I was able to carry my point in each case. This impressed my students a whole lot. Impressed me, too; I'd never really given it any thought before. Also, quite by chance, I'd been reading about the Brasidas-in-Thessaly battle the night before in that copy of Thucydides' *History* I told you about. It was the first time I'd ever come across it, and it was probably that which put the idea in my mind in the first place.

After we'd pushed the idea around for a while, Alexander counter-attacked. 'It's a good point,' he said. 'But what if you've got a general who's so worried about making a big mistake that he's all timid and over-cautious about handling his troops? He's not going to win many battles.'

'I agree,' I replied. 'And that'd be a big mistake on his part. There's a difference between knowing not to jump off the side of a boat with a rock tied to your leg, and never going on a boat in your life just in case someone ties a rock to your leg and shoves you over the rail.'

Alexander frowned a little. 'But what if it's the hundredth battle and the general you're fighting doesn't make any stupid mistakes? Then what happens?'

'You lose, probably,' I said.

'But if I don't make any mistakes either, what happens then?'

I shrugged. 'You keep on fighting each other till nightfall or it starts raining,' I replied. 'Or until your men or his men have had enough and run for it. That's what happens in nine out of ten of the one battles in a hundred.'

'I see,' Alexander said dubiously. 'So you're basically saying, just trust to luck?'

I shook my head. 'Not a bit of it. Luck in war is very like the gods. Never, ever *trust* your luck; just be aware that it exists, that's all.'

In other words I was floundering like hell and in grave danger of being shown up as a windbag and a fraud. Fortunately, before any of those highly intelligent and perceptive young people had a chance to start picking my logic to bits, Leonidas arrived with a big fat scroll under his arm to teach them Homer, and I was able to withdraw in good order, leaving behind me the mistaken impression that I'd taught them something they didn't know already.

★

I tried to put it off for as long as possible, but I knew it had to happen sooner or later. I'd have preferred later, but I didn't have any choice in the matter.

It was my seventh day as a teacher, and I wasn't doing terribly well. My greatest fault as a teacher was a deplorable and pointless urge to show off, to try to impress the students with my knowledge and insight; disastrous mistake. Being the sons of gentlemen, they were too well brought-up to object loudly enough for me to hear, but the embarrassed look on their faces should have been enough to stop me doing it. The wretched part of it was that I knew I was doing it and knew it wasn't the right thing to do, but somehow I couldn't stop myself. Besides which, after seven days it was too late to start again at the beginning. I'd forfeited too much respect, and without respect a teacher can't teach an olive to fall off a tree. I was losing control of the situation and losing it fast; and that's why Aristotle came to see me.

When I heard him scratch at the door and glanced through the crack between door and frame to see who it was, my first instinct was to hide under something until he went away again; but if I'd done that he'd only have come in anyway and started poking about, and the embarrassment of being found by him cowering under an upturned basket was something I didn't want to risk.

'Hello,' I said.

He looked at me as if I'd just crawled out of something he was eating, but all he said was, 'I'd like a word with you, if it's convenient.'

'Come in,' I said. 'Please.'

Before he was even halfway through the door I remembered that spread out on the floor, with bits cut out of it, was the manuscript of *Selections From Aristotle*, or at least all that was left of it after I'd mended a pair of sandals and the folding chair.

'You're busy,' he said, taking in the mess at a glance – by any normal criteria he was too far away to realise it was one of his books I'd been mutilating; but maybe he'd just *know*, the way a mother always knows, regardless of distance, when her child is in pain or danger. 'So I won't stay long. But I felt, as a fellow Athenian—'

I made the standard sit-down-please gesture that all human beings recognise. He nodded in return and sat in the folding chair, right on top of the drying glue and excerpts from his *Analysis of the Constitution of Corinth*.

'Careful,' I said. 'Wet glue.'

Instinctively, he lifted both elbows off the arms of the chair, inspected them and put them back. 'As a fellow Athenian—' he repeated.

'Would you like something to drink?' I asked.

'No, thank you. As a fellow Athenian, I thought you might appreciate a few words of advice about dealing with the Macedonians. The study of other cultures is a special interest of mine, as I believe you already know,' he added, with a deadpan stare, 'so I believe my insights into the Macedonian mind-set are likely to have a degree of validity.'

'That's very kind of you,' I replied. 'Personally, I like these people. What about you?'

He gave me a puzzled look, rather as if he'd asked me what four and four make, and I'd replied 'Sideways.' 'I try and make sure that my personal value-judgements don't intrude on my scientific evaluation of a nation's culture. Also, don't forget, my native city was destroyed by the Macedonians and its people dispersed or enslaved. If I have an emotional response to these people, it's negative rather than positive. But I flatter myself that I can retain my objectivity even under these circumstances.'

I cursed myself for my lousy memory. It was true, Philip had made an example of Stagira a while back; recently he'd also given permission for it to be rebuilt and for the exiles to be allowed home, as a gesture of goodwill to his son's illustrious tutor. 'That's all right, then,' I replied lamely. 'Please, do go on.'

Well, for half an hour or so he told me pretty much everything I'd so far worked out for myself about the Macedonians, together with a few snippets of historical trivia that could never under any conceivable circumstances be of any use to anybody. I sat still and quiet, nodding from time to time and keeping a fixed smile on my face. I was just about to doze off, in fact, when I heard him say, 'But of course, you know all this already.'

I sat up. 'Well, actually,' I said, 'I do. I mean, I did do a little research before the peace mission started, and I've been keeping my ears and eyes open ever since.'

'Of course.' He nodded his head. 'What you don't know is how to convey what you do know to somebody else. And that's what I've just been illustrating for you. I trust you found it helpful.'

'Actually—' I began; but a little voice in the back room of my mind whispered *Why bother? It's not worth it.* After all, it would be far more practical to patch up some kind of working relationship with this man – I was going to have to work with him for several years, and of the four of us on the tutoring staff, he was the only one who might just conceivably turn out to be a useful ally. 'Actually,' I went on, 'I was going to ask your advice about that. Ever since I started work I've had this feeling that I haven't been going about it in the right way. I'm sure you've picked up some feedback from the kids. What would you suggest?'

Aristotle didn't smile, in the same way a tree rarely does somersaults; but the way he dipped his head a little suggested that he acknowledged this small act of deference, as from a young ram to the lord of the sheepfold, declining to start a fight he couldn't win. 'Your attitude is counter-productive,' he said. 'You seem to be afraid of them, which is why you display your knowledge the way a peacock shows its tail. For one thing, I suggest, you simply don't have enough factual information. For another, you should never openly display fear to something you intend to train. If you want a demonstration of the proper way to go about it, may I recommend that you spare the time tomorrow afternoon to go down to the stock-yard and watch young Alexander breaking in horses.'

And on that well-chosen exit line he stood up to leave. Unfortunately, the chair didn't seem to want to let go of him. I found it hard not to close my eyes; the glue on those confounded parchment patches had soaked through and stuck to his gown. He frowned, and tugged; there was a small ripping noise and the chair dropped away.

'Sorry,' I said, but he wasn't paying attention; he'd gathered the torn part of his gown in one hand and was staring at a little parchment scrap that was stuck to it. Plainly legible were the words 'In many respects, the Corinthian assembly resembles that of the Athenians'; not, perhaps, the most memorable line he'd ever penned, but distinctive enough, it seemed.

'Good afternoon,' he said, and left.

So, inevitably, there I was, sitting on the rail with my hat on against the sun, as the first horse was led into the ring.

I have nothing against horses. I know how to ride one, more or less; you sit on the middle facing the end with the ears, it's not exactly difficult. But I've always found it hard to be interested in horses, the way some people are.

Alexander, on the other hand, was obviously a connoisseur, and an expert. Hardly surprising; in Macedon they have both the money and the room for serious horse-rearing, and horses have always been part of the aristocratic lifestyle, so I imagine he'd been riding since shortly after he was old enough to walk. Philip, I knew for a fact, was most definitely a horsey sort of man, and in a way it was significant that a new batch of horses brought him out to Mieza, something the education of his son never managed to do.

And a pretty tedious spectacle I found it, I have to admit. A horse was brought in, the various trainers and horse people persecuted it until it did what they wanted it to, and then they brought in another one. The sight of ten or so men bumping and wobbling their way round a ring on the backs of unwilling animals didn't strike me as either inspiring or amusing, and since I didn't understand the process I didn't feel there was much I could learn from the experience. Still, it would have been the height of bad manners to slope off before the King left, so I was stuck there. I wedged my heels onto the rail below me and let my mind wander.

I was startled out of my reverie by the sound of someone screaming. I looked up and saw one of the trainers, or whatever it is you call them, being dragged along the ground behind a ferocious-looking brute of a tall black horse with a white splodge on its forehead. Somehow the man's foot had got tangled in the reins; as he bumped along the ground, leaving a dark-brown trail of blood in the dust as he went, so with each step he dragged on the left-hand rein, making the horse run in a wide circle. The more they tried to catch hold of him, the faster the horrible creature ran, and I joined the spectacle just before the wretched man's head hit a stone or something with a very definite cracking noise, and he stopped struggling and flopped, like a wooden doll being dragged along behind a small child.

After that there wasn't quite the same degree of urgency about stopping the runaway horse; they stopped trying, and without anybody chasing after it and flapping their hands in its face, the animal soon slowed down and came to a halt long enough for them to dart out and cut the dead man free from the reins.

'Get the damned thing out of here,' I heard Philip shouting; charitably, I assumed he was talking about the horse. But Alexander, who'd been sitting next to him, stood up and raised his hand in a hold-it sort of gesture.

'It's not the horse's fault,' he said.

'Like hell it isn't,' Philip replied irritably. 'Whose is it, anyway?'

I heard someone say that it belonged to a Thessalian called Philonicus.

'Strange,' Philip said. 'I'd have thought he'd have had more sense. It's obviously way past training.'

'I don't think so,' Alexander said, in an embarrassingly clear, distinct voice. 'I say they're just going about it the wrong way, that's all.'

I can only assume he was doing it on purpose. If so, he got the result he was looking for. 'Oh, really?' Philip said. 'And you know everything there is to know about handling horses, and we don't.'

'I know enough to be able to handle this one,' Alexander replied, as cool as you like. That was a habit of his, or a mannerism or whatever; the more heated and excitable the other man got in an argument, the colder and more detached he became. 'Oughtn't to be too difficult,' he said. 'Why, would you like me to show you?'

Philip didn't know whether to shout or roar with laughter; either would have made things worse. It was pretty clear to me as an outside observer that the relationship between these two had reached the crisis stage where one of them was going to have to do something melodramatic and probably regrettable in order to resolve it. It was just a pity that it should have to involve something as horribly dangerous as a rogue horse that had just killed a professional horse-tamer. But from what I know of Alexander, I wouldn't be surprised if this was how he wanted it; the bigger the risk, the bigger the victory, after all. If this crisis had been on the cards for any length of time (and I'm sure it had) it'd be just like Alexander to engineer the breaking-point to be something like that, a very dangerous situation that he felt confident he could handle. Alexander was always a gambler, and he only ever bet on certainties and he never wagered less than his life.

'You're going to break this horse, aren't you?' Philip said, lowering his voice ominously.

'I think I'd like to try,' Alexander replied.

'All right,' Philip said. 'Suppose you fail, and suppose by some miracle you manage not to break your damn neck in the process; what's the bet?'

Alexander thought for a moment. 'I'll buy the horse,' he said.

That took Philip entirely by surprise. 'You will, will you? Hey, you,' he snapped at the man next to him, 'how much does Philonicus want for that horse?'

The man whispered in Philip's ear. 'Louder,' Philip said, 'so we can all hear.'

'Thirteen talents,' the man announced.

(Yes, sorry, I'm losing you again, Phryzeutzis. You don't know whether thirteen talents is the annual revenue of Babylon or the price of a bushel of garlic. Well, let's put it this way. It'd take your average working man, a stonemason, say, or a carpenter, over two hundred years to earn thirteen talents.)

'Still going to buy the horse?' Philip said.

'Yes,' Alexander replied.

'Really. What with?'

Alexander looked at his father without any visible expression on his face. 'Oh, I expect Mother'd lend me the money,' he replied.

Now don't ask me what all that was about; but the way Philip's face tightened showed that Alexander had just said something unforgivable, bad enough that Philip would let him try to tame the horse because he was so angry he wouldn't care if his son did get himself killed. Good tactics on Alexander's part—

(And I thought of what I'd taught him: make the other guy make a mistake. Precisely what Alexander had just done. Whatever the outcome now, Philip would be in the wrong. If Alexander tamed the horse, he'd be quite the young Hercules or Theseus, subduing monsters before he was through potty-training. If, on the other hand, he was killed or badly hurt, then whose fault would it be for letting him do such a crazy thing? The mistake he'd forced Philip into making was losing his temper to the extent that he allowed himself to be put in this no-win position . . .

Did I do that? I wondered.)

'Bet,' Philip said softly, and you can be sure it was quiet enough for everybody to hear. I've never heard so much venom packed into one little word, before or since.

So Alexander hopped down from the rail – it was the lissom

movement of a child, the sort of thing you can't do when you're a grown-up, no matter how fit you are – and walked calmly to the centre of the ring, where the monster horse was standing, radiating hatred and viciousness in all directions. I didn't really want to look; on the other hand, how many chances do you get in a lifetime to see a prince of the blood get horribly mutilated? In Athens there'd have been someone going round with a tray, selling apples.

First he just stood there, looking the horse in the eye; then he walked round it, patted it on the side of the neck, slipped off his cloak and took hold of the reins, turning the animal's head towards the sun. Then he got on its back and rode it round the ring a few times.

You're probably way ahead of me. As soon as I told you that he made the horse face the sun, you reached the same conclusion that Alexander had; the stupid creature was afraid of shadows, and whenever it saw its own shadow, or the shadow of its rider's cloak or anything like that, it bolted. That was all there was to it.

After he'd shown off his horsemanship for a minute or two Alexander pulled up in front of his father, jumped down, looped what was left of the reins over a rail and resumed his seat. For a long time, nobody said anything, or moved; then Philip nodded his head, ever so slightly.

'You noticed that too,' he said. 'Very good.'

'I think I'll call him Oxhead,' Alexander replied, looking straight ahead.

'I see. You think I'm going to buy you this horse, do you?'

'Yes.'

Philip shrugged. 'All right,' he said. 'With luck I should be able to get him for twelve.'

Alexander shook his head. 'He's worth thirteen.'

'All right.'

Now then; assuming one of them set up the other, which was it? At the time I was sure it was Alexander who'd taken Philip; now I'm not so sure. I wouldn't put it past Philip to have arranged something like that, a test so close to the edge that nobody would ever believe it was a set-up. And that, of course, was why it would be such a triumph, the foundation for a legend; nobody in their right mind would ever believe a father would risk his son's life in order that his son could triumph over him in public. Nobody, that is, except

Philip, who was afraid of nothing. If he did plan it, it was one of his best ever pieces of strategy; because that was when Alexander first knew what hitherto he'd only believed.

As for my lesson, Aristotle was quite right, bless his heart. In order to train this boy, you had to turn his head towards the sun and keep him from seeing his own shadow. Understand that simple fact and you could make him do anything you wanted.

By the time I got home that evening, I still liked the Macedonians. But in a slightly different way.

After that, I knew what I was supposed to do. It helps.

Thanks to the books I found in the outhouse, I was able to learn enough to be able to teach. I did a swap with Aristotle, my astronomy and medicine for his lyric poetry and prosodic theory, and learned how to write poetry from Archilochus and how not to from Panyasis; I traded literature for economic theory with Leonidas, and managed to distil enough economics out of the silver-mines franchising pamphlet to bluff my way (actually, any damn fool can work out economics from first principles; you start with 'A has a loaf of bread but no money, B has a silver coin but no food' and carry on from there). As for military history, I had Thucydides' account of the War, the commentary on tactics in Homer and that old favourite, Aeneas' military handbook, so I was spoilt for choice.

Teaching poetry was a piece of cake. None of the Macedonians had any interest in the subject whatsoever, so by mutual consent we whittled the curriculum down to being able to compose lines that scanned in pentameters and hexameters, iambics, dactyls and anapaests, to recognise the dumb-beast basic lyric forms (alcaics, anacreontics, hendecasyllables, sapphics); basic caesura rules, elisions, epic license and archaic forms – yes, I know this means nothing to you, Phryzeutzis; what passes for poetry in this barbarous land works on an entirely different system of lines ending in words that sound vaguely similar, so I won't even try explaining how real poetry works. Let's say that if I'd been teaching them carpentry instead of poetry, they'd have learned the names (but not the uses) of the saw, the rasp and the bow-drill, and which end of the hammer you use to hit the nail with.

I've mentioned economics already. Young Harpalus, the fat kid, was talented and enthusiastic in this field, which was a nuisance, but the rest of the class were happy just to mark time. I based everything on the one bit of economic theory I remembered from my own schooldays, namely Socrates' theory of growth. Actually, like so many of Socrates' theories, it's so full of holes you could use it for straining curds – it's a misbegotten fusion of science, politics and mysticism, which equates the tendency of things in nature to grow (trees and grass and stuff like that) with the practice of lending money on interest, on the basis that money somehow reproduces, like mice in the thatch, and so it's all right to borrow because each silver owl you borrow will hatch out a clutch of little baby owls, which'll pay the interest on the loan and still leave you change for things like food and rent. Piffle; but I made it sound totally convincing, and in due course you'll see what hatched out of it when Alexander and Harpalus eventually came into serious money.

But what they really wanted to learn – and I wanted to teach, because I had three books to teach it from – was military history; so we fiddled about with the curriculum until it ended up like the proportion of wine to water in the mixing bowl during the closing stages of a really evil party. I taught them the battles of the Persian Wars (from memory), the major engagements of the Peloponnesian War (from Thucydides' book), the theory of chivalry and clean warfare (from Homer) and the future of military science (from Aeneas the Tactician; thirty years out of date and still every bit as impractical as the day it was written). I tell you, Phryzeutzis; if I'd been a slightly better teacher, or if they'd had slightly less inherent ability, I could have guaranteed the safety not only of Greece but the whole of the Persian empire.

Leonidas, of course, objected to my teaching Homeric warfare, because Leonidas taught Homer. It was his subject, the only one he knew anything about, the only one that really mattered in the eyes of Philip and the other boys' fathers. I felt it was bitterly unfair that he should be getting at me over this; after all, I loathe and despise Homer, and wanted nothing at all to do with the matter, but the fact remains – teaching war without Homer is like teaching a lad to be a smith while omitting any reference to metal. Can't be done.

The net effect of this was to make me even more rabidly anti-Homer than before; which in turn brought me into conflict with Aristotle, who worshipped the stuff, and by association Alexander, who liked Homer in the same way a fish likes water. All that blood and honour, that simple equation between prowess, exertion and reward – it was the sort of world he most wanted to live in, regardless of whether or not it bore any relation whatsoever to real life.

We fell out over it, in fact. What brought it to a head was a discussion on the role of the archer in various philosophies of war. I'd pointed out that whereas the Greeks had never reckoned much to the bow and arrow, the Persians had won their empire with them. I was just explaining why this was—

'Ibex horn,' I said. 'The only decent bows in Greece are made of ibex horn, and they're difficult and expensive to build, so very few people have them. The majority of the bows we use are just plain wood, and Greek trees make lousy bows. The Persians, on the other hand, make vastly superior bows out of slivers of horn, wood and sinew laminated together; the materials are plentiful and they're good enough at it to be able to make the bows affordable, so everyone who wants one has a chance to own one. So the Persians fight with the bow, whereas we Greeks prefer to fight with spears, in armour; and we prefer to fight that way because we have a different notion of what winning means. For the Persians, winning means killing the enemy. For us, it means making the enemy run away and leave us in possession of the disputed territory. That's what we call *honourable* warfare, and it's purely fortuitous that armoured spearmen can bash the crap out of archers nineteen times out of twenty, because otherwise I'd be telling you this in Persian—'

'Excuse me,' Alexander said. Please note: whatever else I may have failed to do, I'd at least taught him the rudiments of civility. 'But that's not the reason.'

I suppose I should have been used to remarks like that by then; but we were running late and I wasn't in the mood. 'Really,' I said. 'Then maybe you'd care to tell us what the real reason is.'

'Simple,' Alexander said. 'The bow's a coward's weapon. It says so in Homer.'

I took a deep breath. 'It does indeed,' I replied. 'Repeatedly; though that doesn't stop Ulysses from single-handedly exterminating the sons-of-bitches who've taken over his house at the end of the *Odyssey* with a bow, something he'd have had no chance of doing with a sword or a spear. In fact, you'll remember that he proves he's the king because he's the only one who's man enough to be able to string the mighty bow, which implies they weren't quite so snooty about bows on Ithaca, at least. Point of interest, by the way; any bow that's been laid up in the rafters for twenty years and never strung, like Ulysses' bow was supposed to have been, would have snapped like a dry twig long before you could get a string on it, but nevertheless—'

'Ulysses wasn't a man of honour,' Alexander interrupted. 'He was as devious as a fox.'

'Or as we say in Athens, an intellectual,' I snapped back. 'Yes, I'll grant you that. It's not really relevant to the subject at hand, but it's true enough.'

Alexander looked at me, and when he spoke again he'd lowered his voice. Really, I should have known better. 'You don't like Homer,' he said.

'True,' I admitted.

'Well, that's not right,' Alexander replied. 'Even you must see that—'

'You do, don't you?' I broke in. 'You really enjoy the stuff, I can tell.'

'Of course.'

I nodded. I'd been fattening him up for this. 'All right,' I said, 'who would you rather be, Achilles or Homer?'

Alexander smiled. 'That's easy,' he said. 'Homer.'

'Really?'

'Of course. By the time Achilles was your age, he was dead.'

I nodded again. 'Absolutely true,' I replied. 'Eternally famous, yes. The greatest hero of all time, yes. Destined to live forever—'

'Because of Homer,' Alexander pointed out.

'Because of Homer, thank you, destined to live for ever, yes. Dead, yes. And Homer's still alive, I take it?'

'Of course not.'

'I see. Homer's dead too.' I smiled. 'Listen, everybody. Alexander would rather be Homer than Achilles. Tell me this, Alexander, who'd you rather be? The all-comers champion at the Olympic Games, or the little fat guy with a scroll who calls out the names of the winners?'

Alexander didn't like that. Not one bit.

The rest of them did. They tried to keep straight faces; by and large they managed it. But they'd had to put up with Alexander being Alexander for a long time. I'd had enough of it after three or four weeks; they'd had to deal with it all their lives. I made a lot of friends that day.

(Clever me. Just like the man who fell out of the fig tree; he broke his back, but he shook down an awful lot of figs.)

'I take your point,' Alexander said eventually. 'I was wrong. Thank you for pointing out my mistake.'

The look he gave me as he said that made me feel cold all over. Something had happened to him in that moment, and I've been wondering ever since what the hell it could have been.

All right; consider Achilles. He was the son of a goddess and a mortal, forever torn between the limitless possibilities of his mother's divinity and the constraints of his father's gross mortality. When he was little more than a boy, the Trojan War began; almost single-handedly he overthrew the Trojan Empire and brought the war right up to the walls of the city itself. At that point, after fighting always in the front of the battle and achieving every possible objective, he made a mistake; he took offence, fell out with the king on a matter concerning his honour, backed himself into a corner so that he could no longer participate in the war without a disastrous loss of face. So he sulked in his tent, while Zeus gave victory to the Trojans and the Greeks were slaughtered like pigs in the autumn. Only when it was too late to save his dearest friend did he return to the war, kill the enemy champion and avenge his friend; and for his mistake he was punished, dying too soon before the city could be taken, shot with an arrow by a man by far his inferior. Achilles failed; yet he was the greatest hero of them all, and in Homer's *Iliad* he's caught for ever, like a fly trapped in amber mounted in gold on a brooch, everlastingly both pre-eminent and imperfect.

Consider Homer. He was poor and blind, and he was taken prisoner by the enemies of his people, but all the same he won immortality in his old age by creating something that can never die. Homer's life was wretched, and he was a success.

Consider Alexander.

Well, that's my best shot at a theory; at that moment, because of my foolish verbal trap, Alexander made a conscious decision to be Achilles. Consider; when he was little more than a boy, he began the Persian War; almost single-handedly he overthrew the Persian Empire and brought the war into countries that none of us knew existed before he arrived there to conquer them. At that point, after fighting always in the front of the battle and achieving every possible objective, he made a mistake; he fell out with his friends and the Macedonian people over a matter concerning his honour, backed himself into a corner so that he could no longer give up the war without a disastrous loss of face. So he led them into the mountains and the desert, where so many of them died. Only after he had caused the death of his dearest friend did he think of giving up the war, and for his mistake he was punished, dying too soon before the empire could be established, wounded by an arrow shot by some common soldier, dying of a fever resulting directly from that wound.

(And consider me, poor and half-blind among the enemies of my people – no offence, Phryzeutzis, but this city was built by Macedonians in Sogdiana and I'm a long way from home – trying in my old age to make a record of what I've seen, a book that only you will ever read.)

Well, after that the atmosphere was rather strained for a day or so, and I decided I'd better do something to redeem myself, or at least help put that unfortunate incident out of everybody's mind. Fortunately, I'd anticipated that sooner or later there'd be some sort of crisis in the student/teacher relationship, so I'd kept back a choice nugget of comic relief, the sort of thing that dissolves tension in a wave of shared merriment. It was a pity that I was going to have to use it up so soon; but the situation seemed to require it.

I read them the bit in Aeneas the Tactician about the bees.

CHAPTER NINE

I remember once standing in the Potters' Quarter in Athens, chatting aimlessly to someone about something, when quite suddenly I heard the most almighty crash. I turned round and saw that a wall had collapsed. There was a cloud of dust, and someone was screaming, and people were starting to run. In the end, as I recall, they pulled four bodies out of the rubble, all dead. I didn't see a thing, of course. I was looking the other way.

Story of my life, I guess. I was certainly looking the other way while Philip was waging his not-quite-a-war against the Athenian people; I was in Mieza, teaching the next generation of Macedon's best and brightest about the war before the war before last. I was teaching them about the theoretical weaknesses of the traditional Greek heavy infantry formation (I'd figured it all out for myself from first principles; I was ever so pleased with myself) while Philip was training these same kids' fathers and uncles and elder brothers to command the new model Macedonian phalanx, which was designed to exploit those same weaknesses and turn the citizen-soldiers' shield-wall (bulwark of Greek freedom for two hundred and fifty blood-spattered internecine years) into an easy joke.

But we didn't get much in the way of news in Mieza. We were living in an awful kind of cheesy literary epic, pastiche Homer of the worst possible kind, where Aristotle and Leonidas and Lysimachus and I were Cheiron and Peleus and Phoenix and whoever the hell I was meant to be (I objected so strenuously to being Ulysses that eventually I was relieved of duty) tutoring the young Achilles and his comrades, the flower of Grecian youth. In that regard it was all very tasteless and tacky and, to be honest, quintessentially Macedonian. I was constantly reminded of the way the Macedonians periodically tried to put on a play, something famous by Sophocles or Euripides. They made up costumes that were nineteen parts out of twenty accurate and authentic recreations of what the Athenian chorus and actors would have worn, but that remaining one-twentieth was enough to spoil the whole effect. The heels of the boots would be too high or too low, the expressions of the masks too menacingly comic or too ridiculously sad, or one of the colours would be wrong, or (worst of all) some wealthy patron of the arts wouldn't be able to resist fitting out the chorus with genuine purple scarves when the Athenian producer would've found a way to get roughly the same effect with henna. Likewise, they'd speak the lines with passion and feeling, but not quite understand what they were actually saying, while archaic or poetic turns of phrase that they weren't familiar with could cause absolute and hilarious chaos.

I particularly remember one well-meaning, conscientious soul who'd been dragooned into being an actor – in real life he spent his days smearing pitch round the necks of wine-jars – who turned out to have genuine talent and an uncanny insight into what he was saying. He was doing ever such a good job and I was sitting there enjoying the play no end when he came to a bit that he obviously hadn't been able to puzzle out. The line should have been 'After the storm, I see the blessed calm'; but he put the wrong emphasis on the word *galen*, and managed to turn it into 'After the storm, I see the goddamn ferret'. Which was bad enough; but what reduced me to uncontrollable giggling was the way he said it, with a tremendous soaring rush and a both-arms-wide gesture of sheer joy, as the poor fool tried to gloss over the apparently meaningless gibberish with a spectacular piece of histrionics.

Tsk. Macedonians. The fact that they were smart enough to overrun Greece while the majority of us didn't even realise what they were doing pales into insignificance compared with their inability to get a line of poetry right. The point is, they had no business fooling about with poetry in the first place. A lion would look ridiculous pulling a farm-cart.

By the same token, Macedonian princelings had no place sitting under the shade of carefully trimmed beech trees discussing the finer points of Alcaic prosody or the authenticity of the Dolon episode in the *Iliad*. At their age they should have been with their elders on the battlefield or in the camp, polishing armour and carving thick slabs of meat off the whole sheep roasting on the spit. But, being young noblemen, they laboured and strained and excelled themselves, to the point where they could just about have passed for my social equals at an Athenian dinner party.

Case in point; Philip made one of his unaccounted impromptu visits, and made it known that he'd like to hear how Alexander was getting on with his music. So we all trooped into the little theatre (did I tell you we'd dug a little theatre out of the side of a hill? It was small and the seats were just banked-up turf and from time to time a stray goat would wander across during the course of a performance to nibble at the grass growing between the paving-slabs on the stage floor, but by the time we'd finished it was a theatre; or at least, it was useless for anything else) and made ourselves as comfortable as we could. Then, when we were all perching comfortably, Alexander strode onto the stage and started to play the harp.

Needless to say he played it competently; competent verging on well, in fact, because he'd chosen quite an awkward piece with tricky fingering, but he was making it seem much easier than it was.

'Well done,' Philip grunted. 'That's very good.'

Alexander looked up, grinned and started to play something else. This time he played something downright difficult, and what's more he played it not only flawlessly but also with feeling, a genuine interpretation of the music rather than just making a noise that sounded like it. While this was going on, Philip was getting steadily more and more annoyed, until finally he stood up with a scowl on his face.

'That's too good,' he said. 'Aren't you ashamed to be able to play the harp that well?'

At which, as you can imagine, Alexander dropped the harp as if it had just come still cherry-red hot from the blacksmith's forge and stomped back to join the other kids, with not the slightest trace of expression on his face and (to the best of my knowledge) never touched a musical instrument again as long as he lived.

That was, of course, a slap in the face for Aristotle, because music was one of his subjects – oh, he didn't actually teach the harp himself, there was a little man who came in to do that. But Aristotle taught the theory of music, and musical appreciation, and the mathematical foundations on which music is based; and there was Philip accusing him, by implication, of training his son and heir for the life of a four-obols-a-day professional musician, the kind you buy in the slave sales for two-thirds the price of a good quality field hand.

Like Athens and Thebes around that time, Aristotle and I had formed an uneasy defensive alliance against Philip, not because he'd given us cause but just in case he ever did (a bit excessive, you think, Phryzeutzis? You never met Philip) and I remember him coming to see me that evening, after we'd managed to get away from the obligatory Macedonian family feast. If it'd been anybody else my heart would've bled for him.

'What am I supposed to do,' he complained sorrowfully, 'teach mediocrity? Fair enough, if that's what he wants, he has plenty of Macedonians far better qualified than I am. But I just can't do that, Euxenus, I don't know how to teach a boy so much and no more. I wouldn't have the first idea how to go about it.'

I nodded sympathetically. 'Of course not,' I replied. 'It's because you aren't really a teacher. You're a philosopher, a scientist; you have to teach the whole truth because it's all you understand. A teacher doesn't always understand; often as not he doesn't. But he knows how to get across as much of the subject as is good for the pupil. It's a different skill.'

Aristotle sighed. 'There you are,' he said. 'I don't really understand what you've just said. I know what the words mean, but when you examine them carefully they don't make sense. With respect, I feel that you're much closer to your own definition of a teacher.'

I yawned; it was late and I'd had a lot to drink, and I had to be up early in the morning. 'That's me,' I said. 'I'm just a porter who carries knowledge. I pick it up out of the book, lug it across and dump it in the boys' minds, so many basketfuls per shift until I've filled my quota. What's in the basket, I neither know nor care. That's why I'm a good teacher, gods forgive me.'

He smiled. 'You have the knack of putting things in a striking way, with imagery and other pleasing rhetorical touches,' he said. 'I believe you would do well in politics if you ever found anything you believed in. But you don't really believe in anything, I think; that's your Yapping Dog philosophy.'

I stretched out on a couch and rubbed my forehead. 'That's not quite true,' I said. 'I believe quite passionately in the imperfection of all known political theories. I believe that once you've brought them out of Plato's Republic and tried to make them work in the cesspit of Athens, you'll find that none of them can survive prolonged contact with the lowest common denominator, human nature.' I yawned again. 'I don't know, you have this fine slogan, *Man is a political animal*, and I suppose I agree. You can't put three human beings together for more than a week without politics of some description breaking out, like mildew on damp apples. It's definitely part of our nature, I'd never try and argue otherwise. All I'm saying is, it's part of human nature in the same way that greed and violence and vanity are all parts of the mix. It's there and it can't be got rid of, but it's wrong to *encourage* it. And it's doubly wrong to make people believe that if we all sat down and put our thinking caps on and studied enough data and made a big effort, sooner or later we'd be able to come up with the perfect political system. It's like saying that if only we tried really hard we could make ourselves grow wings.'

Aristotle shook his head. 'That's just the Yapping Dog credo again,' he said. 'We are all imperfect, we are all doomed to stay that way, nothing can be done for us. I can't accept that, I'm afraid. Humanity is capable of perfecting itself; if it wasn't, it wouldn't be human.'

I put my hands behind my head and closed my eyes. 'Now we're just swapping slogans,' I said. 'You're welcome to yours and I'll keep mine, and that way we needn't start a fight. Meanwhile, I really am feeling rather tired, so if it's all the same to you—'

I don't think he heard any of that. All the time I knew him he suffered from this terrible intermittent deafness. 'Consider the gods,' he went on, sitting upright and looking at me as if to suggest I really ought to be taking notes. 'Because they're immortal and invulnerable, they can survive and flourish without needing to perfect themselves. Indeed, perfection would be torment for them, since they live forever; they'd be in a permanent state of having reached the end of a journey. Now consider animals, and the lesser forms of humanity that are little better than animals. They lack the resources and abilities that would make it possible for them to perfect themselves; they lack reason and self-awareness and the ability to differentiate between right and wrong, good and bad. Now, between the two extremes, consider Man. He has the ability to rise above the animal, and he has the need to do so, because he is mortal and finite, and because as a mere animal he would be entirely unsuccessful, having no fur to warm him or claws or sharp teeth or thick hide to defend him against the more powerful predators. Consider the means by which he is to achieve that perfection; surely by co-operation, by virtue of the fact that a combination of many men together is far more than the sum of its parts. This is Man in his political mode—'

'Oh, I know,' I said. 'A pile of unlaid bricks is a pile of bricks, but the same bricks put together is a wall. Comes a time, though, when all walls fall down. You show me a wall that's still standing and I'll show you a wall that hasn't fallen down *yet*. Trust me,' I added, with a quite ostentatious yawn, 'I know about walls falling down.'

'I'm sorry?' Aristotle said, puzzled. 'I don't think I quite—'

'You wouldn't,' I interrupted. 'You weren't there. Sorry, private joke.' He'd annoyed me now, and I wasn't feeling quite so sleepy. 'All right,' I went on, 'now it comes down to ways of looking at things. I could say, why build a wall if it's designed to fall down sooner or later? Where's the point? Or I could say, just because it'll fall down in a hundred years' time, or a thousand, doesn't mean to say we shouldn't build it now and keep the sheep out of the newly planted beans. Attitude, that's all. I'm prepared to concede that you've got a good attitude and I've got a bad one, but that begs the question of what's good and what's bad. Your wall may keep the sheep out for a thousand years, or it may fall down tomorrow and kill a bunch of people. Your politics is dangerous, Aristotle, and if it tends to cause more harm than good, maybe you shouldn't play around with it.'

Credit where it's due, he'd been listening attentively and not taken offence. 'I see you sitting on a hillside,' he replied, 'surrounded by stones. You're wet and cold, and sooner or later you'll get fever in your lungs and die. Now, you have the wit and the skill to build a house out of the stones, and to light a fire inside it that'll keep you warm. But you say, no, if I build the house it may fall on me and crush me, and if I light the fire it may throw sparks into the thatch and burn me while I sleep. So you stay out on the hill and die.'

'Maybe,' I conceded. 'Maybe I last twenty years, whereas if I'd built the house and it had fallen on me – Attitudes, you see. Or opinions, if you prefer. The different ways you and I trade off risks and benefits. Maybe the real difference is that you're trying to make me think the way you do, while I'm quite happy to let you do what the hell you like, provided you do the same for me.'

He shook his head. 'Euxenus, plucked to safety at the last moment from a tempestuous sea, complains that I infringe upon his right to swim.'

I smiled. 'Aristotle, who can't swim, imagines that everybody who's in the water will drown if he doesn't save them. And now, with the very greatest respect, I want to go to bed. That way, come morning, I'll be wrong but happy and you can be right and dead on your feet.'

For some time now, Phryzeutzis, I've been hearing your voice at the back of my mind. You're not complaining, exactly; you're just asking in a bemused tone of voice why someone who's led such a quiet and pedestrian life as I obviously have should feel any kind of obligation to make a record of it for future generations. It's not, you point out, as if anything interesting ever happened to me. Oh, sure enough, you add, at various times I met a whole bunch of other people who led interesting lives, but that's not the same thing. Maybe, you suggest, I should forget about telling my life story and tell theirs instead.

I can quite understand. After all, who the hell would want to read the history of just one ordinary man, the annals of how he earned his living, where he lived, who his friends were, who he slept with, whether he ever got ill, what was his favourite sauce to go on pan-fried whitebait. This isn't, I grant you, the sort of thing anybody outside his immediate family would ever conceivably want to know, unless he was someone really important and famous (in which case it might have some bearing on our understanding of the way things happened; he burned such-and-such a city to the ground because its gates were painted blue and he never could be doing with blue; his wife snored, which was why he sat up all night plotting how to overthrow the republic; a little bit of human interest makes history palatable, like a spoonful of honey and grated cheese on top of rough wine).

I understand your puzzlement, and I forgive you for it. You see, my problem is that all the interesting stuff happened in the second half of my life (assuming I don't live to be as old as Nestor, in which case we'd have to make that the second third), but much as I'd like to I can't really skip the tedious early stuff, because you need to have waded through it to understand why things turned out the way they did. When I started this story, I did consider jumping in at the stage I've just reached and then stopping and going back to do the explanations ('And the reason for this was that when I was only a kid . . .'); but that'd just be confusing. The fact is, people don't live their lives like that, starting off in their late thirties, nipping back to catch up on their childhood, then carrying on where they left off – which is a pity, in my opinion. I'm sure I'd make a far better job of my childhood if I could do it now, with the benefit of everything I've learned over the years, instead of having to try to cope with one of the most influential and formative parts of my life equipped only with the shallow and imperfect understanding of a young boy. It's always struck me that asking a kid to cope with being young is like telling a farmer that if he makes a good job of ploughing the field with his bare hands, you'll reward him by giving him a plough.

The truth is, my life never went according to plan, or *a* plan, or anything resembling a plan. It just sort of sprawled. Some lucky people have lives like a new colony, where the public buildings and houses and streets and markets and town walls are all laid out and completed before the first settler moves in. The rest of us are like old villages which grew up haphazard, strung out along a road or squashed in between two mountains. Consider; I was born to be a gentleman farmer, a man who does just enough work to maintain his self-esteem and spends the rest of his time in aimless and harmless enjoyments. Instead, I became a professional liar, a fraudster, a parasite; and my reward for that was to be entrusted with the education of the Prince of Macedon and the next generation of the nation's rulers and noblemen. Now, when I first embarked on a career in lies, the last thing I'd have expected was to find myself in a position of such responsibility, so of course I didn't plan or prepare for anything like that. Instead, I just drifted down the river. My few attempts at living a regular, honest life, such as my marriage, failed quickly and totally, so I stopped bothering. To all intents and purposes, I was living in my sleep, in the same way as other people walk in theirs. By and large, an inoffensive and undemanding way to use up your days, but hardly the stuff of gripping and life-enhancing history.

Then, quite suddenly –

(Here comes the sort of thing you've been waiting for.)

– my life changed and I found myself involved with and initiating momentous and significant events, doing things that will affect the lives of countless people yet unborn, finding myself a place in history. A remarkable, unforeseen change, and all because of an olive.

The olive in question was a small, wrinkled, rather elderly example that nobody had wanted; so it was left in the bottom of the bowl while its younger, plumper brethren were dragged away and eaten like the seven boys and seven girls supposedly sent every year to the Minotaur. Eventually, our sad olive was the only one left; at which point it was scooped up by a greedy individual by the name of Myronides and swallowed whole.

Myronides had the bad habit of talking with his mouth full, and he tried to swallow the sad olive while in the middle of a lively, really quite heated discussion with Leonidas, Euxenus son of Eutychides (me) and General Parmenio, Philip's most trusted advisor. As a result, the olive went down the wrong way, wedged itself sideways in his throat and blocked off his windpipe in the manner of the 300 Spartans who held off the Persian army at Thermopylae. Rather more successfully, in fact; Myronides choked, went an alarming shade of purple, and died.

I'd never seen a man choke to death, and I didn't see it happen this time – I was looking the other way, as usual, chatting to the man on my right because I was bored to tears by Myronides and the rather fatuous argument he'd been waging for the past quarter of an hour. The first I knew of it was when someone said 'Myronides?' in an alarmed voice, and someone else said 'Gods, he's dead!' and people started jumping up and crowding round and yelling for doctors.

If I sound a trifle callous, it's probably because I didn't like Myronides much. He was loud and rude and stupid, but stupid in a crafty way so that he was always able to kid people into going along with his stupid notions. He was, I'm ashamed to say, an Athenian and a philosopher.

The reason he was there, having dinner with King Philip, his chief minister and his tame intellectuals, was that he was pitching an idea; and the real reason why I took an instant dislike to him was that the idea he was pitching was one that I should have thought of myself. In brief, he was there to ask the King to sponsor him in establishing a new colony on the Black Sea coast, where the wheat comes from.

Before Alexander, the Black Sea region was where all ambitious colonists went if they could. A disturbingly large proportion of the bread eaten in Attica was grown there, and reached us by way of the Greek cities of the Crimea; there was plenty of money to be made in those parts, the natives were either friendly or negligible, and the Greek presence had been there long enough to make it something of a home from home.

The other sweet thing about the Black Sea region was that it didn't belong to anybody (apart from the people who lived there originally, who obviously didn't matter). The whole stretch of coastline from Byzantium to Colchis was there for the taking. It was far enough away from Greece proper that you didn't have to get involved in the endless round of dreary little wars between Athens and Sparta if you didn't want to, and the Persian Empire stopped at the Caucasus, with the mountains and the violent, unruly Sarmatians between the Great King and the bit the Greeks lived in.

In consequence, the region appealed to both sections of society from whom colonists are usually drawn; poor, practical-minded people who want an easier living, and woolly minded idealists who want to found a brave new world. It's plain enough that these two types go together like oil and water, having very little in common beyond the vague belief that geography holds the key to human happiness. Unfortunately, most every colony ever founded has been made up of a mixture of the two, and since the idealists are mostly reject or inadequate sons of the ruling class, they tend to be the ones who get put in charge of the venture. Typically, they set out with noble aspirations of founding the world's first *true* democracy, which generally lasts until halfway through the sea voyage out, by which time the fifty per cent of the colonists who underestimated how much food they'd need on the journey have traded their notional five-hundred-acre allotments with their more practical co-settlers for a couple of jars of cattle-feed-quality barley. Again typically, it's the scions of the great and good families who forget to bring a packed lunch; so when they get to journey's end, they tend to adjust the constitution of the Great Experiment a little, usually the parts dealing with land ownership, taxation and representation of the people. Sooner or later there's a civil war of sorts, and since the scions of noble houses are the only ones who could afford to bring along such expensive items as armour and weapons, things generally end up following the pattern everybody left home to get away from, but with the erstwhile younger sons finally having a bit of land to call their own. It's a wonderful system, highly successful and very, very Greek.

That, as I say, is the usual way it's done; but Myronides had something better to suggest.

For some time, Philip had been hiring mercenaries to augment his own troops in his itty-bitty wars. From a purely military point of view, this was good business. Mercenaries generally make better soldiers than civilians, because they fight for money and they only get paid when they're winning. The problem Philip was facing lay in the fact that he now had rather more mercenaries on the payroll than he could afford, and the point at which you thank your paid helpers for their excellent work and suggest that they leave your prosperous, fertile country and go back to their rocky hillsides is notoriously ticklish. Sometimes they don't want to go.

Atypically for an employer of mercenaries, Philip did have enough quality citizen-soldiers to sling them out and make sure they stayed out, if he had to. But why incur such an expense of manpower and resources, both of which he'd need for his next round of itty-bitty wars, if he didn't have to? Myronides' idea was to pack them all off to a colony in idyllic Taurus, where the old Borysthenes river winds lazily to the sea; it'd cost next to nothing, he'd be rid of a nuisance, the mercenaries would be as happy as a pig under an oak tree and King Philip would have a strategically placed outpost on the land route from Greece to Persia, for as and when he had time to extend his interests in that direction. And Myronides, fat, loud, obnoxious and plausible, would be the outpost's first governor.

And would have been, but for that one sad olive.

Like I said, I was looking the other way when it happened. But before that, before I lost interest in it, I'd been taking a lively part in the debate we'd been having about the Ideal Colony. Perhaps you'll recall that I've mentioned before how popular this tiresome and faintly ridiculous subject was back then, as a topic for philosophical debate. If so, you'll remember that it was a favourite subject of mine – not because I was desperately interested in it, quite the reverse, but because it happened to be one I was very good at (and there was also the unmissable opportunity to dance dialectic rings round Aristotle, who took it so desperately seriously, with his mammoth collection of constitutions of city-states and all).

That evening, I'd been on pretty brilliant form until my head started to hurt. Mainly to aggravate Aristotle and get my revenge on Myronides for thinking of my idea before I did, I'd taken it upon myself to rubbish both democracy and direct military rule as ways of running the sort of colony that was being envisaged here. Rubbishing Aristotle was easy enough – after all, it's perfectly true that democracy isn't the way to go in these cases, for the reasons I mentioned just now. I was on rather less solid ground with Myronides' proposal, but Myronides didn't have the verbal skills to win a debate with me if he was trying to argue that fire is hot. Offhand I can't remember what I said, but by the time I lost interest, Myronides had fewer legs to stand on than a flatfish, and was getting rather desperate – hence, I suppose, his carelessness in eating olives. Damn. I hadn't thought of it that way before. It seems as if I was responsible for his death, if you care to look at it from that angle.

Well, for some reason Myronides' demise stole my thunder, and even after they'd towed away the body and mopped up the spilt wine nobody seemed very interested in resuming the debate where it had left off. I made an excuse and cleared off as soon as it was polite to do so. Ironically, it was one of the six nights each month when Theano's husband was away with the horses (didn't I mention Theano? Not much to tell, really. She was the daughter of one of the local tenant farmers, and had married one of Philip's chief grooms in the hope of getting out of Mieza for good; but her husband had fallen in love with one of the boys who worked in our kitchens and had got himself assigned to the royal steading across the valley from us so as to be near him. She found me interesting because I was Athenian and exotic, and spoke with what she maintained was an attractively sophisticated Attic accent. Well, it takes all sorts), but what with death at the dinner table and my bad head I really wasn't in the mood. She shrugged and said she'd hang about for a bit even so; it was a positive pleasure to get out of the house for a few hours, she said, even if only to go and sit in someone else's. I said I didn't have a problem with that, but I wasn't likely to be terribly good company. 'So what's new?' she replied sweetly, and mixed herself a drink.

'You don't mind, do you?' she added, as an afterthought.

I made a vague gesture intended to convey warm-hearted hospitality. 'You go ahead,' I said. 'Finish the jar, if the risk of having all your teeth dissolved doesn't bother you. And to think, I used to reckon Attic wine was rough.'

'Thanks,' she said. 'But I wasn't talking about the wine. What I meant was, you don't mind me hanging around here?'

'Be my guest. Well, strictly speaking you're my guest already, so really what I'm saying is, carry on being my—'

'I'm going to have a baby,' she said.

I thought for a moment before replying. 'That's nice,' I said. 'When's it due?'

She glared at me. 'No,' she said, 'think. I'm going to have a *baby*.'

'That's what I thought you said,' I answered. 'Surely that's a good thing.'

'I don't think my husband's going to see it like that.'

I'm not usually that obtuse, really; but I'd had a long day and a fretful evening, and you know how difficult it can be to think clearly when your head's splitting. 'I see,' I replied.

'You see,' she repeated, and I couldn't help noticing that she used that same flat, expressionless tone of voice that Alexander favoured when he was angry. Probably a Macedonian thing, I told myself. 'Well, that's fine.'

I swung my legs off the couch and sat up. 'All right,' I said, 'I'm open to suggestions. What did you have in mind?'

She looked at the wall a foot or so above my head. 'Oh, I don't know,' she said. 'Hanging myself is probably favourite. They say hemlock's the most comfortable way, but I wouldn't want to try that without some sort of recipe. Maybe you could ask your friend Aristotle if he knows what the recommended dose is. He's heavily into botany, isn't he?'

I didn't like the sound of that; Theano wasn't much given to melodrama as a rule. 'I could ask, I suppose,' I said, 'but hemlock's something of a sore subject with us Athenians, and philosophers in particular. Don't you think you're over-reacting somewhat?'

The Alexander look was replaced with a generous eyeful of pure poison. 'Over-reacting,' she said.

'Yes,' I answered. 'Over-reacting. You may find this difficult to believe, but where I come from, pregnancy isn't usually regarded as some kind of death sentence. In fact, there's quite a few people who wouldn't be here today if someone hadn't got pregnant at some stage. Tell me, has the concept of divorce filtered its way into this delightful country of yours? Or am I looking at a duel to the death, or something equally quaint?'

Her scowl deepened; then she giggled. 'Actually,' she said, 'that's rather sweet of you. But I don't think it'll improve matters if Pisander kills you too. But yes, we do have divorce, and it's only legal to kill an adulterer if you catch him in the act.'

I nodded. 'Same as in Athens,' I said, 'more or less.'

She sighed. 'Oh, you're all right,' she said. 'The worst that can happen to you is an order for damages.'

'What about you?' I asked.

She shook her head. 'He won't kill me,' she replied. 'Dead, I'm not worth anything. No, he'll divorce me and sue you, and that'll be the end of it. It'll probably cost you the price of a couple of good horses but you can afford that, I'm sure. Still, I'm sorry. I didn't do it on purpose.'

I frowned. 'Don't be horrible,' I said. 'Everything's going to be fine, you'll see. I mean, this isn't the first time something like this has happened, and I don't suppose it'll be the last. Just so long as we both take it as it comes and don't panic—'

That made her really angry.

I know, I know. But really, I was completely out of my depth here. After all, I hardly knew the girl. And in Athens, we have a rather more pragmatic attitude to these things. Well, for a start it'd all have been sorted out by men; her father or her brother would have talked to me about it, and we'd have put together some sort of deal for the husband, and then we'd have made arrangements for her and the baby. A nation that's produced some of the finest minds the world has ever known is more than capable of dealing with such minor domestic crises in an organised and efficient manner. Up in the wild and woolly north, however, it seems to be the case that situations of this kind aren't held to be properly concluded without substantial displays of emotion.

'You *bastard*,' she said; and she was clearly about to expand on the subject when someone started banging on the door.

Hell, I thought. 'You told me he was away at the steading,' I hissed.

'He is,' she replied nervously. 'He rode up there this morning with a string of yearlings.'

More banging on the door. 'All right,' I said. 'Go in the back room till I can get rid of them.'

The good news was, it wasn't her loathsome husband Pisander. The bad news was, it was three soldiers.

'Are you Euxenus?' said one of them. 'The Athenian?'

I nodded.

'He wants to see you.'

'Oh. Right.'

You didn't need to be Solon or Pythagoras to work out who *he* was; and it didn't require much imagination to guess what He wanted to see me about. I should have been expecting it, of course. A man drops dead at the King's table, and a fellow guest hurriedly makes his excuses and darts away. Furthermore, said fellow guest had previously been arguing with the dead man; said fellow guest and said dead man were both Athenians. Hell, if I'd been in Philip's place I'd have arrested me before they'd finished sweeping up the spilt chickpeas.

'Can I just get my cloak?' I said, heading for the back room.

'No need for that,' the soldier replied. 'We're only going to the other side of the yard.'

Not that it'd have done you any good, his expression added. Military history and tactics seminar number three: always post a man outside the back-room window. Why they thought I could teach them anything about the subject, I haven't a clue.

'All right,' I said. 'Any idea what this is about?'

The soldier shook his head. 'Sorry,' he added; and the hint of genuine compassion in his voice as he said it was probably the most chilling thing I'd ever heard in my life. When the arresting officer's sorry for you, you know it's not going to be fun.

★

As a fountain of justice, Philip had a certain reputation for flair – when he was sober, at any rate. For example, when sentencing two undesirables to permanent exile, his judgement had been: (to the first undesirable) 'Leave Macedon immediately'; (to the other one) 'Catch him up'. Then there was the old man who was convinced for some reason that Philip had decided the case against him on account of his age; so he dyed his hair and appealed. 'Go away,' Philip said. 'I've already said no to your father.' A laugh a minute, in other words, provided you were sitting in the right part of the room.

As I was led back into the hall, therefore, I wasn't feeling particularly chirpy; and any residual traces of confidence I may have had left melted away when I saw that, as well as King Philip, I was in the presence of General Parmenio, Prince Alexander and a bunch of other high-ranking Macedonians who hadn't been at the dinner. The whole assemblage had too much of an air of justice being seen to be done for my liking, and I was wondering whether there was any point at all in trying to argue that strictly speaking I was still an accredited Athenian diplomat (having never reported to Assembly, filed my accounts and been officially discharged from my duties) when Philip looked up and nodded to the soldiers. They took a few steps backwards, and Philip gestured for me to join the party.

'Not disturbing you, I hope,' he said.

'No, no, not at all,' I replied.

Philip nodded. 'That's good,' he said. 'I was afraid you might have gone to bed.'

I shook my head vigorously, as if denying charges of having murdered my mother. 'Not a bit of it,' I said. 'Wide awake, in fact.'

'That's all right, then,' Philip said, looking as if he was slightly taken aback at the force of my assertions. 'It's been an eventful evening,' he went on. 'And I know you're not one for staying up late.'

That, clearly, was a dig at my habit of sloping off from the communal feasting, which I knew was bad form by Macedonian standards. I couldn't think of anything to say, though, so I just stood there. Philip helped himself to a drink, then went on.

'If you'd cast your mind back to what we were talking about earlier,' he said. 'Before Myronides had his – accident. You remember?'

Here we go, I thought. 'More or less,' I said, trying not to sound too cautious; bewildered innocence was going to be my line, I'd decided (and, come to think of it, I *was* innocent, though in the circumstances I didn't feel innocent in the least. And neither would you, with all those grim-faced people staring at you). 'The proposed colony. And colonies in general.'

'Exactly,' Philip said. 'It's a rather interesting subject. And what you had to say seemed to make a lot of sense.'

'Thank you,' I said.

'Well,' Philip went on, 'we've been discussing the subject, and the consensus seems to be that there's a lot to be said for Myronides' idea, but the points you raised against it were also pretty valid. Good points on both sides, in fact.'

'Ah,' I said.

'Talking of which,' Philip went on, 'I'd forgotten till you reminded me that Archilochus led a colony to the Black Sea. Interesting.'

I blinked. For the moment I hadn't a clue who he was talking about. 'Excuse me?' I said.

'Archilochus,' Philip repeated. 'Archilochus the famous poet. The famous poet you've been teaching to Alexander and his friends.'

'Right,' I said. 'Archilochus. Yes. I found this book of his poetry, you see, it was in an outhouse, and . . .'

With uncharacteristic forbearance, Philip ignored me. 'Very interesting,' he went on. 'I can't help wondering, in fact, with all the work involved in setting up a whole new city, how he ever found time to sit down and write all that poetry.'

'Well, quite,' I said, nodding like a buffoon. 'Still, you know what they say, if you want something done, ask a busy man.'

Philip smiled. 'Are you a busy man, Euxenus?' he asked.

'Me?' My mind went blank. 'I suppose so,' I said. 'Well, not all that busy, I suppose. But fairly busy.'

'Good. Because there's something I want you to do for me.'

Somewhere at the back of my mind I heard a little voice timidly suggesting that possibly I wasn't going to die quite yet after all. 'Anything,' I said. 'You name it. I'd be honoured, of course.'

Philip clicked his tongue. 'You don't know what it is yet,' he said.

'No. No, I don't, that's perfectly true. What can I do for you?'

Philip swigged down the rest of his wine and snapped his fingers for another jug. 'This idea for a colony,' he said. 'As I said, I like the idea but I don't like the problems you pointed out. Tell me, do you think those problems could be sorted out, or is the whole idea not worth bothering with?'

'I don't know,' I replied. 'I'd have to think about it some more.'

'You do that,' Philip said. 'And when you've got an answer, come and tell me. And if it'll help concentrate your mind, if the project's viable and if you want the job, I can't see any reason why you shouldn't be in charge of it. After all,' he went on, 'Alexander here speaks very highly of you; very highly indeed,' he added, with a slight edge to his voice. 'And Aristotle reckons you've got the necessary grounding in economics and politics and all that stuff, as well as a healthy dose of common sense, which is what I'd say is the most important qualification. And Olympias –' he smiled; no, grinned. Definitely a grin '– I know you can count on her support. She'll agree, you're uniquely qualified. So, why not go and get a good night's sleep, and start thinking it over in the morning?'

I felt like a fish who finds a hole in the net just when he's about to drown in air. 'Of course,' I said. 'Right away. That's . . . Well, thank you. Yes. Right away.' And, still babbling, I backed away and got out of there as quickly as I could.

Theano was still there when I got home.

'Well?' she said. 'You're not dead, then. What was all that about?'

I flopped down in a chair and started to shake. 'It's all right,' I said. 'Everything's going to be fine.'

'And what's that supposed to mean?'

I made myself sit up, and looked her in the eyes.

'Go home and pack,' I said. 'We're going to Olbia.'

CHAPTER TEN

꧁꧁꧁꧁꧁꧁꧁꧁꧁꧁꧁꧁꧁꧁꧁꧁꧁꧁꧁꧁꧁꧁

Of course, that was just more melodrama; sure, we were going to Olbia, but not for some time.

Even if you're the king of Macedon, you can't organise something as complicated as the foundation of a new city overnight. Usually, when the Athenians or the Corinthians found a colony, it takes a year or so of debate, deliberations, acrimony and name-calling before the project is even approved by Assembly (and I've never heard of a case where they *didn't* get approval; but if a thing's worth doing, it's worth doing properly and with an appropriate level of public spectacle). Then there's another year to eighteen months of arguing over who the *oecist* is going to be – sorry, I keep forgetting. The *oecist* is the city's official Founder, the man who lays the first stone or ploughs the first furrow, the man whose name gets repeated by smiling children at every Founder's Day festival, whose head goes on the coins, whose soul receives prayers and sacrifices appropriate to a minor deity for as long as the city continues to exist. Doesn't matter a toss if, having laid the first perfectly square stone or clung grimly to the bespoke ivory plough-handle, he immediately hops onto a fast, comfortable ship, goes back home and never sets eyes on the place again; he's now as close to being an immortal god as it's possible for a human being to get, short of shinning up a drainpipe into the castle of Olympus when they've all gone to bed and swigging ambrosia from one of the dirty cups. In this case, of course, we already had an *oecist* (me), but that wasn't the end of it, by any means.

Oh, there's all sorts of things that have to be decided before the expedition sets sail, some of which may even be important; and you can bet your life that every single decision will be hammered out in furious debate between two bitterly opposed factions, while the third, fourth and fifth factions sneak around behind their backs forming alliances and plotting to overthrow them the day after tomorrow. Somehow I'd imagined it'd be different in Macedon, with a strong and autocratic king making all the really significant decisions. True enough, he did; but those weren't the decisions that took time. Rather, it was the trivia he delegated to the proto-colony's provisional ruling council that caused all the fuss, and really, a man like Philip should have known better. For of course these were exactly the sorts of things that I and my fellow babblers had been brought up from infancy to argue over in an appropriately fascinating manner until somebody paid us to stop, and even though we knew that this time we weren't getting paid by the hour, force of habit's a terrible thing and so's professional pride.

Well, at least it gave me ample opportunity to get to know my fellow councillors, although on balance I think it'd have been better for all concerned if the first time we'd met had been at the dockside. These men were the idealist part of the standard colonial mix, the ones who were sailing in the hope of a brave new world and a brighter tomorrow. It's a general rule that cities, like prudent men making gifts to a worthy cause, never give away anything for which they might conceivably find a use one day, and the upper crust of any bunch of would-be settlers tends to be made up in roughly equal proportions of the useless and the malignant. Accordingly, among my Founding Fathers I had two noblemen's sons of such unutterable depravity that I couldn't for the life of me work out how they'd managed to pack so much activity into such short lives without completely ruining their health; a big-time political loser who'd been given the choice between a brighter tomorrow in Olbia and no tomorrow at all in Macedon; five or six extremely earnest, extremely young noblemen who'd read Plato and Aristotle and Xenophon and gods know what else, and who knew for a fact that humankind are basically a decent enough bunch of chaps provided you dredge deep enough, and there's no problem so great that it can't be solved if only men of goodwill are prepared to sit down together and talk through their differences in a rational manner; and one deaf-mute, one kleptomaniac and a congenital idiot.

And so it went on. My colleagues argued and bitched; Philip sent the occasional brisk note asking how much longer he was going to have to keep paying these tiresome mercenary soldiers I'd undertaken to get off his hands; I floundered, banged tables, wheedled, horse-traded and sent replies to the royal court in Pella that weren't exactly lies provided you interpreted them just right; all in my spare time, of course, when I wasn't teaching Young Macedon the correct use of the caesura in Archilochean iambics and the Spartans' blockade of Attica during the Great Peloponnesian War. Just in case this wasn't enough excitement, I also had the joyful prospect of Theano's divorce and Pisander's lawsuit against me to look forward to.

By his own lights, Pisander had been unexpectedly decent about the whole thing. Apart from slapping her about a bit and drawing pretty patterns on her left forearm with a hot iron, he'd accepted the position without anger or bitterness and had come to see me in a thoroughly polite and businesslike manner, as seller to buyer, to open negotiations. Unfortunately, I wasn't nearly as civilised and pragmatically minded as he was. I hadn't actually met him before; as soon as he told me who he was and I realised that he was a head shorter than me and quite slightly built, my rage at his vicious treatment of his wife knew no bounds, and I bounced him off a wall or two before asking him to repeat his opening offer. After that, we negotiated through an intermediary.

Theano herself didn't seem to be inclined to make things any easier for me. She stayed away, didn't answer the notes I sent urging her to leave her husband's house and move in with me; she hadn't even said whether or not she was coming to Olbia with me. When the stage in the divorce proceedings came where she had to leave, she moved back to her father's house, much to his dismay, since he'd recently remarried himself, so there wasn't a vacancy for another female in what was anyway a pretty small, hand-to-mouth household. I went to see him and put it to him that her attitude wasn't doing anybody any good; everything was a mess, and the baby hadn't been born yet. After huffing and puffing for long enough to make sure money changed hands, he agreed with me and said he'd see what he could do to talk her round – an ambitious undertaking in which he was entirely successful, achieving with two short words ('Get out!') what I'd failed to do with several long and extremely well-phrased letters. In my own defence, I should add that she hadn't actually read my letters, mainly because she didn't know how to read. As an Athenian, of course, I'd just *assumed* . . . Well, I learned one valuable lesson from the experience though, as you'll see in due course, a whole bunch of others were entirely wasted on me.

So Theano moved in, and things got very awkward. Now you, my worldly wise young friend, will tell me that anybody with the sensitivity of a stale bun would have realised long before this stage in the game that it wasn't entirely realistic of me to expect her to throw herself into my arms, in a passionate but respectful manner (as befitting someone of her inferior social standing) and thank me with shining eyes for rescuing her from a life of wretched drudgery and lovelessness. And really, I wasn't expecting that, exactly. Neither, however, was I expecting a sharp blow on the side of my head from a hard-thrown pottery cup.

'What was that for?' I asked, dabbing at the point of impact with my forefinger to see if it was bleeding. 'It was just a suggestion, that's all.'

'Go to hell,' she replied.

I frowned. What we had here, I perceived, was a communications problem.

And no wonder. Bear in mind, please, that I was brought up in a traditional Athenian family, and that my mother died when I was quite young. Consequently, I'd never had much occasion to talk to women when I was growing up, and then my wife died young too so I didn't learn the language at that stage in my life, which is when most men find themselves assimilating this uniquely challenging skill. Also worth bearing in mind is the fact that I'd spent a very significant part of my adult life talking to men (and on a competitive basis, at that). I was, by any standards, a good debater, skilled in the logic-based, fundamentally adversarial form which discussion or argument among men generally takes. I imagined that you discussed things with women in basically the same way.

Wrong.

I suppose it's a matter of upbringing as much as anything else; if we taught little girls how to conduct a structured, logical argument in the same way we teach little boys, maybe we wouldn't run into these ghastly problems we tend to come across on those occasions when we find ourselves with no choice but to try to have sensible discussions with women. In practice in normal everyday life, such a need arises so rarely that it wouldn't begin to justify the amount of effort involved, so we don't bother. Upper-crust trophy wives need to be able to talk intelligently, as do the really high-class prostitutes; otherwise it is indeed a prodigious waste of time and resources.

(I'm aware, Phryzeutzis, that things are rather different here, and that men and women share their lives, rather than living parallel lives under the same roof, as we tend to do in Athens. I'm sorry to say, it's an indication of how primitive your culture really is. You see, the same symbiotic relationship does indeed occur in certain sections of society in Greece; but only among the very poor and backward, where it's necessary for the women to labour in the fields alongside the men, doing the same sorts of work, which means that husband and wife are in each other's company pretty much all the time. Once you get away from this basic subsistence level of society, though, you find the regular pattern emerging; men go out to work in the morning and come home at dusk, having spent the day alone or with other men; women stay in the house and do women's work, visit each other, and so on. That's why, incidentally, if you look at the paintings on Greek pottery and woodwork and the like, the men are painted reddish-brown and the women are all white, or a very pale pinky-white; men spend all day in the sun, women scarcely ever leave the house. I wouldn't worry about it, though. As your society develops and matures, so you'll gradually come to adopt more enlightened attitudes, patterns of behaviour and, finally, patterns of speech.)

'All right,' I said. 'I can see we need to talk about this. So why don't you calm down and get a grip and then we might be able to work out just what it is that's bugging you so much.'

She made a curious sort of angry squealing noise. 'I don't *want* to calm down, thank you,' she replied. 'And I know perfectly well what's "bugging me" without any help from you, Mister So-Damned-Clever Athenian.'

'All right,' I said. 'So what's the problem?'

'You are.'

I sighed. A less patient man would have given up long since, but

I'm not like that. 'You'll have to try to be a little more specific if we're going to make any progress here,' I said. 'See if you can't narrow it down a bit. Just what is it about me that makes you lose control and start throwing things? My face? The way I eat soup? The sound of my voice?'

She glared at me. 'All of them,' she said.

I scratched my ear thoughtfully. 'Odd,' I said. 'I've been looking and acting and sounding the same all my life, and yet that's the first time anybody's ever slung the crockery at me. Can you account for that?'

She shook her head. 'They do have crockery where you come from?' she asked.

'My dear girl, we're the biggest producers of fine-grade tableware in Greece.'

'Then I can't understand it,' she replied. 'I'd have thought an arrogant, interfering, manipulative, self-centred bastard like you'd have been dodging flying plates since you were old enough to crawl.'

I was amazed. 'I don't understand,' I said. 'What on earth are you talking about?'

'Oh, go to hell,' she said.

'That's not an answer,' I pointed out. 'You'll have to do better than that if you want me to accept—'

She banged the wall with her fist. 'I don't want you to do *anything*,' she said, 'except get out of my life and stay out, before you do any more damage. Can't you understand that? I don't like you, and you're a menace. Because of you, I've been thrown out of my own house *and* my father's house, I've lost my husband and I'm pregnant. If you can suggest a way that things could possibly be worse, short of having me lose an arm or go blind, it'll be one hell of a tribute to the power of your imagination.' She scowled at me, then added, 'Oh, yes, I forgot. Just to round it all off to perfection, you propose to make it up to me by whisking me miles away from home and stranding me in the middle of nowhere, in a log cabin surrounded by savages, to spend my days as your combination whore, brood-mare and skivvy. That's surely an offer no girl in her right mind would ever dream of refusing.'

She put her hand down on the table not far from the little oil-jug, and I instinctively jerked my head away. It's a well-known fact: once they get a taste for throwing things, they find it quite difficult to stop. She noticed and gave me a look so full of scorn it'd have wilted cress. 'It's all right,' she sighed. 'I'm not going to hurt you if that's what you're worried about.'

'Oh, but you have,' I replied immediately (even I can spot an obvious cue when I see one). 'Hurt me, I mean.' I shook my head sadly, the very model of injured benevolence. 'Just try looking at the situation rationally for a change, instead of letting all those rampant female emotions take you for a ride. We start off with a convenient, amicable business arrangement – one which you first suggested yourself, if you're capable of remembering back that far. All right, so things got a bit out of hand and you found yourself in an awkward position – not something you couldn't have anticipated, unless you had a really weird upbringing, but I suppose you decided to ignore the risk, figuring it'd never happen to you; some people have the ability to do that, and up to a point I almost envy them. I can't, but I'm a born worrier. Anyway, along comes a problem, quite properly you come to me for help—'

'I never—' she interrupted. I ignored her and raised my voice a little.

'You come to me for help,' I repeated firmly. 'I consider the position and come up with an eminently practical way of dealing with it, and what do I get in return? Obstructiveness and hostility, that's what, in addition to all the expense and embarrassment I'm already being put to on your behalf. But that's all right,' I went on. 'I do understand, it's a really difficult and unsettling time for you, you're frightened and upset and so you lash out – at me, naturally, the way a child in that sort of situation would take it out on its parents, the people who're responsible for it and take care of it. It's a perfectly natural reaction, I've observed it many times with frightened kids, and since I've more or less taken over that role in your life—'

At this point she made a loud, unpleasant noise, somewhere between a scream and the squeal of a pig with a burned nose. 'Shut *up*, will you?' she yelped. 'I don't care how bad a state my life's in, I don't have to listen to this. And to think, I found you attractive because I liked the sound of your horrible whining Athenian voice!'

'Theano,' I said; she jumped to her feet, but I was a little quicker and caught her by the arm. Unfortunately, it was the arm her loathsome husband had chosen to practise his pyrography on, and she screamed with genuine, unpremeditated pain. I let go at once, of course, but the harm had been done; the association had already been formed in her mind.

'Theano,' I repeated. 'Look, I'm sorry—'

Waste of breath, of course. She was out of there like a thrush that's managed to wriggle out from under the paw of an inexperienced fox.

I sat down, feeling unaccountably upset. Not by the rudeness and ingratitude – I'm proud of the fact that I'm the easy-going sort, the kind who doesn't take offence unless it's really unavoidable, and besides, there were all manner of extenuating circumstances in this instance, as I'd been trying to explain to her. No, what was bothering me was the fact that she was clearly still distressed, even after everything I'd said to prove to her that I understood exactly what was going on in her mind; which in turn suggested that something else was bothering her, something I just couldn't begin to grasp –

– And me a philosopher. Me, a scientist, a man who hunts the truth to its lair and brings it struggling to the surface, a man who'd been studying his fellow men – that, after all, was what my apprenticeship with Diogenes had been all about – effectively since childhood. And here's me, one of the brightest and the best, unable to get inside something as simple as the mind of a Macedonian peasant's daughter.

I freely admit, it was an uncomfortable moment; like trying to pick up a rock you've been able to lift since you were sixteen years old, and suddenly finding one fine day that it's too heavy for you. I didn't like the feeling one bit, and for a while I was tempted to let her go to the crows and take the problem with her, so that I wouldn't have to try to deal with it again. For two pins . . .

But there wasn't anybody on hand to give me two pins, and my professional conscience wasn't going to let me turn my back on a problem just because it was disagreeably awkward.

Instead, I went to bed. As it so happened, the book I was reading at that moment was the collected works of Semonides, one of my all-time favourite lyric poets; and the line which jumped up off the paper at me like a friendly dog as I pulled down the scroll was:

'*God made women's minds entirely separate from men's . . .*'

True, I thought, and fell asleep.

★

She was back again by the time I woke up, of course; fast asleep on a couch in the main room, with her hair still up and her shoes still on. I left her there, dressed quickly and hurried out without any breakfast; I'd overslept, and a quick glance up at the sky told me that if I didn't look sharp, I'd be late for school.

'Today,' I announced, 'we'll consider what I believe to be one of the most significant military actions ever to take place between two Greek armies; and it so happens that I'm extremely highly qualified to pontificate about this particular slice of military history, because my own grandfather, the great comic poet Eupolis of Pallene, took part in it. In fact, he was so deeply involved in it that it's a miracle I'm here at all.

'I'm referring, of course, to the destruction of the mighty Athenian army sent under the command of General Nicias to conquer Sicily in Syracuse towards the end of the Great War between the Athenians and the Spartans. My unfortunate grandfather was a soldier in the second expeditionary force that was sent out to break the stalemate that resulted from the Syracusans' entirely understandable reluctance to meet an army as huge and ferocious as the first expeditionary force – on its own it was one of the largest armies ever to leave Athens, and once Grandad's mob joined it, it was staggeringly big. Too big, in fact; they didn't bother to bring any food with them, and when they joined their chums under the beleaguered walls of Syracuse, they found them half dead from starvation. The only food to be had, in fact, was the occasional pumice-hard crust or shard of plaster cheese-rind slung over the ramparts by the chubby and prudent Syracusans, either from basic compassion or a savage sense of humour.

'Well, after a couple of disastrously botched attempts to progress matters – a night-attack on the enemy and a sea-battle, in both of which the Athenians contrived to turn victory into heartbreaking defeat with that extreme deftness and sureness of touch that we manage so well – the generals realised that they had no choice but to raise the siege, fall back to friendly territory and get something to eat. Now this clearly was no big deal; in spite of their losses, the army was still enormous, and apart from the garrison of Syracuse itself, the enemy had no field army of any description, let alone one big enough to last five minutes against a force comprising half the male citizens of the largest city in Greece who were of military age and owned enough property to serve as heavy infantry. In other words, the march from Syracuse to Catana was going to be nothing more arduous than a walk in the country followed by a slap-up dinner at a friend's house; what better way, in fact, to spend a day or so?'

I paused there for a moment and looked round. In spite of the family connection, it was entirely possible that these born warriors already knew more about the affair than I did (actually, most of what I was telling them was reheated Thucydides; Grandfather Eupolis scarcely ever talked about the war, so I'm told, except very occasionally in his sleep); in which case they'd be looking bored or smug, and I could skip the rest of the narrative and get straight on to the nice chewy conclusions to be drawn at the end. But no, they all looked revoltingly fascinated and attentive, so I carried on with the story.

'So off they marched,' I said, 'and to begin with they were cheerful and their morale was high. But after a while they began to get a rather creepy feeling, as if someone was following. So they stopped and the generals sent a few men to take a look; and sure enough, trailing along behind them like the village dogs following a sausage-maker on his way home from market was a rabble – I'm being polite calling them that, even – a rabble of Sicilian scruffs and no-goods, hired hands, tenant farmers' sons, city trash, small boys, without a decent helmet or breastplate between them. But what they did have were throwing-spears and bows and arrows and an infinite quantity of good, hand-fitting stones, the size and weight your father told you never to throw at people in case you did some-one an injury.

'It wasn't an army; it didn't have the gear or the social standing to be an army. And since it wasn't an army, it couldn't fight a battle, so it didn't. What it could do, though, was buzz round our resplendent and immaculately polished army like a swarm of angry bees, stinging and buzzing away before they could be swatted. Trying to catch them was a waste of time; you'd feel the *chunk!* of a slab of rock on the back of your bronze-encased head, and down you'd go; by the time you were on your feet again, they'd be nowhere to be seen. The few men who did go scampering off among the rocks in full armour and hot pursuit never came back, of course; twenty or so adolescent thugs were waiting just over the skyline to pull the breathless hero down and tear him apart with their fingernails.

'Nothing for it, then, but to keep marching; in full armour, because of the unceasing shower of stones; in the heat of the day, because they daren't stop; wandering about, herded like goats bewildered by the yapping of small, fierce dogs – they tried to shake them off by marching at night, but they didn't know the way, and the enemy did. The further they went, the further they were driven from the road they should have been following, the one that had wells and streams along it; no water, no food, but lots of dust and heat and the constant nagging persecution of the enemy that wasn't even an army . . .

'In the end, they broke into two sections, one straggling behind the other. The first party staggered down to a river; tortured with thirst, they plunged into the water and the Sicilians killed them as they drank – I gather they didn't make any attempt to fight, they just lay in the water and guzzled it, all filthy with silt and blood, till an arrow or a stone stopped them, or until the Sicilians rounded up the survivors and marched them back the way they'd just come towards Syracuse.

'On the way, they passed the place where the other half of the army had been killed, in a walled orchard on some wealthy Syracusan's country estate. My grandfather was one of a handful who got out of there before the archers and slingers finished off the job. The rest stayed, kneeling behind their shields until hunger, thirst or the unofficial weapons of the Sicilians did for them.

'Only a fraction of the army lived to be taken prisoner; but there were thousands of them nevertheless, and they died of starvation and neglect squashed together in the stone-quarries of Syracuse, the only secure place big enough to hold such a multitude. They died simply because there wasn't enough food or water to spare for such a huge number of men, and nowhere big enough to shelter them.'

I stopped there and looked at my audience. They looked uncomfortable, like children who've just become aware that their father isn't the biggest, strongest man in the world, and that there isn't really a Good Fairy who watches over them while they sleep. In retrospect, maybe it was an unkind thing to do to them, at such an early and impressionable age, to strip them of the comfortable belief that high breeding, solid plate armour and obeying orders without question will always see you right, no matter how dismal the situation. After all, these boys had been raised to be soldiers, and a soldier must have something to believe in, else he'd turn tail and run at the first sight of the sun flashing off the enemy's helmets.

'Right,' I said, 'that's the facts of the case. You don't need me to tell you that it flatly contradicts everything I've taught you so far about military theory. In case some of you weren't listening, I'll just repeat that one basic lesson: in war, the side that doesn't screw up, wins. But in this case, apart from a few logistical problems which they were by no means the first to encounter, I don't think the Athenians made a mistake. They saw they'd bitten off more than they could swallow, so they resolved to withdraw in good order. There was no field army to oppose them. More to the point, there was no *reason* to oppose them, because they were going away, with no suggestion that they were likely to come back. According to basic military theory, there was nothing to be gained by fighting an enemy who's pissing off of his own accord. After all, what did the Syracusans actually gain by the exercise, apart from a lot of healthy exercise burying the dead? They killed thousands and thousands of men; so what?

'And that's the point, surely. The Syracusans *changed the rules*. Up to that moment, everybody in the world knew why people fought wars; it was to decide a simple question, such as who owns this attractively situated plain, or who's going to rule this city. When other means of deciding the issue fail, the question is put to the gods, who hold up a set of golden scales with the fates of each side in the pans – you remember the scene from Homer, no doubt, and very memorable it is, too. We Greeks designed heavy infantry warfare to be efficient and suited to our needs; first, it always gave a clear result; second, it was decided by courage and physical strength rather than the cleverness of individual generals; third, it was relatively safe, even for the losing side; fourth, only the ruling class, the men who can afford armour, are allowed to take part. We've fought this way for hundreds of years without a significant change in the way we go about matters because it works, it does what we want it to do. As a result, war in Greece has never been about killing as many people as possible, which would be infamous and an affront to the gods. So; what went wrong?

'There are many possible answers. You can say that the Sicilians aren't proper Greeks (though, by the same token, neither are you; and you're just as shocked as I was when I first heard the story). You can say that the attack on Syracuse was simply state piracy and utterly unprovoked; and that's true, too, but hardly unprecedented. Maybe you could claim that, after enslaving their fellow Greeks for fifty years, the Athenians were so bitterly hated that something like this was inevitable, sooner or later. You can argue that this all happened at the end of the longest and nastiest war in our history, at a point where one side finally lost its temper and played spite-fully, like a violent child. All sorts of reasons; maybe you can put them all together and end up with enough reasons to make sense of what happened. But that's not good enough for us, because we're trying to learn *history* here, and the whole point of history is to find out how certain things happened with a view to making sure they never happen again. One day, you'll be at the head of an army in hostile territory, and you'll see far away in the distance a big mob of enemy skirmishers keeping pace with you, and you'll think of me then and ask yourself, "What do I do now?"

'All right, here's the answer. Not necessarily a definitively correct one, but something you can write down on your tablets and learn by heart; the side that doesn't screw up, wins; making assumptions is an easy way to screw up. Never assume that the rules will stay the same, that the difficult job is too difficult or the easy job is too easy. My grandfather and his comrades-in-arms assumed that walking to Catana was easy, and destroying a vast army with sticks and stones was difficult; they made assumptions. Now, if I were you, I'd lie awake at nights worrying about what I've just told you. In fact, the night when you can put it out of your mind and go back to sleep should be the night before the day you hand over command to someone else. Any questions?'

I hadn't expected any (I'd *made an assumption*, see?) so I was a little bit put out when Alexander solemnly raised his hand and looked me in the eye.

'Well?' I said.

Alexander swatted away a fly. 'I think it's obvious where the Athenians went wrong. Their army was too big. They had more men than they could feed, and then they sent more men instead of food. And all their soldiers were heavy infantry, with no light troops or cavalry; if they'd had cavalry and archers, they wouldn't have got into such a mess. And they didn't know the way, they can't have or they wouldn't have ended up wandering aimlessly about. That's three mistakes. If they'd have got one of those three right instead of wrong, they'd have made it to Catana without any trouble. So I don't see what the fuss is about.'

I nodded slowly. 'You're right,' I said, 'as far as the details go. But you tell me, why did the Syracusans attack them when they were going home anyway? Why didn't they just let them go and be glad to be rid of them?'

Alexander frowned. 'Easy,' he said. 'If they'd reached Catana alive, they could have come back later; fewer of them, with food and cavalry support and guides who knew the way. They couldn't do that if they were dead. It made sense to kill them all.'

I studied his face for a moment. 'You reckon,' I said.

'Why not?' He shrugged his shoulders. 'What was the name of their general, by the way?'

'Gylippus,' I replied. 'He was a Spartan.'

'Well,' said Alexander, 'if I'd been Gylippus, I'd have done the same thing.'

I smiled. 'And so would I, if I'd been Alexander.'

After class, I went to a meeting of the Town Planning and Statues sub-committee.

It was the seventh meeting we'd had so far, and we'd covered the town plan in the first half hour. That left the statues.

'I don't know why you're making such a fuss,' one of them said to me, his face bright red. 'After all, you know you'll have *yours*, and slap bang in the middle of the market-place too. So I can't see why you begrudge the rest of us a little recognition. After all, we're the ones founding this city, we're entitled . . .'

There's a kind of exasperated noise best described as the sound patience makes when it's been heated to steam and escapes through a gap in one's teeth. I made it. 'I don't want a damn statue,' I said. 'If I have a right to one, I hereby waive it. Now, statues of the gods, yes, we need a few of those; but forty-seven others – have you any idea how much valuable cargo space they're going to take up? Not to mention the expense.'

'Depends where your priorities lie,' someone else said disdainfully. 'You're an Athenian. Wouldn't you just love it if you had genuine authentic statues of Cecrops and Theseus and Aegeus and Alcmaeon, taken from life? Think how proud you'd be, with that kind of tangible proof of your nation's heritage.'

I drummed my fingers on the ground. 'Sure,' I said. 'I really want to be remembered as the *oecist* whose people starved over their first winter because all they had in the holds of the ships were statues of themselves. Tell you what; let's have the statues carved out of hard cheese. That way, when we're done admiring them, we can eat them.'

There was a gloomy silence.

'All right.' My heart sank; Theagenes was speaking, and I'd come to dread his intervention. Whenever there was deadlock, up would pop Theagenes the voice of reason, with a compromise pitched with geometrical precision exactly halfway between the opposing view-points. Unfortunately, halfway between sensible and utterly fatuous is still utterly fatuous. 'All right,' Theagenes said, 'how about this? Instead of lots of separate statues, what about one big statue? A frieze or something like that, with all of us on?'

I shook my head. 'A frieze that big wouldn't even fit on the ship,' I said. 'We'd have to build a ship specially, or buy one of those great big barges they use for shipping marble from Paros.'

Theagenes nodded. 'Fair enough,' he said. 'What about this; we hire a sculptor, take him with us, and he can do all the statues once we get there? That way we'll save all that space on the ship, and we can have as many statues as we like instead of having to decide in advance.'

It took me about three heartbeats to make up my mind to support this proposal with every last scrap of enthusiasm I could fake. After all, no sculptor skilful enough to know which end of the chisel to hit was going to want to leave Greece and go and settle in Olbia; we'd search for one, in vain, until it was time to go, and by then it'd be too late to have our portraits carved – result, no statues. Ideal.

Of course, at that time I hadn't yet formulated Euxenus' Law; namely, never underestimate the perversity of human nature. We found our sculptor all right. His name was Agenor, and he was born on a little chip of rock off the south coast whose name escapes me for the moment. His love for and skill at carving stone led him in time to Corinth, and after a year or so there he started wandering from city to city, staying in one place just long enough to establish a reputation as a highly competent marble-basher and then get himself chased out of town by whoever was running the place, be it a democracy, monarchy or oligarchy. Agenor, you see, was a dreamer, an idealist, a thinker of such deep thoughts that it always amazed me that he didn't bash his own thumb with the hammer more often than he did. Everywhere he went, he found fault with the way the city was governed, and being Agenor he felt it his duty to explain these shortcomings, loudly and in public, whenever he found somebody willing to listen. In Athens, they formally exiled him. In Sparta, they flayed the skin off his back and threw him out of a window; the only reason they didn't hurl him from the city wall is that Sparta hasn't got any city walls. In Megara they dumped him in a cesspit. In Sicyon they tied him backwards on a three-legged mule and let the children chase him out with sticks. In Orchomenus they sentenced him to death and left him in a cell under the citadel with the tools of his trade (an ancient tradition of the city), and he escaped by chiselling out a hole in the rock and slithering through it. In Ambracia they listened to him, and had a brief but highly unpleasant civil war as a result, from which he escaped with great difficulty and the loss of the top third of his left ear. In Pella they found him a job cutting paving-slabs for road-making, and when he said it wasn't quite the sort of work he was looking for they said, tough, make yourself useful or we'll cut out your tongue. Oh, Agenor was delighted to have the opportunity to join us, and after a brief show of reluctance I agreed to take him. After all, I reasoned, he could hardly be more of a pest than most of my fellow Founders, and if I had my way, we'd be laying a lot of paving-stones, so he might come in useful after all.

So we had deadheads, we had enthusiasts, we had idealists, we had the antisocial and the mentally inadequate; we also had some genuine farmers, men whose fathers had had one too many sons, and some craftsmen with useful skills that they were willing to exercise in return for a fair day's pay, and some ex-slaves who knew all there was to know about hard work for little reward; and we had a thousand Illyrian mercenaries, who'd been led to believe that the life they were embarking on was going to be better than the one they were leaving behind. In other words we had Greeks, two and a half thousand of them including women and children. It was a better start in life than many cities get, because we also had food and animals and materials and tools, provided for us by the King of Macedon; we had five ships of our own and the loan of twenty-five others there and back; we had the services of a hundred professional stonemasons for a year, to be paid by Philip in arrears on their return; we had a splendid and extremely long written constitution, composed by a committee chaired by Aristotle himself, of which seven copies housed in shiny bronze canisters were ceremoniously placed in a cedarwood chest in the hold of the expedition's flagship on the day before we sailed – how the mice managed to get at and chew up all seven copies to such an extent that nothing legible remained I simply have no idea, or at least not in front of witnesses. We had all this; and we had me.

And, at the last minute, looking extremely unhappy as her father and two brothers shooed her up the gangplank with my son in her arms, we had Theano; expensive, ungrateful, hard-done-by Theano, who didn't want to go and who'd far rather have worked herself to death washing clothes by the river.

Two and a half thousand idiots and one angry girl, and a fair wind for Olbia.

CHAPTER ELEVEN

𐤀𐤀𐤀𐤀𐤀𐤀𐤀𐤀𐤀𐤀𐤀𐤀𐤀𐤀𐤀𐤀𐤀𐤀𐤀𐤀𐤀

'Excuse me,' you're saying, 'but where's Olbia?' You sound sheepish, perhaps slightly ashamed that you don't know where Olbia is; but it's a good question, and one I really ought to have asked rather earlier than I did.

The sad truth is, I thought I knew. I thought Olbia was a natural harbour at the bottom edge of the almost-island of Chersonesus*, the roughly rectangular chunk that dangles like a spider from the roof of the Black Sea coast at the mouth of the Gulf of Maeotis, with a mountain range on one side and the sea on the other; an area colonised by Greeks for many years, with a pleasant climate and friendly relations with both the neighbouring Greek colonies and the local savages.

There is indeed such a place; it's called Heracleia, and we weren't going there.

Olbia, by contrast, is lodged in the mouth of the Hypanis river like a strand of meat wedged awkwardly between your teeth. It's got a wonderful natural harbour; to the east, there's a promontory very like a folded thumb and pointing forefinger, or a wolf's head with a very long snout. We weren't going there, either; someone had beaten us to it, a mere three hundred years earlier.

The place we were actually headed for** was a little triangular bay nibbled into the coastline between Olbia and Tyras, roughly

---

*The Crimea.
**Between Odessa and Mykolayiv in the Ukraine.

level with the fingernail of the pointing forefinger of land I mentioned a moment ago, which the sub-committee on Names and Public Holidays had, in the comfortable shade of a fig-tree in Mieza, resolved to call Philippopolis en Beltiste ('The city of Philip in the best place anywhere'). In practice, we didn't often refer to it as that. To be honest, if you were to ask me what the most commonly used name for it was, I'm not sure I'd be able to tell you. Some of my fellow Founders actually did insist on calling it Philippopolis-and-the-rest, which made them a joy to listen to after they'd had a drop to drink. (Try it and you'll see what I mean.) The Illyrians called it something unpronounceable in Illyrian. My friend Tyrsenius (I'll tell you about him later) took to calling it Oudama ('nowhere') and the name stuck, at least with some of us. This confused the hell out of the Illyrians and the Callippidae, the local natives; in Greek, you see, the part of the word that means 'no' can be either *ou-* or *me-* depending on whether it's in a principal or a subordinate clause and whether the verb is infinitive or subjunctive, which meant that we'd find ourselves referring to it as Oudama and Medama in the same sentence. The Illyrians firmly believed that there were two colonies being founded simultaneously, and needless to say they'd been sent to the crummy one, which made them very sad. The Callippidae drew roughly the same conclusion, and spent countless thousands of man-hours searching for Medama in the hope of striking a better deal with the Medamites for the sale of their wheat and barley. In fact there was one bright spark who set himself up as the official Medamite commercial attaché in Oudama and got a lot of good business that way, until we caught him at it and asked him to stop.

'In the best place anywhere' was an exaggeration, to be sure. But there were worse places to be, among them Attica and, for that matter, Macedonia. Don't believe what they tell you about the Black Sea climate, all those horror stories about freezing cold winters and roasting summers; it's a little cooler than Greece, but not offensively so. The main difference is in the terrain. It's flat. For an Athenian, used to being surrounded on all sides by rocky mountains, it's a rather dizzy feeling to see land that level or a sky that big. In Attica, and nearly all of Greece for that matter, we grow our food in the thin layer of dust and dirt that covers the lower slopes of the mountains. Olbia is one enormous level, deep-soiled plain, perfectly suited for growing wheat; drop crumbs from your breakfast and they'll take root and grow. Of course, we Athenians have known this for years. For every coarse barley loaf eaten in Athens, we import six medimni of Black Sea wheat, and in return we palm them off with Athenian oil, honey, wine and figs, which we've carefully educated them to prefer to their own.

And who are they, I can hear you asking. The simple and unhelpful answer is, the Callippidae. The name is Greek and means 'sons of fine horses' (and what that's supposed to mean is another matter entirely). The proper answer is that they're Scythians who've packed in the nomadic life, settled down and learned the arts of agriculture and getting cheated by Greeks.

('Ah,' you say, with a smile on your face. 'Like us.'

Yes, Phryzeutzis, very much like you. I mean us. Like our people here, they're renegade descendants of the horsemen of the steppes, who saw the obvious merit in trading a life of mobility, self-reliance, freedom and yoghurt for the security of the same little square of dirt and the uncertain charity of Mother Demeter—

'Maybe they got sick of yoghurt,' you suggest.

Maybe they did. Maybe they just grew tired of moving on. Quite possibly the urge to roam from one set of mountains to the next is the childhood all races and nations go through and grow out of, as soon as they come to know better . . .

'Better?' you ask. 'Define "better".'

I suggest, here in Sogdiana on the Iaxartes river, a place I never knew existed until I wandered here, as far from Attica as it's possible to get.

'Ah,' you reply indulgently, 'but once you got here, you decided to stay.'

Absolutely. This is clearly the place I've been looking for all my life.

Wherever the hell it is.)

Very like us, Phryzeutzis; industrious, slow, suspicious, hospitable, ferocious, incomprehensible – we Greeks have one word for all of that, *barbaros*, barbarian, a foreigner, someone who when he speaks makes *ba ba* noises with his mouth instead of speaking proper Greek. The Callippidae had become a little bit Greekified, in that they lived in houses rather than wagons and dug in the dirt rather than milking mares and ewes. They'd even acquired a taste for Greek delicatessen and some of our showier consumer goods. But *barboroi* beyond question, now and forever.

'Could be worse,' my friend Tyrsenius said, as we leaned over the rail and stared at it. 'Definitely, could be worse.'

Wonderful stuff, optimism. It's like honey; take the lid off the jar and somehow it gets everywhere, clinging to your fingers, smearing on everything you touch. Also, too much of it makes you want to be sick.

'Flat,' I commented.

'And green,' Tyrsenius added. 'Except for the yellow bits. That's corn, presumably.'

'Wheat,' I confirmed.

We looked at each other.

'This could be a nice place to live,' he said.

I nodded. 'I expect the people who live here'd agree with you.'

He shrugged. 'I know these people,' he said. 'They aren't fighters. Warriors yes, but not fighters. We'll get no bother from them.'

My friend Tyrsenius – Tyrsenius the Flamboyantly Wrong, as someone once dubbed him – was the nearest thing we had to a native guide. For years his father had made the long trading run from Elba, off the west coast of Italy, to Olbia; hugging the coast all the way, starting off with a cargo of Italian pig-iron that mutated at every stop he made until it turned into the dried fish he traded for wheat on the shores of the Black Sea, ready to be converted into honey in Athens, honey to crockery in Corinth, crockery to sheepskins in Illyria, sheepskins to timber in Istria, timber to wine in Apulia, wine to cheese in Sicily, cheese to pig-iron on Elba . . . Wizards, they say, can turn one thing into another, can even turn base metal into gold if they're clever enough. My friend Tyrsenius, like his father before him, was a true wizard, though. He could turn iron into wheat.

And he knew these people, or people a hundred miles or so further down the coast who looked and sounded quite like them; 'close enough for a public contract', as he used to say. Warriors, not fighters; I liked the sound of that, though I wasn't quite sure I understood what it meant. Maybe they'd just kill us once and go away.

'You see,' he went on, 'they won't be expecting us to stick

around. They know about Greeks here, you see. Greeks arrive on ships, they buy stuff, they sell stuff, they go. Sometimes they hang about waiting for the winds to change, sometimes they'll even build a city as a base for future operations, but sooner or later they push off, they don't go out into the fields and get their hands dirty. They'll be delighted we've come, just you wait and see.'

I shrugged. I had grave misgivings. I also had a thousand Illyrian mercenary soldiers, whose spears laid all low before them and (further or in the alternative) whose deaths in glorious battle wouldn't draw too many tears from King Philip's one good eye if the worst came to the worst. I clearly had nothing to worry about. Maybe they'd all want Agenor to carve their portraits.

'How long before landfall?' I asked.

Tyrsenius grinned. 'You're learning the technical seafaring terms, I see. Not long.'

'Not long,' I repeated. 'That's another technical seafaring term, is it?'

He nodded. 'That's right,' he said. 'It means I don't know exactly, but not long.'

In fact, a contrary wind kept us hanging about for what seemed like for ever; during which time someone spotted our sail and scampered back to the village to raise the alarm. The reception committee we found assembled on the beach when we finally came ashore didn't look nearly as delighted at our coming as I'd hoped or Tyrsenius had promised.

'They're just shy, that's all,' my friend Tyrsenius whispered to me, as the golden Olbian sun flashed off a scimitar-blade. 'Once they've gone through the motions, a little show of hostility just for form's sake, we'll all get on like a house on fire.'

Not the most comforting of images. Marsamleptes, the Captain-General of the Illyrians, was making grumbling noises as our keel hit the sand. He was probably trying to tell me something or ask me a question, but apparently he still hadn't quite grasped the fact that I couldn't speak Illyrian. He was probably telling me that his boys would eat them alive; that or we didn't stand a chance. One of the two was always a fair bet with Marsamleptes, a straightforward man who tended to chew the ends of his moustache at moments of great stress.

Such as this.

'All right,' I said, 'here we go. No sudden movements, anyone.'

It feels strange, describing to an Eastern Scythian (that's you, Phryzeutzis) what it felt like for the Athenian leader of a largely Illyrian expedition to come face to face for the first time with a Western Scythian. I'm not sure which of us is the funny foreigner, and which of us is Us. The situation at the time was further confused by the fact that, as an Athenian, I was quite used to seeing Western Scythians, but in a less than helpful context.

The City of Athens, you see, has for quite some time now used Scythian slaves as policemen. Sorry, you don't know what that word means; it means men paid by the state to keep order and catch and punish people who break the laws (or at least, that's the theory). We had to use foreign slaves for the job because no self-respecting Greek, let alone Athenian, would dream of doing a job that involved exercising practically unlimited power over his fellow citizens. Quite right, too. Ask yourself; what kind of man would you get volunteering for a job like that? Men who want that kind of power are by definition the last people you'd allow to have it.

So; we imported barbarian slaves, choosing Scythians because they're quick at learning our language, skilled with the bow and arrow – which is why in Athens we just called them 'archers' – and (because of their entirely alien views on what constitutes wealth and happiness) almost impossible to bribe. They did the job well, by and large, but in spite of that – maybe because of it – you'd be hard put to find a Greek with a good word to say about them, or about Scythians in general. Now, I pride myself on being the sort of man who as a general rule isn't particularly bothered about the colour of people's skins or hair or eyes, as witness the fact that I took an almost immediate liking to the not-quite-Greek Macedonians. But a Scythian, with those distinctive cheek-bones and dark intense eyes – I can't help getting the shivers sometimes when I look at them, and a sixty-year-old memory yells at me from the back room of my mind, 'Run for it, here come the archers!'

As if that wasn't enough to contend with, I also had my friend Tyrsenius' last-minute confession about the role I'd assigned him as chief interpreter . . .

'Of course I speak the language,' he told me when I asked. 'Not absolutely fluently, of course,' he added. 'I mean, from listening to me you wouldn't necessarily assume I was Scythian by birth or whatever, but I can make myself understood, most of the time.'

Of the dialect of this particular region, it turned out, he knew about five phrases; things like 'Where are we?' and 'Which way is the sea?' These were, it goes without saying, useless questions to ask, because he had no chance whatsoever of understanding a single word of the reply.

In the event, it wasn't relevant. The chief spokesman spoke excellent Attic Greek —

'— As a result,' he assured me, 'of spending twenty years in Athens as an archer, before I saved up enough to buy myself out and come home.' He looked at me for a long time without speaking, and behind him his escort of tall, solemn-faced warriors allowed their fingers to creep forward and touch the strings of their bows. It was a shall-I-eat-him-now-or-save-him-for-later look, and even thinking about it all this time later still bothers me some.

'I know you,' he said. 'It's a gift I have, I never forget a face.'

That startled me, for sure. 'How can you know me?' I replied. 'We only just met.'

He shook his head. 'Every face I've ever encountered,' he went on, tapping his forehead, 'stored away somewhere, in here. And besides,' he added unpleasantly, 'even if I had a rotten memory I'd still remember *you*.'

I looked at him again; and, though the face was still entirely unfamiliar, I noticed that he did have a significantly crooked nose and a gap in his front teeth. A memory dropped into place.

'Oh,' I said.

(It was a long time ago. I was young, not used to drinking undiluted wine on an empty stomach. And it wasn't just me; in fact, I didn't really participate, I was just tagging along with the rest of them and happened to be the one that got caught—

You want to hear the story, don't you? Oh, all right. Like I said, I was little more than a kid at the time, and we'd been at a fairly boozy party. When it finally wound up, we roamed around the streets for a while, singing abominably and breaking up minor works of civic art, the way one does at that age, until we found ourselves outside the house of some girl that one of us fancied. So we started singing serenades, according to the time-honoured tradition; and when the archers showed up to shoo us off, we made a bit of a fight of it, just to prove we were free-born Athenians who don't take kindly to being pushed around by foreign slaves . . . And one of us, can't remember a thing about him, got a little bit carried away and clubbed one of the archers across the face with the arm off a statue that had got in our way earlier. There was a loud crunch and ever so much blood, and the man went face down; we were sure we'd killed him. At that point, my fellow revellers did the sensible thing and ran like hell. But it was the first time I'd ever seen real, messy violence, and I just stood there staring, a torch in one hand and a walking stick in the other, watching the way the blood trickled out, cutting channels through the dust.

One of the archers told me to put down my stick and my torch – they aren't allowed to lay hands on a citizen unless he hits them first or resists arrest. I heard the words but I wasn't listening, if you see what I mean. He said it three times, then tried to take the stick out of my hand. I was so completely out of it by that stage that I reacted purely on instinct; I smacked him hard across the face, not as hard as the boy with the bit of statue but enough to break his nose and knock out some teeth. He howled and stumbled off into the shadows; the third archer looked at me, and the man on the ground, then slowly pulled his bow out of his quiver, stepped through it to string it, drew an arrow out of his quiver; I knew for a fact that he was going to shoot me. It was something about the deliberate nature of his movements, the fear and wariness in his eyes. It was as if I could read his thoughts, as clearly as if they were cut in marble on a wall. Why should he risk getting killed or mutilated by coming within range of my stick, when he could kill me from ten yards away, with no witnesses to say it wasn't self-defence? I could watch the debate behind his eyes – how would he account for having his bow strung and ready? Obviously he'd thought of something he reckoned would pass muster. Was he certain he could kill me cleanly, without the risk that I'd live long enough to accuse him of cold-blooded murder? He calculated the odds and accepted them, with a tiny nod of the head, and started to draw the bow –

– At which point, I realised that if I dropped the torch I was holding, he wouldn't have enough light to shoot by, and I could escape. So I did; and that was the last I ever saw of him. But the other man, the one I hit with my stick –)

'That's right,' he said.

I chewed my lower lip for a moment. What I really wanted to ask was, 'Did the man die? The one who got hit with the statue?' But I didn't. 'Small world,' I said.

'Very,' he replied. 'And full to bursting with Athenians.'

At this point, I really wished we'd tried to do this through Tyrsenius; in which case, we'd still be at the We-come-in-peace stage. 'Anyway,' I replied, 'we're here as representatives of King Philip of Macedon, on whose behalf I extend friendly greetings from our people to yours. May I ask whether you are authorised to speak on behalf of your people? If not, might I ask you to bear a message to those who are?'

He sniffed. He did that a lot. Something to do with having an awkwardly broken nose, I guess. All those years of sniffing and dribbling snot . . .

'My name is Anabruzas,' he replied. 'What's yours?'

'Euxenus,' I replied, in a very small voice.

'Euzenus.'

'Euxenus,' I corrected him. 'Epsilon, umicron, xeta—'

'Euxenus. Well, that's interesting. Euxenus anything else, or just Euxenus? Forgive my curiosity, but . . .'

'Euxenus, son of Eutychides of Pallene in Attica,' I recited. 'Now attached to the household of King Philip, and duly authorised on his behalf—'

He nodded. 'Thanks,' he said. 'I'd gathered. What do you people want here? Trade?'

I took a deep breath, but couldn't think what to say; at which point, my friend Tyrsenius interrupted.

'Isn't that wonderful?' he exclaimed, shouldering past me. 'That you two should turn out to know each other, I mean. I'm Tyrsenius, son of Mossus, commercial attaché. Now, our objective here is two-fold; first, as you've already guessed, we'd like to trade with you – we have a fine selection of the usual quality goods together with some additional items that I'm sure will interest you. Secondly, we'd like to discuss establishing a more permanent presence here to facilitate further trading opportunities in the future—'

I could see the Scythian's patience draining away, like seed-corn through a rip in the sower's bag. 'First things first,' I said, treading hard on Tyrsenius' foot. 'I'm sorry, I don't think I caught what you said a moment ago, when I asked if you were authorised—'

He gave me a look that wasn't quite a scowl but certainly wasn't a warm and friendly smile. 'I'm the headman of the village over that hill,' he said, jerking his head backwards to one side. 'We have nothing to trade that you'd want, and we don't want anything you've got. Maybe you'd have more luck a bit further down the coast.'

Tyrsenius, the clown, interrupted again. 'Luck is what you make of it, my friend,' he said, flashing a mouthful of teeth, like a panther. 'I'm sure that your people will find something here that takes their fancy; and our prices are probably much lower than you think.'

The Scythian sniffed again. If I were his wife, that constant sniffing would drive me crazy. 'There's an awful lot of you,' he said, 'for traders.' He peered past me at Marsamleptes, who was standing behind me doing pyramid impressions. 'Illyrian?' he asked.

I nodded.

'Right,' the Scythian said; then he sidestepped so he'd have eye-contact, and started making that extraordinary two-cats-fighting-in-an-alley noise that passes for a language in Illyria.

Gods alone know what the two of them actually said; but from what I was able to piece together later, the gist of the conversation was something like,

'What are these arseholes really doing here?'

'We're founding a colony.'

'Oh, yes? You and whose army?'

(Nod in my direction.) 'His.'

(Pause.) 'How many of you are there?'

'One thousand, most of us veteran warriors. If you oppose us, we will kill you all without mercy.'

'Oh. In that case, welcome to Olbia.'

The Scythian took two steps back, and looked at me. Then he shook his head and sighed, and walked away to talk to his followers, who numbered about fifty. I called him back.

'Well?' he said.

'The other man,' I said. 'Was he all right?'

'No. He died.'

'Oh. Thank you.'

'You're welcome.'

He talked for a while with his friends; the discussion was heated, to say the least. He walked away while they were still talking.

'If you want land,' he said, 'we can probably come to some arrangement. We're leaving now.'

'Right,' I said. 'Well, it was . . . Goodbye,' I said.

He looked at me. Didn't say anything. Didn't need to.

'There,' said my friend Tyrsenius when they'd gone. 'I told you everything would work out just fine.'

Under other circumstances I'd have worried myself sick after that. But I didn't have the time or the energy. Too much else to do.

Unpacking a brand new city off a small fleet of ships is a complicated business at the best of times. Uncharacteristically, I'd given the matter some thought, and hit on the inspired idea of organising our disembarkation and the setting up of our temporary quarters in advance. First priority, I'd decided, was to delegate. I'd given responsibility for getting the gear off the ships and onto the beach to one group of Founders, finding and felling timber to another, organising work details to a third, and so on. I'd let the individuals concerned in on the secret and told them what they were supposed to be doing; they told me they understood perfectly and that I could rely on them to make sure everything went as smoothly as a well-fitted hinge.

I was younger then, and rather more naïve.

Alpha Section, in charge of disembarkation, immediately started a bitter dispute with Epsilon Section, i/c putting up our first temporary shelters, over where the stuff was to be piled up on the beach. Epsilon wanted it all piled up neatly *here*, while Alpha reckoned that transferring it to dry land and leaving it where it fell was more than enough to discharge their responsibilities to the community. Before I'd realised what was happening and sprinted up the beach to separate them, they'd already started a fist-fight, and a couple of passionate Epsilons had thrown a load of jars of seed-corn into the sea by way of proving beyond question the superiority of their viewpoint.

While I was dealing with them, a messenger from Beta Section, i/c finding timber, trotted up to inform me that there didn't appear to be any trees in the whole of Olbia. When asked how thoroughly they'd searched, he admitted that they'd gone only as far as the edge of the neighbouring rise, about three hundred yards, so I suggested that it might be an idea to widen the scope of the search a little before we all piled back onto the ships and went home again.

While I was doing this, the fight between Alpha and Epsilon

flared up again, this time involving a couple of the Illyrians who were under the impression that Epsilon were sabotaging food supplies and ought to be killed immediately. In consequence, I was quite busy for a while (none of the interpreters were anywhere to be seen, of course, so I was having to communicate with the Illyrians by waving my arms in the air and waggling my eyebrows) and wasn't on hand to sort out the savage row that erupted in Gamma Section (allocation of work details) over who was going to draw the black pebble and have to try to control the Illyrians. They were throwing stones at each other by the time I got round to them, one of which hit me just above the right ear and forced me to sit down for five whole minutes, during which time I should have been pointing out to Delta Section (unpacking and distributing essential equipment) that we weren't really going to need the ceremonial rostrum quite yet, and they shouldn't be wasting their time setting it up before they'd found the axes we needed to chop down the trees that Beta Section were convinced didn't grow in Olbia.

At this point, Zeta Section (surveying the site of the new city and drawing up plans) reported in to say that the maps we'd been given, on which we'd proudly drawn in the provisional street plan in cheerful red ink, bore no relation whatsoever to the actual topography, and had we in fact landed in the wrong place? It was a fair point, and they deserved better of me than a rudely-phrased suggestion that they try holding the maps the right way up; but I maintain that stomping off and sulking back on the ship wasn't a very mature response, so it was really all their fault that that job didn't even get started. I didn't notice this until some time later because as soon as I could see straight again I had my hands full with stopping one of the Illyrian contingents marching off to the village the Scythian welcoming committee had told us about and razing it to the ground on general business principles.

Then my friend Tyrsenius, seeing that I wasn't really handling things terribly well, decided to help me out by going round the various sections issuing a whole lot of contradictory orders, reinforced by terrifying scowls from the bunch of Illyrians who had for some reason attached themselves to him as a sort of spontaneous royal guard. Thanks to his intervention, Alpha Section found themselves in charge of collecting in the axes which Delta had finally just found and issued to Gamma Section, Red Subsection, and re-issuing them to Beta Section, who'd come back with news of a small stand of nondescript saplings on the other side of the ridge, which could come in handy for tent-poles if we hadn't brought any with us (which we had).

I'd made up my mind to wander off and hide somewhere till nightfall when something truly unexpected happened. Agenor the sculptor – remember him? Well, at various times when he hadn't been able to make a living from pure and unsullied art, he'd filled in as a stonemason, on one project rising to the rank and dignity of assistant foreman. The wise Founders of Gamma Section had assigned him to Subsection Green (utterly useless people, in charge of keeping out of the way) and he'd been standing around for several hours watching things degenerate into a state of primeval chaos, and thinking what a negative turn of events this was. Finally, unable to bear any more, he'd jumped down from the rock he'd been sitting on, rounded up his fellow spectators, led them up the beach and set them quietly and efficiently to work digging trenches, with spades he effortlessly charmed out of Delta Section (who wouldn't have given them to *me* if I'd gone to them on my knees and promised them each their weight in silver money).

One of the sulking Zeta Section Founders, noticing this, strolled across and asked him what the hell he thought he was doing. Digging foundations, Agenor replied. The Founder asked, foundations for what? The city wall, of course. The Founder, managing to keep a straight face, asked him what on earth made him think the wall should go there, when his Section hadn't even found North yet. Agenor looked at him oddly and said that of course the wall went here, because if he cared to look at the map (which Agenor had glanced at a day or so earlier for the first time) he'd see that that over there was the promontory marked on the map as *Promontory*, and that pointy-topped hill was *Hill*, so all you had to do was draw an imaginary line between the two points and start digging.

It took about ten minutes for word to spread that someone had turned up who Knew What He Was Doing; whereupon Agenor found himself surrounded by nearly everybody in the expedition, all demanding at the tops of their voices to be told what to do. It'd have fazed me, and probably Agamemnon and Zeus as well, but you can't fluster an ex-foreman of masons that easily. Bless his heart, he had the courtesy to send someone over to fetch me, and made a show of consulting me while issuing his orders; as far as I was concerned, I was delighted to approve anything he said, on the grounds that he seemed to Know What He Was Doing, and I patently didn't.

From then on, things went rather more smoothly.

Zeta Section announced that we'd come to the right place after all, and set to work with measuring rods, squares and little wooden pegs. Beta found a substantial copse of nice tall pines they'd somehow managed to overlook, and started chopping them down. Alpha unloaded the rest of the cargo and put it at the disposal of Epsilon, who laid the equipment out in neat stacks, nicely convenient for Gamma to collect and take with them to perform the various tasks to which Agenor had assigned them. It was all wonderfully efficient and civilised, and even the Illyrians joined in and worked hard for several hours without killing or maiming anyone.

'There you are,' observed my friend Tyrsenius, sipping a cup of wine he'd managed to find somewhere (drop my friend Tyrsenius out of the sky onto his head in the middle of the Libyan desert and five minutes later he'll have found a chair to sit on, a jug of drinkable wine and a cute girl to pour it for him). 'I told you it'd all go smoothly once everybody knows what they're supposed to be doing.'

'And there was me worrying,' I replied. 'I should have known it'd all be all right.'

Tyrsenius shrugged. 'You need to learn how not to worry,' he yawned. 'It's a basic survival skill for anybody in a position of authority. I tell you, you don't get far running a merchant ship if you spend all your time with your head in your hands, fretting.'

'True,' I conceded, in the hope that it'd shut him up. It didn't.

'Now, if you really want something to worry about,' he went on, 'you could do worse than worry about the Scythians. I don't trust 'em.'

I blinked. 'Wait a minute,' I said. 'Not five minutes ago you were saying how well it had all turned out, and at least we weren't going to have to play dominance games with the natives because they're all so damn friendly.'

He smiled indulgently. 'You know your trouble?' he said. 'You take people at face value too much. You want to watch that, you know.'

I was about to protest that I'd had serious misgivings the moment I first set eyes on them, but I didn't get the chance.

'In Olbia,' he continued, 'the nicer they are to you, the more you've got to watch them. You learn to do that instinctively when you're a merchant, but of course you've never done anything like this before. Now, if I was in your shoes, I'd send a couple of hundred Illyrians down to the village in full armour, just to make a tactful show of force.'

'If you were in my shoes,' I muttered, 'you'd have blisters. Your feet are much bigger than mine.'

He gave me a puzzled look for a moment, then smiled. 'Good to see you've still got your sense of humour,' he said.

A day or so later, as soon as the expedition could be trusted to be left on its own, I led a party to the Scythian village to open a dialogue.

There was me, and my friend Tyrsenius, and Agenor the itinerant sculptor (who'd kindly made the time to come with us) and Captain-General Marsamleptes, and the little man with a squint who was probably the only person in the expedition who could understand what both Marsamleptes and I were saying, and a bunch of Founders, and some particularly villainous-looking Illyrian soldiers in their best armour to add a suitable nuance of menace to the proceedings. And also, for some reason, there was Theano, who'd tagged along on the pretext that she was bored and had nothing to do.

The news that we were on our way to the village was relayed by the inevitable squadron of small boys who were permanently on duty in the patch between the village and the city site, so when we toiled up the hill and got our first sight of our new neighbours, nearly all of them were there to meet us, bearing with them their strung bows and unsheathed scimitars, and other traditional Scythian tokens of welcome. My old friend Anabruzas came out and stood in front of them, flanked by hostile-looking men with helmets and wicker shields.

'You've come, then,' he said.

Well, it was perfectly obvious that we had, but I didn't say anything clever. I just nodded. Taciturn strength, I thought; that's what these people respect.

'All right,' Anabruzas said. 'What do you want?'

'We need to talk,' I replied. 'About land for the colony.'

Anabruzas scowled at me. 'Sorry,' he said, 'none to spare. You'll have to go somewhere else.'

I'd been hoping we weren't going to have to do all that. 'I don't think so,' I replied. 'We just need to rearrange things a little, that's all.'

Anabruzas' scowl tightened up a little. 'You don't seem to get it,' he said. 'There's only so much land, and we need it. You can't grow it on a tree or dig it up out of the ground. Either it's there or it isn't.'

I shook my head. 'Sorry,' I said, 'don't agree. There's only six hundred or so of you, and all this plain; only about a fifth of it's under the plough, and even that's far more than it takes to feed a hundred-odd people. There's more than enough for all of us, provided you're prepared to be reasonable.'

'No,' Anabruzas said.

A fat lot of good being taciturn had done me. 'That's just silly,' I said. 'Look, you're welcome to keep everything you've already got ploughed and planted. The stuff that's just lying idle will do us.'

Anabruzas laughed. 'That's not the way we do things,' he said. 'You ever heard of rotation of crops? One year plough, two years fallow; that's how we get such good yields. We need all this land, and that's all there is to it.'

'I'm sorry,' I said, 'but that's lazy, wasteful farming. Come on, Anabruzas, you've lived in Athens, you know how we do things there. One year under corn, one year under beans, plough five times before planting and use plenty of dung. It works for us.'

'That's as may be,' he said. 'But it's not how we do things. If you want the land, you'll have to fight for it.'

By this time, Marsamleptes had learned to recognise the Greek words for fighting, battles and so on, and now he woke up out of his daydream and started glowering horribly at the Scythians like a dog who can see birds. The Scythians, though plainly alarmed, scowled back.

'If we fight,' I pointed out, 'you'll lose. No question about it.'

Anabruzas nodded. 'Quite likely,' he said. 'But I promise you this. By the time you've killed every last one of us – and that's what it'll take – we'll have taken so many of you with us there won't be enough of you left to found any damn city.'

'It'd be ten to one,' I pointed out.

'Doesn't matter,' Anabruzas replied. 'Better dead than Delos, any day.'

(There I go again, making assumptions. You don't know what or where Delos is; well, it's a small island in the Aegean, famous for two things. One's being the birthplace of Apollo himself, and the other's the slave market; biggest in Greece, they say.)

Well, I suppose it could have been worse. We might have started fighting there and then; if my fellow Founders had had their way, I expect we'd have done just that, and Marsamleptes (who hadn't killed anyone for weeks and was starting to look pale and thin as a result) would undoubtedly have made a thoroughly professional job of it. All I could think of to do was turn away and walk back down the hill, hoping very much that I'd get clear without being hedge-hogged with arrows. I kept on going, and nobody shot at us; didn't somebody say somewhere that any peace conference where you escape with your life can be considered a success?

'You made a right hash of that,' Theano said.

'Yes,' I replied.

'Obviously, tact isn't your strong point.'

'No,' I agreed.

'Of course,' she went on, 'I knew that already. You've got an amazing ability to say exactly the wrong thing at exactly the wrong time.'

'Apparently,' I said.

She walked on in silence for a moment, then continued, 'The worst thing was when you told him he was welcome to keep the land they'd already ploughed and sown – have you any idea how *insulting* that sounded? Or when you told him how much land they *needed*—'

'All right,' I said. 'I think you've made your point.'

She smiled. 'Just so long as you know,' she said. 'After all, I know from bitter experience, you're so damn ignorant, maybe you hadn't actually realised—'

'Thank you,' I said.

'Because,' she went on, 'I can't see how somebody could know they were doing something like that and keep on doing it. I mean, it just doesn't make sense—'

'Thank you for your input,' I said. 'I'll try and bear it in mind.'

*

You didn't have to be anybody clever – Aristotle, say – to work out what the likely sequence of events would be. Messengers would go out from the village to other settlements all over the Olbian hinterland; men with bows and scimitars would assemble like ghosts in the grey dawn, and we'd be jerked out of our sleep by the screaming of women and the hissing of fire on the thatch. We wouldn't stand a chance. It'd all be over before we had time to put our shoes on.

So Marsamleptes organised the defences, and none of us got much sleep for the next week or so. We scrabbled together huge piles of brushwood and lit them at sunset; we posted sentries; we all took our turn to peer anxiously at the border of the light and the darkness, imagining stealthy shapes where the shadows were longest; we worked in armour until every scrap of clothing we possessed was dripping with sweat and snagged to ribbons, and the swords dangling from our shoulders got in the way of everything we did, digging trenches and hauling masonry blocks and putting up scaffolding. We were exhausted and uncomfortable and very, very short-tempered with each other, but we were ready for them.

Of course, nothing happened.

Our scouts, creeping up to the skyline to spy on the activity in the village, reported back that they appeared to be going about their business as if nothing had happened. *They* weren't clanking about the place like refugees from the *Iliad*, or sitting up all night screaming, 'Who goes there?' at quietly scuttling foxes. 'Lulling us into a false sense of security,' my friend Tyrsenius called it; of course, he'd clambered into his armour the moment he got back from the peace conference and set about ringing his tent with a wonderfully intricate system of tripwires linked to five enormous cow-bells (where he got them from, gods only know; but Tyrsenius always had everything), the incessant clanging of which really started to get on our nerves after the first couple of hours. After a week of not being killed, though, he was strolling around the place (still head to toe in shining bronze, of course) announcing that we were over-reacting quite dreadfully and he'd said from the very beginning that there was absolutely nothing to worry about from that quarter.

The work, meanwhile, slowly began to take shape.

It's remarkable how small a large copse can be, when you cut it down, trim its branches off and hammer its component trunks into the ground to make a stockade. By my system of reckoning, any stand of trees large enough to get lost in is a wood, probably even a forest; but the small forest we located on the first day was all used up by the time we'd built the first gatehouse, let alone any wall for it to be a gate in. Given our nervous state, we didn't dare send any logging parties out of eyesight of the camp without an equivalent number of armed escorts, and of course we also had to make sure the camp itself was never without an adequate garrison. This didn't leave too many bodies over to do any productive work, and the few who actually did some soon began to harbour uncharitable thoughts about their fellows who spent all day lounging about leaning on their spears, watching and occasionally making helpful suggestions. Nevertheless; up the stockade went, our first priority, and after that we felt just a little bit more secure, enough to allow ourselves the luxury of taking off our breastplates while we worked.

Originally, the idea had been that instead of wasting money buying stone (I mean, who'd be stupid enough to buy the stuff when all you need do is chip it off the sides of cliffs?), we'd quarry it ourselves from the nearest exploitable seam of granite or sarsen.

It was an understandable mistake, bearing in mind that we were Greeks, brought up on the tiny patches of flat ground squeezed in between enormous bare mountains. We never imagined for a moment that stone might be hard to come by, just as a fish probably can't understand the concept of a desert. After we'd wasted a lot of valuable time and manpower in prospecting for suitable material, we gave up and asked Tyrsenius if he knew where we could get building stone from; and in due course, purpose-built barges trundled along the coast from Odessus, riding low in the water under their burden of neatly trimmed modular sandstone blocks. The cost was staggering, so we sent a ship back to Macedon for more money, one thing we could be sure we wouldn't run short of so long as Philip was alive.

'If we'd only done this in the first place,' announced Tyrsenius, formerly our self-appointed Director of Quarrying Operations, as he checked the manifest of the latest stone barge, 'we'd be a fortnight further on by now. I do wish people would listen to me now and again; it'd save you all a lot of time and effort.'

Agenor, now firmly established as Director of Works, suddenly remembered that not long ago he'd been a professional sculptor and demanded marble instead of sandstone for the façade of the gatehouse, which we were building directly behind the gate in the stockade. I told him to go to the crows with that idea, whereupon he appealed to the Founders and explained that if at some point he was going to decorate the gatehouse with a commemorative frieze depicting the founding of the city, he would need not just marble but good marble, a point which the Founders held to be entirely valid. I told them to go to the crows too. We held a number of quite passionate Works committee meetings, noted the objections form- ally on the record and told Agenor to shut his face and get on with his work, which he did once I'd promised him all the marble he could use once the city was built and priorities could be reassessed.

There was a moment – I can't remember when, exactly, but it happened quite suddenly, while none of us were watching – at which point it stopped looking like a huge, random mess and started looking like a baby city. Not Athens, that's for sure, or even Pella; but a city. There were streets, or narrow strips where you could believe streets would one day be; we stopped walking all over the place and kept to them. We even gave them names; Main Street and Gate Street and South Street and West Street, none of which appeared in the list previously agreed by the relevant sub- committee, but if you said 'the plot two thirds of the way down West Street on the left as you face the sea', people would know where you meant. It was a bizarre feeling, once we allowed ourselves to acknow- ledge that it had happened. And time went on, the Scythians didn't attack, the money didn't arrive from Macedon but the barges kept coming from Odessus, we arranged further credit with Olbia City for more food, tools, canvas and rope, we found more timber a day's walk away, we stopped wearing armour and sending armed escorts, we finished the first well, we completed the preliminary land survey and began drawing lots for who was to get which parcel of land, still the money didn't come, we broke up the palisade because it was getting in the way and we needed the timber for other things, we finished the first house, we started the first temple, we held countless endless meetings, we made our first plough, we laid the foundations of the granary, the money arrived but there wasn't nearly enough, the fourth house fell down in the night and we started it again from scratch, we looked up and found we'd been there a year—

Theano and I got married; something of an afterthought, fitted in on a spare afternoon while we were waiting for the plaster to dry before making a start on the roof. The Scythians hadn't attacked yet. We were still here. And the next day. And the day after that.

I began to record the history of the city, on a piece of parchment that had come wrapped round a large cheese. I recorded our first harvest, the first couple of deaths and births, the first major theft, the first rape, the first sale of land—

It wasn't anything special, in fact it was mostly downright primitive. But it was alive.

Extraordinary . . .

CHAPTER TWELVE

𝍢𝍢𝍢𝍢𝍢𝍢𝍢𝍢𝍢𝍢𝍢𝍢𝍢𝍢𝍢𝍢𝍢𝍢

When my son was a year old, I chose a name for him. I'd left it rather late, putting off the chore for a variety of insubstantial reasons – perhaps at the back of my mind I believed that if I ignored his existence he'd go away. Why I should want to think like that I have no idea; I wasn't conscious of not wanting the child, or not feeling the usual degree of paternal affection. Maybe it had something to do with the fact that Theano and I weren't getting along particularly well, though there's no logical connection there that I can see. On the other hand, logic doesn't usually have much to do with anything in such circumstances, as far as I can tell.

I named him Eupolis; nominally after his great-grandfather, the Comic poet, but really because Eupolis means (or can be made to mean) 'from the best of cities'; it was a propitiatory sacrifice, an act of dedication for the colony itself, as well as a pun on the high-faluting 'official' name the Founders had chosen. As such, it was well received and taken by my honest neighbours as a vote of confidence, or an act of faith. Something like that, anyway.

Fair play to us; we built that city quickly and well. I believe that a large measure of our success was due to the fact that the Founders, having settled every last theoretical detail from the names of the streets to the colours the statues were to be painted before the expedition left Macedon, left us alone once we actually got there, and we were therefore able to ignore everything they'd decided, which was a great help. As for all that wonderful theorising about the ideal form of government for the ideal colony, all the model constitutions and draft law-codes we drew up and then tore to bits over someone else's wine and chickpeas, in practice it all turned out to be about as much practical use as a tiny, pearl-encrusted gold pickaxe. We didn't bother with any of that stuff; no need. The problem we had wasn't deciding how best to impose the orders of the ruling class on our subordinates; quite the reverse. Where we ran into difficulties was in finding anybody who was prepared to give any orders at all.

Odd? Well, it was an odd set-up, I suppose. What made the difference was that, whether by random chance or disguised good fortune, we arrived on the Black Sea coast with a profound shortage of expertise. We had farmers, and a handful of people who knew a bit about building things, and that was about it; all the other technical knowledge pooled between us lay in the fields of killing and toss-arguing, and neither discipline (we quickly acknowledged, thank the gods) helps much when you're trying to put a roof on a barn or mark out a wall in a straight line.

Now, if we'd all been as useless as each other, I expect we'd have wiped each other out in bitter feuding within a week or so, as each faction of opinionated ignorance tried to bring its rivals round to its way of thinking by force of arms, like they do in real cities. But we did have experts, though not nearly as many as we'd have liked, and so pretty soon we had a workable system of government. Each expert was in charge of the project that needed his expertise and the rest of us kept our faces shut and did what we were told. As *oecist* I theoretically had the right to interfere, veto and command; but as they say, just because you've got ten fingers doesn't necessarily mean you can play the harp. Like every farmer I knew a bit about everything, just enough to be able to see that there are some things you've got to entrust to the man who knows what he's about.

The system worked because none of our experts wanted to give orders – after all, who wants responsibility when he's got to live with the consequences himself? Agenor the sculptor, for example, knew about dressing stone, and as much practical architecture as a site foreman needs to do his job. He wasn't an architect; but we made him be one. The first thing he did, accordingly, whenever called upon to build anything, was to make it clear that he wasn't an architect, and that he'd much prefer it if somebody else told him what to do ... Having reluctantly accepted the commission, he proceeded with extreme caution, like a cat walking along a branch of a thorn tree, happily listening to all relevant suggestions and actively canvassing opinions from anybody foolhardy enough to express them. In short, quite by chance, we'd hit upon that golden mean we philosophers had been babbling about for generations: a society where the people who didn't want power were landed with it, and all decisions were reached cheerfully by consensus. Trust me; it works. Whether you could make a go of it in any context other than that of a completely new settlement, a bunch of people with tools standing on a grassy field with no food or shelter apart from what they contrived to make for themselves, I have no idea. That, by the way, was another beneficial side-effect of the settlement process; it cured me for ever of the pernicious urge to speculate about things I don't know spit about.

The Founders, meanwhile, kept pretty much to themselves, as I mentioned a moment ago. By some happy chance, they realised of their own accord that they were hopelessly out of their depth here, and that any prospect of getting fed, clothed and housed depended on the efforts of the rest of us, who'd do a far better job of providing for them if not interfered with.

'We have a problem,' my friend Tyrsenius informed me, as we shared a jug of wine under the shade of the east wall of our nearly completed temple.

(Temple, singular; where the original Foundation plan had provided for no fewer than fourteen temples, we'd edited and modified a bit, coming to the conclusion that the gods were going to have to muck in like everybody else in this colony, share a house and learn to get along with each other without squabbling.)

'Really?' I said, with my hat over my eyes.

'You bet,' Tyrsenius replied. 'If only you'd listened to me earlier, of course—'

'Quite,' I said. 'Refresh my memory. What's the matter?'

Tyrsenius sighed. 'We're broke,' he replied. 'Worse than that, we're up to our ears in debt. I was going over the accounts this morning, and—'

I sat up and pushed my hat back. 'We've got accounts?' I said, startled.

'Of course,' Tyrsenius replied irritably. 'I'm your treasurer. What do you think I do all day?'

I shrugged. 'That's wonderful, Tyrsenius,' I said. 'And what's in these accounts of yours?'

'Our borrowing,' he replied grimly. 'What we owe to the other cities, Odessus and Olbia City. Think about it; we've been buying food and building materials and gods know what else from them since the day we arrived here, on the assumption that King Philip'd bail us out and send money.'

I yawned. 'Which he has done, bless him,' I said. 'Thanks, in no small part, to the incredibly persuasive letters I send him every month—'

'Well, you haven't been persuasive enough,' Tyrsenius replied. 'To be precise, you've failed to carry conviction to the tune of twelve talents, three minas. And that's what I'd call a problem.'

I poured a little more wine. 'The cities don't seem all that worried,' I said. 'They keep supplying the stuff, and I haven't noticed them badgering us for money. Don't worry about it.'

He scowled at me. 'Of course they aren't badgering us,' he said. 'It's all secured on land. Our land. And interest is running, let me remind you—'

'So?' I shrugged. 'What do you think is going to happen? Are the Odessans going to show up one morning with spades and buckets and dig up all the land and cart it back to Odessus? Don't see it myself. If they want more land, all they've got to do is go out and take it, right in their back yard. There's more than enough for everybody. You're thinking like we're still in Greece, my friend.'

He shook his head. 'You're telling me their security's worthless, then.'

I nodded. 'For all practical purposes,' I replied. 'It comforts them to know there's mortgage stones all over the fields here; I suppose it helps them balance their books and all. But in real life they know they're going to have to wait till we're on our feet and producing before they get their money. They trust us. Everything's all right.'

Tyrsenius blew out through his nose, like a horse. 'You reckon,' he said.

'Sure,' I replied. 'One thing they won't do is anything that'll make life difficult for us – like trying to call in the debts. If we go under, they'll never get paid. So they've got to keep supporting us. Good for us; in the long term, good for them. Plus, they've got King Philip as guarantor at the end of the day, and his credit's good, I'm sure.'

'You think so? You think he'll hold still and be sued if we default on a loan?'

I smiled. 'What an enticing mental image that is,' I said fondly. 'But no, that's not what I mean at all. Be realistic. What they're getting in return for goods and services delivered is the most valuable currency in the world – Philip's awareness that they're doing him a favour. Have you been listening to the news from Greece lately?'

Tyrsenius looked puzzled. 'Not sure I follow,' he said.

'All right,' I said. 'Suppose you lived in Sicily or somewhere like that, where they have those villages perched on the rim of a giant volcano. Now, suppose that the next time the volcano starts rumbling and burping fire and generally giving notice that it's about to play war, you're in a position to whisper in its ear, so to speak, that you've been going out of your way to be nice to the volcano's pet nephew; the volcano recognises this, so when it erupts, the other villages get swallowed up in the lava flow, but you don't. Worth a few bad debts, don't you think?'

Tyrsenius thought about it for a moment, then snuggled his back against the wall and put his hands behind his head.

'My point exactly,' he said.

I'm not going to write the history of Philip's piecemeal gobbling-up of the Greeks. It's a long and tortuous story, and to be honest with you I'm not sure I can remember the details after all this time, particularly since I wasn't there when it was happening. What you need to know is that my royal patron had worked his way down through Greece, stirring up trouble and then stepping in to stop the resulting brawls; and once he was in somewhere, it proved rather difficult to get him out again. He was everywhere, the voice of sweet reason, agreeing with everybody at the same time. His operating system reminded me a lot, in fact, of those same Scythian archers who kept the peace back home. When a fight broke out, they didn't rush in and intervene, thus uniting the warring factions in the common cause of beating the shit out of them. Instead they waited till the fight was over, and then stepped in and arrested anybody who was still standing. That was Philip's way, except that he'd also started the fight.

It was, of course, that wonderful diplomatic skill of his that made it possible, and somehow everybody played along, though they must have seen for themselves what he was up to. In Athens, for instance, my old colleague Demosthenes harangued Assembly nearly every day with ferocious, entirely accurate accounts of Philip's evil cunning. I gather that Demosthenes' speeches were so popular that the City ground to a halt, with everybody who could manage to squeeze into the Pnyx hanging on his every word. When he'd done they'd applaud him till the ground shook – then proceed to vote down his proposals and do what Philip wanted, for the simple reason that if they didn't, it might give him a pretext for declaring war, and that would be that.

The only city that openly defied him was Sparta; and he only tolerated them, I think, out of sentiment. You see, Sparta wasn't the world-class power it had been in Grandfather's time. It had, quite simply, grown old; it was a little, wizened shadow of what it had once been, and Philip made a point of treating it with the respect due to an honoured but rather senile ex-hero, tolerating its tantrums and threats with a broad smile that told the rest of Greece that he knew exactly what the realities of the situation were. At least the Spartan sense of humour was still alive and kicking; when Philip sent a long and beautifully reasoned letter to the Spartan high council, demanding various concessions and backed with a delicate infusion of blandishments and threats, the Spartans duly considered it and sent back a reply, which read *In reply to yours: no.*

But plucky little Sparta was an exception. The rest of Greece knew what was going to happen, but there was nothing they could do. They were on the edge of the volcano, roasting chestnuts in the glowing ash while they could and waiting for the sky to turn red.

The other day I came across one of the letters Alexander wrote me at about that time – I was patching my oldest and most highly prized pair of boots, not for the first time, and when I came to peel off one of the many layers of parchment I've pasted on the underside of the uppers over the years, there it was; three-quarters legible, and the rest easy enough to guess from the context.

There was nothing special about that letter, beyond the fact that it had managed to survive so long and so much; just like me, I suppose. It's absolutely typical of the letters he sent me while he was trailing round Greece acting as Philip's adjutant; my theory is that he treated his letters to me as practice exercises, to make sure he didn't forget how to conduct a formal correspondence with a respected elder of lesser rank. They read like the examples you get in those *Complete Letter-Writer* books, the sort that provide a model letter for every conceivable occasion – letters from fathers to sons; letters from ambassadors to kings; letters from creditors to debtors, class one (apologetic), class two (dismissive), class three (overbearing and arrogant); letters from husbands to wives; letters from recently appointed stewards to their masters informing them of increased annual yield or reports of dishonesty among the casual labour – but I knew for a fact that Alexander was far too proud to copy out forms and precedents written by somebody else, because when I told him to back in Mieza he flatly refused, and told me why in no uncertain terms; so I guess he was in effect writing his own and using me as a kind of quality control.

His letters were always meticulously constructed:

1) Formal greetings;
2) Conventional enquiries about my health and brief report on his own;
3) Admirably lucid and concise precis of the state of play in the current campaign – excellent practice for writing dispatches, and clearly showing that he'd taken to heart what I'd taught him when we did class exercises in military prose composition back in the old days;
4) Interesting and informative observations on matters of geographical, political, anthropological and botanical interest that had come to his attention since his previous letter; why he sent these to me rather than Aristotle (who liked that sort of thing) I don't know, unless he wrote the same letter to both of us, changing only the name at the top and the address on the outside;
5) One amusingly whimsical anecdote, human interest story or similar lighter note, also serving to reiterate some point or

statement made earlier in the letter about some major current topic, thereby completing the structural loop;

6) Exhortations to reply and best wishes.

Of their kind, they were perfectly good letters – easily B, often rising to B+, and always a straight A for presentation and hand-writing; I'd dutifully reply in the appropriate manner, singling out the good bits for elegantly muted praise and tactfully drawing his attention to omissions or infelicities of style ('I was fascinated by your account of the black sticky substance the olive-growers of Thessaly use to protect their trees against rats, but I think I may have missed the part where you say whether it actually works or not. Does it?'); throughout our correspondence, which lasted until Philip died, I can't say I learned anything about Alexander that I didn't know already, or ever read a word that couldn't just as fittingly have been written to somebody else.

We had one good harvest, followed by a bad one, followed by one that was just about good enough. The problem, we found, was the seed-corn; Greek seed wasn't used to the rich and productive soil, and something went wrong with it in the second year. For the third year we bought about half our seed from Odessus; by a strange coincidence, about half the crop came up.

In the third year we cut down all our olive trees and burned them. It was obvious they weren't going to come to anything, and we needed the space. It was at this point that someone pointed out that the Greeks bought their Black Sea grain with olives, because olives didn't grow here.

That apart, there wasn't much for me to record in the official history. We carried on building and borrowing, we gradually ploughed up more land without any protests from the Scythians, who stayed out of our way so completely that we wouldn't have known they were there. The days were full, and at night we were too tired to do anything except go to bed.

Like everybody else, I'd been allotted thirty acres, with the right to stake a claim on any unclaimed land I liked provided I ploughed and sowed it within a year. Like nearly everybody else, I had my work cut out coping with thirty acres. For one thing, it wasn't like thirty acres in Attica, which would work out on average as seventeen acres of usable soil and thirteen acres of bare rock. I only wish my father could have seen it; so much flat, fertile, deep-soiled ground, enough to provide a good living for a whole damn dynasty.

But I was out of practice; it had been years since I hung off the handles of a plough from dawn to dusk or spent a week bashing clods with a mattock or digging trenches. Embarrassingly, there were some things I'd just plain forgotten how to do; rather than ask, though (an *oecist* has his pride, after all), I guessed, and usually got it wrong. I sowed my beans too thick and my borage too sparse. I cut timber when Sirius was rising – it should be overhead – and got plagued with woodworm. I built myself a cart, but made the felloe too narrow (two spans instead of three). I began ploughing when I saw the first cranes in the sky, which would have been right in Attica but not here; I ploughed at the winter solstice, after the Pleiades had set, but luckily it rained just enough to fill in the hoofprints of my oxen shortly afterwards, and so I got away with it. I pruned my vines when Arcturus first appeared at dusk, which was fine, but I cut them back too fiercely and did them no good at all. In fact, there wasn't an awful lot that I did get right, and I suppose that if I'd been back home I'd have come to grief. But a poor harvest in Olbia was better than a good year in Attica, when all was said and done, and at least I made a point of learning from my mistakes.

What with buggering up the ploughing and making a hash of the pruning, I didn't see much of my wife and son, which in retrospect was a good thing. The less she saw of me, the less I could get on her nerves, while the normality of everyday life did a lot to smooth over her sense of having been badly used. After all, spinning and carding and grinding flour and keeping house are pretty much the same wherever you do them, and in most ways she was no worse off than she'd been before she met me. When our paths did cross we treated each other more like good neighbours than anything else; a few friendly words of greeting and encouragement in the morning, polite enquiries about each other's day in the evening, and so forth. When I wanted my tunic darned or she wanted me to rehang a sticking door, we each helped out cheerfully, the way you or I would do if the man next door came and asked for the loan of a pruning-hook or a hand with driving in a row of posts. Mind you, that was pretty much the prevailing attitude throughout the colony; we were all neighbours and we did our best to get on with each other on the grounds that sooner or later we'd need a favour.

The fourth harvest was pretty good; good enough that we'd be able to put away a year's supply of grain, which is the minimum an Athenian farmer wants to have squirrelled away before he can start sleeping at night, and still have a surplus we could sell for cash. I'd finished my cart by then, new full-width felloe and all, and I started picking up when Orion first put in an appearance, exactly as I was supposed to. In fact, there wasn't much left that could go wrong; except that, while I was loading the cart, I lifted a heavy stook awkwardly and felt my back give way. There was nothing for it but to slide agonisingly to the ground and wait for someone to walk by.

Now in Attica, where we all work little tunic-sized scraps of land, it's very rare to be out of sight of at least one other person. Here, in the abundant vastness of Olbia, you could go for hours at a time without having anybody intrude on your privacy; particularly at a busy time like that, when everybody was bustling back and forth from their fields to the barns, with too much to do and not enough time to do it in. I tried crawling, but I didn't get further than about twenty yards before I gave it up, on the grounds that I was in enough trouble already.

Needless to say, in my misery I couldn't help thinking of my father (you'll recall that he died under not dissimilar circumstances); and from there I started to worry, the way you do. If I died, what would happen to my son? Who'd work the place till he was old enough to inherit? In Attica my wife would have bought a slave, but thanks to our damned principles we'd resolved that we wouldn't bring any slaves to Olbia, it was going to be a true republic of free men, purged of decadence by the ennobling effects of self-reliant labour; and besides, there wasn't enough room on the boats for both slaves and oxen, and if things get really tough you can eat an ox. So if there was nobody to work the land, presumably Theano'd have to give it up and make a living by prostitution or doing laundry, in which case my son's only way of claiming his inheritance would be to wait until he came of age and then file a lawsuit; maybe Tyrsenius would take him on as an apprentice (an image of my father, looking serious and saying, 'Teach a boy a trade and he'll never starve' filled my mind like a wild bees' nest in the crack between your lintel and the wall); but when I thought about that for a while it didn't cheer me up too much. Sure, I'd trust Tyrsenius with my life, but that's not quite the same as trusting him with my money, let alone my son's birthright; in addition to which, the man was an idiot, and likewise I really didn't like the idea of my son fooling about on ships, which can sink, particularly if they're owned by idiots who probably haven't got the sense to tar them in the off season . . .

'Why are you lying on the ground?' someone asked.

It was Theano. She was the last person I'd expected to see (all right, hear; I was lying on my face, and all I could see were her toes); she never came out to the fields, because women don't, in the same way that dogs rarely if ever fight in the front rank of the phalanx.

'Hurt my back,' I said.

'What?'

'Hurt my back,' I repeated.

'Oh. How'd you manage that?'

'Lifting,' I said. 'Look, can you help me up?'

'All right,' she said. 'What do I do?'

At first, she did more harm than good; but eventually I was able to explain (between the screams) the correct technique for helping a man with a bad back, and somehow we got me up and lying in the back of the cart, on top of all that nice soft straw.

'Now what?' she said.

'Drive the cart home,' I told her.

'All right. How do you do that?'

Nothing's ever wasted, they say; my experience teaching the young nobility of Macedon how to scan an iambic pentameter had taught me the rudiments of communicating information, enough to explain to Theano the approved method of driving a cart.

'Grab that stick thing,' I said. 'Now get on the cart and give the ox a smack round the bum.'

'Done that,' she replied, as the cart suddenly lurched forward.

'Only,' I added, 'not quite so hard. Now, you see those leather straps?'

She sighed. 'I do know what reins are,' she said. 'There's no need to be—'

'Grab them,' I said. 'Pull the left one to make him go left, and the right one—'

'Yes, I know all that. What about stop?'

We got home, somehow; and as luck would have it, the Founder

Archestratus (who hadn't been near me for eighteen months) had chosen that evening to come round and bitch about the colour the walls of the temple were being painted. With hindsight, a three-legged dog would have been more use, but there's never a three-legged dog around when you want one; so he helped Theano get me indoors, then delivered his harangue and went away.

'This isn't good,' Theano said, looking at me critically as I sprawled in the chair. I had the feeling that I was making the room look untidy, but I couldn't help that.

'No, it isn't,' I replied. 'By the way, where's the boy?'

'Next door,' she replied. 'You don't think I just put him away in the clothes-press when I go out, do you?'

'Sorry,' I replied. 'No, it's a disaster,' I went on. 'Next year's food's lying out there feeding the rooks, and there's bugger-all I'll be able to do about it before it all goes mouldy and rots.'

'Oh,' she said. 'What do you expect me to do about it?'

I shrugged. 'Don't know,' I replied. 'Picking it up and carting it to the barn'd be a good place to start, though.'

She frowned. 'What, on my own? You must be joking. I'll go round your friends a bit later on, I'm sure they'll lend a hand once they know—'

I shook my head, though that wasn't a good idea. 'Think,' I said. 'They've all got their own stuff to get in, it's one of the busiest times of the year. You may get a few promises of help, but I don't suppose any of 'em will actually turn up. Which is understandable,' I added.

She didn't seem to believe me, and went out. An hour or so later she came back, looking angry.

'Fine friends they turned out to be,' she said.

I sighed. 'You weren't rude to them, were you?'

'I told them what I thought of people who'd let a man's harvest rot because they're too selfish and bone idle—'

'You mean, yes, you were?'

She shrugged. 'Friends like that you can do without,' she said. 'So now what?'

I was lying on something (turned out to be a little wooden horse I'd made for the boy). When I shifted to get comfortable, I felt as if I were a fish, being gutted while it was still alive.

'Lie still, for gods' sakes,' Theano snapped. 'It'll never get better if you keep wriggling about like a maggot on a fishing-line.'

I gave up and lay still, the horse's nose sticking into my backside. 'If they won't help and I can't move, who does that leave?' I asked sweetly.

'You want me to do it,' she said.

'Yes.'

'All right,' she said.

And she did.

To be fair, Tyrsenius rolled up on the first day and watched her for an hour, making helpful comments; and a few others showed up too and helped for as long as they could in the intervals between getting in their own cut grain. Mostly, interestingly enough, they were Illyrians, men whose names I didn't know and couldn't have pronounced if I did. Later on I found out that they, like Queen Olympias, were devout snake-worshippers, and once the word got out that I had this sacred snake in a jar . . . Never mind; they helped, and eventually the job got done, which was just as well; I was laid up unable to move for ten days, and it was another three days after that before I could do any useful work and make a start on the winnowing.

'Thanks,' I said.

'That's all right,' she replied.

We'd been married for four years at this point, and those were the nicest things either of us had ever said to the other. After that, however, things started to get a little easier between us. On her side, I think it was mostly time and acceptance – the further away she got from the things she perceived as grievances, the less they seemed to matter. For my part, I couldn't help but respect the way she'd handled the crisis, which could have been far more serious than it turned out to be if she hadn't put herself out to the degree she did. We started talking about things more; she took much more of an interest in the work of the farm, and I found it was worth listening to what she had to say. Often she'd surprise me by knowing the answer to a problem that had me foxed, or remind me of some elementary thing I'd completely forgotten, such as cross-ploughing (plough twice; once up and down, the second time side to side).

When the plough we'd brought with us finally shook to pieces at the end of the season and proved to be beyond repair, she helped me build a new one. First we searched the woods till we found an elm sapling of the right height and thickness, which we bent down with ropes, trussed up to a former to take the shape of the stock, and left there for a month. When it was ready, we fitted the eight-foot ash pole to the stem of the stock, with mould boards and double-backed share-beam. Then we cut a linden sapling for the yoke, and she whittled down a billet of beech for the handle and put it up in the rafters to smoke until it was time to put the bits together. Finally we salvaged the iron ploughshare from the broken plough, heated it up enough to make the metal expand, then cooled it to shrink the iron onto the wooden beam. It was a lovely job when it was finished, though I say so myself.

There have been parts of my life when it's felt like I've been asleep.

Sleep's a curious thing, if you stop to think about it. You lie down and close your eyes, your brain still reverberating with the various issues and projects of the day – must remember to fix that broken floorboard tomorrow before it does someone an injury, wonder if the sinew from the old plough-ox is cured yet, I'd have time to card it tomorrow, why are the Scythians so damned quiet, and just what is Tyrsenius up to with those seventy jars of quicklime? – and before you know it, the whole tedious and unproductive night's over and there's suddenly enough light to carry on where you left off the day before. Sleep cuts out the boring bits of life, so we don't go mad sitting still in the dark.

With my life, though, it's generally been the other way around. I've tended to sleep through the good, quiet bits and only woken up when something's going wrong, or there's a fresh tranche of shit to be waded through. For example; I was ten years in Olbia. When I arrived I was twenty-eight years old, supposedly at the height of my strength and abilities, old enough to have got past the awkward, ignorant part of youth, but not so experienced and work-hardened that I couldn't do a full day with the mattock and still be fresh the next morning.

When I next opened my eyes I was thirty-six; almost completely bald on the top of my head, grey flashes in my beard on either side of my chin, rather less flexible in the back and legs, the joints of my left hand just starting to feel cramped. I had a ten-year-old son, old enough to be useful at last, who'd recently started working with me during the day. I was getting to know him, though that was some-thing of a disappointment; on the rare occasions when I'd thought about what my son would be like, I'd always assumed that he'd be something like I was, reasonably bright with an enquiring mind and a taste for words. While I'd been asleep, however, he'd grown up into my brother Euthyphron, a perfect little farmer, whose interest was wholly confined to thirty specific acres out of the whole world.

As we worked together I tried to teach him things – poetry, history, philosophy, science, even (gods forgive me) Homer. He was a polite lad and he humoured me by pretending to listen, but I could see he wasn't interested in the slightest degree by anything that wasn't obviously useful or relevant. When I told him all I could remember of what I'd read about foreign lands in Xenophon or Herodotus, he looked away, his mind on what he was doing or just at rest, that trance-like state that only farmers at work can achieve. Only if I happened to mention, say, the fabulous oxen of the Egyptians or the incredible fertility of the mud of the Nile delta would he look up and actually take note of what I was telling him; and even then I could see him thinking: So what? That'd be worth knowing if we were in Egypt, but we aren't, so who cares?

I tried telling him the history of our family, their experiences in the wars; but of course, he'd never seen Athens or lived in Attica. I told him stories of the gods and heroes, but he quickly reached the conclusion that the gods and heroes were a load of rich bastards who never did a day's real work in their lives, and so were beneath contempt. I explained to him Socrates' theory of the origin of rain, how the sun is supposed to suck water up off the sea and drop it on the mountains, whence it flows back down the rivers and returns to its source; that caught his attention for a little while, but he soon realised it wasn't important enough to bother with. After all, who cared why rain fell so long as it kept falling? Now, if I knew how to make it rain or how to stop it raining, that'd be great, but I didn't; forget it. As for Homer – well, there were a few bits he managed to learn, mostly the parts where he describes men working in the fields. They stuck in my son's mind because (in his expert opinion) they were pretty silly ways to go about things, and we knew a whole lot better, so why did we bother to learn by heart stuff that was just plain wrong? Didn't make sense. The only poems he learned were the *Works and Days*, which he thoroughly approved of – dates for ploughing and planting and pruning and pricking out, help-fully condensed into easily remembered hexameters, though the old-fashioned diction bothered him a lot. He'd go into a study and then re-emerge to say that he'd thought of a way to change such and such a line so that it wasn't old-fashioned any more but still scanned, maybe even included some additional snippet of information that the old fool had left out; when I tried to explain that, actually, he was missing the point, he'd cast his mind adrift once again and let me babble to myself without further interruption.

'Maybe I should find him a trade,' I suggested to Theano one evening. 'Learning a trade broadens the mind, as well as giving you something to fall back on.'

She made a little dry laughing noise. 'Like you learned a trade, you mean?'

I frowned. 'All right,' I said, 'so that didn't work out the way it was planned. But in the event it achieved the desired result. If I hadn't learned my trade with Diogenes, I'd be earning my living voting in Assembly and eating nothing but dried fish and barley-husks. It was my trade that got me here, doesn't matter *how* it got me here.'

She thought about that for a moment as she threaded a needle. 'You remember that game you tried to teach me, the one with the bone counters and the chequered board?'

'Draughts,' I said.

'That's the one.' She narrowed her eyes and licked the end of the thread. 'All I remember is that instead of going up and down the board, the little counters move sort of sideways, across the corners of their squares—'

'Diagonally,' I said.

'Whatever. Well, it seems to me you've lived your life like those counters move – making progress, but never straight ahead the way you planned to go, always – what was that word again?'

'Diagonally.'

'Which means,' she went on, 'that you've come a hell of a long way, but not the way you'd ever intended to come. Am I right?'

I thought for a moment and nodded. 'You could say that,' I replied. 'Though maybe you're bending the facts a bit to make them fit the comparison. So what do you think?' I went on. 'Should we find someone to apprentice him to?'

'I'm not sure,' she said. 'It'd be a big step. And a lot depends on who you had in mind.'

I took a deep breath. 'It crossed my mind,' I said, 'that we could send him back to Athens, where he could learn pretty well anything. He could go with Tyrsenius' friend, you know, the dried-fish man—'

She looked at me as if I'd just suggested that our son would go down well as a pot-roast, with leeks and maybe just a touch of marjoram.

'No,' she said.

'But think of the advantages he could have in Athens that he'd never have here,' I said. 'He could live on the farm with Euthyphron or Eugenes, and go to the City to learn law or banking or medicine – we haven't got a half-competent doctor here, he'd make a good living—'

'He'll make a good living off thirty acres,' she replied severely. 'What else could he possibly ever need?'

I rubbed the back of my neck, where the muscles were always stiff. 'There's so much he's missing here,' I said. 'Dammit, he'll grow up just like the other kids here, not even properly Greek. I mean, apart from the language we speak and a taste for olive curd, what difference is there between us and the Scythians in the back country? That's an awful lot to lose, you know, everything that being Greek stands for—'

'Oh, yes?' she said. 'Such as what?'

'Such as . . .'

Obviously I knew the answer; all the things I'd tried to teach him that he didn't want to know. But for some reason, I realised, Theano didn't value them either. I was rather shocked.

'You want him to be like you,' she went on, in that calm voice that meant she was getting ready to be seriously angry. 'You want him to learn all that clever, white-is-black, I'm-right-and-you're-wrong trouble-making stuff. What the hell is wrong with living quietly and making an honest living? Why does he have to be Greek, and not just a human being?'

For a moment I couldn't really understand what she was trying to say. 'Everything we know,' I replied. 'All the science and poetry and philosophy—'

'But it's all bullshit,' Theano interrupted. 'Euxenus, you made a living by pretending you had a magic snake that told you the future. You *know* it's all bullshit, else you could never have done that. What the hell's so important about bullshit that you want our son to go to Athens to learn it?'

I shook my head, trying to keep my temper. 'I thought you understood,' I said. 'After ten years of living with me, I thought you'd be able to understand by now.'

A moment later, I saw that I'd said something really bad. For one thing, she didn't even answer, just looked at me . . .

'Come on,' I said, 'that's what all this has been about. A fresh start, a whole new city, a chance to build the perfect city with Greek ideas and all the advantages we've got, but away from the stony soil and the dry, barren mountains—'

She was breathing out through her nose by this point, a sure sign of impending volcanic activity. 'Oh, really,' she said. 'That's what it's all about, then. It's – what do you call it? – scientific research.'

'In a way.'

'Like cutting open dead bodies to see where the bones go. And what's going to happen when your scientific research is over, Euxenus, and you report back to whoever the hell it is you report back to, some bunch of idle old men sitting under a tree in Athens? What're you going to do *next*, for your next experi- dammit, what *is* that word?'

'Experiment,' I told her.

'Thank you, yes, experiment. Are you going to see if you can make a pair of wings to fly with, or pull the moon down into a bucket? Or are you going to find another stupid peasant girl to cut up, to study how she works?'

I confess, I didn't see the logical connection there, and I still don't. 'Come on,' I said soothingly, 'you're laying it on a bit thick, aren't you? What makes you think I've even considered going back to Athens? Ever? There's nothing for me there.'

She glared at me as if she was trying to set light to my beard by sheer eye-power. 'Then why in the gods' names do you keep on and on about the horrible place?' she said. 'To me, to Eupolis, to everybody who can be bothered to listen. In Athens we did it like this, of course if we were in Athens all we'd have to do is ask so-and-so—'

I shook my head. 'Athens is where I grew up,' I said. 'That's where I learned to do things. So when I say that's how we did such-and-such, I'm saying this is the way I know how to do it. That's all.'

'Like hell,' she snapped. 'You know what, Euxenus? You aren't really here at all. All that's here is like – like a diplomatic embassy you've sent out to gather information and carry out an experi-mence—'

'Experiment.'

'Oh, shut up. The real Euxenus is still back in your damned Academy with all those old men, and you're an . . .' She closed her eyes, dragging the right words out of her memory with a violent effort. 'An accredited observer,' she said triumphantly, 'like the students your friend Aristotle used to send to other cities to write reports on their laws and their government stuff. And you know what the joke is, Euxenus? You play the philosopher and the scien-tist like this, but it's all lies anyhow. You were never a philosopher, you were a fraud. You never hung out with all those clever old men,' she went on. 'You lurked round the market square selling your snake in a bottle. With no snake,' she added vindictively. 'Well, the hell with you. You can do what you like, but Eupolis isn't going to Athens and he isn't learning any trade.' And with that she stomped off into the back room and slammed the door.

I've heard great orators. I knew Demosthenes personally. But none of them could get one tenth of the condensed nuances of meaning into two hours of speech-making that Theano could cram into the slamming of a door. It's a wonder the hinges lasted as long as they did.

CHAPTER THIRTEEN

There are days when the world changes. Between sunrise and sunset, something happens, and nothing is ever the same again. I always had a suspicion that if such a day happened during my lifetime, it'd be on the day after I'd been out all night at a really obnoxious party, which'd have left me so hung over and drained that I stayed in bed all day and so slept through the great event that changed the world, and would have to rely on other people's accounts of what happened for ever after.

Well, for once I beat my own low expectation of myself. On the seventh day of the month Metageitnion* during my tenth year in Olbia, in the slack period following the harvest and the mad panic of getting the year's corn threshed and stored, I was down at our newly finished jetty helping to stow thirty-seven jars of my surplus grain on board a ship bound for Athens. It was the start of the trading season; the sea was relatively calm and predictable, nothing much to do on the farm for five or six weeks, prompting the industrious man to better himself by seeking opportunities away from home, either in person or through the proxy of his merchandise. Thirty-seven jars was substantially more disposable surplus than I'd had before, so I was feeling bright and cheerful. I almost wished I was going with them, to see Athens again, maybe even look up my brothers, find out what they'd been up to, inspect the crop of nephews and nieces, walk the familiar fields and pontificate on how much better everything was in Olbia . . .

*August–September

But going home would involve being on a ship, and I've never felt comfortable on the wretched things (and me an Athenian; for shame!), so I suppressed the impulse and went home.

It was early morning, about the time when people were leaving the city to walk to the fields. Always a cheerful time of day; you'll see parties of neighbours going in the same direction, chattering away with early morning enthusiasm about the prospects (which are always good on the walk out to the fields, and dismal on the way back) until they're joined by some other neighbours, who join in the conversation until they run into a group from another part of the city heading in the same direction. At this point the scope of the discussion widens to include anything anybody happens to have on his mind, from the comedies at last year's Lenaea to the price of nails to the political situation in Thrace – doesn't matter that none of them know the first thing about what they're discussing; Athenians have never allowed mere facts to stand in the way of a good opinion.

On the seventh day of Metageitnion in the tenth year since the founding of the city of whatever it was we'd resolved to call it that week, I fell in with a mixed bunch of neighbours on my way to work. It was a fairly typical mixture for our city. There were two Macedonians, Ptolemocrates and Amyntas, whose land backed on to mine; a Corinthian called Pericleidas, a nodding acquaintance from over the other side of the valley; a Milesian by the name of Thrasyllus, who played the flute quite well; and five Illyrians, whose names I still didn't know after ten years. One of them could speak excellent Greek and he told me his name was Illus; like his friends, he went to work with his quiver on his belt and his bow in its case over his left shoulder. When I commented on this, he explained that it was mostly force of habit, understandable in a forty-year ex-mercenary who'd first gone to the wars at the age of fourteen. Two of the Illyrians and Amyntas and Pericleidas had their sons with them, so add another five to the group, ages ranging from six to nine. We were all carrying our mattocks, and Ptolemocrates and an Illyrian called Bassus or something such had spades as well. It was early, an hour after dawn, and the day promised to be hot and sunny. Most of us were wearing our broad-brimmed hats, apart from Amyntas and his two boys, who were wearing felt caps copied from the local design.

We'd almost reached the point where Thrasyllus and Bassus the Illyrian were going to turn off when we noticed that one of the boys had stopped in his tracks and was staring at the horizon, as if watching something absolutely fascinating. It so happened that his father, an Illyrian, had been boasting about the boy's remarkable eyesight earlier on, and Ptolemocrates, who'd been sceptical about the man's claims in this regard, decided to conduct an experiment and asked him to describe what he could see.

'Horsemen,' the boy replied.

Ptolemocrates frowned. 'Where?' he said. 'I can't see anything.'

'Over there.' The boy nodded. 'Look, there was the sun flashing on something.'

'He's right,' I put in. 'I saw something flash just now.'

Ptolemocrates was impressed. 'Well I'm damned,' he said, 'I do believe he's right. I think I can just make something out myself; but I wouldn't have known they were horsemen.'

We'd stopped by now to look for ourselves. 'I can see a couple of dots,' said Illus. 'And I guess they're going too fast to be on foot, and if they're carrying something metal, they can't be cattle or deer. So the boy must be right. But he figured it out, he can't actually see more than a couple of tiny specks.'

'Yes I can,' the boy replied, 'they're all wearing yellow, so I guess they're Scythians.'

(The local people did wear rather a lot of yellow, for reasons I never could grasp. Something to do with some plant or flower which grew all over the shop up here and made an excellent dye for wool.)

'Are you sure?' I said.

'Sure I'm sure,' the boy answered.

'All right,' I said. 'How many of them do you think there are?'

The boy nodded his head and muttered under his breath as he counted. 'Fourteen,' he said.

That threw me. 'Are you sure?' I repeated, knowing as I said it that I was doing a fairly good impersonation of a cross between an idiot and a tree. The boy didn't waste any more words on me, just nodded.

'Out hunting, I suppose,' someone remarked.

Illus shook his head. 'Not this time of year,' he replied. 'Nothing to hunt. Could be rounding up strays, but why so many?'

Having disposed of alternatives two and three from the mental checklist we'd all prepared, we were left with alternative one, something that none of us liked the thought of very much.

'War party,' Amnytas said at last. 'Raiding cattle from their friends up the valley, maybe?'

'Don't think so,' said the boy. 'They're heading in this direction, actually.'

'You sure?'

'*Course* I'm sure,' the boy complained. 'Why does everyone keep asking me that?'

'Be quiet,' ordered the boy's father. 'See if you can tell more about where they're headed.'

The boy scrambled up into a low ash tree to get a better look. 'Right this way, it looks like,' he called down.

'You sure? I mean, they're not headed towards the city, are they?'

'No,' the boy replied. 'Don't think so.'

Oh, I thought. I'd wondered if it might be an embassy from the village with its escort, but that scuppered that particular theory. We were using up the nice comforting speculations like a starving family eating the seed-corn. 'I don't suppose you can see if they're armed,' I asked.

'Not from this distance,' the boy answered. 'Most of them have got stuff that flashes in the sun occasionally, but they'd have to be a whole lot closer before I could say what it is.'

We stood in silence for a while, waiting for the boy to come up with some more details. It was pretty obvious what we were all thinking.

'Maybe we shouldn't be standing out in the open like this,' said Pericleidas the Corinthian nervously. 'Well,' he added, 'if it *is* a war party, and it's headed this way—'

He was only saying what we were all thinking; problem was, we were in open, flat country, where we could see and be seen for a long way. Nowhere much to hide.

'Look,' the boy called out, 'there's some people just coming up out of the dip.'

'Scythians?' I asked. 'Or can't you see?'

'They're on foot,' the boy said. 'I guess they're our people.'

I had a bad feeling, and I wasn't the only one. 'Could we signal them, do you think?' someone asked.

'No point,' Illus replied. 'If we can see the Scythians, so can they. More to the point, maybe the Scythians haven't seen us yet. If that's the case I'd like to keep it that way.'

I thought for a moment. 'Our best bet'd be to keep still,' I said. 'Put down your tools and anything that might catch the sun, then stand under the tree.'

Everyone did just that. 'They've seen the men on foot,' the boy announced. 'Definitely seen them, they're changing course a bit and riding towards them.'

'What are our men doing?' asked Thrasyllus. 'Can you tell?'

'Just standing there, I think,' the boy answered.

'It's not as if there's anywhere they can go,' someone said unnecessarily; the same was true of us. I was beginning to wish I was an Illyrian, who always carried his bow with him even when he went for a shit in the woods. I'd got my mattock, of course; wouldn't want to be hit with one of those. But the Scythians fought with arrows mostly; arrows from a distance, then close with the lance and scimitar to deal with anyone left standing. I began to feel sick.

'Any ideas?' Amyntas asked nervously.

Nobody replied.

'They're really close to our people now,' the boy said a bit later. 'They're breaking into a gallop, charging at them. I can't see – I think they're going to ride round them in a circle.'

'What, they're going to leave them alone?' said Thrasyllus.

'No,' the boy replied.

By now, we could see fairly well for ourselves, though the boy continued to call out a commentary, like some people do when they're watching the Games. At that moment, oddly enough, I thought of Alexander; *Who'd you rather be*, I asked him, *the all-comers champion at the Olympic Games, or the little fat guy with a scroll who calls out the names of the winners?*

It went like this. The Scythians rode round our people – there were five or so of them – and shot arrows, killing a couple. Then they rode in. One man just stood there and was chopped down. The other two ran a little way. The Scythians left them where they fell and then carried on heading for us.

'Did you see that?' Thrasyllus demanded. 'They just—'

'All right.' I pulled myself together, though it wasn't easy. Never seen violent death before, you see. 'That's enough. Illus, you're a soldier; is there anything we can do? Or do we just stand here and wait?'

Illus shook his head. 'Nowhere to hide and no cover worth spit. I don't see how we're going to get out of it this time.'

Marvellous, I thought; but what I said was, 'We'll see about that. Illus, I want you and your friends with the bows to shoot down as many as you can. You never know, if we sting them a bit they may go away.'

Illus looked at me. For a moment there he'd thought I was actually going to come up with something clever, but I'd disappointed him. 'If we shoot a couple it'll probably only make things worse,' he said. 'We could try surrendering. If we tell them who you are, maybe they'll spare us to keep as hostages.'

I shook my head. 'I don't think so,' I said. 'Just do as I say.'

I remember watching them get closer, changing from small shapes of horsemen into people, with discernible faces. They were young – sixteen to nineteen; I remembered reading somewhere that young Scythian warriors aren't admitted to full manhood until they've killed someone, and I'd always assumed that was just sensationalist rubbish, like the stories about the crocodiles of Egypt or the island in the far north where at times the sun shines at midnight. But the faces of those men, or boys, or whatever they were, seemed to me to be filled with fear, every bit as much as ours; they were facing something they knew they had to do but which terrified them. They were new to this sort of thing, the same as I was, and they were well aware that they were about to play a game with us which had no rules, no guarantee of safety. They were afraid of getting killed, the same as we were.

At seventy-five yards they broke into a gallop and shifted formation, flowing round us like a river bursting its banks. One of the Illyrians drew his bow and loosed an arrow; it missed. The Scythians were drawing their bows now; a couple of shots went wide, then Pericleidas the Corinthian staggered and sank down to his knees. He'd been hit, and there was an arrow sticking out of his stomach about a thumb's length above the navel, a little to the right of centre. He wasn't dead, but the pain and shock were so great he couldn't speak or even make a noise, only mouth the words, as if he didn't want the enemy to hear. I was staring at him, trying to think what to do, when Ptolemocrates suddenly swore loudly and keeled over, shot through the heart. A moment later I heard the sound of something heavy crashing through tree-branches and a heavy bump as it hit the ground; they'd shot the boy down out of the tree. One of the other boys, who was standing quite close to me, started to scream; he had an arrow through the middle of his left hand. On my other side, an Illyrian was bending his bow, taking aim, when an arrow hit his jaw about halfway along. The bow flew from his hands and the arrow cartwheeled sideways; I stared at the arrow sticking straight through his face, the broad barbed head standing a hand's breadth clear of his cheek on the other side. He was still on his feet, looking groggy with shock; he tried to speak, and as he did so the arrow bobbed up and down.

And that, I'm thoroughly ashamed to say, was enough for me. I'd never seen actual fighting before, though of course I'd speculated endlessly about what it must be like. Let's say it wasn't at all like I'd expected, and leave it at that.

The wounded Illyrian's bow had landed a foot or so from where I was standing. I grabbed it, then pulled a handful of arrows from his quiver. He saw what I was doing and tried to say something, making the feathers on the arrowshaft sticking out of his face waggle about in a ludicrously comic fashion. What he was actually trying to say, the gods only know.

An arrow flew past dangerously close, a foot from my right shoulder, if that. I couldn't help it; I ran. At least two of them called out my name, but I didn't want to hear what they were saying. I ran.

I went about eighty yards without looking round. Then I heard hooves drumming, not a terribly long way behind. I had no idea what to do.

There was one Scythian horseman, a kid of seventeen, bearing down on me. He'd stowed away his bow and was holding his lance. I only saw him close for a very short time, six or so heartbeats, at which point I realised that I wasn't running. I was down on one knee, bending the bow I'd taken from the Illyrian, with one of his arrows on the string. I was never any good at shooting arrows, as a boy or later on in life; it's always been one of those things that other people make seem easy, but which goes by me entirely. At the actual moment when I relaxed my fingers and let the string pull off my hand, I may even have had my eyes shut (I've been told that's what I do when I loose the arrow, though I've never been aware of it). If I did, I opened them in time to see where my arrow had gone. By fluke, luck or providence, it had punched through the boy's thigh, pinning him to his saddle. Needless to say, the horse was going mad, prancing and thrashing about, trying to shake loose whatever it was that was causing all that unexpected pain. Ordinarily the boy would have been thrown clear, but the arrow pinned him tight in his seat. His eyes were huge and round, and his mouth was nearly a perfect circle.

I left him to get on with it, dropped the bow and carried on running. I was the only one who tried to escape, just as I was the only one who got away. You hear stories about men who're the only ones to survive out of this or that mighty army; they're supposed to be crippled with guilt and remorse for ever after, and I can understand that, in a way. But as I ran, I was praying to all the gods, *Let them kill the others and forget about me, concentrate on the others, maybe they'll exterminate each other so there aren't any left to chase me.* I'm not proud of it. The number of things I've done in my life that I'm proud of you could count on the fingers of one badly mutilated hand.

I was never a great athlete, but I ran a good race that day, and I only stopped when I tripped over something and found I couldn't get up. I'd twisted my ankle and I couldn't move. Now that was a horrible feeling, that helplessness, that feeling of clumsy, lethal stupidity. I managed to drag myself round so I could look back towards where I'd come from; I couldn't see any horsemen coming. There was a dip and a slope in the way, so I couldn't see the fighting. For a moment, in fact, I wondered whether any of it had actually happened, until I caught sight of a thin red weal across the inside of my left forearm, where the bowstring had hit me. Apparently, so competent archers assure me, that's a sign of a sloppy loose, holding the bow all wrong with your left hand.

I tried crawling, but it hurt and I got only a few yards before I gave it up as a bad job; I was too far from home for that. The ridiculous thing was that I *was* home, I was in our fields, a piece of land owned by an Illyrian called Bardylis (he had the same name as one of their national heroes, who was killed fighting Philip at the age of ninety – imagine that, I thought as I lay there, ninety years old and he still couldn't escape from this shit, you'd have thought a time would come when you didn't have to do it any more, but apparently not) and any moment now, assuming the whole plain wasn't crawling with marauding Scythian war-parties, Bardylis might appear over the brow of the hill, looking for somewhere out of the wind to eat his lunch, and find me. He'd stare and ask me, in atrociously bad Greek, what the hell had happened to me; and what was I going to say to him?

In the event, it was a war-party of our own that found me. Apparently, someone else had seen the whole thing and scampered back to the city to raise the alarm. He went to my house, but of course I wasn't there; Theano sent him to find Marsamleptes, who wasn't there either, so he went home, got his horse (being a sensible sort; his name was Lytus, an Illyrian) and rode out to Marsamleptes' holding, which was only a short way out of town. Marsamleptes knew exactly what to do; he'd been quietly and hopefully planning, and so was able to mobilise an early response unit – I think that's the right jargon – in under an hour. They rode to where the fighting had been, but all they found were dead bodies. It was sheer chance that they stumbled across me, following what they'd mistakenly thought was the trail of the retreating Scythians (in fact, it was a goat-track). A couple of them took me home on a spare horse, while Marsamleptes continued the search. He came home late that after-noon looking thoroughly miserable; he'd found neither hide nor hair of the Scythians, just the bodies of the men we'd seen being killed before the horsemen turned on us, and a courting couple who'd sneaked off into a small copse on the edge of our territory and been spitted with lances and left to die. He found two dead Scythians at the place where my group had been killed, both shot with arrows; no trace of a young lad with an arrow in his thigh, or a dead or wounded horse.

It didn't occur to anybody that I'd been with that group; they assumed that I'd been on my own and that the Scythians had tried to ride me down, and I'd somehow got away from them. Many of the Illyrians regarded my miraculous escape as proof that the sacred snake was watching over me; I gather that there was this story about how as I was lying there with Scythian lancers all round me poised to strike, a monstrous snake sprang up out of the earth and coiled itself about me, protecting me from the spear-thrusts with its impenetrable scales and driving the attackers away with spumes of poison (or, in some versions of the story, fire) sneezed out of its nose. In any event, my standing with the Illyrians went up considerably, and Marsamleptes, a superstitious man, took to averting his eyes when he spoke to me and treated me with great respect, in spite of several requests to pack it in. Needless to say, I never contradicted any of it, not even the snake stuff, and this is the first time, Phryzeutzis my friend, that I've ever told anybody the truth about what happened there. After all, where the hell is the point of lying to you? For all you know, I might be making the whole thing up, just to make my story a little bit more interesting.

Now, you're thinking that this unprovoked attack by the Scythians was what I was talking about when I said that that day, the seventh of Metageitnion in the tenth year of the colony, was a day that changed the world. Not a bit of it. The truly significant and memorable event of that day took place in Greece, at a place called Chaeronea, which is between Thebes and Delphi. There, King Philip, ably assisted by Prince Alexander and the other young Macedonian nobles who'd been brought up with him, fought a battle against the Greeks who still resisted him and utterly defeated them, thereby effectively making him the ruler of the whole of Greece. A thousand Athenians died that day and a further two thousand were taken prisoner; among the dead were my brothers Eudorus and Euthyphron. My brother Eudemus lost an eye, but escaped; Eumenes and Eugenes were both captured, but were later released unharmed along with the rest of the Athenians.

According to the reliable accounts of the battle, it was Alexander who led the charge that broke the Theban Sacred Band, the best soldiers in all of Greece. As well as directing his troops with outstanding skill and flair, he forced his way into the thick of the fighting and turned the tide of the battle by the sheer ferocity of his onslaught; he was like an Achilles, they said, something out of Homer and the old stories, utterly regardless of his own safety, and he came back to his tent after the battle almost unrecognisable for blood, spattered on his face and hair, his own blood and that of the men he'd killed. They say that Philip didn't know what to think; his heart was bursting with pride at the outstanding prowess of his son, but at the same time he was furiously angry that on the day of his crowning achievement Alexander had eclipsed him and taken all the glory for himself. Personally, I have a clear mental picture of the scene, as Philip looks at his tall, handsome young son all covered in dried blood, like something not human; he looks at him for a while with his one good eye and says nothing. After the battle, they say, Philip got more drunk than he'd ever been before; he danced up and down the battlefield, kicking the bodies of the dead and singing (loudly and off-key; Philip couldn't sing):

> *Demosthenes,*
> *Son of Demosthenes,*
> *Of the parish of Paeanea, proposes these—*

– Which is how the heralds at Assembly made the formal announcement each time Demosthenes had got up to urge the Athenian people to resist Philip, in those immortal speeches of his. Demosthenes, they say, ran like a hare almost as soon as the battle started. He'd bought a new shield especially for the occasion; it had the words GOOD FORTUNE painted on it in huge gold-leaf lettering. He threw it away when he bolted, and Philip used it as a chamber-pot for weeks until the leather rotted away.

Interesting, I've often felt. I mentioned earlier that remark I made, about Homer and Achilles, *Who'd you rather be, the all-comers champion at the Olympic Games, or the little fat guy with a scroll who calls out the names of the winners?* Now, the Olympic Games, like the battle of Chaeronea, is a time when all the Greek states send their finest men to compete together for honour and glory and all the dearest values of free Greek citizens; and on the day when Alexander took part and came away the all-comers champion, I was at another battle, of which I'm the only surviving witness, the only one who can call out the names of those who took part. At the time, I also gave a certain amount of thought to the fact that I was the only son of Eutychides who wasn't at the battle, the only son of Eutychides who got home that night, albeit with my own little consolation prize of a twisted ankle. It bothered me, I have to say, and not just because the seventh of Metageitnion turned out to be a bad day all round for the Eutychides boys; to be the only one left (or left out), twice in one day – you can't help thinking about things like that, even if you're not a great and notorious philosopher.

I don't know. The best rationalisation I've heard so far is the story about the enormous snake, and I don't believe that for a moment.

*

What I dislike most of all about catastrophic tragedies is the amount of extra work they cause. They hauled me back to my house, propped me up in a chair with my twisted ankle on a footstool and started arguing with each other. A Founder by the name of Agesilaus (as soon as the news reached the city the Founders had suddenly materialised, like monsters in a bad dream, and scampered round to my house in a flock; they were all there, looking impatient and helping themselves to wine and figs, when I was carried in) immediately demanded that we abandon the colony and return to Macedon, before the Scythians swooped down and massacred us all; to hear him talk, you'd think the whole plain was carpeted in Scythians squashed together heel to toe, with scarcely any room to breathe, let alone draw a bow. About two-thirds of the remaining Founders all started jabbering at once; we were here to stay, we weren't going to be chased out of our homes by a bunch of renegade savages, immediate retribution employing the maximum degree of force, where was Marsemleptes when he was needed, something must be done. I'd have been quite happy to let them babble themselves hoarse, even though it was my wine they were lubricating their throats with; but my friend Tyrsenius, who'd also appeared out of nowhere or who might have been there before they arrived, saw fit to intervene at this juncture, pointing out that even as he spoke Marsamleptes was out hotly pursuing the marauders and would doubtless return at any moment with their heads woven into a string, like onions. At this, the other third of the Founders boiled over, like an unwatched pot on the fire – on whose authority, how dare he escalate the incident and risk bringing the whole Scythian nation down on our heads, he would be held personally responsible, although in accordance with the chain of command ultimate responsibility lay with the *oecist*—

'Hey,' I objected feebly. 'All of a sudden it's my fault. Did I miss something?'

A pointy-faced Founder called Basiliscus nodded enthusiastically. 'As *de facto* commander-in-chief—' he began; but he didn't get any further, because at that moment Theano, who'd been hovering in the background with a big basin of steaming water and a bandage, sprang at him, emptied the bowl over his head and bundled him out of the door. He was too stunned to resist.

'And the rest of you,' she said, scowling horribly. 'Get out. And you, Tyrsenius. Go on.'

If it'd been a band of marauding Scythians, they might just have hung about and tried to argue the toss. Since it was Theano in full Cerberus mode, they did the only sensible thing and left without a word.

'Thank you,' I said. 'I think.'

She frowned. 'What the hell do you think you've been playing at?' she replied. 'Sit still.' She swept out into the inner room and came back with the basin refilled. 'Let's get this ankle strapped up first.'

'I have an idea,' I said, as she wrapped the bandage round, 'that throwing the city council out into the street is a severe breach of protocol.'

'Good. And besides, if anybody's going to get into trouble for it, it'll be you. The chain of command, and all that stuff.'

'That's all right, then,' I said.

'Glad you think so. Now, is that too tight?'

'What, the bandage? No, not really.'

'Then it's not tight enough. Hold still while I just—'

'Hey!'

She pulled the bandage tighter still and tied it off. 'If you had any sense you'd rest it,' she said, 'but I never yet saw a man who had that much sense. Just try and go easy on it, or it'll be months before it's right again.'

They were back before very long, but this time they asked nicely before they came trooping in. This time, they had Marsamleptes and a couple more Illyrians with them, plus Tyrsenius (honorary interpreter), one or two farmers and Ptolemocrates' widow. There weren't enough seats, needless to say, so Tyrsenius sent my son and a couple of other lads to borrow chairs, trestles and saw-horses; meanwhile, the later arrivals had to make do with standing or crouching on the floor.

Marsamleptes, who looked very tired, made his report in incomprehensible Illyrian, and one of the men with him translated it into passable Greek as they went along. There were a few raised eyebrows, sharp intakes of breath and other histrionics as he reported that they'd found no trace of the raiders beyond the two dead Scythians, but I ignored them pointedly.

'All right,' I said, summing up. 'Looks like it might well have been a cattle raid or a spur-of-the-moment lark by some of the young braves. Quite likely it wasn't officially sanctioned in any way. Any suggestions as to where we take it from here? Sensible suggestions,' I added.

'Sure,' replied one of the Founders, whose name escapes me for the moment. 'We should retaliate. They'll think better of bothering us again if we burn a few houses and run off their horses.'

A farmer by the name of Chersonesus replied to that. 'Maybe that's exactly what they said when they were planning the attack,' he said. 'And if we attack them, what's the odds they'll feel obliged to reply in kind? Next thing we know we'll have a war.'

'And there's more of them than there are of us,' someone else pointed out.

'All the more reason for giving them a really nasty jolt,' answered one of the Illyrians. 'Look at it the other way. If we do nothing, what kind of message is that going to send them? I say we've got no choice; hit them hard, and then try talking.'

'Agreed,' said a Founder. 'People like that only understand one thing.'

Before the debate could develop further, the extra chairs arrived, and we were held up for a minute or so while the people who were standing fought over them. In the end there was one singularly rickety-looking saw-horse left over, and three men who preferred to stand rather than trust it.

'We're getting out of control here,' I said. 'This is probably how the Trojan War really started, and any other war you care to name. I agree that we can't just ignore what's happened, that'd be asking for trouble. So would responding to an unofficial attack with an official one. No, the sensible thing would be to talk first, and fight only if that doesn't do any good.'

'Wonderful,' jeered the Founder Agesilaus. 'Give them notice we're going to attack, so they've got time to get ready. Was that the kind of military theory you taught back when you were a schoolmaster? If so, gods help Macedon.'

I shook my head. 'They'll be expecting an attack right now, don't you worry,' I replied. 'I'm afraid the element of surprise is a luxury we just don't have. Look, what we're doing here is setting a precedent for whatever troubles we have with them in the future –

and there'll be trouble, mark my words, so we might as well use our brains here and see if we can't come up with something a little bit more advanced than starting a fight. After all,' I couldn't help adding, 'I thought this was supposed to be the Ideal City. If we're really superior citizens, let's try acting the part.'

Ptolemocrates' widow didn't like the sound of that. 'Excuse me,' she burst out, 'but it's my husband who's just been murdered, and you're the people who've got to do something about it. I can't believe I'm hearing this; talk nicely to the people who slaughtered my husband—'

That was more the sort of thing the meeting wanted to hear. I wasn't having any, though. 'Oh, fine,' I said. 'You just lost your husband; let's see if we can't widow a few more women too, to keep you company. Yes, all right,' I added quickly, 'that wasn't a nice thing to say, I'm sorry. But sometimes the truth can be ugly. We've had a terrible shock – dammit, I was there, it could just as easily have been Theano as you making that particular speech. But we've got to use our heads now, if we don't want to throw away everything we've worked for these past ten years. Otherwise we might as well do what Agesilaus here suggested when the news first broke and pack up and go back to Macedon – I notice he's changed his tune since, for which I'm grateful. Or is there anybody else here who thinks we should do that?'

Nobody said anything.

'All right,' I said, 'here's what I suggest – and it's only a suggestion, nothing more; this is a free city, and we'll abide by our principles. We send a mission to the Scythians and demand that they hand over the men who did this. We make it absolutely clear that if they don't, they're going to regret it. Then we see what happens before we do anything we might have cause to regret later. My guess is they're absolutely terrified right now, expecting us to come tramping across the fields in full armour with burning torches. Let's show them we're not savages, and maybe we'll find out they aren't savages either. Well? Anyone got anything to say?'

Nobody had; and, to my intense relief, they went away and left me to the serious bout of delayed shock I'd been needing to get out of my system for the last hour or so. Please remember, this was the first time I'd been involved in fighting, or seen violent, deliberate death. It was all right for the Illyrians, and most of the Macedonians as well. They'd been soldiers, they knew about this sort of thing, whereas I knew about it only to the degree that I know about Ethiopia – I've read about it and on balance I believe that it exists, and I have a vague, probably entirely false mental image of what it's probably like. I suppose it was just as well that I had the familiar, almost comforting business of sorting out the idiotic squabbles of my contemptible fellows to take my mind off it all. If I'd been one of them, with someone else to load the responsibility onto, I expect I'd have been scared out of my wits.

Once I'd pulled myself together and dealt with the urge to crawl under a couch and curl up into a tight little ball, I forced myself to figure out what needed to be done.

In theory, we Founders were merely the representatives of the colonists, and any major decision should have been put to a full Assembly and argued out until a consensus was agreed. The hell, I decided, with that; time was of the essence here, and what the colonists really wanted was to be told that everything was under control and nothing like this would ever happen again. Failing that, of course, they'd all want their say (or their shout, more like) and if the embassy idea didn't work, I was quite happy to indulge them, if only to avoid having to take responsibility for the management of what could turn into a genuine war.

I thought it over for a few minutes, then yelled for Theano, who was still in the back room.

'Did you hear all that?' I asked.

She nodded. 'It says something when the most sensible, practical person among this city's leading citizens turns out to be *you*,' she said sweetly. 'On balance, maybe packing up and going home really would be the best thing—'

'Do me a favour,' I interrupted. 'Go and fetch Agenor and Marsampleptes, tell Marsampleptes to get twelve good, reliable men, with their armour on but under their big cloaks, swords only. Tell Eupolis to get the horse saddled up. All right?'

She nodded. 'Just those two?' she said.

'Who else would you suggest?' I asked.

She considered for a moment. 'Polybius,' she said. 'I know he's a Founder but he's too meek and wet to interfere, and you'd better take one of them with you or the others'll play war.'

'All right,' I said. 'That's sensible. Anyone else?'

'Tyrsenius.'

I scowled. 'Oh, come on,' I said. 'I've got enough on my plate as it is . . .'

She shook her head. 'For one thing,' she said, 'you'll need him as an interpreter for the Illyrians—'

'Balls,' I interrupted. 'I know more Illyrian than he does. Come to think of it, so do you. So does Anthemius' daughter's pet ferret, come to that.'

'Also,' she went on, rather rudely ignoring me, 'the Scythians know him and trust him, it'll be useful to have someone they—'

I held up my hand. 'Hang on,' I said. 'What do you mean, "know and trust"? How the hell can that be? We haven't had anything to do with them for years.'

Theano frowned a little, as if she'd realised she'd been indiscreet. 'Tyrsenius has,' she replied. 'He is a merchant, remember, he's got to have someone to trade with. He's been dealing with them for ages.'

'Really,' I said. 'What's he been dealing in?'

'Corn for oil, wine, dried fish, pottery, a few other bits and pieces—'

'What other "bits and pieces"?'

She shrugged, just a little bit too vigorously. 'Oh, you know. Jewellery. The odd piece of furniture. Cloth. Metalwork. The usual things.'

I looked at her. 'Metalwork,' I said.

'Sure, metalwork,' she said. 'Big bronze mixing-bowls. Lamp-stands. Ornamental breastplates. You know the sort of—'

'You mean armour,' I said.

'A few bits of armour. That ornate, decorated stuff, status symbols really. Only a few pieces.'

I breathed out through my nose. 'Fine,' I said. 'Tyrsenius has been selling armour and weapons to the Scythians for – how long did you say?'

'I didn't. And you said weapons, not me.'

'A considerable time, then. Years rather than months.'

'It's a very popular line. And it's not as if they don't have perfectly good weapons of their own. Better, in fact.'

'Oh, so I'm right about the weapons, then.'

'You're blowing it up out of all proportion,' she said angrily. 'He hasn't sold them anything they can't make for themselves; and if they didn't buy from him, they'd get the stuff from Olbia City or Odessus. And really, it's just expensive toys for a few of the top men.'

'Armour and weapons,' I repeated. 'And you've known about it all this time and never saw fit to mention—'

'So? There's all sorts of things I don't tell you. And you know why? Because they aren't important. Euxenus, I saw a thrush today. Euxenus, Calonice bought a jar of sprats the day before last. Euxenus, one of the straps has gone on my second-best pair of sandals . . .'

'All right.' I held up my hand again. 'We'll talk about it later. Is it your considered opinion that I should take Tyrsenius with me?'

'Yes,' she said.

'All right, fetch him as well, though it's against my better judgement. Anyone else?'

She nodded. 'Me,' she said.

'You?' I snorted. 'Don't be ridiculous. If they get the idea that we let women participate in making decisions—'

'Actually,' she said coldly, 'many Scythian tribes have women elders, it's quite usual in many parts of the region. But that wasn't what I meant. I think you need someone to carry the jar.'

'Jar?' I furrowed my brow. 'What jar?'

'The one with the snake in, of course. Do you know why the Scythians have left us alone all these years? Well?'

I stared at her. 'You don't mean—'

'Of course. Once they heard the colony was led by a great wizard with a familiar serpent . . .'

I groaned. 'Marvellous,' I said. 'All right, you come along as the high priestess or whatever. Now go and round the rest of them up, quick as you like. There's no time to waste if we're going to get all this sorted out.'

Once she'd gone, taking the boy along with her, I tried to concentrate on the job before us, but it was hard going. Instead of focusing on what I was going to say or the possible excuses they might come up with, I found my mind slipping back to this strange image of my wife Theano and my friend Tyrsenius . . .

. . . None of which had anything much to do with the present situation. Yes, I knew that. But once you start thinking about that it's really difficult to stop, and the more you try the harder it gets.

By the time the party was ready to leave I'd become all quiet and preoccupied, which must have been quite impressive. At least it took my mind off the desperate nature of the crisis we were facing . . .

Theano. And Tyrsenius. Tyrsenius, my so-called friend . . . I snapped myself out of it. 'Right,' I said, 'listen to me. When we get there nobody – and I mean that, nobody – says a word unless and until I ask him a question, all right? You can say what you like before and you can say what you like after. While we're there, keep it shut and don't pull faces.'

Tyrsenius nodded. 'Absolutely right,' he said (and I thought, *You bastard. Bloody fine friend you turned out to be*). 'You can rely on us, Euxenus. We won't let you down.'

I sighed. 'All right,' I said. 'Let's go and get this sorted out, once and for all.'

CHAPTER FOURTEEN

༄༄༄༄༄༄༄༄༄༄༄༄༄༄༄༄༄༄༄༄

It was agony getting on the horse, and worse getting off again. My ankle had stiffened up, the way they do, and there was no way I could put any weight on it; I hung from the shoulders of two of the Illyrian soldiers like a drunk being helped along by his friends. How I was going to get back into the saddle to go home I really didn't know. I had visions of swaying home slung over the horse's back like a sack of onions; this particular mental picture competed fiercely with the Theano/Tyrsenius image, with the result that I was in a foul mood by the time we got there, and in no mood to take any crap from anybody.

As we hobbled into the village, the people stared at us as if we were harpies or the demon warriors who sprang out of the ground when Cadmus sowed the dragon's teeth, then scuttled back into their houses and slammed the doors. If my old acquaintance Anabruzas, the former City archer, had turned up ten minutes or so later than he did, we may well have given up and gone home.

But he showed up, with ten or so venerable-looking whitebeards and a bunch of scared-looking men with bows. Anabruzas himself didn't look too happy, either.

'There you are,' I snapped (the hanging about hadn't helped my temper). 'Right, you know why we're here.'

Anabruzas nodded. 'I've got a pretty fair idea,' he said. 'You want to hear our side of it?'

'Not really,' I replied. 'Your people killed some of my people.

They tried to kill me. Now, it may be that your lot has some legitimate grievance against our city, but whatever it was, it doesn't justify murder. So here's the deal. You hand over the murderers to us, no fuss, no rhetoric. In return; first, I'll do what I can to keep my friends from coming over here with torches and setting fire to your village – and that's going to take some doing, but I promise I'll do my best. Second, if you want to file a formal complaint about anything you say we've done, I'll listen and I'll try to make them listen too. Otherwise – well, it'll be out of my hands.'

Anabruzas was quiet for some time. 'I'm not authorised to make deals like that,' he said. 'I can't order anybody to do anything, that's not the way we do things. It's up to the head of each household—'

I shook my head. 'Sorry,' I said, 'I'm not interested. Some day, when I'm writing a book about Scythian laws and customs, I'll come back and you can tell me all about it. Right now, I'm holding you personally responsible, because I know your name and you can speak Greek. Unless you personally want a war, you personally do something about it.'

He gave me a look of pure fear and hatred, roughly half and half. 'I can't,' he said.

'Pity,' I replied. 'Because my friend here – his name's Tyrsenius, I think you know him – my friend here can make himself understood in your pathetic excuse for a language, and in a minute he's going to announce in a very loud voice that Anabruzas has refused our demands and we have no alternative but to declare war. I think you might find life a bit interesting after that.'

Anabruzas' expression didn't change. 'I'll do my best,' he said. 'How does that sound?'

'We're getting there,' I said. 'Bear with me a moment, will you?'

I got my two supporters to take me back a yard or so, then called Tyrsenius over.

'Listen,' I said. 'Can you really talk their language?'

'Yes,' Theano put in, before he could open his mouth. 'Not too well, but well enough.'

'All right,' I said. 'And does he really know any of these people?'

She nodded. 'The head man, for one.'

'You mean him? Anabruzas?'

She nodded again. 'For what it's worth,' she added, 'he's telling the truth about not being able to order the heads of house to give those men up. He just hasn't got the authority.'

I shrugged; difficult, when both your arms are round the shoulders of tall men. 'Someone's got to,' I replied. 'Tyrsenius, I need to ask for a couple of hostages. Who do you suggest we ask for?'

Tyrsenius thought for a moment. 'Anabruzas' wife and daughter,' he replied. 'Sorry, I don't know their names. But I know they exist, because he had me get them each a Phoenician mirror – you know, the ivory ones with the carved backs—'

'Sounds good to me,' I said. 'Right, you two, take me back over there.'

I told Anabruzas that I wanted his wife and daughter as hostages until the murderers were handed over. At first I thought he was going to lose control altogether and attack me, but he calmed down – I could almost see him suppressing the anger, it was like watching a piece of iron cool down from bright red to cool grey – and eventually agreed.

'Wait there,' he said.

The ten or so minutes that followed, after Anabruzas had gone stomping off, leaving us alone with a bunch of scowling elders and utterly expressionless guards, were thoroughly awkward and embarrassing. I had the distinct feeling that I'd overplayed my hand and set rather more store on the threat of war with us than was actually merited, and if Anabruzas had come back with a war-band, I wouldn't have been in the least surprised. But when he returned, he had with him a short, sullen-looking woman of about his own age, and a fourteen-year-old girl who walked with a limp.

'Is that them?' I asked. Tyrsenius nodded.

Anabruzas tried to shoo them in our direction, as if he was herding goats across a fast river. The girl didn't seem to mind too much, but the woman was swearing at him and waving her hands furiously in the air.

'The girl's a bit simple,' Tyrsenius whispered. 'The limp's because she fell off a horse and bust her leg, and the bones didn't set straight. You want to watch yourself around the wife, though. She'll have all the skin off your bones.'

We went home after that. An awful lot of people came to stare at the hostages, and it was comical to watch them standing in the doorway of the barn we put them in; the older woman ranting and shaking her fists, the girl solemnly waving and smiling. Together they served the useful purpose of beguiling the colonists into forgetting just what it was that had caused them to be there; they were a freak show of the highest quality, and nothing calms down an over-excited bunch of people better than high-class entertainment.

A day or so later I was at home, trying to mend a broken mattock handle with newly boiled rawhide and glue, when someone came and told me there was a deputation from the Scythian village waiting to see me. I quickly washed the glue off my hands and went to see what they wanted.

It was Anabruzas. With him were a couple of the silent old men and a boy. I recognised the boy; I'd have known his face even if he'd been able to walk.

The wound from the arrow I'd shot into him had gone badly septic, and they'd had to amputate the leg four inches above the knee. Gods know why he hadn't died, of the amputation as much as the wound itself. Clearly the Scythians knew a thing or two about medicine. He looked thoroughly wretched, as was only to be expected. They'd carried him in on a stretcher, and he just lay there and stared up at the sky.

'All right,' I said, trying to look stern and uncompromising, 'that's one of them. Where's the others?'

Anabruzas gave me a filthy look. 'That's all you're getting,' he said. 'Sorry.'

'That's not good enough.'

'Tough.' He gave me a smile that had nothing to do with friendliness. 'I told you, I can't give orders to my people, I'm not a king or a magistrate or anything like that. The only people who can give orders are the heads of households.'

'Really,' I said. 'So what's he doing here?'

Anabruzas looked at me for a moment. 'I can order him,' he said. 'He's my son.'

There was a long and awkward silence, filled with all the unfortunate history we'd somehow contrived to share over the years.

'I see,' I said.

'Well?'

'Well what?'

'Well, do I get my wife and daughter back now?'

I frowned. 'That's the deal, is it? You trade me your son for your wife and daughter. What charming people you are.'

Once again, I could see him visibly not getting angry. 'It's common sense,' he said. 'His life is ruined anyway, they're both reasonably healthy, fit for work. All right, the girl's a liability, but she can still card wool.'

I nodded slowly. 'That's how you see people, is it? Strictly utilitarian.'

'Sorry, I don't understand long words,' Anabruzas said. 'I'm trying to prevent a war, and this is the best I can do. I can't think of anything else I can offer. If you've got any suggestions, I'm listening.'

Suddenly I felt tired and not terribly nice to know. 'Take your wife and daughter and go to the crows,' I sighed. 'I'll do the best I can. No promises.'

He smiled again. 'That's all right,' he said. 'I wouldn't trust them if you made any.'

Once the story got about, the sheer melodrama appealed to my people so much that they almost forgot about our own dead, they were so entranced by it all. This was tragedy come to life, and Anabruzas made a wonderful tragic hero. What with that and the freak show as well, they seemed to feel, the Scythians had paid their debt in pure entertainment. Even the families of the men who'd been murdered admitted that they couldn't ask a great deal more, especially once we'd concocted a false confession in which the poor lame bastard supposedly admitted that he'd been the driving force behind the whole raid, and the others had just been following his orders (we made him out to be some kind of high-ranking commander of the Scythian armed forces; a sort of Alexander to Anabruzas' Philip).

On the day we put him to death, everybody turned out at first light and hung around the market square for hours so as not to miss a thing. Some of them brought garlands and offerings of flowers, bread and fruit. Quite a few of the women were in tears, which goes to show what a soft-hearted lot we Greeks can be. There was a moment of pure farce just before the actual business – Marsamleptes' men dropped the poor kid as they lifted him off the stretcher to carry him to the chopping-block, and the stunned look on his face was highly comical, in a sense. There was a muted cheer as the axe went down, but nobody seemed particularly cheerful as the head was ceremoniously carried to the steps of the market hall and hung up in the temple porch; it all seemed fairly pointless somehow, and afterwards people drifted quietly away, much to the disappointment of those who'd brought along wine and sausages to sell.

After three days we took down the head and sent it back with the body to the village in a cart. They didn't seem particularly interested – they don't go in for funerals to nearly the same extent as we do – and the carter told me it was almost as if they were doing us a favour taking the bits off our hands.

We heard about what had happened at Chaeronea some ten days after this, from the captain of an Athenian grain-freighter. Obviously, he didn't tell me about what had happened to my brothers; I only found that out when my friend Tyrsenius got a letter from one of his business associates back in Athens. He turned up on my door-step late one evening, put the letter in my hands and walked away without saying anything.

I was pretty much out of things for a day or so after that, and so I missed the next development in our relationship with the Scythians. As far as I was able to piece it together afterwards, however, it went something like this.

There was an old man in the Scythian village who had a very fine horse. The son of an important man in the next village along saw this horse one day, found out that its owner was too old and sick to ride it more than once or twice a month, and asked if it was for sale. The old man said no; sure, he didn't ride it, but he just liked owning such a beautiful animal. That didn't suit the young man, who reckoned it was a waste and a crying shame. He kept increasing his offers until he was offering a ridiculous amount for the creature, but the old man wouldn't have any of it. He was too old, he said, to be interested in money, he just wanted to own a really exceptional horse, and would the young pain in the bum please stop bothering him? The young man was starting to get obsessive about the horse. He felt it was a personal affront, and he was going to have the horse if it was the last thing he did. One of his father's hangers-on smelt money, so he crept out one night, stole the horse and brought it to the village.

When the young man's father found out what had happened, he quite understandably went berserk. Stealing horses is a very serious crime for all Scythians – I don't know why I'm bothering to tell you this, Phryzeutzis; you undoubtedly know more about the nuances and implications of all this than I ever will – and the thought that he'd been party to horse-theft, even without knowing it, was enough to stop him sleeping at night. He immediately had the horse killed, chopped up into small bits and burned; then he did the same with the poor fool who'd stolen it, and sent his worthless son off to live with some cousins a couple of villages away. He felt a bit better after that, but he still couldn't sleep; the theft of such a fine horse was big news, and he knew it'd only be a matter of time before people linked the theft with his son's excessive offers and general bad behaviour. So he put about the story that the Greeks from the colony had stolen the horse, as a way of getting back at the villagers for the killings.

Now, one of the men who'd taken part in the original escapade (who was still, of course, very much at large, though extremely nervous at all times) heard of this and decided to try to make something of it. He hated us anyway, which was why he'd joined the raid in the first place, and after what had happened to Anabruzas' son he was convinced that unless he did something quickly it'd only be a matter of time before he met with a pretty unpleasant end. He'd been trying to nerve himself to leave the village; but that would have meant being parted from his wife and children, because his father-in-law had made it perfectly clear that if he left the village he'd leave it alone, and he didn't want that. The business with the horse (which was, for all he knew, perfectly true) seemed to him to be a first-class opportunity for stirring up the villagers against the Greeks and launching a proper attack that'd make us go away once and for all.

That may sound like extremely wishful thinking; but the villagers had some pretty odd notions about us at the best of times. Try as they might, they could never understand how anybody could willingly leave his home, the place where he'd been born and brought up, to go hundreds of miles away and make a new home somewhere else. That wasn't something they could ever imagine doing; for better or worse, they reckoned, a man belongs where he's born, and that's where he stays if he possibly can; which is why exile is a far more cruel punishment than death among these people. Accordingly, they figured that we were either mad or else had been banished for some awful crime; in either case, it wasn't going to take much to shift us, since we'd already abandoned one home and were therefore capable of abandoning another, if only we were given the incentive.

The fact that the original raid had happened at all proves how high feelings ran in the village. We hadn't known a thing about it, but the only reason we'd had ten years of peace was because of an old witch (every village has a witch; she gets drunk, breathes in the smoke of strange poisonous herbs, and rides on an eight-legged horse into the spirit kingdom to ask the advice of the ghosts there. They take it all very seriously, and the village witch is as near as they get to a community leader) who refused to let them do anything to us. The ghosts, or her own good judgement, had warned her that tangling with the Greeks could only end in disaster; even if they managed to dislodge us, it'd cost so many lives and so much property that the village would cease to be functional. Accordingly, whenever she was consulted about us (fairly regularly, it seemed) she made it unequivocally clear that as long as she was alive, anybody who picked a fight with us would get no help from the ghosts in this world or the next.

But she died, about a month before the raid, and when the villagers met to choose their new witch it was pretty clear that the successful candidate would be someone who talked to a different bunch of ghosts or could get them to give a different answer on this subject. Predictably, the new witch came back from the spirit world with the news that the ghosts had revised their views about the Greeks, to the effect that they were now extremely unhappy with anyone who *didn't* help drive the offcomers into the sea with all due dispatch.

That there wasn't an immediate all-out attack was, it appears, largely due to my old acquaintance Anabruzas. Every time the subject was raised, he'd stand up and say that he didn't give a toss about what the ghosts said, he wasn't going to have anything to do with a war with us, for the simple reason that he knew Greeks the way none of the rest of them did, and a war could have only one outcome; namely, that the ghosts would suddenly have so much new company out there in the spirit world that they'd be hard put to it to find a patch of grass to graze their horses on. The villagers believed in the ghosts, but they also knew and respected Anabruzas; he'd gone away and come back a rich (by their standards) and wise man, he'd learned all manner of strange and incredible skills in the city of the Greeks, he knew how to cure diseases and make things, he'd picked up a wonderful way with words. He now argued that it didn't make any sense that the ghosts should have changed their tune to such a drastic extent just because one witch had died and another had taken her place. They all knew, he said, that the new witch was telling them what they wanted to hear, which wasn't necessarily the same thing as the truth. He knew all about that sort of thing, he told them, after living in the city of Athens, where the people met every day in Assembly to do democracy, which is the art of telling each other what they want to hear and then taking a vote to turn it into the truth. The Athenians, he said, were perfectly capable of passing a law stating that the sea is pink, if that's what they wanted it to be; but the sea wouldn't be noticeably pinker as a result, if they voted till they were blue in the face. The Athenians didn't usually go that far, of course; but they did vote that everybody should be happy and well fed and rich and that there wouldn't be any more stealing or fighting in the streets and that Philip of Macedon would crawl down a hole and die; and if the villagers believed that the ghosts were telling them that it was now all right to attack the Greeks, they'd be demonstrating that they had no more of a grip on reality than the people of Athens – and if that was the case, then the ghosts have mercy on them all.

But Anabruzas had a son; a foolish, rather crazy kid who didn't get on with his father and was at that age where he'd do anything provided it was what his father didn't want him to do . . . It occurred to one of the leading anti-Greeks that if Anabruzas' son got involved in an attack on the colony, it'd force his father to stop opposing the war and that'd be the main obstacle out of the way. So they talked the kid into coming with them and set off to do just enough damage to start a war.

It was supposed to be a quick, safe job, but of course it didn't turn out like that. Two of the raiders were killed, another badly injured, in an attack on a small group of supposedly unarmed farmers walking out to the fields. The Greeks, in other words, appeared to be every bit as dangerous a proposition as Anabruzas and the old witch had said they'd be, and it was a matter of cold fact that we outnumbered them at least four to one. Enthusiasm for the war melted away like a candle on a bonfire, particularly when

Anabruzas tore into the raiders in the meeting that followed and set an awful example by handing over his son to us to be killed.

So that was the situation the anti-Greek faction faced when the horse-stealing affair came about, and the man I told you about who'd been on the raid was trying to rally support. Obviously, he needed to find something to change the odds significantly in the villagers' favour; and, because of the business with the horse, he found it.

The difference was, of course, the rich man in the next village who'd started the horse-theft rumour. What he wanted most of all was to be able to fetch his son home again. If the Scythians went to war with the colony, then his version of what had happened would be accepted as the truth essentially by default, and he wouldn't have to worry about accusations of horse-stealing. Since he was as influential in his village as Anabruzas was in what I'm going to call our village, he didn't have much trouble in whipping up a nice anti-Greek froth on the surface. But he knew that when it actually came time to do something about it, it might well be a different story. His people had heard about how very formidable these Greeks were – by this time the facts were starting to grow ears and whiskers, the way they always do; the number of raiders had grown, the number of Greeks had diminished, the Greeks tore the dead raiders apart with their bare hands, it was more like twenty dead rather than two, and so on; furthermore, the King of the Greeks was under the direct protection of a ghost-snake who accompanied him wherever he went in the form of a beautiful but ferocious yellow-eyed woman (you know, except for the fact that Theano's eyes were dark brown rather than yellow, I'd say there was more than a germ of truth in that part of it) and any attack on them was doomed to ignominious failure.

The rich man – I wish I knew his name, but I don't; I'm sorry – didn't give up. Instead, he thought it all through quite carefully and came to the conclusion that what he needed was proof that these Greeks weren't nearly as tough as people now thought they were. He'd taken pains to find out what had actually happened by talking to the man who'd been on the raid, and when he analysed it carefully he saw that the only reason there'd been any casualties at all was that the raid had been poorly planned and carelessly executed, as you'd expect from a spur-of-the moment escapade by a bunch of young hooligans.

Fortuitously, about that time, a party of Scythians from much further north arrived in the area. Unlike our Scythians, they were true nomads who'd had to leave their tribe on account of one of the messy, complicated blood-feuds that break out up there every now and again. These men were to all intents and purposes professional soldiers; what with cattle-raids and counter-raids and ambushes and hot pursuits, they'd gained an impressive amount of experience in small-scale warfare, and were now at a loose end, badly in need of a job. The rich man took them into his household and spent a long time with them, asking their advice and listening to what they had to say.

But he still wasn't going to rush into anything. He knew that if something went wrong, or if the exhibition turned out not to be sufficiently impressive, he'd only make things worse for himself and his ally in 'our' village. What he really needed, he decided (and his nomad friends were very much in agreement) was some good, solid military intelligence. For example, some of the Greeks had their bows with them wherever they went, others didn't. Some of them were trained soldiers, others were apparently as soft as butter. What he needed was someone who could give him reliable information, sufficient to make intelligent plans. This was going to be awkward to achieve now that there was active hostility between them and us; but there was still one man in the colony who kept up apparently friendly relations with the Scythians, namely my very good friend Tyrsenius. The rich man decided that he was the likeliest prospect, and set out to find a way of establishing contact without being too obvious about it.

When I finally climbed out of the dark hole the news from Athens had dropped me into, almost the first thing I saw was an enormous soppy grin on the face of my friend Tyrsenius. It made me wonder whether I hadn't been better off down the dark hole.

'Where the hell have you been?' he barked at me, grabbing me by the elbow and marching me from my front door towards the market square. 'Really, you ought to have more consideration than to go wandering off when there's work to be done. Still, here you are at last, so that's all right.'

I should point out that the big soppy grin was quite unlike Tyrsenius' usual predatory, slightly leering grin, which was such a fixture on his face that it always reminded me of the old story of Medusa's head, which turned people into stone. My favourite theory was that Tyrsenius had been unlucky enough to encounter the Gorgon's petrifying visage as a young boy while on the point of eating a particularly lush, sticky honey-cake he'd just stolen from a smaller, less quick-witted child. Theano, on the other hand, held to the view that he'd had a nasty shock while relieving himself after a long and uncomfortable bout of constipation. Her version was more arresting but I prefer my own, if only because it's more literary and cultured.

'What's going on?' I asked.

'You may well ask,' Tyrsenius replied helpfully. 'Come on, you can see for yourself.'

I was intrigued, I must admit. It wasn't the level of animation that caught my imagination; Tyrsenius was always hopping about, like a sparrow on ashes, until you got dizzy and sick watching him. It was more the irresistible cheerfulness that wafted from him, like the reek of a tanner's yard. Only two things could have had this effect on him; money and love. If it was money, it meant he'd struck some particularly juicy deal, and for some reason he rarely required my official presence as *oecist* when he was cooking up his famous juicy deals – quite the reverse, in fact. That only left love. I groaned audibly, but he didn't seem to notice.

'Tyrsenius,' I said, grabbing onto a doorpost to stop him swirling me away, 'what's going on? You're in love again, aren't you?'

He scowled at me. 'Rubbish,' he said.

'Don't mess with me,' I sighed. 'I was there the last time, remember? And the time before that. And the time before that. And . . .'

'Don't be ridiculous,' he said. 'You make it sound like I fall in love every other day.'

I didn't say anything. The plain fact was that Eros had shot my friend Tyrsenius so many times with his pernicious little arrows that it was a miracle he didn't leak when he drank a cup of water. Over the last six months, for example, there had been the niece of one of the deadlier Founders, Marsamleptes' daughter, Marsamleptes' son, the night-soil boy, the Olbian dried-fish merchant's wife, the cute little Illyrian girl who cleaned the guts for her father the sausage-maker, the girl with the gammy leg who was betrothed to one of

Tyrsenius' business partners in Odessus, Agenor the stonemason's apprentice and (I suspected, though I didn't have any proof) my wife Theano. It said a great deal for Tyrsenius' invincible amiability that people didn't try to cut his throat as he walked across the square, let alone continued to trade with him and regard him as a friend. But that was Tyrsenius all over; ill-will simply dripped off him, the way water refuses to adhere to the waxy belly-feathers of ducks.

'Not every other day,' I conceded. 'Every other week.'

He didn't dignify that cheap shot with a reply. Instead, he yanked me free of the doorpost (he was deceptively strong for a man of his build) and carried on marching me across the square.

'There,' he said magnificently, as if introducing me to Zeus.

Scythians, I thought; *what joy*.

A second look confirmed that the four wretched, grumpy-looking people huddled together on the steps of the market hall were indeed Scythians of some kind, though not any kind we'd encountered before. For one thing, they were seriously overdressed; it was a warm day, and they were swaddled up in the traditional Scythian cold-weather gear; tall, conical felt hats with drooping earflaps that reached to the collar-bone, tight-fitting jackets and trousers of heavy patterned cloth, deeply lined with felt. I could see the sweat glistening on their foreheads. And it took only one glance at their nervous, hawklike faces to tell that this was the first time they'd ever been inside a Greek city, possibly even a permanent settlement of any kind.

'Who are these people?' I asked.

'They're the Budini,' Tyrsenius replied in a low whisper.

Remarkably, the name was familiar. 'I've heard of them,' I said. 'Or at least, I think I read about them somewhere. Aren't they the ones who're supposed to eat fir-cones?'

Tyrsenius looked blank. 'I don't know,' he replied, 'you'd have to ask them that. The point is, they're here to trade and – get this – to make an alliance with us against the village people.'

I stood still for a moment and thought about that. 'Where did you say they came from?' I asked.

'I didn't,' Tyrsenius said. 'You didn't ask. But as far as I can tell, they live way up north in the frozen country, just under the lee of a big range of mountains.'

I nodded. 'And they've come all the way from the frozen country on purpose to pick a fight with the inhabitants of a small Olbian village. Yes, that makes a lot of sense, I can see that quite clearly now you've explained it to me.'

'Not this particular village,' Tyrsenius said wearily. 'That'd be silly. What I meant was, they'll help us if we help them. It's got to be the most wonderful opportunity.'

'You mean for selling them things?' I asked. 'I reckon they live so far north that they won't have heard the warnings about you yet.'

He looked worried for a moment until he realised I was joking. 'Very witty,' he said. 'Now come on, Euxenus. Even you should be able to appreciate—'

Then I happened to catch sight of one of them and everything fell into place. The youngest member of the party was a girl; a pretty one at that, if you like that slim, boyish, ambiguous look (which Tyrsenius notoriously did; Theano always reckoned that what he liked was the uncertainty of not knowing for sure whether it was a boy or a girl until he'd actually got them home and unwrapped them, as it were). I looked at her, then back at Tyrsenius. The poor fool definitely had it bad this time.

'It's a girl,' I said. 'Trust me on this and save yourself a lot of time and hassle.'

For a moment I was afraid I'd really upset him, but I needn't have worried. Just as it was impossible to be angry with Tyrsenius for more than a minute or so, he never really seemed to take offence no matter what you said to him. 'I can see that,' he said. 'What I don't see is the relevance. Here we are on the brink of what could be a turning-point in our history, and all you can do is babble about girls.'

I sighed and gave up. 'All right,' I said. 'What do you want me to do?'

At his insistence I invited these peculiar people into my home (Theano took one startled look at them, grabbed our son and shot out of the house; can't say I blame her) and spent the best part of the morning trying to communicate with their leader, a granite-faced character called Bossus or something like that, while Tyrsenius twittered round the girl like a wren trying to scare off an elephant. I'll say this for the man; he never ever seemed to worry about the language barrier – I imagine that's a necessary trait for a trader. It was patently obvious the girl didn't understand a word he said to her, but then again, you didn't need to be Aristotle to work out what he was after. Whether or not he was getting anywhere I neither knew nor cared. Bossus, on the other hand, could just about make himself understood in Greek, something I should have found suspicious if I'd had my wits about me.

He said that his people lived Far Away (he pointed; apparently they came from somewhere just left of the sun) and they'd been driven from home by Bad Cold and they wanted to come and live down here, where it was warmer. The fact that the region was already heavily settled didn't seem to bother him (we are Fighting People; Fighting is Much Honour) and he seemed to regard our neighbours as decadent and depraved because they'd abandoned the nomadic habits of their ancestors and taken to staying in one place. Obviously this blanket condemnation of the settled life didn't apply to us, because he seemed only too happy to commit his entire nation to a war of aggression against all the non-nomadic Scythians in Olbia, but declared that with us he only wanted to live in peace.

Fair enough, I thought, assuming this clown is for real. That, however, didn't seem all that likely. For all his vagueness about where Far Away actually was, I could see no obvious reason why he should have set his heart on this particular piece of territory to the exclusion of other alternatives that might prove easier to acquire. The clincher, as far as I was concerned, was that he was prepared to sit still and natter away at me while not two yards away, a degenerate Greek was doing his level best to debauch his daughter, and do nothing about it. Even I knew that this wasn't the Scythian way, and as soon as our honoured guests had been induced to shove off back to the guest quarters Tyrsenius had requisitioned for them (in my name, which I thought was a bit much), I raised this point.

'Not the Budini,' he replied. 'They're completely relaxed about that kind of thing. They believe in open, non-exclusive communal relationships; you know, like in Plato's *Republic*.'

Now, I knew for a fact that the only copy of Plato's *Republic* that Tyrsenius was likely ever to have looked at carefully would have been one wrapped round a bundle of fish; however, I really couldn't be bothered to labour the point. Indeed, the prospect of Tyrsenius being chased round the square by a party of enraged Scythians with long, sharp knives was, at that moment, rather attractive. 'I see,' I said. 'Well, there you go. When you've finished with these people, please make sure they leave. I don't mind them, but there's a lot of people in town who get very nervous at the sight of Scythians these days.'

He made a sad noise and proceeded to lecture me for several minutes about openness, trust and the desirability of setting his new friends on the people of the village like a pack of wild dogs. Eventually, when he'd gone, I put my hat back on, picked up my mattock and went out to do some work.

After the raid and the events that immediately followed it, there was an understandable wave of paranoia. People took to going out to the fields in full armour again, or at the very least with helmet, spear and shield; and although that didn't last more than a few days before the sheer impracticality of trying to fresh out ditches clad head to toe in shining bronze made people revise their security arrangements, the attitude persisted.

Nearly all the Illyrians had bows and knew how to use them. Greeks, however, don't really hold with bows and arrows, preferring to trust in heavy metal and physical strength. Back home, where you're never out of sight of your neighbours, it wouldn't have been nearly so bad. Here, where we all had so much land, a man working in the fields was pretty much on his own, and that feeling of isolation was bad enough at the best of times. With the constant threat of attack present in everybody's minds, it began to have a serious effect on our lives.

It was Agenor the stonemason who first suggested hiring the Budini to guard us, and I must say I'd have expected better from him. Once he made the suggestion, it caught on like a brush-fire, and Tyrsenius (who had, incidentally, succeeded with the girl in the face of all the odds) at once opened negotiations for setting up a rent-a-guard agency, to be organised by himself, on an almost-but-not-quite-non-profit basis. I tried to talk them all out of it, but I'd left it too late. Not long afterwards, bands of boiled-looking men in heavy wool and felt started drifting into the city, to be marshalled by Tyrsenius and allocated to a particular household. When not guarding, they lived in a huge sprawl of tents outside the wall (we had stone walls now in place of the stockade, and very proud of them we were). Nobody knew how many of them there were, except presumably my friend Tyrsenius. Nobody cared much, either. It had all the appearance of a logical and satisfactory arrangement that could carry on indefinitely.

And after a while, I stopped worrying about it. I'd been expecting to wake up one night to the sound of rampaging Budini sacking the city and massacring Greeks in their beds, but so far this hadn't happened, or if it had they'd been very quiet and discreet about it. Even I, with my unique talent for looking in the wrong direction whenever anything worthy of note happens right under my nose, would have noticed something like that.

My personal guard (the Founders insisted that I had one, though I objected like hell) was called Azus, though I didn't find this out until he'd been following me around for the best part of a year. The most striking thing about him was the smell – not unpleasant, just very, very noticeable; he smelt of a combination of smoke, hemp and violets. I'm no dwarf myself, but Azus towered over me like a mountain looming over a valley, and until the novelty wore off Theano and I amused ourselves no end exchanging tall-bastard jokes. He didn't speak Greek and I didn't know more than a dozen words of the Budini dialect of Scythian – which I doubt whether you'd be able to understand, Phryzeutzis; it's full of bizarre archaisms and peculiar dialect words, and the syntax is so complicated it's a miracle that young Budini manage to learn to talk before they're forty. He used to stand there all day while we were out in the fields, just watching me work; big broad-bladed spear in one hand, heavily recurved horn-and-sinew composite bow in the other, with an expression of total detachment on his face, as if it was all a strange, incomprehensible dream. Finally one day, when I'd been wrestling with a huge log for half an hour without making any progress beyond wrenching my back, I lost patience with him; I grabbed him by the arm, led him across to the log and made frantic gestures, until he carefully laid down his bow and spear and grabbed the other end of the log. Together we had no trouble at all shifting it, and when we'd done I smiled and nodded thank you. To my amazement he smiled back.

The next day I borrowed the young son of one of my neighbours; he'd been learning Budini for some reason and could interpret for me. Thanks to him I found out Azus' name, and learned that he'd been only too delighted to help; it was horribly boring, he said, standing about all day with nothing to do, and he'd never been able to understand why these crazy Greeks never allowed them to lend a hand, even when it was patently necessary.

We got on much better after that; the boy taught me how to say, 'Help, please,' and I did the rest in sign language. Gradually – very gradually – I picked up a little of his language and he learned rather more Greek, until we were able to hold a sort of conversation, though it was a major effort for both of us, and we frequently talked for a long time without realising we were completely at cross purposes. He told me that the reason Bossus had given for leaving the tribe's ancestral pastures wasn't quite the truth; the fact was that he and his small contingent of followers had been thrown out after a blood-feud had got badly out of hand, even by Budini standards, and that they'd ended up here not because of any grand plan of carving out *lebensraum* for themselves among the effete plains-dwellers, but because they'd had to come this far to get beyond the reach of their enemies, who had friends and relations all over the place. Contrary to what we'd been told, there weren't any more of them waiting for the call to come sweeping down from the high pastures; it had taken all Bossus' skill and tenacity as a leader of men to keep them together this far.

Above all, Azus said, he wanted to make the point that compared with the traditional life of the nomad, the life they had here was little short of the earthly paradise, and in order to have this good a time back home, you had to be virtuous and honourable all your life and then die. About the only thing we'd been told that was true, in fact, was what Tyrsenius had told me about the Budini attitude to personal relationships; and that was because there were so few adult male Budini (because of the blood-feuds) that more conventional arrangements would have been pointless and led to the rapid extinction of the race.

If you're thinking back to what I told you about the rich Scythian's plot, and wondering when the Budini are going to stop pretending to be our friends and start butchering us in our sleep, I'm afraid you've got the wrong end of the stick. The truth is (though of course we didn't know this) that the plan had gone badly wrong. Sure, he'd arranged for the displaced nomads to ingratiate themselves with us, specifically using the girl as bait with Tyrsenius; but he hadn't anticipated that they'd find their new life with us so entirely agreeable that they'd forget all about the deal they'd made with him and come over to us. Maybe I should have suspected something from the way Azus and some of the others kept harping on about how treacherous and deceitful our settled-Scythian neighbours were, and how we ought to be constantly on our guard in case of further sneak attacks; but we all assumed that they were just playing up the hazards so as to keep their jobs, and paid no great attention.

Meanwhile, to everybody's amazement, Tyrsenius married the Budini girl, shortly after the birth of their second daughter. Once they were married he gave up trying to pronounce her real name (they'd been together two years and he'd never managed to get it right) and announced that henceforth she'd be answering to Callixena (which means 'beautiful foreigner'; for a man so entirely given to flights of fancy, Tyrsenius had the imagination of a small rock). She didn't seem to mind. In fact, she seemed genuinely fond of him in a mildly contemptuous sort of way, while he calmed down to a remarkable extent and appeared to have given up falling in love almost entirely; perhaps as a result of the Budini custom whereby married women wore a razor-sharp two-edged dagger as part of their everyday dress. Anyway; since I can't remember what she was really called, I shall refer to her as Callixena, not that it really matters a damn after all these years.

CHAPTER FIFTEEN

Oh, I almost forgot; a year or so after Chaeronea, Philip of Macedon was murdered.

After the battle, it didn't take Philip long to break up what little resistance remained. He awarded himself the title 'Captain of the Greeks', a delightfully nebulous term which suggested that he was merely the temporary head of a coalition of great and equal partners joined together to accomplish some mighty purpose. Imagine everyone's surprise, therefore, when it turned out that he really did have a mighty purpose in mind.

And purposes don't come much mightier than the one Philip had selected. For reasons that better men than I have speculated endlessly about, he'd decided that the vast and invincible Persian Empire, which extended eastwards from the Hellespont to the very ends of the earth (to here, in fact), was decadent and ripe for conquest; furthermore, that he was the man who could do the job.

And, as usual, he was right. By virtue of its very size and the diversity of the nations that it comprised, the Empire was the next best thing to ungovernable at the best of times. As soon as one rebellion was put down in one province, another broke out – the old joke has the Great King starting each day by asking his chamberlain which provinces he still ruled – and ever since the civil war in which the celebrated Xenophon took part (you may remember I told you about it a while back) the King had come to rely more and more on Greek mercenaries rather than his own levies to do the day-to-day work of a standing army. The logic behind this was impeccable; he couldn't trust his own people further than he could sneeze them out of a blocked nose, but Greek mercenaries were legendary for their loyalty so long as they got paid, and since they got paid as long as they were winning, they tended to do a good, professional job.

The key word, of course, is professional. By rights, a Greek heavy infantry army shouldn't stand a chance on Asian soil against Asian cavalry and archers. But it's a fact of life that a trained and determined army of professionals will defeat unwilling amateurs every time, even if they're outnumbered ten to one and armed with sticks of celery, because there's always that moment when the two sides face each other, and one side weighs the advantages of victory against the perils of defeat, and realises that war, even if you win, is a mug's game and no occupation for a sensible man.

Philip of Macedon (who hired *me* to teach his son military history) knew all about this, which was why he spent his life perfecting the Macedonian professional army. If you want to, you can interpret everything Philip did from the moment he became King as leading up to the invasion of Persia, and all the facts will fit that view. He united Greece, he trained and developed a magnificent army; in his dealings with the Greek cities he conquered he went out of his way to be nice so as not to alienate them and lose them from the grand design. And, if he'd lived, I believe he'd have achieved a substantial part of his objective, maybe even ending up after twenty years or so of war as ruler of a quarter of Asia.

He never got the chance. Shortly before the expedition was due to set off, he staged a magnificent wedding for his daughter Cleopatra, who was marrying the King of Epirus. It turned out to be a long, hard wedding, with days of good old-fashioned drinking lightly seasoned with mandatory cultural events befitting the taste and discrimination of the Captain of the Greeks, some of which Philip even attended. It was at one of these, an athletic contest held in the theatre at Aegae, that a young guardsman called Pausanias stuck him through the ribcage with a Celtic-pattern broadsword, rendering him as comprehensively dead as it's possible for a man to be in just one lifetime, before running away, tripping over a trailing vine and falling smack on his nose in front of gods know how many thousand utterly stunned people.

Pausanias didn't live very long after that. He certainly didn't survive long enough to answer any questions, but that was all right because, apparently, it was common knowledge that he had a personal grudge against the King – lots of suitably squalid stuff about a clandestine love-affair that resulted in a gang-rape and all manner of prurient details; interestingly enough, the story struck me as remarkably familiar the first time I heard it, and it didn't take me long to work out why. It was basically the same as the hallowed tale of Harmodius and Aristogiton, the two young heroes who killed the tyrant Hipparchus and set Athens free a century or so back. For some reason, this made me think quite hard about Aristotle, a man who knew a good story when he heard one and had a very good idea of the sort of thing that catches the public imagination. If I'm right, the parallel between Philip and the lecherous monster Hipparchus was a singularly deft touch, which would compel me to raise my estimation of Aristotle by a significant factor.

Once the show was over (I assume they must have carried on with the wedding, because Cleopatra did marry the King of Epirus) and everybody had finally accepted that what they'd seen was for real, the speculation began. Favourite for the role of First Murderer was Olympias the Queen, and there's no denying that she had a pretty substantial motive, because not long before, Philip had married a young and beautiful girl (also confusingly called Cleopatra), apparently neglecting to divorce Olympias first but in all other respects indicating that he'd had enough of her and her bloody snakes and was proposing to start over with someone a bit less exhausting to live with. This Cleopatra lived longer than the man Pausanias but not by much, and there were all sorts of rumours flying about that Olympias, far from denying her involvement, was worried in case other people stole the credit for her great accomplishment.

Entirely possible; but I don't think so. The Olympias I knew could easily have smashed Philip's skull with a chair-leg in the heat of an argument. She might even have poisoned his soup, if he'd done something that really upset her (and I don't see going through a form of marriage with some girl as being enough to do that). But a public execution involving accomplices wasn't her style at all; she was far too direct and self-reliant to bother with anything like that, and it seems pretty obvious that the whole purpose behind killing Philip at that particular time in that particular place was to stop

Philip leading the army into Persia and starting the war with the Great King.

Nor do I believe that the Persians had anything to do with it, though that too would have been entirely possible; or the Athenians, come to that, though they rather crassly voted that Pausanias should be awarded the posthumous rank of Hero of Athenian Freedom, and Demosthenes showed up at Assembly in a flamboyant new outfit designed to represent Great Joy, even though his daughter had died a few days previously. Both the Persians and the Athenians would have realised that killing Philip wouldn't solve anything as far as they were concerned unless Alexander died with him; and Alexander didn't die. Oh no. Not one bit.

Alexander, in fact, became King; quite unexpectedly, while in the full flower of his youth and brilliance, which would otherwise have been wasted as he served his time as his father's loyal lieutenant and second-in-command. If Philip had lived to a reasonable age, Alexander wouldn't have succeeded to the throne much before his fiftieth birthday – by which time, quite possibly, all the best bits of the mighty purpose would already have been accomplished, and Alexander would've been stuck with the rotten job of consolidating and keeping in one piece the mighty empire Philip had carved himself out in the East. A fifty-year-old Achilles; I can't see it, somehow. And I don't believe that the Alexander I knew ever had the slightest intention of living to be fifty, if there was any way it could possibly be avoided.

Yapping Dog history, take it or leave it; none of it matters much now, in any event. If you're ill-mannered enough to insist that I offer some token scrap of evidence to back up my wild innuendoes, consider this. The man Pausanias was a guardsman, one of the Companions. I don't remember him from my time at Mieza, but Pausanias was a fairly common Macedonian name at that time, so who knows, maybe the poor fool was a student of mine. One thing that's certain is that the young Companions had been raised from birth to be unquestioningly loyal to Prince Alexander, to do whatever he ordered them to do regardless of the consequences to themselves. Of course, it's possible that one of these carefully prepared young noblemen could have been so obsessed with sexual jealousy over a middle-aged one-eyed drunkard that he broke clear of everything he'd been brought up to revere to the extent of stabbing his lord's father to death on his daughter's wedding day; anything's possible where human nature is concerned, as witness my friend Tyrsenius and Callixena, or Anabruzas and his son. But I was taught to yap like a dog when I was a boy, and I've come to the conclusion that it's as good a way of looking at the world as any, and probably better than most. So sue me.

In the twelfth year of the colony we finally got a decent growth of grapes, and I was pleased and proud to announce, in my official capacity as *oecist*, that henceforth, for the first time in its history, our city was going to be self-sufficient in booze.

Naturally, we had to celebrate; but instead of letting us have a cheerful spur-of-the-moment party, our noble Founders decided that it would be more appropriate to combine our first vintage with a ceremony of thanksgiving to commemorate our tenth anniversary. This was an eminently reasonable thing to do in our twelfth year (by Founder logic, at any rate), and the highlight of the affair would be the official dedication of the city, something we'd unaccountably forgotten to do twelve years back, preferring to fritter away our time on building stockades and digging latrines.

The slight difficulty was that, in order to dedicate a city, you really do need to have a name for it, and we still hadn't got round to thinking of one.

Instead, we'd thought of several. The Nowheresville joke had worn thin by now, and most of us simply referred to the place as Polis, 'the city'. Our Greek neighbours called us Nea Polis ('the *new* city') or Macedones ('the Macedonians'), or just Houtoi ('Oh, *Them*'). After Philip's death, the Founders stopped calling it Philipsville-in-the-best-of-all-possible-worlds, for some reason, and found ways of phrasing their remarks so as to avoid naming it at all. What the Scythians called us we didn't know for sure, though we could guess.

So, for a month or two before the planned vintage party, we talked about nothing else but what we were going to call the city. It was a game that everybody could play, and once the obligatory jokes were out of the way, we took it surprisingly seriously. I guess it was a sign that we'd finally stopped thinking of ourselves as Macedonians or Athenians or Corinthians, or even as Illyrians or, come to that, Budini; we no longer regarded stories of what was going on as news from home, but rather as strange and rather irrelevant happenings in places we used to know, in a part of our lives that was getting more and more distant and improbable-seeming with every successive harvest and winter. We were, in other words, all starting to think of ourselves as citizens of *something*, so it's logical, I suppose, that we should take an intelligent interest in what *something* was going to be called.

Tyrsenius, in a fit of that nauseating sentimentality that was becoming an increasingly dominant facet of his personality, proposed that we call the place Callixene, after his wife. On another level, of course, it could be interpreted as meaning 'beautiful foreign city', but that didn't do terribly much for the rest of us, because of course it wasn't foreign any more, it was home. A Founder called Menippus suggested Apoecia, which means both 'colony' and 'home from home'; neat, but too slick for us. We wanted something plain but substantial. Another Founder suggested Euxenopolis – a triple meaning; 'city friendly to strangers', 'city on the Black Sea' and 'city founded by Euxenus', but I persuaded him to withdraw the suggestion by offering to cut his throat for him if he didn't. Nobody seemed to care much for my suggestion, Alexandria ap'Olbia. Obviously, this was blatant patronage-seeking, just the sort of minor toadying that Alexander would appreciate – our balance of payments position wasn't getting any worse, but it wasn't improving much, either, and rather too much of the silver money we earned from selling our surplus grain to our better-established neighbours (for resale to the old country) tended to stay with them as interest on their original loans to us from a decade ago. For the price of our self-respect, we might be able to coax Alexander into letting us have some of the money his father had promised us and never sent, which would make it possible to clear off some of the overhead and start building up a little working capital of our own. When I tried to explain this idea, however, the eyelids of my fellow citizens began to droop and the eyes beneath those lids began to glaze, and I gave it up before I made myself unpopular.

In the end it came down to two contenders; Apollonia, because our temple was nominally dedicated to Apollo (and the reason for that was that Agenor the sculptor happened to have a statue of Apollo on his hands, as the result of a cancelled order, and offered it to the temple wardens at next best thing to cost); or Antolbia ('Just across the way from Olbia'), a suggestion which, for all its manifold and obvious faults, at least had the virtue of being both accurate and useful for traders who wanted to visit us but didn't know where to look for us.

We settled on Antolbia – it turned out there was another Apollonia near enough to cause problems – and moved on to the next phase of the job in hand, namely getting ready for our vintage party.

Well, the first thing you need for a successful vintage party is wine; so we made some of that, quite a lot of it, in fact. Needless to say we made our wine Greek style, and since (if the muck in the cup in front of me as I write is anything to go by) you people still have a lot to learn about this noble art, I think I'd better describe how we go about it. This isn't a hint or anything; but the duty of a historian is to record things which may prove useful or inspiring to future generations, so pay close attention.

Now then; it's early autumn, Arcturus is rising and the grapes are the right size and shape. Having secured the services of everybody in your community who can walk but not move fast enough to get out of the way when you come round recruiting, you hasten to the vineyard, taking with you an ample supply of large wicker baskets, fine-meshed nets and the makings of your pressing-box. If possible, induce the others to do the hot, back-breaking work of filling the baskets with grapes. You'll be far better off assembling the pressing-box, which consists of a block of timber about four feet square, with raised sides, four legs (the front pair shorter than the back pair) and a spout at the front for the grape-juice to drain through. Willing helpers then take the bunches of grapes from the baskets and load them into a dirty great bag made out of light, flexible wickerwork, which fits nicely inside the pressing-box. You then scramble up into the box and start crushing the grapes through the bag, starting off by using your knees, then standing up and squeezing out the remaining juice with firm, even pressure from the soles of your feet. The juice drains off down the spout into jars, which you later load onto your cart, take home and decant into your large fermentation vessels, where it stays for at least six months, until you've finished all your pruning and Arcturus starts rising at dusk; only then do you tap it off into small jars, seal them with resin and either drink it or sell it to the unwary. This method produces a light, sharp white wine that you can drink all night in a half-and-half mix without dying or having to be taken home in a wheelbarrow.

The other method we sometimes used, which is vastly inferior but still better than yours, is to cart the grapes home and crush them in a huge baked-earth vat, big enough to hold your entire crop of grapes and at least three people, and fitted with a tap or spigot a foot or so above ground level. You leave the skins and pips in with the juice, cover the vat over with dressed hides and go away for six months or so, until it's time to draw off the dark, murky result of your endeavours into jars. This method gets you a heavy red wine that tastes of decay and death, and which is best drunk neat, with plenty of honey and grated cheese, by people who lead unhappy lives in some distant town.

Well, we made our wine by the first method, and settled down to wait for it to perform its small miracle. We had plenty of work to be getting on with in the meanwhile; ploughing and sowing, getting the beans in, followed by late ploughing at solstice and breaking up the fallow to let the frost in. As the summer faded, it became cool enough to sit out in the sun at midday, so we were able to catch up on the backlog of lawsuits we'd had to hold over during the hot season. That year, I recall, we had the Attack Rainwater case, which has stuck in my mind for no great reason other than the incredible ferocity with which it was waged by the two fools involved in it.

The fundamental premise was reasonable enough. If your neighbour's land lies above yours on the hillside and it's been an unusually hot summer (as this one was) there's always a risk that if it rains heavily, the run-off will come cascading down the slope in a flood and wash out anything you've planted that happens to get in its way. The defendant in this case had anticipated this contingency when he first moved in and took the place in hand twelve years previously; he'd dug a conduit to run the water across the side of the hill and down to his barns, where it could be used for watering the animals and do some good. But there hadn't been any flash floods for the next ten years, and in the meanwhile his neighbour (the plaintiff) had been rather careless about letting his goats wander, so the defendant built a stone wall on his downhill boundary to keep the four-legged pirates out. In building this wall he blocked the (by now forgotten) conduit; so when the rains came after our long, hot summer and the water was pouring down the hill in sheets, instead of being led safely away into docile captivity it dammed up at the foot of the wall, overflowed and rampaged through the plaintiff's onion patch like a Spartan army.

There followed a sharp and forthright exchange of opinions between the parties, followed in turn by a punch-up and litigation. It wouldn't have been so bad if the defendant (an Illyrian) hadn't convincingly won the punch-up, thereby changing the nature of the conflict from a dispute between neighbouring farmers into a rematch in the eternal battle between good and evil.

If ever there's a vacancy among the Judges of the Dead, and I'm co-opted to fill it, the first thing I'll do is recommend that they punish people who've been very wicked indeed in this life by making them members of a jury hearing a dispute between two farmers. It's a fine irony that, whoever wins or loses the case itself, the people who suffer most are the poor fools who have to sit still for the best part of a day and find some way of staying awake while, for example, a small, excitable Greek and a large, taciturn Illyrian share their feelings for each other in a public place. The plaintiff, a man who seemed to believe that the more often you say something the truer it gets, alienated me so badly while presenting his side of the argument that I'd have unhesitatingly found for the defendant if the court had risen immediately after they turned over the clock. Once the defendant started to speak, however, I quickly revised my judgement. Where the plaintiff had told a simple tale at insufferable length, the defendant tried to compress a bewilderingly complicated narrative into a few incomplete sentences and a succession of inarticulate grunts. As far as I could reconstruct what he was actually trying to say, his argument was that he couldn't be charged with Blocking A Watercourse Recklessly Or With Intent (which was what he was accused of in the statement of claim) because there had never been enough rain in previous years to cause a sufficient overflow, and so water had never actually coursed down the said conduit, which meant it had never been a watercourse within the meaning of the statute; further or in the alternative, he'd been more or less forced to build his wall by the ferocious onslaughts of his neighbour's goats, which had frequently done more damage in an afternoon than the water had wrought in the space of a month; 'furthermore,' he'd added, 'what was I supposed to do with all that water anyhow? Drink it?' This wasn't really what you'd call a convincing legal argument, but at least I could see the point he was trying to make without having to twist my imagination at right-angles to my brain.

Clearly the fair and equitable thing for me to do as a juror was to ignore the evidence of both sides and go with the version of events as set out in the pleadings, which reduced the whole thing to a straightforward question of law. Now, it's a sad but universal fact that when people are sitting under a tree on a pleasantly warm afternoon dreaming up laws for their city, they tend to devote most of their time and ingenuity to the exciting stuff, such as murder, rape and assault. By the time they get around to considering civil suits, particularly those likely to have a rural setting, it's late and the wine ran out an hour or so ago and the fun is wearing a bit thin; they tend to skimp and rush through, and when these laws come to be put into practice, this weakness shows up with a vengeance. We'd gone a stage further down the road to chaos and confusion by basing our farm law on the models set out by Plato in one of his perfect-society pamphlets, a decision we came to regret quite quickly. Stickler for annoying detail though he was, Plato never went so far as actually to define a watercourse; was it a ditch or trench through which water actually passed, or a ditch or trench intended to be used for the transmission of water, whether or not water actually ever came in contact with it? I agonised over this point without reaching any decision until it was time for the jury to start voting, at which point I asked myself the simple question, *Which of these two imbeciles would you least like to live next to?* I went with my instincts, and gave judgement for the defendant.

In fact the plaintiff won, though there were only four votes in it. There was a much closer consensus on the amount of damages; we awarded him the value of his ruined onions, less the value of the damage done by his goats, resulting in a net award of the price of a medium-sized jar of dried figs. Personally I'd have gone further and included an additional award against both of them for wasting a specified proportion of my life in a manner likely to cause aggravated pain and suffering; but I don't suppose either of them could have afforded to pay such an enormous sum.

Well now, Phryzeutzis, I'm sure that by now you've tumbled to the fact that I've been trying, in my heavy-handed way, to give you some idea of what real life in this perfect society of ours was like, twelve years into its history. You'll have noticed that it was by no means perfect, and it didn't have much in common with those high-minded and carefully crafted model constitutions we used to play around with after dinner back in Athens. I don't know if that was a good thing or a bad thing; we had no real government to speak of, just the Founders (whom everybody ignored as a matter of course) and me, who tried his level best to avoid doing any governing unless compelled to do so by force. We had no foreign policy, because it never occurred to us that we were grown-up enough to need one. As far as economic policy went, we had my friend Tyrsenius, the man who sold overpriced ornamental armour and unserviceable weapons to our potential enemies, and urged us to borrow money from our neighbours that we never had a hope in hell of ever paying back. We had just enough law and order to discourage us from cutting each other's throats. As for politics; well, we had better things to do with our time. And yes, we made a hash of quite a lot of things, we drifted far enough away from our original intentions that not only the Illyrians but some of the Budini were able to fit in and make themselves at home. We produced no literature, art, science or philosophy. We had no time to spare for the finer things in life. What's more, we didn't care. It wasn't Athens (but in Athens you could be put on trial for blasphemy, or slandering the City in front of foreigners, or failing to farm your own land to an acceptable standard of husbandry; you could be put to death for proposing a law to repeal another law, if you went about it the wrong way; you could be executed for refusing to take either side in a civil war; and every year we had a ballot to exile a certain number of people, not because they'd done anything wrong but just because nobody liked them very much); and it wasn't Macedon either. By a process of elimination, we were forced to the conclusion that it was Antolbia; nothing more, nothing less.

That, then, was the opinion most of us had of ourselves while we were planning our monumental civic thrash in honour of a dozen years of nationhood; and by and large, we liked what we saw in the mirror. There's a part of me that wishes I could have taken that young Prince Alexander I once helped to capture a hive of bees on a leisurely tour round Antolbia instead of trying to teach him the art of war and the knack of scanning elegiac couplets. There were things he'd have seen there that might just have answered some of the questions he tried to resolve by leading the Macedonian army to the very edge of the world, and possibly the answers he'd have come across with me would have been a hair's breadth closer to the truth. By the same token, if I was made of pottery and had smaller ears, I'd be a jar. It's hard enough writing history without trying to rewrite it as well.

The Founders wanted to kick off with a procession – lots of smiling children with their faces washed and their hair combed – carrying baskets of freshly baked bread and seasonal fruits from the place where the first ship landed to the temple. This would be followed by communal singing of the Homeric Hymn to Apollo and selections from Pindar, after which we could relax with a recital of flute and harp music and an athletics contest.

The rest of us felt that if that was the Founders' idea of a big time, then good luck to them. What we wanted to do was drink excessively and make a lot of noise, and possibly even round the celebration off by smashing up a few redundant statues (such as the one of me that had been plonked down, much against my will, in an alcove round the side of the market hall. On many a dark night I'd tried to nerve myself to go and do mischief to it with a big hammer; I just couldn't bear the thought of the look on the Founders' faces if one of them had caught me at it).

In the end, we compromised; procession, edited highlights of the Homeric Hymn, and a big vat of booze in the middle of the square for everybody to dip a cup in. My contribution to the success of this consensus was persuading Founder Perdiccas to donate three sheep and three goats for sacrifice and subsequent barbecue, a result I achieved by thanking him in public for his exceptionally generous offer without asking him first. A highly effective ploy, that, and one I recommend to you.

Early reports on the wine suggested it was going to turn out drinkable, though of course there'd be no way of knowing until we actually racked it off. There was a degree of apprehension among the gloomier of the self-professed experts; they held that the richer, deeper soil and milder temperature of Olbia might tend to produce a more watery, fruity wine without the subtle malice of Greek vintages. Up to a point, their concern proved to be justified when the first jars were opened; the stuff tasted sweet and bland, prompting them to reduce the water in the mix from a half to a third. The consequences of this experiment were dramatic; you drank a pint or so of the stuff to no apparent effect, and a quarter of an hour later you fell over. On balance, we decided that this was a good thing, the stuff that truly heroic binges are made of.

'Wake up,' Theano said to me, just before dawn on the day of the festival.

I grunted. 'Why?' I said. 'Is it that time already?'

'No,' she replied. 'But I want to get the house straight before we go, and you're making the room look untidy.'

My son Eupolis was one of the basket-bearers in the procession. In essence, his job was to walk from A to B without tripping over or dropping the basket, and both Theano and I had grave reservations about whether he'd manage it. However, he seemed quite relaxed about it all when we finally managed to prise him out of his bed and chivvy him into his clothes (specially made for the occasion and almost a good fit) so we worried about me instead. As *oecist* I was not only reciting some of the magic words during the formal part of the ceremony but also reputedly making a keynote speech, after the Hymn but before the drinking started. As you can imagine I'd given this speech a great deal of thought. The first draft was about twenty minutes long and packed with references to the wisdom of the Founders, the unreliable protection of the gods and other lofty themes. The final version was a loose paraphrase of 'Drinks on the house!', which at least had the merit of giving the people what they wanted to hear.

'You're not proposing to go out looking like that, are you?' Theano said.

'Yes,' I replied. 'Why not?'

'For one thing,' she said, 'it's too small. For another, there's a dirty great patch just above the left shoulder, and it isn't even the same colour.'

I frowned. 'I wore this same tunic on the day we made landfall,' I said. 'I thought it'd be a nice touch if I wore it today, just to demonstrate—'

'What a scruffy slob you've become. No thank you. People always blame the wife, and it's not fair. Go and change.'

She also insisted that I take the jar – you remember, *the* jar, the one that didn't have a snake in it. Actually, I didn't object; it was Olympias' belief that there was a snake in it that had led to all of us being here, so it seemed appropriate, in a twisted kind of way.

Against all expectations, I enjoyed the procession. Meaningless civic rituals have never done very much for me, but just for once I was able to kid myself that this one wasn't meaningless. And yes, dammit, I felt ever so slightly proud when I saw my son toddling along at the front of the line, grimly clinging to his basket, eyes determinedly forward, like the spearman at the apex of a wedge formation going into battle. Sure, it was cheesy and sentimental; but the bread in the basket and the basket itself had been made in Antolbia, and it was high time we showed our gratitude to Apollo, on the off chance that he really did exist. You'll gather that I'm not a particularly religious man, but there are certain times when the act of religion is far more important than whether or not there really is an Apollo or a Zeus. Maybe it's moments like that which create gods. Who knows?

We shuffled up into line to sing the Hymn.

We left the gate open.

Well, it didn't seem important.

There's a certain comic irony in the fact that the line we were singing at the moment when it started was, *I will remember and not be unmindful of Him who shoots from afar,* because we hadn't, of course. We'd clean forgotten. Like most of the survivors I've talked to, I can clearly remember what I was thinking the instant before the first arrow struck; I was thinking that since the grapes we grew in Olbia were fatter and pulpier than the average Greek grape, it stood to reason that with a little care we ought to be able to make a genuinely sweet white wine, like the stuff you occasionally get from Phoenicia. The image in my mind was of a big, plump grape, its skin just starting to split under the pressure of a man's knee in the pressing-box. I could see the first big teardrop of juice oozing out of the split and running down the side of the grape, cutting a channel in the dusting of yeast.

Then somebody screamed. We all looked up, wondering what was going on.

I was at a picnic once, out in the fields at Phyle. We'd gone out on the pretext of making an offering at the shrine there – I can't have been more than seven years old – and we children were playing running-about games when some fool threw a stone and hit a hollow tree that happened to house a swarm of wild bees. Out they came, like cavalry appearing unexpectedly on your unprotected flank; and at once the picnic party broke up in wild, grotesque panic – people running backwards and forwards, their hands over their faces, crashing into each other, knocking over the jugs and jars, breaking crockery, swearing, squealing. I'd never actually encountered wild bees before and I just stood there like an idiot, trying not to get trodden on. Because I stayed put and didn't identify myself as a target the bees left me alone, but the rest of the party got thoroughly stung. At the time I thought the whole thing was rather amusing and wonderful.

It took a while for us to realise that there were people behind us, shooting arrows. We couldn't imagine who'd be doing such a thing until we actually saw them; genuine wild Scythians, tall men on rather undersized horses, performing the hardest of all martial manoeuvres, shooting from the saddle. Amazing, the skill of these people; they drop the reins completely and guide the horse with nothing more than gentle pressure from their knees, while using both hands to draw and aim their bows. I don't suppose I'd ever have been able to learn the trick; it must be something you're born to. I've even seen them string the bow at full gallop, one-handed.

I saw Melanthius, one of the Founders, stagger and drop to his knees. I never liked Melanthius much. I saw Eurygye, the wife of a man whose name I've forgotten but who helped me build my first barn, trying to haul herself along the ground on her elbows because an arrow had lodged in her spine. She was sixty if she was a day, and so badly troubled with arthritis that she found it hard to get about freely at the best of times. I saw Azus, my Budini bodyguard, struggling to string his bow without even trying to pull out the arrow that was lodged between his collar-bone and neck tendon. I saw Agenor, the stonemason, pushing people down and shouting. I saw Perdiccas the Founder running at a Scythian horseman with a meat-cleaver in his hand; but the Scythian saw him first and sliced off the top of his bald head with his scimitar, like a fussy man tackling a boiled egg. I saw Theano, sensible girl, ducked down behind an overturned table, holding up a bronze meat-dish like a shield. I saw Bollus, an Illyrian who once returned a stray goat of mine, shoot a Scythian from his saddle at seventy-five yards. I was just standing there, quite still, clutching my jar that didn't contain a snake, and nobody seemed very interested in me. I've said this before; whenever something happens, I'm always on the sidelines, though just for once I wasn't looking the other way. I saw Jason, the Illyrian wheelwright who was such an expert on the diseases of sheep, pinned by an arrow to a door, while his wife threw plates at the Scythian who'd shot him; he was coming back for her with his scimitar, but she hit him in the face with a plate, it broke and drew ever such a lot of blood; he wiped it away and so was able to see, and then she hit him again – but he killed her before she could throw again. I saw my friend Tyrsenius, with one arm hanging limp and useless at his side while he hacked a fallen horseman to death with the captured scimitar he held in his good hand. I saw my son Eupolis running towards our house, and I watched the arrow that killed him all the way from the bow.

I didn't see Marsamleptes and Charicles the Founder lead the counter-attack that finally drove them off; apparently they went for them with sticks and pots and their bare hands (I saw a bee-keeper once capture a wild swarm with nothing but an empty honey-jar; he judged the moment just right and swiped the whole swarm out of the air and into the jar, and he didn't get stung). Nothing bad happened to me while all this was going on. Afterwards, people said the snake protected me, same as bloody always.

I suppose the attack lasted about the time it takes to bring a basin of water to the boil; it seemed longer, while at the same time it was all over in a moment. Someone shut and bolted the gate, while others manned the wall. People were running or walking, calling out names, screaming, sobbing. Agenor, who didn't know much about medicine but who'd seen his fair share of nasty accidents while he was working as a stonemason, was organising people to see to the wounded, sorting out the dying from the merely damaged. The basic principles of looking after badly injured people are calm and patience; I once watched Agenor piecing together a shattered vase that I'd simply have given up on and thrown away. Of course, it's that bit harder to throw away people, but the temptation's there all the same.

I went over and looked at the body of my son, who was every bit as dead as Philip of Macedon (why did I think of that, I wonder, at such a moment? Sure, I wasn't thinking straight; it was like the time I stood up sharply under a low beam and gave my head the most almighty crack. For a long time, everything seemed to be very slow and far away, and I remember wondering whether I was still alive, and being pleasantly surprised to discover that I was).

They were using the wine to clean out scimitar-wounds. I saw two children standing very still, looking down at a dead body. They were just as still as I was; then one of them kicked the body, which was almost but not quite dead, presumably because it was Scythian – only it wasn't, it was Budini, and he'd died with his axe in his hand, trying to fight the enemies of his people. Made no difference really, of course, a kick in the head from a child was neither here nor there in his condition, but it was the total lack of expression on the boy's face that lodged in my mind, like the barbed sting of a bee.

I'd never known Theano go all to pieces before. Hardly surprising, of course; but like I said I wasn't thinking straight. I expected her to be cold and hard, to lock her feelings out or shove past them, like a bad-mannered man in the fish queue. But she didn't; she broke up into tears and rages, and I'm ashamed to say I left her to get on with it.

As for myself I was – we have this expression for someone who's blind drunk, 'feeling no pain'; that was me. It was very much like being drunk, that aimless, drifting, out-of-it feeling when you're using everything you've got just to keep your balance and not fall over, nothing to spare for anything less immediate. In a sense, you're never more intimately aware of being alive, because all the things you usually do without thinking take so much conscious effort. Yes, that was me. Feeling no pain. I was completely out of it. I guess the snakes protected me.

Whenever you get really huge disasters, there's always so much work to be done afterwards, so much clearing up and mending, digging graves and covering for the people who've been injured and can't milk their own goats; so many strategy meetings and heads-of-department meetings – just when we could have used the Founders, we had five dead and seven seriously wounded – and who knows what else. As an excuse for staying out of the house, they were just what the doctor ordered. I really pulled my weight over the next few days.

Azus, my bodyguard, died on the fourth day after the attack, of blood poisoning. I was with him when he died, and all he could talk about was how he'd let me down, how he hadn't done his job, how he should have saved my son's life. I told him not to worry about it, but he didn't want to listen. He died with tears running down his face, trying to think of the Greek word for honour. Oddly enough, I couldn't remember it either.

CHAPTER SIXTEEN

'Kill the bastards,' they told me. 'Kill all of them. Every one.'
'Believe me, I'd like to,' I replied. 'Nothing would please me more. Now, if someone would just suggest a way of going about it that won't get all the rest of us killed—'

'Wrong answer.' My friend Tyrsenius shook his head. 'If you say that, some hothead's bound to stand up and say he's got a plan that'll bring 'em to their knees by the end of the month, and everybody'll start cheering and waving their arms; and either you'll have to hand over command to him or take it yourself. Either way, it spells disaster.'

'And what if it was one of the Illyrians,' Prodromus the Founder added, 'and he actually took command and he won? We might as well turn over the government of the city to them now and be done with it. That's exactly how Cleon grabbed power in Athens during the Great War, when the Spartans were on Sphacteria.'

That sounded like typical Founder talk to me, but I wasn't in the mood to play political games. 'All right, then,' I sighed. 'So what do you suggest I tell them? Anybody?'

'Easy,' said Tyrsenius, getting in ahead of the others by a comfortable margin; years of practice in business negotiations. 'They say, Kill the bastards. You say, We will. We're going to. We're working on it right now. Obviously it's going to be a while before we're in a position to make our move, but you can rest assured that as soon as the moment's right we're going to make them pay. Something like that,' he added. 'There's absolutely nothing anybody can object to there, and you haven't committed yourself to anything.'

I shook my head. 'Sounds to me like I've just committed myself to military action against the Scythians,' I said. 'They're not fools, you know; that line might get them off our backs for a week or so, but they aren't going to forget all about it as soon as there's something new to talk about. And the longer I hang about, the weaker my position's going to get.'

Tyrsenius thought for a moment. 'All right,' he said, 'let's try this. It's an old trick, but I've never known it fail. You say, Yes, of course we're going to attack, we're going to attack straight away, just as soon as the rest of the alliance are ready, which'll be any day now. And whoever's asking the question'll look bewildered and say, Alliance, what alliance? Ah, well, you'll reply, I wasn't planning on making an announcement on this until it was all agreed a hundred per cent, but I've been talking with our neighbours in Olbia and Odessus; basically the only thing we've still got to agree on is the precise number of ships they're going to send. That way, you see,' Tyrsenius added, 'when time goes on and nothing happens, it'll be their fault in Olbia and Odessus, not ours. And then finally, when you've played it along as far as it'll go, you make an announcement that the alliance isn't actually going to happen, because the other guys have pulled out at the very last moment; and by then, of course, they'll be so used to the idea of the alliance that they won't want to take the risk of just us going in alone. And the whole thing'll blow over, which is what we want.'

Prodromus looked up sharply. 'No, it isn't,' he said.

'Don't be ridiculous,' Tyrsenius snapped. 'We aren't getting tangled up in any war with the Scythians. Why the hell would we want to do a stupid thing like that?'

I closed my eyes for a moment. 'Tyrsenius,' I said.

'Oh, come *on*,' he replied incredulously. 'Don't say you've actually been taking this nonsense seriously.'

The very same Tyrsenius who'd demanded, a mere four days earlier, that when we took the village (*when*, mark you, not *if*), we should burn down all the houses and plough up the site, and distribute the land between our citizens. I knew where he was coming from then; he was already looking ahead to buying up all this extra land cheap, once everyone had realised it'd be completely impractical to try to farm a large additional holding a day's ride from Antolbia, with a view to selling it dear to the next wave of settlers he was already planning to bring in once the Scythians had been dealt with. It was gold to bronze he had an equally sound commercial reason for this latest change of heart, but I really wasn't interested in hearing about it.

(The very same Tyrsenius who killed four Scythians during the raid, pulling them down from their horses and hacking them to death with one of their own scimitars; all this in spite of having been shot through the left bicep in the first volley of arrows, losing so much blood that when it was all over he passed out and nearly died in the night. I, of course, just stood there and did nothing, while the sacred snake shielded me in its coils and flicked flying arrows away from my head with its tongue.)

'I can't believe I'm hearing this,' Prodromus was saying meanwhile. 'Euxenus, for gods' sakes, the whole future of the colony's at stake here. How the hell can we be expected to get on with our lives with the threat of something like this hanging over us every day till we die? You've got to do something and it'd better be soon. Two more families are talking about getting on the next ship out. Soon there'll be nobody left here but the Illyrians.'

He was making me lose my temper. 'That's what's really bugging you, isn't it?' I said angrily. 'You're afraid that unless we true-born Greeks take control of the situation, the Illyrians are going to lose patience and go off on their own to do something about it; and then you won't be a Founder any more, just some Greek who's got to work for a living.'

'I resent that,' Prodromus replied, predictably enough. 'I think you'd better take that back, before—'

'Hey,' I said. 'That'll do. As it happens, I agree with you, not Tyrsenius. I *want* to kill the bastards, every last one. It's them or us; there's no way we can live peacefully together after what's happened, and I wouldn't want to if there was. All I'm saying is, unless we do it right they're going to massacre us.'

'That's nonsense,' Prodromus said. 'Isn't it?'

The last part of his remark had been directed at Marsamleptes, who'd been sitting there still and quiet as a log, through all Prodromus' comments about the shifty and treacherous Illyrians, without once taking his eyes off the sconce on the opposite wall.

'No,' he said. 'Euxenus is right. If we attack, we must do it properly.'

'If?' Prodromus repeated. 'Don't you start. It's bad enough Tyrsenius here wants to pretend nothing's happened. For pity's sake, Euxenus, just for once take your responsibilities seriously and tell him—'

I held up my hand for silence and, much to my surprise, I got it. 'When we attack – shut up, both of you, or you might miss something important – *when* we attack, we're going to do it properly. Now, so far I haven't heard any suggestions as to how we should go about this that make any kind of sense at all. Until I see a plan of action that's got a better than seventy-five per cent chance of success, we aren't going anywhere, because if you think things are bad now, you wait and see what they'll be like if we attack and get well and truly beaten. That really would be the end, and I've come too far to take chances like that just because you Founders want to be the first in line in the fish queue.'

The homely image was intended to annoy him, and it did; nothing put Prodromus' back up more than the thought that he wasn't being taken seriously. That said, he was one of the brighter Founders, and I much preferred dealing with him than, say, Perdiccas—

(Whose brains I'd seen on the steps of the market hall; four days later, there was still a brown stain. When we buried him we tried to fit the top of his skull back on, but the scalp had shrunk. We had to bind it on with a strip of cloth in the end; he went into the ground looking like an old woman with her shawl pulled up over her ears.)

'All right,' Prodromus said. 'I'll take that as a definite commitment to action, and I'll tell the rest of them that I've heard your proposals for action and I'm prepared to go along with them. But I warn you, if I find you're playing for time and you don't really have any intention of carrying the war to the enemy, I promise you there'll be trouble.'

I rubbed my eyes; four days with very little sleep. 'I'll take that as agreement,' I said. 'Not that I'm all that fussed whether you agree or not. Now then, Marsamleptes; how about some basic facts? What sort of army can we put together?'

He thought for a long time before answering. 'We are strong in heavy infantry,' he replied, speaking slowly as ever, 'very weak in everything else. My people can mostly shoot well with the bow, but they will want to fight with the spear. The Budini are fine archers, but there are so few of them. We have no cavalry. If we mean to fight, we must lead to their strength and find a way of overcoming it.'

'I see,' I replied. 'And their strengths are?'

'Cavalry,' he replied. 'Cavalry and archers. I cannot tell how a battle between horse-archers and heavy infantry would be, because I have never seen one, but I think the horse-archers would win if they were well led.'

'Not necessarily,' Tyrsenius interrupted. 'Look at Leonidas at Thermopylae. Or the Greeks at Plataea. Or Xenophon—'

I frowned. Of course, none of the examples he'd quoted had involved horse-archers fighting against heavy infantry. 'Marsamleptes,' I said. 'If you had to fight such a battle, how would you go about it?'

Once again, long pause for thought. 'Tyrsenius talks about the battle at Plataea,' he said. 'When the Persians shot at the Greeks, the Greeks knelt down behind their shields and made themselves small, and the Persians grew impatient and attacked them with the spear. That was a mistake on their part.' He looked up at the roof. 'Maybe the Scythians would make a mistake too. I doubt it, having seen them. It would be hard to attack them in this way, of course.'

'I'm not so sure,' Tyrsenius chimed in. 'Think of the Carthaginians at Himera.'

That reference was so obscure I didn't even bother considering it. 'You want to make them attack us, I take it,' I said.

'Which they will not do,' Marsamleptes went on, 'unless they make another mistake. There are more of us. Why would they choose to attack a larger army?'

'I can see your point,' I conceded. 'You'd better go away and think about it some more. Prodromus, I want you to calm your people down as much as you can. Tyrsenius' idea about sending for help to Olbia's a good one. Tyrsenius, I want you to write to your friends in Olbia, just in case they might be prepared to help us. I know, they haven't got any quarrel with their neighbours, but you might play up the idea that once they've got rid of one Greek colony, they might like the idea of getting rid of them all. And you might make enquiries about mercenaries; light infantry, archers, maybe even some experienced Thracian cavalry if there's any at a loose end.'

Tyrsenius shook his head. 'I doubt it,' he said. 'Anybody who's any good will have gone with Alexander. You should see what he's paying.'

That's right, I'd forgotten; Alexander had set out with his army to conquer the world.

You know all about it, of course, Phryzeutzis, you were brought up on it. When you were little, your daddy told you stories about the great warrior who founded this city. Later on, you listened to the recital of the official history on Founder's Day, the day when all the children get given an apple and a honey-cake, to bribe them to be good citizens when they grow up. I'll bet you can name the great battles, in places you've never been to, in countries you can't imagine; when you were a child, I expect you recreated them in places you knew, so that the stream that runs down off the mountain became the Granicus, and the brook through the town meadow became the Issus. You staged the siege of Tyre here in the city; it must have been a tight fit, all those hundreds of thousands of men crammed into our dusty little market square, with Alexander's vast siege ramps and assault towers poking their noses over our low, burned-brick wall. Where did you see Gaugamela, I wonder? Don't tell me; either the temple lot, before we started the building work, or the patch of scrubby orchard behind the water-tanks. Of course your Alexander will have been dark-haired and black-eyed, with a tall felt cap on his head as he rode his short-legged, round-nosed pony in the cavalry charge at Arbela – was Arbela the battle with the cavalry charge, or am I thinking of the Granicus? My Alexander, you see, is getting fainter as the years go by, while our civic Alexander gets bigger and bolder and more godlike as each year passes, as each year of children meet him for the first time on Founder's Day, with the cake sweating honey through their hot little fingers. The day will come when I won't recognise our Alexander at all, the way a senile father forgets his own children.

But we're not there quite yet; so indulge me and put aside your personal Alexander for a moment, or try to think of the man I'm going to talk about as someone else who coincidentally had the same name.

Before setting out on his great adventure, Alexander of Macedon cleared up all his father's outstanding business in Greece. He had four of his relatives murdered; they were too close to the throne to be left behind, and they weren't wanted on the journey. They were the two brothers of the King of Lyncestis, a bastard son of King Philip's and the son of Philip's elder brother, as whose regent Philip had been crowned in the first place.

Alexander went to Corinth with an army to be officially installed as Captain of the Greeks in his father's place. While he was there, so they tell me, he paid a visit to one Diogenes, known as the Yapping Dog, who'd moved to Corinth from Athens a few years earlier for the good of his health. Now, it may be that he remembered some of the things his old tutor had told him about Diogenes, or maybe the great philosopher (who I thought had been dead for years at this point) was included on every sightseeing tour; in any case, Alexander summoned Diogenes for an audience. Diogenes didn't turn up. So Alexander went to see Diogenes.

'Hello,' he said. 'My name is Alexander.'

Diogenes (or at any rate, *my* Diogenes) grunted and said nothing. He was sitting, naked as the day he was born, on a flat stone half a mile outside the city, staring up at the hills. As I picture him, he must have looked pretty much like a thin brown lizard. Alexander studied him for a few minutes, as if getting ready to write an essay for his next tutorial, while behind him the soldiers of his bodyguard shuffled their feet and the Corinthian civic dignitaries cringed with embarrassment and wondered how in hell they were going to get out of this in one piece.

'Are you all right, sitting there?' Alexander asked eventually.

'Mphm.'

'Is there anything I can do for you?'

Silence.

'Is there anything at all I can do for you? Anything you want? Just name it.'

Then this long brown lizard of mine turned his head and opened one lidless reptilian eye. 'Since you ask,' he said, 'there is.'

Alexander's lips curled in a small smile, an *I-thought-there-might-be* expression. He might have remembered being taught when he was a boy that power, like money, works rather like magic, because it can make people do things they normally wouldn't, and can make possible things that normally aren't. 'Name it,' he said, 'and you'll get it. You have my word.'

The lizard nodded. 'In that case,' he said, 'move a bit to the left. You're getting in my light.'

At which, so they tell me, this Alexander was bitterly offended, and it was only his respect for the grand old man of Yapping Dog philosophy that kept him from losing his temper and having the old fool punished. 'That's no favour for a king to grant,' he said.

'All right,' Diogenes replied. 'If it makes you any happier, give me a thousand talents in gold.'

Alexander smiled; a very thin smile, probably. 'That's no gift for a Yapping Dog to receive,' he said.

Diogenes nodded. 'Good answer,' he replied. 'I can see the time I spent on you hasn't been entirely wasted.'

Alexander raised one perfect godlike eyebrow. 'I don't follow you,' he said.

'What?' Diogenes sat up, resting on one elbow. 'Oh, sorry, for a moment there I thought you were someone I used to know.'

It was probably at this point that the Corinthian civic dignitaries suggested that now would be a good time to go and look at the new aqueduct.

After that, Alexander took an army into Thrace and Illyria and beat hell out of the natives there, for reasons that doubtless made a lot of sense at the time. He pushed up as far as the Danube – we heard about him from the Scythians (it was before the trouble started), who seemed to blame us for all the disturbance and bother their south-eastern cousins were having, though we assured them that Alexander was no fault of ours. He very nearly died up there, as a result of carelessness and overconfidence, but he pulled himself out again with some brilliantly imaginative improvisation that wouldn't have been needed if he'd been paying attention when we did Brasidas' northern campaigns . . .

But news of his supposed death reached the ancient and powerful city of Thebes, which for a while, in my father's time, had been the most important power in Greece. Immediately, the Theban government resolved to throw off the Macedonian yoke and restore their city to its former glory – a bit like the mice declaring war on the grain-bin once they've heard the cat is dead. At least one of their politicians urged a degree of caution; wait a week or so, he suggested, just in case. 'After all,' he told them, 'if Alexander's dead today, then he'll still be dead tomorrow. Who knows, he may even still be dead the day after tomorrow; and *then* we can declare war on Macedon.'

But nobody listened; which was a pity, because when Alexander came back to life again, he stormed Thebes, massacred the citizens and had the place levelled – except for the house where Pindar, the celebrated poet, was supposed to have lived a hundred years or so ago; it's nice to see that all those hot, dull afternoons scanning iambic pentameters under the fig-tree in Mieza turned him into a man of culture and refinement.

After that he went back to Macedon, where his mother had just murdered his father's second wife by roasting her alive over a charcoal brazier, to discover that he had inherited from his father a balance of payments deficit of three million drachmas, which, as I understand it, is roughly how much it would cost to build the Great Pyramid in Egypt.

To say he was annoyed would be an understatement. Imagine how Achilles would have felt if, having killed Hector under the Scaean Gate and stripped him of his armour, he'd had that same armour impounded by the bailiffs on account of unpaid forage bills. As far as Alexander was concerned, *his* Alexander wasn't supposed to have to bother with stuff like that, so he did the only honourable thing and pretended he hadn't heard. Instead, he borrowed a further five million drachmas (I have no idea who from) and marched into Asia with forty thousand men. His first stop, they tell me, was Troy, where he broke open the vault of the temple and helped himself to a shield that was supposed to have belonged to Achilles—

'Achilles was lucky,' he told someone at the time. 'He had Homer to praise him.'

What the other guy said is not, for some reason, recorded.

In spite of Tyrsenius' dire warnings, we did manage to hire some mercenaries; a hundred Budini horse-archers and fifty or so Thracian light cavalry. The Budini were very much like the ones we'd already met, but the Thracians were a miserable bunch, mostly men who'd been thrown out of their villages for antisocial behaviour of one sort or another. Nobody liked them very much, but they kept to themselves and only bothered those of us who hung around their camp looking for trouble. Nevertheless; we were paying them by the day and they weren't cheap, which was a further incentive to us to make a move.

Even so, I persuaded my colleagues to restrain their enthusiasm for a little longer, simply because the longer we left it, the better our chances would be of taking them off-guard. We needed the element of surprise. With our deficiency in cavalry, we couldn't mount the sort of lightning raid they'd hit us with, and besides, we had something rather more permanent in mind than killing a few people at random and torching a handful of buildings.

After endless meetings, discussions, debates, councils of war and other exercises in communal futility, I made a decision. I wasn't the best person to decide the matter, gods know, and I'm not entirely sure to this day whether I actually had the authority to be quite so unilateral about it, but what mattered was that nobody else knew I didn't have the authority. If I hadn't forced the issue, I console myself, we'd probably still be arguing about it now; or at any rate, our grandchildren would.

My idea was to send the Thracians on a make-believe cattle raid. If they were sufficiently convincing (and I couldn't see any reason why they wouldn't be; in their particular dialect of Thracian, the words for 'soldier', 'hero', 'cattle-thief' and 'unmitigated bastard' are all the same) this would have the effect of turning out the able-bodied and warlike inhabitants of the village *en masse*, leaving the way clear for us to walk in through the front gate. When the village warriors realised they'd been had, of course, they'd turn back and ride like hell for home, knowing perfectly well what the diversion was in aid of; at which point they'd be ambushed by the Budini and the infantry reserve, with the Thracians coming in at the end to murder and rob the walking wounded. Finally, the ambush contingent would join the main body of the army to help with the demolition work.

Two days before we were scheduled to go, I was sitting in the back room of my house polishing my armour. If you could have seen me then, you'd have got a very good idea of the priority that matters military had had in my general view of things up to that point, because my helmet and breastplate were as green as the lush grass of the Vale of Tempe, the clip in the left-hand greave had gone soft, and the little patch that had been brazed over the hole in the backplate, through which Death had come to visit the armour's previous one careful owner, had come away on two sides and was curling up like a dry leaf. That armour was worth exactly what I paid for it, which is another way of saying it was junk.

'Someone to see you,' Theano said. She had an expression on her face that I just couldn't place, though I could deduce enough to know it wasn't a happy one.

'All right,' I sighed, putting the breastplate down. 'I'll come through.'

As I walked into the main room, I nearly fell over.

'Well, you've got a nerve,' I said, as soon as I felt able to speak. 'What the hell are you doing here?'

Anabruzas, my old acquaintance, stood up. As he did so, the three men Marsamleptes had set to watch his every move started forward and grabbed their daggers. I frowned and shook my head, and they backed off, looking disappointed.

'Thank you for the welcome,' Anabruzas said. 'Is there any point trying to talk to you?'

I took a deep breath, nodded and told him to sit down. 'I'd always rather talk than fight,' I said. 'I suppose that's the difference between us. Now, what's on your mind?'

He looked at Marsemleptes' men, then at me, and sat down, rather as if he expected the chair to come alive and bite him. 'I told them not to do it,' he said. 'You know by now that I can't stop them doing something they've set their hearts on doing, but I did hope I could talk sense into them. I couldn't, so there it is.'

'I see,' I said. 'So you're telling me you have absolutely no authority to negotiate any kind of settlement.'

He rubbed his eyes, like a very tired man. 'What they're saying,' he replied, 'is that there's no point trying to talk to you now because after what happened, you're never going to listen. If I can go back to them and tell them otherwise, I might be able to make them see sense.'

I looked at him, then said, 'And if you do go back and tell them we're ready to talk, what makes you think they'll trust either of us?'

He smiled sadly. 'They know me,' he said. 'And they've dealt with Greeks long enough to know that they take this sort of thing seriously – you know, treaties and oaths and honour, the sort of thing you make laws and write poems about. Oh, you'll bend the law right back on itself if it gives you an advantage, but you'll stick to the letter of it. A wise man from one of the other nations of my people once said that Greek laws are like our bows; they're designed to be bent almost indefinitely but never to be broken.'

'That's neat,' I said. 'I must use it myself some time. And if I try really hard, I suppose I could interpret that as a compliment to our integrity. Now, do you have anything specific to propose, or is this just an exercise in vague hand-wringing?'

He shook his head. 'I have a very specific proposal,' he replied. 'I propose that we pay blood-money for your people who were killed, as if this was a family feud between us; then we join together to build a wall between your land and ours, which we both undertake never to cross without the other's leave. And, since you have no particular reason to trust us without some sort of security, we'll send you the second sons of each of our leading families as hostages; hereafter, for every Greek who's killed by one of us, you'll be entitled to execute five of our children.'

I nodded. 'That's a very favourable ratio,' I said. 'But personally I'd rather you simply gave up killing Greeks.'

'So would I,' he replied angrily. 'I still have one son left—'

'Which is more than can be said of me,' I broke in. I felt guilty for saying it, though I'm not sure why. It was as if it was cheating to equate his son with mine, because he'd loved his son . . . The thought made me frown.

He looked at me. 'I'm sorry,' he said, and I knew he meant it. 'But you must try to understand, we don't think the way you do, and I'm trying to be realistic. With the best will in the world I can't guarantee there won't be any more killings. If I pretended otherwise, I'd end up being proved a liar, and then there'd be no hope of peace after that. All I can do is try and arrange matters so that, if there is any more violence, we know that we'll come out of it far worse off than you. If there's anything else you think I can do, please tell me.'

I didn't say anything; I was thinking, what a remarkable man this was, a man who'd sent his own son to be ritually slaughtered by us the first time he'd tried to make peace; and here he was again, asking to be allowed to send us his other son, fully expecting that there'd be a time when we slaughtered him, too. This man was no philosopher, he didn't profess to disregard the material world as an unimportant illusion. There are philosophers and holy men who offer up their lives and the lives of those they love for the good of others because they put no value on life, and so they offer something they don't care much about. That's cheating, of course. And I've heard that among some of the Scythian tribes, when their king dies his wives and servants and companions are pleased and honoured to have their legs and necks broken and be buried in the same mound as their lord, because it means they'll go to the pastures in the land of the dead that are specifically reserved for kings and great lords, instead of the cold steppes where commoners go. That's cheating; it's haggling with death for a better deal, getting a higher price for what you've got to trade than it's actually worth. And those men who die in battle, whose names are read out before the people and whose sons are honoured on Remembrance Day with laurel crowns and suits of armour provided at public expense; everyone dies eventually, but at least they've bought something with their death, obtained an advantage that they haven't necessarily deserved. But I couldn't see where Anabruzas was taking his profit in this deal; he was paying out and there didn't seem to be anything in it for him. A strange man, and one I couldn't help admiring, insofar as it's possible to admire a fool.

'I'll tell you what I'll do,' I said. 'I'll talk to my people. I'll try to make them understand. I'm making no promises; that way, I won't be made a liar either. But please, bear this in mind. We don't want to have to fight you, or anybody. We don't like fighting, we don't have the same notions of honour and glory as you do; basically, we just want to know we're going to be left alone. If we have to defend ourselves, we'll do so as thoroughly and effectively as we possibly can, but we look at this sort of thing as if we were keeping accounts. Every dead Greek is a net loss, and we get no profit from killing any number of your people.'

He looked at me as if he expected me to say something else, as if what I'd been saying was obviously incomplete. 'That's all,' I said. 'Now you go away and do your best, and I'll do what I can. You never know, we might get out of this mess yet.'

An hour or so after he'd gone, Prodromus the Founder came bustling in with a face like thunder.

'I don't believe it,' he said. 'After everything we'd agreed. You gave your word.'

I had my hands full with a broken greave; I was trying to solder a new clip, but the fire wasn't hot enough to make the solder run. 'What are you babbling about now, Prodromus?' I asked.

'You made a deal with the Scythian,' he said. 'One of the guards who was here with you came and told me. You're betraying the trust of the whole city, I hope you know that.'

I sighed. 'Balls,' I said. 'I'm doing no such thing.'

He was speechless for a moment. 'Euxenus, you can't lie to me, I've heard everything that was said in this room. You told that man you'd do everything you could to promote a peaceful settlement.'

'I know,' I said. 'I was lying.'

'What did you say?'

'I was lying,' I repeated. 'I have absolutely no intention of trying to talk you and the rest of them out of attacking the village; partly because I know it wouldn't work, but mostly because I want to see that village burned to the ground and the heads of the men who killed my son stuck on poles among the ashes.'

Prodromus looked at me as if I was talking Persian. 'I don't understand,' he said. 'You told that man . . .'

'That's right. And he's gone back to his village, and right now I expect he's telling all the people how the Greeks are willing to talk, and this is their last, best hope for peace. With any luck, he may even convince them. Which'll make our job that much easier the day after tomorrow.'

I don't think I've ever seen anybody look as shocked in all my life. 'Euxenus, for the love of the gods,' he said. 'You can't do that, it's . . .'

'Clever,' I said. 'Is that the word you were looking for?'

'It's *inhuman*,' he shouted. 'It's disgusting. I refuse to have anything to do with it.'

I smiled. 'I can't remember asking you,' I replied, 'so that's all right. Oh, for pity's sake, Prodromus, we've all solemnly agreed that the day after tomorrow we're going to attack their village and kill the lot of them. Compared with that, a little white lie is neither here nor there.'

He stared at me as if I'd grown an extra head. 'I can't believe I'm hearing this,' he said. 'Not from an Athenian.'

'Ex-Athenian,' I reminded him. 'Now please, unless you're any good at soldering, shove off and stick your conscience where it won't get in the way. And if I were you, I'd keep my face well and truly shut for the next couple of days; that's unless you want the Scythians to learn what we've got planned for them. I have a feeling that our security isn't everything it should be, or how did they know the gate was going to be left open?'

He opened his mouth, then closed it again and went away without another word. And, in case you were wondering, I got the solder to run perfectly well after that. I suspect that before I hadn't been using enough flux.

The average Thracian, when you get to know him, is probably a decent enough fellow. I expect they herd their sheep and goats the same way we do, plant their barley and their beans, argue with their wives, spoil their children, fall out with their relatives, grumble about the weather, grow old and die exactly the same way as everybody else. By the same token, the average Thracian, like the average Greek, is born, lives and dies in his native village and never goes more than twenty miles from it in his whole life. It follows that the Thracians we hired weren't average Thracians, just as we weren't average Greeks.

So I can't justify a statement along the lines of 'All Thracians are worthless, treacherous bastards'; I must reserve my hatred and abuse for the particular bunch of Thracians I had dealings with, and that's all to the good; the fewer of them, the more hatred there is to go around.

Worthless, treacherous, *cowardly* bastards; they took our money, we gave them a relatively safe and perfectly simple job to do, and they cocked it up. I don't subscribe to the theory, popular around the city of Antolbia shortly after the events I'm about to describe, that their actions were deliberate, if only because they were far too stupid to have done what they did on purpose. If they'd been trying to screw up the operation they'd have got it wrong, and things wouldn't have turned out nearly so badly for us.

You'll remember the plan, Phryzeutzis; my plain, simple, logical plan whereby the Thracians were to drive off the Scythians' livestock, drawing the main war-party out of the village and leaving it open to our main army; meanwhile, once they'd realised they'd been tricked, the war-party would hurry back towards home and run straight into the ambush we'd set for them.

Well now. What could possibly go wrong?

On the day, I'd chosen to go with the reserve, who had the job of ambushing the war-party. Partly this was because that engagement was the only one that could possibly go wrong (the attack on the undefended village would just be a massacre, and you don't need to be an Alexander or a Brasidas to organise the slaughter of women and children), mainly because I didn't really want to be there when the non-combatants got killed. I know; hypocritical and pointlessly squeamish, but what the hell.

The Thracians set off just before dawn, and we followed almost immediately, since we had to get to the ambush site on foot. We arrived and were in position when the war-party set out. We watched them galloping furiously up the nicely conspicuous trail the Thracians had left, made a rough estimate of their numbers, which tallied nicely with what we knew of the fighting strength of our enemies, and did our best to keep calm and stay quiet while we waited for them to come back.

We waited.

A long time.

Noon came and went. Noon is a very hot time when you're crouched behind a rock in full armour, and as we hadn't anticipated being there for nearly that long, we hadn't burdened ourselves with much drinking water. If we stayed put, not only were we going to fry to death, we were also missing out on what was happening elsewhere – for all we knew, the Scythians had caught and obliterated the Thracians and, flushed with success, were sweeping down on unguarded Antolbia; if we moved, we ran the risk of being caught out in the open by the war-party and severely handled.

It was at this point in my reasoning that I gave up. Either way, I could picture myself facing an angry mob of Founders, all saying, 'How could you have been so *stupid*—?' It was bad, but not nearly as bad as finding out you've been sitting behind a rock all day while your friends and neighbours were being cut down where they stood by barbarian horsemen.

'Back to the city,' I ordered, 'quick as you like. You –' (referring to the hundred-odd Budini horse-archers) '– split up; fifty towards the city, fifty towards the village. Find out what's going on, send me a message, and do whatever you can to help if you're the ones who find the enemy. Got that?'

The Budini captain nodded, and gave his orders while I sat down again and rubbed my left calf in an attempt to disperse a savage attack of pins and needles. Not long after that we set off for the city at the double.

We'd gone about half the distance when a rider from the Budini contingent I'd sent to the city came galloping up with the news that the city was safe and the survivors of the attack had been coming in about the time he got there. I didn't like the sound of that word 'survivors' one little bit; but although the man's Greek was first rate for a Budini nomad, I couldn't make any sense of his attempts to clarify. In any event, whatever had happened appeared to have happened; there was no need to break our necks scrambling over rocks in a desperate rush to get home. We marched the rest of the way at normal speed.

'Where the hell were you?' they shouted at me as I led my men through the gate. It wasn't so bad. I'd been anticipating worse.

It was all the Thracians' fault. They'd dawdled, basically; they'd pottered along with the livestock so slowly that the war-party had caught up with them far earlier than expected, and came on them by surprise, taking them in flank and rear. This sort of thing could only be construed as proper grown-up fighting, which our expensive professional cavalry hadn't been expecting. They promptly panicked and broke away; but instead of carrying on down the road they swung north, in effect leading the war-party back towards the village. They managed to outrun their pursuers (when it came to serious, no-holds-barred running away, I have to concede that the Thracians did a spectacular job); but so fast and far did they run before shaking the Scythians off that the war-party arrived home at almost exactly the moment when our army appeared in front of the main gate of the village, anticipating a jolly time among the weak and helpless rather than a battle with an over-excited and extremely confident Scythian cavalry detachment.

In the event, Marsamleptes and his men gave a good account of themselves. They'd been practising anti-cavalry drill ever since the first raid, and once they'd recovered from the initial shock they did their drill-masters proud. Furthermore, instead of holding off and shooting at them, the Scythians tried to press home a charge with lance and scimitar, and they emerged from the resulting scrimmage quite definitely in second place. I forget how many of them we claim we killed; rather more to the point, we came out of it with none killed, four seriously injured (one man lost his left hand, another lost an eye; the other two recovered. The man who lost his hand was a young Greek by the name of Chrysippus; he'd recently been taken on as an apprentice by Agenor the stonemason. Agenor himself was slashed across the face with a scimitar after his helmet had fallen off; the cut healed, but the scar was spectacular and his beard always grew funny afterwards).

This wasn't nearly the same sort of thing as chasing terrified Thracians, and the war-party pulled back, regrouped and rode in a wide loop until they were able to take up a position directly between our men and the village. Marsamleptes, commanding our forces, decided that he'd done enough for one day and ordered a withdrawal in good order, which the Scythians let go without any further bother. Finally, when the fifty Budini showed up some time later, the war-party (who were still milling about in front of the gates at that point) saw them off with a volley of arrows and a charge, but our men had the good sense to get out of there quickly and in several directions at once, and so sustained no casualties.

In short, it was a banjax, but a non-lethal one. It made me think of military history lessons in Mieza; most battles are lost by the loser rather than won by the victor, and this was no exception. In fact, we claimed it as a victory and did the usual Greek thing of piling up a trophy of captured weapons (only we hadn't captured any weapons, so we hunted around for souvenir bows and scimitars and borrowed a few from the Budini; they sneaked out after dark and retrieved them, and nobody commented, so I don't suppose they noticed). After all, we'd engaged the enemy and killed a substantial number of them ('substantial': military jargon meaning 'at least one') without loss to ourselves. In practice we'd proved that we were incompetent strategists but formidable fighting men, and trying to charge our heavy infantry formation was a mug's game, so I suppose we did more good than harm, at least in the short term.

Well, once the debriefing and the gripe session were over, we'd posted a guard on the wall and built that damn trophy, there was nothing left to do but go home. In my case, this would have meant going back to my house, with Theano sitting staring at the wall or pacing up and down or bolting herself in the inner room and dissolving into floods of tears; not the most attractive prospect for a man who's spent a long hot day crouching behind a rock. So when a couple of the Illyrians came sidling up and asked me rather diffidently if I'd like to join their thanksgiving celebration, I thought, 'Why not?' and agreed.

I was expecting something rather raucous and Illyrian, with lots of booze and banging of fists on tables and throwing of bones. In fact, it was an eerie and rather beautiful ceremony, most of it conducted in dead silence except for the pattering of dancers' feet on the baked earth of the dancing floor. It's an odd phenomenon, the Illyrian tendency to dance without music, but quite effective (and to be honest with you, the absence of what the Illyrians think of as music is a blessing at all times), and the oddest part of all was watching these rather stolid ex-mercenaries, quite a few of whom I now knew to talk to and some of whom I thought of as actual friends, dancing their silent, intricate courses in the pale moonlight. Merely by virtue of the light, the silence and the tradition they followed, they stepped out of context and into a state of almost instant grace, until the dance came to an end and they trooped back to their places laughing and complaining about how sore their feet were.

The last dance, they told me, was something special; if I possibly could, I should stay and see it. Well, I had nothing better to do, so I stayed.

It was, of course, a snake-dance; I might have guessed when they were at such pains to invite me. A young Illyrian called Boizas danced the snake, while ten or so of the older men danced the evil spirits the snake drives away. There was music to go with this one, which spoilt it rather, but in spite of that I must admit I was entranced.

First the snake came out of his lair and did a solo, a very still, quiet piece that would have been plain dull if it wasn't for the exceptional degree of intensity that young Boizas brought to it. When he moved, it was as if he was laden down with some particularly heavy load, so that the slightest movement of an arm or a foot was an achievement to be applauded. At the height of this part of the dance, the evil spirits appeared and bore down on him, ringing him round with their arms raised as if to strike, so that he was completely hidden behind them. The spirits' dance was fast and lively, they seemed to flicker and dart like flames; then, when they'd completed the circle and were so closely packed together that I thought they must be standing on poor Boizas, he jumped up, somersaulted and landed with a foot on one shoulder of each of the two tallest spirits. He then proceeded to perform a quite remarkable dance, hopping from shoulder to shoulder, leaping, somersaulting in a manner I'd never have thought possible, until he jumped high in the air, landed neatly between the circle and the spectators, and set about chasing the other dancers away in a rearing, swooping set of movements that was just like every snake you ever saw in every respect apart from actual motion, if you see what I mean; he managed to convey everything there is to notice about a snake without once doing anything that imitated how a real snake acts. It was bizarre and no end impressive; and he concluded it by cartwheeling across the dancing-floor, vaulting to his feet right in front of me, reaching down and pulling a large and bad-tempered looking snake of indeterminate species apparently out of the fold of my gown. He held this thing up for a moment in both hands – you could see it was a real live one by the way its tongue kept flicking in and out – then let it curl round his arm and slither up into his sleeve, at which point he pulled off his tunic and threw it in the air, and no snake fell out. Indeed, when he brought the tunic to me there was no sign of any snake, either inside the tunic or wrapped round Boizas (and since he was wearing nothing but a very short kilt there was nowhere he could have hidden it). Then he bowed and danced away, and as I raised my hands to join in the applause, I found that same snake sitting in my lap, where Boizas had found it in the first place.

Oh hell, I thought; then, extremely slowly and carefully, I grabbed the snake firmly below the head, the way I'd seen it done, lowered it into a large pottery jug and slapped the lid on as fast as I could. I found out afterwards that it was – well, I can't remember what the Illyrians said its name was, but it's so deadly poisonous that even a tiny smear of the stuff on an open scratch or cut would kill you before you can count to ten.

CHAPTER SEVENTEEN

╗╔╗╔╗╔╗╔╗╔╗╔╗╔╗╔╗╔╗╔╗╔╗╔╗╔╗╔╗╔╗╔

Talking of remarkable people, Phryzeutzis; I once knew a man who had this amazing, astounding, reality-distorting ability to lose hats. He was bald as an egg, which didn't help matters; he had to wear a hat, because otherwise there'd have been nothing between the fury of the Attic sun at noon and his poor, squidgy brains except a thin layer of bone. But hats simply left him; they'd blow away in sudden gusts of wind, or snag in the low branches of trees, or slip noiselessly past his eyebrows when he was bending over to peer down a well. If all else failed they subtly attached themselves to whoever he happened to be with; you'd be sitting chatting to him under a tree, and then you'd look up at the sun and see how late it was getting, scramble to your feet (reaching instinctively for your hat as you did so) and hurry back to work before your goats had a chance to stray into someone else's pasture. Later on, when it was time to go home, you'd notice something was strange; you'd reach up to pat the top of your head, and there a hat would be, though you knew for a certainty you left the house that morning without one. I'm not saying that hats hated this unfortunate man, or feared him, or anything like that. In the short space of time his hats spent with him, I seem to recall he treated them kindly. But after a day or so, they all seem to have come to the conclusion that it was time to move on, and they left him.

With him, hats; with me, women. Not, perhaps, to quite the same extent; I don't drop them down wells or carelessly leave them behind when I visit other people's houses. But sooner or later there comes a time when I look round to say something to them and there they aren't. No doubt they have their reasons; and if I could understand what those reasons were, I would understand women far better than I do, and maybe they wouldn't leave.

What I'm trying to say is that Theano left me. As a historian, I have a duty to record all the facts; she became very friendly with a Syracusan cheese merchant, a month or so after the failed attack on the Scythian village, and when he left, so did she. It's a logical assumption that they left together, although I can't put that down as a fact since I didn't witness it myself. He was tall and very fat, this merchant; older than me, bald (like the hat-man) and with an unusually curly beard. I get the impression, though, that what really attracted her to him was the fact that he wasn't me.

Well, it wasn't quite the elopement of Helen of Troy, and I'd be lying to you if I pretended that I was terribly upset about it. But I was still feeling no pain after the death of my son Eupolis; and besides, our marriage had been a mistake from the very beginning. One aspect of the matter that does puzzle me even now is the timing of it all; I mean, one moment she was sobbing herself to sleep over the death of her only child, and the next she was swept up by an overwhelming passion for a tubby, bald-headed cheese vendor with skin as pale and flaky as the plaster rind of his wares. Tyrsenius reckoned that the role of the cheese man in all this was simply as a provider of transport; since she couldn't very well ask me for the price of a passage out of Olbia, she had to make what arrangements she could and pay her fare with what she had at her disposal. Maybe; I don't know, and I'm not much bothered. All my life I've found it too much of an effort to take an interest in things I know I don't understand.

The Thracians, very sensibly, never came back; but the Budini we'd hired for the attack stayed on, first as soldiers, then as settlers. They didn't ask for land, of course; which was just as well, since the Founders would never have let them have any. They didn't even admit that they intended to stay permanently. They just stayed, and made their living as hired labourers, a commodity much in demand. For all our noble professions that we had come to Olbia to work with our own hands, we were getting a little bit jaded after twelve years of high-minded nobility. It was nice to be able to watch some-one else being uplifted by manual labour for a change, especially from under a shady tree with a cup of wine in one's hand.

I suppose about six months must have passed; six or seven, since the abortive raid. I remember that we heard the news of the great battle between Alexander and the Persian King at the river Granicus, where the Macedonian heavy infantry with their absurdly long pikes and Alexander's heavy cavalry between them humiliated the Persian army, and where Alexander, fighting always in the front rank, twice breaking his spear, his horse shot dead under him, somehow failed to get himself killed in spite of everything. He was Achilles that day for sure, except for the happy ending; and when he raised his trophy of captured armour and weapons, I doubt whether he had to borrow swords and lances from his own men to get it to a respectable height.

Maybe it was hearing about the battle, I don't know; but there was a general feeling among us all that we should finish what we'd started with our neighbours, before the first anniversary of our first vintage came round with our dead still not yet made comfortable. The Illyrians in particular were all for taking some strong action; so too, unaccountably, were the Budini, though it may just have been a way of dealing with the fact that they'd been stuck in one place for so long. Most curiously, our fire-breathing Founders weren't nearly so enthusiastic as they had been. Prodromus actually tried to talk me out of organising an attack; he said that it would be much better to wait until we'd got the harvest in, because otherwise we'd be vulnerable to reprisals when we were out working in the fields. I told him he'd missed the point; that if we did a proper job this time, there wouldn't be anybody to make any such reprisals, and so the consideration wasn't valid. He didn't like the sound of that very much, and accused me of being bloodthirsty and blinded by my personal tragedies to the moral implications of what I was pro-posing. I told him to go stuff his head up something dark and wet, and on that note we parted.

Well, the cattle-raid stunt wouldn't work again, so we had to think of something else. Marsamleptes pointed out that we'd done best when the enemy had tried to press home a charge against our heavy infantry; if we could provoke them into making the same mistake twice, there was no reason why we shouldn't take them on in the open field, rather than resorting to some over-elaborate stratagem.

My first inclination was to tell Marsamleptes to take a cold bath and think again; but then I thought of Alexander and the Granicus battle. Once you pared away all the Homeric stuff, what you were left with was a disputed river-crossing. The Persian infantry took no part in the battle; it was their cavalry who lined up on the other side of the river and tried to stop Alexander from struggling through the ford. In other words, Alexander had kidded the Persians into using their cavalry as infantry; and when it comes to infantry fighting, a man sitting on a horse is at a significant disadvantage.

So, I thought; the greatest threat to us was the speed and manoeuvrability of the war-band and their ability to shoot their bows from the saddle. Trick them into standing still, and you deprived them of their advantage, while tilting the balance in favour of our well-drilled, disciplined heavy infantry. All that was needed, I realised, was a suitable river-crossing; and as luck would have it, I knew the very place.

It was a hot day. You know what it's like when you've had to wake up earlier than you'd have liked, and as soon as you open your eyes the brightness of the sun makes you wince. I overslept, like a fool, and by the time I came to it was well past dawn. Of course, nobody had thought to come and wake me up.

By the time I'd struggled into my armour and stumbled out into the bright sunshine, I had a blinding headache, which didn't go well with the upset stomach I'd failed to shake off by not eating anything the day before. Anything less than a battle or harvest and I'd have stayed in bed, but an *oecist*-cum-commander-in-chief doesn't have that option, no matter how dodgy his tummy might be.

By the look of it, I wasn't the only one who didn't really feel in the mood for mortal combat that day. We marched slowly, coughing and grumbling as we breathed in the dust we were kicking up into a towering cloud. In my capacity as general, however, I didn't mind the dust-cloud. In fact, I was counting on it to attract their attention and get them to come trotting out to meet us. Timing, of course, was important. If we wanted to fight them in the place we'd chosen, it was fairly crucial that we got to the river first. If the enemy crossed over before we arrived, we'd be facing another kind of battle entirely, and one I didn't really want to be involved in.

But somehow we reached the ford, and in reasonable order too.

We didn't have to wait very long before the enemy cavalry put in their appearance; and, just as I'd wanted them to, they spread out along their side of the river and waited to see what we had in mind.

This was the point during the battle of the Granicus at which Alexander launched his cavalry charge, to hold off the enemy while his heavy infantry waddled across the ford. Characteristically of Alexander's military planning, it was a bold, innovative and highly successful manoeuvre, and nobody could ever deny that it worked like a charm –

– Which is why we were all at a loss to know why it didn't work nearly so well for us. The situation, after all, was more or less identical – river, cavalry on one side, heavy infantry on the other; it was as if we'd taken the ingredients for honey-cakes, mixed them together in the prescribed manner, and ended up with cheesecake.

I remember the stone in my boot, which I hadn't had a chance to get rid of all the way from the city to the ford. I remember how the headache made it such an effort to think at all, let alone try to revise my plan in mid-flow. I remember thinking, right in the middle of the fighting, that unless I managed to control my irregular bowel movements until the battle was over and I could snatch a few moments behind a bush somewhere, it was all going to be terribly sordid and embarrassing. I clearly recall the high curtain of water thrown up by the hooves of the Budini's horses as they clattered into the ford at a brisk, jarring trot. I have a whole library of pictures in my mind from that battle, dozens of little scenes and observations, all as self-contained as the black and red pictures on the sides of fancy pottery. Quite a few of them I'd be delighted to get rid of, such as the sight of the entire front rank of our cavalry charge sliding dead off their horses into the water as the Scythians poured a volley of arrows into our ranks from about fifteen yards away. Those horses; I can see them clearly, trotting up the opposite bank of the river, as if they knew that without the burden of men on their backs they were safe, they were welcome as being valuable commodities, not just martial scrap to be heaped up on a trophy. Of course, I'm proud to recall how our line of spear-points hardly wavered as the infantry line crossed the river, though that image isn't as sharp as the others. What I do remember is how wet the water was when we knelt down in the river, taking shelter behind our shields from the next volley of arrows. I can feel the claggy wet cloth of my kilt against my skin, and the singularly disagreeable sensation of water running down the inside of my legs as I stood up afterwards. I can remember the colour of the water; briefly muddy with kicked-up silt and the blood of the dead Budini.

These images are all so sharp and immediate, in fact, that it amazes me that I've never come across them or others like them in the great battle-scenes in Homer, which are supposedly about men fighting each other. It makes me wonder; did Alexander get wet and shivery as he crossed the Granicus; or did the water somehow fail to soak into whatever he was wearing that day? Perhaps kings and heroes have a special dispensation that lets them off getting wet when they fight battles in the beds of shallow rivers. I don't know; and although over the years I've had plenty of opportunities to ask people who were in a position to analyse what happened and what went wrong, I've never quite been able to deal with it.

Most curious of all is that when I've talked about that battle to other people who were there, they claim to have noticed an almost completely different set of observations and impressions, as if they'd been at a different battle in the same place on the same day. There can't have been another battle, can there? I'm sure I'd have noticed, and so, I assume, would they, unless it started half an hour after I'd gone home. But they reckoned they saw me there, and most of them were far too unimaginative to have made up something like that.

We were about halfway across the river when they fell back, pulling their horses' heads round and cantering off a hundred yards or so towards their village. They were conceding the crossing to us. They weren't meant to do that. The whole idea was that they were meant to see that we'd made a tactical error – trying to cross an awkward obstacle in the face of the enemy, it's suicide, ask any general – and that they should immediately press home their advantage before we had a chance to recover, let alone get across the damn river. This would mean riding down onto the riverbed to fight us, or at least holding their bank against us, which from our point of view would mean they'd lose all their advantages as cavalry and accordingly succumb to our superior infantry, just the way it had happened at the Granicus.

But they didn't. I can only assume they were too stupid to see the obvious advantage, or too cowardly to dare to seize the moment.

Instead, they waited till we'd pulled ourselves out of the water and started shooting at us again. The fools.

Fortunately, we were ready for them, thanks to all those hours of foot drill. We dropped down on one knee, lifted our shields, same as before; they scratched and dented a lot of expensive metalwork, but they didn't kill anybody. After three or so volleys they stopped, worried about running short of arrows. We got up and started to advance. They let us come on seventy-five yards or so, then rode off another hundred yards and started shooting again. We knelt, waited, got up, advanced, a hundred or so yards at a time. It was slow and painful stuff, not to mention embarrassing – by rights, we should have killed them all by now, whereas we hadn't got close enough to make out the colour of their eyes, let alone hit anybody. At this rate, it'd be a long, dangerous crawl to the village, provided that their arrow supply held out.

It was at this point that someone quite unexpectedly did something intelligent. Corus, the captain of the remaining Budini (he wasn't their regular leader; he hadn't made it), suddenly led a frantic charge, apparently at right-angles to everything that was going on. It was as if he'd caught sight of that other battle I was speculating about just now, the one that everybody else but I could see, and had gone racing off to join it. The enemy lowered their bows and stared, unable to fathom what the hell was going on; we were staring too, come to that. If it hadn't been for the drawn scimitars and levelled lances, I'd have sworn they were running away. But they weren't. After they'd galloped about a quarter of a mile, they abruptly veered off to the right and swung back; they'd gone just far enough to be behind the enemy's line, provided they could reach it before the enemy had a chance to get out of the way.

It was close; the war-party had to back and shuffle before they could turn round to face the incoming attack, which was closing at a hell of a rate, and that was when I saw it, the complicated manoeuvre in the face of the enemy – the mistake. I scrambled to my feet and yelled for an immediate attack; Marsamleptes was way ahead of me, and he had the wit to give the order to the trumpeters, who blew the charge. In the event, I did well to keep up and not get trampled on.

When they saw us coming, the enemy tried to turn back again, thereby getting themselves hopelessly tangled up. It was more by luck than judgement, but both charges, cavalry and infantry, went home at more or less the same time. We were holding them like a piece of hot metal in a pair of tongs. They couldn't shoot or run. It was just like the Granicus, only better.

Being rather slow off the mark, I ended up in the fourth row of the infantry formation, where I couldn't see anything past the helmet of the man in front of me, and couldn't contribute anything beyond my body-weight. As to what actually happened, therefore, I have no idea; I didn't get to see any of the cut and thrust of hand-to-hand combat, the lunging and feinting and parrying, the footwork and shieldplay. My experience of the battle was something like being caught in a big, over-excited queue, like when you're lining up to get into the theatre or Assembly, and they open the doors and everybody surges forwards at once, sweeping you along with them. I was scared, no question, but not of the enemy; the immediate threat to me (and a very real one too) was from the butt-spikes on the ends of other people's spears, the terrifying risk of slipping and getting trodden into the dirt, or being crushed like a bug between two ranks of armour-clad bodies. In fact, I only have other people's word for it that we engaged the enemy at all. I didn't see any of them, certainly, unless you count one or two dead bodies I trod on when something suddenly gave way and for a few short, scary moments we were all stumbling forward out of control. They must have been the enemy, those dead men, because they weren't wearing armour; but that was all I had time to notice about them.

It's not as if I gave a damn, anyway. Fighting and killing were the last things on my mind just then.

From what other people told me, I gather that we sort of squeezed them into nothing, as if you took an overripe pear in your hand and crushed it, till the pulp squirted out between your fingers and you were left holding the core and the pips. It was something like a hundred and seventy-odd killed, as many again captured, while our losses were in single figures, apart from the Budini shot down in the river (seventeen killed, twenty or so wounded). Anyway, people who knew about this sort of thing reckoned that it was a good closing score and we'd done well, and there was plenty of stuff for a proper trophy this time. But the rest of them got back inside the village and shut the gates, and after we'd caught our breath and sorted ourselves out, there was nothing else to do but go home again. Complete waste of time, if you ask me.

'We did well,' Tyrsenius said, 'considering. Of course,' he went on, 'we'll have to be very careful from now on. Very careful indeed.'

I yawned; it was late and I was very tired after all that frantic pushing and shoving. 'What you're saying is,' I replied, 'we've attacked them, provoked them, killed nearly two hundred people, and sooner or later they're going to attack us again.'

'That's a rather negative way of looking at it, don't you think?' Tyrsenius said. 'After all, we've just won a rather splendid victory.'

'Which achieved nothing,' I said. 'If anything, we've made things worse. You know what I'd do if I were in charge in that village? I'd send messages to every Scythian community in reach, saying, Dire warning, unprovoked attack, we must all band together now and get rid of these Greeks once and for all, or else we don't stand a chance. After all,' I added, 'isn't that what we did?'

Prodromus the Founder looked at me. 'I thought you were the one who wanted this war,' he said.

I leaned back and let my head rest against the wall. 'I wanted to wipe out the village,' I said. 'No village, no more problem. It serves me right, I suppose, for thinking you can do that sort of thing.'

'Sounds good to me,' Tyrsenius said. I ignored him.

'All right,' Prodromus said. 'So now what are you saying? We should give up the war? Try to negotiate peace?'

I nodded. 'We've made our point, at least,' I said. 'And sure enough, we've thinned out the war-party, got rid of a lot of the young braves who were spoiling for a fight. We've got the anger out of our system too, I hope. What I'd like to do is go back to the terms Anabruzas proposed that time, and see if we can make anything out of those.'

Marsamleptes stroked his beard with the ball of his thumb. 'That's if those terms are still open,' he said. 'Maybe now it's their turn to be angry.'

I shrugged. 'I'd have hoped we've killed too many of them to let them afford the luxury of being angry,' I replied. 'Even though we lost control of the battle right at the outset, they still weren't able to do us any real harm. We've proved they're no match for us in a pitched battle.'

Marsamleptes dipped his head a little. 'Maybe they aren't figuring on having any more pitched battles,' he replied. 'It's not the way they do things, left to themselves.'

I saw his point. If we were going to thump them every time we met in the open field, the sensible thing from their perspective would be not to go to the open field any more. But they could still launch surprise attacks, ride down our people as they walked home from work, and then dart back behind their gates before we could do anything about it. Then we'd have to follow suit, they'd step up their attacks; and when, in the middle of all this, would any of us find the time to do any farming? 'So what's your idea?' I asked him.

'Gather more men,' he said. 'Hire more soldiers. Then we lay a siege and destroy the village.'

I sighed. 'Back where we started, only harder,' I said. 'In fact, we've achieved nothing.'

Marsamleptes shook his head. 'Things have changed since we started,' he said. 'Back then, we could have come to an agreement. Now, we have to see it through.'

Nobody said anything after that, and the meeting broke up. Marsamleptes went off to organise guard duty; his work wouldn't be over much before dawn. We weren't supposed to be doing all this; it was summer now, but soon it would be autumn; vintage, harvest, ploughing, sowing. In Greece, the campaigning season has always been very rigidly defined, wars don't drag on into vintage and get in the way of people's work. But in Greece, everybody knows what wars mean, they understand the meaning of a victory or a defeat. It's like judgement in a lawsuit, and if the judgement goes against you, you don't complain or try to wriggle out of it, you pay up and get on with your life. How would it be if every dispute over who owned which side of a ditch or who was responsible for breakages in a consignment of jars of honey had to be carried through until one or other of the parties was dead? That was the lesson of military history: only fight battles if you're prepared to abide by the result.

That didn't seem to work here, which made the point. We weren't in Greece any more. We'd left all that, moved on.

Pity.

I crawled out of my clothes, which had dried on me twice that day – once from the river-water, once from the sweat – and slumped onto my bed. I was used to being alone in the house now, it was remarkable how quickly I'd adapted to it. Everything had gone wrong, one way or another, and I'd accepted it without really noticing.

I woke up in the middle of the night and realised that I'd decided to leave Antolbia.

In a sense, there was nothing left to leave. My Antolbia was firmly based around the notion of home, family, farm, the life I should have had if only my father hadn't screwed everything up by having so many sons. Now my own son was dead, my wife had fled to Sicily with a cheese magnate, I didn't dare go to my farm for fear of getting shot; that didn't leave much. The ideal society had gone the way of all such experiments – it had lasted longer than some, and I had the consolation of knowing that the forces tearing it apart were mostly external, but it was still a fundamentally impossible project, as close to real life as Homer's version of battle. The truth was quite simple; we'd tried to found a Greek city that wasn't in Greece, in a place that was already somewhere else by the time we got there. When Greeks founded Miletus and Syracuse and Cyrene and Croton and Odessus, the world was still soft and plastic, like a ball of wet clay that could be moulded and shaped. By the time we went to Olbia, it was already too hard to work.

The only question was, when would I be free to go? Perversely, if everything had been going well I could have walked away without a second thought (but if everything had been going well, I wouldn't have wanted to). True, I had no material ties worth bothering with, and thanks to Philip of Macedon and the battle of Chaeronea, I was the rightful heir to substantial property in Attica – following the deaths of Eudorus and Euthyphron, half my father's original estate; I'd have to fight hard in the courts to get it, of course, and on that score the sooner I left Antolbia and started my campaign, the better. But leaving at that particular moment, either the beginning or the middle of the war, but most certainly not the end, was something I couldn't bring myself to do. Don't get me wrong; it wasn't anything to do with obligation or responsibility or honour. It was more a matter of wanting to be looking in the right direction when the main event happened, just for once in my life –

My fellow Antolbians, it is with a heavy heart . . .

– And partly, of course, cowardice, because I didn't have the nerve to stand up in front of them and make that speech. No, if I wanted to leave now, I'd have to sneak out of town on some pretext, like the man who tells his wife he's just going up to the market to buy a quarter of whitebait, and is next heard of ten years later, as a captain of mercenaries in Libya.

After a sleepless night (more to do with rough wine and anchovies than mental turmoil, I suspect) I decided on a compromise. When we'd erased all traces of the Scythian village, I'd be free to go. Even while I was formulating the proposal, I couldn't help wondering what had happened to me over the last dozen years, to bring me to a state where I predicated my personal redemption on the whole-sale slaughter of innocents. But I explained that by saying that I was merely reverting to type. What we'd have called genocide in Olbia would have been considered in Athens a sensible business pre-caution.

I went to see Marsamleptes.

'I'm not sure,' he replied, in answer to my question. 'If we had the resources, I'd want catapults and battering-rams, plus at least three hundred specialist archers.'

'Sorry,' I said. 'I can't afford the money, or the time. What can we do with what we've already got?'

He thought for a while longer. 'Attack by night,' he said eventually. 'In the dark, they can't see to shoot. If we can force the gate before they realise what we're doing—'

I shook my head. 'Is that likely?'

'No,' he admitted. 'Not really.'

I chewed my lower lip for a moment. 'What if someone opened the gates for us?' I said. 'Would that be enough, do you think?'

As always, he considered his answer carefully before replying. 'Yes,' he said, 'I think it would. Basically, we'd have to use the village stockade like a net, as if we were lamping for hares. Surround the stockade but leave the two side gates unblocked. Put in an assault party through the main gate, with torches, setting fire to everything in reach and making it look like there's more of them than there really are. Once they realise what's going on, they'll try to bolt through the side gates. That's where we catch them and kill them.'

I looked doubtful. 'Isn't that over-elaborate?' I asked. 'Judging by how things went the last two times, we'd better assume that anything that can go wrong, will.'

He looked at me with a very faint smile. 'I'm a soldier,' he said. 'I always assume that. Unfortunately, it doesn't solve much. Just because you know a thing's the weak link in the chain doesn't mean you can do anything at all about it. No, we'll just have to make sure that we make as few mistakes as possible.' He looked at me steadily. 'Do you really think you can find someone who'll be willing to open the gates?' he said.

I nodded. 'I think so,' I said.

He looked older than he had the last time I saw him. His broad shoulders were starting to get bony, the muscles of his forearms were shrinking, so that he wore the bones like an old man wears a tunic that fitted him like a glove twenty years ago. His hands looked bigger, and they shook a little. But he still had the scar I'd given him all those years before, and the look in his eyes was exactly the same as always.

'Peace,' he repeated. 'I don't think you people know the meaning of the word.'

'We don't,' I replied. 'That's why it's got to be done this way. Look, Anabruzas, I'm being absolutely straight with you. If you don't open the gates and let us occupy the village, calmly and peacefully while everyone's asleep, then we'll come along with catapults and battering-rams and break in during the day; and I promise you, you won't like that.'

'I'm sure,' he said. 'And if I felt I could trust you, it'd be a different matter. But I don't. How can I, after what you did the last time?'

I shrugged. 'If you don't co-operate,' I said, 'we'll definitely storm the stockade and kill you all. If you do what I'm telling you, there's a chance I might keep my word. Even half a chance is better than none at all.'

Anabruzas gave me a look of pure contempt. I wondered what I'd done to deserve it.

'If I do open the gates,' he said, 'what will you do? Just how will you go about it?'

I smiled. 'Do I look like I'm stupid?' I said. 'I'm not going to tell you that. Listen, will you? I'm talking about a chance to save lives; your people's lives, mine as well. I'm trying to be practical, for all our sakes. I'd have thought that you, of all people . . .'

He turned away, as if he couldn't bear the sight of me any more. 'For your information,' he said, 'my son – my *other* son – was killed in the battle. I'm too old and too tired to raise any more. Do you know the story of the woman who was captured by the Persians?'

I blinked. 'No,' I replied. 'At least, I don't think so. Is this a time to be telling stories?'

He took no notice of that remark. 'Once,' he said, 'the Persians attacked some of my people and captured a village. A Persian officer saw a woman he liked the look of. Since she wanted nothing to do with him, he rounded up her whole family and told her he was going to kill them all, unless she did what he wanted her to. If she co-operated,' he went on, stressing the word, 'he promised he'd spare one of her family. Just one; it'd be up to her to choose.'

'Interesting story,' I said. 'Go on.'

'She accepted the offer,' Anabruzas continued, 'and told the Persian that she wanted him to spare her brother. The Persian was as good as his word; later, though, he told her that he was curious to know how she'd arrived at her decision.

'"It was a matter of logic," she told him. "I didn't choose my husband, because one day I might find myself another husband. I didn't choose my children, because if I marry again I might bear more children. But my mother and father are dead, so I can never have another brother, and that's why I chose him."' He sighed, and looked at me. 'I used to wonder,' he went on, 'whether anybody could ever reach the point where they'd be able to make a choice like that. I honestly didn't think it'd be possible; you simply couldn't bring yourself to figure something like that out in such a cold, rational way. That, however,' he went on, 'was before you Greeks came.'

I frowned. 'Are you going to do it, or aren't you?' I said. 'I really don't care enough either way to be kept hanging about.'

'Oh, I'll do it,' he replied. 'I can't see that I've got any choice, logically. Tell me; the people you capture. Don't you Greeks sell your prisoners as slaves?'

'Sometimes,' I said. 'But we don't believe in slavery in Antolbia. I'd have thought you'd have noticed that.'

He acknowledged what I'd said with a slight bow. 'That's true,' he said. 'You don't. We don't either. Other Scythian nations do; the

Budini and the Massagetae and the others whose names I don't know, who live at the other end of the world. We never have, for some reason. It's not an idea we're comfortable with.'

I shrugged. 'Owning slaves makes a society weak and decadent,' I said. 'Where you have rich men with armies of slaves, the ordinary farmers and craftsmen can't make a living. Also, you've always got the problem of keeping them in order; that's the sort of thing that can ultimately wreck a society, the way it did for the Spartans. All through their history, everything they did was motivated by the fear that their slaves might get loose some day and kill them all. You can't live with something like that hanging over you.'

'Oh,' he said. 'Different reasons. Do you promise that if I open the gates, you won't put my people in chains and ship them off to – remind me, where is it you have your big slave market?'

'On the island of Delos,' I replied.

He nodded. 'Isn't that where you have the big temple?' he asked.

'That's right. We believe Delos is where the god Apollo was born.'

'I see,' he said. 'You take a holy place and turn it into a slave market. Clearly you Greeks are more complicated than I thought.'

'You have my word,' I said. 'Once the village has been levelled, you'll be free to go.'

He stood up, slowly and painfully, like a man with a bad back. 'I'll open the gates,' he said. 'And when you've done what you have to do, I'll never see you again. Do you promise that as well?'

'I can't see any reason why we should ever meet again,' I replied.

He smiled. 'That's all right, then,' he said. 'It's just that I had this horrible premonition. I thought I'd died, and travelled to the place in the far north where we go when we die; and the first face I set eyes on when I got there was yours.' He walked towards the doorway, then stopped and turned back. 'One last thing I wanted to ask you,' he said. 'Is it true what they say, that you keep a magic snake in a jar that brings you victory and tells you what people are thinking?'

'No,' I replied.

'Oh. Oh, well,' he said. 'I should have known it wouldn't be something that simple.'

I'm not claiming to be some sort of mystic or visionary here, but there's one point on which I feel confident that I'm able to interpret the wishes of the gods. As I see it, the setting of the sun and the shrouding of the world in unspeakable darkness is intended as a hint to mortal men to stay home until morning.

If you must insist on going out after dark, the one thing you should avoid doing at all costs is taking part in any sort of military operation. The plain fact is, at night, you can't see where the hell you're going. Now, that's bad enough when the worst thing that can befall you is an unsuspected tree-root and a skinned knee. When you're shuffling along in a packed wedge of bodies, with the spear-points of the men behind and the butt-spikes of the men in front threatening you at all times, it ceases to be a foolhardy adventure and becomes sheer insanity.

I remember my father telling me the story his father told him about the notorious night attack the Athenians made on the Syracusans during the Great War. My grandfather took part in that debacle, and if it hadn't been for either fool's luck or the direct intervention of the god Dionysus, our family history would have ended right there, Phryzeutzis, and you and I would never have met. Perhaps because of this, antipathy for fighting battles at night runs in our family. Unfortunately, on this occasion blind stupidity, which also runs in our family, must have run a whole lot faster and got there first, because this attack, my first and only experience of the technique, had been my own damn stupid idea.

The men gathered in the market square at nightfall; apart from a very few with legitimate excuses, the entire male citizen body of Antolbia, together with the surviving Budini and a small band of Triballian javelin-and-buckler artists, the only additional mercen-aries we could get at such short notice – not nearly as useless as they looked, as it turned out. There was a curious feeling about the assembly; extreme nervousness bordering on terror, which was quite right and proper under the circumstances, mixed with an involuntary thrill of excitement and, for want of a better word, fun. I guess it was something to do with everybody being in the adventure together, with the additional spice of it being at night – after all, you can't help associating nocturnal gatherings with booze and exuberance and socially acceptable acts of boorishness and vandalism.

The closest thing I can remember to that feeling was the big organised boar-drive that I went on while I was at Mieza; a massive social occasion, with the whole court there, all kitted out in big boots to ward off the thorns and undergrowth as we plunged about in the forest trying to flush out the wild boar. As it turned out, the whole thing was a complete waste of time; we found nothing, got tired and scratched and bad-tempered, and trudged home again feeling very sorry for ourselves. But the atmosphere as we set out was extraordinary; we were off for a grand day's sport, a wonderful chance for relaxation and camaraderie, enormous fun, with a small but significant chance of being ripped open from the groin to the chin by the most dangerous wild animal in the whole of Greece.

Marsamleptes had divided our people into three groups. The first to leave was the encircling party, whose job was to throw a cordon round the village, with special reference to the two side gates. I went with the main party; we were the ones who were going to walk in through the open gate. The remaining section, made up mostly of the Budini, the Triballians and the best of the Illyrians, were a mobile reserve, who'd follow on closely behind the main body and stand ready to reinforce the other two groups as and when necessary.

We were late setting off. Marsamleptes had sent two Budini to creep up on the village and make sure everything was quiet; they didn't come back when they were supposed to, and we immediately began to worry. If they'd been caught, there was a fair chance the enemy would be ready for us, and there's nothing on earth quite as vulnerable as an ambush party walking into an ambush, with the possible exception of a baby hedgehog on its back. When at last they finally showed up, the news they brought wasn't encouraging. Apparently they'd been pinned down by groups of Scythians wandering about in the darkness, calling out to each other and seemingly carrying out an organised search.

(What had actually happened was that a little girl had had a blazing row with her parents and run off. There was no sign of her inside the village, so her family turned out and started searching outside, afraid that she might meet up with a bear or a wolf or – ha! – a band of marauding Greeks. Then she turned up in somebody's hayloft, and they called off the search and went home. But we, of course, didn't know that.)

In the end, Marsamleptes decided to send more scouts; and, by the time they came back and reported that as far as they could see everything was quiet and there were no signs of additional sentries, it was well past midnight; we'd have to get a move on if we weren't to get caught out by the dawn.

The encircling party set off. They were doing their best to be as quiet as possible, and they'd muffled their boots with hanks of felt and wrapped wool round their sword-hilts so they wouldn't clank against their armour; but as they marched into the darkness, I was convinced they were making enough noise to be audible in Byzantium.

Once they'd gone, the jovial adventure atmosphere dissipated a bit, and the rest of us stood about, leaning on our shields and trying not to fidget as we waited for it to be time for us to follow on. It was while I was standing about that it suddenly occurred to me – you can tell I wasn't thinking straight, I should have seen this hours before – that because we were so far behind schedule, there was a good chance that Anabruzas had either given up waiting and gone home, or he'd opened the gates anyway, the treachery had been discovered, and the enemy would be waiting for us with arrows nocked on their bowstrings.

I pointed this out to Marsamleptes and demanded that we scrub the whole show. He got angry and said that he already had a third of his army in position; was I suggesting that we just leave them there till dawn, or were we going to try to pull them out, which would inevitably lead to the alarm being raised? If the gate wasn't open when we got there, he said, we'd just have to bash it in with a log or a big stone; compared with the difficulties involved in trying to abort the operation at this late stage, the gate being shut was no big deal. If the worst came to the worst, we'd use an assault on the main gate as a diversion while he put the mobile reserve in through the side gates and carried the village that way.

There was no point in trying to argue with him; now that the operation was under way, he was the man in charge and nobody was going to listen to me, even if I had a witnessed deposition from the gods telling us we were all going to die.

Now that was a long march, Phryzeutzis, that night-march from the city to the village. I kept going by fixing my eyes on the back of the head of the man in front of me; I could just about differentiate between the shades of black, though as far as seeing where I was going was concerned, I might as well have had my eyes shut. As luck would have it, there was cloud over the moon and stars, which meant that even after I'd been walking for a long time I still wasn't seeing any better than when we set off. How Marsamleptes found the way I just don't know, and because I'd lost all track of time I thought we must have come too far and walked straight past the village. In fact, I was just screwing up the courage to break ranks, find him and point out this obvious error when the man in front of me stopped abruptly and I only just managed to avoid walking my knee into the butt-spike of his spear.

I was in the third rank, so although I didn't see a thing, I heard the hinges of the gate creak. *Good old Anabruzas*, I caught myself thinking, *I knew he wouldn't let us down*; then I just had time to castigate myself for being a sick bastard before we moved off again.

There was light inside the gate; only a couple of lamps, but after our journey in the dark it was like noon. I took a very deep breath as I walked into the light – I felt stretched and squashed up, both at the same time, and I couldn't keep my mouth from lolling open. We were in. I made a solemn oath to take as small a part in the proceedings as I possibly could.

'What the hell kept you?' a voice hissed to my left. I looked round; it was Anabruzas, his eyes glowering at me from under the brim of an absurdly wide Greek hat.

'Sorry,' I whispered back.

I thought he'd go away, but instead he skipped along at my side; it reminded me of something I'd seen back in Athens one time, when a division of men were being marched off to some war. One of the men apparently owed money to his neighbour, because I watched the creditor scurrying along beside the column, trying to keep up while he ranted and yelled at this poor man, calling him all the names under the sun, while the soldier stayed rigidly eyes-front and in step, all the way down the road where the Long Walls used to be and halfway to Piraeus.

'Go away,' I whispered.

'Oh no,' he replied. 'I'm coming with you.'

Once the whole unit was inside the gates, Marsamleptes gave the order and we split up into platoons. We'd practised this bit several times so as to be sure to get it right, but of course we'd practised it on an open, uncluttered drill-square, rather than a village street. Now, as we tried to carry out the operations we'd learned so carefully, we found to our horror that there were houses and carts and a well in the way. We blundered about, knocking over jars and making a hell of a racket.

'Forget it,' Marsamleptes shouted. 'Push down through, and try and keep in line.'

(Did I mention that habit of his? Marsamleptes was hopeless at giving directions. He knew exactly what he meant, of course; but what he'd say would be something like, 'I'll go on down over, and you follow me up through and we'll meet up on the other side.' Gibberish; and totally misleading, if you made an attempt to understand it.)

I could feel Anabruzas' hand gripping my arm. 'What are you doing?' he said.

'Let go,' I replied.

'Tell me what you're doing, I want to know.'

'Not *now*,' I said; honestly, we sounded like an old married couple. 'Get out of my way.'

They'd lit torches off the lamps in the gateway, and thatch was beginning to flare up, splashing wavering yellow light over everything. 'What are they doing?' Anabruzas said. 'Tell me, what's going to happen?'

I lost my temper and shoved him away; he staggered back a step or two, then slipped and fell over. I hoped he'd stay out of the way, but he didn't; he rushed up and tried to grab hold of the torch in a man's hand; he was just about to set light to the eaves of a roof. The man didn't know who Anabruzas was; he had his spear in his other hand, and stabbed him underhand, driving the blade in under the ribs on the left-hand side. There was that sucking noise as the blade came out again, and the whistling noise of a man breathing through a punctured lung. That was the last I ever saw of him.

(I think of him, Phryzeutzis, even now. I find it disturbing to think that here was a man, a good and very unlucky man, whose life was marked by disaster and sorrow at every turn, and each and every one of those disasters and sorrows was directly caused by me. I was the author of all his misfortunes, right from that night in Athens when I bashed his face in and left him sprawling in his own blood. I led my people into his homeland, I made him send one son to be butchered, ordered the battle in which his other son died; I forced him to betray his village in the name of saving it, and made him become the traitor on whose hands the blood of all of them would lie. And yet I'm not a bad man, Phryzeutzis, I've never been more than careless or insensitive, never evil or malicious; and everything I did in Olbia I did for the best.)

Things were getting lively now. I didn't have a torch of my own, so I held my shield over one of the men who did. There were people running in every direction, bundling out of the houses as we set fire to them, bumping into us and jostling us out of the way as they ran in terror from the flames, or crashing into our shields as they blundered out, their arms full of their precious possessions. Most of them acted as if we weren't even there, as if they had far too much on their plate already to be bothered with us; but there was one old man, white-haired and stark naked, who jumped at me with a big wooden spade and started smacking my shield with it, making a deep booming noise, like a drum. After he'd done this five or six times I tried to prod him off with the butt of my spear; but he either stumbled or charged forward at just the wrong time, and the butt-spike slid into his groin like a wooden spoon going into the whey. He dropped down when I pulled the spear out, and I didn't hang around to see what became of him.

The fire was doing our job for us, which was just as well, since we'd got completely out of line and were wandering aimlessly about, like visitors who've come to Athens on a grain-boat and want to see the sights. There were no arrows, no fighting; all we were doing was gently pushing people down the street towards the side gate, like shepherds driving a flock down a wide road. I gather that the encircling party took their duties rather more seriously than we were doing.

Quite soon the fire started to spread of its own accord, which made the village a bad place to be. I heard Marsamleptes shouting to us to withdraw, but only because he was standing quite close to me; you can't hear much at the best of times when you've got a thick, well-padded helmet down over your ears, and there was so much noise inside the village that I was lucky to have heard him at all. The only casualties we suffered that night, in fact, were four men who didn't hear and got caught too far inside the village when the fire got completely out of hand.

Sorry, there were five. Right at the last moment, as he was ushering us out of the main gate, counting under his breath to make sure we were all there, Marsamleptes was hit in the face with an arrow, probably the only one shot that night. He'd taken his helmet off so we could see who it was and hear his orders better, and the arrow hit him on the lower rim of the eye-socket on the left-hand side. He dropped down without a word or a movement.

When the encircling group heard from the mobile reserve that the enemy had killed Marsamleptes, they got very angry. The Illyrians loved and trusted him – they're quite an emotional people, when you get to know them – and even the Founders had come to respect him over the last dozen years. All in all, killing him was the worst possible thing the villagers could have done just then, and they paid the price of their ineptitude. When the killing stopped at dawn (I don't know why it stopped then, but it did) both of the side gateways were pretty well bunged up with bodies, and because of the blockage, a whole bunch of people hadn't been able to get out of the way when the main granary went up, right in close to the stockade. We didn't bother raking through the ashes so I can't put a figure on it, but to judge from the noise they made there were quite a few of them.

We didn't kill them all, of course; nothing like. We grabbed a few of the survivors at random, and left the rest standing around staring at the carnage and the mess. I was out of it by then; I'd breathed in rather too much smoke, and spent a long time while the action was at its most intense doubled up just outside the main gate, coughing my lungs up; so yes, I suppose I was looking the other way once more, as I always seem to be. Just for once, though, I wasn't particularly sorry to have missed the main event.

I was free to go. I'd done what I'd undertaken to do, and there was nothing to keep me in Antolbia. Just for once, I'd managed to see something through to the end, to a successful result. Maybe it would have been nicer if it had been something a bit more positive than genocide, but losers can't be choosers, as we philosophers say.

The news that I was going back to Athens spread quickly enough, and wasn't well received. I suppose it was a bad time to make an announcement like that, immediately after the death of Marsamleptes. Of the two of us, there was no question who was the greater loss; he'd been an efficient and competent soldier and the effective spokesman of the Illyrian majority, in which capacity he'd shown a modest flair for diplomacy and what for the want of a better word I think I'm going to have to call statesmanship. Besides which, people liked him. I'd liked him. What was there not to like?

'You aren't liked and respected the way he was, obviously,' Tyrsenius tried to explain. 'People could – I don't know, people reckoned he understood what they were thinking and feeling, that he was one of them. You've always been the *oecist*, however much effort you've put into that man-of-the-people persona of yours. But that's not the point. You're the *Founder*. You're the man who founded the city, it's your name on all the inscriptions and records, your name in all the laws: "Euxenus the *oecist* and the people decided that . . ." You're like a statue in the market square, or the figurehead of a ship; people *need* to see you there. And if you deliberately decide to leave – just think how that makes people feel.'

Not for the first time, I wondered how Tyrsenius had ever managed to sell anything to anybody. 'It's really sweet of you to say all these nice things about me,' I said, 'but my mind's made up. I just don't want to live here any more. It's different for you, for most of them in fact. All they expected from the place was somewhere to live, some land to farm. It was always supposed to be more for me.'

'The perfect society,' Tyrsenius said. 'Quite. Actually, I don't see what the problem is there. Look at us; we've got no faction fighting, no oligarchic tendency slugging it out with the mob, no military dictator screwing everybody for taxes. We've got Greeks and Illyrians living quite happily side by side; we've even got Budini. Isn't that your perfect society, Mister Philosopher?'

I shook my head. 'Tyrsenius, the only reason we haven't got those sorts of problems is that we're too small. Everybody knows everybody else, we've all got roughly the same amount of land, we've just fought a war against a foreign enemy; obviously we're all united and filled with brotherly love *now*, you'd hardly expect anything else. And I'm not leaving because the experiment's failed. I'm leaving because it's over. Do you understand?'

He nodded. 'I think so,' he said. 'I think you were never part of this community to start with. You came here to study, to see what it'd be like. You've done that, and now you're off to study something else. You know what? I think you really are a philosopher after all.' He frowned. 'And to think I reckoned you were an honest charlatan, a genuine confidence man with a snake in a jar to prove it.'

'What's wrong with being a philosopher?' I asked.

'If you don't know, I don't think I'm up to explaining it to you,' he said. 'Just take it from me, there's a place in decent society for snake-in-a-jar operators. Philosophers; well . . .'

I thought he was making a joke, but he wasn't. And when I thought about it, I could see his point.

It turned out I wasn't the only one who was ready to leave. Agenor the stonemason asked if he could share the journey home with me; he'd always fancied trying his luck in Athens, he said, where people really appreciated fine sculpture and works of art.

'Sure,' I said. 'But what's the matter? I thought you were nicely settled here.'

He looked at me as if I'd said something offensive. 'You can't be serious,' he replied. 'You know what I've been doing virtually since the moment I got off the ship? I've been building houses, and barns, and city walls, and wells, and gods only know what else. As soon as I've finished one building job, someone comes up to me and more or less demands I come and build something for him. And I hate building work, Euxenus; it's hard, dirty, boring, degrading work and I've had enough of it.'

'But think what you've achieved,' I said. We were standing in the market square; I pointed, and swung round in a circle. 'You see all this? You did all that, Agenor. What you didn't build with your own hands you designed or supervised; if anybody deserves to be remembered as the Father of the City, it's you. Don't you feel good about that?'

'No,' he said. 'It's crude, ugly, makeshift stuff. The materials are rubbish, I'm ashamed of some of the techniques I used, it's a miracle most of it's still standing. Just look at that,' he went on, pointing at our little temple. 'See those proportions? All wrong. Height's all wrong for the length, which means the pillars had to be too close together, and too thick. If I had my way, we'd pull the whole lot down and start over.'

I was shocked. 'I didn't know you felt like this, Agenor,' I said. 'And I can't see anything wrong with it. I think it's beautiful.'

'I know,' he said. 'So does everyone else. That's why I'm finally leaving. Twelve years of living with your own sloppy work is bad enough; knowing it'll probably never be put right is just too much. I want to go somewhere they'd pull something like that down *tomorrow.*'

I couldn't think of anything to say. After all, his complaint was more or less the same as mine. 'All right,' I said, 'but why now? If you hated it so much, why did you stay so long?'

He shrugged. 'Laziness,' he said. 'Tried to kid myself into thinking that I was doing a good job. You probably noticed, I've always been the one who's tried to help, got involved wherever I thought I could make myself useful; I tried, Euxenus, I really did. But this war – I didn't like that. I'm not saying it was wrong,' he went on, before I could interrupt. 'On the contrary, it had to be done or we'd never have had a moment's peace. But my apprentice; you remember, he lost a hand in that raid? He was going to be a *good* builder, he had the knack; he'd have been able to do *good* work with this lousy crumbly stone and all the little annoying things that I could never see how to get round. Now he's as good as dead and I don't want to train anybody else.' He breathed out and looked around. 'I just don't like living here any more,' he said. 'I suppose you could say that if I've got to live in an imperfect city, I'd rather it was one that someone else has cocked up, not me.'

There was nothing more to say, so I walked home. The house was dark and quiet, and every part of it seemed filled with me; I was sick and tired of having nothing but my own personality around me all the time. Once I'd had a wife and son living here with me, only I hadn't appreciated them for what they were. Most of the time I tried not to notice them, because who they were and what they wanted didn't seem relevant to what I was trying to do. At that moment, I could cheerfully have lit a torch and set fire to the place.

It comes to something when you can walk away from twelve years of your life with nothing more than you can carry in a small goatskin bag. In fact, I was hard put to it to fill the bag. Most of the weight was coined money; I'd sold my armour and my plough and the tools that were worth having, and some of the furniture (though most of it wasn't fit to give away; I've never been bothered about things like that) and Tyrsenius had advanced me the value of my harvest and my small flock of goats, as well as giving me free passage on his ship as far as Athens. I had enough money to get home and to live on for a few weeks while I got my lawsuit under way; I had more money deposited with a bank in Athens to pay for the rest of the suit, left over from my relative affluence as a respected teller of fortunes. I wasn't worried about what I was going to do when I got home; if necessary I was sure I could go back to my old trade of cheating gullible businessmen. In fact, I wasn't worried about anything, because in order to worry you first have to care.

As well as the money, and of course my lucky snake-jar, I took a comb that had belonged to Theano (after all, a man needs a comb), a set of knucklebone dice I'd made for my son (because a man can virtually make a living playing dice on board a ship, provided he knows which way the dice are going to fall; and my dice were utterly predictable, because Eupolis always got so upset if he lost), a knife, a razor and a scraper, and a roll of mostly blank Egyptian paper, on which I'd started to write the history of Antolbia, back before it was ever called that. I'd intended it for Aristotle, as a contribution to his vast database on matters political, and as a smug and offensive lesson in how a perfect society is perfectly possible, if only you're prepared to get out there and *do*, rather than just sitting on your backside and talking about it.

It was a very long, excruciatingly boring journey. The ship crawled along the coast from city to city, converting figs into honey at one port of call, honey into iron ore, iron ore into dried fish, dried fish into olive oil, olive oil into figs (about thirty per cent more figs than we'd started off with), figs into hides, hides into grain . . . There was nothing to do but sit on deck, staring at the coastline as we sailed by and trying not to get under the feet of the sailors. At first, Agenor and I talked all the time about a whole range of things – philosophy, art, religion, history – but I found that talk like that irritated me now; when we disagreed I lost my temper, where once I'd have relished the chance of a good debate. We decided it would be better if we didn't talk any more, and for most of the journey home we sat at opposite ends of the ship, me staring in one direction, he in another. In the end, he couldn't face any more of the tedium and discomfort and left the ship at Scione; he'd see if there was any work going there, he said, and if not he'd carry on to Athens as originally planned. As and when he got there, he promised to come and look me up; after all, in spite of the fact that we'd fallen out on this long, boring sea journey, we'd still shared a dozen years of important experiences, and were really the only friends either of us had now, outside Antolbia. As he walked down the gangplank at Scione we waved to each other; I shouted out, 'See you in Athens,' and he called back, 'Count on it.'

Needless to say, I never saw or heard of him again.

As soon as we crawled into Piraeus I hurried thankfully up the road to the City to treat myself to an indulgence I'd been promising myself every day I had to spend on that grotty, uncomfortable ship: a proper Athenian haircut and shave.

To my delight, my favourite barber's shop was still there, and it had hardly changed at all since I'd been away. The barber didn't recognise me after all that time, but I recognised him; last time I'd seen him he'd been an eleven-year-old boy, sweeping up and whetting the razors while his father saw to the customers. Suddenly I felt overwhelming joy mixed with desperate sorrow; I'd been away far too long, but I was home.

While I was sitting in the chair, basking in the glory of just being there again, I listened to the gossip. There was only one topic of conversation. News had just arrived that the Macedonian colony of Antolbia on the Black Sea coast had been overrun by the local savages and utterly destroyed. There were, it seemed, no survivors.

CHAPTER EIGHTEEN

꘡꘡꘡꘡꘡꘡꘡꘡꘡꘡꘡꘡꘡꘡꘡꘡꘡꘡꘡꘡꘡꘡

I won my lawsuit. It took me a year and an infinity of patience and effort; I had to learn the law, for one thing. There's an awful lot of it, and surprisingly nobody seems to know what it is; the more closely you study it, the more aware you become of this, as each new aspect you address turns out to be yet another 'grey area', which is lawyer's talk for 'We haven't a clue, and if we did we wouldn't tell *you*'. I ended up with the conclusion that about sixty-four per cent of Athenian law is known by nobody at all; which is odd when you consider that if you happen to break it, ignorance isn't an excuse.

While I was fighting the case, I earned my living the way all poor Athenians do, by hanging round the law-courts and Assembly. Three obols a day for sitting on a jury, the same for attending Assembly; it's a living, but by the gods you meet some insalubrious people when you're a professional citizen. Traditionally, juries are manned by deadbeat old men without families to care for them who're too old or too crippled to go to work. Half of them are stone deaf, half of the remainder are crazy or senile, so that they can't remember their own names, let alone the points made in the previous speaker's deposition. But if you're on trial for your life, they're the ones who'll be sitting in judgement over you, and you can tell what sort of justice you're likely to get by looking at their fingernails; you can always tell a professional juror by the thick clots of wax. When the accused is found guilty, you see, the jury votes on the severity of his punishment by scratching a line on a wax tablet – the longer the line, the harsher the penalty.

It's the same crew of dead and desiccated corpses who sit in Assembly when they can't get on a jury (jury work's better, because the hours are shorter; kinder to an old man's bladder, though the experienced juror takes his chamber-pot with him. It's disconcerting, to say the least, when you're winding up into your closing speech and all you can hear is the steady trickle of piss on pottery) and it's a great comfort to think that these are the men who wield the sovereign power in the Athenian democracy, the fairest and most perfect democracy the world has ever seen.

I particularly remember one day in the law-courts; I was on the jury for a complicated fraud trial, and the evidence was about as boring as it's possible to get. I must have been the youngest man on the jury by about twenty years. Sitting behind me were a couple of regulars – we called them the Living Skulls because they were so old and shrivelled that you could clearly see the bone under the skin of their faces – who'd been having the same conversation for the last ten years. As soon as the proceedings started, they began to talk. When court was dismissed for the day, they broke off in mid-sentence and went home. The next day they picked up exactly where they'd left off. Nobody could figure what it was this marathon conversation was actually about. It was something to do with a quarrel between their sisters, long since dead, but since they kept drifting off on side-issues, it was impossible to follow. The man next to me was fast asleep; not the only one, by any means. On my other side was an old boy who hummed softly under his breath all day; asking him to stop had no effect, and neither did jabbing him sharply in the ribs with your elbow. Directly in front of me was another old man who talked to himself, and beside him was yet another celebrated jury personality, nicknamed Ocean because he never seemed to run dry (but it was his habit of emptying his chamber-pot at random over the benches below him that made him really famous).

It was early in my legal career and I was actually trying to make sense of what was going on; but what with the snores and the tinkling and the humming and the muttering and the earnest voices of the Skulls, not to mention the heat of the sun and the hardness of the bench, I got hopelessly lost after the first half-hour. When the time came for the vote, the usher went round prodding awake the sleepers and chivvying us all off the benches towards the voting urns. A white pebble for not guilty, black for guilty; except that we had to provide our own pebbles, and white pebbles are harder to find; anyway, we voted and the verdict was Guilty, so we were sent back to decide on the punishment. My neighbours didn't take long about it; they dug their nails in hard and ripped, like a cat laying open a dead mouse; straight lines across the tablet, the death penalty. When this was announced, the lawyer who'd been acting for the accused got up and tried to explain that the death penalty didn't apply for this particular offence; it was a fine, or at the worst, exile. No sooner had he sat down than his opposite number bobbed up and asked us to convict his learned friend for contempt of court, in that he'd challenged the decision of a duly constituted jury. So off we went to vote once again; and since it was the last case of the day, we'd all used up our last remaining pebbles on the previous vote. But the usher saved the day; he found a man selling beans and confiscated his stock, then issued them to us to use instead of pebbles. Now these beans were a sort of dark brown colour, as near black as made no odds; so the lawyer was found guilty, and the usher passed round the wax tablets. A few minutes later, he announced that the jury had decided on the death penalty, which was a valid punishment for contempt; what had happened was that there were no more unmarked tablets, so they simply reissued the ones used for the last vote, without explaining that what we were meant to do was turn them on their sides . . . After the case was over, just out of interest, I stopped one old boy and asked him innocently what scratching a full line across the tablet meant.

'Means he's guilty, of course,' the old man said.

'Really? I thought we used the pebbles for that.'

'Oh.' The old man thought for a moment. 'No,' he said, 'you're wrong. Least, I been coming to this court forty years and I always done it that way, and nobody ever told me different.'

Gradually, I found out what had happened at Antolbia.

There had been one survivor – one. He was an Illyrian who'd hidden in a grain-pit. When they set fire to the barn, the roof fell down in such a way as to create a pocket of air that lasted until the fire burned itself out, so he was saved from the smoke; but he was down there for two weeks, pinned down by a fallen beam and unable to move, until quite by chance some Odessans who'd come to see if they could salvage any grain happened to open up the barn and found him. He'd survived by eating the raw grain and catching drips of water from a mill-stream that had been diverted when a house fell into its course, sending it down across the barn floor. Because the floor had been stamped hard, the water ran off it instead of sinking in, and enough drips fell over the side of the pit and into his mouth to keep him from dying of thirst. He was so firmly wedged in by the beam that they had to cut off both his feet before they could get him out of there.

When he was able to talk again, he told them what he could remember, which wasn't much. He'd been out drinking the night before, and hadn't made it all the way home; the furthest he'd been able to stagger was a friend's barn, so he crawled in and collapsed on a pile of straw. When the attack began, he'd been woken up by the shouting and screaming; he guessed at once what was happening, and all he could think of to do was to dive into the pit and hope for the best. As it was he fell in head first and nearly drowned in the grain; it was like swimming through mud, he said, and that far down he could scarcely breathe through a mouth and nose filled with grain.

All in all, he said, he wasn't surprised at what had happened, bearing in mind that the General had just been killed and the *oecist* had vanished a day or so later, taking the city's lucky snakes with him. Obviously, he said, the snakes had warned the *oecist* about what was going to happen and told him to get out while he still could.

It took longer to find out the Scythian background. In fact, a year went by and I'd pretty well given up hope of ever knowing when quite by chance I met a Scythian policeman (he arrested me for sleeping off one of my regular drinking bouts in the market square). When he found out I could speak quite a lot of his own language he was mightily impressed and let me go; then he asked me where I'd learned Scythian. I told him and he looked rather thoughtful.

The attackers, it turned out, were his people, the Sauromatae; to be precise, a rogue war-party that was escaping after a defeat in some civil war or other and had turned south, through the land of the Alizones and down into the settled region. He hadn't been with that particular party, but a cousin of his had, and he'd heard the story from him.

It was then I found out about the rich man whose son stole the horse, and all the rest of the story. When we burned the village, the rich man went around the other villages stirring up trouble, promising that they'd be next. Everyone was very worried, as you can imagine, but none of them wanted to be the ones to take us on, since we were so very warlike and ruthless. Then, quite by chance, these outlaw Sauromatae turned up, and were immediately approached to undertake the task of attacking the colony. They replied that they'd fought their own people, the Royal Scythians, the Alizones and the Persians; they certainly weren't afraid of a few Greeks. There were about seven thousand of them, I believe, all with their own horses.

Before attacking, they sent infiltrators down into the city, pretending to be mercenaries looking for someone to hire them. They were told to go away, since with the General dead and the *oecist* gone, there wasn't anybody dealing with security or defence right then; it was supposed to be the elders' job (the Founders, I suppose he meant) but they hadn't been able to decide between them who was going to do it, and meanwhile there weren't even any sentries on the wall, because there wasn't anybody to organise a rota.

The attack, my policeman friend told me, was pretty much an anticlimax, much to the disgust of these warlike Sauromatae. They'd taken the job as much for the pleasure of matching themselves against the invincible Greeks as for the pay (which wasn't much, since the villages were at little better than subsistence level at the best of times), but when they made the assault, at midday, they found the gate left open and met with no resistance whatsoever. After they'd killed and burned everything inside the city, they combed the surrounding fields, rounded up the livestock and burned off the crops before reporting back. After they'd gone, the villagers who'd formed the alliance against Antolbia held a meeting and decided that they couldn't stay where they were; there were bound to be reprisals from other Greeks, and the Sauromatae had moved on and wouldn't protect them. So they did what the Scythians have always done in the face of concerted invasion; they destroyed all their permanent structures, burned their crops, poisoned their wells, packed everything they owned into wagons, and set off north, into nomad country.

A little after that, I learned that Olbia and Odessus had decided to take no action; after all, the Scythians had gone, and the whole region was now empty. But, since Antolbia had nominally been a Macedonian colony, they sent a petition to Alexander asking him to avenge the massacre by sending a punitive expedition. Alexander got the message and acknowledged it, but nothing was ever done; Alexander was a long way away and had other things on his mind.

Well, I hope the rich man was able to get his son back in the end. It'd be truly sad if he went to all that trouble and expense for nothing. I never did find out his name, and as a historian I regret that. The duty of a historian is to ensure that the momentous deeds of men whose actions shape the world are never forgotten, and I guess that if anybody qualifies under those criteria, he did.

A month or so after the end of my lawsuit, when I was sure that my ninth-cousin-fifty-times-removed had finally packed up and slung his hook, I went back home to Pallene.

It's an old house; my father was always talking about pulling it down and building something better, but he never got round to it, and while I was growing up there it was still basically as it had been when my great-great-grandfather built it. In the middle there's a courtyard, closed in on the southern and western sides by plain mud-brick walls and on the other two sides by the two flat-roofed blocks of the house which meet at right-angles at the north-eastern corner, comprising the main room (facing north) and the inner room (facing east). The gate's in the east wall, with a verandah on the outside. The northern half of the courtyard is shaded by the roof of the portico. That's it, basically.

As I walked down the hill, the first I saw of it was the flat roof of the inner room; that was where we all used to sleep during the hottest part of the year, when it was impossible to sleep indoors. A little further down the trail, and I caught sight of the tower, a separate building a few yards behind the house itself, masked from the path by a little curtain of apple trees. These trees had grown a lot since I'd been away – nobody could be bothered to prune them, I guess – so it was only when I left the path and wound my way past the two big rocks we called the Gateposts that I was able to see the house itself. Apart from the overgrown trees it was exactly the same as I remembered it. Even the half-dead old fig-tree we'd pegged to the outside of the south wall when I was just a kid was still there, still lolling off the pegs like a drunken man leaning on the shoulder of a long-suffering friend. The fallen-down barn we'd kept promising ourselves we'd restore was still standing, no more and no less dilapidated than when I'd last seen it. The old cartwheel my father had hung from a branch for us to play on was still propped against the pear-tree, still missing the same two spokes. Even the two bee-hives were exactly where they'd been the last time I conjured the place up in my mind's eye.

I was home. Fact.

I walked into the verandah, lifted the latch and gently pushed the door. It opened a hand's span or so, then stuck. I put my shoulder against it, forced it open enough for me to squeeze through, and went into the main room.

There was nothing there, of course. My defeated rival had taken all the furniture and movables with him when he left, and for the first time in my life I could see all four corners of the room at once. It was much smaller than I'd remembered, the doorways were lower, the hearth narrower. It was darker, too.

I was about to turn round and go outside when I heard a faint scuffling noise from the inner room. I tiptoed across and jerked the door open.

'Who's there?' I asked.

The inner room had been stripped bare too, of course, and it was even darker. Under the shadow of the far wall I could see something that looked like a bundle of old cloth.

'You,' I said. 'Who are you?'

'Euxenus?'

I took a step closer. The voice wasn't familiar exactly, but I had an idea I'd heard it before. 'Who are you?' I repeated.

'It's me,' the voice said. 'Don't you remember?'

It was an old man's voice, quite quiet, with an accent of some sort. 'On your feet,' I said. 'This is my house now, and you're trespassing.'

'Euxenus? It's me, Syrus.'

For a moment my mind was as blank as a fresh wax tablet; then I remembered.

'Syrus?' I said. 'I thought you were dead.'

You remember the slave who hurt himself during the olive harvest, and thereby indirectly caused the death of my father? That was Syrus. 'No,' he replied, 'not so's you'd notice.'

I moved closer, and he lifted his head. It was Syrus all right. He'd gone bald and his beard was white and scraggy, he was painfully thin – he'd been a stout, round-faced man when I last saw him – and the folds of empty skin around the sides of his eyes and chin made me think of sacks dumped on the floor. He'd gone blind, I realised.

'What the hell are you doing here?' I asked.

He looked at me – well, about a yard to my right, actually; it was rather disconcerting. 'Nowhere else to go,' he replied. 'You remember, in his will your father set me free.'

'That's right,' I said. 'You were going to go into the rope-making business.'

'I did,' he said, nodding. 'Worked for fifteen years in a ropewalk in Piraeus, till I saved up enough to start up on my own. I was doing all right, too.'

I waited for a moment, then said, 'What happened?'

'There was a fire,' he said. 'My wife, my boy, the two lads I had working with me, the house, all the stock and materials – it's tricky stuff, rope. Actually, it's the tar we put on it to keep it from rotting. One spark and the next thing you know—' He smiled; or at least his lips pressed together and widened, and his body shook a little. 'They fished me out, but they shouldn't have bothered. It's nothing but a waste of good food keeping me alive now.'

'I'm sorry,' I said. 'So why are you here?'

He shrugged. 'Well, nobody was going to keep me back in Piraeus, I'd have starved. But I thought, the boys back at the farm, they might look after me for old times' sake. Of course, when I got here I heard, they're all . . . Except Master Eudemus, and he's no better off than I am really. He lost an eye, you know, in the battle.'

'I know,' I said. 'That reminds me; do you happen to know where he is?'

Syrus turned his head towards me. 'Didn't you know? He – I'm sorry, Euxenus, he's gone too. Some kind of illness, I never heard any more.'

I sighed. 'That's it, then,' I said. 'It looks like it's just me. And you,' I added. 'So you got here and you found they were all dead. What then?'

'Your cousin, Philocarpus; he let me sleep in the barn and eat with the hired help. That was kind of him, he didn't need to do anything like that. But he only laughed and said I went with the land, like some old tree-trunk it's easier to plough round than dig out. Then he came and told me he was having to move on back to Priene, because you'd won your case. He didn't make it sound like I could go with him, so I stayed here.'

I thought for a moment. 'Is there anything at all you can do?' I asked.

He shrugged. 'I'll be straight with you, Euxenus, there isn't much.' He lifted his hands; I could see the scar tissue from the burns even in that poor light. 'I can grind, and turn the olive-press, if someone else fills the hopper. That's about it.'

'I see. Fine inheritance you turned out to be.' I opened the flap of my satchel and pulled out a small, half-empty jar of rough wine that had been keeping me company as I walked out from the City. 'Here,' I said, 'help yourself.' He found the neck with his hands and drank deeply, spilling wine down his chin. 'Just you and me,' I repeated. 'And I've come ever such a long way to get here.'

He frowned. 'I don't follow,' he said.

'Don't worry about it,' I replied. 'Look, you can carry on dossing down in the barn, and I'll see you don't starve. What do you do all day?'

'Not a lot I can do,' he said. 'I sit, mostly.'

'Sounds pretty boring.'

'It is,' he said. 'But there's worse things than boring. Thank you, Euxenus.'

'Forget it,' I replied. 'Doesn't sound like I'm doing you any favours, at that.'

He smiled again. 'Remains to be seen, doesn't it?' he said.

And that, my young friend, is how, after a lifetime of wandering and striving after achievement, I finally attained what had always been my heart's desire, the life and dignity of an Athenian gentleman. Curious; if I'd known that all I had to do was manage to reach the age of forty-one without dying, I'd have stayed at home and kept myself amused with pottering around the market square, telling lies for money, rather than educating the sons of kings or founding cities, and maybe an awful lot of people would still be alive today; Scythians, Illyrians, Greeks . . . Not to mention a fair number of Persians, Medes, Bactrians, Cappadocians, Armenians, Gedrosians, Drangianae, Fish-eating Ethiopians (so called to distinguish them from the other Ethiopians, who live in Africa), Arians, Massagetae, Egyptians and Indians whose deaths are probably partly my fault as well. I remember hearing once about some savage king of somewhere or other who had a road running the length of his empire paved with the skulls of his enemies. I can go one better than that. I travelled from Pallene to Pallene by way of Macedon and Olbia, walking a road paved with the dead bodies of my family and friends.

'Self-pity, Euxenus,' you're muttering at me, Phryzeutzis, as you smile the patronising smile of the tolerant young. 'You're exag–gerating for effect again. That's not the way to write history.'

I won't argue with you; thirty years ago, now, and you'd have had a real dialectic fight on your hands, but these days the sound of my own voice raised in debate simply makes me feel tired. So I'll con–cede the point, if it makes you feel any better. Anyway, I don't need to use any philosopher's tricks to make my point. Picture me and Syrus, sitting opposite each other in the empty house in Pallene; that'll be far more eloquent than I ever was, even when I was young and fiery.

So we won't overplay the melodrama. During the day I didn't crouch in the ashes like a heroine out of Euripides; I went out into the fields – my fields – and I worked, bloody hard. For a while I was an inspiration to my neighbours. 'Up before dawn,' their wives would tell them, 'and off with the team or the mattock, never comes home till dark, and he's got that place looking as good as it was in his father's day, all on his own. Why can't *you* be more like Euxenus?' And yet, in spite of that, they were still prepared to talk to me. They wanted to hear all my fabulous tales of far away, about King Philip's court and the boyhood of Alexander ('Is it true that when he was just a baby, he strangled two snakes in his cot?'), about desperate battles against the cannibal Scythians, and of course my opinion about the latest news from the East. 'We heard Alexander's reached Pasargadae,' they'd say to me, 'where's that?' Whereupon I'd smile knowingly and reply that they didn't want to go believing everything they heard (which is good advice at all times, though as a matter of fact Alexander had indeed reached Pasargadae, wherever the hell that is, and had turned north-east towards Ecbatana). That would impress them no end, though I don't imagine they had a clue why they found it impressive, and maybe they'd even buy me another drink.

In short, I became a prosperous and well-respected citizen; you might almost say a model citizen, the sort of person you'd want living in your perfect society. I got the vineyards back into shape, put some heart into the soil by ploughing five times a year and growing beans in the off year; I repaired my walls and trellises, pruned back my trees, shored up my terraces, interplanted barley between my rows of olive trees so that not a square yard of good soil went idle. I saved up and bought a couple of slaves, good, strong middle-aged men who worked long hours silently and never gave me any bother. I was as near as you'll ever get, in fact, to the Good Farmer, that enigmatic character you read about in the books on good husbandry that people like Aristotle are so fond of writing; 'the good farmer,' they say, 'takes the trouble to sow vetch and lupins on the fallow, both to put heart into the soil and provide winter fodder for his livestock.' When I was young I used to picture this paragon of virtue, trying to imagine the expression on his face as he carefully lifts a crumb of soil to his tongue on the tip of his little finger, to ascertain whether it's too sour for growing wheat, or his quiet smile of satisfaction as he inspects the flourishing shoots he's grafted onto his vines to boost their productivity. But I never quite managed to get a fix on him until one day I was looking something up in one of those damned manuals, and realised, with rather mixed feelings, that he was me.

Now, they're all well and good, those books, but they never tell you enough. They don't tell you what this good farmer does the rest of the time; at night, when he's finished repairing broken tool-handles by wrapping them with saturated rawhide or plaiting himself a useful rope out of the loose hairs he's saved off the curry-comb; when it's late and the house is empty, and he sits alone in the dark instead of going to bed. On reflection, though, that situation wouldn't arise for the good farmer, because he married a good wife in chapter three (industrious, good at spinning and weaving, capable of helping with field work in the busy season, not inclined to drink or gossiping with other women) and their union was blessed in chapter five by the birth of three strong, healthy sons (four is too many, placing too much strain on the farm's resources; two isn't enough, because one of them may die young and leave the farm short of manpower), who will presumably inherit come chapter twenty-nine, when the good farmer dies, surrounded by family and friends, with a finger stuck in the book to mark the place in case he needs to refer to it for instructions before the end finally comes. Maybe I wasn't the good farmer after all; or maybe he never actually existed. You know, the more I read, the more sceptical I get. I never met the man who farms like the good farmer, or the soldier who fights like Achilles or the heroes in Homer, or the citizen who participates in the ideal society, or even the great historical personage who bears any resemblance to the description in a book of history; even, I hasten to add, this book of history, as written by me.

We finally made a start on patching up that old barn. The incentive was a freak rainstorm – we get them every ten years or so – which washed the last of the thatch off the roof and nearly drowned old Syrus and my two slaves. Now, the Good Farmer naturally takes care of his slaves; they are, after all, his most valuable perishable asset, and if they die of pneumonia or even if they miss work for a week or so because they're ill, it's a dead loss. Accordingly, he makes sure that their quarters are dry and warm, and that they're adequately fed and clothed. You'll find specifications for the ideal slave rations in those excellent books, the perfect balance of nutrition and economy; an ideal to which, I confess, I never aspired. They knew where the grain-store was, and they helped themselves. I suspect that if I'd taken the trouble to follow the ideal, I'd have spent more on fancy padlocks and Molossian watchdogs to keep them from pilfering than I'd ever have saved on barley, cheese and figs.

The stones were mostly still where they'd fallen; we'd used a few over the years to patch up walls, but not many. All we had to do was figure out how they fitted together and put them back. Simple.

In theory. It's a basic rule of nature that putting something back together is always a hundred times harder than taking it apart; as witness that barn. It was so easy to bring it down that the wind and weather managed it without human assistance. If I'd thought of it, I could have hired a Thessalian witch to catch the wind in a bag and ask it if it remembered how the stones fitted. But I didn't; I tried to figure it out for myself, and as a result arrived at Euxenus' Law of applied geometry, which states that just because things fitted together once, it doesn't follow that they'll fit that way again. It's a good law, that, and I think you'll agree if you've been paying attention to this story that it doesn't just apply to dry-stone walling.

After two frustrating days of skinned knuckles, wrenched backs and foul tempers, we decided to adopt a more radical approach, involving cold chisels and big hammers. I borrowed the necessary tools from my neighbours and we set to work, trimming and shaping the stones to make them fit. Although I hadn't actually done any masonry work myself, I'd stood and watched Agenor a score of times over the years, and he always made it look easy. Without scribing a line or taking measurements he'd simply tap-tap a couple of times with the chisel, then give one sharp, hard tap and split off the irregular chunk of stone, leaving a smooth, flat face that would lie nicely flush against its neighbour. The waste material came away like rust flaking off an iron ploughshare; the desired shape was already in the stone, and all he had to do was strike off the encumbrances. He never swung the hammer in great double-handed sweeps; just those little woodpecker taps up and down a convenient fault-line. Definitely the way to go; nothing to it.

For some reason it didn't work that way when we tried it. Either we got nowhere, scarcely even marking the stone, or else it exploded under the hammer into a shower of razor-sharp fragments, like the results of the technique they use in the quarries when they heat the rock with bellows and a brazier, then throw vinegar on it to make it shatter. Unfortunately for all of us, this total lack of progress annoyed me so much that I resolved to persevere and succeed at all costs. Match the intransigence of stone, I said to myself, against the infinite flexibility of the human mind, and eventually you'll get a row of neatly dressed masonry blocks, together with the immeasurable satisfaction of knowing you've won. True, my philosopher's brain had proved itself not to be entirely up to the task of building the ideal city, but a simple thing like chipping out a few blocks of stone, something that an unlettered and uneducated man like Agenor could do so easily, ought to be well within my capabilities.

'Keep at it,' I commanded. 'And keep your mind on what you're doing.'

They looked at me, wiped sweat ostentatiously from their foreheads, and renewed their assault on the stone. They may possibly even have lost their tempers just a little, or perhaps they were playing the game we all play when we've got a tedious job to do that involves hitting or slashing, and imagined that the rock was me; in any event, the chips started flying in all directions, and I, being a prudent man as well as a philosopher, muttered something about measuring up and retired to a safe distance.

I was fooling about with a measuring rod when I heard one of the slaves – Sclerus, his name was, or at least that was the name I'd given him; he was a Celt, from Galatia, and what they call themselves is nobody's business but their own – yelp loudly enough to make me drop my rod, and then start swearing in Galatian.

'Now what?' I said.

'Got something in my eye,' he replied.

I looked round, and saw that he was crouched on the ground with his hands over his face. He'd stopped swearing and started making a sort of whimpering noise, which was most unlike him.

'What happened?' I asked.

'A bit of that damned stone,' replied his colleague, a Sicilian I called Aeschrus. 'It flew up and hit him in the eye.'

'Let me see,' I said; but Sclerus didn't want to take his hands away from his face. I could see blood trickling down his cheek. 'Aeschrus, hold his hands,' I said. 'This is no time for melodrama.'

Aeschrus was a big strong lad; Sclerus was tall but thin and bony. So Aeschrus twisted his arms behind his back and I held his head still. I could see the splinter easily enough; he'd had his eye shut, but the splinter had gone right through it, pinning it to the eyeball. 'That looks bad,' I said. 'Get him into the house.'

I broke a thin piece of bronze off the rim of a wooden bowl and bent it double to make a pair of tweezers, with which I was able, eventually, to pull the splinter out. It wasn't easy; the splinter was an awkward shape and I couldn't get a grip, and every time I tried Sclerus would roar with pain and thrash about like a deer that's run into the nets during a forest drive. When eventually it did come out, a lot of blood came with it, and the poor man fainted. While he was out I washed the wound with hot water on a clean bit of rag until the bleeding stopped; then I gave Aeschrus some money and told him to run to the City and see if he could find a doctor.

He came back that evening with the money but no doctor. He'd tried four, he said, but they were all either busy or not at home. I don't think a doctor could have done any good, in any event. The wound stayed fresh, which was something; gods only know what would have happened if it had turned septic. I tried to treat it with a poultice, but whenever I went near him with the stuff Sclerus would start to bellow and cower, so I gave up and left him to it. Aeschrus made him an eyepatch out of very fine goatskin, because even though he couldn't see through it, strong sunlight made it hurt terribly.

We gave up on the barn after that.

It occurs to me, looking back, that I should have known better. The project contained all the elements of my previous disasters; trying to make life better for other people, trying to restore a bit of the life I'd left behind when my father died, trying to build something, trying to make something that wanted to be one shape into another. When I was a boy I heard the story of an enthusiastic but entirely talentless boxer; when he died, they said, his family and neighbours had a gravestone carved showing this man standing in the ring, his hands bound up for fighting, his arms raised to strike; and underneath, the inscription 'In memory of Polydamas, of whom it can truly be said, he never harmed his fellow men'. You know, I feel a bit like that Polydamas, only the other way round. He tried to hurt people but never managed it. I've tried to do good, on and off, my whole life, and I've left a trail of dead and mutilated bodies behind me wherever I've gone.

Now, in that excellent book, I expect it says that if one of the good farmer's slaves gets damaged in a way that affects his performance of his duties, the only sensible course of action is to cut one's losses, sell him for what he'll fetch and buy a replacement, rather than compound the loss by feeding and providing for a slave who does less work but eats the same amount. I didn't do that, however, which meant that Syrus, Sclerus, Aeschrus and I had five good eyes between the four of us, and people started calling us the Graeae, after the three witches in the old stories who have one eye between them, which they pass from hand to hand. (That, by the way, is the sort of thing that passes for wit in rural Attica, along with tying burning twigs to the tails of dogs and shoving drunks down wells.) So, with Syrus unable to do anything much and Sclerus restricted to light duties only (when we finally managed to get hold of a doctor, he warned that too much exertion could mean he'd lose the other eye as well), I ended up having to work longer and harder to put bread on the table for my slaves than I'd ever done before I bought them.

In the end I hired a couple of lads from a neighbouring farm to knock down what was left of the old barn and build a new one. It took them three days. They made it look easy.

'You could have done that,' they said to me as I paid them their money.

'Probably,' I replied. 'But you know how it is.'

They looked at me. 'Come again?' they said.

I grinned, thinking of Diogenes and the magic talisman that made people do things for you, the silver coin. 'Why do a job yourself when you can get someone to do it for you?'

'Right,' they said. 'Like, you keep three men and do all your own ploughing. No wonder you packed in being a philosopher.'

I nodded. 'Get off my land,' I said, 'before I set the snake on you.'

Time passes at a different rate, depending on where you are. A week in some strange place seems to last for ever, while you can lose a year at home as easily as a forgetful man misplaces his hat. I can't say I was really aware of time passing; someone would mention something that happened a while ago, and I'd say, 'Yes, that was the year the crows got in the laid patches in the barley.' And then I'd think, when was that? Not last year, because the barley stood up well right up till harvest. Not the year before, because I got Aristodemus' boy to stand guard with his sling and a bag of pebbles, and after a week he told me he'd killed thirty-seven of them. So it was either the year before that or the year before that – and suddenly I'd taken note of the passing of four years, which had sneaked by me like an adulterer creeping out of the window while his girlfriend keeps the husband talking in the front room.

While I was drifting aimlessly between harvests at home, Alexander of Macedon was marching from victory to victory, as unstoppable as a cart running down a hill. I could give you a battle-by-battle account of the campaign, I suppose, but it'd only be a rehash of what I've read in books; I wasn't there, remember, I was in Antolbia, then Attica, where the glorious achievements of the son of Philip were as remote and as irrelevant as the Trojan War. As far as we were concerned in Athens, Alexander had marched off the edge of the world, and the further he went away from us, the better we liked it. Sure, he wasn't hated and feared the way his father was. Truth to tell, he left us pretty much alone, and there were days you could go from dawn to dusk without anything reminding you of the Macedonian presence in Greece, or the effects of the battle of Chaeronea. If any of my neighbours knew I'd been to Macedon, been the boy's tutor, they were too tactful to mention it. Just occasionally, though, something reminded us of his existence; news of another glorious victory, rumours that he was dead ('Alexander dead?' someone said on one such occasion. 'Don't you believe it. If Alexander was dead, the stench would fill the earth') or had been captured by the enemy, or had ascended bodily into the heavens to rejoin his real father Zeus; there were rumours that he'd listened to bad advice and marched his army into a vast, waterless desert, where most of them had died of thirst. There were rumours that he'd finally gone mad, and was demanding that everybody worship him as a god. He'd married the daughter of the King of Persia, there was to be peace and Alexander was to succeed to the Great King's throne; he'd been shot in the chest while storming a fortress, and was hanging onto life by a thread; he'd murdered his best friend in a fit of drunken rage and burned down the capital city of the Empire in an excess of guilt-ridden insanity; he'd decided to merge the Greek and Persian races, and soon we'd all be shipped off and forcibly resettled in Asia, each of us being required to take at least one Persian wife, and wear trousers, on pain of death. Oh, there were always rumours; and of course we ignored them, or half-accepted them, not caring whether they were true or not – it's like when you read books about faraway lands, and you're told that beyond the great deserts of Africa there live people whose faces are in their bellies, whose ears are so long that they trail on the ground as they walk. You read, and you neither believe nor disbelieve, because even if you live to be a thousand years old, there's no possible set of circumstances whereby things like that could ever be relevant to you. If it's all lies, then so what? It's a pretty story. If it's true, then your belief or your scepticism aren't going to alter anything; it doesn't matter. Whichever way it goes, the fact that there may or may not be people in Africa who have one enormous foot instead of two normal-sized ones isn't going to make it easier or more difficult for you to cut your late barley before the crows flatten it, so you dismiss such things from your mind with a shake of your head and get on with your work. Similarly, the fact that at least three-quarters of the rumours we heard about Alexander turned out in the end to be true was neither here nor there. So what? Nothing, the gods be praised, to do with us.

Indeed. It'd have been nice, I guess, if it had stayed that way.

They called for me a couple of hours before dawn, in the early autumn of the eighth year after I came home. I'd made a start on the pruning the day before; I was tired out and fast asleep, so I didn't hear them ride up. The first I knew about it, in fact, was when Aeschrus grabbed my shoulder and shook me awake.

'There's soldiers outside,' he said, in a terrified whisper.

'What are you talking about?' I mumbled. He'd pulled me out of an all-too-familiar dream, the one in which I'd decided not to leave Antolbia after all; curiously enough, he woke me at the point in the dream where Theano usually shook me awake to tell me the Scythians were overrunning the city.

'Soldiers,' he repeated. 'In armour, on horses. Can't you hear?'

I listened. Someone was kicking the door. 'Get out of sight,' I told him, swinging my legs off the bed and discovering that I had pins and needles in both of them – well, I wouldn't be running far like that. No escape option; well, it simplified matters. 'And get the other two under cover as well,' I added, as he scurried off. 'I'll keep them talking if I can.'

I suppose I was scared; most of all, though, I was just plain sleepy and bewildered. It was perfectly possible that I had enemies, considering everything I'd been responsible for over the years, but I couldn't think of any who were in a position to send soldiers to get me.

I didn't have to wait long before I found out the answer. They were Macedonians; to be precise, they were troopers from King Alexander's mobile reserve.

'Are you Euxenus?' one of them asked, as I opened the door a little wider.

No point in denying it, I thought. 'That's right,' I said. 'How can I help you?'

'You're coming with us,' the soldier said. 'If you want to pack some stuff, be quick. We haven't got time to hang about.'

I stayed where I was. 'Where are we going?' I asked.

The soldier grinned at me. 'India,' he said. 'Are you taking anything with you or not?'

'India?' I repeated.

'You heard me.'

Of course, I didn't have the slightest intention of going to India, or anywhere else for that matter, in the company of these ferocious-looking men. They were a sight to see, no question, standing there in their armour – Macedonian-pattern helmet, breastplate and greaves; if you looked closely you could see dozens of small repairs, where a dent had been raised or a hole had been patched and brazed. Their clothes told the same story – here bleached by the sun or by being soaked with water, there darned and patched, all neatly done (a soldier may be reduced to wearing rags, but they'd better be neat rags if he doesn't want to find himself pulling extra latrine-digging duty). I could well believe that they'd just come from somewhere like India, and in a hurry too.

I tried to think of a plan of campaign, a way of getting away from them and keeping away until either they gave up and left me alone or neighbours showed up in force and rescued me. Unfortunately, both versions of a happy ending were no end improbable. I had no way of calling for help, and these people didn't look as if they'd just go home again if they didn't get what they wanted.

'Who sent you?' I asked. They didn't reply; instead they surged forward into the house, pushing me gently but firmly out of the way. 'Could you at least tell me what it is I'm supposed to have done?' I added.

The soldier looked at me oddly. 'You haven't done anything,' he said. 'At least, not anything wrong. Alexander needs you for something, that's all I know. And that's enough, too.' He picked up a small terracotta statue of a man riding on the back of a bird, examined it as if checking to make sure there wasn't a company of archers hiding in it waiting to ambush him, then put it back. 'All right,' he said, 'time's up. Your things'll have to be sent on later. I expect the Colonel'll see to that for you.'

One of the soldiers took hold of my shoulder. His grip didn't hurt, but it was firm, like a well-trained dog retrieving a hare in its mouth. 'Colonel?' I hazarded.

The soldier nodded. 'Colonel Eudaemon,' he said. 'Your brother. The one who's going to be living here now you're going to India.'

CHAPTER NINETEEN

The soldier's name was Colonel Timoleon, and as soldiers go, he wasn't so bad. Once we were safely on board the ship and there wasn't any likelihood of my getting him into trouble by escaping or wandering off, he relaxed a little.

'Colonel Eudaemon,' he said. 'We served together for years, off and on. Of course, he was mostly in the rear of the line of march, being an engineer.'

I looked out over the dark-blue sea, the same view I'd got so thoroughly sick of on the long journey back from Olbia. 'I haven't seen him for – oh, twenty years at least. In fact, if you'd asked me I'd have told you he was probably dead. He was just a kid when he left home.'

Timoleon nodded. 'It's easy to lose touch with home when you're in the service,' he said. 'Me, I've been away sixteen years, and I wasn't with the original army, the first lot who crossed into Asia and fought at the Granicus. Most of them have never been back – the ones who're still alive, that is. Even losing as few men as the King does, the casualties mount up over twenty-odd years. And that's just the ones who get killed in the actual fighting,' he added. 'Mostly they die of disease, bad water, bad food, that kind of thing.' He smiled bleakly. 'Truth is, the enemy's always the least of your problems.'

I shrugged. 'I suppose so,' I replied. 'I've never been a regular soldier, so I wouldn't really know.'

Timoleon turned his head to watch a seagull flying low. 'I heard about what happened in Antolbia,' he said. 'Bad business. One of these days, he'll sort them out for what they did, you can count on that. After all,' he added, 'it's one of the few parts of the world he hasn't been yet, so he's bound to go there sooner or later.'

The way he said that impressed me. 'Tell me,' I said. 'Do you believe Alexander will end up conquering the whole world? Every last bit of it, I mean?'

He nodded. 'Don't worry about it,' he said. 'You look at the rate he's been going. In ten years he's taken in the whole of Asia; and next year, once he's finished tidying up in India, he'll reach the far ocean, which is the end of the world, you just can't go any further than that. Then he'll head back north-west, clean up those Scythians and bits and pieces up there; then it'll be Africa, and afterwards on to Italy and Spain; and everyone knows, they'll be easy as squashing grapes compared with the East. I reckon he'll have conquered the whole world by the time he's forty. Just think of that, will you? The whole world, one end to the other.' He shook his head, then grinned. 'Then maybe we can all go home,' he said. 'Unless he goes ahead with this idea of settling us all down in these new cities and creating this ideal society everyone's always banging on about. Can't see it ever happening myself. Still, I expect they said the same about the idea of conquering Asia.'

I looked away so that he couldn't see my face. 'I heard rumours about that idea,' I said. 'But we get so many rumours in Athens, it's hard to know which ones to believe. So that's really a serious proposition, then, planting Greek colonies all over Asia?'

'Too right,' the Colonel replied. 'Only it's more than that. He reckons that the only way there'll ever be peace and harmony between us and them is if there isn't any more Greeks and Persians, just one big happy family. So we're all going to be given land and wives in Asia, and they're going to ship most all of the people out of Greece and settle them down all over the world. Greeks and Persians, Greeks and Egyptians, Greeks and Italians when we get there, Greeks and Indians, Greeks and Scythians—'

'Been done,' I interrupted. 'Didn't work too well.'

He shook his head. 'That's because it wasn't done right,' he said. 'No disrespect to you and your people,' he added quickly. 'Don't get me wrong, I don't really know enough about all this to have an opinion, I'm just a soldier, me. But you've got to admit, if it can be made to work, it's got to be a bloody good idea.'

'Ideal,' I said. 'Wonder where he got the notion from?'

Timoleon looked at me oddly. 'From you, of course,' he said. 'Else, why's he sent me all this way to fetch you?'

'I'm sorry?'

He raised a shaggy eyebrow. 'He wants you to lead his new colony,' he said. 'In Sogdiana. It's to thank you for how you inspired him, when he was just a kid, gave him the burning ambition to create the perfect society.'

'Me,' I said.

'Yes, you.' He grinned. 'You look surprised.'

'I am surprised,' I replied. 'I don't remember ever mentioning it. And if he thinks I'm going to get involved in that bloody game again—' I shook my head. 'I'm sorry,' I went on, 'really, it isn't your problem. But I think you've probably had a wasted journey.'

He looked at me for a long time before he spoke again. 'If he says you're going to lead a colony in Sogdiana,' he said, 'you're going to lead a colony in Sogdiana. Bet on it.'

'Thanks,' I said, 'but no.'

'Bet on it,' he repeated.

I thought for a moment. 'A drachma,' I said. 'Athenian.'

'Done.'

I owe Colonel Timoleon a drachma, Phryzeutzis. When I die and you clear out my things, you'll find it in the little cedarwood box beside my bed, along with Theano's comb. It's the only genuine Athenian drachma I've got left. I'm sure I can rely on you to travel all the way to Macedon, track down Timoleon or his next of kin and hand it over. Be sure to get a receipt.

We made landfall at Ephesus, where I found a letter waiting for me. It was written on best-quality Egyptian paper and was presented to me by the Macedonian prefect's first adjutant in person, as I staggered down the plank feeling like death. I read it in a quiet corner of the public baths the next day, and I've still got the wretched thing somewhere, still in its dinky little bronze tube embossed with prancing lions; but I know it by heart, so I won't bother looking for it now. It went:

Alexander son of Philip to Euxenus son of Eutychides; greetings.

This message is twenty years overdue, my dear Euxenus; please forgive me, I've been busy. You left before I could say goodbye, and what with one thing and another I've never got around to writing.

Do you remember those bees? There are times when I'm ready to believe the gods sent them, just to make sure our paths crossed that day. The debt I owe you is incalculable, and hardly a day goes by when I don't think about the things you taught me. I can't believe it's been so long since we sat together under the trees at Mieza; it only seems like a week or so ago that you were handing out our study assignments, or explaining to us about the battles of the Great War. In a very real sense, anything I might have achieved so far in my life is largely due to you. Without your teaching and, to an even greater extent, your example, I don't suppose I'd be where I am today. You opened my eyes, my dearest friend and mentor; you showed me that life can have a purpose, that it can mean something. What greater treasure could anybody possibly give, or receive?

Above all, it was the example of what you set out to do in Olbia that fired my imagination all those years ago, Now, I expect you've long since despaired of me; you think that all I'm interested in is fame and glory, and extending my kingdom from one end of the earth to the other. I can picture you shaking your head sadly. 'You're missing the point,' I can hear you say. And if it were true, if all I was interested in was making a name for myself, you'd be right. Everything I've done would pale into insignificance compared with what you nearly achieved at Antolbia. But it's all right, I promise you. I hadn't forgotten, though I'll admit I've been dreadfully slow off the mark. But it's time now.

I have to tell you, I can't spare the men or the time to come with you back to Antolbia, avenge the terrible loss you suffered, and rebuild the city. I'm sorry; it'd be a far nobler deed than what I'm doing here, but please understand, I have to finish here before I can do anything else, otherwise there's a terrible risk that everything here will just fall to pieces, with nothing to show for all the lives it's cost for me to get here.

So I'm going to do what I hope is the next best thing; in fact, in some ways I hope it might even be better, because this time it's going to be that much closer to your original dream. I'm asking you to lead my new colony in Sogdiana.

This one isn't going to be anything like any of the other cities I've founded, or which have been founded in my name. This time, Euxenus, we're going to put into practice everything we talked about all those years ago, that day when I sat spellbound at your feet listening to you telling us about your wonderful ideas for the ideal society. That's why I've waited so long; I had to find the right place, the right people. And Sogdiana, Euxenus – I knew at once when I first came here, this is the place we've been dreaming of, this is the perfect mixture of people to make it work.

How did you put it? The perfect fusion of opposites; that's what we've got here. These people here, they're so different from us and so alike at the same time. Here's where we're going to find that perfect fusion; Greek and Scythian, settled and nomadic, urban and rural, pure intelligence and raw energy, all the elements you said we'd need. You know, I really wish it could be me undertaking this wonderful experiment. I've said this so often over the years, Euxenus, but never to you, the one person it matters that I say it to; if I couldn't have been Alexander, I'd have wanted to be Euxenus. Well, here's another perfect fusion, my friend; you and me, fused together in a joint act of creation.

Well, that's enough of that. I'm sure you remember how I always used to get carried away – brevity, Alexander, brevity; isn't that what you used to tell me when it was my turn to say something in class? There's nothing worth saying in twenty words, you said, that can't be said better in ten. Come and join me, Euxenus. Together, we can make your dream a reality at last. Anyway, there you have it; better late than never, as we say back home.

If all goes well, you should arrive in Ephesus just as Eudaemon's getting there. Be warned; he's changed a lot since you used to know him. He'll explain the background.

Goodbye, Euxenus. Here's one last promise: as soon as the foundations are laid, I'll come and say hello properly, and we can sit together under a tree in the sun and talk over old times and new dreams. Keep well, my friend, and may the gods favour you.

And what all that's about, I confess I have no idea. I've ransacked my memory scores of times over the years, but however hard I try I simply can't recall any of those cosy chats in the shade back in dear old Mieza that the letter refers to. I don't know; maybe he was getting me confused with somebody else, or maybe he'd recreated me in his mind as the wise old mentor he felt he should have had.

And the tone of the thing; I've asked around, at the time he was dictating that lot (it was far too neat to be his own handwriting), he was issuing edicts to his loyal fellow Macedonians requiring them to fall on their faces in his presence and worship him as a god. Of course, there's a perfectly good explanation for the god business; the Persians expect to be required to worship their kings as gods, and if they saw the Macedonians treating him as an equal, a mere mortal, he'd lose their respect. Perfectly valid argument, by which I'm not in the least convinced.

I was tempted – ye gods, I was tempted – to write back telling him where he could shove his colony and his perfect society and all the rest of it, but fortunately I had more sense. I told myself that I'd never have dared say anything like that to Alexander even when he was just a kid; disobeying his orders now that he was effectively the ruler of the world simply wasn't an option. Now I'm not so sure. There was always a side to Alexander that positively invited the apparently humiliating rebuff from people who were entirely in his mercy; as witness, for example, the way he allowed himself to be insulted by Diogenes. On one level, it was shrewd public relations, demonstrating his humanity and self-assurance; after all, Alexander is always the hero of these stories, which make great play of his humility and sense of humour (and Alexander had just enough of both of these qualities to fill a small nutshell, provided the nut was left in place). Maybe if I'd written back a churlish, ill-mannered refusal he'd have smiled indulgently, handed the letter to a nearby hanger-on and let it go at that. On the other hand, maybe the last thing I'd ever have seen was the inside of the sack they put over my head as they rowed me out to sea and tipped me over the side. Someone capable of writing a letter like that would be capable of anything.

Well, then; I was going to Sogdiana, wherever the hell Sogdiana was – and by rights, Phryzeutzis, that's the end of the story, because here I am still. It turned out, quite by chance, that Sogdiana is probably the nearest thing to a home I've ever had since my father died. At the time, though, I wasn't to know that. I assumed I was being sent off to some crack in the mountains to live among monosyllabic Macedonian veterans and cannibal natives. You can guess, I wasn't very happy about it.

I left the baths, where I'd gone to read the letter, and started to walk back to the garrison barracks, where I was staying. It was a warmer than average evening, and I had a hill to climb, so I was taking it slowly, my mind still full of Alexander and his letter. Consequently I wasn't paying much attention to the people around me and didn't notice the man in a military cloak and helmet who came bustling up behind me until he'd rammed me in the back like a warship and sent me sprawling on the ground.

He went down too, and I distinctly heard a crack, the unmistakable dry-branch-snapping noise of a human bone breaking. At once he started to curse and groan. I untangled my feet from the hem of his cloak and got up.

'Are you all right?' I asked, rather foolishly.

'No, I'm bloody well not,' he replied. 'You clown, you've broken my leg.'

'I'm sorry,' I replied. It wasn't the most intelligent thing I could have said, I grant you, but I meant it for the best. He wasn't impressed, though.

'Sorry's not damn well good enough,' he gasped, and then let out another roar of pain. 'Well, you're going to regret this, I promise you, because I'm a colonel in the King's army, and nobody . . .'

'Eudaemon?' I asked.

He jerked his head round and glowered at me. 'Do I know you?' he said.

'Eudaemon, it's me. Euxenus.'

'What?'

'Euxenus,' I repeated. 'Your brother.'

'Oh, for gods' sakes.'

Just then a couple of soldiers happened to pass by; they helped Eudaemon up off the ground, prompting yet another leonine roar of agony, then told me I was under arrest.

'Don't be so damn stupid,' Eudaemon wheezed. 'This idiot's my brother, apparently.'

The soldiers weren't quite sure what that had to do with anything; brother or not, I was still a civilian who'd apparently caused grievous bodily harm to a serving Macedonian officer. Before they could hurl themselves at me and start tearing up flesh, however, Eudaemon started giving them orders; you could almost hear the click as they disengaged their brains, allowing their superior officer's voice to act directly on the muscles, nerves and tendons of their bodies. They picked him up and carried him, his arms around their shoulders like a drunk being taken home, in the direction of the barracks. I followed.

The surgeon wasn't in his quarters; he was out to dinner. Eudaemon sent someone to find him, and we were left alone, in a courtyard outside the surgeon's office.

'Hello, Eudaemon,' I said. 'I thought you were dead.'

He frowned. 'Really,' he said.

I tried to think of something else to say. 'How are you keeping?' I asked.

'Not so hot,' he replied. 'Some damn fool just pushed me over and broke my leg.'

I looked at him. He was a little shorter than I remembered, but considerably more massive; whatever he'd been doing over the last twenty-odd years had invested him with an enormous amount of muscle and flesh. His shoulders, arms and chest were huge, and his belly sagged over his belt in a bulging fold. Even his fingers were enormous; my hand would disappear into his, like a child holding hands with its father. His cheeks were round, like an apple, and his beard came up almost to the sockets of his eyes. I've never seen such a thick neck in all my life. Under all that beard it was hard to see anything of his face, except that he'd developed an exaggerated version of our father's long, flat nose. On the inside of his left forearm, almost exactly midway between his wrist and his elbow, there was a suitably large and spectacular scar, the residue of a severe burn – I saw something similar once on the shin of a blacksmith, who'd stumbled while holding a billet of white-hot bronze and ended up kneeling on it for a brief, agonising moment.

'What happened to your arm?' I asked.

'Cave-in,' he replied, in a detached, almost bored voice. 'Siege operations at Tyre. We'd dug a shaft under the wall, and we were burning out the gallery props to collapse it and bring the wall down. Some fool had skimped on the job and it came in too bloody early. I got buried, and six foot of burning beam landed on my arm. Of course, I couldn't move, just had to lie there till someone came back and hauled me out. No fun,' he added, with a small, grim smile. 'Anyway, how about yourself? I gather you moved back home. How is the old place?'

His tone of voice as he asked was one of forced interest, such as you'd use when asking after the health of a distant and rather disreputable relative.

'Not so bad,' I replied. 'It hasn't changed much since your day. I've tidied it up, put things in some sort of order.'

'Mended the hole in the scullery roof?'

I nodded. 'But the store-room door still sticks,' I added.

'Really? I can't remember.' He tried to shift a little, but the pain made him wince. 'Really, Euxenus, you're a bloody menace. Haven't seen you in twenty-six years and the first thing you do is cripple me. You always were a clumsy bugger.'

'I didn't do it on purpose,' I replied, guilty-irritable.

'I never said you did,' he said. 'But you never did look where you were going. I remember that time when we were kids and you dropped that ladder—'

'Eudaemon,' I interrupted, 'you're amazing. We haven't seen each other in gods know how long. I really thought you were dead. Dammit, I thought *all* our family was dead. And then suddenly, out of the blue, you come to life again and all you can say is, Euxenus, you always were a clumsy bugger. Really—'

'Do me a favour,' he said. 'Look, if you're telling me you really didn't know I was still alive then I'll believe you, though I find that hard to credit. So all right, you've lost touch with me. Not the same the other way round. Oh, no. I've been hearing about you so long you're lucky I don't break your foul neck. Dammit, if it wasn't for you—'

I held up my hand. 'Hold on,' I said, 'you've lost me.'

'The celebrated Euxenus,' he went on. 'Euxenus the philosopher. Euxenus, the wisest man I ever knew. Euxenus, without whom none of this would ever have been possible. I tell you, brother, there were times when for two pins I'd have shaved my beard, changed my name and deserted just so I wouldn't have to hear any more about wonderful, sun-shines-out-of-his-bum Euxenus. And to cap it all,' he added angrily, 'as if you haven't done enough already, the first thing you do when finally our paths cross is break my goddamn leg. Figures,' he concluded bitterly. 'On reflection, if the worst I end up with is a bust leg I reckon I'll have got off light.'

'Slow down, will you?' I said. 'Just what exactly am I supposed to have done?'

He laughed unpleasantly. 'That's bloody rich, that is. Euxenus the Great Sage, teacher, mentor and living inspiration of the divine Alexander, son of Zeus, stepson of Philip. For gods' sakes, brother, you're one of the most famous men in the Empire. And,' he added with a shrug, 'I'm your kid brother. Wonderful.' He let go a long, measured sigh. 'Well,' he said, 'by the look of you it hasn't all been wine and honey-cakes. You look pretty bloody awful, brother, no offence.'

'Thank you so much,' I said.

Just then the surgeon bustled in. He was wearing a fancy dinner gown with red wine spilt down the front, and as he walked through the door he masked a cavernous yawn with the back of his hand. I don't know, there was something about him that didn't inspire confidence.

'What the hell was so urgent,' he said, 'that I had to be dragged from my dinner . . .?'

He'd made a tactical mistake. He'd got just a little bit too close to the bench my brother was lying on, and before he could finish his sentence, Eudaemon reached out with his enormous left paw, grabbed the surgeon's gown where the folds hung round his neck, and dragged him to his knees. Sweetly done.

'You're drunk,' he said.

The surgeon was too shocked to answer; so would you have been, I reckon, if you suddenly found yourself kneeling at less than arm's length from my brother's savage, staring eyes. Eudaemon held him there for a count of five, then relaxed his fingers and let him go. He stood up and backed away a couple of paces.

'Are you drunk?' I asked.

'No, of course not,' the surgeon replied.

'You've got booze all down your front,' my brother said. 'If you can't even find your face when you're sober, you must be a bloody rotten surgeon.'

'It was an accident,' the surgeon said, rather desperately. 'Look, do you want me to set your leg or not?'

My brother made a soft, growling noise in the back of his throat. 'I'm not sure,' he said. 'I used to think I was a pretty tough character; I mean, I've fought the Persians and the Bactrians and the Medes and the Indians and a whole lot of other people whose names escape me right now, and they didn't bother me too much. But I've got to admit, this clown scares the shit out of me.'

'That's enough,' the surgeon said. 'I'm going.'

'Stay where you are.'

The unfortunate man froze in mid-step. I'd have done the same. My brother had the perfect parade-ground voice, not so much loud (though it was loud enough) as densely packed with a lifetime of contempt, weariness and disgust.

'Please,' the surgeon said, 'make your mind up. Either you want me to treat you or you don't.'

My brother sighed. 'Get on with it,' he said. 'And do a proper job, or you'll wish you were never born.'

Now, I've never had a broken bone, so I don't know from personal experience, but people I've met who've had bones set say it's probably the most intense pain there is, though women tell me childbirth is worse. I'll admit, the click as the surgeon put the thing back where it belonged was enough to make me want to throw up. But Eudaemon didn't make a sound, apart from a tiny grunt, the sort of noise you'd expect from a fieldmouse belching. As for the surgeon, he looked scared to death. I had the feeling his evening wasn't going quite the way he'd planned.

'Well,' Eudaemon said, after the surgeon had packed up his things and gone, 'that wasn't nearly as bad as I'd thought it would be.'

'You don't like doctors, do you?' I said.

'Whatever makes you say that?' Eudaemon replied. 'True, half of them are butchers and the other half are frauds, but by and large they've never done me any harm. Though I've always done my best to stay well clear of them, I'll be honest with you there. Anyway, you'd better help me back to my quarters. And this time, try not to break anything else. I really don't want to have to go through all that again.'

Luckily, Eudaemon's quarters weren't too far away. He had a place to himself, smaller than a cowshed but much larger than a clothes-press, say, or a beehive. Inside it was sparse, to put it mildly. Stacked against the wall, his armour – expensive breastplate and helmet, lavishly decorated with enamel that had been chipped and scraped into worthlessness, a small shield with a large letter A painted on it, and a pair of battered silver-plated greaves – and beside it a goatskin pack with the hair still on, the strap frayed and repaired with rawhide cord. There was a plain cord-mattress bed, the type common to all the quarters in the place, and a folding three-legged stool with a patched rush seat. That was it.

'So this is home,' I said, as I lowered him off my shoulders onto the bed.

'Of course not,' Eudaemon replied. 'I'm not planning on staying here, or at least I wasn't. Now I guess I'll be stuck here for however long it takes the bone to knit. Thanks again.'

I sat down on the stool and leaned forward, my elbows on my knees. 'All right,' I said. 'Maybe now you'll tell me what's going on. I got this crazy-sounding letter, apparently from Alexander himself—'

'No apparently about it,' Eudaemon interrupted. 'I know all about your precious letter, thank you very much. Seems like I've got you to thank for being elbowed out of the service.'

I shook my head. 'Don't blame me,' I said. 'First I knew of all this was when a couple of soldiers turned up outside my house and told me I was going to Asia.'

Eudaemon was silent for a moment. 'Figures,' he said. 'It all sounds a bit like Alexander arranging things for the best. You know, that man's a miracle. He can do more damage with a good intention than twenty thousand of the Great King's crack guardsmen let loose in a crowded marketplace.' He turned his head and looked at me. 'From what I gather, you're pretty much the same, though on a suitably low and primitive level. I don't know; maybe it's one of the things that marks you men of destiny out from the rest of us.'

I let go a long, deep sigh and shifted the stool back a few yards. 'All right,' I said. 'Now you can start explaining what's behind that and all the other snide little cracks you've been making ever since I laid eyes on you. And before you start lashing out and trying to strangle me, you'll please observe I've had the sense to move out of range.'

'Good thinking,' he replied with mock approval. 'Obviously a certain rudimentary tactical ability runs in our family. You really think I'd hurt you, my own brother?'

I nodded.

'Also,' he added, 'an ability to judge character at a glance.' He wriggled a little, trying to get comfortable, and groaned. 'You know, you're not the same man as the one I've had cluttering up my memory all these years. At least,' he added with a sigh, 'I guess you were both one and the same person, but you've sort of grown apart, like we have. Figures; my version of you has been all round the world with me, seen things you'll never see if you live to be a hundred and twelve.'

I nodded. 'Which of us do you prefer?' I said.

He thought about that. 'Hard to say,' he replied. 'I mean, my version's a right bastard, done me no end of harm over the years. But he never went so far as to bust my leg.'

'Tell me,' I said, 'about this Euxenus of yours.'

'All right,' he said. 'Draw up a seat, I'll tell you all about him.'

I'd actually shifted the stool an inch or two before I saw it. 'No thanks,' I said. 'What did you call it? Basic tactical ability?'

'Rudimentary was the word I used. Sounds better. Longer.' He shrugged, then regretted it as a spike of pain made him shudder. 'Please yourself, then, and stay where you are. This Euxenus I know is an arrogant, thoughtless, self-centred jerk who doesn't give a stuff about anybody except himself – not really bothered about himself, even, or at least not in the way most people are. Doesn't really care about money or position or pleasure or even comfort. He's the sort of cold, dead bugger who cares about ideas, not people. Dangerous sort, that; they tend to be horribly persuasive, people listen to them and get all fired up with these ideas of theirs. They attract disciples, like honey attracts wasps. Give one of these arseholes a disciple or two and he can burn down cities.'

'Or found them,' I added with a smile.

'Same difference,' he said. 'You need the same mentality for both. Now me,' he went on. 'I've been a soldier all my adult life—'

'Yes,' I interrupted again. 'What about that? Last I knew, you were hanging round that man – what was his name? The one who made you read the book about the bees.'

Eudaemon looked at me, then burst out laughing. 'Bias,' he said. 'And the book was Aeneas the Tactician. Now there were two more inspirers-of-disciples. If I had my way, the whole lot of you'd be rounded up like sheep and strangled with your own intestines.'

'Probably wise,' I admitted. 'Go on. You were a sort of apprentice to the man Bias.'

Eudaemon sighed. 'We went to join the service of the King of Macedon,' he said. 'Or at least, I did. I'd saved up a bit of money – thirty drachmas, I think it was – to pay my passage and travelling expenses to get there and buy some extra kit, and Bias told me he'd make the necessary arrangements for us both, so I gave him the money and I never saw him again; at least, not for years. But by the time I twigged, of course, I was on board this ship going up the coast, and without so much as a dud copper obol to pay for my fare. The master wasn't at all pleased, as you can imagine.'

'How far had you got?' I asked.

'Bias told us both he'd be joining the ship at Oropus – why he said that and why we believed him I have no idea. Anyway, there we were at Oropus, and no sign; so that bastard of a ship's captain slung me out, kept my sword and spear for payment, which was a total rip-off, and sailed away. I had a breastplate, a helmet, shield and a pair of greaves (all second-hand, and the greaves didn't fit worth a toss) but no weapons and no money; so after a day or two of moping about in Oropus getting laughed at when I went looking for work I did the sensible thing, sold the rest of my gear for what I could get – second-hand armour was a real drug on the market back then, of course, because of all the kit taken off dead people after battles; you'd be amazed how cheap people let their armour go for when they're dead – and then bummed around a bit more trying to decide what to do.

'Couldn't bring myself to slink back home; nobody wanted to hire me as a mercenary soldier, or anything else much, at that. Finally I decided I'd had enough of sitting in the shade eating my capital, so I set off to walk to Macedon. Turned out to be far less hassle than I thought it'd be – straight roads all the way, not much bother. Didn't have much to eat, of course, or anywhere to sleep, but there's always a wall or a tree when you want one, and it toughened me up, got me used to long marches, short rations and sore feet. Arrived at Pella, found Philip wasn't there, off beating the crap out of the Illyrians or some such improbable race; but they were hiring men for General Parmenio and the home guard, weren't all that fussed about who they took. I pretended I was a veteran of gods know how many campaigns – made half of 'em up, and nobody knew the difference – so they took me on, issued me with some kit and the mighty sarissa; now there's an evil device if ever there was one. I'll tell you about it some time if I can be bothered. Anyway, that's how I came to be a soldier; and I was chugging along quite nicely, worked my way up to junior captain of auxiliary infantry, thought of myself as more of a Macedonian than I'd ever been an Athenian, when suddenly King Philip dies and King Alexander takes over, and somehow – gods know how – word reaches him that Captain Eudaemon is the brother of his old schoolmaster, Euxenus of Athens. At which point,' Eudaemon said, with a dreadful scowl, 'my life stopped being a slow but steady progress towards self-improvement and became a steaming lake of shit. Thanks to you,' he added, with a nod.

'Me?'

'You.' He shook his head. 'Of course, you'd buggered off by then, off to Olbia with your happy band of idealists. And of course you'd left behind this amazing impression in the mind of young King Alexander. Gods know what it was you said to him when you had that long, inspirational chat under the fig-tree at Mieza—'

'I swear to you,' I interrupted, 'I can't remember anything like that. He mentioned it in his letter, but it was news to me, really. I think he was mixing me up with someone else.'

'Balls,' Eudaemon replied. 'You've just forgotten, obviously. I know it happened, because King Alexander told me so himself, and a man like me always believes what his commanding officer tells him; so you're wrong and he's right. In any case,' he went on, 'I refuse to believe that anybody could ever get you confused with a brilliant thinker or a silver-tongued orator. It'd be like confusing a duck with an ox. So if it wasn't somebody else, it must have been you. That's what we call logic,' he concluded cheerfully, 'in the army.'

I shrugged. 'All right,' I said, 'maybe I did say something that took root in Alexander's mind, I don't know. Anything's possible. But that doesn't explain how being my brother ruined your life.'

Eudaemon yawned and stretched, until the movement jarred something and he winced. 'Isn't there anything to drink in this rat-hole?' he said querulously. 'My throat's dry as shield-leather.'

'I can't see anything,' I replied.

'Well, in that case,' Eudaemon said, 'one of us is going to have to trot down to the mess and get a jar of service-issue red. Which one of us is best suited to the task, I ask myself?'

Basically (Eudaemon told me, after I'd come back with the jar and two cups) it was gratitude, or respect; that's what screwed up my life. If you'd never been born, or you'd died before you were weaned, or if you'd managed to find yourself a proper job when you were a kid instead of preying off the gullibility of the feeble-minded and foreigners, everything would have been just fine. When Alexander became King, he'd have launched his expedition and I'd have gone along as Captain of Auxiliaries, done my bit for the cause, earned my pay and got my share of the plunder, probably by now I'd be a Colonel of Auxiliaries, maybe even sub-prefect of a province, with a bunch of secretaries to do my work for me and nothing to do all day but lie on my back boozing and making myself obnoxious to the local women. All by my own unaided efforts, please note; not bad for a man who walked into Macedon in a pair of raggety sandals and a third-hand tunic.

Instead, I had to be your brother. It wasn't my fault, it was something I had absolutely no say in, but I got dumped on all the same. I hate things like that.

I was sitting outside the mess hall playing draughts, I remember, when they came looking for me. Staff bastards, they were, gilded belt-buckles and cream-white tunics, sprigs of your full-blood Macedonian nobility; anyway, they told me Alexander wanted to see me immediately, so off I went, wondering what the hell it was I was supposed to have done, and whether I was going to make it back to my tent alive.

Needless to say, I'd never actually met him before. Oh, seen him, yes; everybody's seen him, at a parade or a march-past or a public occasion. Goes without saying, of course, that the Alexander you see from a distance over some other bloke's head is quite different from the man you sit and talk to. Your public Alexander; well, you'd have to be a pretty bloody cold fish not to be in love with him. The looks, the poise, the style, the speaking voice, the instinctive air of command – you'd follow him to the ends of the earth, and a hell of a lot of men have done. Fair play to them. That Alexander's a man who merits following. That's as close as nine hundred and ninety-nine men in a thousand ever get, and that's as close as you want to get, because when a man's as well-nigh perfect as your public Alexander is, anything further you find out about him can only be a disappointment, a smudge across the illusion, and who wants to serve a man he knows is less than perfect? I tell you, Euxenus, if you hadn't made me meet Alexander I'd be as happy as a mule in the bean-helm believing he was perfect; you know, like worth fighting and dying for, worth spending your whole life dragging up dusty mountain roads with a gut full of dysentery for. But no; I have to meet the real Alexander, I have to get to know what he's really like. Lucky me.

So; they keep me hanging about in this dismal little courtyard for most of the evening, and I'm just nodding off and trying to find some way to get comfortable on a hard stone bench when some assistant deputy to the deputy assistant secretary comes out and says, 'The King will see you now.' So I go in, and there he is, sitting on the step in front of the throne, yapping away while some old bugger scribbles down everything he says. And part of me's saying, *What's wrong with you, you fool? You haven't done anything wrong, so what's there to be afraid of?* And the other part's saying, *Well, actually, if you care to consult the records you'll find I've done any one of a dozen things that'll get me dismissed from the service according to regulations, and one or two that just don't bear thinking about* . . . I am not, in short, the happiest of men at that particular moment. Looking back, of course, I realise it's my soldier's highly developed sense of the presence of mortal danger; and what the fuck's the use of a hair-trigger instinct if you don't listen to it?

So I stand there, to attention – I'm telling you, wild dogs could have eaten my feet and I wouldn't have shifted without being told *At ease* – until he's done with the letter he's dictating and notices me, like as if a six-foot man in armour's difficult to spot in a room that size.

'Captain Eudaemon,' he says, 'at ease, please. Sit down. Thank you for coming.'

You know another thing I hate? It's when a superior officer talks to you like you're the lord mayor or the Persian ambassador or something. You don't know what to do. If you carry on being all regulation and by-the-drill-manual, it looks like you're being rude. But if you say, 'Thanks, don't mind if I do,' and flop down in a couch with your feet up on the table, you can bet the next thing you'll be hearing is the adjutant reading out the charges. Anyhow, I sit down, as if on a big row of six-inch spikes, and wait for him to say something.

Which he proceeds to do. He says that of all the remarkable men he's been privileged to meet (or some such crap) Euxenus of Athens had done more to shape his thinking on the critical issues that really count than anyone else alive or dead, and that he owes said Euxenus more than he can possibly ever repay. I'm sitting there thinking, Well, that'd be fine if I knew who this Euxenus is, when it hits me like the roof caving in, he's talking about my brother Euxenus. Not to put too fine a point on it, you. But this is so far-fetched, I have to interrupt and check it out.

'Excuse me, sir,' I say, 'but may I just ask; you mean Euxenus son of Eutychides? My brother?'

'Of course,' he says, frowning a little as if he doesn't like my tone of voice. 'I'm not ashamed to say it, Captain, that man's been more than just a mentor to me, he's been . . .' And he stops, because mentor's exactly the word he wants to use, but he can't because he's used it already. 'When the history of these times is written down,' Alexander says, 'people will begin to realise just how important a man he was, the kind of extraordinary things he achieved.'

'Sir,' I say.

'Which is why,' he goes on, 'I want to honour what he's done for me by doing something for you. You see,' he says, 'I know the sort of man he is, he doesn't care for money or position or rubbish like that—'

('He said that?' I interrupted.

'His exact words,' my brother replied.

'Hellfire,' I said. 'All right, carry on.')

'Rubbish like that,' he says. 'How can you insult with money the sort of man who thinks nothing of abandoning all his worldly wealth and ties just to accept the position of a lowly tutor, and then rejects all suggestions of reward from his patron in order to lead a colony to the ends of the earth? I'd be ashamed, my friend, to offer money to such a man. It'd be a betrayal.'

Wisely, I didn't say anything to that; just carried on sitting there like I had a twelve-foot lance up my arse. Actually I was thinking, maybe Euxenus was this bloke's tutor, that's how come he learned to be so incredibly goddamned pompous. I mean to say, I could see him sitting there listening to himself. Not a pretty sight, brother, I assure you.

'So,' he goes on, 'since I can't reward him in person, the least I can do is extend my favour to his brother, don't you think?' And I'm keeping very still and *not* saying that if he thought like that, then maybe it'd have been a nice gesture not to have wiped out most of our bloody family at Chaeronea – yes, I heard about that; these things happen, you know? And he sort of smiles and says, 'You know, Eudaemon, you and I are very much alike, I think.'

Well, this one really gets past me. 'Sir,' I say, and I think I was putting it mildly.

'Both of us,' he goes on, 'have seen our path in life; our way is service, my friend, service to something that goes beyond what's here and now. We aren't men of the moment, but of all time. Would you agree?'

'Sir,' I say.

He nods, as if I've just said something really clever. 'So I know,' he goes on, 'that the best reward I can give you is a chance to serve in the noblest, most productive way you can; and that, of course, is where your brother's teaching comes in yet again. I'm sure you're familiar with his theoretical work on the art of war, with particular references to siegecraft.'

'Sir,' I say.

'Brilliantly innovative,' he goes on. 'Quite wonderful, how a man without a conventional military background can have such insights.'

(You'll remember, by the way, that all this stuff's being spouted at me by this kid; he's what, just turned twenty years old? And your most deadly boring old farts in Assembly were never as turgid as this. Credit where it's due, brother, clearly you taught him everything he knows about the effective use of words.)

'When we march into Asia,' he goes on, 'I intend to take with me a siege train organised and equipped in line with Euxenus' principles of static warfare, incorporating all the advances he's developed in this aspect of military science. And I want you, Eudaemon, to be part of this. After all, you must be more familiar with his approach than anybody else in the service – he's your brother, after all, it'd be the next best thing to having him there in person. So I'd like to make you a formal offer of the position of Colonel of Engineers, with direct command of counter-insurgency operations.'

Well now I thought, as I was marched out of there by some secretary; not so bad after all, as the man said when he shot an arrow at a wolf, missed and hit his wife's mother. Obviously young King Alexander is a very strange man indeed, but Colonel of

Engineers, at my age, and a job that's practically staff, whatever way you slice it, that can't be anything but a piece of the good stuff. Of course, I was really puzzled by all this talk of Euxenus of Athens and his amazing contributions to the art of war –

('Me too,' I pointed out.)

– but being a practical sort (Eudaemon went on) I put all that out of my mind and went on a colossal piss-up to celebrate, the way any rational man would. Next morning, feeling a bit fragile and frayed round the edges, I handed over my company to my replacement in the auxiliaries and reported to the Chief Engineer's office.

I knew as soon as I walked in the door that he wasn't pleased to see me. He had that face on that shows you here's a bloke who's getting on with his job, doing his best, when the bloody brass reach down from on high and dump some irrelevant shit on him that he's got to pretend he likes while he works out how to stop it getting in the way of the smooth running of his department.

'So you're Eudaemon.' he said.

'Sir,' I replied.

'Right,' he said. 'The bee man.'

This time, I really did feel like I'd been woken up in the middle of a particularly crazy dream. 'Excuse me, sir,' I said, 'but what did you just say?'

'You're the man who's going to be in charge of the bees,' he said, and then he grinned at me. I didn't like that. 'Well,' he went on, 'all I can say is, the very best of luck. Just try to keep the horrible things from stinging anybody.'

Well now, brother, I hope you're feeling really ashamed of yourself, because your sins have finally bloody well found you out; and if you hadn't broken my leg, I'd be breaking your bastard neck right now, so maybe you weren't such a fool after all. When I reported to my duty assignment a few minutes later, I realised exactly what you'd done. You'd taken that stuff about the bees out of Aeneas the Tactician, and you'd passed it off as your own damn idea; and it had so impressed that clown Alexander—

('Bees?')

'Chucking hives of bees down mineshafts to chase out enemy sappers. And to think; it was me first told you about it—'

'I swear to you,' I broke in, 'on my son's grave, I never did anything of the sort.'

'Alexander said you did. Well,' he amended, 'you know what I mean. He said it was your idea.'

'Oh, sure,' I replied angrily. 'And he said I was his mentor and the wisest man he ever met. On that basis, you're going to take his word over mine?'

Eudaemon looked at me for a moment. 'I'd like to believe you,' he said, 'but I know you too well. A man who earns his living with a tame snake in a wine-jar isn't going to be fussy about attributing his sources. And if we're going to get along, I suggest you stop lying to me. It makes me angry, being lied to.')

Anyway (Eudaemon continued), there's your answer. You asked me what you'd done to screw up my life, and I've told you. Because of you I went from being a successful, competent professional soldier and in the twinkling of an eye I became the bee man. And all I can say about that, dear brother, is thank you. Thank you ever so fucking much.

CHAPTER TWENTY

'All right,' I said, 'I can see how you've got hold of this idea that your getting this post in the engineers is somehow my responsibility. That's still quite a way from "screwed up your life", though.'

He scowled at me. 'You just don't know,' he said. 'You really haven't got a clue. The question is, have I got the patience and energy to tell you?'

I shrugged. 'Please yourself,' I said. 'Obviously, I'm dying to hear what you've been up to all these years, but if you're holding some sort of irrational grudge—'

'"Irrational grudge",' he repeated, shifting his weight slightly to ease the pain in his broken leg. 'You know, it'd be easier if I had a walking-stick. A bit of broken spear-shaft would do. Anything long enough to reach over to where you're sitting so I could smash your stupid face. Listen, Euxenus, I haven't got an irrational grudge, as you so charmingly put it. It's an entirely rational grudge, and the thought that by the time I'm up and about again, you'll be safely away in Sog-bloody-diana, where I won't be able to get at you, is enough to make me—'

I sighed. 'All right,' I said. 'Tell me all about it. Maybe talking about it'll calm you down.'

'Wouldn't count on it, brother,' he yawned, and I noticed that he was missing two front teeth. 'Still, I suppose it's only right and proper you know what you've done. Then, if you've got even a tiny shred of decency left in you, you'll piss off and hang yourself, and save me a job.'

Consider, dear brother (Eudaemon said), the life of the bee. Now, you're the philosopher, and I wouldn't presume to teach you your trade, if you can call it that; but haven't you ever stopped to think that, apart from minor details like size and flying ability, man and bee are as close as – well, brothers? To judge by that dumb look on your face, obviously you haven't, so I'll explain it to you.

Men build. So do bees. Men live in communities. So do bees. Ideally, men work together to accomplish the common goal, the good of the many, the well-being of the commonwealth. So do bees. Men sometimes make the ultimate sacrifice and give their lives for their home and family. So do bees. Men have territories, and like to beat the shit out of invaders and interlopers. So do bees. Human societies have the workers at the bottom, the better sort of people in the middle and the big boss at the top. So do bees. Truth is, for as long as there's been cities, people have been trying to live as much like bees as they can possibly manage; the order, the dedication, the diligence, the selflessness, not to mention the annihilation of indi-vidual liberty and the blind intolerance of every other living thing. So far at least, humans can't fly and their leaders aren't females; apart from that, all that separates man and bee is a trivial matter of scale; and like they say, size isn't everything.

Basically, I don't like bees; never have, certainly never will. Partly it's because the buzzing sets my teeth on edge and I don't like getting stung, but it's not just that, by any means. What really gets to me, I think, is this depressing resemblance between them and me. It's like what Dad used to say to us when we were kids and he was dragging us off to be apprentices; work hard, study carefully, observe, learn, one day you could be just like him. Well, I look at Brother Bee, with his smart uniform and his chain of command and his manifest destiny and his regulation spear jammed up his arse, and I see me. Then, if I'm quick enough, I tread on him.

My first day as Colonel of Bees, a sergeant took me over to an enclosure on the far side of the camp, where nobody ever seemed to go, and introduced me to my new command. There were something like ten million of them, divided into twenty-five hives, each under the command of a queen who, presumably, reported directly to me.

The first thing they did was chase me three times round the enclosure and sting me on the legs. It was then I discovered, rather to my disgust, that I'm allergic to bee-stings.

I should have known, of course. You may remember, when we were kids – I think I was about eight or nine at the time – one summer I got stung by a bee just under my chin, and the whole of my neck swelled up like a wineskin and for about a week everybody was certain I was going to die. Seems I'm one of those people who can get really seriously ill from bee-venom, because by the start of my second day as Colonel of Bees I was so badly crippled up I could only just crawl out of bed far enough to fall on the floor and lie there on my face.

Well, for two pins I'd have packed it in then and there, and so what if it meant the end of my career with the Macedonian army? But before I was well enough to crawl to His Majesty's pavilion and turn in my command, my sergeant showed up with a couple of Scythians in tow. Really evil-looking types they were – well, you'd know all about them – and I was just about to ask the sergeant what the hell he thought he was doing filling my quarters with bloodthirsty cannibals when he said that these Scythians were experts in everything to do with bees, including how to deal with a bad reaction to getting stung.

To cut a long story short, these Scythians gave me a big jar of stuff to put on the stings which drew the poison out before it could do me any real harm, and another jar of a different kind of stuff to stop them coming anywhere near me in the first place, and both of these worked fine, believe it or not, though the smell was something else. It'd have been just fine if they'd left it at that, but they didn't.

Oh, did I mention that apart from making me swell up like that, the bee-stings were also quite amazingly painful? Well, they were. Every bit of me seemed to hurt like I had bits of sharp gravel trapped inside my joints, and next day I mentioned this to those two wise Scythians, who looked at each other and nodded.

'We can help you there,' they said.

I was so impressed with the other stuff they'd given me that I'd have tried anything they chose to recommend without a second thought. But I'll say this for them, they did try to warn me.

'These leaves,' they said, 'are a great medicine among our people. When we're sad or unhappy, we throw a few handfuls of them onto the campfire, and a few minutes later we're all dancing and singing and laughing, as if we hadn't got a care in the world. It's a bit like being very drunk,' they went on, 'except that we've noticed before now that from time to time a man will get so happy because of the smoke that he'll trip over as he dances round the fire and fall into it, and unless his friends pull him out he'll just stay there, lying quite happily burning to death. The magic smoke, you see, makes you feel no pain; and that's why we're a bit wary of giving it to foreigners who aren't used to it. You'd be amazed,' they went on, 'how effective it is. A man can lose his wife and see his children die before his eyes, and still he'll feel no pain, just sit there grinning and muttering happily to himself. So be careful with it, that's all we're saying. A man who doesn't feel any pain at all can be a real danger to himself and other people.'

'All right,' I said. 'Point taken. Just so long as it takes away the pain of the bee-stings, it'll do me just fine.' So they gave me a big jar of these leaves, and as soon as they'd gone I pitched a handful on the fire and waited to see what would happen.

Brother, it was amazing. After a few minutes, all the pain in my joints was gone; in fact, I didn't seem to have a body at all. In fact it reminded me a lot of Plato –

('You read Plato?' I asked.

Eudaemon frowned. 'Yeah, well,' he said. 'A bloke I served with had a copy once. Sometimes it gets so boring on campaign you'll read any bloody thing. And it made a welcome change from "Produce of Attica" on the necks of wine-jars.')

– That bit in Plato where he talks about the perfect or ideal state of being, where we've purged ourselves of the body and all its worldly concerns and we exist as creatures of pure thought, which I guess is what you philosophers reckon is a good time. A load of crap, obviously, when you stop and think about it; but after I'd been breathing in that smoke for a bit, that's just how I felt, and in a strange way I could see the attraction. Anyway, it sorted out the bee-stings, and an hour or so later the effects wore off and I gradually came back to normal. Of course the stings started hurting again after that, but not so much, because the other stuff was doing its job; at least I could get about, and I could walk from my quarters to the mess hall without bursting into tears.

*

Now that I had a way of at least surviving, I knuckled down and started learning about bees. And believe me, there's a lot to learn. Luckily, I had those two Scythians to teach me; I had a word with their commanding officer and got them seconded to my command. They were happy enough; it got them out of serious soldiering, and I upped their pay a bit, too; anything to keep them sweet and take the load off me.

Anyway, they taught me how to make and repair beehives, either by sewing together tree-bark or weaving osiers, and smearing clay in the cracks to keep the little buggers nice and warm. You've got to be particular about what kind of bark you use, mind; some kinds of tree don't agree with them at all, like yew or crab-apple. They taught me which kinds of leaves and plants you need to gather and dump about the place to keep them sweet and make sure they keep coming back; balsam, saffron and honeywort really draw them in, which only shows there's no accounting for tastes. Even more important, they taught me how to sort them out when they get all stroppy and start swarming – all you do is, you scoop up a big handful of dust and throw it over the swarm, and they calm down just like that. Amazing, the first time you see it. And they showed me how you recognise the queen by her size, and how you pull her wings off to stop her flying away and leaving the hive; a dirty trick, if you ask me, but that's war for you.

They made me this smock thing, with a big hat and a veil to go with it, and that helped keep the bastards from stinging me to death; but I still got stung in spite of all the fancy dress, whereas they never got stung at all. So I asked them about it and they said, No, the bees left them alone because they understood each other. After a while, they said, you learn how to communicate with bees, on a very basic level, of course. It's all to do with the way you move, they said; if you're relaxed and calm and don't make sudden movements or anything like that, they stop seeing you as a threat and quit stinging you. Of course, I reckoned that was all a load of cock; but bugger me if it wasn't true, and gradually it became second nature to me. They stopped bothering me, took no notice of me at all, even when I was up to my wrists in them. I promise you, it'd make you swear off drink for life to watch me groping about inside a seething mass of bees, with them crawling right up my arms and all over my face, and never getting stung once.

So; thanks to extreme dedication and diligence on my part, I'd gone from being more or less completely ignorant about bees to the point where I could probably keep a household in honey and beeswax. Pretty impressive, don't you think? Except that that wasn't the point. King Alexander didn't want honey and beeswax; he wanted a secret weapon that'd cut a swathe through the great walled cities of Asia. On that score, my two Scythian friends weren't any use to me. Nobody was. Even if Aeneas the Tactician were still alive (he may be, for all I know, though I hope for his sake that he isn't, just in case he runs into me some dark night) he wouldn't have been able to help me, for the simple reason that neither he nor anybody else had ever done anything of the sort before. If Alexander was to have his secret weapon, I was the one who was going to have to figure out how to make it work.

'You're mad,' said Anacharsis, the elder and gabbier of the two Scythians, when I broke the news to him. 'It can't be done.'

'Oh,' I said. 'Why not?'

He rolled his eyes. They're good at that, Scythians. 'Well,' he said, 'for a start, the King wants you to move the bees, yes?'

'More than just move them,' I replied. 'Wherever the army goes, they go too.'

'Out of the question,' Anacharsis said. 'If you load the hives onto a cart, you'll lose the bees. They'll fly out, and when they return the hive won't be there any more. They won't be able to find it.'

I thought for a moment. 'All right,' I said. 'How'd it be if we sealed the hives up with wax or mud while they're in transit?'

He shook his head. 'They'll die,' he replied. 'Either they'll fight among themselves and kill each other, or they'll just curl up and go to sleep. Forget it.'

I rubbed my cheeks with the palms of my hands. Helps me concentrate. 'All right,' I said, 'I take your point. But we've got to find a way round it, somehow or other. Put that on one side for now; any other problems?'

He nodded. 'Feeding them,' he said. 'If you let them out to gather pollen, they'll fly away. Now suppose you find some way of keeping them in the hive without killing them; they'll just starve to death instead.'

My head was beginning to hurt. 'Honey,' I said. 'We buy up all the honey we can lay our hands on and feed them on that. Money's not a problem, remember.'

He sighed. 'This is ridiculous,' he said. 'Bees are meant to make honey, not consume it. The whole idea's unnatural.'

'Agreed,' I said. 'But we're lumbered with it, so stop being so damned negative and help me find a solution, unless you want to find yourself reassigned to a suicide squad come the first battle.'

Then his mate Bobas, who usually never said a word from one new moon to the next, lifted his head off his chest and looked at us both. 'Siege towers,' he said.

We waited for him to enlarge on this oracular statement, but he didn't oblige. I shook my head. 'How about—' I'd started, when Anacharsis grabbed my arm.

'He's right,' he said joyfully. 'Do you know, that's brilliant. Exactly what we need.'

I scratched the back of my head. 'Could one of you explain it to me?' I said. 'I'm lost.'

Anacharsis looked at me as if I were feeble-minded. 'Siege towers,' he repeated. 'You know, the portable scaffoldings with wheels they use to attack walls and towers . . .'

'I know what a siege tower is, thank you very—' I broke off. I'd seen the light. Just like the man said, it was brilliant.

Now you, dear brother, have spent your life skulking about in well-fortified cities or following a plough, so I don't imagine you're all that familiar with siege towers and how they're made. Basically it's a platform perched right up high on a scaffolding tower, all resting on a wagon-bed with two pairs of small, very solid wheels sticking out of the corners. The idea is, the top of the platform's level with the top of the battlements of the city you happen to be picking a fight with at that particular moment. The assault party stands on the platform and a whole bunch of other guys push this contraption tight up against the wall.

Now then; obviously the thing's got to be made on site since no two city walls are the same height and if you're too high or too low – well, forget it. But some of the components are interchangeable, one-size-fits-all sort of thing; for example, the big wicker shields they hang on the front and sides to keep the enemy arrows off the assault party. Actually, they aren't worth a light when you come down to it, but there's one very special thing about them I might not have mentioned yet. They're made of either hard bark or thick osiers woven together with a very fine weave, which makes them strong enough without being too heavy. In practice, they make the weave so fine that nothing gets past or through, except an arrow at point-blank range. They're certainly bee-proof. And they're big. Just what the doctor ordered. Cut 'em up and build what's effectively an enormous hive, one with enough space for the little bastards to fly about inside and keep from going nuts or dying of boredom. We made them the same length as the bed of a great big long wagon, with a trapdoor in the side so we could get in and out.

Simple idea. The bees stay in this hutch contrivance, which bounces along on a wagon with the rest of the siege train. A couple of times a day, someone climbs in to keep the feeders topped up with honey and change the leaves and foliage, make sure they're all right. And there you have it. Mobile beehives that'll go wherever you can take a long wagon and a dirty great long train of mules. Simple, yes?

Simple idea, hideously complicated to build in real life. We ended up tying the parts together with fine-filament rope, the way they make the hulls of ships in Egypt. It worked, is all I can say. It stayed in one piece and it kept the bees happy, or at least not as mad as they'd have been cooped up in a closed hive. We loaded it onto a wagon bed and took it for a twelve-mile hike just to test it, and it survived and so did we, and so did the bees.

'Crazy,' Anacharsis said, as we brought it back into the camp.

'Maybe,' I replied. 'But it works.'

'So far,' he answered gloomily. 'We're going to look real idiots if these things fall apart somewhere in the mountains of Ecbatana and all the bees fly away.'

'True,' I conceded. 'But at least we'll have lived that long. And besides, remember what it is the King's got in mind for us to do. Chances are we'll all have been cut into rashers by the Persians long before we get to Ecbatana, so nobody'll ever know.'

Does that sound unduly pessimistic to you, brother? Well, you've got the wonderful advantage of hindsight. You know that in spite of the odds and some truly shameful acts of bad soldiering, King Alexander pretty well strolled through Asia, with the Persians either running away or impaling themselves on our spear-points like moths buzzing burning lamp-wicks. Now that's not how it was either, but I don't suppose I'll ever convince you of that, because all you know of the story is the outcome. You know we won, and we won easily, so as far as you're concerned there can't have been anything to it.

But I tell you, brother, those weeks when we were getting ready to set off, the only way we kept from going crazy with fear was by single-mindedly thinking about something else. We *knew* that what we were about to try to do was utterly impossible. We knew we were probably all going to be dead inside three months. Believe me, if I'd thought I'd still be lugging around those idiotic bee-hutches ten years later, I'd never have dreamed of trying something so dumb; I'd have applied my mind and thought of a better system. As it was, I didn't care all that much. The hutch idea was, as they say, good enough for government work, so that's what we did. And if ever I started worrying about it, I had those excellent Scythian leaves to take the pain away. Wonderful medicine, that; cured you of life, which at times is even more painful than bee-stings.

Now, according to King Alexander, dear brother, you're the world's greatest living authority on military history, so obviously you don't have to be told about the Persian war by a mere eyewitness. You know it all already. In fact, you ought to be telling me.

Actually, to be straight with you, I wouldn't recommend that you put a lot of faith in my testimony even if you weren't a mighty historian. Truth to tell, I was out of it a lot of the time, in more senses than one. While the King and the fighting army were off tanning the hides of the Persians, we were plodding along with the siege train or standing about waiting while the engineers slowly and painfully dismantled the wagons to get them through some narrow mountain pass or other, then put them slowly and painfully back together again. We spent hours like that, watching other people work, with the convoy of mules and wagons stretched out behind us, nothing to do but listen to the soft chink of distant hammers driving out axle pins. It was *boring*, and boredom is a very acute form of pain, let me assure you. Fortunately, I had plenty of medicine; so it won't come as too much of a surprise when I tell you that I haven't a clue about a lot of the places we went to, what they looked like, whether the houses were flat-roofed or thatched, whether they kept sheep or goats, the names of the rivers and the location of the fords, where the snow-line was, how many days it took to get from one particular poxy little village to another. You can read all about it in one of the books, you don't need me to tell you. So I won't. Now I could tell you some pretty damn fascinating stories about some of the things I did see and some of the people I spoke to, often for hours at a time, but you see, they weren't real, and therefore of only incidental interest to a dedicated historian like yourself. In a way, of course, I'm sorry I missed the show; but that's me all over. I was always the kid who was so excited at the prospect of going to the theatre that he lay awake all through the night before and then fell asleep immediately the play started.

Yes, brother, that's soldiering for you; well, partly. Actually there's more to it than that. There's also the long days in the murderous heat, when you're manhandling the baggage over trails where the wagons can't go, in your breastplate and helmet (because there's a one-in-ten-thousand chance that there might be renegade Hyrcanian infantry units hiding out in the hills, and you know that the one time you don't wear your armour is the time they'll attack), with the sweat trickling off your forehead into your eyes, no skin on your palms because of hauling on dry papyrus cables with sweaty hands, your head pounding from the cruel brightness of the sun – and then, just when you reckon you're about done, the load gets wedged fast between two rocks, or an axle pin shears or a mule refuses to budge or some fool gets his leg trapped under a fallen boulder or an A-frame pops its dowels or some other bloody thing goes wrong; nobody else is going to fix it but you, and you aren't going anywhere till it gets fixed, so although you're so weary you can't stand straight, let alone think, you've got to force yourself back into problem-solving mode, find that last scrap of energy you were saving for taking your boots off, and deal with it, as quickly and efficiently as possible.

Soldiering is about climbing for two days up the only pass through the tallest mountains you've ever seen in your life, only to find that you've reached a defile so narrow you can't get the hutches through even if you turn them on their side, so you've either got to unship the pickaxes and widen the bugger, chip by bone-jarring chip, or trudge back down the way you came and go the extra seventy miles south that'll take you round the mountains, even though it means losing contact with the rest of the column. Soldiering is about breaking open the five jars of flour that are going to have to last you the three days it'll take to get down the mountain, only to find there's been a cock-up somewhere in Supply, and your five jars of flour are in fact three jars of lamp-oil and two jars of shield-dubbin. Soldiering is getting to the top of the next lot of mountains and looking down to where there should be a big, wide river where the barges are waiting to carry you the next sixty miles; but not only are there no barges, there's no damn river. Soldiering is furious arguments with some other poor bastard just like you over who was supposed to have checked with Intelligence that the barges were going to be there, and finding out that really it was your fault, and the whole miserable mess is your responsibility, nobody else's. Soldiering is dysentery, unexplained fevers that you simply haven't got time to indulge, wrenched muscles you ignore until you're so used to the pain you don't notice it any more; it's men under your command having their hands torn off by badly secured loads shifting on the crane, or falling off narrow tracks down steep gullies and breaking their backs, and you have to leave them and keep going on, because if you stay and wait for them to die, the water or the barley for the mules is going to run out, and everybody's going to be in trouble.

Oddly enough, you historians tend to skip over most everything that makes soldiering what it is, in favour of battles and plans of campaign and a whole lot of other stuff that happens on the edges of soldiering – it's as if you really believe that any one man, one general, is in control of the things that happen to an army as it blunders and lurches along from one wretched, inconvenient foul-up to the next, or that battles turn out the way they do because two great men in red cloaks sit down to play a game of draughts with the bodies and lives of a hundred thousand people. Obviously you don't believe anything of the sort, because nobody that gullible ever learned to read, let alone write a book; and yet you put it down in the scroll, and people who've been soldiers and know what it was really like will listen to your book being read and nod their heads, maybe muttering to the man sitting next to them, 'Actually, I was on that campaign; I'd forgotten all about that skirmish till he mentioned it just now.' You know, you're almost as bad as Homer and the poets for not mentioning the painfully obvious. I suppose it's some sort of literary convention, like the way that throughout a hundred thousand verses of the *Iliad*, with all the fighting and speechmaking and roaring about the place in chariots, nobody ever needs to stop what they're doing to go for a pee.

Sorry, brother, am I boring you?

That's all right, then. I saw you yawn, and I thought you might be getting bored. Just in case you're only being polite, I'll tell you about something truly interesting, shall I?

There's a city called Tyre – you've heard of it? Oh, good. I'm not surprised; after all, it's one of the biggest cities in the world, maybe the most important seaport and trading centre in Asia. This would be – what, two years after we left Greece? Something like that. King Alexander had resolved to capture Phoenicia, to get hold of the Persian fleet and so secure his seaborne supply-lines, or some such thoroughly intelligent plan. Anyway, it was winter and in Syria, in winter, it rains. Believe me, it rains. I've seen wonders all right, on these travels of mine; staggering rock formations and vast rivers and amazing animals and people, but for someone like me, coming from Attica where it rains twice a year, just about enough to fill a small cup, that Syrian rain was the most amazing sight of all. Have you ever been soaked to the skin by rain, brother? Well, it's an experience. It gets in your eyes and your mouth, it trickles down between your neck and the rim of your breastplate, it turns the dust to oily black mud that sticks to your boots and makes your feet so heavy it's unbearable to lift them. Well, while we were struggling through all that, Alexander was picking a rather genteel fight with the city fathers of Tyre, in the hope of making a pretext that would allow him to attack the city with honour.

Basically, Alexander wanted to find a way of *not* attacking Tyre. It was far too big and far too well defended to take by storm, and if we tried to lay siege to it we'd starve to death long before they did, with their ships unloading a thousand tons of grain a day into the town granaries. So he was trying to do what his father had done so well: scare them into giving up without a fight. All he really needed was a token of submission, nothing much; merely entering the city would do, at a pinch. So he wrote to the governing council to tell them he was proposing to visit the temple of Melkarth, of which he'd heard so much. The Tyrians wrote back saying that in fact the city temple wasn't anything like it was cracked up to be; if he wanted to see a real cracker of a temple, he should do himself a favour and visit the one ten miles or so down the coast, where they had some absolutely stunning bas-reliefs. Alexander replied that he'd set his heart on seeing the city temple, and he'd take it as a personal favour if they'd just confirm that such a visit would be in order. He got no reply to that, and declared war at once.

'It's obvious what he's up to,' somebody said to me, as we huddled underneath the bed of a wagon for shelter from the rain. 'Tyre's the home base of the fleet the Persians would use if they were going to send help to anti-Macedonian rebels in Greece. Now then; Sparta's openly at war with the Macedonian presence in the Peloponnese, Athens is just waiting for someone to give the lead, and they'll pile in too, and if Athens rebels, half of Greece will be up in arms, provided they can get money and supplies from Persia. From the Persian viewpoint, opening a second front back home in Greece is about the only thing they can think of that'd get Alexander out of Asia. So; unless Alexander takes Tyre, he could lose this war in a matter of days.'

It sounded eminently sensible under a cart in the middle of a flash rainstorm; Tyre's a problem, get rid of Tyre, problem solved. Unfortunately, the nearer to Tyre we got, the harder it became. For one thing, Tyre isn't on the coast; it's on an island, or at least the old town is, and that was the part we needed to capture. When I say island, I mean a proper island, not just some splinter of rock; but Tyre old town covered every part of it, and the sprawl of the new town lay just across the straits on the mainland. Since the Tyrian navy controlled the sea, we couldn't try an amphibious attack even if we'd wanted to (not that we'd ever want any such thing). All in all, the expression 'hiding to nothing' took on a whole new dimension of complex and sinister undertones in this context. The only logical course of action was to pack our things, send a polite note to the King of Persia apologising for any inconvenience, and go home.

I can't remember, brother; when you were Alexander's tutor, was logic part of the curriculum? If it was, you made a really poor job of it. He took one look at the island, decided the sea had to go, and ordered us to fill it in.

It was such an awesome piece of arrogance and folly that nobody had the heart to object. That bit of sea's in your way? Grab a spade and shovel dirt into it. So we did. To be precise, we set about building a causeway to link Tyre island with the mainland. To give you an idea of what was involved—

'Eudaemon,' I interrupted, 'I'm sure this is going to be absolutely fascinating, but it's been a long day and I've got to be up at the crack of dawn tomorrow. Do you think we might possibly . . .?'

He gave me a look that would have turned milk into cheese instantly. 'Fuck you, brother,' he said. 'We haven't seen each other for twenty-five years, after tomorrow we'll probably never see each other again, I'm explaining to you in detail exactly how you buggered up my life, and all you can think about is sneaking off to your pit. Well, the hell with you, brother. You can damn well sit there and listen, and if you so much as nod, I'll take this jug and smash it over your thick skull. Understood?'

I shrugged. 'Since you put it like that,' I said, 'go on, please. Though I still don't see why it's my fault that Alexander ordered you to build a causeway across the straits of Tyre.'

Eudaemon smiled sourly. 'Ah,' he said, 'that's because you will insist on talking rather than listening. Well, the less you interrupt, the sooner I'll be done, so shut your face and pay attention.'

Where was I? Oh, yes. To give you an idea of what was involved, think back to that time when we were kids and that rich bastard – now what was his name? The old bloke with the young wife and that incredibly ugly *thing* on his nose, damned if I can remember – yes, that's it, Philochorus – that rich bastard Philochorus was terracing that parcel of mountain land he'd inherited from his uncle. Well, think back to when he was going round borrowing every slave and day labourer he could find for the job of carting the rubble and spoil for the terraces up the mountain. It all had to be lugged up there in baskets, remember, and so he was scrounging baskets too, every last hamper and backpack and pannier in Pallene; only there weren't enough, so he had to go to the Market Square and buy every blessed scrap of wickerwork he could find; and as soon as word got around that Philochorus the Nose was desperate for baskets, the prices climbed so high they were having to crane their necks to look down on Olympus.

And, dear gods, do you remember the performance when he

actually got around to starting work? All the organisation; the relay teams and who was going to be foreman of which shift and who was going to report to who and the water-carriers and the muleteers suddenly coming over all snotty when they found out the masons were getting an obol a day more than they were and the masons talking back to the foreman because they weren't being given enough time to do the shoring-up before the earth-moving crews started pouring in the dirt. Wasn't that the best show we'd ever seen in our lives? Well, picture that in your mind's eye, and then try to imagine what it was like doing a similar sort of job, only with a hundred thousand workers instead of a hundred; then factor in the complications of the sea and the constant hail of missiles and arrows from the ramparts of Tyre, and maybe your imagination might just get a toe wedged in the door of what it was like.

Not, of course, that I had any part in it. I was, as we say in the army, standing by; which means I was sitting on my bum where I'd been told to sit, all poised and ready just in case I might be needed at some undefined future stage in the proceedings. The first few days, of course, I really didn't mind at all. Our family have always relished watching other people work, and the spectacle of all those poor fools in full armour humping enormous baskets of rubble on their backs while trying to dodge catapult bolts without falling into the sea was fairly engrossing, I can tell you. The amazing, the utterly astonishing thing about it was the rate of progress. You wouldn't have believed it possible that ordinary men and women chucking one basketful of dirt at a time into the sea could have achieved so much in such a short space of time. There was something utterly inhuman about it all; it was like watching a tree grow. Maybe that's what it's like for the gods; when they're feeling lazy after a good meal, do they lie on their stomachs in the sun watching forests sprout or rivers dig themselves valleys between the hills? No wonder the gods don't seem to care too much about us. We must move so fast, they couldn't even see us if they tried.

After a few days, though, I was so twitchy and uptight I couldn't keep still any longer. I broke the cardinal rule of military life, and volunteered. The staff bastard in charge shook his head and told me I wasn't allowed to; I was specialist technical crew and I had to carry on standing by, whether I liked it or not. He added that if I volunteered again he'd have me suspended from duty on grounds of insanity, so I gave it up and went back to the tree-stump I'd been sitting on for the past three days.

As it turned out, he'd done me a big favour, because by that point the Tyre garrison had stopped gathering on the walls to laugh themselves silly at us, and were getting pretty damn nervous. So they decided to stop us; they stepped up the interference fire from the walls, they sent out war-galleys in continuous shifts to stand off a hundred yards on either side of the causeway and shoot up the work crews – which meant, in effect, that our people were under fire on three sides; they were dropping like olives off a tree, though that didn't constitute a valid reason for not working, and besides, they were only local civilians, so it didn't matter. It was only much later, when the rate of progress had slowed by about a quarter, that Alexander realised he was going to have to divert some manpower from the job to deal with these bastards; but that was all right from my point of view, because finally I was allowed to do something.

The idea was that we'd unship and assemble two of the mobile siege towers that we carried disassembled in kit form, and wheel them up to the top of the causeway to provide cover. Well, we set to with a vengeance, and there really was a lot to do.

They were a fairly new addition to our stores, those towers; it was only when we reached Lebanon that we were able to find timber long and strong enough to build these particular designs. That meant, of course, that we'd never actually had to unship and assemble the damned things before; we hadn't even worked out the drill in theory, let alone smoothed out the wrinkles in practice. I'm here to tell you, it was a hell of a job to have to do on the fly. Those things were *enormous*, they had to be in order to bear the weight of the full-size long-range catapults that Alexander wanted installed at the top of each tower. First we had to raise the uprights; of course, we found out at this point that half of the tenons didn't quite fit the mortices, because the green timber had moved a bit since it was cut, so we had to plane and shave and chisel out on site, up to our ankles in dust and mud and shavings, while our people were being slaughtered by the dozen a few hundred yards away. Helps you concentrate, something like that.

Anyway; we got the frames up, laid in the ties and braces, put in the flooring and the rails, finished up by stretching any number of green raw hides over the frames to stop the arrows and catapult shot, and handed them over to the teams who had the job of deploying the things. We'd done well, no doubt about it; and those things worked, too. They were tall enough that the guys inside them could get clear shots at the enemy on the wall and in the ships, and robust enough not to fall to bits no matter what got slung at them. We'd had the sense, you see, to stretch those hides pretty slack, so that arrows and such just flopped off them instead of going through.

To cut a long story short, things were going pretty much our way by this stage. The towers were doing their job, and to increase the protection for the work crews we'd made up rawhide fences that ran the whole length of the causeway, so not a lot was getting through one way or another. Just when we thought we'd cracked it, in fact, those bastards on the island turned round and showed us we hadn't. Let me tell you about that, brother, if you can spare the time.

It was early one morning, and there was a good stiff westerly wind blowing; we noticed two Tyrian warships cracking along at a hell of a lick, towing this enormous fat old hulk of a horse-transport. It was so broad in the beam it was practically round, and it was sitting up in the water like a dog begging. Oddest thing about it was two thin masts right forward; they looked like thin, bare saplings and they had round cauldrons hanging from the yard-arms, like apples on the branches of a tree.

We were staring at this thing thinking *What the hell?* when the warships towing it veered off on either side of the nose end of the causeway, cut cables and buggered off at top speed, letting the hulk carry on under its own momentum so that it crashed into the front end and actually rode up on the causeway broadwalk, for all the world like an otter or a seal. Under the impact the two flimsy masts bust, and those cauldrons went toppling down; turned out that they were full of this mixture of pitch and naphtha – that's a kind of lamp-oil they draw off out of the rocks in those parts, and boy, does it burn well; doesn't just catch fire like olive oil or lard tallow, it goes up *whoosh!* and the next thing you know is, people are staring at you and saying, Sorry, didn't recognise you without the beard – along with this other secret ingredient they've got that actually catches alight when it comes in contact with water. Result, the mixture slops all over the wooden planking and the props and struts, not to mention the towers, the hide fences and quite a lot of people, then drains over the side into the water and wham, flares up like hell, and suddenly everything's on fire.

Meanwhile the two warships had come back, along with a whole load of other boats, all of them with archers and catapult crews squeezed in right along the rails; first they shot the guys jumping off the burning causeway into the water, then the other guys who didn't dare jump for fear of getting shot, and the fire took care of the rest. By the time the Tyrians had disembarked their assault parties on the causeway, there wasn't anybody left alive to fight. So they knuckled down to their job of breaking up the causeway, while the ships covered them against our reinforcements. Between them and the fire, they did as thorough a job as you'd ever want to see, and before what was happening had really started to sink in properly, down the causeway slid, its own weight letting it simply melt down into the water.

Enough to make you spit, really. Everything we'd worked at so hard for all that time ended up at the bottom of the straits along with gods know how many dead workers and the charred scrap of our two beautiful siege towers. It was one of those moments of total and abject failure that takes it all out of you, all the stuff inside your head and your heart that makes you keep going. For my part, I cooked up a big hot fire of my own and started sprinkling my beautiful medicinal leaves in big handfuls.

It was only the day after, though, that the full implications became obvious enough that even I, with my head full of smoke and painlessness, could get the drift of it. While we'd been farting about trying to fill in the sea, the King of Persia had been putting his army back together again in Armenia, and he was coming to get us. The Tyrians had been deliberately playing us along, letting us fritter away our time with our buckets and spades so as to give the Great King a chance to get his act together. When word reached them that the Great King was ready, they cleared up the mess we'd made, like grown-ups putting away the toys. We'd fallen for it, complete in every part. At last, finally, Alexander had made a big mistake; a super-jumbo-sized, war-losing mistake that was going to get us all killed.

And that, brother, is why if I wasn't stuck on this damned bed unable to move, I'd be up on my feet throttling you right now; because when the general staff urged him to give it up and get out while there was still a slim chance of getting away, he stared at them with those ice-cold blue eyes and said no, certainly not, because that wasn't the way he'd been taught the art of war, and anybody who even suggested pulling out would pretty soon be reckoning that the Great King was the least of his problems. So what if the enemy had pulled down the causeway? We'd build another one; only bigger, and wider, with room for lots more siege towers. True, thousands of our conscript workers were now dead and at the bottom of the straits, leaving us with something of a labour shortage, but that wasn't really a problem; plenty more where they came from, plus all the specialist masons and carpenters and engineers he'd had rounded up in Cyprus and Phoenicia. History, he informed his open-mouthed heads of staff, would remember Tyre as a shining example of Macedonian siegecraft (that is, he implied, if History knew what was good for it).

At this point, a nervous young man called Hegelochus, who held a command in the Horse Guards, cleared his throat pointedly and asked what, if anything, led Alexander to believe that he'd have any more luck the second time round than he had the first. Now, I wasn't there, so this is all hearsay; but a man I used to play knucklebones with had a cousin who was in the same cockfighting syndicate as the younger brother of Callas, the commander of the Thracian heavy cavalry, who was there; so what I'm telling you now is as close to absolute Platonic truth as you're likely to get in this sadly imperfect world, and Callas said that Alexander didn't like the implications of that question, not one bit.

'Something's bothering you about this, Hegelochus,' he said, in that level, calm voice of his that sent people who knew him scurrying off in search of abandoned well-shafts to hide down. 'I'd like to know what it is.'

That young fool Hegelochus cleared his throat again. 'With respect, the whole thing bothers me,' he said, 'because I've got the strangest feeling I've been here before.'

Alexander smiled. 'Is that so? Now that's strange, my friend, because we've known each other since we were both six years old, and I don't ever remember you going abroad even, let alone to Phoenicia. When was this?'

'When we studied together in the school at Mieza,' Hegelochus replied. 'That time when Professor Euxenus was telling us about that battle – sorry, can't remember the name of it now – where the besieging army sat under the walls of this impregnable city grinding themselves down to no effect until the relief force came and scrunched them up.'

'Syracuse,' Alexander said. 'You're thinking of when the Athenians tried to take Syracuse in the Great War. Euxenus told us his grandfather was in that army.'

Hegelochus nodded. 'That's it,' he said. 'He was one of the very few survivors, wasn't he?'

Alexander scowled at that; he'd been made to play the straight man, something he hated unless he'd deliberately set it up himself. 'Sure,' he said. 'And I'm sure you remember the moral of the story. Euxenus said that if he'd been the Athenian commander there, he'd have kept pegging away till he found a way to take Syracuse, because that was the only way the army was going to get out of there in one piece. And then one of us – wasn't that you, Cleitus? – one of us asked how he'd have proposed going about that, since everything they'd tried had failed. And Euxenus just smiled, that way he did, and said, "Simple. I'd have waited for them to make a mistake. They always do, you know. All wars are lost by the loser, not won by the victor."' He paused for a moment and looked at Cleitus, his head slightly on one side. 'You haven't forgotten that, have you?' he went on. 'Or are you saying Euxenus was wrong?'

('I don't remember saying that,' I interrupted.

Eudaemon gave me a long, cold stare. 'Don't you indeed,' he said.

I thought for a moment. 'Well, bits of it,' I replied. 'That tag about wars being lost by the loser – that was a favourite line of mine, I admit. I thought it was pretty neat, and it seemed to impress the kids, so I used it a lot to save myself the trouble of thinking. But that actual conversation, about what I'd have done at Syracuse; I don't remember that at all. Sorry.'

Eudaemon shrugged. 'Maybe you don't,' he said. 'After all, who'd expect you to be able to remember every damn thing you said to a bunch of kids when you were teaching them? Maybe you never actually said it at all, in so many words, and Alexander remembered it wrong. Doesn't matter. *Alexander's* Euxenus said it, and it very nearly got us all killed. And Alexander's Euxenus was more real to him – and, as a result, to me – than you'll ever bloody be. In fact,' he added, glowering at me, 'of all the Euxenuses there are or were, I'll bet you're about the most insignificant of the lot.')

So that was that. Hegelochus and Cleitus were in disgrace, we were staying, the siege continued, with us trapped up against Tyre like a billet of red-hot bronze between the hammer and the anvil. The Tyrians started building up their walls with wooden towers so they could shoot fire-arrows directly down into the working parties. We stumbled on – there were people getting shot down or squashed flat by rocks from the catapults every minute of every day, and we were just supposed to ignore it – and in the meantime Alexander got bored and wandered off, with his boyhood chums and his pet light-infantry brigade, to go hunting tribesmen in the hills. Of course, the bloody clown nearly got himself killed; there was this old fool called Lysimachus, who'd been a teacher at your school –

('I know Lysimachus,' I interrupted.

'No doubt.')

– And he'd insisted on tagging along on this adventure. Seems they were playing at being people in Homer, they were always doing it; Alexander was Achilles, Lysimachus was the old tutor, Phoenix. Anyhow, Lysimachus strayed off and got left behind. The tribesmen were all around, dogging the column's footsteps, never coming to grips, just making sneak attacks, shooting arrows and throwing javelins and then melting away; a lot of our people got killed, and there was bugger all our Achilles and his Homeric knights could do about it; I guess the tribesmen hadn't been to your classes, didn't know to conduct themselves in a fitting manner. Well, everybody was terrified out of their minds; all except Alexander, who was absolutely furious. They were spoiling his game, you see, there wasn't anything in all of this for him.

Anyhow, when Phoenix went missing, Alexander freaked out and said they had to go back and find him. None of the others wanted anything to do with that, understandably enough; they were in enough shit as it was. But no, Alexander insisted, he'd caught a whiff of honour in the breeze and went off after it like a bad dog after a hare. So there they were, completely lost, surrounded by these tribesmen who were knocking them off like ducks on a pond; and night falls, and everybody knows they aren't going to see tomorrow, because the tribesmen have started up their spirit dance, which means they're going to attack and finish the job, and there's thousands and thousands of them out there, according to a friend of mine who was on this jolly. Our boys know they've got no chance, because they haven't been able to get a fire going – sudden downpour of rain, all the kindling soaked through – so they can't see spit, they're completely at the mercy of the enemy. At this point, when it really couldn't get any worse if it tried, Alexander gets up without a word, takes his cloak with the hood and a long dagger and walks away. Twenty minutes later, he's back; he's only snuck up on the nearest enemy camp, scragged a couple of sentries, lit a torch in their fire and come bouncing back with an absolutely enormous grin on his face, like a boy who's just killed something. Think about it, brother; the king of the known world, prancing about stalking sentries; everybody else was scared out of their wits and he was off *playing*.

But he'd got a torch, and they were able to light a fire and see to keep a lookout, and what with one thing and another the enemy didn't attack; and the next day, by the purest fluke, they stumbled across old Lysimachus, curled up in a bush and whimpering with fear. Alexander didn't like that, completely out of character for his role in the make-believe game, but he'd got what he came for and they headed back. Made it, too, though they left a lot of their own behind, littered all over the trail like bits of crust and apple-cores a bunch of untidy kids leave behind them as they go. And of course, Alexander's the great hero who single-handedly saved everybody's life, and the fact that the whole trip was a disastrous failure – well, History knows better than to record that. But old Lysimachus, who's desperate to get back in the lad's good books after disgracing himself, he stands up at the next council of war and starts going on about how Alexander's really braver and better than Achilles ever was, and how even Homer himself wouldn't have been able to find words to tell the story like it should be told; and Alexander's face melts into this huge self-satisfied smirk.

Well, now he's back Alexander calls a council and says there's been a change of plan. Forget the causeway, he says, it's obviously not going to work, any fool could have told you that. Nobody says a word; and Alexander goes on and says that the only way to take Tyre is to fit out special warships with battering-rams mounted on them and go smash in the seaward walls. So we do that, and it's an absolute disaster. The ships just can't get in close enough, the water's too shallow, except in one place, and the enemy've realised this and dumped huge great rocks there to obstruct the shallows and keep ships from coming in.

But Alexander won't be beaten. He's really away with the wood-nymphs now; sometimes, when he isn't thinking, he's calling the place Troy instead of Tyre, every day he's sending heralds demanding single combat with the enemy's champion – they're just standing there in their watchtowers looking *embarrassed* – and when they tell him about the rocks he just frowns and says, 'Well, if they're in the way, you'd better fish them out again.' Bugger me, Euxenus, he was *serious*; so we had to build ship-mounted cranes for hauling up these rocks – under fire all the time, remember, and the rawhide screens we'd used on the first causeway to keep the arrows off were useless, because these new towers the enemy had built meant they could shoot right over the top. Also, the enemy sent out ships and boats of their own, and soon they were fighting ship to ship; they'd sent in these little ships that were all planked in to protect their men from our archers, and they'd nip out, cut the anchor cables of the dredgers and scoot off again before we could do anything about them, though eventually we swapped the cables for chains, and that put a stop to it.

So Alexander called a council of war and said the ships weren't working, time to finish off the causeway, which was clearly their only hope of taking the city. So we finished the causeway – we were using the rocks the dredgers were pulling up out of the shallows, and if that wasn't the dumbest thing; pulling trash out of the sea at point A and slinging it back at point B – and we set up battering rams on it, but they don't do any bloody good, the wall's made of huge blocks of stone cemented together.

So Alexander called a council of war and said stuff the causeway, concentrate on the ships. Finally, after we'd nearly filled up the hole the dredgers had excavated with the bodies of our dead, we managed to bash a hole in the seaward side. Before we could get the ships with the portable drawbridges in, they'd sealed it again – a whole ship full of workers and engineers got caught out then, and the lot of them were killed when the enemy set their ship alight. So we tried again next day, the whole army (except me; I was standing by); and somehow those crazy Macedonian infantry managed to get across the jerry-rigged drawbridges and into Tyre. The whole of the first wave got themselves killed in the breach; and Alexander saw this and went charging in there himself, waving his sword and yelling like a lunatic. Should've been killed just like all the others. Wasn't.

So we stormed Tyre. Killed eight thousand civilians, sold thirty thousand more to the slave dealers, along with some of our surplus labour – we needed the money, we were hopelessly over budget after all this fooling about, the cost of materials alone was enough to have bankrupted a city. But we won. I guess.

Oh, and that Persian army I was telling you about? They got held up. Pure fluke; bad roads, rivers in spate, that sort of thing. Instead of sweeping down on us when we were at our most vulnerable and butchering us where we stood, they were backing up in narrow mountain passes that had got blocked by freak rockslides, or frantically repairing bridges that had been swept away by flash floods. When they realised they weren't going to make it in time, the Great King sent Alexander a message with a peace offer – 10,000 talents cash and half the empire, everything west of the Euphrates, provided he'd piss off and leave Persia alone. They had a council of war to discuss the offer. 'I'd take it, if I were you,' said old general Parmenio. 'Sure, so would I,' said Alexander, 'if I were Parmenio.' Then he told the embassy what they could do with their offer, and told us we were going to conquer Egypt.

In all the excitement, of course, he'd completely forgotten the reason he'd wanted to sack Tyre in the first place; the Persian fleet, which was all poised and set to sweep down on Greece while our backs were turned. But that turned out all right; the Byblians and the Sidonians fell out with the Persian admirals over something or other and buggered off in a huff, the Cypriots joined them, and a whole bunch of ships changed sides and came over to us, asking for a job. And that was the end of the Persian fleet, our part in its downfall being exactly nothing.

'Oh, well,' my mate Peitho said to me, when we heard about this. 'We needn't have bothered with Tyre after all, then.'

'Apparently not,' I agreed, and I chucked some more leaves in the fire.

'How come you stayed out of the fighting?' Peitho asked me. He'd been hit twice, once during the dredging operation, once during the assault, and the second arrow had put out his left eye.

'I was standing by,' I replied.

'Fair enough,' Peitho said, breathing in deeply through his nose. 'Grows on you, this stuff, doesn't it?'

'Very good for bad backs and sprained ankles,' I said.

'Quite likely. Hey, I wonder if Alexander realises all that business with Tyre was for nothing?'

I thought for a moment. 'You tell him,' I said.

CHAPTER TWENTY-ONE

'That's a really amazing story,' I said, stifling a yawn. 'And now, if it's all the same to you, I really must go and get some—'

'Shut up,' my brother said.

It was after the siege of Tyre, and because of the siege of Tyre, that my friend Peitho and I realised that there was something we could do to make the world a better place, yank the human race back from the brink of an abyss, and win ourselves an honoured place in history at the same time.

We could kill Alexander.

Now then, brother, before you turn white and start screaming for the guards, I ought to point out that when we reached this conclusion, Peitho and I had been kippering ourselves in that wonderful Scythian smoke more or less non-stop for a couple of weeks (Peitho had really bad toothache, the sort that gets to you so completely that you can't think of anything else, and I felt it was my duty as a fellow human being to do what I could to alleviate his misery), so we were both as crazy as a jarful of polecats or we'd never even have considered the idea for a moment. After all, enough innocent, harmless men had their throats cut because of entirely mythical and non-existent plots against Alexander to make a sane man think very seriously indeed about embarking on a *real* one. But we, medicated as we were from the soles of our feet to the tips of our ears, were above such mundane considerations as fear or common sense.

Really, brother, I wish I had some of that stuff left, it'd do you a world of good. Maybe even loosen you up a little, if that's humanly possible.

Now, it's all very well to say, 'I know, let's kill Alexander and then everything'll be sweet'; but getting close enough to him to stick a knife in his back wasn't going to be easy. First off, he was surrounded day and night by his lifelong companions, the young Macedonian nobles you prattled away to in dear old Mieza; animals, the lot of them, who'd cleave your skull without a moment's hesitation if they didn't like the way you wiped your nose. I put this point to my fellow conspirator one evening, when we'd pitched camp for the night and were sharing a sociable lungful or two of medicine. He thought about it for a while, while I shovelled another double handful of leaves on the fire.

'All right,' he said. 'Fair play to you, Eudaemon, you've got a point there. No way we can get to him while the Companions are about. They'd slice us up like bacon.'

'You bet,' I agreed, nodding. 'Our heads'd be rolling on the deck before we got close enough to smell his sweat.'

Peitho frowned. 'All right,' he said, 'there's no need to get all negative about it. Like the philosopher said, a problem is just a challenge in disguise.'

'Oh.' I thought for a moment. 'Which philosopher was that, then?'

'My cousin Gelo,' Peitho replied. 'He wasn't a professional philosopher, mind, it was more like a hobby with him.'

'I see.' I paused, filled my lungs with smoke, held my breath for a count of five and breathed out again slowly. 'What about poison?' I suggested. 'Don't have to be anywhere near for that.'

Peitho scratched his head. 'Doesn't he have all his food tasted before he eats it?' he asked.

'Sure,' I replied, 'but that's no problem. Use a slow poison. Something that doesn't start working till the next day. Then, by the time the taster goes bright purple and keels over, it'll be too late to do anything about it.'

Peitho yawned. 'All right,' he said. 'So you know all about poisons, then, do you?'

'No,' I admitted. 'Haven't a clue.'

'Me neither,' Peitho said. 'Know anybody we could ask?'

'Not really,' I replied. 'Besides, you go around asking people about poisons, they'll want to know why. Maybe there's a book about it we could read.'

'Probably,' Peitho said. 'There's books about heaps of stuff. Who do we know who's got a lot of books?'

I sat back on my chair – one of those three-legged folding efforts, as I recall – and tried to think. Wonderful insight those leaves give you, though your mind does tend to go racing off on side-issues. 'How about Anaxarchus?' I suggested. 'He's got a whole box of the things.'

Anaxarchus was one of Alexander's tame philosophers; he had two of them with him on the trip, Anaxander and Callisthenes (who was the nephew of Aristotle, who was – oh, of course, you've met him, haven't you? All right, you know about Aristotle). I'd only met Anaxarchus a couple of times, barely spoken a dozen words to him, but if ever there was a man who was likely to own a book about different types of poison, it'd be Anaxarchus. Not that he'd have had any use for it, in the same way that a dagger'd be wasted on a shark.

'All right, then,' I said. 'First thing in the morning, you go round there and ask him.'

He looked up at me, eyes narrowed. 'Why me?' he said.

'You're a Macedonian,' I replied. 'He'll trust you.'

'Why? He's isn't Macedonian.'

I sighed and poured myself another drink. Actually, my Scythian friends had advised me not to drink booze while using the medicine; the combination, they claimed, could sometimes have the effect of making a man somewhat light-headed. Never had that effect on me, though, or not that I was ever aware of.

'Doesn't matter,' I said. 'He'll trust you because you belong to the ruling class. The elite.'

'No I don't,' he objected. 'My dad works seventeen acres on the Paeonian border. My mum isn't even a citizen.'

I shook my head. 'Missing the point,' I said. 'The Macedonians are the chosen people, the beloved of the gods. They shall inherit the fucking earth. While a poor bloody Athenian like me goes in some philosopher's tent asking to borrow his copy of *Poisoning for Pleasure and Profit*, next thing I know, my body'll be waving at my head and telling it not to be a stranger. Besides,' I added, 'I don't think he likes me.'

'Really? Why not?'

'Because my brother was Alexander's tutor.'

'Really?'

I nodded. 'When he was a kid.'

'Your brother?'

'Alexander. When Alexander was a kid. Anaxarchus is jealous because he's only come on the scene recently, he's got to sit there listening to how Euxenus said this and Euxenus said that. Cramps his style. Wouldn't lend me the wax out of his ears, let alone enough poison to wipe out half of bloody Asia.'

Peitho tipped his head up and down, like a man leaning to and fro in a chair. 'All right,' he said. 'Suppose I'd better do it. What if he says no?'

I raised an eyebrow. 'Why'd he do that?'

'Maybe he hasn't got a book about poisons,' Peitho pointed out. 'No reason to think he has, when you get right down to it.'

I sighed. 'Well,' I said. 'Only one way to find out. Ask the bastard. Just go in there, look the bastard straight in the fucking eye, and ask him. He'll tell you, I promise you.'

'All right.'

'How's your tooth?'

'Much better, thanks.'

Now, as a rule, going to bed and sleeping for a bit tended to dissipate the effects of the medicine; but we were both of us so utterly fumigated with it that it no longer seemed to wear off the way it had at first. Accordingly, Peitho did go to see Anaxarchus, and afterwards he came to see me.

'He hasn't got one,' he told me.

'Buggery,' I replied. 'So that's that, then.'

Peitho shook his head. 'Not necessarily,' he said. 'He thinks he knows who might have one.'

'Ah. Right. Who?'

'Callisthenes.'

'Oh.'

'Because,' Peitho went on, 'Callisthenes has got copies of all his precious uncle's books, and it so happens, or at least so Anaxarchus reckons, that Aristotle's done a poisons book.'

'Really?'

Peitho nodded. 'Apparently. Well, it's more your general book about plants, but in it he seems to remember there's a lot of stuff about which plants are poisonous and what the poisons do to you. It'd be a start, anyhow.'

'Better than a kick in the head,' I agreed. 'All right, then, you'd better go and see Callisthenes.'

He didn't seem too happy about that. 'Why me?' he asked. 'Why not you?'

I had an answer ready for him. 'Because,' I said, 'my brother Euxenus—'

'The tutor.'

'That's him. My brother Euxenus is Aristotle's deadly enemy. They hate each other's guts. I'd have no chance.'

'I see.' Peitho thought for a moment. 'Is there anybody in this man's army your brother Euxenus hasn't pissed off in some way?'

'Don't know,' I replied. 'It's a big army, mind.'

Callisthenes did have a copy of *The Natural History of Plants*, and when Peitho spun him some yarn about wanting to look up some wildflowers he'd recently gathered beside the road, he lent it to him gladly. That evening, after we'd pitched camp and I'd fed the bees, he brought it round to my tent and we went through it together.

'You sure there's stuff about poisons in here?' I asked, after we'd been at it an hour. 'Mostly it's garbage. Can't make head nor tail of it. Here, what do you make of this?' I screwed up my eyes – it was a badly written copy, all abbreviations and poncified lettering, with notes scrawled in all the margins and over the tops of the lines. '"And it would be thought that a man is acting more under compulsion and involuntarily when his object is to avoid violent pain than when it is to avoid mild pain, and in general more when his object is the avoidance of pain than when it is to gain enjoyment. For what rests with himself means what his nature is able to bear; what his nature is not able to bear and what is not a matter of his own natural appetition or calculation does not rest with himself."' I looked up and shrugged. 'What the hell's that got to do with the price of fish?'

Peitho scowled thoughtfully, then leaned forward and craned his neck over so as to look at the page. 'You clown,' he said, 'you're reading the wrong book. The plants book's further on in the scroll. This is something about ethics.'

'Oh,' I said. 'Well, fuck ethics.' I rolled the scroll down a whole lot and tried again. 'How about this?' I said. 'Here's a bit all about lupins.'

'Lupins aren't poisonous, are they?'

'No, but at least they're plants, so we're in the right book. Now then, let's see what we can – Ah, now that's more like it. The roots of the white hellebore, it says here, produce a poison so deadly that death is practically instantaneous—'

'I thought we wanted a slow poison.'

'Oh bugger, so we do. Hey, this is turning out to be harder than I thought.'

Peitho was starting to look thoughtful, like a duck trying to hatch out a stone. 'You know,' he said, 'maybe this wasn't such a good idea after all.'

'It'll be in here somewhere, I'm sure. Just a case of reading it through carefully—'

He shook his head. 'No, I mean this whole killing Alexander thing. Come on, it's a bit drastic, isn't it?'

'No,' I replied. 'Look, he's got to go, we both agreed. He's a bloody menace.'

Peitho bit his lip. 'Well,' he said, 'to judge by that performance when he rescued old Lysimachus, chances are he'll go on some dumb adventure and get himself killed while we're still trying to make sense of this goddamn book. Shouldn't we just leave well alone and let the gods do it for us?'

I looked him squarely in the eye. 'The gods,' I said, 'help those who help themselves. So if it's all the same to you—'

'Actually,' he interrupted, 'you're wrong there. They don't. In fact, they come down on them like a ton of bloody bricks. Look at Daedalus.'

'Fuck it, Peitho, it's just an expression, doesn't mean anything.'

'Then if it doesn't mean anything, why the hell say it?'

I closed my eyes for a moment. 'The point I'm trying to make is, we can't just sit tight and wait for things to happen, we've got to get up off our bums and—'

'Or what about Prometheus? Or Theseus? Or Hercules, even? Or Paris; he surely helped himself, and look what happened to him.'

'Yes. Thank you.' I put the book down. 'I say we cut his throat while he's asleep. What do you think?'

'You know what I think.'

To cut a long story short, we didn't kill Alexander that day; nor the day after. And then we found ourselves at a place called Gaza, where there was another fortress – nowhere near as big or as grand as Tyre, but the governor, a man called Batis, was the Persian King's good and faithful servant, and all the time we'd been fooling about at Tyre, he'd been getting ready for us. He'd reinforced the mud-brick walls, hired a mob of Arab mercenaries, built up a stash of food and supplies that would last for well over a year; and when our engineers surveyed the position, they reported back that the hill on which the fortress stood was so steep, it was physically impossible for battering-rams to reach the walls.

Alexander didn't want to hear that. 'The more impossible it is, the more I'll do it,' he snarled, as he gave us the pre-mission briefing. 'I always do the impossible, remember; that's why they fear me.'

'You're right,' Peitho whispered to me as we stood in the ranks, listening. 'Got to go.'

'Knew you'd see it my way in the end,' I replied.

And so, there we went again, building bloody great causeways to bring the siege engines up to the walls; or, in my case, standing by. Mind you, for a week or so I really thought I might actually be needed, when Alexander suddenly woke up in the middle of the night convinced that the Gazans were digging mines under the causeway to collapse it, and sent a team of our sappers to counter-mine them. But there weren't any enemy sappers, and all that happened was that our countermine came up right under the weakest part of the causeway, which promptly subsided down the hole, killing the miners and a few dozen workers on the surface and wasting a week's effort. But eventually it was completed; the engines rolled into place and started pounding shit out of the walls. Batis and his Arabs refused to surrender; although it was now pretty well a foregone conclusion, they counter-attacked, set fire to some of the engines and actually forced a company of Macedonian regular infantry to give ground down the hill. Cue, needless to say, heroics; Achilles to the rescue. Alexander led the charge in person, his sword flashing in the sun, his head bare so that everybody could see it was him – and then *wham!*, a bloody great big catapult-bolt from an engine on the walls smashed through his shield and breastplate and knocked him clean off his feet onto his bum. Just for once I was actually watching, I actually saw it happen; it was like the hand of a god swatting a wasp. *Fuck me*, I thought, *he's dead, no bugger could've survived that.*

There was a moment when everything was still; everybody, even the men who were hacking at each other with swords, stopped what they were doing and stared, as if a herald had just announced the end of the world. I remember thinking, *So now what?* But then Colonel Hephaestion and the bodyguards rushed forward and picked him up; someone yelled out, 'It's all right, he's alive!' *Fuck*, I thought; then the battle started again, with the Arabs hurling themselves at us like madmen, trying to cut off Hephaestion's party and get to Alexander before we did. I promise you, brother, I never saw human beings fight so savagely; they were slashing at each other, not bothering to protect themselves with their shields, so that they were trading slash for slash, the last one to die being the winner. I saw a Macedonian and an Arab whittling each other to bits, they just didn't give a damn; it was as if Alexander's life being in the balance had removed every last Arab outside the walls, for what little good that did. There were only a few of them, and once we'd done that we were back where we were. Nothing had changed. Some smartarse bastard of a doctor patched Alexander up somehow; the day after next he was hobbling up and down the lines while everybody cheered and shouted and whistled to show how clever they thought he was for still managing to be alive. I was still alive too, but nobody seemed terribly impressed by that.

So up came the big siege-engines we'd used at Tyre, and down came the walls. We had to make four sorties, mind, and even then those stupid bastard Arabs wouldn't give up. We killed them all, except for some of the women and children.

Oh, Himself was back in action in time for the last assault, and once again he got clobbered by a catapult shot; but this one only whacked him across the shins, not even hard enough to break them, and by now it was painfully obvious that nothing as mundane as artillery was going to be enough to kill Alexander. In fact, it was a moot point whether anything could, which depressed Peitho and me no end.

Poor Batis, the good and faithful servant, was taken alive – alive on balance, let's say; he didn't give up easily – and frogmarched in front of Alexander, who was just coming round after being hit by the engine. As a result he wasn't in a good mood.

Anaxarchus was duty philosopher that day, and they were playing the Iliad game. I can't remember who Anaxarchus was supposed to be – Nestor or Phoenix, someone like that; Alexander was being Achilles, of course, and little Batis – he turned out to be this short, fat, bald guy, this man who'd held us up for two whole months, made us look like clowns, nearly killed Alexander; I got a good look at him and he reminded me of what's-his-name, Craterus, the funny little chap who used to come round with a handcart mending broken crockery – Batis was immediately cast as Hector; typecasting, you might say. Now, if you recall your Homer, you'll remember that when Achilles killed Hector in front of the Scaean Gate of Troy, he had his body dragged behind his chariot seven times round the city walls.

'Do it,' Alexander commanded.

'Just one thing,' someone pointed out. 'He isn't dead.'

Alexander looked at him. 'So?' he said.

Well, if he wasn't dead at the start, he was at the finish. They cut slots through his feet with a carpenter's chisel for the ropes to go through, and Alexander drove the chariot himself; since he couldn't stand, they had to sort of tie him into it, to make sure he didn't fall out when cornering sharply. In the event he did eight laps, one more than Achilles (well, naturally; anything you can do, and so forth); and when they untied him, they found the restraints they'd tied him in with had ripped all the skin off his knees and thighs. He didn't seem to notice; enjoying himself too much, I expect. He stayed in character right through. He was brilliant like that. If he hadn't been a soldier, he'd have made a wonderful actor.

After we'd finished smashing up Gaza, he went through the spoils looking for nice presents for his mum and his kid sister back home; really considerate, I call that. He sent his mother a lovely ivory dressing-table set, all matching (used to belong to Batis' wife) and he chose some really pretty silk fabric for his sister to make tapestries for the family dining-room at Pella. He even sent old Leonidas five hundred talents' weight of frankincense and a hundred talents of myrrh, on the grounds that when he was a kid, Leonidas told him off for being wasteful with expensive spices and teased him, saying he'd have to wait until he'd conquered the

Kingdom of Spices before he could afford to chuck the stuff around like that.

('Hang on,' I interrupted. 'Did you say Leonidas?'

'Yes. Are you deaf as well as clumsy?'

'That wasn't Leonidas,' I said. 'That was me. I made that joke, the first time I met him.'

Eudaemon smiled. 'Be fair,' he said, 'it was an exceptionally forgettable joke.'

'Agreed,' I replied. 'And absolutely typical of him that he remembered it.'

– And typical, Phryzeutzis, that he remembered it well enough to send his extremely thoughtful and staggeringly generous gift to the wrong bloody tutor. But that was Alexander for you: every bad thing he did came out right, and every good thing he did was ever so slightly wrong.)

When we met up that evening (Eudaemon continued) Peitho was in an unusually assertive mood. 'Definitely,' he said. 'Got to go. No question.'

I think we were the only two sober people in the whole camp; ironic, because we'd been as prodigal with the leaves as the boy Alexander had apparently been with the frankincense. I shook my head doubtfully.

'Not sure it can be done,' I replied. 'How can you kill a bloke who survives direct hits from heavy artillery?'

Peitho scratched his head. 'I wasn't suggesting we bombard the bugger to death,' he said. 'I still think poison's the way to go, personally.'

I made a rude noise. Aristotle's book had proved to be a complete and utter wash-out; not one slow poison from beginning to end. Yards and yards and miles and miles of meaningless philosophical drivel ('We could bore him to death, easy,' Peitho said gloomily, 'only we'd never get him to sit still long enough'); but actual recipes a bloke could use? Bugger all.

'Slit his throat,' I said, 'it's the only way. Unless the bastard's some kind of god, that'll kill him, you mark my words. The only question is, how?'

Peitho frowned. 'I never heard it was difficult,' he said. 'You just sort of get a knife and—'

'How do we get close enough to do it,' I said, 'without some bugger catching us? I mean, selfless heroism's one thing, but I'm fucked if I'm going to get myself killed just to free the world of a pest.'

'Well,' Peitho said, and poured himself another drink.

He had a point there, of course. The trouble was, Alexander was never alone. Not ever. Apart from his faithful bodyguard-buddies, there were always people trooping in to see him, make reports, get orders, explain themselves, pitch ideas, beg favours; not to mention all the philosophers and poets and local celebrities and general hangers-on that buzzed round him every hour of every day in a sort of shimmering cloud, like those tiny midges that you get by the thousand on cow-pats. Even when he was asleep there were ten or so blokes in the tent with him, lying at his feet like big soppy dogs.

'Got to be poison, then,' I said after a while. 'No other way.'

'There's fire,' Peitho said. 'We could set fire to the tent.'

'Nah.' I shook my head. 'They'd rescue him quick as spit through a trumpet. Poison. Put something in the pea soup. Kill the lot of 'em.'

Peitho frowned. 'I'm not sure we should do that,' he said. 'Alexander, yes, but poison the whole retinue—'

'So what?' I said. 'They're all Macedonians.'

'I'm Macedonian,' Peitho pointed out.

'Yes,' I replied. 'But not a real one, you said so yourself.'

'True.' He stopped, then looked up with a big grin on his face. 'The honey,' he said. 'We could poison the honey.'

I looked at him. 'You know,' I said, 'I don't think I'm going to let you share my fire any more. The smoke's doing things to your brain.'

'Oh, shut up, Eudaemon. No, listen. It's perfect. You know how when they sit around in his tent after dinner with a big bowl of booze, and they always have a jar of honey to sweeten it with? Poison the honey. What with the honey and the booze, they'll never notice the taste; and everybody'll think it was the wine that was poisoned, not the honey, or at least they'll never be able to prove anything, since it all gets mixed up together anyhow. It'll work, I promise you.'

I leaned back and rubbed my chin thoughtfully. 'All right,' I said. 'But that still doesn't answer the question; what do we poison the buggers *with*? We still haven't got a clue.'

Peitho shook his head. 'No, no, you're wrong. They taste the food but they never taste the wine; no point, they all drink the wine and Alexander always assumes that anybody who'd want to kill him would be an upper-class Macedonian. Anybody who poisoned the wine would have to drink it himself.'

He had something there. 'So we wouldn't have to use a slow poison,' I replied.

'Not at all. Quicker the better, really; the first drink's always a toast to the gods, they all drink simultaneously, so – what's so damn funny?'

'Sorry,' I said, as soon as I'd managed to get a grip on myself and stop laughing. 'It's just the picture that came into my mind just then, all those fucking great long-haired Macedonians swilling down a toast and then hitting the deck at precisely the same moment—'

Peitho sighed. 'You're a sad bastard, Eudaemon,' he said. 'Come on, let's think. What was that poison you found in the book the other day?'

'White hellebore roots,' I said. 'One dewdrop'll kill an elephant. Good stuff.'

He nodded. 'Sounds just the ticket. Where do we get some from?'

'Search me,' I said, shrugging my shoulders.

'All right, we can dig some up. What does it look like? Where does it grow? Come on, you read the book.'

'It didn't say,' I said. 'It's a crummy book.'

'Obviously.' Peitho slumped forward, his cheeks cupped in his palms. 'Why is nothing ever bloody straightforward?' he said.

We made no further progress that night, mainly because I fell asleep; next thing I knew it was morning, and we were moving out. We talked a little more about it over the next few days, but what with one thing and another – we were getting ready to invade Egypt, and everybody was suddenly busy, except me, of course – there wasn't really much time for sitting about.

Alexander's conquest of Egypt was the biggest non-event ever. The Persian governor, a man called Mazaces, surrendered before we even asked him to; poor bugger, he had no army, and the thought of what had happened to Batis obviously troubled him. We crossed the desert between Syria and Egypt in a week and headed straight for Memphis, the capital, where Alexander was officially crowned.

It's an odd thing with the Egyptians; they believe their kings are the eldest sons of their chief god, or maybe the same eldest son born over and over again, I'm not sure – no, that doesn't make sense, because then how could the reigning king and his son and heir both be alive at the same time? Actually, I don't think they worry about things like that. They don't think about these things in the same way we do. In fact, I'd go further and say they're all as crazy as fruitbats, the lot of 'em. Anyway, it didn't bother them at all that one moment Darius of Persia had been the only begotten son of god and Alexander the next. I think the argument went something like, everything and everybody is god to some degree or other, but some people and things are a bit more god than the rest, which explains why some people have to work for a living and others don't. Anyway, they were pretty confident that Alexander was a whole heap of god and therefore not only qualified but eternally predestined to be King of Egypt; which was convenient, bearing in mind that he had a large and ruthless army standing by to kill anybody who said otherwise.

'How do I look?' he's supposed to have whispered to his buddy Hephaestion, immediately after the coronation. 'I've never been a god before.'

'Your nose is maybe a bit longer,' Hephaestion replied. 'Apart from that, pretty much the same.'

So there we were in Egypt, the richest, oldest and weirdest country in the entire world. Everything in Egypt is weird, brother, everything. We were in the Kingdom of the Weird. It was, I think, where we all deserved to be.

I ask you; it's a country that's mostly burned desert, but every year the river floods and drowns out all the farms and villages, leaving them covered in thick slimy mud – and that's great, because if you spit a grape-pip into Egyptian mud, ten minutes later you've got a mature vine. In Egypt, dead people live in huge triangular palaces without windows, while the living don't even bother to build proper houses, because where's the point if they're going to get buried in mud anyhow? In Egypt, it's compulsory to drink wine but illegal to make it; that's why we Athenians have been selling them our rot-gut stuff for a thousand years. In Egypt the King never dies, and god is every stray cat and white cow you see as you walk down the street.

People just don't care, in Egypt; they don't care about anything, because life is just an illusion and you don't really start living till you're dead. They don't grow wheat because it's their living, they do it because it's a religious act, and it's got to be done the right way, with priests supervising everything, or it doesn't count. In Egypt they write everything down, but once it's written down nobody reads it because it doesn't matter (nothing matters). In Egypt, they don't run away when a crocodile slides up out of the water, because a crocodile is god and has every right to eat anybody He chooses. In Egypt, they'll fight you to the last drop of blood one minute and let you walk all over them the next. As far as I could tell, they didn't really seem to notice we were there, like we were invisible or something. They did everything we told them to do; but when we were talking to them they appeared to be listening to somebody else we couldn't even see.

Personally, I liked Egypt. I could fancy living there.

Alexander decided to found a city. The pretext was that a replacement was needed for Tyre; it had been the commercial centre of the whole Near East and now that it was nothing but a pile of rubble, people hadn't got anywhere to buy and sell things. This wasn't actually true; the market was in the new town, which we hadn't really touched. I think Alexander (who absolutely adored Egypt, for some reason) just wanted to found a city there. There was something distinctly fishy about Alexander and founding cities. He founded cities every bloody place he went, he left them behind him like a trail of broken wine-jars. As is tolerably well known by now, Alexander had no sex-life whatsoever, and my theory is that he got his fun doing to countries what normal people do to women, cities being the tangible outcome. At least, that's part of it; the other part, brother dear, is that you left him to found the perfect city, so obviously founding perfect cities is what really great men do. And to think; I could have strangled you when we were both kids, and I never knew it was going to be important.

The name of this city was to be Alexandria; hardly surprising, since all the cities he founded were called Alexandria. Anyway, for a long time he was utterly obsessed with the project and wouldn't tolerate anybody even mentioning anything else (such as the war or the King of Persia; but that was all right, because every time the Great King tried to rally his enormous army and come after us, something went wrong; a general died or a province rebelled or plague broke out or a river flooded or a supply-train was robbed by suddenly materialising nomads or the omens were bad, so nothing ever got done. Incompetence and rotten luck every step of the way; a one-legged dwarf could probably have conquered Persia at that time).

The Egyptian priests advised Alexander to visit the holy shrine of Ammon. Actually, not true; they told him he'd *already* visited the holy shrine of Ammon, in a sense, and unless he hurried up and actually went there in person, with his physical body, it was going to upset a lot of things and throw the whole balance of cosmic forces out of kilter. So off he went, with a packed lunch and an entourage of hundreds of soldiers and thousands of Egyptian priests (who claimed they knew exactly what had happened when he went there, but politely changed the subject when he asked them to tell him).

The shrine of Ammon is at a place called the Oasis of Siva, in the middle of the unspeakably awful Libyan desert. Needless to say, they got lost; the Egyptian priests knew the way all right, but when Alexander set off in the wrong direction they didn't say anything, assuming that since he'd been there before he knew the way too. When they were all about ready to drop dead of heat and thirst, apparently they happened to bump into two enormous serpents blessed with the power of human speech, who told them to turn left at the next big sand dune and follow their noses; whereupon the heavens opened, it poured with rain for two whole days and they all got soaking wet. It was either talking serpents or a couple of camel-drovers; accounts differ. You're the historian, you choose.

Well, they found the place eventually, and in he went, and out he came again.

'How'd it go?' they asked.

'I heard what I wanted,' he said, and that was all they got out of him on the long trudge back to Alexandria. As a justification for a long and hazardous journey, it doesn't amount to much; he could have done that just as easily if he'd stayed home, where a substantial number of the officers on his general staff devoted their lives to making sure he only heard things he'd be likely to want to hear. What's not in doubt, however, is that whatever it was he heard out there in the desert had a significant effect on him. One school of thought regards it as some kind of spiritual rebirth, while others hold that even if you do have a magnificent head of long golden hair, if you insist on going several days in the desert sun without a hat, you get what's coming to you.

At first, the changes were subtle, and could easily have been due to something else; he was worried about something, or preoccupied with profound matters of state and strategy, or just pissed off and in a foul mood. He didn't talk all the time like he used to, there was less of the obvious delight he'd always taken in being leader of the pack. Most of all, he started wanting to be alone occasionally, which he'd never shown any sign of wanting before. People who'd been close to him, or reckoned they were, went around muttering about the bad effect Egypt was having on morale generally, and how it was time to move on and find someone new to kill, rather than moping about boozing and enjoying ourselves.

But for once, Alexander wasn't the sole focus of attention, every hour of every day. It was announced that a concert party was on its way from Athens to entertain the troops, and for a day or so nobody could talk about anything else. In retrospect there's nothing surprising about that; we're Athenians, grandsons of Eupolis, we grew up with it, but for provincials (I'm being nice here, calling them that) the thought of seeing genuine Athenian theatre was rather more exciting than pyramids and crocodiles and the singing statue of Memnon, Son of the Dawn. Indeed, people even started taking notice of me, what with the family connection and all, and it was no use my saying I was completely out of touch and I'd never been all that keen to start with, they automatically assumed I was a theatre buff, drama critic and boyhood chum of every Athenian actor they'd ever heard of. They made me recite everything I could remember, from Grandfather's stuff right back to the slabs of Aeschylus that Father made us learn when we were kids, and when I'd run out and told them I couldn't remember any more they just got snotty and accused me of being stand-offish.

When the concert party finally arrived, I expected there'd be a riot. Instead of the flower of the Attic stage, we'd been sent the trash, the dross, the understudies' understudies. You remember Telecritus, that doddering old ham we saw a few times when we were kids? I'd assumed he'd died years ago, and the performances he gave while he was there didn't do much to convince me otherwise; but the Macedonians loved him. They thought he was marvellous, even when he forgot his lines and started making them up, or patching in bits from other plays. Honestly, I thought it was a rather clever skit and was laughing quietly to myself, when some big hairy joker sitting next to me told me to shut my face or he'd push it out my neck for me.

I'll tell you who was in that company, though. I don't suppose you'll remember him, but I knew him quite well at one stage – Sostratus, our neighbour Achias' eldest boy.

'Hello, Sostratus,' I said, having walked up quietly behind him. 'What're you doing here?'

He jumped about twice his own height into the air, then spun round. 'Sorry,' he said. 'Do I know you?'

'Eudaemon,' I replied. 'Eutychides' son. Our fathers shared a boundary in Pallene, remember?'

'Oh,' he said, and his face fell like a bucket down a well-shaft. 'You.'

I grinned. 'Nice to see you too, Sostratus. How's the nose these days?'

He scowled. 'Still not right,' he said.

'After all these years,' I replied, 'fancy. That's a shame. How's things at home?'

'Awful,' he replied. 'That's why I'm here. Anything to get out of the City for a month or so.'

'In what way awful?' I asked.

He made a vague, all-encompassing gesture; far better than anything he'd done on stage, where he acted with all the style and fluency of a ploughshare. 'Every way you can possibly think of,' he said. 'Harvests have been pathetic, prices through the roof, goddamned Macedonians chucking their weight around, nothing in the shops, everybody at each other's throats in Assembly—'

'Fine,' I said. 'Good to see some things never change. So you're an actor now, are you? Since when?'

He sighed. 'Since I gave Orestes my share of the farm. No point both of us starving to death, after all.'

'I see,' I replied. 'And how is your brother? Did he ever marry that tart from over the Mesogaia he was so crazy about? What was her name, now? Callipyge, something like that.'

Sostratus looked at me. 'No,' he said, 'I did.'

'Oh. And how's she keeping?'

'She died last year.'

'Ah. That's too bad.'

'Not really,' Sostratus said, with another sigh. 'She was an evil bitch.' He studied me for a moment down the full length of his nose. 'So,' he said, 'what's it like, working for the Macedonians?'

'Not so bad,' I replied. 'It's a living.'

'You were probably wise to clear out when you did,' Sostratus said. 'Things have been getting steadily worse all the time. Oh, by the way.'

'Yes?'

'You remember Megasthenes? He was in our gang when we were boys.'

I smiled. 'Of course I remember him. Never been anybody who could imitate a dog being sick like Megasthenes could. How is the old son of a—?'

'He's dead too,' Sostratus said. 'Got stabbed to death by robbers on the way home from the City. In broad daylight, too.'

You've no idea how much meeting Sostratus cheered me up. I've always found other people's bad news has that effect on me; you listen to a catalogue of woes and then think of your own troubles, and you come away all happy and grateful. What really bucked me up, though, was the thought that if I'd stayed in Athens and taken my rightful share of the family property, I could well have ended up just as miserable as Sostratus. In fact, he made me feel so good about myself that I decided to do something for him.

'What're these?' he asked, as I pressed the gift into his hands.

'Just dried leaves,' I told him. 'You chuck them on the fire and they make the room smell nice.'

'Oh.'

'All the way from Scythia,' I pointed out.

'Oh. Are they valuable?'

I shrugged my shoulders. 'Depends,' I said. 'If you mean valuable as in selling them for money, probably not. On the other hand, how can you put a price on happiness and a general sense of well-being?'

He looked at the leaves for a moment as if he expected them to try to steal the money out of his mouth. 'I could do with something like that, actually,' he said. 'That bastard Coenus has started a tannery right across the street from our house, and you wouldn't believe the stench—'

'Try the leaves,' I said. 'Just the job.'

He thought a little longer, then said, 'Thank you.' I think he was almost as surprised as I was to hear the words come out of his mouth. 'Well then, this trip won't be a complete dead loss, then. Almost,' he added, 'but not quite.'

I frowned. 'Aren't they paying you, then?' I asked.

'Oh sure. Not much, but something. Trouble is, I spent most of what I've been paid already on what I thought were genuine bona fide goods, and it turns out they're worthless.' He grinned wretchedly. 'Just my luck,' he added.

'Sounds like it,' I said. 'What happened?'

'Oh, I was in the market at Ephesus, we stopped there a day or so on our way here, and I saw this stall selling jars of honey. Dirt cheap; of course, if I'd had the sense I'd been born with I'd have suspected something was wrong then and there. Anyhow, I bought the stuff, twelve jars of it, and stowed it under my bench back on the ship. Turned out later – and of course I only found this out after we'd set sail, when it was too late to do anything about it – this honey was made by bees who fed off this special sort of shrub you only get in that region; big bushy job with glossy leaves, purple flower in late spring. Can't remember the name offhand. Anyhow, the point is, honey made with pollen from that stuff's deadly poison. Eat so much as a finger's wipe of it and you're dead, just like that. Talk about a narrow escape; I could have wiped out half of Attica with that lot. Although,' he added, 'the way things are there right now, maybe I'd have been doing them a favour, at that.'

I waited for a moment before saying anything. 'This honey,' I said. 'Where is it now?'

'Still on the ship,' he replied. 'When I've got five minutes I'll dump it into the sea and wash out the jars. Might get a few obols for them, you never know.'

'That's all right,' I said. 'I'll take them off your hands for you.'

'Why?'

'Sorry?'

He scowled at me. 'What do you want with twelve jars of deadly poison?'

Well, he had me there. 'I'll give you what you paid for them,' I said.

'Answer the question, dammit. What do you—'

'Mice,' I said. 'And wasps. They can be a real pest, out here in the desert.'

'I don't know,' he muttered, looking away. 'What if someone ate some by mistake and died? Wouldn't people say it was my fault?'

'Doubt it,' I replied. 'And anyway, I'll take full responsibility. But nobody's going to die, I promise you. Not any more.'

'What do you mean "any more"?'

'Do you want to get rid of the stuff or don't you?'

'Oh, all right. But you'll promise me you won't—'

'I promise.'

Well, we hauled the stuff back on a cart. Then I gave Sostratus the slip and went to look for Peitho.

'Poisoned honey?' he said.

'That's right.'

He bit his lip thoughtfully. 'How do you know it works?' he said.

I frowned. 'Well, it's not as if he was trying to sell it to me. Why'd he say it was deadly poison if it wasn't?'

'Maybe he was just exaggerating,' Peitho said. 'Maybe it just makes you ill, gives you the runs or something.'

I considered this for a moment. 'So what do you suggest?' I said. 'You want to test it on somebody first, is that it?'

He looked at me all strange. 'No, of course not. Well, not on some*body*. Some*thing*.'

I couldn't see any harm in that. 'Such as?' I asked.

'I don't know. It'd have to be something big,' he went on. 'If we use a dog or a sheep, that wouldn't prove anything.'

I had a brainwave. 'I know,' I said. 'What about a camel?'

'That'd do,' he replied. 'Where are we going to get a camel from?'

I clicked my tongue impatiently. 'This is Egypt,' I said. 'Everywhere you look, there's bloody camels.'

'All right,' he said. 'You find us a camel.'

So I did. I marched straight down to the livestock pens, grabbed the smallest and most hapless-looking Egyptian clerk I could find and started yelling at him, hoping he wasn't one of those annoying cosmopolitan Egyptians who can speak Greek. Fortunately he wasn't, so I was able to terrify him into letting me book out a camel without actually stealing it. Works every time, that trick; if you're annoyed and you outrank them and they can't understand a word you're saying, all they really want to do is get out of your way. Understandably, of course; the Macedonian reputation for unmitigated bastardry is entirely merited.

The camel hit the deck like a windfall apple off a tree; I'll swear its stupid, ugly mouth was still churning away when it went splat. Don't think I've ever seen anything taken dead that quickly since my first campaign in Illyria, when the man next to me in the line had his head taken off by a catapult bolt.

'It works, then,' Peitho said.

'Looks like it,' I replied.

He prodded the camel's nose with his foot. 'What are we going to do with this?' he asked.

I hadn't really given the matter any thought. Under normal circumstances, I'd simply have called over the nearest couple of squaddies and told them to clear up the mess; as it was, I didn't want to do that, just in case. Well, you never know; people remember things, they put two and two together. And if that sounds paranoid, fair enough. When you get into heavy stuff like regicide and treason, paranoia's a useful survival tool.

'Bury it?' I suggested.

Peitho gave me a pained look. 'You bury the bloody thing,' he grumbled. 'Look at it, it's huge.'

I shook my head. 'It's not that big,' I said. 'If you go steady, don't try and rush it, won't take you more than a couple of hours.'

'Me? Why me?'

'Bad back,' I said (which was true; bad experience dismantling and manhandling carts the day before).

'Get lost,' Peitho said, looking around. 'We'll drop it down a well.'

I frowned. 'Can't do that,' I said. 'Mortal sin, that is, in these parts; hardly the way to stay inconspicuous. Go on, bury it like I told you. The sooner you make a start . . .'

The flies were starting to gather. 'I know,' Peitho said, 'we'll send it to the mess tent. We'll say it got delivered here by mistake, nothing to do with us. They'll cut it up and stew it, problem solved. Besides, it's wicked to waste good food.'

'You're crazy,' I said. 'You saw the way it went down, the bloody thing's full of poison. You could wipe out half the bloody camp.'

'I'm not burying it,' Peitho said firmly. 'For gods' sakes, I'm a Captain of Engineers, Captains of Engineers don't bury camels. If anybody saw me, they'd know at once I was up to something.'

I scratched my head. 'All right,' I said, 'we'll leave it here.'

'What?'

'Just leave it. Walk away. There's nothing to connect us with it. Nobody's seen us except that Egyptian clerk at the pound, and we all look alike to them.'

Peitho looked worried. 'I don't know,' he said. 'I don't like it.'

A big fat fly settled on the camel's naked eyeball and started to get busy. 'Fine,' I said. 'I'll bring you a spade.'

'We'll leave it,' Peitho said. 'Nothing to do with us.'

'Agreed. And if anybody did see us with it, we'll just tell the truth. We checked it out of the pen, it suddenly keeled over dead, we left it there and walked away. What does that make us guilty of? Untidiness. They don't chop heads off for being untidy, even in this man's army.'

Peitho rubbed his temples, in the manner of a man who has a bad headache coming. 'I suppose that is the truth,' he said, 'in a way. I mean,' he went on, 'most of it is actually true.'

'All of it,' I said. 'Which is more than you can say of History.'

I don't think anybody would deny that Alexander's rapid and well-documented slide into weirdness began not long after the visit to the Ammon shrine at Siva. The big question is, did he catch weirdness there, like some kind of nasty tummy bug, or did it just bring out the weirdness that had always been in there somewhere? Like most big questions, I'm not sure it matters a damn, but for what it's worth I'm inclined to go for the latter option.

Don't get me wrong; I'm not saying his trip to Ammon had nothing to do with it. But a man doesn't walk into a place believing he's a mortal and come out again believing he's a god unless there's at least a slender core of weirdness in him already.

What's the matter, Euxenus? You look like you've just swallowed a wasp. Didn't you know? Oh, for gods' sakes, I thought everybody knew. One thing it was never intended to be was a secret.

Yes, it's perfectly true; and I don't mean History true, I mean *true*. During his time in Egypt, shortly after his interview with whatever it is they've got tucked away in that shrine at Siva, Alexander let it be known that with effect from such-and-such a date he was a god and that all diplomatic and administrative protocols were to be amended to take account of this development.

The official explanation was that it was all for the benefit of the Egyptians, who believe that all their kings are gods; if Alexander went round saying he wasn't a god, he couldn't be King of Egypt, and we'd suddenly find ourselves with a horrendous rebellion on our hands. Perfectly valid point; the Egyptians are like that. Go into the market, round up a hundred people at random and cut off their heads, and nobody'd dream of making an issue out of it. Accidentally run a cart over a sacred cat or a sacred dog and they'll come for you with scythes and hayforks, and they'll keep coming till either you or they are wiped out. Really, you've got to admire a people who take their faith that seriously (actually no, you haven't; people who take their faith that seriously are dangerous nutters. Still, we as a race do tend to admire dangerous nutters, so I don't see why we shouldn't admire the Egyptians. They're pretty much like us, when you get right down to it, except that they're completely different).

Well, that was the official explanation, and it was logical and comforting in a look-at-these-funny-foreigners sort of a way; at first it was all a great big joke, with Alexander joining in absolutely as much as he was able to, given that he had the sense of humour of a sandal. In the mess-hall, they're serving dinner; everybody else gets their usual monster serving of bread and roast beef, Alexander gets an empty plate. 'Where's mine?' he asks. 'You're having prayers,' they reply. It starts tipping down with rain, everybody's getting soaked; Hephaestion gives Alexander a filthy look. 'Pack it in,' he says. 'Sorry,' Alexander replies, looking sheepish. 'Told you you shouldn't have had the watercress,' says Cleitus, shaking his head. Everybody laughs.

Except me, of course. Well, you understand why; but Peitho, poor bloody Macedonian that he was, couldn't see why I was being so uptight about it.

'It's an Athenian thing,' I said. 'You wouldn't understand.'

'So explain,' he said.

I shrugged, and stoked up the fire. 'It's how we Athenians

honour the gods,' I said. 'We make fun of them. It's our sincerest expression of faith.'

Peitho raised an eyebrow. 'Get away,' he said.

'Straight up. That's how the comic plays started off, actually; the priests and the congregation making fun of the god. It's our way of showing affection, which is so much more important than faith.'

'You're an odd lot, you Athenians,' Peitho said.

'A lot of people think so,' I admitted. 'Blasphemy, they call it; to which we quite rightly reply that the biggest blasphemy of all is saying that the gods haven't got a sense of humour. Which,' I added, 'they quite patently do. You look at the way human beings reproduce, or remove waste materials from their bodies, and then try to tell me the gods haven't got a sense of humour. Pretty basic one, not to mention a bit sick; but nobody's perfect.'

Peitho thought about it for a moment. 'All right,' he said, 'I can see where you're bothered, you being an Athenian. But Alexander isn't; he's Macedonian.'

I nodded. 'But he was brought up Athenian, to all intents and purposes. Educated Athenian. Made to learn Athenian plays. Don't think for a moment he isn't seeing all this exactly the way I am. And that worries me. It's as bad as the Egyptians falling flat on their faces whenever he looks at them. Worse. The Egyptians are just funny foreigners; the people cracking the jokes are Greek.'

Peitho breathed in, held his breath and blew out slowly. 'All right,' he said, 'I can see why you're worried. Doesn't change anything, does it? I mean, if we were going to kill him when he was relatively sane, we ought to kill him even more now he's gone potty. Well,' he added, 'you know what I mean.'

'Sure,' I said. 'But here we are talking about it, not doing anything.'

'What's that supposed to mean?'

'Oh, come on, Peitho. What I mean is, what're we waiting for? We've got the poison honey, there's never going to be a better time. Why don't we just do it?'

He blinked several times, rapidly. 'What, right now?'

I shrugged. 'Why not?'

He rubbed his cheeks with the heels of his hands, as if he was sleepy and trying to wake himself up. 'All right,' he said.

'Right now?'

'Right now.'

'Right.' I felt a shiver go right through me. 'You don't think we should—'

'What?' Peitho looked at me. 'You just said we should do it now. You just said.'

I shook my head. 'That's not what I said,' I replied. 'I said I couldn't see a reason why we shouldn't do it now. Doesn't mean to say there isn't one.'

Peitho frowned. 'You've lost me,' he said.

I stood up, took a few steps forward, then back, then sat down again. 'Let's face it,' I said, 'we aren't very good at this. It was only the other day we were wetting ourselves trying to think what to do with a dead camel. Now you're saying we should murder the King of Macedon and half the court.'

'You've changed your mind,' Peitho said. 'You're scared.'

'I'm bloody not.'

'You bloody are.'

'Yes, of course I'm scared,' I said. 'If I wasn't scared, I'd be crazier than he is. Scared is a precious gift the gods gave us to stop us doing bloody stupid things that'll get us killed.'

Peitho nodded. 'Perfectly true,' he said. 'But the whole point of killing Alexander is to stop him getting us killed. What you might call a higher plane of scaredness.'

I slumped forward in my chair. 'You're right,' I said. 'I don't know. Maybe we should either do this thing now or not do it at all.'

'Now you're talking,' Peitho said cheerfully. 'After all, what's the worst thing that could happen to us?'

'Are you serious?' I said. 'We could be caught and horribly tortured to death.'

'All right,' Peitho said. 'And if we don't do it, if we leave it and for some reason it becomes impossible, like we move out or suddenly we can't get to him, what then? We could be killed in a battle, or get wounded and die slowly and painfully of blood poisoning, or catch some terrible disease; or the Persians might get us and peg us out in the desert to die, or—'

'Oh, shut up, for gods' sakes,' I said. 'You're not helping.'

'I'm just saying,' Peitho replied. 'There's no way of knowing what's going to happen, so what's the point of worrying ourselves sick about it? Just makes it harder on ourselves.'

I thought about it for a moment. 'So what you're saying is,' I said, 'we should do it now. Right – now.'

'Yes.'

I sighed. 'All right,' I said.

'You'll do it?'

'Didn't I just say?'

'Sure. All right, let's do it.'

'Right.'

We both stood up – a little bit shakily, but that was the medicine, it catches you sometimes if you move suddenly. 'The honey,' I said. 'Where'd you stow it?'

'In the supply tent, of course,' he said. 'You don't think I'd keep it here, do you?'

'Why not?'

'I get caught with twelve jars of poisoned honey and they ask me what I want it for, I'm going to have a job explaining,' he replied, reasonably enough. 'So I stashed it in with the rest of the stores, at the back where it won't hurt. Then, if anybody asks, it's nothing to do with me.'

I frowned. 'Small point here,' I said. 'How the hell are we going to know which jars are the poison? Dip a finger in and suck?'

He looked annoyed. 'You think I'm stupid,' he said. 'I marked the jars so we'd know them again. Scratched a big P on the necks.'

'P,' I said. 'For Poison, right?'

'They've all got batch numbers on,' he replied. 'I checked. The last batch in was Small O, and the batch they're drawing now is G, so there's no danger they'll draw the poison stuff by mistake. You see,' he went on, 'if you do things carefully and methodically, you don't make mistakes.'

So we went to the supply tent. It was late, dark as a foot up a bag, so there was nobody about. I'd brought an oil lamp with a little stubby wick.

'I'd have thought you'd have known about the batch numbers,' Peitho was saying. 'It's your bloody clerks who do the drawing.'

I shook my head. 'I just let 'em get on with it,' I said. 'No good ever came of telling a clerk how to do his job.'

'True,' Peitho said. 'Right, here's where I left them, behind the corn bins, under some old sacks.'

I lifted the lamp. 'No you didn't,' I said.

'What do you mean?'

'Look,' I said. 'Old sacks, yes. No jars.'

He scowled. 'Bugger,' he said. 'Someone's moved them.'

'Some bastard of a clerk,' I said. 'They're always tidying stuff, it's a miracle anything ever gets found.'

He nodded, and lit another lamp from mine. 'Just as well I had the good sense to mark the necks, isn't it? Otherwise, gods only know what might have happened.'

'Very true,' I said. 'All right, you look on that side and I'll check these ones here. I still say you shouldn't have put them in here in the first place.'

'Relax,' he called back out of the darkness. 'This is the army. A place for everything, and everything in its – Right, here we are.'

I breathed out; I'd been more worried than I'd realised. Silly, really; after all, we were only planning to poison the entire general staff. 'Make sure you count them,' I said. 'Just in case.'

'Of course I'm going to—' He stopped, didn't finish the sentence.

'What's the matter?' I asked; though of course I knew.

He didn't say anything for a minute or so. 'Well,' he said at last, 'I can find ten.'

'Wonderful,' I said. 'What about the other two?'

'They're here somewhere,' he replied, a little shakily. 'It's just some bugger's put them in the wrong – Make that eleven,' he said. 'Are you looking your side?'

'Yes,' I told him. 'I've got A to M here.'

'Check them all,' he snapped.

'I am doing,' I replied irritably. 'And they're all A to M, like I told you.'

I watched the pale glow of his lamp coming towards me. 'There's a jar missing,' he said. He looked awful.

I took a deep breath. 'The main thing,' I said, 'is not to panic. Right, what's the drill? Who checks them out? If I know clerks, there'll be a register, stock-book, something like that. You can't draw a breath in this man's army without sealing for it.'

'Stock-book,' he repeated. 'You're right, there's got to be a stock-book. Where do you think it'll be?'

'I don't know, do I? Where do the clerks sit?'

He pointed towards the door. 'Over there,' he said, 'on those barrels.'

I nodded. 'Then I'll bet you that's where you'll find the stock-book. Logic, you see.'

Sure enough, next to the barrels the clerks sat on we found a stack of wax tablets. They were covered in little rows and columns of tallies, crossed through and double-crossed, each line and row marked with one or more letters. Meaningless, of course, unless you're an army clerk.

'I can't read this,' I said.

Peitho shook his head. 'We need a clerk to explain it,' he said.

'Oh, fine. We go round and wake one up. Excuse me, we say, we seem to have mislaid a jar of lethally poisonous honey, would you mind checking your records so we can see who we've murdered? That'd really finish us off, that would.'

He glared at me. 'So what do you suggest?' he said.

'Walk away,' I replied.

He looked shocked. 'You can't be serious.'

'Watch me. It's just like the bloody camel,' I went on. 'Nothing to do with us.'

'Eudaemon, hundreds of people could die—'

'All right,' I said. 'I know. And it's very sad. But life is like that, particularly in war. Hundreds of thousands of people die in wars and nobody seems too fussed about it most of the—'

'Eudaemon,' he said. 'We've got to do something.'

'Yes,' I said. 'Walk away, that's what we've got to do. After all,' I went on, 'it's not like we actually put the poison in the honey our-selves. It's naturally poisonous. Really, it's just a tragic accident, this tainted stuff getting in with the good stuff. It's like when the Thracian cavalry got the shipment of tainted wheat. There was no way any-body could know just by looking at it.'

He grabbed my arm. 'We know,' he said.

'Nobody can prove that,' I pointed out.

He stared at me. 'We know,' he repeated.

I looked into his eyes until I had to look away. 'All right,' I said. 'Look, this can't be the only register, it's just a stock list, tells 'em how much of everything they've got at any one time. There's got to be another one somewhere that says who's been issued with what.

You know, the one we have to seal when we draw stuff.'

Peitho thought for a moment. 'You're right,' he said. 'Doesn't seem to be here, though. Well, of course,' he went on, 'they wouldn't keep it here, would they?'

'I don't know,' I said.

'Think about it. All that sort of thing's got to go through to the Quartermaster's office. I'll bet you what happens is that each set of stores hands in their returns to the QM's clerks every night, so they can keep the tally up to date. That's where those tablets'll be,' he went on, 'in the Quartermaster's office.'

I sat down on a barrel. 'Fantastic,' I said. 'That's that, then.'

He sat down beside me. 'Not necessarily,' he said. 'We're looking at this the wrong way, you know.'

I looked up. 'We are?'

'Sure,' he said, with a decisive nod. 'We're looking at it from the point of view of two evil bastards who've managed to lose a jar of poison they were planning to kill people with. That's not how it is at all.'

'Explain.'

'How it is really,' he said, 'is, we – or rather you, you're the one who knows all about fucking bees - you have reason to suspect, because of something you've heard just now, you have reason to suspect that the latest batch of honey might be tainted. Maybe even dangerous, so, being a responsible and conscientious officer, you're going to dump the whole consignment, just to be on the safe side.'

'Of course,' I said. 'Well, it's what anybody would do.'

'All right, then. Imagine your dismay when you find that one of these jars has somehow already been issued—'

'Issued out of turn,' I pointed out. 'Against regulations.'

'Quite. Some clerk's going to get his arse kicked for that, if there's any justice.'

'Heads will roll,' I agreed. 'A mistake like that could have cost hundred of lives.'

Peitho looked up. 'Still might,' he said. 'Come on, you'd better get yourself over to the Quartermaster's, quick as you can.'

'All right,' I said. 'Why me?' I added. 'You're coming too.'

He shook his head. 'Nothing to do with me,' he replied. 'You're the fucking bee supremo. How would I have got involved?'

I sighed. He had a point there. 'All right,' I said. 'I'll meet you back at your tent when I'm done.'

'Better not,' he said. 'Just in case. I mean to say,' he explained, 'if something has gone wrong and half the camp's dead already, I think I'd rather not be associated with you just now. You do see, don't you?'

'Perfectly,' I said.

'Logic,' he replied.

CHAPTER TWENTY-TWO

A nd that, dear brother, is how I came to be a hero of the war, a
man who saved the lives of hundreds of his comrades. As
someone pointed out to me, on a strictly arithmetical basis, number
of lives saved, I was among the top five great and glorious heroes of
the war, because most of the jokers who got awarded the laurel
crown and the desirable giftware for saving lives only saved one or
two, or at the most five or six, in some battle or other. True, they
risked their lives, got themselves carved up, whatever; but if you go
by end result rather than circumstances surrounding the act of
heroism in question, they were nowhere compared with me.

The reason why I was such a great and glorious hero was that if I
hadn't raised the alarm, that jar of deadly poison would have gone
in the wine for drinking the Queen Mother's health on her birthday,
and the consequences of that would've been drastic, to say the least.
Hundreds, in fact, is quite definitely an understatement. Make that
thousands.

So great and glorious a hero was I, in fact, that it wasn't enough
for me just to get my laurel crown and desirable giftware from my
superior officer (a man by the name of Diades, Chief Engineer; nice
enough man in his way); no, I was to receive my rewards and
honours from the hand of Alexander himself—

'Perfect,' Peitho said, when I told him.

I frowned. 'Actually,' I replied, 'I'd rather there wasn't any fuss at
all. In fact, the sooner the whole thing's forgotten about—'

'I'm not talking about your stupid fucking laurel crown,' Peitho said testily. 'I'm talking about killing Alexander. You do remember, don't you? Our plot to assassinate the King of Macedon?'

'What are you talking about?' I said.

'Gods, are you dumb or what? Here's a golden opportunity, handed to us on a plate by some god who loves us—'

I was shocked. 'You're not suggesting I kill him while he's giving me my award?' I said.

He looked puzzled. 'Why the hell not?' he said.

'Well . . .' Unusually for me, I found I had trouble putting my thoughts into words. 'It wouldn't be right,' I said. 'Not when he's being so—'

'Nice?'

'Well, for want of a better word, yes.'

Peitho stared at me as if I'd just sprouted wings out of my ears. 'I don't believe it,' he said. 'A bunch of dried leaves and a three-obol tripod, and you go from being the man who was prepared to wipe out a whole generation of Macedonian aristocracy in one hit to some sort of Ideal Soldier. Dear gods, Eudaemon, if this wasn't so bloody serious I'd wet myself laughing.'

He was starting to annoy me. 'It's nothing to do with the damned crown,' I said. 'And yes, I still believe Alexander's got to go. I'm really behind that, every step of the way. I just can't see how I'm going to murder him face to face like that.'

'Why not? Afraid of hurting his feelings?'

I kicked over a stool. 'All right,' I said, 'you tell me. There I am in his tent. When do I stick him with the knife? Before he hands me the laurel crown or after? I know; it's his mother's birthday, he might offer me a drink to toast her health. I could slash his throat out while he's pouring me a cup of wine with his own hands. Or should I wait till he's turned his back to pick up the tripod he's going to give me?'

Peitho shook his head. 'All right,' he said, 'it's a bit cold-blooded. That's how it goes. I'm afraid there just isn't a polite way to murder someone.'

I folded my arms and looked away. 'Besides,' I said, 'if I killed him there and then, I'd never get out of there alive. What makes you think we'll be alone in the tent, for one thing? He's never alone. These days, when he goes for a crap behind the mess tent, there's half a dozen ambassadors with him, not to mention the duty philosopher.'

'All right,' Peitho said, 'you may have to take out a bystander. Big deal. You're a soldier, that's what soldiers do. They kill people.'

I shook my head. 'This is getting worse and worse,' I said. 'And even if I do succeed in killing Alexander, and six assorted staff officers, what then? Standing over the bodies with a dirty great knife in my hand, it's not the sort of thing you can bluff your way out of.'

Peitho thought for a moment. 'All right,' he said. 'You're in there, getting your award for being a great hero. While you're there, some clerk or adjutant goes berserk and kills the King. You're too late to stop him, but at least you manage to wrestle the knife out of his hand and cut him down before he manages to escape. Who knows?' Peitho added sourly, 'Maybe they'll give you another laurel crown for that.'

'Nobody's going to believe it,' I said. 'I'd be committing suicide, and you know it.'

He glowered at me. 'You're the one who's so desperate to be a hero,' he said. 'Why not be a real one instead of a bloody fraud?'

'I resent that,' I said. 'And you're beginning to get on my nerves.'

'So?'

I could see that things were getting out of hand. 'Look,' I said, 'it isn't helping matters us being at each other's throats. At this rate we'll end up killing each other before we so much as lay a finger on Alexander. Just accept it, I'm not going to kill him when I go to get my award.'

'Fine. A wonderful opportunity wasted.'

'Not necessarily,' I said patiently. 'What I can do while I'm talking to him is to try and set up a real opportunity. One that won't get me killed.'

Peitho heaved a long sigh. 'All right,' he said, 'let's hear it.'

'Try this,' I said, leaning forward. 'While he's giving me the crown I whisper to him that I've got to see him alone. Urgently.'

'You going to give any explanation? Or just rely on your silver tongue?'

I marshalled my thoughts. 'I'll tell him I know all about a plot against his life,' I said. 'That'll do the trick. He's always ready to listen to stuff like that. Imagines plots and conspiracies everywhere, he does.'

'What, like ours, you mean?'

I ignored that. 'Then,' I said, 'when we've got him on his own, with no guards or adjutants or hangers-on, no witnesses – That's how you do these things, must be. Careful planning. Thinking about it first. Not like that crazy bastard who assassinated King Philip.'

Peitho didn't say anything for a moment. 'All right,' he admitted, eventually. 'I can see the logic. Well, I'll leave you to it. Best of luck. You'll need it.'

'I've always hated it when people say that.'

I never could be doing with polishing armour; oil and sand and a little twist of rag, round and round till your wrists ache. It all seems so pointless, somehow; the plain fact is, bronze isn't meant to be all golden and shiny, its natural state is that sort of dull, rich brown, like oxtail soup. The patina is nature's defence against verdigris and corrosion; scour it off and there's nothing between the bare metal and the malice of nature.

Still, I polished up my armour, and the rest of my gear, till I looked like one of those rich-kid soldiers who have five slaves employed full-time bulling kit. Don't know why; perhaps I thought that Alexander would be more likely to trust a well-turned-out soldier than a scruffy one, or maybe I just needed to keep myself busy while I waited for my interview.

Wasn't the first time I'd been in The Presence, face to face – well, you know that, because I've told you. But I knew as soon as I put my head under the tent-flap that something was drastically different.

For one thing, the tent was next best thing to empty. I remembered thinking, the last time, how the great man's quarters were only just on the tidy side of cluttered – everywhere you looked there were things, bits and pieces he'd acquired in the course of his great adventure – the Shield of Achilles he'd pinched from the priests at Troy, for example, the severed ends of the Gordian Knot, the swords of mighty Persian warriors he'd slain in hand-to-hand combat, gifts of rare and precious tableware from kings and governors, relics (he was a sucker for those; shinbones of giants, genuine dragons' teeth in a little jar, Hercules' toothpick, Perseus' left sandal, Theseus' toenail-clippings, you name it, some toerag had palmed it off on Alexander of Macedon). Now there was nothing but a bed, a big wooden box the size of a coffin, and a single service-issue folding stool.

And Himself, of course. He was sitting on the bed, staring blankly into space, his mouth slightly open. He stayed that way for about as much time as it'd take to count to forty.

'Eudaemon,' he said, eventually, without turning his head. 'Euxenus' brother. Come in, sit down.'

You know that feeling you get when you know something's badly wrong? I had that feeling. Hey, do you remember that old man who lived up near Acharnae, the one whose house we went to when we were lost up that way one time? Yes, of course you do; seemed quite normal, till he pulled out that trunk from under his bed and in it was his dead wife. I expect you remember how he insisted on introducing us, like she was still alive. Well, it was that kind of creepy, I-want-to-get-out-of-here-now feeling. Can't say why I felt like that, exactly; maybe it was just the sight of that big wooden box that brought back the old memory. Gods only know what he'd got in there. His clean clothes, probably.

Well, I sat down, perched on that folding stool like a pigeon on a thin branch, and waited. He was still staring into space. Carried on doing that for a very long time, until one of the men who'd brought me in, can't remember who it was but it was one of the inner circle, made a sort of coughing noise and said, 'Alexander.'

'Yes, I know,' he replied, still staring into thin air. 'All right, dismissed.'

I could tell the man didn't want to go, but he couldn't very well disobey an order. A moment later, there was just me and Alexander. I'll be straight with you, Euxenus, I was scared. Well, you know I've never liked creepy stuff.

'They tell me you've done a very great thing,' he said, 'saved the lives of your fellow soldiers. That's good.'

I didn't say anything. Didn't seem like I was expected to say anything. I just sat there.

'It's a good feeling,' he went on. 'I think I'm supposed to give you something now.' He turned his head and looked me straight in the eye. 'Do you think he knew?' he asked.

'Sir?'

'Oh, never mind. I expect he did. A man like him, he'd have seen it. Doesn't matter. You're very fortunate, you know. We've both been very fortunate, to have known him. Still, you'd have thought he'd have mentioned it. Unless he was supposed not to, of course.' He smiled at me. 'It's been hard for me, you know, coming to terms with it. If he'd said something, just given me some sort of a clue, maybe I'd have been able to cope with it a little better. Anyway,' he said, 'that's enough of that, where's that crown thing I've got to give you?' He looked around. 'Doesn't seem to be here. Would you be terribly disappointed if we forgot about that? After all, it's the thought that counts, isn't it?'

I nodded stiffly. I knew I had to do my bit now, the speech about the conspiracy I'd so carefully worked out; but all I wanted to do was get the hell out of there. 'Alexander,' I said, 'there's something I have to tell you. It's really important.'

He looked up at me. 'All right,' he said. 'Go on.'

I looked round, the way I'd practised. 'I need to tell you when we're alone.'

'We are alone,' he pointed out. 'Fire away.'

I remember one time when I was a kid and I'd scrambled up into that old apple tree in the top corner of the big field at Pallene. There was a big fat apple all on its own right at the end of a long, thinnish branch, and I'd set my heart on that apple. I remember the feeling of utter disgust when suddenly I wasn't in the tree any more, I was on the ground with a broken branch between my legs and my head feeling like someone'd just belted it with a big smith's hammer.

'Go on,' he said.

I looked round again. I suppose I was trying to create the impression that even though we seemed to be alone, there were hidden listeners hiding everywhere. Hiding behind what, gods know, since the place looked like it had just been raided by the bailiffs.

'It's a conspiracy, isn't it?' he said.

It felt just like being punched very hard in the pit of the stomach; dizzy, frightened, couldn't breathe, couldn't move. Just sat there.

'It's all right,' he went on. 'I know. I know all about it.' And he smiled.

'You do,' I repeated.

'Oh, yes. I've known for some time. Really, I'm sorry for them. It's so pointless, isn't it?'

He'd said 'them', not 'you'. I looked at him. He broadened the smile, till you could have dried fish in the warmth of it.

'Poor Eudaemon,' he said, 'you look so worried. But really, there's nothing to worry about. They can't hurt me. Nobody can. That's why I haven't done anything. At least,' he went on, frowning slightly, 'not yet. I've been wondering about that, actually.'

'Oh, yes?' I said.

He nodded. 'It's awkward,' he said. 'Really, I should know the answer to this, but I can't seem to clarify my thinking. Ever since I've known, it's been – well, disorientating, I suppose you could call it. I feel like a child who's suddenly found himself inside a man's body, it takes some getting used to. No, the thing I can't decide is, ought I to do anything about it? I mean, if their silly plot can't possibly succeed – and it can't, of course, we both know that – then ought I to punish them for it? Should you punish someone for try-ing to do something that's wicked but actually physically impossible?' He rubbed the tip of his nose with the knuckle of his thumb – dammit, brother, he picked that up from you. I knew it was bugging me, where I'd seen someone do that before.

'I suppose I've got to,' he went on. 'I mean, my father does. He punishes blasphemers and perjurers and people who desecrate His temples. If my father does it, I suppose I've got to do it too; for their sake, really, not mine, otherwise if I don't, how can they possibly have any faith? I don't know, it just seems so unnecessary, somehow. So petty, if you know what I mean.'

I nodded. 'So you know who's in the plot, then?' I asked.

'Of course I know. I've always known.' He grinned. 'I guess it's a bit like people who get hit on the head and lose their memory, and then a while later it slowly starts coming back. Yes, that's a good way of putting it; there's all these things I've always known, and slowly I'm beginning to remember them. Explains a lot, really; like how I've always known exactly what to do in a battle, without really knowing why.' He frowned. 'That's a point, actually. Since I'm – well, what I am – do you think there's any point in carrying on with the war? I mean, it all seems so unfair. They can't possibly win, can they?'

I realised that I'd stopped breathing some time ago. 'Well, no,' I said. 'Of course not.'

'Maybe I should stop, then,' he said. 'Except, I can distinctly remember a whole lot more battles, ones we haven't had yet. There's going to be one quite soon, in fact, once we've crossed the

Tigris. I wouldn't remember if it wasn't going to happen, it stands to reason. There's all sorts of odd things I can remember, you know. I can even remember dying, which is a really strange sensation, let me tell you.'

'It must be,' I said.

He sighed, and shook his head. 'That's the trouble,' he said, 'I'm blundering about, not really having the faintest idea what I'm doing, and of course there's nobody I can ask, which is what's really annoying. You'd have thought my father would have told me by now, or sent somebody. But I assume that's all part of it, working it out for yourself. It's very lonely, you know? I've never been alone before, I'm not sure I like it. There's so much I don't understand yet. Still, that's my problem. I've enjoyed talking to you, though. It's almost like talking to your brother. We must do it again. Often.'

'Sir,' I said.

He stood up, and I stood up too, just in case he was about to bite me. 'I've been thinking of sending for him, you know. I can't think of anybody else who might possibly understand. But I don't think I should, really. It'd be unfair on him, for one thing. And really, I do have to deal with this on my own, there's no getting away from it. He'd say the same thing if he was here, I know.'

'Thank you, sir,' I said. 'Am I dismissed?'

He nodded; then, before I could get out of there, he went on, 'I think I'd better punish them after all. For one thing, it's what I would have done – you know, before. And I've decided that until I've remembered a bit more and I've understood what I'm supposed to be doing, it'd probably be better if I carried on as if nothing had happened. Otherwise it might upset people. What do you think?'

'I don't know,' I said. It seemed safest, somehow. And true, of course.

'I think it's best,' he said, with a slight nod of his head. 'Until I really know what I'm doing and what I'm about, I'd better keep it to myself; otherwise I'm just going to make myself look ridiculous. I'll send for you when I want you again.'

'Sir.'

'That's all, then. I'm sorry about the bees, by the way. It was an accident, obviously. We'll get some more in a week or so. They do say the African ones are much fiercer, so in a way it's all for the best.'

I got out of there as quickly as I could, which wasn't nearly quick enough. As I sneaked back across the camp, I felt as if someone had scratched the word IDIOT across the back of my mirror-burnished breastplate in very big letters. My first instinct was to head back to my tent, stoke up the fire but good with medicine, and try to get away from it for as long as possible; but something prompted me to go to look in on the bees first, so I did.

Wish I hadn't; because when I got there, I found my two Scythian friends standing inside one of our specially adapted siege-tower frames, with the lid flung open and a noticeable absence of angry, buzzing bees. The old boy was in tears, and his sidekick not much better off.

'What's going on?' I asked.

The old boy looked up at me, great fat teardrops rolling down his face. 'They're all dead,' he said.

I tried to look surprised. 'What do you mean, they're all dead?' I asked.

'Dead,' the old boy replied. 'I can't understand it. When I looked in on them a few hours ago they were fine. When I came to give them their honey just now, they were all—'

I walked over and looked in. He was standing up to his ankles in dead bees. Damnedest sight you ever saw.

'How did that happen?' I asked.

The younger Scythian shrugged. 'No idea,' he said. 'It wasn't cold or hunger or smoke. They just died.'

'Don't be daft,' I said. 'Bees don't just die, surely. Nothing just *dies*. They die *of* something. What've you two been doing to them? And what the hell are we going to tell Diades?'

They didn't reply, either of them. Just then, they couldn't be bothered with me. Reasonable enough, I suppose; the deaths of literally millions of living things, even bees, is liable to scale things down a bit. Really, I was glad they were preoccupied. Otherwise they might have noticed how calmly I took the news; like I'd been expecting it or something.

'Get rid of them,' I said. 'I'll put in for some more. We can buy locally. I do hear the African variety's a whole lot more aggressive than the Greek strain, anyway.'

I walked away, but the picture went with me; all those dead bodies, heaped where they'd fallen, like men surrounded by the enemy in some battle, hemmed in till they couldn't move and cut down. Alexander's battles were often like that.

All right, then; let's say there were a million dead bees, at a very conservative estimate. Now let's think how many people Alexander killed – and I'm not talking about those he killed with his own hands, or who died in his battles, I'm thinking of every man, woman and child who died because Alexander decided to invade Asia; killed in battle, died of disease along the line of march, died of starvation and exposure after our army had marched through their land, died in a wide variety of ways because of him. A million? Very conservative estimate. Now then; imagine them piled up in one place, the way the bees had been. Lay them out on the mountain and from a distance they'd look like a forest or a city. Dump them in the sea, and people would think it was a new island. Think of the bee-keeper standing over his ankles in dead bees, or the god in dead men. Enough to put you off your porridge, it really is.

I asked myself as I walked back to my tent, *How did the fucker know?* And there were only two answers; either he had them killed, or he really was—

Peitho was waiting in my tent when I got there. 'Well?' he demanded.

'Bastard killed my bees,' I replied.

'What?'

'He killed my damn bees,' I repeated. 'Why'd anybody do a thing like that?'

Peitho half-rose from his stool, then sat down again. 'What the hell are you talking about?' he asked. 'Did you see him? Have you set up the meeting?'

I shook my head. 'It didn't work out that way,' I replied.

'You did go, didn't you? You didn't lose your nerve and not turn up?'

I shook my head. 'Of course I turned up. It didn't work, that's all. We'll have to think of something else.'

'Oh, for—' Peitho scowled and screwed up his eyes. 'It was the perfect opportunity. What was it; wouldn't he go for the conspiracy thing?'

'Reckons he knows all about it already,' I said. 'He's gone mad, by the way. Completely off his head. Here, look, you nearly let the fire go out.'

Well, we got the fire going again, and we were just building up a nice head of fog when the tent-flap was thrown open and in stalked a couple of guardsmen. Startled the life out of me, as you can imagine.

'Which one of you's Peitho?' the officer said.

Peitho looked round. He was pretty far gone with the medicine, which was unfortunate. 'Me,' he said. 'Who wants to know?'

'You've got to come with us.'

I wanted to do something, but between fear and medication I was pretty well paralysed. Peitho stood up, staggering slightly. The guards officer was coughing and pulling faces, but he didn't say anything.

'Where are we going?' Peitho asked.

'Am I coming too?' I added. Gods know why.

The guards officer shook his head. 'Just him,' he said. 'All right, move it along. You,' he added, looking at me, 'stay there.'

So I stayed there, until my eyes grew heavy and I fell asleep. When I woke up, there was light flooding in through the tent-flap and the smoke-hole, and some bugger in armour shaking me by the arm.

'What?' I asked, noticing that my head was splitting.

'Come *on*,' the man said. 'He says he can't start the trial without you.'

I stood up. 'Remembered something else, has he?' I asked.

'What?'

'Forget it,' I said.

Twice in so many days; most soldiers'd give their right arms to be commended by the King himself for two separate and distinct acts of conspicuous merit on two successive days. But for me, he said, this terrible plot might have succeeded. But for me, the army, the kingdom, the empire would now be an orphan child cruelly bereft of its father, a ship without its rudder, a people wandering in the dark. But for me.

Of the six poor buggers standing up in front of the tribunal, three I'd never seen before in my life; the other three were Callisthenes, the philosopher nephew of Aristotle who'd lent us the book; my junior Scythian bee-keeper; and Peitho, my friend.

It was a chilling tale, right enough. The three staff officers, companions of Alexander since childhood, brought up as his brothers, educated with him under the shade of the same tree at Mieza, had conspired to kill Alexander and divide the empire between them. To this end they'd suborned the other three; Callisthenes, who did the research in his extensive library of books about poison and murder, the bee-keeper, who acquired the poisoned honey, and Peitho, who co-ordinated the whole operation. Mercifully, they made the fatal mistake of confiding their terrible scheme to a loyal, honourable man who, in spite of his friendship with all three of them, never hesitated to put his duty before his personal feelings, and revealed the whole sordid business to the King.

Brother, everybody's scared of dying; but as I stood there in front of the tribunal hearing all this, I could think of worse things. There was a part of me that wanted Peitho to turn round and say 'It was him, it was all his idea' – honestly, if he had, I'd probably have admitted it then and there. As it was, I was too shit-scared and ashamed to move at all. Peitho didn't even look at me. The Scythian called out to me – 'Eudaemon, tell them it's not true, tell them I never even saw the poison honey' – but I pretended he wasn't there. Callisthenes just included me in his general bewildered stare. They were found guilty, of course. Then everybody went very quiet, as Alexander stood up to announce the sentence.

Well, there weren't any surprises; death by hemlock for all six, sentence to be carried out forthwith. The Scythian and one of the Macedonians started shrieking and kicking; the guards bashed them on the head and dragged them out by their feet. The other four just walked away, and that was the last I ever saw of them. Alive, at any rate; dead, it was rather hard not to see them, since their heads were put up on poles and planted at the corners of the drill-square, in the usual manner. As soon as it was safe to go, I walked away fast; but someone ran up behind me. It was another of those damned guardsmen.

Here we go, I thought; but instead the man pushed a wreath of leaves and a small brass tripod into my hands. 'Alexander says you forgot to take these,' he said. 'You left them behind, remember?'

I thanked him, took them and went back to my tent. Someone had been in there and taken away the rest of the leaves, which was a blow, but there was still plenty of wine left, at least when I started on it. Not so much later on. I chucked the laurel crown on the fire, but its leaves turned out to have no perceptible medicinal value.

Afterwards, we marched for a long time and fought a battle. We won. I say 'we'; I spent the battle standing by.

They never got me any more bees. Apparently there were difficulties in Supply; the purchasing clerks didn't get the necessary docket, or they got the docket but it was sealed at the beginning instead of the end. Something like that. It didn't matter, anyway; as a reward for my part in unmasking the evil plot I was promoted to acting adjutant to the Chief of Countermines (there was no Chief of Countermines) and issued with a garish red sash for standing by in. Since by this stage the Department of Bees consisted of me and the old Scythian, who quite sensibly deserted the day after they killed his friend, the Department was consolidated with Livestock and Stores and never heard of again. I had absolutely nothing to do now except ride a horse while the army marched and hang around in my tent all evening on the off-chance of being summoned to a staff meeting. I asked for a transfer back to the auxiliary infantry, but the Macedonian in charge of establishments and personnel told me that my request couldn't go through unless it was sanctioned by my immediate superior. When I explained that I didn't actually have one, since there was no Chief of Countermines, I was told, no superior officer, no sanction; no sanction, no transfer. I tried to explain that this meant I was drawing pay and eating up rations and not doing a hand's turn in exchange. 'Aren't you the lucky one?' he replied, and ordered me to go away.

So please, don't ask me what it was like in the front line at Gaugamela, or the charge of the wedge at Arbela, or the day Alexander rode into Babylon, or the tight corner in the defile among the Uxians, or the bypassing of the Persian Gates; I wasn't there, or I can't remember. Don't look for me in the wall-paintings and marble bas-reliefs; I won't be there, unless the patron of the arts who's commissioned them is so thorough that he's even had his store-room and outside privy done, to depict the long, straggling baggage-train limping along a day or so behind the interesting bits of the army. I was at Persepolis when Alexander set fire to the royal palace of the Persian Kings with his own hands, after a long, hard night with the local wine, but the part of town I was billeted in was so far away that I didn't even see the glow in the sky. I was around when General Parmenio's son Philotas was accused of treason, and father and son were put to death as blithely as we'd wring the neck of a goose for the table, but I only heard about it a day or so afterwards. I marched to India all right, but mostly what I had to look at was the ruts in the road left by our carts and the arse of the horse in front. I wasn't important enough (thank gods) to be one of the officers at the staff meeting where Alexander announced out of the blue that from now on, the Macedonians as well as the Persians and the other conquered peoples were expected to fall on their faces and worship him as a god. All this stuff, this history, passed me by. Which is probably just as well.

The plain truth is, by this stage I wasn't feeling quite myself, if you see what I mean. It was something to do with the medicine I'd been taking. I'd assumed, no more bees, no more medicine, but it didn't quite work like that in practice. I found that not taking the medicine left me feeling much worse than the bee-stings ever did; I was dizzy, muddle-headed, irritable, nervous, shaky and sometimes quite horribly depressed, and I couldn't begin to imagine why, since there wasn't anything wrong with me. So I asked around until I found some Scythian auxiliaries – they were full-time horse-breakers, attached to Livestock – and asked them if they knew how I could get some more medicine. But they just looked sad and said they knew exactly how I felt; the bush or tree the leaves came from simply didn't grow in Persia, and that was all there was to it. However, they went on, they'd been making their own enquiries and they'd found out about a local Persian medicine that was probably almost as good, and as soon as they got hold of some they'd let me know so I could give it a try.

They were as good as their word. It was completely different stuff; for a start it was some kind of root rather than leaves, and you chewed it rather than burning it, and if anything it was a good deal stronger than the leaves had been. Anyway, it certainly did the job as far as getting rid of the dizziness and the shakes and all, so I got them to make me up a big, big batch of the stuff.

At first I was as happy as a lamb; happier, in fact, since lambs don't go around smiling all the time or occasionally bursting out laughing for no apparent reason (which I'm told I did, frequently). But then I started getting the weirdest dreams; first when I was asleep and then, annoyingly, when I wasn't.

The dreams were always different, but they generally started off with me asleep; but I wasn't at the war, sleeping in a tent, I was back home in Attica, and the bed was an old one that had been in our family for generations, and I was the head of the family, which wasn't even our family, if you see what I mean. Anyway, I'd wake up and remember that I was a prosperous Athenian farmer with a beautiful young wife and three fine sons; and then I'd roll over and see on the pillow next to me a dead body, shrivelled away into a skull, with the dried skin shrunk tight to the bone and a fine, full head of snow-white hair. This always scared the shit out of me, even though I knew it was coming. Anyway, I'd get up and go into the next room, and there on the floor under a blanket would be three more skin-and-bone corpses of very old men. By this time I'd have worked out that the one in my bed was my wife and the other three were my sons, and that I'd somehow been turned into a god during the night. Well, a good night's sleep for a god is longer than a mortal lifespan; while I'd been asleep my wife and sons had slept with me, and in that long sleep they'd grown very old and died.

In fact, so had everybody, except me. As the dream went on, so I'd remembered more and more; before I was a god I was a soldier, part of the army that conquered the world with Alexander. So I'd go and see if there was anybody I knew there; but when I found them they were all dead too, all shrivelled up in their beds and cots and hammocks. Then I'd remember that Alexander had been a god, just like me, so I'd go to look for him; and I'd find him, dead in his sleep and dried up like strips of fish in the sun, until his skin was as hard and brittle as the bark of a dead tree and his hair snapped off if you touched it. I'd search the whole world, in fact, but they'd all be the same. I'd outlived them all, in one night, every living thing in the world. The only other person I ever found in these dreams was Peitho, who was every bit as dead as they were, but not dried up or shrivelled, so somehow he could talk to me and move about.

'Hello, Peitho,' I'd say.

'Hello,' he'd reply, and salute; or sometimes he'd do the full Persian obeisance routine that Alexander had such trouble getting the Macedonians to do. And I'd know as soon as I looked into his eyes that he was plotting to kill me, because I'd become a god; and that wouldn't do, since it's bad for morale if junior officers start murdering gods all over the shop. So every time he tried to poison me, I'd have him executed, and the next day there he'd be again, until eventually he'd be there all the time, just like he is now. Of course, he was younger then; now he's grown old and shrivelled just like the rest of them. The only one who hasn't changed is me.

Of course, I know he isn't there really, he's some kind of nasty side-effect of the medicine, just like that damn buzzing sound, like a swarm of bees, that I hear nearly all the time now. Interesting, the bees. You see, I don't know if you know this but bees are immortal, too; not individually, of course, but as a group, a bit like a city. It's that old thing about the component and the whole; the small parts die and perish but the thing they make up endures for ever; like some city founded by a mighty hero to perpetuate his name, for instance, or even an empire such as the empire of the Kings of Persia or Alexander of Macedon.

Components die; components don't matter, they aren't worth spit. Only the whole, the unity, the thing made up out of the parts, really exists. Not the man, only the god he becomes. The Egyptians told Alexander that everybody is part of the god; then that he was the god that they made up. Now, I can't say I quite follow that line of reasoning, though it does sort of tie in with what I've noticed over the years, about the difference between who people are and who they become through the eyes of other people; like you became this great wise philosopher who'd taught Alexander the meaning of everything. Well, quite. I rest my case.

Sometimes, in fact, Peitho is the bees and the bees are Peitho; I look at him closely and he sort of melts down into the swarm, so closely packed together (dead but not really dead, because the swarm can't die) that from a distance they look like a single man. Oh, it's all right, he isn't like that now, he's just ordinary, dead old Peitho. Best friend I ever had, till he started trying to kill me.

And, of course, all this is imaginary, the side-effects of the medicine, which the Scythians told me I'll have to keep taking for the rest of my life if I ever want to be really cured. I've got a big jar of it. They gave me exactly enough, they said; when I come to the end of it, that'll be the time for me to die. I find it reassuring to know I'll never run out of the stuff; by now, I guess, without it I'd be seriously ill. But it gets to you after a while, knowing deep down that however they appear on the surface, everybody you meet or talk to is actually dead, that all I'm seeing right now is my memory of you, and that we're not having this conversation, I'm simply remembering history, a conversation we had years and years ago, before you died.

CHAPTER TWENTY-THREE

꙰꙰꙰꙰꙰꙰꙰꙰꙰꙰꙰꙰꙰꙰꙰꙰꙰꙰꙰꙰꙰

N ext morning, we went our separate ways; Eudaemon back
to Attica, to the family farm I'd been keeping warm for him,
with his jar of medicine and his invisible companion; me on into
Asia, heading East towards Sogdiana, with my empty jar and my
invisible snake. The last I saw of him was the back of his head as he
slept; with his broken leg he couldn't come down to the post halt,
and to be honest with you I wasn't too sorry. It would have been
awkward saying goodbye to him now that I knew he'd gone completely crazy. I'm afraid I get terribly embarrassed around people
with disturbed or damaged minds.

The Persian system of post roads is, sorry, *was* little short of miraculous. In King Darius' time, before the Greeks let it go to rack
and ruin, the royal messenger service maintained a straight, well-
surfaced road all the way across the Empire, with inns at regular
intervals, fresh horses standing by, cavalry escorts to get you across
dangerous or debatable territory, everything a traveller in a hurry
could possibly want. For all I know, I could have been one of the last
people to use it to go right across the Empire and so get the full
benefit of it. Now, of course, with what was the Empire split up into
several rival kingdoms and parts of it effectively outside anybody's
control, the messenger service has gone and the road's in a sorry
state. A pity, but there it is.

Since it was fairly obvious from pretty early on that my horsemanship simply wasn't up to the standard needed to make proper

use of the road, the couriers who went with me organised a carriage – well, more of a cart, really, except that it was drawn by horses rather than oxen or mules, and it had a sort of vestigial leather hood to keep off the worst of the sun and the weather. Nevertheless, the feeling of being a consignment of olives on their way to market was depressingly strong. The motion of the cart made me very drowsy, and I slept on and off for most of the journey; even when I was awake during the day, I kept well in the shade of the canopy and out of the blinding sun. As a result, I missed the scenery and the points of interest and the remarkable sights, as usual.

Instead of sightseeing and taking an intelligent interest in my surroundings, as a good historian should (think of Herodotus, with his magpie mind and his tape measure and his incessant questions), I spent a lot of time thinking with my eyes shut; a proceeding which greatly puzzled the couriers, until the Macedonian courier explained to the two Persians that in the small, plain jar in my luggage was a magic, fortune-telling serpent, and I was communing with it. After that, they left me well alone, except for a few tentative enquiries about romantic encounters and gambling strategies.

I thought a lot about jars, as it happens, and the contents thereof; jars of bees hurled into mineshafts to flush out the enemy; jars of wine and grain being meticulously counted by the keepers of the Athenian census, to ascertain which property class a man belonged to; jars of various sorts of produce stacked up in the hold of my friend Tyrsenius' ship; jars of arrows bumping along in a supply train on their way to the war; empty wine-jars littering the floor of the house of a man who's given up bothering; jars of poison for the body and the mind; jars of wisdom and prophecy. Most everything that moves about from one place to another in this world travels in a jar – it's the handiest, most convenient container of all, waterproof, of a fixed and easily regulated volume, easy to stack, easy to keep track of if you simply scratch a few letters on its neck. According to legend, the greatest of all the heroes, Hercules, escaped from the murderous Cercopes by hiding in a jar. Seal the neck with wax or pitch and the contents will stay fresh indefinitely, like the words of a historian in a book. If you're so minded, you can hire a painter to embellish the outside of your jar with unreal images of legendary and long-dead people, drawing out of his imagination the way they ought to have looked (which is not necessarily what they were actually like; but who's to say which is the more valid image, the way a man was or the way he ought to have been, or the way he seemed to be to those around him, those influenced by him?). Oh, your humble jar has a fair claim to being Man's best friend, if you discount the first ever jar, the one the gods gave to Pandora, with all the troubles and evils of the world packed inside; but she didn't know that and clawed away the wax that stopped the neck, releasing all the evils and the troubles into the air, like a swarm of buzzing bees, and leaving behind only one, the most pernicious of all – blind Hope, the queen bee, who has lived at the bottom of jars ever since.

And so, after a long and uneventful journey (I got sunstroke once and dysentery twice; a wheel came off the cart at the Caspian Gates, fortunately before we struck out across the desert; between Bactra and Nautaca one of the post inns had burned down, so we had to sleep in the cart and eat field rations; otherwise nothing to speak of), I arrived here, where the Scythian mountains run down to the Iaxartes river, wherever the hell that is in relation to anywhere else. As I perceived it, a day came when the cart stopped early, a courier woke me up and said, 'We're here,' and, having no reason not to believe him, I got out and unloaded my luggage. I suppose it's possible that he played some kind of practical joke on me and this is in fact Italy, or southern Libya, or the country north of the Danube. Of course that'd mean you were in on the joke too, Phryzeutzis; but you'd tell me, wouldn't you?

Don't answer that.

Assuming that this is Sogdiana, it's the furthest north-easterly point where the wilderness of the Scythian nomads (that's you, my young friend) impinges upon the settled, mundane world of farmers and city-dwellers. Is it just me, or do you Scythians lie at the edges of everything, as the Ocean is reckoned to encompass all the dry land? Go north off the edge of the map (Aristagoras' engraved bronze map, that bamboozled the Athenians into the First Persian War . . . Maps have a lot to answer for) and it seems to me that wherever you go, from northern Greece to India, you'll find yourself among Scythians; an unlikely race to have had such a significant effect on the lives of my brother and myself, but a pretty pervasive influence all the same. Maybe you Scythians (sorry, *we* Scythians, I keep forgetting) surround the other nations of the earth the way darkness surrounds the light of a flickering lamp; or maybe Scythia is the rule and the bit in the middle is the exception; the small exception, maybe – does anybody know how big Scythia actually is? For all I know it could be so huge that all the countries of Darius' and Alexander's Empire put together are tiny in comparison, like a single fallen leaf in the market square of a busy town.

The walls were already up when I arrived here; the streets were laid out, the public buildings more or less complete, the water supply connected up. Apparently, because of Alexander's habit of founding cities like a dog pissing against trees, the engineers had made it a rule always to have the basic components of a city to hand, all neatly stored in jars, numbered, ready to slot together at a moment's notice – modular unit Ideal Societies, where the temple roof from Alexandria-in-Arachosia would fit the temple in Alexandria-on-the-Caucasus should they ever happen to need a spare. They'd got putting the bits together down to a fine art, they could put up a city almost as quickly as their colleagues in the siege and assault department could tear one down. My old friend Agenor the stonemason would have hated that.

So there was precious little for me to do, apart from 'stand by', as my brother would say (but all my life I've been a bystander, though never, gods know, an innocent one). I had to dedicate the temple, where the statue of the god (god, unspecified, marble, service issue, one) bore an uncanny resemblance to Alexander of Macedon, until a thrice-blessed workman contrived to chip off half of its nose while installing the head on the shoulders. Now our god stands there in an inspiringly martial pose, one hand outstretched to aid and succour, the other upraised to strike, looking like one of those professional boxers we used to get at country fairs who's lost one too many fights for the good of his health. They were supposed to send us a new head, all the way from the main factory at Abydos in Egypt, but it got sent to the wrong Alexandria, and since they had a perfectly good head already, they spirited it away and stuck it in the nearest lime-kiln; so now it's helping the crops grow, just like a good god should. The factory's closed down now, of course. King Ptolemy (General Ptolemy, as was) had it turned into a plant for making catapult-balls. I gather they're very good, too.

A day or so after I'd dedicated the temple, I was standing by in a hammock in the courtyard of the really rather fine house I'd been allocated as governor when the major-domo waddled in and announced that there was a deputation waiting to see me. I wasn't expecting visitors, let alone any deputations, but there was always the off-chance that it was something important, so I told the man to bring them in.

'We'd like you to dedicate the shrine,' their spokesman said.

'Already done that,' I replied.

The man shook his head. 'Not the temple,' he said, 'the shrine. We built it specially as soon as we knew you were coming.'

I frowned. I didn't like the sound of that. 'Sorry,' I said, 'this is the first I've heard about any shrine. Whose shrine is it, specifically?'

The man looked confused. 'For the sacred serpent,' he said. 'You know, the one you carry about with you in the jar. We've built a permanent home for it, just past the corn exchange as you go up the hill. It's very nice.'

I was silent for a very long time. 'Let me just make sure I've got this right,' I said. 'You want me to give you my snake.'

He looked worried. 'It may seem like that at first sight,' he said nervously, 'but it isn't, really. We just thought the serpent might be happier if it had some kind of permanent home.'

I shook my head. 'He's a nomad, my snake,' I said. 'Just like your cousins to the north. Just like me, I guess,' I added; it hadn't occurred to me before but yes, in my time I've been every bit as nomadic as your average full-blooded Scythian. 'He doesn't want a permanent home. He likes the freedom, you see.'

'The freedom,' the spokesman replied. 'In a jar.'

'A jar that's been all over the world,' I pointed out. 'Just because he's stayed inside the jar doesn't mean he hasn't been to all those exotic places. I'm sure he'd have paid proper attention to them if he'd ever stuck his head up above the rim.'

But it obviously meant a lot to them. So, in spite of my serious reservations about the whole idea, I said I'd do it. This left me with a problem, of course; inside the jar – no snake. Well, I couldn't very well buy one, in case people put two and two together and got upset. Nor could I find one, however hard I looked (and usually the trick is not finding one, as you walk the fields in your bare feet). So; no buy, no find; all that was left was to try making one. That may sound daft to you, but when I was a kid we used to find cast-off snakeskins in the fields, stuff them with wool and use them to frighten the life out of people by leaving them lying about (in the clothes-press, for instance, or buried in someone's clothes while he was swimming in the sea). With a little practice, we were able to get them looking ever so lifelike, and they had the tremendous advantage over the real thing of not being able to bite and kill you.

Well, of course, I didn't have a snakeskin either; but I had an idea where there might be one. You may remember that when I was in Macedon, Alexander put a snake in my jar; it popped out at an embarrassing moment, if you recall. I'd noticed recently when I'd been moving the jar around that there was something small and light rattling around in there; my guess was that Alexander's snake had taken advantage of the quiet and privacy of my jar to slough its skin. Anyhow, it wouldn't cost me anything to turn the jar out and have a look.

So I stood on a stool and reached up to lift it down from the hook in the rafters where I'd hung it; but it was a very old, tired stool. I heard a sharp crack, just as I'd lifted the ear of the jar off the hook, and the next thing I knew was that I was sitting uncomfortably on the floor, one leg folded underneath me at a very unusual angle, feeling extremely sorry for myself. Strangely enough, it was my right leg I broke, whereas my brother broke his left.

I was too preoccupied with screaming and sobbing with pain to pay too much attention at first to what had become of the jar; but after I'd yelled myself hoarse and nobody came (major-domo and cook down at the market, shopping; housemaid and gardener off together somewhere), I calmed down a bit and saw that the jar had smashed. That shook me, I'll admit. The jar had been with me a long time, it had been my living and a tremendous influence on the lives of myself and others – think; if I hadn't had the jar, Queen Olympias would never have wanted me to tutor her son; if I hadn't tutored Alexander . . . Well. And now it was broken; and there among the small, sharp potsherds I saw the dried-up remains of a dead snake, curled up tightly like a coil of coarse rope, as perfectly preserved as an Egyptian king.

Well, they do say that snakes are immortal too; instead of dying as we do, they simply slough off their old bodies and slither away. I wonder; as they break out of death like a chick out of an egg, do they remember the life ahead of them, or do they have to wait for it to come back piecemeal, like us ordinary gods? I have no idea; I never knew the answer to that one, or else it's slipped my mind. I'm getting terribly forgetful these days, Phryzeutzis; I can't remember anything unless I write it down somewhere.

The broken leg was a perfect excuse for not dedicating the shrine; and one day while I was laid up waiting for it to mend, the gardener came rushing by with a basket in one hand and a long stick in the other. I asked him what the fuss was about.

'There's a snake got into the storeroom,' he said. 'Thrassa's doing her block, so I'm going to get rid of it.'

I propped myself up on one elbow. 'Do me a favour,' I said. 'When you've caught it, don't kill it; sling it in a jar and stuff the neck with straw. I've got a use for a live snake.'

He looked at me as if I was crazy; then again, he always looked at me as if I was crazy. 'All right,' he said. 'Where do you want it put?'

'Oh, anywhere,' I said. 'Just see that nobody disturbs it.'

So the shrine got its snake, a little wriggly green bugger that slid away out of sight as soon as I pulled the straw out. The assembled local worthies were no end impressed, and took care to stand back as I passed so my shadow wouldn't fall on them. For two pins, I think, they'd have started worshipping me as a god.

The Macedonians have a law, or at any rate a tradition, that you don't start a war during the month Daisios (that's roughly the Athenian Thargelion; gods know what you people call it. At any rate, it's between the rise of the Pleiades and solstice, about threshing time, and if you haven't finished digging over the vineyards, you're way behind). In the middle of Daisios in the thirteenth year of his reign, when he was thirty-two years old, Alexander was in Babylon, all ready to set off and conquer Arabia, a huge and worthless desert away to the south. On previous occasions, he'd taken the trouble to sidestep the tradition by having his astronomers repeat the previous month, Artemisios; this time, however, he couldn't be bothered. Besides, he argued winningly, the intercalated second Artemisios had clearly been spurious, which meant that in the eyes of his fellow gods he'd gone to war in Daisios before and got away with it, so there was no reason why he shouldn't do the same thing again.

A day or so before the scheduled departure date, Alexander went to a party given by a man called Medius. It must have been a good party, because he woke up feeling awful, so he ordered the domestic staff to shift his quarters from the palace to a house in a park on the posh side of the river, where it was quiet and peaceful and a man could recover after a long night with a jar. There was a swimming pool at this house, and he decided to sleep beside it, under the stars; apparently Babylon's like an oven at that time of year, and it's nice and cool by the water.

Next day he was a little feverish, so he had a bath and spent the rest of the day at home with Medius, some other friends and a hair or two of the dog, since he wanted to be sure to be fighting fit when the army moved out in a couple of days' time. He didn't sleep well that night, and the next day the fever was a little worse. The general staff started making plans for postponing the expedition, but he wouldn't hear of it, even though the next day, which was when the fleet should have sailed, he was no better. But the day after that he was almost fully recovered, and put in a full day's work catching up on what he'd missed while he'd been ill. Maybe he overdid it; he was so bad the next day that he had to be taken back to the palace.

He lived for another four days. Most of the time he was too weak to say anything, and when he wasn't he was wandering in his mind, calling out all sorts of strange, delusional gibberish, the way people do when they're out of their heads with fever. He did have a lucid spell near the end, but when his chief officers and ministers of state tried to talk to him about the succession he didn't appear to remember who they were. When he was dying, he kept shouting that there were snakes on his pillow, but it was all right; he'd strangled them, because he was the infant Hercules and just about to be born. Then he said that Aristotle had had him poisoned, because Aristotle didn't believe in gods and thought there shouldn't be any; he'd got the recipe for the poison out of his nephew Callisthenes' book, the one Eudaemon had told him about, and the poison had been served to him in a cup made out of the hoof of a mule, because half-breed gods can't have children. He gave orders for Babylon to be burned to the ground, followed by the whole of the earth, because he remembered that last time he'd wiped out the human race with a great flood and it didn't do to repeat one's effects. Then he sat upright and asked for someone to read to him out of Euxenus' book about the war, since he wanted to know what had happened in the end. They told him Euxenus hadn't written any books, and asked him which of the generals he wanted to have the empire after he was gone. 'How should I know?' he answered angrily, 'I haven't got to that bit yet,' whereupon the generals had the room cleared.

Some people say he died screaming, or in tears; that he went to bed just before he died; that in the last moment of his life a mighty eagle swooped in through the window and carried his soul away to Olympus. Other people will tell you that he didn't die at all, that the embalmed, imperishable corpse that lies buried in Alexandria in Egypt (perfectly preserved, like a dried snake in a jar) is somebody quite other, a body he sloughed off when it started to fray, and Alexander is still alive somewhere, waiting for some unspecified event which means it's time for him to return and continue where he left off. Some people would have you believe that he will never die, that he lives on in the group mind of the swarm of Macedonians and Greeks that are buzzing all through Europe and Asia these days, gathering nectar and nesting in every crack and corner of the world, even as far out as the eastern border of Scythia.

Personally, I think he's dead, and bloody good riddance.

If history were to end there, with the death of Alexander and the collapse of his empire, it'd be a poor show; a great deal of work would have been wasted with nothing to show for it, and generations yet unborn would make pilgrimages to piss on our graves. I don't intend it to be that way. I may be old, but I'm not so old that I can't still dream about the ideal society, or at any rate the perfect city.

It started a year or so ago, when that Lydian merchant showed up with his little cart full of plunder from some battle or other. Odd creatures, your Lydians; they're about as Greek as the river Ganges, but they've had Greeks living next to them for so long that the colours have run, so to speak, and to listen to some of them talk, you'd almost believe they were as Greek as I am. This Lydian was like that; he called himself Theocles or some such Greek name, and if you believed his sales pitch everything in his cart that wasn't made in Athens was made in Corinth or Megara or Thebes. Anyway, in among the bloodstained boots and the slightly war-damaged armour (one careful but unfortunate owner) there was, he told me, something he knew I'd want to buy. In fact, he said, once I knew what it was I'd be so desperate to buy it I'd undoubtedly offer him far more money than I could possibly afford, so as a favour to me and a token of respect for the memory of the divine Alexander he'd offer it to me for a mere ten staters, sight unseen . . .

Needless to say, I told him to go forth and multiply, whereupon he gave me a very sad look, the sort of look Lydian faces were expressly designed for, and said that the price was now twelve staters. This intrigued me; so I said that if he told me what this thing was, I'd give him half a stater, local coin. His face lengthened a little more, his hand turned palm upwards, and he told me it was a book.

'A book?' I said.

'A book. A *Greek* book,' he added.

He was right; I was interested. 'What sort of book?' I asked.

'About so long,' he replied, 'so much round, in its own brass tube. Tube's extra,' he added quickly, but not quickly enough.

'Fine,' I said. 'But what's it about? Who's it by?'

He shrugged; a complicated, multi-dimensional folding of the shoulders, as if he was about to take his arms off and put them neatly away. 'Does it matter?' he said. 'It's a book. In Greek.'

I thought about it for a moment. 'I might be interested,' I said. 'For three staters.'

Honestly, I thought he was about to burst into tears. 'I'm sorry,' he said; then he fished about under his tunic and produced this book-tube, with the very dog-eared edges of a book poking out. He pulled it from the tube, unwound about a hand's span, tore it off and ate it. 'Fifteen staters,' he said.

I wanted to see how this was going to turn out. 'Seven,' I said.

He unrolled and ate another span. 'Seventeen,' he said.

'Done.'

'You won't be sorry,' he said, spitting out a wadge of half-chewed Egyptian paper. 'And three for the tube.'

'You know what you can do with the tube,' I told him.

As I'd feared, the book turned out to be the goddamned bloody *Iliad*, messily copied by an illiterate scribe somewhere in Egypt, at a guess. Still, a book's a book, so that afternoon, when it was too hot to do anything else, I sat down under a tree and started idly scrolling through, more interested in the footnotes and the little comments scrawled by previous owners in the margins than Homer's actual immortal words. When I reached the end, I saw there was something else after it; the scribe, having cramped his writing up really small, had been left with blank space at the end and had to fill it up with something else. The text he'd chosen was new to me; it was *On Death*, by someone called Pherecrates of Cnidus. Quite by chance I'd stumbled across a treasure richer than gold: a book I'd never read by a man I'd never heard of. My lucky day.

That afternoon, I got to know Pherecrates of Cnidus pretty well. He wasn't a difficult man to understand; a gentleman farmer like myself, who made use of the idle parts of the year by renting space on his rich neighbour's ship, loading up his surplus produce and a few bits and pieces he'd bought in specially, and cruising up and down the coast between Rhodes and the Hellespont. Men like Pherecrates don't usually tend to trouble history, and Pherecrates himself would never have been an exception to this rule if he hadn't come ashore one day at a something-and-nothing little town on the island of Chios, whose name he couldn't even remember. He did reasonable business there in the morning, trading figs for cheese and cheap silver hairpins for cheap bone combs, but in the afternoon nobody much was about, and he was thinking of packing up and heading back to the ship when a man came up to him offering to sell him a pair of shoes.

They were, according to Pherecrates, very old shoes, shoes that could well have walked to Spain and back, and Pherecrates said he didn't want them. The man said fair enough, but showed no signs of wanting to go away, and for lack of anything better to do Pherecrates started chatting to him.

How the subject came up, Pherecrates couldn't quite remember; it was something to do with some historical figure, and the man happened to comment that he'd seen this man once, years ago.

'You can't have,' Pherecrates objected. 'He died sixty years ago.'

'Oh, I saw him all right,' the man replied. 'Why, are you calling me a liar or something?'

Pherecrates shook his head. 'No offence,' he said, 'but you simply couldn't have seen him. Like I said, he died sixty years ago, and you're obviously not a day over fifty-five.'

The man grinned at him, revealing a perfect set of teeth. 'I'm eighty-seven,' he replied.

Well, that made Pherecrates very curious, not to mention sceptical. 'And what's more,' the man added, 'I'll prove it to you. Stay there.'

'I'm not going anywhere,' Pherecrates said; and a little while later, the man came back with two other men, who both looked like slightly younger copies of him.

'This is my son,' the man said, 'he's sixty-six; and this is my grandson, who's just turned fifty. Isn't that right, boys?'

They offered to go and fetch the rest of the family; great-grandson and great-great-grandson, but Pherecrates assured them there was no need. He believed them. 'That's remarkable,' he said.

The son smiled patronisingly. 'No it isn't,' he said. 'Just sensible, clean living.'

'Oh, yes?' Pherecrates said, expecting to be sold something if he wasn't careful.

'That's right,' the old man said. 'I've always lived clean, and my boys here have always lived clean, and look at us. Never had a day's illness in our lives.'

Pherecrates frowned (or I imagine he did; he doesn't say so in his book, but it'd be human nature to frown at this point). 'When you say "live clean",' he said, 'what exactly do you mean by it?'

Then the old man explained. Ever since he was a boy, he said, he'd had a phobia about dirt; couldn't abide it, he said, made him go all queasy. So, when he built his own house, he went out of his way to make sure everything was always clean. He moved the privy away from the house, downstream on the little brook rather than upstream; he made sure the house was swept clean once a day and that any food that had gone off was thrown out or given to poor travellers, rather than left to moulder in the store-room; he insisted that all the family's clothes and bedding were changed and washed regularly; he banished the animals from the house and built a special stall for them instead, well away from the house and the water supply. If anybody cut himself or got dirt in an existing cut, they had to wash it out immediately and put on a clean bandage. In short, he was utterly obsessive about it. And nobody in his house ever seemed to get ill.

Well, Pherecrates thought no more about it at the time. But, as the years went by, what the old man had told him snagged in his mind, like a hook in a fish's throat, and he started to think, and use his eyes. When he went abroad, to the towns and cities where he bought and sold, he looked about him and made connections – an epidemic in Priene, where the nightsoil from one quarter soaks away into another quarter's water supply; a man in Ephesus who died of a poisoned flea-bite; old men's stories of their fathers' experiences in the Great Plague at Athens; deaths here, deaths there, deaths everywhere – until he came to the conclusion that shocked him like nothing had ever done before.

Half the people who die, he now firmly believed, die of diseases caused or aggravated by dirt. Incredible numbers of people troop down to the Styx ferry and stump up their two obols to the ferryman simply because they don't, as the old man he met on Chios put it, live clean. According to Pherecrates, from the people who wouldn't die if you cleaned up the water in Greece, you could raise an army large enough to conquer the world, found colonies in every province, and still have enough left over to have hunger riots. If only half of the wise men, philosophers, scientists, poets, statesmen who die of infections, blood poisoning and other dirty deaths were to be spared, mankind would soon be so wise and so powerful that the gods wouldn't stand a chance. We could exile them to the Arabian desert or the frozen wastes out back of Scythia and run the world ourselves. All it would take to make the difference would be a few aqueducts, drains and cesspits and a weekly wash-and-brush-up around the home, and we'd have stolen a prize so valuable as to make Prometheus stealing fire from Heaven seem trivial. According to Pherecrates.

Now, he was sceptical at first, just as I was and you are. For instance; how can bodily waste be so dangerous and poisonous when it comes out of our own bodies? It didn't kill us while it was still inside us, so why should it be so desperately lethal after it's left us and seeped into the village well? And dirt, honest dust and mud; dirt and mud are what we grow our food in, and once we've grown it, we eat it. If dirt and mud are so deadly that a little getting into a cut or a scratch can kill you, how come food isn't deadlier than my brother's poison honey? Isn't it far more logical to assume that diseases and deaths are what we've always believed they are, supernatural entities that roam and buzz unseen among us, looking for unlucky or doomed people to pick on, rather than perverted products of the good earth and our own bodies?

Pherecrates couldn't answer that; all he could do was set out his evidence and suggest that the conclusions he drew from them were worthy of serious consideration. At which point the book ended, and Pherecrates stepped out of my life back into the darkness he'd so miraculously appeared from.

Yes, I know. It sounds like the demented ravings of a man with an obsession, like those people you try to avoid in the market square who do their best to convince you that the King of India's sent assassins to murder them, or that the stars are eating their brains. But what if he's right? What if there's even a tiny scrap of truth in his notion? The only way to know for certain, I suggest, is to try it and see; build a city with all his fussy ideas put into practice and count how many people drop down dead and how many don't. As great experiments go, it's no daffier than Alexander's pet project of forcing a thousand selected flowers of Macedonian manhood to marry a thousand hand-picked Persian girls, with a view to breeding a master-race he could use to repopulate Asia. Of the two great leaps of faith, why not choose the one that causes least inconvenience to the subjects of the experiment and has the most potential for good, in the unlikely event that it's successful?

So here I am, Phryzeutzis; in my old age, an old fool who should know better, once again trying to play god and create an ideal city. Maybe it's a disease of the elderly and underoccupied; certainly it's the sort of thing I could imagine the Founders at Antolbia coming up with (and I'd have told them, politely, but firmly, to go and stick the idea where the sun never shines, because people with work to do in the real world simply don't have time to get involved in wild idealistic schemes – or if they do it turns out an utter disaster, like Plato's bad experiences in Sicily when he went out there to found the philosopher kingdom). So what? In theory, under the charter Alexander gave this place when he set it up, as proxy *oecist* I have absolute power here, so I probably ought to use it once in a while, if only to show the people here how lucky they are to have me, rather than someone who rushes about *doing* things all the time.

This city won't last, of course. How can it? Greek city, founded on a whim by a great king who was briefly a god but who's now dead, populated by savages and ruled by a crazy old man. I remember a city so very much like it that these days I have trouble telling them apart. There are times, Phryzeutzis, when I think you're really my friend Tyrsenius, or my Budini bodyguard, and that this is Antolbia, and that any moment now Theano'll come out of the house with a big jug of wine with honey and cinnamon; or that any minute, the other savages will come bursting through the gate with arrows on their bowstrings and kill us all. I sit here sometimes, Tyrsenius, and I seem to be remembering some specific small incident that happened at the old city, rather than watching it happen again here in the new one. History, of course, is the setting down in writing of the deeds of great men and the happening of great events, so that they shall never be forgotten, and so that the manifold and grievous errors of the past can be recognised and avoided by those that come after us; so, by writing history, I'm pinning this time down, so that we'll know it's not the time before or the time after. It's a trick to stop myself going crazy, I guess. If I can look it up in a book, I can know for certain that this is something that's happening, not something I'm remembering.

And, like most tricks, it doesn't work.

Lately I've been getting this pain in my right hand, where the joints are chalking up; and that very nice woman from the vegetable market who thinks that if she mothers me and looks after me I'll leave her money when I die, that very nice woman gave me something to take away the pain. What she gave me was a little box of dried leaves; you sprinkle them on a fire and breathe in, and next thing you know the pain doesn't hurt any more. Well, she's absolutely right, I feel no pain now; but whenever I sit by the fire with a cloth over my head, breathing deeply, I seem to see someone sitting next to me, also breathing in and enjoying the smoke. I have no idea who he is; I can't see his face clearly through the smoke, and his voice is fuzzy and indistinct, like the hum of distant insects. Sometimes I think it's my father, or Diogenes; at other times it's Alexander or Aristotle, or Tyrsenius or Agenor the stonemason, or Theano, or one of my brothers, or my grandfather Eupolis, or Pherecrates the drainage enthusiast, or Eudaemon's friend Peitho (who of course I never met). Sometimes, when I'm drowsy and not thinking straight, I think it's you, and that you're reading my book, and I'm the book sitting there being read.

I suppose I ought to be worried. But it's too late for that. These days, I'd gladly trade a blurred edge to my sanity for something that'll take away the pain. Sanity's a wonderful thing, but it isn't a patch on a good night's sleep, or being able to take a piss without feeling like someone's hammering a tent-peg into your kidneys. All my life I've felt no pain, as I've bounced happily along with death and destruction at my heels like happy dogs being taken for a walk, eating up everybody around me and, in general, leaving me alone. It's a small price to pay, the company of some indistinct figure who vaguely resembles the way I think some long-dead person I can barely remember ought to have looked, in order that he fits the character I've drawn for him in my book of history. As the man said after he'd been in solitary confinement for fifty years, it's a pain having to share this cell with the devil, but it's better than being alone.

THE WALLED ORCHARD

Tom Holt

'Read *The Walled Orchard* so you can tell your descendants,
"I was there when the historical novel started holding its head
up with the rest of literature"'
The Washington Post

The hero is Eupolis, weary, cynical and believing only in comedy.
The heroine is Athens, at the height of her schizophrenic glory.
A startling mixture of comedy and tragedy, *The Walled Orchard* is
the poignant, charming story of their turbulent relationship.

'Witty, ironic . . . and achieves a deeply felt authenticity'
The New York Times

OLYMPIAD

Tom Holt

The incredible story of the first-ever Olympic Games –
a compelling new historical novel from the acclaimed author of
The Walled Orchard.

Two thousand, seven hundred and seventy-six years ago a group
of men ran between two piles of stones, and invented history.
If, that is, history can be believed.

The first ever Olympic Games in 776BC were apparently so
memorable that all Western chronology is based on them.
All we know about them is the name of the man who won the
race. Over two and a half millennia later, it's about time
somebody told the story.

Olympiad is an enthralling and beguiling historical novel full of
adventure and misadventure. It will confirm Tom Holt's place as
an innovative, challenging and wonderfully entertaining
writer of historical fiction.

THE LAST ENGLISH KING

Julian Rathbone

In 1066, a 'jumped-up little Norman and his bunch of psychopaths' cross the water and alter the course of English history. Three years later and Walt, King Harold's only surviving bodyguard, is still emotionally and physically scarred by the loss of his king and country. Wandering through Asia Minor, headed vaguely for the Holy Land, he tells his extraordinary story.

'Fascinating'
Guardian

'There are scenes of such solidity that no reader
will easily forget them'
The Times

'Gripping . . . a rattling good story, told in strong,
clear prose . . . unforgettable'
Spectator

'Powerful'
Sunday Telegraph

MASTER GEORGIE

Beryl Bainbridge

'Truly extraordinary, heart-breakingly good'
Sunday Telegraph

When Master Georgie – George Hardy, surgeon and
photographer – sets off from the cold squalor of Victorian
Liverpool for the heat and glitter of the Bosphorus to offer his
services in the Crimea, there struggles behind him a small caravan
of devoted followers: Myrtle, his adoring adoptive sister; lapsed
geologist Dr Potter; and photographer's assistant and sometime
fire-eater Pompey Jones, all of them driven onwards through a
rising tide of death and disease by a shared and mysterious guilt.

Combining a breathtaking eye for beauty and a visceral
understanding of mortality, Beryl Bainbridge exposes her
enigmatic hero as tenderly and unsparingly as she reveals the filth
and misery of war, and creates a novel of luminous depth
and extraordinary intensity.

'It is hard to think of anyone now writing who understands the
human heart as Beryl Bainbridge does . . . *Master Georgie* is brief,
intense, and remains seared on the mind long after reading'
The Times

THE REQUIEM SHARK

Nicholas Griffin

It is the eighteenth century's Golden Age of Piracy, and William Williams is a forced apprentice to Bartholomew Roberts, slaver turned pirate captain. Enlisted first as a musician, then as the captain's biographer, Williams chronicles the conflicts with merchantmen and whores, the tribesmen and soldiers that populate the ends of the known world.

Captain Roberts's goal is the capture of the treasure ship *Juliette*, a quest that finds the *Fortune* scouring the coasts of Africa and the Caribbean; a search made ever more precarious by the pursuit of two British men-o'-war. Rich in historical detail, *The Requiem Shark* is a gripping maritime adventure set in an environment dominated by gold, disease and blood.

'Remarkable . . . a vivid and authentic picture of life at sea that is second to none . . . There is more than enough action and adventure, blood and guts, disease and death, love and cruelty, acts of loyalty and deeds of deceit to keep all but the most squeamish turning the pages'
Daily Mail